By the author

Fireheart, Volume One of the Chay Trilogy
Whitefire, Volume Two of the Chay Trilogy
Firesoul, Volume Three of the Chay Trilogy
Bloodfire, Prequel to the Chay Trilogy

Copper Snake, Volume One of the San Francisco Trilogy
Voices of Angels, Volume Two of the San Francisco Trilogy
Out of the Ash, Volume Three of the San Francisco Trilogy
Bloodline in Chiaroscuro, Prequel to the San Francisco Trilogy

Saguaro, Volume One of the Arizona Trilogy
Crucifixion Thorn, Volume Two of the Arizona Trilogy

All photographs including cover shot courtesy
of author Gloria H. Giroux.

CRUCIFIXION THORN

VOLUME TWO OF THE ARIZONA TRILOGY

GLORIA H. GIROUX

iUniverse

CRUCIFIXION THORN
VOLUME TWO OF THE ARIZONA TRILOGY

This is a work of fiction. All of the characters, names, incidents, organizations, and dialogue in this novel are either the products of the author's imagination or are used fictitiously.

iUniverse books may be ordered through booksellers or by contacting:

iUniverse
1663 Liberty Drive
Bloomington, IN 47403
www.iuniverse.com
1-800-Authors (1-800-288-4677)

Because of the dynamic nature of the Internet, any web addresses or links contained in this book may have changed since publication and may no longer be valid. The views expressed in this work are solely those of the author and do not necessarily reflect the views of the publisher, and the publisher hereby disclaims any responsibility for them.

Any people depicted in stock imagery provided by Getty Images are models, and such images are being used for illustrative purposes only. Certain stock imagery © Getty Images.

ISBN: 978-1-5320-5199-9 (sc)
ISBN: 978-1-5320-5200-2 (hc)
ISBN: 978-1-5320-5198-2 (e)

Library of Congress Control Number: 2018907852

Print information available on the last page.

iUniverse rev. date: 07/03/2018

MAP OF
ARIZONA
Population——40,440
Area sq. miles__113,929

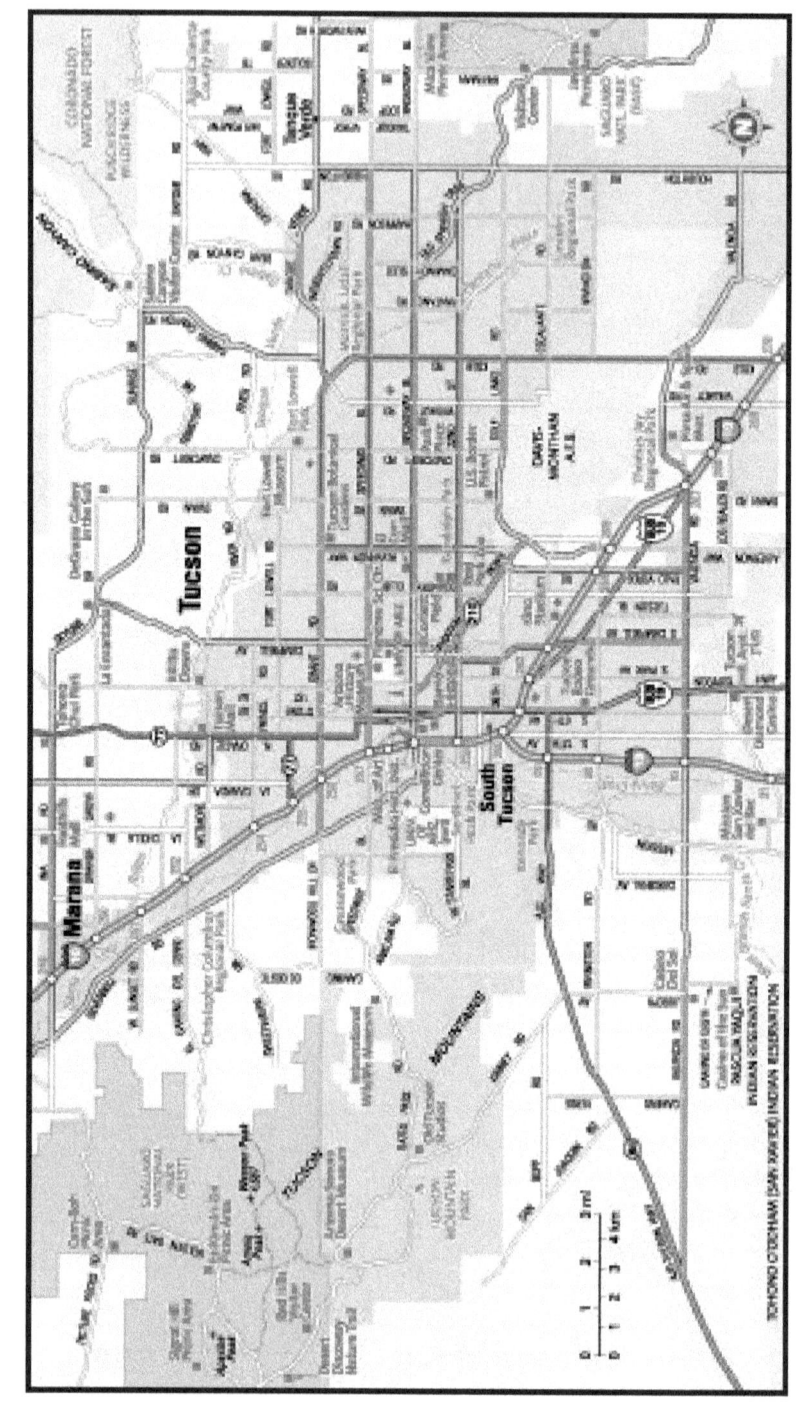

Author's Foreword

I am a writer. It's who I always have been and who I was always meant to be. Writing is as intrinsic to my genetic composition as the DNA that produced my brown hair and hazel eyes. I cannot imagine my life without translating my thoughts into the written word, as I cannot imagine not nourishing this vital part of me through education and life experiences.

There hasn't been a moment in my long memory when books were not part of my life, beginning with those my single mother read to me and encouraged me to read. She placed the highest premium on education, and I strove to acquire as much structured education as possible, in addition to personal education through my city's library. As a teenager I visited that bastion of learning and peace at least once per week, and the two books that truly initiated my love of literature were *Silver Chief: Dog of the North*, and *A Place Called Saturday*. As I progressed through middle school and high school, my thirst for knowledge was slaked by the excellent choices of textbooks I studied in my English, History, and Social Studies courses. I was able to translate my understanding and appreciation of my studies through interpretative and researched term papers that were well-received by my educators. I began my creative writings through the medium of poetry; I wrote my first poem at thirteen.

There was never any consideration of not going to college—that subject wouldn't dare be discussed in our household. After I graduated Hartford's Bulkeley High School with honors, I applied to and was accepted at three colleges: the University of Connecticut, Southern Connecticut State College, and North Adams Teacher's College. I chose the University of Connecticut for its extensive and well-respected English and History programs and matriculated in September 1971. I did not do well in my first semester, primarily because my high school never prepared any of its students for the vast academic differences between high school and college. I learned the hard way what I needed to do to succeed, and in my second semester turned my grades around and made the Dean's List. I performed very well for the remaining tenure of my time as an undergraduate, placing a high emphasis on English literature and personal enlightenment through studying fiction and nonfiction books. I fell in love with Shakespeare. At that time in history, there was no internet or e-books, and reading was restricted to physical books. To this day, I prefer to read such books. Also, since high school I have collected a vast array of paperbacks and hardbacks and have a large personal library in my home.

1975 was a problematic year for job-seeking college graduates—engineering graduates often found their first jobs pumping gas. I decided to forego my Master's right away since I placed a higher imperative on relieving my mother of working two jobs to support both of us as well subsidizing a secondary college education. Unfortunately, I was unable to find any kind of job, so I decided to go back to school to learn a trade whose marketability would secure employment. To that end, I took out a loan and attended the Computer Processing Institute in East Hartford, Connecticut, where, surprisingly, I found myself enjoying and being good at computer programming. After graduation, I applied for a technology job at a Hartford insurance company. I found that I thrived in the early days of computer programming, where primitive tape drives and keypunch cards dominated storage and processing. I acquired quite an intimacy with beepers going off at 2 AM. Although today's technologists would consider that period the dinosaur age, I feel that the restraints of those computers and systems mandated that programmers truly understood logic and could research and resolve issues with intelligence and good reasoning rather than with clicking an icon and letting a machine do the "thinking."

I was part of the technology landscape for forty-one years before retiring in 2017 and have worked at a number of companies in many capacities: programmer, senior analyst, manager, consultant, project manager, and technical writer, to name a few. I have worked with global partners and have traveled all over the world to meet with them and develop the computer systems they required. One may think that such work does not entail many forays into writing: not true. Communication is the linchpin of any successful relationship, business or personal, and a large part of my duties entailed writing documents, e-mails, and other textual components to develop and maintain efficient technology. It is sad to see the dearth of proper English and expression of thoughts in today's technology work; I frequently cringe when reading an e-mail or analysis report. In the last few years I took it upon myself to develop a communication course and present it to several groups to assist them in learning how best to express themselves in verbal, written, and body-language manners. This has been especially necessary due to the many non-American coworkers for whom English is a second language.

In addition to my consistent drive for professional and personal reading and writing, I have made it a goal in my life to travel to and explore as many cultures as possible. To date I have visited thirty-six countries on six continents (I don't do cold—Antarctica is out) and have experienced such remarkable snapshots of life as riding a camel at the pyramids of Giza; ascending fifteen hundred meters up in a hot air balloon over the volcanic region of Turkey; and climbing the Harbour Bridge in Sydney, Australia. My current "Bucket List" goal is to visit forty countries by the year 2020. I purchase and study books from each country so that I can understand the culture and language of each place. I ensure that I learn to speak key words and phrases before I arrive in any country, and actually studied Hindi and Arabic via CD.

My travels serve another purpose—material for my fiction novels. One day in 1987 I couldn't get a thought out of my mind, and simply sat down at my IBM-Compatible computer (5 ¼-inch floppy disks) and began typing. This effort resulted in my first manuscript, which was published years later as *Copper Snake*. The same thing happened on my second novel, *Fireheart*, which became the first entry in a science-fiction trilogy. In both cases, as well as those of my other nine novels, I did not have an outline, or any idea what I would write and how the story would turn out. I sat down, and I wrote. People have asked me where I come up with the plots, characters, and dialogue. I answer honestly—I don't know. The words just come. The plots just come. The characters just come. The dialogues just come.

Crucifixion Thorn is my tenth novel, the second in my Arizona trilogy. I have a third and either a sequel or prequel to go before closing out this series. And then?

I'm a writer—what choice do I have but to continue writing ...

This book is dedicated to family and friends who have supported and encouraged me, and who—in some cases—have wound up in my novels in one way or another. Thank you.

Cast of Returning Characters[1]

Michael "Quint" Quintana:	P.I. in Union Jack Investigations in Tucson, Arizona
Wilde Sinclair:	P.I. in Union Jack Investigations in Tucson, Arizona; life partner to Victor Renard
Victor Renard:	P.I. in Union Jack Investigations in Tucson, Arizona; life partner to Wilde Sinclair
Deliverance Dane:	Partner in Union Jack Investigations in Tucson, Arizona; wife to Michael Quintana
Alejandro "Alex" Dane-Quintana:	Quint's and Deliverance's son; twin to Aislinn
Aislinn Dane-Quintana:	Quint's and Deliverance's daughter; twin to Alejandro
Crescent "Cress" LaChoisi:	Criminology professor at Saguaro Western College, Tucson, Arizona; brother to Phaedra and Constantine and life partner to Gray Kingston
Gray Kingston:	Head of the Anthropology department at Saguaro Western College, Tucson, Arizona; Cress's life partner
Erzsébet "Bliss" Báthory:	Head of the History department at Saguaro Western College, Tucson, Arizona; specializing in cultural witchcraft
Malachi Dillinger:	Head of the Criminology department at Saguaro Western College in Tucson, Arizona; husband to Bliss Báthory

---

[1] Please see the novel *Saguaro* for background on these characters.

Charity Dane:	Deliverance's mother, from Salem, Massachusetts
Nicolae Blaskó:	Deliverance's father, from Salem, Massachusetts
Constantine Black Wolf:	Anthropology professor at Saguaro Western College Tucson, Arizona; brother to Phaedra and Cress
Phaedra Black Wolf Begay:	Owner of a Native American art gallery in Tucson, Arizona; sister to Constantine and Cress
Moon Wolf Begay:	Navajo silver artist in Tucson, Arizona; husband to Phaedra Black Wolf
Reichardt Belzer:	Police Detective in Tucson, Arizona
Aloysius Munch:	Police Detective in Tucson, Arizona
Rupert Ferdinand:	Police Captain in Tucson, Arizona
Santiano Bronson:	Publisher of the newspaper *Old Pueblo Sentinel* in Tucson, Arizona
Laurel Bollmeier:	Reporter on the newspaper *Old Pueblo Sentinel* in Tucson, Arizona
Don Bollmeier:	Police Officer in Tucson, Arizona; husband to Laurel
Mike Beckham:	Police Officer in Tucson, Arizona
Pete Murphy:	Police forensics expert in Tucson, Arizona

Cast of New Characters

Vikki Dane-Quintana:	Quint's and Deliverance's second daughter
Shayne Bulkeley:	Union Jack Investigations Associate in Tucson, Arizona
Turner Jackson:	Union Jack Investigations Associate in Tucson, Arizona
Thayer Burton:	Union Jack Investigations Associate in Tucson, Arizona
Judie Sutphin:	Reporter on the newspaper *Old Pueblo Sentinel* in Tucson, Arizona
Yale Cornell:	Police Detective in Tucson, Arizona
Forest Baxter:	Police Detective in Tucson, Arizona
Mike Welsh:	Police Detective in Tucson, Arizona
Keene Swansey:	Police Detective in Tucson, Arizona
Josie Ross:	Police forensics expert in Tucson, Arizona
Danny Sinclair:	Wilde Sinclair's brother
Raine Sinclair:	Wilde Sinclair's niece by his brother, Danny; computer expert
Beckett Renard:	Victor's thirteen-year-old grandnephew from New Orleans
Bechet (Beh-*shay*) Renard:	Victor's ten-year-old grandnephew from New Orleans
Storm:	Six-year-old orphan
Fox Newberry:	Lawyer working for & at Union Jack Investigations
Tucker Townsend:	Number Eight
Iris Flynn:	FBI agent located in Phoenix, Arizona
Liberty Adams:	FBI agent located in Phoenix, Arizona
Nicholas Lisbon:	FBI agent located in Phoenix, Arizona
Josh Wyllys:	Helicopter pilot in Tucson, Arizona
Rafe Spencer:	Manitou Security Solutions bodyguard in Tucson, Arizona
Honora Waring:	Psychologist in Tucson, Arizona

Cast of Additional Characters[2]

Norah Maguire: Writer, Publisher from San Francisco

Adam Manzone: Private Investigator in San Francisco; Norah's husband

James Danziger: Publisher of the *L.A. Daily Record* newspaper in Los Angeles

Gregory Garrison: Newspaper reporter on the *L.A. Star Herald* in Los Angeles

Griffin Wilder: Newspaper publisher of the *L.A. Star Herald* in Los Angeles

Donna Pallone: Computer master from San Francisco; works for Norah Maguire

Lee Jernigan: Private Investigator in Los Angeles; Adam Manzone's business partner

Richard Ballard: FBI agent located in San Francisco*

Gilead Blackledge: Antiques dealer in New York City

Charlotte Blackledge: Antiques dealer in New York City

---

[2] Please see the novels *Voices of Angels*, *Out of the Ash*, and *Bloodline in Chiaroscuro* for background on these characters. *Please also see the novel *Saguaro* for this character.

PROLOGUE

January 15, 1947, Los Angeles, California

The weather in Los Angeles is temperate in January, ranging from a high of around 64°F down to a low of 46°F, with the average hovering at 55°F. The sea temperature averages somewhere in between, usually around 59°F. It's a fairly rainy month, with rainfall normally reaching 79mm for a total of perhaps six days during the month.

Unfortunately for Angelenos this January and this day were enduring the effects of an unusual cold wave that had gripped the city for several days. Young mother Betty Bersinger, a pretty brunette with thick, wavy hair who wore her locks up in a high, tight twist, and her three-year-old daughter, Anne, were bundled up as they traversed the streets in the Leimert Park section of Los Angeles. The middle-class neighborhood was originally projected as a master-planned community by its progenitor, Walter H. Leimert, in the late 1920s. It was envisioned as a self-contained community with residences, businesses, and cultural events. The community plan was designed by the Omstead Brothers architectural firm established in Brookline, Massachusetts.

Although a significant part of the master plan was successfully executed over the years, there were still sections that were undeveloped. The Bersingers were taking a morning walk around 10 AM and were passing a vacant lot at 39th and Norton Avenues when Mrs. Bersinger spied something white in the bushes. At first, she thought the object was a discarded mannequin; as she went closer she gasped in shock—the object was something entirely different and certainly unexpected. Scared to death, she dragged her daughter away and went to a house where she banged on the door, gasped out her story, and used the resident's telephone to call the police. She was so flustered that she forgot to identify herself.

Gregory Garrison, a twenty-seven-year-old reporter on the *L.A. Star Herald*, was half-listening to his short-wave radio in his car as he drove east on Santa Monica Boulevard towards his small apartment off Wilshire. His radio was the most expensive that could be purchased by a civilian, and his whip antenna was dauntingly long. He had pulled an all-nighter on the Hollywood crime beat and was exhausted. He hated working nights, especially as a newlywed, but he had a living to make, and he worshipped his gruff but honest and fair boss, Griffin Wilder, whose generous employment offer had lured him away from accepting a job on the *L.A. Times*. He snapped to attention when he caught "Code Two" and "a 415;" the 415 indicated indecent exposure and the Code Two meant that it related to a drunk woman. He was close to going home to his loving wife, Amelia, but on a hunch, he swung south on Sepulveda until he hit Slauson and headed east towards Arlington, where he turned north and made his way to the address that came over the air.

There were already several cars and a few dozen people milling about the location on South Norton. He spied a reporter from the *Los Angeles Times* as well as Aggie Underwood of the *Herald-Express*, and Will Fowler and Felix Paegel of the *Los Angeles Examiner*. Aggie was a legend in the business, making great strides for female reporters in this post-World War II cutthroat media world. At a seasoned forty-five she had the energy of a twenty-year-old and had garnered widespread respect when she scooped all other L.A. newspapers with her Amelia Earhart interview, her very first assignment on the *Herald*. She was known for writing about murder and other death cases in the city, and in L.A. in the forties, there was plenty of material to tantalize readers.

Today on this chilly morning she was dressed in a light dress and matching coat, with dark high heels. Her nylon lines were impeccable. She waved to him but basically ignored him as she went about gathering facts and snapping photographs. She was standing in a vacant lot over a couple of lumps of white, scribbling madly as her rapaciously intelligent eyes took in every aspect of the scene. Still, he thought, as he got out of his car and locked the door, she did tend to write text somewhat infused with purplish prose, using garish adjectives to paint colorful pictures of her stories. He doubted that this situation would be any different.

Garrison nearly forgot to take his Leica III camera out of the front seat, but he grabbed it and headed over to the object in the lot. Unlike Will Fowler, he didn't have the luxury of a dedicated photographer. He wrote his own copy and took his own snapshots.

He moved carefully past another reporter to view the woman.

He heard a siren and looked over to see a black-and-white police car pull up and disgorge two uniformed patrolmen.

The closer he got the less likely he thought that this had anything to do with a drunken woman; the lump on the hard-packed earth was … something else. When he got close enough he gasped; his stomach turned over violently. He had been in the war and had seen his share of mayhem and cruelty during his tour in the South Pacific. He had been assigned to write about the January 1945 liberation of the Bataan Death March prisoners in the prison camp at Cabanatuan City in the Philippines; many were living skeletons, many were missing limbs, teeth, and eyes. He had seen the remnants of atrocities committed throughout the Pacific by Japanese forces, including a baby impaled on a stick in a burned-out village. He had cried along with prepubescent girls who described their gang rapes at the hands of soldiers of the Empire of the Sun.

But this … this was something else.

This was no mannequin.

The dead, naked young woman lay sprawled in the dirty lot.

But not in one piece.

The corpse was bisected at the waist, severing the vertebrae and the intestines, the two pieces about a foot apart with the intestines tucked under the top half of the torso out of which peeked part of her liver. It was easy to understand why Mrs. Bersinger thought the body was a mannequin: it was drained of blood, leaving the skin a pallid white. The lack of visible blood around the body suggested strongly that the woman had been killed elsewhere and dumped here. The body itself was mutilated, with large strips of flesh cut away from her thighs and breasts. Her face, framed by blood-matted, dyed black hair extending out from chestnut roots (Garrison recognized this; his wife, Amelia, was a part-time hairdresser while she went to secretarial school) was brutally slashed to mimic the infamous "Glasgow smile" (also known as the "Cheshire grin"), two side slashes from the corners of the mouth to the ears. She was missing several front teeth. She might have been pretty in life; she wasn't in death. Her eyes were initially closed, but someone bent down and pulled back one eyelid and Garrison could see that they were light blue under well-plucked, symmetrical eyebrows.

The body itself had clearly been posed, with the legs grotesquely spread-eagled and her hands thrust up over her head. Whoever had killed her wanted to ensure that she suffered the most humiliation even after death. Garrison felt nothing but pity and horror, and he was certain that his plain face showed his emotions. Aggie and the other reporters seemed impervious to emotion as they snapped pictures and scribbled madly and talked amongst themselves.

More reporters and looky-loos were descending on the scene, and shortly an unmarked police car pulled up. Garrison recognized the two men who got out of the car: LAPD detectives Harry Hansen and Finis Brown. He'd interviewed them before and considered them tough, smart, and honest. Hansen had been on the force for twenty years, joining in 1926 after he gave up on an unimpressive career in vaudeville. He had a long, thick nose and people told him that he looked like Jimmy Durante. Brown was also a longtime officer in the LAPD along with his brother, Thad, who it was said had aspirations of someday becoming Chief of Police. The men had been born in Missouri but had made Los Angeles their home decades earlier. Brown was a sergeant and would oversee the investigation. A bulky man with a long, oval face, eyeglasses, and a warm smile, he was well-regarded within the department.

Garrison figured that crackerjack forensics specialist Ray Pinker would be called in on the gruesome crime. If any team could find the monster that decimated the poor girl on the ground, it was that team.

He managed to snap a half dozen photos before the detectives had the body covered with a blanket, which masked her disarticulation but left her head and feet sticking out. Even so reporters and police officers were tromping all around the death scene, obliterating, Garrison thought, any relevant tire marks or footprints that might help the investigation. That was the downside to the relationship between members of the Fourth Estate and law enforcement; the upside was that there was an intimate camaraderie between them that provided much insight and many inside tips to police investigations. Garrison admitted that he partook of the lackadaisical bond. He had bought three of his favorite detectives and one uniform expensive bottles of whiskey just this past Christmas and the one before and had reaped the benefits when he was given a tip in July 1946 about the discovery of Gertrude Evelyn Landon, thirty-six, a missing Los Angeles woman who was found half-buried in a gravel pit in the Wilmington Shipyard. Garrison's incisive, well-researched article garnered him a five-dollar-a-week-raise.

Garrison remained at the site for the next hour as the crowd swelled and many law enforcement personnel descended. He had a brief conversation with Aggie, who was eager to get back to her office and write up her article. She mentioned using a "werewolf" allusion to the perpetrator. He couldn't wait to read her text any more than he could wait to get back to the *Star Herald* and start pounding away on his own Royal Quiet Deluxe typewriter, one of the last models to roll off the assembly line before production suspended temporarily due to World War II. Production had started again, but he liked his 1040 model for the office; Amelia had bought him a new one for home just this past Christmas.

He meandered around the neighborhood trying to find anyone who might be a witness, but he had no luck. He'd wanted to interview the woman who called in the body, but the police had apparently whisked her off for their own interrogation. He managed to sneak past a uniformed officer and have a few words with the resident who'd let the woman use his telephone to call the cops. All he got from that was a description of the lady and her kid, and a few tidbits about her shocked demeanor. He might be able to weave those impressions into his article, but he liked to keep away from emotionalism and stick to cold, hard facts. At least the guy was nice enough to let Garrison call his wife and say he wouldn't be home any time soon.

The coroner took the body away and Garrison tried to get a quote from Hansen or Brown, but to no avail. He noticed that they were polite and jovial to Aggie and Fowler. They probably thought of him just as an upstart kid. Someday he'd prove them all wrong when he owned and published his own newspaper.

He drove to the *Star Herald* office. The usual morning crowd was there and most waved to him as he got a cup of strong coffee and dropped down into his uncomfortable swivel chair, which was on its last legs. He glanced to his left; Wilder wasn't in his office yet but should be there any time. He dialed the photography department and had them send a kid up to retrieve his film and develop it pronto. He threaded a piece of paper into his typewriter and stared at it for a moment, trying to decide on the headline he wanted. He thought about, "Murdered Woman in Leimert Park;" that would be the least salacious combination of words that would indicate the basic nature of the crime. Still, it wouldn't catch the eye. He kept thinking, then finally sighed, and typed out the headline one slow letter at a time: "Horrific Torture Slaying of Innocent Young Girl." He hated the purple prose-like infusion of the grim adjective, but, as Griffin Wilder said, they were there to sell papers, not be the moral arbiters of the reading public.

The body of the article came fast and furious, although in his haste he made several typos and had to ruin the cleanliness of the paper with cross-outs and handwritten inserts. He had barely finished the first page when he sensed a figure looming over him and his neck snapped around to see a cigar-chomping Griffin Wilder scowling down at him. Without a word Wilder tore the paper out of the typewriter and scanned it, his facial expressions ranging from a deep scowl to surprise as he relentlessly chewed on his cigar.

Death came to a quiet neighborhood named Leimert Park early this morning with the gruesome discovery of a woman's ravaged body. Neatly bisected in two, the marble-white corpse was once a young woman in her early twenties. Possibly beautiful in life with curly, dark hair and once-symmetrical features, her murderous killer not only took her life but her beauty as well. Her face was savagely slashed, as were her extremities. Her internal organs ...

This murder was beyond shocking, beyond cruel, beyond any semblance of humanity.

Police are attempting to identify this poor young woman, and any help the public can provide would be ...

He handed the sheet back to Garrison.

"Identity?" Wilder barked.

"Unknown. I'll give Beltran a call after I finish the first draft." Roderigo Beltran was a rookie cop from East L.A. with an abundance of enthusiasm tempered by a deep well of cunning and the willingness to sell information for a price; Beltran had given him the tip on the Landon murder. "You want this to go out tomorrow morning?"

"You think the *Herald-Express* or the *Examiner* will wait? Hell, no. They'll put out a special afternoon edition and that's exactly what we're gonna do. Get that copy down to Roger right now and have him set it with the most gruesome photo you took. The broad naked?"

"Very naked. Very dead."

"Shit. Then show her from the neck up but no tits or snatch, got it?"

"Got it, boss."

"Put a subtitle under it askin' if anyone knows her and print our phone number next to it. Maybe we'll get lucky." With that Wilder whirled around, stubbed out his cigar on entertainment reporter Cal Bean's ashtray, and went into his office, slamming the door.

Garrison finished the story in five minutes and ran it down to proofreading where he stood over a middle-aged woman who read faster than he ever could and used her red pen to swipe across typos and rearrange grammar and syntax. She shoved it back to him and he ran to Roger who already had a set of photos. They selected one that showed part of the corpse but no real nakedness.

Garrison was done with his part and breathed a sigh of relief. He called Amelia and told her he'd be home by eleven and he was starving. She said she'd have his favorite beef stew ready and waiting. Christ, he thought—he loved that woman. He couldn't wait to have a family with her.

He finished up a few tasks and called Beltran, who told him that the detectives had already started pulling in dozens of men to interrogate. The FBI had been contacted to see if they had any hits on the dead woman's fingerprints, which had been transmitted to them with that newfangled machine called Soundphoto. Beltran said he'd call Garrison if anything broke, especially since the autopsy was scheduled for the next day.

Garrison went home to Amelia and her cooking. He finished two huge bowls of stew and nearly a quart of orange juice before he slipped off his shoes and lay down on the couch for a brief nap. She awakened him four hours later when the afternoon edition of the newspaper came out with his story on the front page. She said that Wilder called and said the edition had nearly sold completely out.

A couple of hours later Beltran called and whispered that the victim had been identified. He hedged about providing the name, but they quickly settled on a case of tequila and fifty bucks.

The FBI had come through more quickly than anyone thought. They identified the woman by a set of prints from a 1943 arrest for underage drinking at a Santa Barbara bar. Nineteen–year-old Elizabeth Short was born as one of five daughters in Boston, Massachusetts, although her mother lived in Medford and that was where the authorities sent the teenager when they released her. Somehow, at some time, she had returned to California and had met her fate. Beltran said more details would follow, and to put the five ten-dollar bills in an envelope in the usual drop-off place. Garrison thanked him and called Wilder, who told him to get his ass into the office and write an article for the morning edition. Reluctantly, Garrison kissed Amelia goodbye and went back to work.

The wet-behind-the-ears, eager office gofer smacked a few newspapers down on Garrison's desk and he scanned the various stories. As he'd thought, Aggie had purple-prosed her article with tantalizing adjectives and assumptions.

The modern counterpart of a medieval torture chamber, in which a slim, attractive young girl writhed for hours before her brutal murder by a maniacal "werewolf" killer, was sought by homicide detectives today.

The butchered torso, hacked in two at the waist, was found yesterday in a vacant lot in a Los Angeles "lover's lane."

Like the victims of predatory killers assuming the form of a wolf in ancient folklore, the body was gashed and mutilated almost beyond recognition.

Garrison grinned at the article; Aggie was one of a kind. Will Fowler's article in the *Los Angeles Examiner* was titled "Girl Tortured and Slain." He shook his head, hating himself for falling into the trap of salaciousness that garnered headlines, but that was his job. Now his job was to find out everything he could about the victim, Miss Elizabeth Short.

Over the next few days he and every reporter on the crime beat were diving into the same background territory. He'd gathered quite a lot of material on the victim; born in Boston on July 29, 1924, she'd died at the tender age of twenty-two. Subject to bronchitis and asthma, she relocated to a warmer climate for health reasons part of each year, living during the winters in Miami. Her father, who had abandoned the family when she was a child, lived in California and Elizabeth—better known as Betty—moved in with him. It didn't go well, and after her arrest she spent a little time back in Medford but found that Florida was a better match for her temperament and life in general. She became engaged to an Army Air Force officer who died before they could be married, and once again she found her way back to the City of Angels where she worked as a waitress while waiting and hoping to become a movie star.

Over the week after the discovery of the body and its identity, law enforcement and the press had explored dozens of avenues for clues to the mysterious young woman and her possible killer, or killers. Aggie Underwood as well as other intrepid reporters tried to make a connection between Short's murder and those of not only Landon, but other murdered women whose killers had not been found, such as Ora Murray and Georgettte Bauerdorf.

The last known sighting of Elizabeth Short was at the Biltmore Hotel in Los Angeles, where a married lover had dropped her off to meet her visiting sister. From there, she vanished into notoriety and history. Although law enforcement had promised an early resolution to the identity and punishment of the killer, the killer was never identified let alone found. Whoever he was, he, too, faded away into history, perhaps to wield his special brutality somewhere else.

Gregory Garrison followed the story for years, writing his last article on the murder nearly three years later at the tail-end of the 1940s decade. He considered the article his best, the result of years of research and probing. The day before the article was to be published, it was quashed, and he was fired for the second time by one James Danziger, who bought out Griffin Wilder (with underhanded tactics, Wilder groused to anyone who would listen to him), assumed control over the *Star Herald* and changed its name to the *L.A. Daily Record*. Danziger fired a number of longtime employees, including Garrison. The reporter's work was the "property" of the newspaper, so he couldn't take it to another publication as he removed his typewriter, his framed picture of Amelia, and other miniscule items from his desk and was walked out of the building under guard. He was angry and frustrated, but he had other fish to fry as he pursued his career. The article and the murder faded from the forefront of his mind, although it was never fully eliminated from that honeycomb cell in his brain that cataloged and stored every story he'd ever worked on, every victim, every injustice. He managed to write and sell a freelance article on the fifth anniversary of the murder, and he was interviewed about the crime by a young writer, Helen Bean, who was writing a book on the event and the aftermath. He thought of Elizabeth Short every so often, but he thought of her by another name.

The name that had been bestowed on the victim by her pre-death physicality—particularly her dyed ebony hair—and those who remembered her from various locations around town, including a soda shop in Long Beach, would remain written in notoriety, especially since her murder was never solved.

The Black Dahlia.

BOOK ONE

"Land of extremes. Land of contrasts. Land of surprises. Land of contradictions. A land that is never to be fully understood but always to be loved by sons and daughters sprung from such a diversity of origins, animated by such a diversity of motives and ideals, that generations must pass before they can ever fully understand each other. That is Arizona."

Arizona: A State Guide, compiled by Workers of the Writers' Program of the Work Projects Administration in the State of Arizona, 1940

Crucifixion Thorn, Scottsdale, Arizona

1

CHAPTER ONE

September 16, 1983, Tucson, Arizona

Wilde Sinclair stretched under the bedcovers as he awakened Friday morning, turning over on his side as he sighed and thought that he just wanted to stay in bed. He heard a soft giggle and opened one eye to find two identical pairs of sapphire-blue eyes staring at him, wide grins on two five-year-old faces framed by coal-black, silky hair; hers, down to the small of her back and his just at shoulder-length.

"Told ya he was awake," Alejandro Dane-Quintana said to his sister, Aislinn, as he elbowed her in the side just before he climbed onto the bed and snuggled between Wilde and his life partner, Victor Renard. In two seconds he was followed by Aislinn, who cuddled close to an awakening Victor. She threw her arm over Victor's chest. He was her favorite and the adoration was mutual.

"Mommy said to get your butts in gear and come over for breakfast," she said.

"Those were her exact words?" Victor asked laughingly as he hugged the little girl and made her squeal by rubbing his close-cropped salt-and-pepper beard against her soft cheek.

"No, she said asses. Daddy said to use butts," Aislinn replied. She sprang up and tried pulling Victor's hands. "Up, up, Uncle Victor," she exclaimed. "The pancakes will get cold." She jumped out of bed and hopped around, joined by her kinetic brother as they chanted "Up! Up!" over and over again.

Wilde grinned and threw his long legs over the mattress, yawned, then rose and told them he was going to take a fast shower and then he and Victor would come over for pancakes. He shooed them away and they ran screaming out of the house and back to their own next door.

"Petits lutins," Victor said, shaking his head as he slipped out of bed, shrugging out of his tee-shirt and boxers to reveal the still-ripped physique of the fifty-year-old black man who could have come off Mount Olympus if Mount Olympus was deep in the heart of Africa—or New Orleans, Victor's hometown.

"Imps doesn't quite cover it." Wilde laughed as he went into the bathroom, stripped, and turned on the shower. He smiled as he sensed his lover come up behind him. Victor put his arms around Wilde's waist and nuzzled his neck.

"May I join you?" Victor asked.

"If I have no other choice," Wilde sighed melodramatically.

"You don't," Victor said as he stepped around Wilde and into the steaming hot deluge.

The two longtime life partners spent a solid ten minutes washing each other before ending the shower with a quick but satisfying bout of lovemaking. They dried off, Wilde shaved, and they dressed in their best business garb—Victor in his favorite three-piece charcoal suit with a lavender shirt and purple silk tie, and Wilde in navy-blue pants and jacket with a white shirt, maroon tie, and red suspenders (or braces, as he called them). They were usually a little less formal, but when meeting a new client for the first time they always put on their best front. Of course, getting Quint to put on his "best" was generally a losing battle; their partner thought that crisp new jeans, a checkered gingham shirt, and a bolo tie constituted "getting dressed up."

They walked next door to the Dane-Quintana house where their business partners in the private investigation firm, Union Jack Investigations, lived with their twins and their two-year-old second daughter, Charity Victoria Erzsébet, named after Deliverance's mother, Victor, and Bliss (her real given name).

As soon as they entered the back sliding door which opened to the great room and the kitchen they smelled the delectable scents of Deliverance's cooking. She had a top-of-the-line kitchen, gradually updated from the original one when she and her husband, Michael Quintana, bought the house in 1978. This was her domain, and Quint stayed as far away from the culinary hubbub as possible, choosing instead to concentrate on the "manly" tasks of maintaining the property and doing cosmetic work such as painting and building bookcases and shelves per his wife's demands. The previous weekend he had been struggling and cursing up on the roof as he installed a huge new state-of-the-art TV antenna; the next day he repeated the process up on Victor's and Wilde's roof.

Deliverance scowled at the two men as she bustled about her kitchen, flipping pancakes and tending to the succulent, thick-cut bacon. Her husband was a die-hard meat-eater, and he never felt really satisfied at the morning meal unless he had bacon, ham, or sausage piled high on his plate alongside a mountain of scrambled eggs and two thick slices of rye bread toast.

"Sit," she commanded her friends and they immediately complied. Even though she was still a callow twenty-eight and only reached five-foot-nothing in heels, the tiny terror was a force with which to be reckoned. She kept her men and her kids in line with an iron hand, but had a soft, gooey side to her that mitigated their basic fear of retribution. And, she was a psychic Wiccan, more facets to her unusual life and personality.

But what made them toe the line this week was that it was "her friggin' cycle" (as Quint called it) and Deliverance with hormones raging was most definitely something to be feared. She was even wearing a custom tee-shirt that made her mood very clear: "I Have PMS and Can Turn You Into a Toad. Any Questions?" With her eerie amber eyes and her waist-length, honey-blonde hair swirling about her head like a demented version of the old Farrah 'do, she gave the appearance of a mad valkyrie ready for battle.

One twin jumped up on each lap as they usually did when Wilde and Victor came over for a meal. Their titular uncles were a dedicated part of their young lives since birth, and since Wilde and Victor were gay and couldn't have children of their own, the two men showered their affection and care on the twins and their baby sister. Aislinn's full name was Aislinn Maximiliana Luisa, after Quint's mother, late aunt, and late cousin. Alejandro's middle names were Carlos Wilde, after Quint's late uncle and, of course, after his friend and business partner of many years, the man who had introduced him to his wife. Little blonde-haired, brown-eyed Vikki was sitting peacefully in her highchair, focused on manually grabbing her scrambled eggs and shoving them into her mouth—or all over her face, as the case might be.

"Where's your other half?" Wilde asked as Deliverance flipped three humongous pancakes onto his plate before moving her pan and spatula over to Victor. He reached over the table and snagged the warm maple syrup. He noticed the bookmarked hardback on the table next to her plate: *The Long Storm*, by critically acclaimed writer and publisher Norah Maguire. He knew that she had picked the book up at Bookmans the previous day and was already halfway through it. Their friend, Norah, had written the bestseller about a stunning nonfiction tale of adultery, vengeance, kidnapping, murder, and decades-old consequences relating to one of her friends, photographer Zack Lassiter (now Zack Prescott) and his family.[3] Norah's husband, Adam Manzone, was a former 'Nam-mate of Quint's.

"He's in the garage changing the oil in his new baby and blasting Michael Jackson's *Thriller* at the top volume of his stereo. If I hear *Beat It* one more time, I'm gonna throw him out of the house," she replied as she flipped one pancake onto each child's plate and told them to scoot to their own places. Reluctantly they did; no one messed with Mommy as they learned from a short lifetime of experience.

Quint's "new baby" was his brand-new, beige-colored Dodge 400 convertible. He refused to give up his 1972 Cougar, but he'd seen the Dodge in a dealership window and couldn't resist even though technically he had been looking for a good station wagon for his wife since her Cutlass had died a natural death. He didn't discuss the purchase with his wife, who, upon seeing him pull into their driveway with the new car, top down, gave him a disapproving scowl then loaded the kids into the back seat and told him to take them for a ride. They drove up the Catalina Highway to Mount Lemmon, and by the time they returned Deliverance told him he could keep the car. He went back the following week and picked up a light-blue Plymouth station wagon for her. She was appropriately mollified.

As Deliverance poured syrup on her kids' pancakes she asked Alex, "What's the word of the day?" Deliverance taught them a new word each day when they woke up to stimulate their imaginations.

"Phantasmagoria," her son said. He took a bite of his pancake.

"Spell it," she said. He complied without hesitation—and accurately. She rubbed his hair, and he preened.

"And your word?" she asked Aislinn who had just stuffed a huge piece of pancake into her mouth; syrup was dripping down her chin. She quickly wiped it off and replied, "Onomatopoeia." Before

---

[3] Please see the novel *Copper Snake* for the Lassiter/Prescott story.

her mother could ask *that* question, she admitted, "No way in hell I can spell that, Mommy."

"Where do you pick up that kind of language?" Deliverance snapped.

"Yeah, I wonder," Victor whispered loudly to Wilde. She threw him a disapproving frown.

"You both have your outfits ready for tonight's party, right?" she asked. Today was the celebration of Mexican Independence Day, and the extended family was scheduled to join a few old friends for dinner, dancing, and music. Little Victoria would be left in the care of a babysitter, but the twins would accompany their parents, dressed in full Mexican regalia as homage to their father's paternal ethnicity. His maternal ethnicity was honored on St. Patrick's Day when the kids were dressed as leprechauns.

"As if we'd dare be unprepared," Victor mumbled as he chewed a blueberry pancake swathed in maple syrup and melted butter and mentally ran over his outfit in his mind: a Spanish bullfighter, complete with floor-length red cape. He had stubbornly chosen the outfit despite Deliverance's scowl and tart jab at his choice to appear as a "murderer of innocent, terrified animals." He checked his watch. "We need to be at the office by nine to meet a new client."

"Fine, if you're not interested in finishing the pancakes I slaved over a hot stove to prepare," she said as she whipped Victor's plate out from under his fork with one hand and Wilde's plate with the other.

"Hey," Wilde said. "I'm not in a rush. I wish to finish those magnificent efforts of your hot stove. Please," he pleaded with big, blue puppy-dog eyes that sometimes made him look like a callow teenager instead of a forty-two-year-old British expatriate. He ran his fingers through his long auburn hair and hoped that his outfit, that of an Aztec warrior, would meet with his partner's approval.

"I'd like to finish, too," Victor said, contrite.

"I thought so," she said, slamming the plates back down.

The front doorbell rang and Aislinn screamed, "I'll get it!" and scampered off to see who was ringing the bell at such an early hour. She was gone for about five minutes before her mother yelled out to her.

Aislinn tromped back into the kitchen carrying a small, square cardboard box. "Someone left this on the doorstep, Mommy," she said. "I didn't see no one around."

"Anyone," Deliverance corrected automatically. As a star in her college English class she was determined that her kids would use proper grammar. She had quit high school at sixteen and always regretted the disruption of her education. Her kids would never experience that situation and regret or be forced to get a GED instead of a regular diploma. She had already set her sights on Harvard for both twins, and Stanford for Vikki. She was setting an example for them and achieving a goal for herself: she was halfway through the curriculum necessary to acquire her Bachelor's degree in Psychology at Saguaro Western College.

"Give that to me, Aislinn," she said, stretching out her slender arms.

Aislinn pouted but handed the box to her mother. Deliverance looked down into it and shrieked and dropped it, backing up into the refrigerator, her face a mask of shock and revulsion.

The decapitated head rolled out of the box and came to rest face-up against the island cabinet. Wilde and Victor shot out of their seats.

Alejandro slid off his chair and ran over to see. "Cool," he said. He looked at his sister with rapt anticipation. "Any more body parts out there? Wait'll Daddy sees this."

"Just this," Aislinn said shyly. She held out a severed finger and handed it to Victor.

Victor gingerly took the finger and looked at Wilde. "I think we'd better get Macho Man in here. Kids," he said, looking at the rapt twins who were eagerly focused on the head, "maybe you should head off to your room and get ready for school."

"Aww," the twins chimed in unison.

"Haul ass," their mother snapped, and they ran like hell. She turned to Wilde. "Go out and drag my old man in here. I want him to see this before we call the cops." An evil smile curled her lips. "We'll call Belzer and Munch. Aloysius hasn't had any exciting cases since the ax murders."[4]

---

[4] Please see the first novel in this trilogy, *Saguaro*.

Wilde absconded to do her bidding as she and Victor stared down at the head.

"Shit," she said. "This better not fuck up our dinner plans tonight. I got me a hankering for a chimichanga." She looked at her partner. "You want another pancake?"

Aloysius Munch was a creature of habit. He liked being a creature of habit; reveled in it, actually. He watched the *Today* show every weekday morning and was comforted by the soothing synchronicity of hosts Jane Pauley and Bryant Gumbel, news anchor John Palmer, and weatherman Fred Willard. He watched the *NBC Nightly News* each night, and was just getting used to anchor Tom Brokaw, although he did miss David Brinkley. His Sunday night was centered around *60 Minutes*, and he worshipped Andy Rooney, who had a persnickety personality quite similar to his.

His wife made meatloaf and mashed potatoes for dinner every Thursday (except Thanksgiving); they had other regular dining options for a few other weekdays and went out to dinner on Sundays. He took his coffee strong and black, drank whiskey like an Irishman, and thought wine was for women and sissies. He loved apple pie and celebrated each Jewish holiday in temple. He donated to his temple regularly, had performed an act of tzedakah several times, and volunteered four times a year at the neighborhood soup kitchen. He held the United States Marines and his service within in the highest esteem and had a Marine Corps tattoo spread across his upper right arm. He had never lost his craving for a good Coney Island knish, the kind he used to eat regularly during his childhood and youth in Babylon, New York. If he had one serious complaint about living in the desert southwest it was that decent delis were few and far between.

He had three basic loves in his life, in this order: his wife, his children, and his job. He had been married to Pamela for twenty-four years, and they had three children: Belinda, twenty-two, an ER nurse at the Sisters of Mercy Hospital; Karin, twenty, a junior at Saguaro Western College studying communications; and Aloysius, Junior, seventeen. He adored his daughters, but his son—his son was the center of his paternal universe. Five years earlier the young man had gone through a savage bout of cancer and chemotherapy, and against all odds had survived. He was in his senior year of high school and planned on matriculating at the University of Arizona the following year. Aloysius, Junior wanted to study medicine, and become an oncologist. Aloysius, Senior longed for the day when he could proudly boast, "My son, the doctor."

Aloysius also loved his longtime partner, detective Reichardt Belzer, with whom he'd been paired for thirteen years. People often referred to them as "Mutt and Jeff" because of their disparate physicality: Belzer was tall and had a physique like a beanpole; Munch was shorter and stockier. Both had receding hairlines and secretly resented men whose locks were thick and healthy, like those damn partners in Union Jack Investigations.

Both men also shared steel-trap, sharp minds and overwhelming compassion for victims and their families. Both men presented professional, objective faces to the world as they did their jobs, but each cried in the privacy of his homes for those they could not save, those victims who were doomed from the first moment a predator set his sights on them.

Today, his beloved *Today* show was interrupted by a telephone call from private investigator Victor Renard, who politely requested his presence in the Quintana kitchen. He grumbled and cursed because he was riveted to the show as the news spilled out about the aftermath of the Soviets shooting down the South Korean airliner on September 1st. He didn't trust the Russkies, never had; they were all "Russkies" to him no matter where they were in the Soviet Union. President Reagan was on the money when he called it "the evil empire." As if that wasn't bad enough, it appeared that the country he loved might be embroiled in covert operations in the Nicaraguan war. And, the U.S. negotiators still hadn't arranged a cease-fire between the Lebanese Army and Syrian-backed Druse militiamen. The world seemed to be going as crazy as it had been during the Vietnam War.

Pamela soothed his ruffled feathers by promising to video tape the rest of the program on their new VCR, a JVC HR7100 that he had yet to master. Thankfully, his wife and son were more technically inclined, and had enjoyed programming the beast with their super expensive VHS tapes, which cost a stunning $20 apiece (Pamela had splurged on his birthday and had bought a VHS movie for him for

9

a whopping $69: *First Blood*, with Stallone; he loved Stallone). He had wanted to buy a Betamax machine, but he had been overruled, and since it appeared from recent newspaper and trade magazine articles that beta was going to fall under the VHS onslaught, he had probably lucked out.

Pamela kissed him goodbye, and he scowled his way to his beautiful and treasured banana-yellow 1980 Cadillac El Dorado coupe. Sure, it was probably too much car for a lowly detective, but he fell in love with it in the police impound lot and bought it in a moment of uncharacteristic emotion. Pamela had frowned at him when he brought it home, but that only lasted until their first smooth drive in it up to Phoenix to watch Aloysius, Junior, play in a high school basketball game.

Munch drove over to the Quintana house alone. Belzer was nowhere to be found and wasn't answering his beeper. He wished they were together when he knocked loudly on the door and Michael Quintana admitted him into the inner sanctum. He had been to the house several times before, twice on business and twice for a holiday barbecue.

Quint led him into the kitchen where the other Union Jack partners were gathered around the kitchen island. Deliverance was petting her weird, green-eyed black cat, Pyewacket, who was curled up on the island licking his double paws and ignoring the silly humans. The two Quintana dogs, a chocolate lab named Cocoa and an Irish setter named Cork, were lounging by the back door, longingly eyeing the back yard where a hapless bunny was sitting and nibbling on sunflower seeds that the mistress of the house had dispersed the night before, unaware that he was being scoped out as an entrée.

Munch stared down at the head on the floor, taking in the salient points. It appeared to be a woman's head, with long black hair and mascaraed eyelashes (on the other hand, Munch thought sourly, the hair and makeup didn't rule out men nowadays if that UK fella, Boy George, and that rock group, Aerosmith, were any indication of the new fashion look for men). There was only one eye—the left one had been completed gouged out. He gently edged the other one's eyelid back and the semi-milky eye seemed as if it might have once been dark blue.

The head was neatly severed with about two inches of throat showing; the decapitation was close to the collarbone. There were traces of blood around the severance, but none on the face itself. There were no bruises on the face; however, there were upward slashes at each side of the mouth, aimed towards the ears.

Munch sighed theatrically. "You couldn't just call 9-1-1, could you? You had to call me."

"We couldn't think of anyone better to handle a weird case," Wilde said amiably, "and we knew you'd be craving one since the Axewoman killings. Face it, Aloysius—you're a danger junkie, a man who needs excitement, thrills—"

"A taste of the bizarre," Victor interjected.

"Blood, guts," Quint added. "We figured that you could use a little professional boost."

"I don't need excitement, thrills, or dead bodies. Especially dead heads," Munch grumbled as he walked over to the kitchen phone and began dialing. He threw Quint a nasty look. "I hate you." He hung up the receiver after he sent Murphy a beeper message.

"I know," Quint replied sympathetically.

"All of you," Munch added just as Pete Murphy called back. "Pete? Get your crime scene analysts over to the Quintana house. I have a job for you. Be discreet—no sirens. What? No, nothing to do with axes. Just get your mick ass in gear." With that he hung up and faced Quint.

"So, who found the head?" Munch asked as he eyed the plate of cold blueberry pancakes on the table.

"Our daughter," Deliverance said. "Someone rang the front doorbell. She went to answer it and found the box and brought it back in."

"The kid okay?" Munch asked, sincerely concerned. A five-year-old finding a decomposing head could be traumatizing.

"She's fine," Deliverance said. "She's a tough kid. Didn't even faze her or Alex." She reached into her apron pocket. "Here. She found this, too." She handed Munch the severed finger encased in a plastic baggie.

"Jeez," Munch said as he took the finger and stared at it. He frowned at Quint. "Any more body parts?"

11

"Not that we know of," Quint said. "Wilde and I scoured the front property and the rear and found nothing. Aislinn said she didn't see anyone around when she picked up the box. Since she would have seen a car take off, I'm assuming our gift-giver made off on foot at least for a distance. By the way, where's Belzer?"

"Not a clue. I beeped him a coupla times. Don't you trust me to work this solo?" Munch grinned.

"I have as much trust in you as you do in me," Quint replied casually. They had once worked together before Quint resigned his detective shield after his own partner's murder, fell off the grid for a few months, then joined Wilde Sinclair in the latter's private investigations firm to solve a series of vicious ax murders that held Tucson in thrall for eighteen months.

"I'll let that one go," Munch said. He squinted at Deliverance. "Any … impressions from the box? You held it, right?" Munch was skeptical—always would be—but Deliverance was a self-professed psychic who did seem to have odd insights when least expected. Five years ago, when Junior was battling cancer she told him without any hint of uncertainty that the boy would be all right. She'd also had quite a few dead-on insights into the ax murders case that couldn't be explained away rationally.

"Not really," she answered. "Maybe if I touched the head."

"Not a chance," Belzer said as he walked into the kitchen. He smiled tightly. "The door was open, so I invited myself in. What time did the kid find the box?"

"Seven thirty-six," Deliverance answered. "What? I noted the clock when the head fell out. Oh, good, more fuzz," she sighed as Pete Murphy and two of his forensic associates joined the growing kitchen crowd faster than they'd expected.

"It's always nice to be appreciated," Murphy said. "Josie's outside processing the stoop and yard. We were only a mile away at another scene. Burglary and vandalism. Second one in the neighborhood."

"Any media in sight?"

"Not yet."

"Great," Deliverance said. "So, finish up fast so you can all leave. We have work to do and a party to get ready for." She stopped dead still for a brief second as an odd rush of electricity ran up her spine. She shook her head; probably just a reaction to this weird situation.

"You having the Independence Day celebration here?" Belzer asked absently as he studied the head. He and Murphy were squatted down next to it; Murphy was taking photos.

"Mariposa Linda's," Victor said. "You and your wives want to come?"

"Not me, but thanks," Munch said. He didn't much care for Mexican food anyway, and Friday night was deep-fried cod and chips night at the Munch house.

"I …" Belzer began, then stopped. "Thanks, but I … I have a commitment. Let's get this wrapped up so we can leave these poor people to what's left of their breakfast." Like Munch, he eyed the cold pancakes. He nodded towards them. "Mind if I nosh?"

"Feel free," Quint said. He turned to Victor. "Can you drop the kids off at school?"

"Sure." At the top of his voice he called out to the twins. "Allons-y, les enfants, maintenant."

"They speak French?" Munch asked, surprised.

"I'm teaching them," Victor said. "By the time they're ten they'll sound like Parisian natives. I'm also teaching Alex piano."

"Lucky kids," Belzer said just as the twins in question dashed into the kitchen. He chewed on a rolled-up pancake that he'd swiped through a pool of maple syrup. He thought that he needed to talk to Quint privately about something that had no relation to this situation; maybe at the station when they were alone.

"Cool," Alex said. "The head's still here. Can we touch it?"

"No," his father, mother, uncles, and the police said at the same time.

"That sucks the big one," Alex muttered.

"Alejandro Carlos Wilde Dane-Quintana," his mother admonished. "Don't use that kind of goddamn language, hear me?"

"Yes, ma'am," her son muttered faux-contritely.

"All right. Off you go. And Alex—I don't want to have to come down there and extract you from the principal's office because you stuffed little Darren's head in his desk again. Scoot."

Victor grinned and ushered the kids out back where he led them through their mutual yards to his car. The school was only five blocks away. He'd head over to the office right after he dropped them off.

Belzer stood over the head as Murphy continued processing it before they'd take it to the lab for further examination. He squinted at Deliverance. "We're going to need statements from all of you. Think you can grant me the honor of your presence at the station right now?"

She nodded. "I'll go but you'll have to wait for Quint's and Wilde's statements. They have to go to the office." At that moment Yolanda Rojas, their nineteen-year-old babysitter for Vikki, walked into the kitchen, saw the head, screamed, and fled, slamming the front door in her wake.

"Well, fuck," Deliverance said. "There goes another one. Looks like the Vikster is going to be spending the day at the office with us. And we'll need to find another babysitter. I don't think number five is coming back."

CHAPTER TWO

Indian summer is a period traditionally associated with autumn, when the weather is unusually warm and dry. Autumn was a few weeks off on this bright Tucson day, but Victor thought that the weather was everything it could be as the weekend encroached and the holiday celebrations would kick off and probably last until Monday. On the other hand, he thought, the typical Indian summer weather was typical Tucson weather after the dog days of August; warm, sunny, pretty damn perfect.

He was also aware of and agreed with the secondary meaning of the term, relating to a period of happiness, contentment, or success occurring in one's later life. At fifty, he was experiencing an early Indian summer in the air and in his life.

He dropped the Dane-Quintana twins off at their kindergarten, then headed off to the office where he'd been part of the Union Jack team since 1978. Deliverance had moved them from their original tiny offices in a strip mall on Broadway to a larger suite of rooms on Swan south of Sunrise. When their business began growing after they'd solved the shocking set of ax murders in 1977-1978, they needed increased personnel and personal space. Rather than move again, the building itself came up for sale and she negotiated a sweet deal with the owner. The other tenants' leases were up soon, and Deliverance choose not to renew them, taking the rest of the two-story building for their operation. Under her direction and redecorating choices (none of her men chose to argue with her) she rearranged the offices on the second floor for the four partners, knocking out a few walls to double the sizes of all four partners' work spaces. She hired an architect to redesign the offices on the first floor for their subsidiary sections, including new associates' smaller offices, a darkroom, and a business center complete with state-of-the art computers and word processors. The occasionally needed "babysitting" room was upstairs and adjoined her spacious office, which had the best view of the Santa Catalina Mountains in the north.

Deliverance had upgraded their burgeoning technology with new personal computers for herself, the men, and two of their new associates just the previous year. None of them, of course, had the faintest idea of which machine was best, but Quint remembered that Adam had said his wife, Norah Maguire, had established a computer firm called Maguire Computer Solutions (MCS). Quint and Norah talked and came to a business agreement and the next day an unusual woman named Donna Pallone appeared on the Union Jack doorstep; tall, raw-boned, frizzy-haired, big-eared, wearing huge eyeglasses and a Klingon tee-shirt and carrying a *Star Trek* tote out of which peeked a few furry tribbles and comic books, she was not what anyone would expect of a technology professional. She cloistered herself with Deliverance for a half day as they discussed company needs and finances. They decided that they'd upgrade the Union Jack offices with the same computers that Donna had used for Norah's companies and Adam's private investigations firm.

Donna ordered nine brand new IBM personal computers (six for the office, and one each for Wilde, Victor, and Deliverance to use at home; Quint was useless with technology) complete with the main processors, monitors, keyboards, and printers for a massive $1,565 each, and two extra Apple III personal computers as backups as well as a stock of hundreds of 5.25" floppy diskettes. Deliverance pooh-poohed the cost when Wilde weakly protested: it was the company's top-of-the-line computer and had four central processing units offering up to sixty-four million characters of main memory and forty-eight channels. None of the Union Jackers had even the remotest clue as to what that meant, but they grudgingly began to learn how to use the machines and appreciate some of the new techniques and abilities of the burgeoning technology. Donna had also ordered a half dozen extra keyboards since she knew from experience with one of Adam's colleagues, Duke Ondigo, that frustrations would likely cause immediate execution or savage mutilation of said keyboards as angry fists banged into them. Wilde "executed" three keyboards in the first week, their deaths accompanied by particularly ubiquitous British cursing; Victor knocked a few keys off his keyboard but generally kept it in working condition. Quint tried to avoid using his computer, but Deliverance mastered hers in days and was fast becoming the office guru for state-of-the-art technology. She was even teaching her twins how to use the machines with the one she ordered for her home office, and Aislinn was showing real aptitude.

Donna stayed for an entire week, bunked out in Quint's elegantly appointed guest casita, then handed Wilde the bill, collected a check, and flew home to reassume her place as the queen of MCS and of her husband, *Seraphim* editor and writer Bruce Peterson. Quint was surprised that she was the wife of the man who had interviewed them in 1978 after the denouement of the series of ax murders. He couldn't imagine any more disparate set of spouses, unless he considered himself and Deliverance. And maybe Wilde and Victor.

Norah had given Donna a full-page computer tips section in her magazine, *Seraphim*, under the title *Pallone's Pithy Processing Points*. As a gesture Norah had given Union Jack Investigations a free subscription to the magazine so they could keep abreast of improvements in the growing technology field. Deliverance also ordered subscriptions for the current magazines dealing with computers: *Compute!*, *80 Micro*, and *PC*. She had established a weekly staff meeting in 1980 and added technology updates as an agenda topic. She also devised a series of procedures to transfer all their paper files to floppy disks, and she took monthly copies of said disks to store in a safe deposit box at Merabank. She had hired a young college student to help her transfer the data, and they were about 75% complete. The girl hinted none too subtly about obtaining a permanent position, but Deliverance wasn't too sanguine about that possibility.

Victor pulled into the parking lot, admiring the lengths of acacia bushes and cacti that provided a certain privacy from the street. They had a landscaper that came in monthly to trim and weed, and the office building and its surroundings were always clean and elegant, presenting an aura of professionalism and care that the team felt also represented their approach to their jobs and clients. He noticed that there were three cars already parked, including a long, brand new Cadillac limousine. The other two cars belonged to the college student and the new lawyer who was sharing space with them and performing routine legal chores for the various cases. He was running fifteen minutes late due to the unexpected morning surprise and hoped that their new client wasn't too put out by the tardiness. Being punctual was one of Victor's hot buttons, and he especially loathed any diversion by himself. He didn't think that anyone arriving in a limo would be very tolerant of being kept waiting. He flipped open his notepad and checked the appointment again: 9:00 AM, 9/16/83, one Dan Vincent of Philadelphia. Something vague about a background check.

He parked in his designated space, grabbed his briefcase, and hurried up the stairs. He opened the door to the lounge and found Fox Newberry having what appeared to be a pleasant conversation with the young college student, Santina Smith. She was a giddy creature, susceptible to flattery and attention from anyone wearing pants and having a penis. She wasn't promiscuous, but she wasn't particularly adept at choosing sexual partners who might stick around for more than a night or two. She had made overtures to Fox, but he backed off immediately, not desiring another scandal in his life; the last one had practically derailed his professional life and sent him careening west from his hometown of Charleston. She had also made advances towards their newest associate, Turner Jackson, but he wasn't having any of her salaciousness, either. Victor was relieved that this was Santina's last week before her services were no longer necessary.

The two associates looked up quickly as Victor entered and smiled at him. Fox slid off the edge of Santina's desk and nodded towards the hallway.

"Hey," Fox said in his sugary South Carolina drawl. "I put Mr. Vincent in the Saguaro Conference Room and got him some coffee." He pronounced the "I" like "Ah."

"What's he like?" Victor asked as he put his briefcase down on Santina's desk. "Pissed about me being late?" He picked up the copy of the *Old Pueblo Sentinel* and automatically turned it to the last page where the crossword puzzle waited for his attention. A devout cruciverbalist, he took that challenge and the one in the *New York Times* every day.

"Nah, he seems, cool," Santina said. "Nice-looking for an old guy. Polite." She grinned salaciously. "Bet he's rich, too. I saw the limo."

"Down, girl," Fox warned, not altogether humorously.

"Just sayin'," she shrugged as she noisily dragged the last ounce of iced coffee out of her cup straw.

18

Wilde Sinclair walked into the office at that moment and after a quick nod rushed over to the Mr. Coffee and poured a large mug. He handed it to Victor then tossed an Earl Grey teabag into his own mug and poured boiling water on it.

"Where's Quint?" Victor asked as he blew on the steeping brew.

"Ah, long story, but they lost another babysitter and he decided to accompany Deliverance to the station to give both of their statements. Took Vikki with them and they'll be in later."

"What's that—number four?"

"Five, I think."

Victor laughed, and they headed down the hallway and entered the conference room. Vincent had his back to him as he stared out of the window at the desert scene, the west side of the Catalinas presenting a beautiful view of red rock and eerie cloud patterns wafting lazily across the imposing jagged peaks. He was sipping his coffee casually.

"Mr. Vincent?" Victor said. "Victor Renard and Wilde Sinclair. We apologize for keeping you waiting." He walked around the table to sit down facing the client and froze as he came face to face with the man. He regrouped quickly, sat down, and sipped his coffee. "Or unless you've changed your name, may I say Mr. Danziger?"

James Danziger smiled lazily and took another sip of his coffee. "Apology accepted, if you'll accept mine for the … shall we say, subterfuge?"

"Perhaps an understated term," Wilde said as he sat down next to his partner. He took a moment to study the man before him, a man who had had a significant if unknown impact on their lives years earlier.

Santina had called Danziger "old." Technically, she was correct. He was in his late sixties, but looked years younger, and was as fit as any man of fifty. He was sitting, but from old photographs Wilde knew he was tall, over six feet. His silver hair, still threaded through with sable streaks, was swept back, thick and silky. His skin was unblemished, and his green eyes were clear and sparkling with amusement and perhaps a touch of sarcasm; the crow's feet at their edges did nothing to detract from his attractiveness. He was wearing what Wilde recognized as an Armani silk suit, three-piece, dark navy, with a baby-blue, French-cuff shirt and sapphire-blue silk tie; if Wilde had to guess, Danziger had probably gone to Milan to have the suit custom-made for no less than $1,000. The man reeked of elegance and money, and perhaps just a bit of danger.

"So, Mr. Danziger," Victor said slowly, "what can we do for you? And why did you feel it was necessary to pretend you were someone else?"

Danziger brushed off an imaginary piece of lint from his arm and smiled. "My pretense seemed to be necessary since previous overtures under my real name resulted in rejection and often a lack of response. You even refused my request for an *L.A. Daily Record* interview at substantial compensation after everything came to light, and yet you allowed Norah Maguire's magazine to have the exclusive story." His voice turned cold. "I don't like being ignored."

"And we don't like being lied to," Wilde said just as coldly, his clipped British accent cutting through the conference air like a knife. He stood. "Goodbye, Mr. Danziger."

Danziger smiled slightly and sipped his coffee. He ignored Wilde and locked eyes with Victor. "I'll just keep annoying you until I'm satisfied. Perhaps it would be better for all concerned if you simply dealt with my presence and questions now instead of postponing the inevitable."

Victor gently waved Wilde back down and Wilde sat, glaring at the man across from them.

"I'll repeat myself. What can we do for you, Mr. Danziger?" Victor said evenly.

Danziger leaned forward slightly, his eyes intense. "You can tell me everything you know about Willow Cheney."

"She's dead," Wilde snapped. "End of story." Willow Cheney had been murdered by Trent Plaine, an old newspaper associate who held her responsible for the gang-rape and suicide of his only daughter.

"Thanks for clarifying that," Danziger replied, never deigning to look at Wilde. He kept his eyes focused on Victor. "Now tell me why she seemed to be so focused on the late Cheyenne LaChoisi, AKA the Axewoman of Tucson. According to her last letter they were close friends and she made efforts to hide what she suspected and knew about your infamous series of murders a few years ago."

"They were friends," Victor replied.

"Willow didn't have any friends. She was a rapacious, self-centered woman who used people."

"Then you must have had a lot in common," Wilde sniped.

Danziger smiled. "Oh, yes, we had a lot in common. What I'm wondering about is what else we might have had in common." He was clearly dancing around any direct implications.

"You tell us," Victor challenged. Would this be the moment that he and his partners had long anticipated when they'd have real proof that James Vincent Danziger had fathered Willow Cheney's quadruplets? Proof beyond the engraved gold cufflinks that rested in their safe deposit box.

Danziger ignored the challenge. "Tell me about Cheyenne."

"She's dead, too," Wilde said.

"I hadn't realized that by the newspaper articles and books written about the subject. It's my understanding that your firm had a great deal to do with uncovering and resolving the situation." Danziger reached into his suit jacket pocket and withdrew an envelope. He handed it to Victor.

Victor opened the envelope and withdrew a cashier's check. He showed it to Wilde without any facial expression of surprise or awe. He looked at Danziger. "$50,000? Nice retainer. I'm afraid we can't accept it though. We have nothing to offer you in return." He put the check back in the envelope and slid it over to Danziger on the table.

Danziger tapped his finger on the envelope but didn't pick it up. He casually extracted another envelope, put it on the table, and flicked it over to Wilde. Wilde opened the envelope and smiled slightly. He showed the check to Victor, then returned it to the envelope and gently placed it on top of the other one.

"Thanks for the offer, Mr. D, but we're not for your hire under any circumstances," Wilde said. "Even for $100,000. Have a nice day." Wilde and Victor rose at the same time, with Danziger following suit as he smoothly retrieved the envelopes and put them back in his jacket pocket.

Danziger smiled at them, although the smile didn't reach his startling green, cold eyes. "I've done my research on you and your firm. You have good reputations, albeit slightly off the normal professional kilter. I found it intriguing that a Brit, a southerner, a semi-disgraced ex-Tucson detective, and a psychic witch managed to come together and form a rather unusual firm. By the way, I have dossiers on each of you, very, very … thorough dossiers. Some things should be left to the imagination eh?"

"I think that's a good rule to follow, Danziger," said Quint who had just appeared at the door with Deliverance by his side, a snoozing Vikki in his arms. She was watching Danziger quietly, studying his face, his posture, trying silently to find any physical hints that he was indeed the late Cheyenne's biological father.

"Michael Quintana, I assume?" Danziger said. He extended his hand, but instead of Quint taking it Deliverance did instead. She shook his hand tightly, then suddenly grasped his hand in both of hers. Instead of pulling away, he let her keep hold and watched her expressive face curiously. He was fascinated as ripples of emotions cascaded across her beautiful heart-shaped face like waves washing against the shore. He was momentarily taken aback when one of those emotions—just a nanosecond flash, really—revealed a hint of sadness.

"Mrs. Quintana," Danziger said politely.

"Ms. Dane," she corrected before letting go of his hand.

"My apologies. I'm sorry you weren't here a few moments earlier. I was making a proposal to your partners that had a very substantial amount of compensation attached to it."

"How substantial?" Deliverance asked, her chin slightly tilted upwards. She had changed into a casual cream business suit with impressively broad shoulder pads, white silk blouse, and high heels, which still left her over a foot shorter than the man to whom she was speaking.

Danziger withdrew the second envelope and handed it to her. She opened it, and Quint whistled in appreciation over her head as they stared at the $100,000 check.

"Okay," Quint said slowly. "That would qualify as substantial. And what do you want for that exceptional paycheck?"

"Everything you know about Willow Cheney and her relationship with Cheyenne LaChoisi." He spoke to Quint but kept his eyes on Deliverance.

"And if we know little or nothing more than what's been printed in the papers and books?" Quint asked.

"Then without much effort you get to take off the first half of 1984 and spend it on a beach in Tahiti, courtesy of my largesse."

"I've already told him no," Victor interjected.

"We'll take you up on your offer," Deliverance said to the shock of her partners. Before any one of the three could argue, she went on. "You're right, Mr. Danziger. We know more than we've told. However, there's a caveat."

"Which would be?"

"You will return here after the first of the year and we'll sit down and tell you everything. No sooner. If what we tell you doesn't meet with your expectations, you get your money back. Deal?" Deliverance stuck out her hand again and after a few seconds' hesitation Danziger took the hand and shook it firmly.

"Deal," he said quietly. He grinned like a Cheshire cat at the rest of the Union Jack team. "I'll meet you here at 9 AM sharp on January 2nd. Good day, folks." With no other word he ambled out of the conference room, and a moment later they heard the front office door close.

"Are you barking mad?" Wilde asked Deliverance furiously. "We agreed to keep those secrets, not wait to sell them to the highest bidder."

"And if we were to expose the truth, the C's should be the first ones to learn that truth," Victor agreed. Neither Cress LaChoisi, Phaedra Black Wolf, nor Constantine Black Wolf knew who their biological father was, although they had learned that Willow Cheney was their mother, and as quadruplets had been divvied up as two sets of "twins" to two separate adoptive sets of parents. Cheyenne was Cress's "twin," and had been shot and killed by Deliverance before the madwoman could kill her, Quint, and their own twin babies. The team referred to them collectively as "the C's" since all of them had first names beginning with "C," the leading letter of Willow's last name; Phaedra's first name was actually Cassandra. Although they and the Union Jack family, Belzer, and Munch knew the truth of their sibling relationship, the world at large did not since those facts were kept out of the official story. It was generally known, however, that the three were "half" siblings since they'd been given up for adoption and "found" each other through investigation once they'd learned that they were adopted. It was a delicate balance to keep the truth from getting out, but so far after five years the obfuscation seemed to be holding.

"Agreed," Deliverance said, "but it's a moot point. I'm going to Merabank and cash this now." She turned to leave but her husband grabbed her arm.

"Why is it a moot point?" Quint asked.

"Because we'll never have to tell him the truth. He's going to be dead very soon, well before the first of the year. The man is saturated with doom, doom from someone close to him. I sensed it, and, quite frankly and practically, if he's pushing up daisies he won't need the hundred grand. I'm sure his heirs are well-provided for." She paused. "Did you see his eyes? Constantine has his eyes and his nose. Gotta go," she said as she waved and left the office.

"Think she's right?" Victor asked Quint. "Think his clock is ticking down?"

"She usually is right about things like this. Worst comes to worst, her psychic whackadoo is off and we give him the money back."

"What about the C's?" Wilde asked. "Is it time to tell them the truth? I mean, especially if what our little witch says is true. It may be the last time to give them the chance to meet their father."

"I hate these philosophical arguments," Quint groused as he deposited his daughter on a leather chair. "I knew this whole thing would circle back around to bite us in the ass someday. Guess someday is here. And as if we don't have enough grief with a dead head miraculously appearing on my doorstep."

"Why are you back so early anyway? Get frustrated and shoot Munch?" Wilde grinned.

"Don't think I wasn't tempted," Quint said. "We made a basic statement, but Vikki was getting cranky, so we blew it off and promised to go in later today to finish up."

"So how do we handle this situation with the C's? If we're taking a vote, I vote for letting them know the truth," Victor said.

"I'm on the fence," Wilde said.

"Me, too," Quint agreed, "but I'm leaning to the truth-telling side."

"We need la petite sorcière to help make this decision," Victor said.

"You know what?" Quint said. "I'm off the fence. I'd want to know about my past no matter what the facts or consequences."

"Yeah, yeah, you're right," Wilde grumbled. "I'm off the fence, too."

"So regardless of what Witchy Woman thinks, we present a united front of truth-telling," Victor said.

"Are you going to tell her that her position is actually moot in this matter?" Quint asked his partner, his eyebrow arched, his lips threatening a wide grin.

"No, mon ami, you are," Victor said. "She's your wife."

"Coward."

"Oui. C'est vrai. I have a keen sense of survival."

"Do you think there are any legal ramifications to keeping the truth hidden, including the proof?" Wilde asked. Even their "buddies" in the police force, detectives Belzer and Munch, didn't know about the damning cufflinks with James Danziger's initials on them. They had been part of Cheyenne's stash of trophies, but Wilde had filched them before the police could uncover their existence.

"I think we have a lawyer at our beck and call, so we can check that out," Quint replied. "In fact, since we have time let's sit down with Fox and talk about this now." With that Quint left the conference room and a few minutes later returned with Fox Newberry, who confirmed that everything they told him was confidential.

They sat him down opposite the three of them and for the next hour laid out a long, complex story. At the end of the tale silence fell over the room, and Fox got up wordlessly, left the room, and returned with a bottle of Jameson's and four shot glasses.

Fox thought that he had found himself in something of a calm, safe cocoon when he was hired by Union Jack Investigations after a recommendation by his long-ago fellow law student, Barnaby Lucas.

He had no idea that the partners' histories were so damn fascinating and exciting.

Damn, life was good.

If only he could find a restaurant that made decent grits and could truly fry bacon to a charcoal consistency.

CHAPTER THREE

On September 17th Vanessa Williams became the first black Miss America when she was crowned in Atlantic City, New Jersey. Constantine Black Wolf had been babysitting his five-year-old niece, Persa, and her two-year-old brother, Black Wolf (or, cloyingly, "Wolfie," as his parents and grandparents called him), while his sister, Phaedra, and brother-in-law, Moon Wolf, were out on the town enjoying a childfree night of dinner, dancing, and a movie. They were going to the Foothills Mall off Ina where the Plitt Foothills 4 Cinemas was showing *Strange Invaders*, a science fiction movie. Phaedra said it probably wasn't the best movie, but it beat out the other offerings, *Vigilante*, *Revenge of the Ninja*, and *Nightmares*, and she and Moon Wolf just needed a fun night away from family obligations.

That left Constantine to play with the kids and watch whatever was on TV Saturday night. At least the Begay house wasn't too far away from his own townhouse. He was glad that they had sold Phaedra's old house in south Tucson and bought something larger in north Tucson, not too far from him and from their art gallery. A new townhouse development had opened just the previous year on North Oracle past Ina and he was one of the first buyers. At fifteen hundred square feet on a single story, the home provided all the space that Constantine needed, including a spacious home office. As a full professor of Anthropology at Saguaro Western College, he was always on his computer writing and devising curricula. His sister and his brother, Cress, always chided him about working too hard and not having much of a personal life. He didn't disagree, but he blithely told them that he liked his life that way. They reiterated that at twenty-eight he was becoming a curmudgeon. Again, he didn't disagree.

Just as Williams was being crowned he glanced over and smiled—his niece and nephew were sleeping soundly on the floor; Wolfie was lightly snoring. He returned his attention to the console TV set and thought that Americans of color were finally coming into their own. As a man of mixed blood, he'd experienced his share of bigotry and limitations; but at least some of the barriers were being broken down. Slowly, but surely. He hoped by the time Persa and Wolfie were grown that their color and heritage would be transparent and mean nothing in terms of educational, social, and personal constraints.

Persa wouldn't have any trouble on first glance; despite her mixture of black, Native American, and white blood, she was a light-skinned redhead with brilliant green eyes. Her biological father, Luke Wheeler, was white, but had been murdered before she was born. Moon Wolf, Phaedra's husband, was a full-blooded Native American, and little Wolfie had black hair, brown eyes, and skin the color of dark cinnamon. Moon Wolf had adopted Persa when he married Phaedra; Persa's full name now was Cassandra Persephone Wheeler Begay.

Constantine carried first one child then the other to their beds and tucked them in. He sat on Persa's bed and studied her as she slept. He absolutely adored his niece and pushed away the sorrow he felt at losing his expected child five years ago. The unborn baby had died when its mother was shot to death. Its mother—his own sister, whom he didn't know was such until just before she died. If that wasn't bad enough, she had been a serial killer that had terrorized Tucson with a series of ax murders over an eighteen-month period. Perhaps it was just as well that the child had never been born as a result of incest and a mother who was utterly mad and vicious. And a father who was arrogant, intolerant, and, yes, curmudgeonly.

He turned off the TV set and put a jazz album on the stereo. He poured himself a glass of anisette, sat down on Moon Wolf's luxurious recliner, closed his eyes, and mellowed out to the music. He wondered what his brother, Cress, and Cress's longtime lover Gray Kingston were doing tonight. He'd seen them at the Mexican Independence Day dinner last night and they had been exuberant and chatty and had made every effort to draw him into their conversation. They had a trip planned to Australia in November for Gray to study aborigine culture, amongst other interesting things. They were traveling with Victor Renard and Wilde Sinclair. Apparently, Victor had always wanted to go to the land Down Under, and he and Wilde had a swath of exciting milestones to plough through during their stay. They had planned to travel to Australia in August of 1981, but their flight was canceled along with hundreds of others when President Reagan mass-fired 11,000 air traffic controllers. Cress would spend some time with them while Gray was studying and visiting several tribes, and his brother had been enthusiastic about visiting the Blue Mountains, Manly on the Tasman Sea, and Hunter Valley, Australia's answer to Napa. A visit to Ayers Rock and the Great Barrier Reef were also on the agenda, and Gray planned on being part of the latter experience. All told the two couples would be gone for three to four weeks, but back in time for Christmas.

Constantine turned on his word processor and opened his file on the Native Americans of the mid- to late-1800s. He had written his doctoral dissertation on a topic that his late sister, Cheyenne, had been starting for her own PhD dissertation before she was killed. She planned on exploring the anthropological concepts of white captives of Indian tribes, how they had been taken, how they were treated, their offspring, and what happened if and when they returned to white society. She had devised an outline and a couple pages of notes, but she'd never pursued it further. Constantine thought that the subject matter was intriguing, and although he hesitated at first to pick up where she left off, his academic curiosity and ambition overrode those doubts. He had met with the committee and explained where he'd come up with the idea and how far she had gotten—which was pretty much nowhere except for the idea itself. After much discussion he was given the go-ahead, and his dissertation had achieved his last academic goal—he acquired his PhD and could now be called "Dr. Black Wolf" by his colleagues and students. His brother, Cress, had also achieved his doctorate in Criminology, and became Dr. Crescent LaChoisi.

His dissertation was extensive, but he felt that it could be expanded into a full book, and he was in the process of doing so. He had even come up with a title for the book: *White Captive, Indian Heart*. He was currently in the chapter that dealt with the mixed-breed offspring and how they were treated both by their Indian society as well as white society when some of them accompanied their freed mothers back into their world. Being mix-blooded himself—black, white, and Native American—he was totally focused on the subject and this was turning out to be one of the more detailed, intense chapters. Phaedra told him that he needed to back off a little and enjoy life rather than committing it strictly to studying, teaching, and writing. He was only twenty-eight, and should be indulging a personal life with dates, movies, restaurants, and an occasional drink in a bar. He promised he would, but he rarely did. He understood that he was still affected by what had happened five years ago. Like Cress, he had attended therapy sessions, but he found no enlightenment or peace with those and after six months abandoned them. Cress found more satisfaction in his therapy, which lasted for a year. By all accounts and purposes Cress seemed fine, but Constantine knew that he, his brother, and his sister still struggled with emotional demons that might very well last a lifetime. He knew through Gray that even after five years Cress still needed a nightlight on to sleep, an aftereffect of being trapped underground in darkness for a week.

He wondered if those demons would spread their reptilian wings and claws and come flying in their faces when they met with their Union Jack friends Monday. Wilde had called each of them asking for a meeting at 10 AM. He hedged about the reason, but said it was important and might impact their futures. Intriguing, so each sibling agreed to meet. Constantine had a ten o'clock class, but his best grad student agreed to take it over.

He typed several pages, edited them, and fixed the grammar. He printed out his pages on Phaedra's dot-matrix printer, and spent a few minutes making corrective red slashes across things he'd missed. He was in the middle of the last page when his sister and her husband came home. He quickly stored his papers in his briefcase and tried to look innocent of spending some family time on work. Hell, the kids were asleep after all.

"You were working on your book, weren't you?" Phaedra asked, almost laughing. She knew him too well.

Constantine blushed and sighed, then confessed. "Just a little after I put the kids to bed. I'm pressing a deadline."

"Whose deadline—yours?" Moon Wolf asked incisively.

"That's the only deadline that counts," Constantine grumbled.

"You're hopeless," Moon Wolf replied then walked off to check on his children.

"He's right, you know," Phaedra said. "You are hopeless. But I still love you." She bent down and kissed the top of his head before following her husband into their kids' room.

While they were gone he packed up his stuff and slipped on

his jacket. It was late but his favorite restaurant, The Happy Spartan, was still open, and he could pick up a takeout order of spanakopita to nosh on at home. Maybe he'd get a full meal of moussaka and the fixings for tomorrow since he planned on spending all day at home polishing up his last few chapters. His sister returned and saw that he was ready to go. She knew better than to try to tempt him into staying.

"So, we'll see you Monday?" she asked.

"Yup. Ten sharp. Gotta go. Bye." He kissed her cheek quickly and left without another word.

"We need to get him a girlfriend," Moon Wolf said as he came into the living room. "It's way past time." He kissed his wife's cheek and rubbed her midsection, where their third child was aborning.

"I know," Phaedra sighed. "He has to stop punishing himself for something that wasn't his fault to begin with."

"Your crazy sister really did a number on his head."

"Yeah, on a lot of heads. But she's dead, and it's been five years. He needs to, well, get over it." She craned her neck to look into his deep-set brown eyes. "You kind of like him, don't you, Tonto?" She used the derogatory term that Constantine had first used on her husband when they met. A full-blooded Navajo, Moon Wolf looked like an Indian warrior of old with his height, physique, waist-length black hair, deep-set, dark chocolate brown eyes, dark cinnamon complexion, and sharper than sharp cheekbones.

"Let's just say I'm used to him. I refuse to admit that I like him."

"He adores the kids."

"His primary saving grace. That, and his devotion to you and Cress."

"He's handsome, educated, articulate—"

"Arrogant, annoying."

"—devoted to his family, kind, compassionate."

"A big, fat marshmallow in curmudgeon clothing."

"Someone has to be out there to get his romantic life back on track." She arched her eyebrows at him. "Got any cousins or friends that need a boyfriend?"

"Um, no one I'd be willing to throw under a bus."

31

"That's mean."

"Fine. I'll root around. Don't hold your breath."

"Thank you. I'm exhausted. Bed time?"

"Shower time, then bed time, then ..."

"Yes?"

"I'll leave that to your imagination."

With that he took her hand and led her into the shower. They were about to fall into bed together and explore each other's imagination when they saw that the kids had invaded their bedroom and were snuggled under the covers. They sighed in unison, put on some nightclothes, and slipped into bed. Moon Wolf wrapped his arms around Persa while Phaedra cuddled her son to the warmth of her body. All four Begays were asleep in minutes.

Well, four and a half.

Constantine arrived home forty-five minutes later, fortified with two days' worth of food from his favorite Greek restaurant. He had been raised on good old southern cooking and Greek food thanks to his parents, Alexandra and Dionysus, a proud Greek expatriate. He pulled his car, a fire-engine-red Camaro, into the garage, got out, and locked it before lowering the garage door. He studied the car, which was in mint condition for a 1977 model. The car had belonged to his dead sister. He had asked Cress to sign it over to him after Cheyenne's estate—minuscule though it was—was settled. He didn't know why he wanted it. He just did. And five years later he was still driving it. Phaedra told him he needed to get rid of it and get a new car all his own. He knew he should, but he had been bucking her. Maybe bucking her for too long. Yes, he needed to divest himself of the last tangible reminder of his dead psycho sister/lover. Monday he'd put an ad in one of the Phoenix newspapers. He didn't want anyone in Tucson to buy it so that he'd never have to encounter it again.

One of Moon Wolf's voluminous cousins owned a Ford dealership on the south side of town. Perhaps he'd head on down there and pick up a new car. He'd browsed the car sale circulars and saw that White Hawk Begay had a lovely new Mustang GT convertible for sale, canary yellow with a black top. He could make do with that. It was pricey at $13,479, but Moon Wolf had hinted that his cousin could knock the price down by ten percent. He could make that work with a down payment from the sale of his current car. Of course, practically speaking, getting a hardtop would drop the price down to around $7,500, but, hell, he deserved to have a nice car and had waited too long to make the decision.

He set the food down in his kitchen, then went to the front door to collect the evening paper. The *Old Pueblo Sentinel* had started putting out an abbreviated evening edition, and he preferred that to the morning one. The newspaper was rolled up and secured with a rubber band. As he bent to pick it up he noticed that something was stuck in the rubber band—a flower. He took the paper inside and gently freed the flower. It was pretty and looked like a big carnation with volumes of thin petals that were a rich, deep pink with white tips.

He wondered if the newsboy had stuck the flower in for some reason but discounted that; the teenager was surly at best and unlikely to do anything nice for anyone. It wasn't his sister, and he couldn't imagine Cress dropping by to give him a single flower.

He put the flower in a small vase of water, then dropped the newspaper on his desk for perusal the next morning. He showered and dropped into bed, tired. He was looking forward to a Sunday of relaxation, relaxation being working on his book and the curriculum for the spring semester. He was asleep almost as soon as his head hit the pillow.

CHAPTER FOUR

"Thanks, Deliverance," Belzer said as she refilled his coffee cup. It was his third cup of the morning, and probably two more than he should have had. But, his sleep patterns had been disrupted and he had to jump-start his ageing body with some kind of stimuli. He sipped. "This your usual blend?" he asked.

"Nope, changed brands," she replied as she sipped her Makaibari Indian tea. "So done with Folgers. This is a special blend from that new coffee shop that opened up on Prince. Comes from Ecuador from the western foothills of the Andes."

They were sitting in the Saguaro Conference Room, the largest of the three in the Union Jack offices. There was a second one called the Crucifixion Thorn Conference Room on this floor, and one called the Devil Cholla Conference Room on the first floor. They had all been named after desert flora, but this one was homage to the case that had brought the partners all together.

Belzer took one more sip before he put his cup down and continued with his details on the head that had been delivered to the Quintana residence a few days earlier.

"We've determined that it's a woman's head, hair naturally dark brown but dyed black, eyes light blue, blood type A, maybe around twenty to twenty-five. The head was neatly severed with a sharp object, possibly a circular saw. There's no way to tell her measurements, how tall she was, her weight, or how she died. The head was removed postmortem."

"What about the finger?" Wilde asked. "Any fingerprint match?"

"It was in good enough shape to take a print, but we didn't find any match in any database."

"So, we have no identity yet," Victor sighed.

"Nope. But we've sent it off to the fibbies and maybe they can come up with something. They're also checking to see if any crimes match this one, if it actually is a violent crime."

"Why wouldn't it be?" Deliverance asked. "Someone cut off her head."

"Yes, but it could have been a natural death and some weirdo just disposed of the body. Of course, that's a crime, but it doesn't mean it was murder," Belzer said as he rose and went over to pour himself a fourth cup of coffee under Quint's curious eyes. He went on. "What is still baffling us is why the head and finger were delivered to your house specifically."

"No clue," Quint said. "We've checked our files and none of our clients or people related to their cases seem to match your dead girl."

"Anyone in particular pissed off at you? I mean, besides in the overall law enforcement community?" Belzer asked.

"Oh, a few people," Victor said. He looked at Wilde. "There was that midget who was incensed about our ruining his ménage-a-cinq with those secretaries. And the doctor who was molesting his patients and got his license revoked."

"Don't forget the engineer that got booted from his job when we proved he was conspiring to do industrial espionage, or the guy that failed his background check at Saguaro Western when we found out he'd been fired from his last seven positions," Wilde added.

"That doesn't even count the three phony evangelists that we proved were skimming off the donation buckets. And didn't that UFO hunter swear to get even when we proved his photo was actually a doctored Frisbee?" Quint said.

"So, you see, Belzer," Deliverance said smoothly, "we've pissed off a lot of people, but no one we think could kill or decapitate someone. Of course, that doesn't count Aloysius, who turned the air blue when we sent over a dozen beignets and a cheesecake the day he started his new diet."

Belzer nodded. "That was a good cheesecake. Okay, well, if anyone sends you any more body parts, you'll let us know, right?"

"I saw the story in the *Sentinel* and it was just a couple of paragraphs," Quint said. "Glad you didn't mention whose house it got delivered to. Laurel Bollmeier would've been camped out on our doorstep to get a quote. And Del, here, doesn't want to waste another slushie."

"Keeping the details close to the vest," Belzer said. "You know, to forestall any false confessions. Well, gotta go," he said as he rose. He hesitated, then said to Quint, "I need to talk to you privately about a … personal matter. When you have the time."

"Sure. I can come over to the station later, say, about four?"

"Good, thanks. Bye all." With that Quint walked Belzer out of the conference room just as the C's and their significant others were entering the vestibule. Belzer gave them a short nod then left. He knew why they were there, and he didn't want to be around if they exploded all over the Union Jackers.

"Thanks for coming in on such short notice," Quint said as he shook everyone's hands. He looked over at Sage Thompson, who was manning the reception desk since Sarita was off on some personal errand. "Sage, could you please bring some coffee into the conference room?"

"Not a secretary, Quint," she said absently as she kept her focus on the computer screen that displayed her essay on the Economic Recovery Tax Act of 1981, which lowered tax brackets from the top of the scale to the bottom. Reaganomics were a complex suite of financial policies that were either loved or hated by the American population. She was pursuing a Master's degree in economics at the U of A and often lost herself in the concept of the professional versus the personal.

"Not an employee any more, Sage," Quint said evenly as her head snapped up. "Or would you like to forestall that dire situation by accommodating a polite request by the man who writes your paychecks?"

Sage rose abruptly, her jaw set. "Christ, fine. I'll bring the coffee in." She turned and stalked to the lounge room where the coffee counter was waiting for her actions.

"She's a charmer," Phaedra said. "Do you need a flute and some Indian music to make her behave?"

"I was thinking more of an Indiana Jones bullwhip, but so far that hasn't been necessary. Come on in." He led his five guests into the conference room where Victor and Wilde stood as the women seated themselves.

Cress grinned and said, "That was a great dinner Friday night. Loved the costumes." He had been wearing a buckskin outfit reminiscent of a frontiersman.

"It was fun," Wilde agreed.

"Why was Belzer here?" Constantine interrupted. "Does it have anything to do with the reason this meeting was called?"

"Not at all," Victor said. "Totally different matter." He looked at Quint and Deliverance, who nodded slightly in a go-ahead. "Did you see the article in the *Sentinel* about the severed head the police found?"

"Think so," Gray replied. "Wasn't there a finger, too? It didn't say where they found it. I'm assuming out in the desert."

"I wish," Quint muttered. All eyes were on him. "Somebody deposited it on my front doorstep in a cardboard box. My kid found it."

"Oh, my God," Phaedra exclaimed. "Do they know who it is?"

"They haven't identified her or why my family was the happy recipient of such a lovely decomposing gift. Ah, good," he ended as the door opened and Sage brought in a tray with nine filled coffee cups on it. She deposited it on the table with a bang and ignored the thank-yous as she left the room.

"You might want to reconsider that bullwhip," Moon Wolf said. "Smearing her with honey and staking her out on an anthill could be a viable alternative."

"Don't tempt me," Quint said. "Okay. To the purpose of this meeting." He glanced at his partners, who seemed ready to leave the story to him. He took a deep breath and plunged in. "Look, we've kept something from you from the case that brought us all together. We kept it secret because, well ... we didn't know if we should tell you since it was the result of investigation and supposition. We didn't have any definitive proof, and Willow never confirmed it outright."

"Willow?" Cress said. "Please don't tell us there are more C's out there."

"No, no, not that we know of. But ..." Quint stopped and looked helplessly at his wife.

Deliverance rolled her big amber eyes and took up the tale. "We believe we know who your biological father is. We should have told you our thoughts years ago, but—"

Constantine flashed a genuine grin, something the dour young man rarely did. "Are you trying to tell us that James Danziger is our father?"

Phaedra jumped in. "We knew that a long time ago."

"Yup," Cress said, nodding. He laughed out loud at the shocked looks on the partners' faces.

"What? What?" Wilde babbled.

"You guys aren't the only ones who can investigate," Cress said. "We decided to backtrack Willow's life, especially after we compared the phony birth certificates with the paper that had Madame LaVache's notes on our births. They said we were actually born on May 19, 1955. We figured that even if we were, say, a month or so premature because there were so many of us, that she probably had to get pregnant in September or October of 1954. It's documented that at that time she was working on the *Times* in L.A., and we know from your notes and articles that she was having an affair with him for a few months, although we're very grateful that those facts were never part of the official record. So, unless she was banging some other white guy at the same time, he was a good bet for Daddy."

Constantine took up the story. "So, I went to L.A. and covertly, well, stalked him and took some photographs, and even got up close to him in a restaurant. You know, I have his nose and both Cress and I have his eyes. That time he was with his daughter, Sarah—who, by the way, seems like a real solid-gold bitch. So, when we discussed everything we were maybe 99% sure that he was our bio dad."

"Wow," Victor breathed softly.

"Didn't you want to make contact with him?" Deliverance asked curiously.

"We thought about it," Phaedra said, "but our investigation showed that he wasn't the kind of father any of us would want. From all accounts he was ruthless, dangerous, and generally considered cold as ice when it came to business and personal relationships."

"He's rich as hell," Victor said. "You could have been set up for life if he believed you were his children."

"Not interested," Cress said as he finished his coffee. "Money's all well and good to some degree, but, well, we all have really good lives and are happy with them as they are. We have wonderful parents that love us. We don't need his money, his drama—"

"Or getting a bitch of a sister. From what I saw, she's a little off," Constantine said. "We've already had a sister that was more than just a little off. Thanks, but no thanks on a sequel."

"Are you mad at us for holding out on you?" Quint asked. He jiggled the cufflinks in his pocket.

"Nah," Cress said. "You had good intentions."

"I've got something for you," Quint said slowly as he withdrew the cufflinks from his pocket. He handed them to Constantine, who stared down at the tangible proof of his paternal bloodline.

"Did Cheyenne have these?" Constantine asked softly.

"She did," Wilde confirmed. "They were in her stash of trophies and I nicked them before the cops could see them up in the Summerhaven cabin."

"Oh, my God," Cress said quietly. "I remember now. I remember seeing cufflinks when I found her stash in her house just before she knocked me out. I'd forgotten all about them until now. I never registered the initials." He felt Gray squeeze his leg in sympathy. He felt chilled to the bone as he remembered waking up with a savagely throbbing head in a filthy, cold root cellar, manacled and gagged, and set to be yet another victim of his "twin" sister.

Constantine handed the "J" cufflink to Cress and said, "Phaedra and I will keep the other one."

"Look," Deliverance said. "I know you don't want to make contact with him, but there's something I've got to tell you, something that might change your minds."

"Okay," Cress said carefully as he absently rubbed the cufflink between his fingers.

"He was here last Friday. He used a phony name to get an appointment. He wanted to know about Willow and Cheyenne. He gave us a massive retainer—"

"Which we initially turned down," Victor said pointedly.

"But," Deliverance went on patiently, "I accepted it a little rapaciously—"

"A little?" her husband interjected. She elbowed him.

"I accepted it and told him that we'd spill the beans after the first of the year and no sooner. I said that believing that we'd never have to tell him."

"Why?" Phaedra asked.

"Because … because when I shook his hand I sensed … I sensed that he was going to die before that." She slumped a little in her chair, grateful to get that prediction out to the people to whom it would matter the most.

"Die?" Cress said in disbelief. "I know you have some sort of … power to sense things, but … couldn't you be mistaken?"

"I hope so. That's why I'm telling you now and why we decided to let you in on the whole Danziger connection. So that you'd know about your biological father and have the opportunity to meet him before—if—my prediction comes true." She fell silent, then added. "We're happy to give you the retainer to split up as you see fit. A hundred grand." She didn't add that she had also purloined the $150,000 that Cheyenne had blackmailed Willow out of; Deliverance had kept the bagful of money after she killed their enemy, and used part of it to buy her home, present her partners with expensive gifts, and pour the rest into buying the building that housed their firm.

The C's and their mates were quiet, so the Union Jackers let them digest this latest information. Constantine finally rose and said, "We need to discuss this amongst ourselves." He looked at Deliverance. "Any timeframe on this demise?" He had once considered her a carnival fake psychic and had been derogatory and insulting, but over the years he had come to respect and even like her and saw that some of her predictions were spot-on. He had even apologized to her for his behavior, and that had been a difficult pill for him to swallow, but, he was glad that he had done it.

She shook her head. "I just felt it would be before the new year. Also, I sensed that … that he would die at the hands of someone close."

"Okay," Cress said, rising. "We'll talk about it and let you know. Look, thanks for being honest. It couldn't have been easy to hold onto that secret, not knowing what to do."

"No, it wasn't," Quint admitted as he led them out to the front office where Sage was glaring at her screen and typing madly. She gave them a bare glance but said nothing and kept typing.

The C's left. Deliverance whirled around, furious at the young woman with no sense of propriety, tact, or courtesy.

"Sage," Deliverance said flatly.

"What?" the woman in question snapped as she cursed at a typo and angrily hit the backspace button.

"Miss Thompson," Quint barked loudly, finally managing to get her attention. "Thank you," he said acidly. He looked at his wife. "She's all yours." With that he stepped back and waited with his amused partners.

"Sage," Deliverance began, "I don't want you to take this the wrong way, but you're fired."

Sage's mouth dropped open and she abruptly stood. "What?" she said in a strangled voice.

"Let me rephrase: You're fucking fired. Now, you have five minutes to get your crap together and get out of this building."

"You ... you ... you can't fire me," Sage exclaimed.

"Of course I can. This is an at-will state, and I can fire your ass without a reason or a second's notice. However, should you like a list of reasons, here are a few: You're lazy, you're arrogant, your so-called professional courtesy is somewhere south of a dung beetle's, your personality, well, sucks, no one likes you, and I personally am sick of you using company resources to bolster your academic aspirations. I hope that you have the intelligence to realize that there won't be a good reference forthcoming for any future employers, and that any derogatory remarks on your part about this firm will result in either a libel or slander suit, depending on the medium. Now—Get. Out."

Sage stuffed her newly printed essay pages in her tote bag along with her floppy disks, and practically hurled herself out of the office. They heard her footsteps pounding down the stairs, a door slamming, then the screeching of a car's tires as she tore out of the parking lot.

Deliverance looked at her amused men and said, "That was something I've been wanting to do for weeks. Although I don't normally think of myself as a cruel person, I'd really have preferred to beat the snot out of her."

"Looks like we need a new associate," Wilde said.

Deliverance winked at her friend. "Thanks for volunteering to find one."

CHAPTER FIVE

Sabino Canyon on the northeastern side of Tucson is a favorite hiking place for tourists and residents alike. Located in the Santa Catalina Mountains in the Coronado National Forest, it is replete with high, lush mountains, deep valleys, and granite boulders that dot the land after they were dislodged during the 1887 Sonora earthquake. Sabino Dam was built during the Depression along with nine bridges that straddle Sabino Creek. Bear Canyon Trail is a favorite hiking choice, and it is bordered by high peaks along with standard desert flora such as saguaro cacti, scrub brushes, palo verde trees, acacias, prickly pears, and crucifixion thorns. Its endpoint marks the trailhead to go to Seven Falls, a marvelous cascade of water over a tall granite rock face, along with quiet pools surrounded by rock terraces. The usual blend of mammalian and reptilian creatures dart to and fro as they search for food and shelter; they generally avoid humans. Huge, flat rocks dot the valleys and flatlands, and comprise steps throughout the babbling streams that push clear spring water through its banks. In the winter the top peaks are usually dusted with snow. The delicately balanced ecosystem is a scenic wonder.

Sabino Canyon is inarguably a spectacular place to enjoy the desert, and never presents the same experience to any hiker, even if he or she goes back any number of times. It is a constant place of beauty, and yet is ever-changing. There is an almost four-mile paved road that leads into the canyon. Private vehicles used to be permitted along the road, but in 1978 they were forbidden, and a tram is now used to move people in and out.

Chandler Hooker was considered by many to be a bon vivant. He was born to a wealthy manufacturing family in Avon, Connecticut, and although he graduated Yale with a Bachelor's degree in Astronomy, he didn't have to work for a living; that was fortuitous since he had no desire to work. His doting parents bestowed a remarkably generous trust fund on him the day he graduated, and he used that to travel the world and to develop exquisite tastes in food and drink. He proudly boasted that he had eaten a full, sixteen-ounce Kobe steak in Tokyo (twice), fried crickets in Bangkok, the finest gnocchi on the planet in Florence, firinda dürüm in Antalya, Turkey, and haggis in Glasgow, Scotland, to name just a few. He kept a journal of his culinary explorations, and it was hundreds of pages long. He was currently on the page where he had started his hike through the eateries of the southwest. He had started in Santa Fe and worked his way down through New Mexico and into Arizona, where he planned on trying the cuisine that Tucson had to offer before he tramped up to Phoenix and Sedona. From there he wasn't sure in which direction he'd go: north to Nevada, or northeast to Utah. He was leaning towards Nevada.

He had made a list of the restaurants at which he wished to dine, starting with the Hidden Valley Inn on Sabino Canyon Road. Its façade was reminiscent of an old-west building, and it was considered by all to be a true Tucson treasure. Famous for its steaks and ribs, its décor was definitely attuned to the mystique of cowboys and the old west. Saddles, spurs, branding irons, and boots shared space with an old-west diorama and wall photos of cowboys, Indians, and cattle, from historical to present times. It had opened in 1977 and was an immediate hit, especially with out-of-towners.

Chandler had partaken of lunch there about an hour before he arrived at the Canyon and was satisfied but not overly impressed with the prime rib meal he had ordered. The gravy was not up to his standards, the bread crusts did not snap and crackle as fresh bread should, and there was a miniscule amount of ice in his watery Coke. He looked forward to writing a detailed critique on the eatery and sending it into both the restaurant and the Tucson Visitor's Bureau. He planned on eating dinner at Gordo's Mexacateria on Broadway. He had seen the rather cheesy commercials on television where owner Diego A. Valenzuela had asked his potential customers, "Do you like chimichangas? I mean do you r-r-r-really like chimichangas?" He didn't hold out much hope for the quality of said chimichangas, but he was a daring, dashing bon vivant and he thought he'd give it a try. He decided that tomorrow he'd come back to the area and stop at the Tack Room on North Sabino Canyon Road, which, according to the saying on its infamous yet gaudy, forty-ton, concrete-and-steel welcoming boot, had "elegant dining" and cocktails. He had a sweet tooth and had marked Austin's Old Fashioned Ice Cream on

Broadway for an early evening treat. He did not, however, plan on ordering their famous pickle ice cream.

His palate sort of sated by his meatloaf meal, he was ready to work off the fat and carbohydrates by a brisk walk through Sabino Canyon. He was perfectly dressed for the occasion. He shopped for his outdoor activities' clothing solely at L.L. Bean. The offerings were pricy, but of top-notch quality. He was wearing their finest hiking boots, made in top-grain leather since 1912; a softer-than-soft flannel shirt; and cargo shorts just above the knee. He carried a canteen of purified water, Foster Grant sunglasses, a pair of binoculars, a brand-new Sony Walkman, and a small Nikon camera in case he came across any worthy floral or faunal subjects. His one nod to the state was a baseball cap denoting the University of Arizona Wildcats.

It was the second week of October and the mornings were quite chilly, which is why Chandler decided to start his hike around 1 PM. He had planned to enjoy his nature agenda the week before, but a deluge of rain had turned much of the Tucson area into rivers of rushing water and mud. Like many people ignorant of the amount and causes of water in the desert, he'd had no idea that all of a sudden a river like the Santa Cruz could wash over and cake with mud a residential community like the one at Prince and the I-10. He was agog at the photos in the *Arizona Daily Star* that showed "the Floods of October" and their devastating consequences. The water surges under the St. Mary's Road bridge from the Santa Cruz River looked like tidal waves that had surrendered to their savage instincts. The flooding had even hit the town of Summerhaven far up on Mount Lemmon; the main street was crumbled near the Alpine Lodge and looked as though it had disintegrated through a dynamite explosion. Sabino Canyon had its issues with some flooding but was safe enough now to traipse through and mark off as a completed task.

He drove his rental Cadillac up the paved canyon road as far as he could take it, then parked it in a small side lot a little too close to a sad-looking Chevy. He locked the car doors, double-checked to make sure the canteen was filled, and slid a cassette of classical music into his Walkman. He affixed the earphones to his head over the cap, checked his trail map, and set off on what he hoped would be a leisurely walk in the wilderness. He had dismissed the idea of taking a tram up the trail. He was not, after all, an arrogant dilettante. Then he could check that task off his must-do list, return to his suite at the Westward Dream, wash up, change, and head off to Gordo's.

He passed quite a few other hikers going his way and returning to the parking area. He waved courteously when necessary but tried to tune everything out with his music and his careful attention to where he was walking. He snapped a few shots, a javelina family scuffling through the underbrush, a young rattlesnake hissing and tightly curled under an acacia, a pair of hummingbirds delicately dipping into cactus flowers. About ninety minutes in he cursed his stupidity for not using the restroom in Hidden Valley. Well, he was in a fairly desolate area and there was no one around, so he went off-trail for a few yards until he came to a copse of ironwood trees sheltering a crucifixion thorn bush nearly ten feet tall. He gave one last look around, unzipped his shorts, and let loose a dark yellow stream of urine. He let out an audible ah, then zipped back up. As he turned around, he caught his foot on something and tumbled over backwards, coming to rest on something hard and sharp.

He pulled his hand away and saw that he was bleeding from a long, deep scratch. He cursed angrily, then swiveled around to see what he had landed on. He froze and stared. He stared for what seemed to be an eternity but was only a few seconds.

Then he started screaming and scrambled to his feet and ran haphazardly back to the trail and back down the route he had come. He nearly knocked over several hikers who yelled at him but got out of his way. Somehow, he managed to get back to his car, gasping, threw his accouterments into the car, then wobbled over to a tour guide who was getting ready to accompany a small group through the trails. He babbled about a dead body and bones and—he managed to get a few distinct phrases out, and then Chandler Hooker, scion of a wealthy New England family and self-described bon vivant, crashed to the ground unconscious as the park ranger scrambled to call the police.

Detective Reichardt Belzer stood a few feet away from the forensics team that was processing the body over which poor Chandler Hooker had fallen. Munch stood beside him, chewing on his ever-present Teaberry gum. They had arrived on the scene in the same car and had noticed two very critical things about the skeletonized remains: one, the head was missing, and two, the body was disarticulated at the waist; there were two distinct portions of the body, about twelve inches apart. The skeletal legs were spread wide, and there were gnaw marks on them, no doubt from critters that found a wonderful feast when the body was dumped. Only a few patches of decomposing skin were attached to the bones; Belzer wasn't sure they could get a blood grouping, but he'd leave that to the magnificent abilities of Pete Murphy.

Belzer watched Pete scrape a few strips of skin from an arm bone and put it into his plastic evidence bag.

"Find any hair samples?" Belzer asked Pete.

"Give me a chance, Belz. I've only been working this scene for twenty minutes," Pete groused without looking up. He snagged a big black bug nestled under a rib and dumped it into a small plastic jar. He smiled as he took a few seconds to study it. He had been taking Entomology courses over at Saguaro Western to learn the ins and outs of bugs and was fascinated by them. He'd had plenty of off hours to move forward academically since Ben Deuel had been promoted over him as "king" of the forensics lab months earlier. He tried not to be bitter about working for a man with less experience and seniority than he; sometimes, he was successful at doing so.

"I thought you were related to the Amazing Kreskin and could do anything fast," Munch said.

"Distant ninth cousins. He got the psychic powers and I got the looks." Pete was an average-looking guy in his late-thirties with brown hair and grey eyes, of average height, and was relatively unremarkable. However, he did have an uncanny ability to interpret crime scenes, and there wasn't a single person in the Tucson Police Force that didn't respect and admire him.

Pete said, "I can tell you that I'm pretty certain this is a female by the structure and size of her pelvic bones. The pelve is wider, and so is its pelvic inlet bone. The ilia crest is lower. See here?" he asked as he pointed to a section of pelvic bone. "The inlet's oval, and a male's inlet is more heart-shaped. I can confirm that when we get her back to the lab."

Belzer and Munch moved a few yards away and left Pete to his tasks.

"Think this is the body that's missing the head that Quintana got dropped on his doorstep?" Munch asked as he unwrapped another piece of gum, folded it, and stuck it in his mouth.

"Highly likely, but not definitively," Belzer replied. "We find a lot of bodies out in the desert and mountains, although not usually without heads." He called over to Pete. "Check the hand bones. Any fingers missing?" He and Munch waited an agonizing minute while Pete very carefully brushed leaves away from the hands that rested above the absent head. His actions were being carefully filmed by his assistant, Josie, with the new camcorder that the department had bought for him.

"Nine fingers, right index finger missing," Pete announced.

"Shit on a stick," Munch said. "Guess that proves that we found Little Miss Bodyless's body."

"I guess," Belzer sighed, dejected. At least that meant that they weren't in possession of two female bodies, one without a head and a finger and one without a body. He looked at Munch. "You want to re-interview the weenie hiker? He gave a statement, but we might be able to tease a few more details out of him once he gets over the vapors."

"Do I have to?" Munch said.

"No, I can do it, but I will effect retribution for your reluctance at some point in the future when you least expect it. Think Don Corleone. No pressure, though."

"Right, no pressure," Munch said sourly. "Fine. I'll give it another go." With that he shuffled off towards the trail and wound his way back to their car, which had been permitted entrance since they were investigating a crime scene. He grinned; let Belzer walk all the way back to the trailhead. His partner was breaking in a new pair of Florsheims and the walk wouldn't be pleasant.

Munch tried to elicit a few more details from his reluctant witness, but Hooker had basically dissolved into a puddle of uselessness, his tears supplemented by his vacated bladder and bowels. Munch took pity on him and said that a uniformed officer would drive him back to his hotel and another would follow in the rental car. He was told to stay available for a couple of days and to not discuss the event with anyone. The uniformed officer threw Munch a look of distaste when the smelly witness parked himself in the back seat of the patrol car.

Munch watched Belzer traipse down the road from the location of the dead body. Belzer had a scowl on his long, thin face, and it was all Munch could do to not laugh. He hid his grin behind his hand and faux-coughed, but he could see that Belzer wasn't fooled.

"Nice," Belzer remarked as he walked past his partner and slid into the passenger seat of their car.

Munch got behind the wheel and said, "Where to?"

"I want to question the Quintanas again to see if anything shakes loose with this find. Pete promised he'd have something by tomorrow morning. I told him to keep a lid on this for the time being. Last thing we need is a panic with people thinking we might have another crazy serial killer on the loose. The Axewoman's path of destruction is still pretty fresh in everyone's mind, even after five years."

Munch started the car and shifted into drive, pulling away slowly past a couple of patrol cars that were causing a crowd of tourists and hikers to wonder what was going on. "Don't think there'll be much of a chance to keep this under wraps," Munch said as he pulled onto Sunrise and headed west.

Belzer was silent. That wouldn't be the only thing difficult to keep under wraps, he thought. His wife kicking him out and taking up with a younger guy wouldn't be a secret much longer. He was hoping that Quint could uncover something illicit about her relationship that could give him an edge in divorce court. She wanted the house, the furniture, the cars, everything. And he wasn't about to give her that satisfaction even though those things meant little to him. She sure as hell wasn't going to get any of his pension. He was holed up in a cheap studio apartment off Speedway. He'd slept in his car for several nights before finding that place. He had a mattress on the floor, a hotplate, and a tiny black-and-white TV. At least he took the dog when he left. She could burn in Hell before he'd let her have the tiny beast; Thumper, a skittish black Chihuahua, was the second love of his life and now, maybe the first.

Munch kept up a steady stream-of-consciousness babble on meaningless things as they drove along Sunrise. He and Pamela were going to the cinemas at the Foothills Mall on Saturday to see the new James Bond movie, *Never Say Never Again*. The following Saturday they were going to see *The Osterman Weekend*. He'd heard that there was going to be a witches' convention at a small auditorium on Halloween. He wondered if Quint's wife and her friend, Bliss Báthory, were arranging the festivities to celebrate her fifth wedding anniversary and Deliverance's fourth.

When they arrived at the Union Jack offices and got out of the car, Belzer suddenly turned to his partner and said, "Margie threw me out."

Munch sighed and looked sad. "Yeah, everyone knows."

"Shit," Belzer said, dejected that the secret apparently was no secret at all. "Shit."

CHAPTER SIX

Dr. Malachi Dillinger was doing double duty today, half of his efforts expended on his Criminology courses at Saguaro Western College, and half as the devoted dad to four-year-old (almost) Angelique, the child of his heart and soul. The little girl, with her golden-blonde curls and sea-blue eyes, was the reason he bounded out of bed in the morning, ready to face the world. Well, his daughter was half the reason—the other half was his wife, Bliss, who had changed his life forever five years ago when she married him first in a Wiccan handfasting ritual and then in a traditional Presbyterian ceremony. Every day he woke up wondering what that beautiful intelligent, fascinating woman saw in him. He didn't mull that over too closely— he just accepted and reveled in his good fortune.

Today their babysitter was sick and unable to pick Angel up after nursery school, and Bliss was off campus planning the celebration for not only their fifth wedding anniversary, but for a major witches' sabbat, Samhain, on October 31st. She was waffling on location but was leaning towards Sabino Canyon. She was having an informal meeting with all her coven members today, including Deliverance Dane, her best friend and fellow wedding anniversary celebrator. With exactly two weeks to go, Malachi thought that they'd better nail down the specifics quickly or it might be chaos like last year's. He tried to put out of his mind the police and fire sirens, the yelling and cursing, the general free-for-all between the Wiccans and "normal" people, and the joyous bounty several bail bondsmen encountered. Three members of the coven were arrested for disorderly conduct; luckily, neither Bliss nor Deliverance was in that group.

He glanced over at the corner of his office where Angel was sitting on the floor and playing with a Ouija board. She had put aside her tarot cards, telling her father that she wanted to wait to play with them until she and Alejandro could play together. Deliverance confided to Bliss that although she'd hoped that her daughter would inherit her psychic powers, it appeared that little Aislinn had none, unless they were latent. Her son, however, was showing inklings of intuition that exceeded the norm for a child his age.

Malachi turned his attention to the outline for his January

curriculum for Unsolved Murders, Unknown Killers. He had always been fascinated with crime, particularly since he shared a name (but no bloodline) with an infamous gangster of the 1930s. He had tried a career in law enforcement, but that was short-lived. Then he became a teacher back east and wound up in Tucson after a failed romantic relationship. That turned out to be fortuitous, since now he was the head of the Criminology department, the husband of Dr. Bliss Báthory—the head of the History department—and the father of the most wonderful child in the universe.

He had outlined the course nearly a year earlier, but his current commitments had prevented him from pursuing the topic until recently. He had compiled a very lengthy list of unsolved crimes over the past two centuries and whittled it down to a manageable twelve. He let his finger roam down the list of old cases that he planned to explore during his course. He planned on presenting the overview of the victims and crimes and throw it out for discussion and essaying about how law enforcement could have proceeded to unravel the cases if they had the resources and technology of today. He divided his course into three sections: the 19th century, 1900 through 1949, and 1950 to the present day.

For the 19th century he selected four cases: Benjamin Nathan, a philanthropist who was found beaten to death in his home in New York City in 1870; the Whitehall Mystery, an 1888 slaying, dismemberment, and dispersal in three separate locations of an unknown woman; the Gatton siblings in Queensland, Australia in 1898; and the Borden murders in Fall River, Massachusetts, in 1892.

The cases he selected for the first part of the 20th century were Elsie Sigel, a twenty-year-old who was strangled and stuffed into a trunk in an apartment in New York City's Chinatown in 1909; Mary Phagan, a thirteen-year-old who was raped and strangled in 1913 (a supposed perpetrator was caught, convicted, and lynched by a mob that broke him out of jail, but it was later considered a horrific miscarriage of justice); William Desmond Taylor, an American actor and director who was shot in the back in his bungalow in 1922; and, of course, the infamous 1947 "Black Dahlia" murder of aspiring actress Elizabeth Short in Los Angeles.

Cases that would be dissected from 1950 to the present

day were Albert Anastasia, a mafia boss who was gunned down in a barbershop in 1957; Louis Allen, a black man who was shot to death in 1964 when he tried to register to vote and to provide information on the murder of another black man by a white state legislator; Sister Catherine Cesnik, a twenty-seven-year-old Catholic nun who was missing for two months before being found in 1970 in a garbage dump with a fractured skull; and the "Lady of the Dunes," whose unidentified body was found in Provincetown, Massachusetts, in 1974.

He decided to break down his student class into four groups, each of which would be assigned to one case per time period. He hadn't been this excited about a course in a long time and was especially looking forward to having Deliverance in the course that semester. She was majoring in Psychology with a minor in Criminology, both of which would be beneficial to her not only intellectually but also for the business in which she was a partner. He had become close to Deliverance through the young woman's relationship with Bliss, and through her also with the other partners in the Union Jack firm. He was always pleased when they asked him to consult on a case, and they also used Cress LaChoisi as another reference.

Deliverance was due any moment to take Angelique off to Costumes, Costumes, Costumes with Alex and Aislinn while Bliss and another Wiccan planned on going to an alternate Samhain site to check it out. He hoped that his daughter wasn't going to return with another witch costume as she had for the last two years. Deliverance made sure her kids chose a different costume each year. This year, she mentioned that they might dress as Alexis and Blake from *Dynasty*. He didn't even want to imagine that fashion horror. He was hoping that Angel would be a little Princess Leia or a pirate of Penzance.

As he closed his folder there was a knock at the door and Deliverance came in, her twins screeching and running towards Angelique where they plopped down next to their friend and started ranting about Halloween. Deliverance slipped her petite frame into his guest chair.

"You girls have a fun meeting?" Malachi asked.

"There were a few tussles about, well, everything, but Bliss kept them in line."

"Not surprised. She keeps me in line quite well." Malachi looked over to where the children were playing. He saw that Angel and Alex had their fingers on the planchette and seemed to be moving it slowly around the Ouija board. Bliss had commissioned the wooden inlaid board (cedar, walnut, and cherry) from a Wiccan back in Salem, and it truly was a work of art. She didn't want Angel learning the process on a cheap "toy" model. Bliss made it very clear that there were definitive, imperative rules to follow when using a Ouija board: no evil spirits will emerge if you place a silver coin on the board; never, ever leave the planchette on the board when you're not using it; and if you need to destroy the board you should break it into seven pieces, pour Holy Water on it, and bury it—if you try to burn the board, it will scream.

He went on. "Bliss confided in me about the head you guys encountered last month. Any progress on that?"

"The cops are keeping it pretty much close to the vest and thankfully we haven't been bothered by any reporters. You must have read about the body they discovered up in Sabino Canyon?"

"Yeah, gruesome. They said it was headless. So, is your head her head?"

"Seems to be according to the M.E. They still haven't identified her and are scouring missing persons' reports from all over the southwest, and even from California. No joy yet."

"They kept any intimate details out of the papers, it seems. I guess I'm just nosy, but do you know anything special about the body that would titillate me?"

"According to Bliss, it doesn't take much to do that." Deliverance laughed.

"You know my lips are sealed. And if I did reveal anything told to me in confidence my wife would tear me a new one."

"Scared of her?"

"In an adoring sort of way."

She was about to confide something she had seen in the crime scene photos that Belzer had shared when Angelique yelled out.

"Daddy, Daddy," the little girl called loudly.

"What, baby?" Malachi said.

"What's a dahl?" she asked.

"Honey, you know what a doll is—you have a dozen," Malachi said patiently.

"I know that," she huffed, "but it's spelled different on the board. See?" She walked over to him and thrust out a piece of paper on which she'd written "dahl."

"Hmm," Malachi mused as he showed the paper to Deliverance. "Mean anything to you?"

"Afraid not." She asked Angelique, "Honey, any other letters come through?"

"No, Aunt Del. After the 'l' Alex let go of the pointer and I didn't feel anything anymore."

"Well, maybe you guys can play again this weekend when your mom brings you over to the house to swim." Deliverance stood up and clapped her hands hard. "Okay, mini-Quints—time to go. You too, Angel-bug." While the kids scrambled to get ready she glanced down at Malachi's desk and saw the folder marked "Unsolved Murders, Unknown Killers." She nodded towards it.

"That the new course I signed up for in January?"

Malachi's happy grin fairly split his pleasant but unremarkable face in two. "Sure is. Want to see the outline? Gotta promise not to do any preliminary research on any of the cases, though." Without waiting for an answer, he whipped out the outline and handed it to her. She scanned the paper from top to bottom, stopping for a split second halfway down.

She forced a neutral smile at Malachi. "Mind if I have a copy to show my old man? Think he'd be intrigued."

"Sure, sure," he said and walked over to his Xerox machine and made a copy of the page. He placed the original in his folder and handed the other one to her. "Gonna bring my little witch home before five?"

"Absolutely. Gotta go," she said as she ushered the three kinetic children out of Malachi's office and down the stairs to her Plymouth.

After she buckled the kids into the back seat an animated Aislinn whined, "Are we goin' to the costume store, Mommy? Are we?"

"No, not today. Tomorrow, maybe." She spoke over the

harmonious aw's. "We're going to someplace even more exciting—the public library." Any further words were drowned out by louder aw's as the disappointed kids grumbled in the back seat while she drove to the Tucson Public Library's main building on South Sixth Street. She unstrapped the kids and led them into the library where she took them to the children's literature section and grabbed a few books, then led them to the nonfiction section where she sat them down and told them to read. Since all three liked to read, they settled down and gave her the freedom to look for a few volumes on Los Angeles in the 1940s. She pulled a couple off their shelves and sat down and flipped through them. Two had what she wanted, so she gathered the kids up again and checked out the books they were reading and the ones that she needed.

Deliverance saw that she still had plenty of time for the costume store even though she was chomping at the bit to get back to the office. She hustled the kids into the store, and when they left thirty minutes later both Angel and Aislinn were Princess Leias (complete with light sabers) and Alex was an Ewok. She was glad they hadn't chosen the Carringtons.

She dropped Angel off at home where Bliss had just arrived. They kissed cheeks and Deliverance said she'd talk to her later and rushed her twins out to the car. She headed east on Skyline to Sunrise, then turned at Swan and parked in her office spot. She followed her kids up the stairs to her office where she was happy to see that all three of her partners were bullshitting about the last game of the World Series, which had taken place the night before for their viewing pleasure on ABC. The Baltimore Orioles had crushed the Philadelphia Phillies four games to one; to add insult to injury, the Phillies had lost that crucial game at their own Veterans Stadium. Her men were arguing about how first-year Orioles manager Joe Altobelli had pulled it altogether and gotten his team to their third championship, the first two occurring in 1966 and 1970, and whether his momentum could bring them a fourth win next year.

Quint was the first to break their conversation and greet his wife and twins. "Hey—get the costumes?"

"Yeah," Deliverance said distractedly. "We're doing a Star Wars Halloween this year. You're Darth Vader." She hit the intercom and asked Fox to come in. A moment later he appeared and took charge of the children and led them into his office where he distracted them with a Newton's Cradle. Just before the door closed she heard Fox ask Alex, "What's the word of the day?" He responded right away, "Sacerdotal." Without being asked Aislinn piped up, "Inorganic."

"What's up?" Wilde said, noticing Deliverance's serious expression.

She smacked the two books she was holding down on her desk triumphantly.

"Ever hear of Elizabeth Short?" she asked.

"Uh, no," Wilde said.

"I don't think so," Victor said.

"Sounds … a little familiar, but I can't exactly put my finger on it," Quint said.

"How about the Black Dahlia?" she asked.

"Doesn't ring a bell," Wilde said.

"It sort of rings a bell," Victor said, frowning.

"Yeah, it does," Quint said slowly, recognition dawning on his thoughtful face. Suddenly his eyes opened wide and he stared at his wife. "L.A., the 1940s."

Deliverance opened her desk drawer and withdrew a set of crime scene photos to which Belzer had granted them access. She selected the full-body down shot and slapped it on the desk. Then she opened one of the books to a page she had marked and placed it next to the photo. Her partners came closer and started down at the two images; one a skeleton with its legs spread and its arms over where the head should have been, and the other a dead, naked woman whose limbs were in the same pose and whose midsection, like that of the Sabino skeleton, had been bisected at the waist. She tapped her fingernail on the gruesome photo in the book.

"Meet Elizabeth Short, aspiring actress, waitress, originally from Boston, emigrated to Florida and California, and on January 15, 1947 wound up dead, naked, and bisected at age twenty-two in a vacant lot in L.A."

"Was she decapitated?" Wilde asked; the grainy black-and-white photo didn't show enough of her neck clearly. He had never heard of the case since he hadn't even hit the American shores until 1969.

"No, but according to the newspaper articles in this book she had black hair and blue eyes like our head, and that so-called 'Cheshire grin' carved onto her face, again, like our head. No finger removal, either, but pretty damn scary that her corpse and ours have so much in common."

"Yeah, it is," Quint said quietly as his mind turned over the possibilities. "I can't remember—was the killer ever caught?"

"Nope," Deliverance said. "It's one of those fantastical unsolved cases."

"It was thirty-six years ago," Victor mused. "Not out of the question that it's the same killer. Unlikely, but possible. Should we loop Belzer and Munch into this?"

"We have to, otherwise I'm looking at the possibility of being thrown into jail yet again," Quint sighed, remembering Belzer's reaction years ago when he had kept a critical aspect of the ax murders' case from the police.

"Christ, I hope this isn't a repeat of that case, with bisected dead bodies popping up all over Tucson," Wilde said.

"Well, at least this time we found out right away instead of four months down the line," Deliverance said.

"Should we call Belzer now?" Wilde asked.

"Nah," Deliverance said. "We'll ask him when we get home."

"Home?" Victor said.

"Yeah, he and his dog have temporarily moved into our guest casita," Quint informed him. "He and his wife split, and he was living in a dump with a hotplate. I took pity on him."

"Sound familiar?" Deliverance asked Wilde and they both laughed; Quint had been living somewhat in that way when they found him in San Francisco after he surrendered his detective shield and left Tucson for a few months after his partner, Luke Wheeler, was murdered. He was broke, had hocked his wristwatch and sold his beloved '64 Mustang, and had also spent a couple of nights in the San Francisco jail after a rousing bar fight.

"So, let's pack it up, grab the kids, stop for a couple of large pizzas, and head off to the old homesteads," Quint said.

"Do you have to feed him, too?" Victor asked, his rich chocolate eyes twinkling.

"No, he has a kitchen of sorts, but I'm feeling magnanimous," Quint replied. As though by telepathy Fox opened the door and the twins rushed in. "Get your sh- stuff together. We're going home," Quint said to his son and daughter.

"Can I have a tarantula?" Aislinn asked, all seriousness.

"No," her mother said.

"Why not?"

"Because I said so."

"That's what you always say to Daddy."

"And that's why Daddy always backs down," Quint said affably.

"Exactly. Butts in gear, now." Deliverance clapped her hands together hard and the kids scrambled out to the reception area.

The extended family bustled out behind them and stopped dead. A tall, beautiful, elegantly dressed redhead in her mid-twenties—with sparkling violet eyes—was parked on the edge of the desk filing her nails and grinning. An overstuffed suitcase was at her feet. She stood quickly and threw her arms out from her lithe, six-foot-tall frame.

"Hello, Uncle Wilde. Glad to see me?" Then Raine Sinclair threw her arms around Wilde and hugged him tightly.

"Bloody hell," Wilde exclaimed happily.

CHAPTER SEVEN

Belzer and Munch munched on their own pepperoni pizza as they huddled in Quint's casita and pored over the two books Deliverance had lent them. The casita, linked to the back patio of the family room by a wide, serpentine brick pathway, was octagon-shaped with a red tile roof over its vaulted ceilings. It was had a comfortable five-hundred-square-foot interior comprised of a small bedroom; a kitchenette with an electric stove, a small fridge, a tiny microwave, and a large living room with a ten-inch color TV and a small boom box to play cassettes. It was tastefully furnished in pure southwest style including a lodgepole bedroom set and a comfy sofa/loveseat set with a red-brown-orange Native American pattern. The coffee table was roughhewn maple wood and matched the two square end tables. Twenty-by-thirty-inch posters of prints by southwestern artists Amado Peña, G.E. Mullan, and Deborah Hiatt decorated the stark white walls.

As the Union Jackers had done earlier they put the books' photos side-by-side with the Sabino crime scene photos on the coffee table and admitted that there were too many aspects of the scene to be a coincidence. Neither of them held much truck with the two crimes being the work of the same killer; a copycat was the most likely scenario. And, the last thing they wanted to deal with was a repeat performance of a new serial killer reproducing the acts of an old one—they'd had their fill of that with the Axewoman of Tucson replicating the crimes of the Axeman of New Orleans.

Munch cursed as he dripped a thread of oil on his shirt. Pamela was going to be pissed. He tried to wipe it off but gave up. He realized that Belzer was saying something to him. "What?" he asked.

"I was saying that the next steps should be to fully investigate the 1947 killing by going to L.A. It's all well and good to read about it, but if we can talk it out with people we might glean something useful. Sound like a plan?" Belzer said.

"Yeah, I guess. Are you suggesting that you go out there? 'Cause I'm good with that. You know I don't like to travel."

"Yeah, I know. And, it's not like I'd be disrupting my home life by going."

"Heard anything from Margie?"

"Since she filed the divorce papers? No, not really. You know, I hired Quint to look into her recent past and see how long that affair was going on and if there's anything I can use as leverage to not get taken to the cleaner's in divorce court."

"He find anything?"

"Coupla things. We're working out a strategy." Belzer paused. "You know, Quint's been really kind about my situation. He's even letting me live here rent-free for a month or so until I get back on my feet." He flashed his teeth. "I guess he's forgiven me for throwing him in jail."

"He's okay. He was always a good cop. Wife's a little weird, though. But she was right on the money about my kid surviving the cancer." Munch grinned widely. "He's applying to Harvard and Princeton as well as the U of A. His guidance counselor says he's got a good shot." He cocked his head thoughtfully. "You ever regret not having kids?"

"Sometimes." He didn't elaborate or tell Munch about the two miscarriages early in his marriage. He had brushed off the grief and disappointment when he was thirty, but now at fifty-four he regretted not having kids or grandkids to dote on. "Okay. Let's finish up these last two chapters and hit Captain Ferdinand about my idea. I wonder if he'd be willing to hire Quint to accompany me and help?"

"Oh, sure. Ooh—look out the window—pigs are flying."

"Cute," Belzer said sourly, then he stiffened and cocked his head. "Did you hear something outside?"

"What? No. Probably just a raccoon or a coyote."

Belzer got up and opened the door and stared outside at the darkness. He did hear a very distant coyote howling, but he was sure that he'd heard something closer by. He walked carefully over to the garbage can and noted that the lid was off. He stared down into it and even in the dark under a blanket of stars and a sliver of moon he could see that something had rummaged around. Yeah, a damn raccoon, he thought. Next time the critter was going to meet his maker.

An affectionately amused Victor watched the two animated, redheaded Brits, who pretty much hadn't stopped talking in their heavily accented, ethnic-particular slang since they all arrived at the

Quintana house. He had met Raine four years earlier when he and Wilde visited his family in Hove, England, shortly after the Halloween wedding ceremony of Quint and Deliverance. The Sinclairs had had a rousing 21st birthday celebration for Raine on November 8th at Wilde's favorite pub, The Druid's Head in Brighton. Wilde's parents, Davey and Mamie, his brother, Danny, Danny's wife, Arabella, and their two sons Brett and Roger were in attendance, and the toasts, ale, bangers and mash, and fish and chips flew around their rowdy table. What amazed and heart-warmed Victor was that Wilde's family seemed to breezily accept who he was and welcomed Victor into their family circle. A wave of sadness passed over his soul as he thought about how his parents and nephew were still at odds with him for his "sinful lifestyle." He hadn't been back to New Orleans in two years, and phone calls were few and far between, and always strained. Times like that, he missed his older brother, Shaun, so much it was hard to bear. Shaun had been his rock, and Victor had lost him in January of 1978 when Shaun was murdered by the late Willow Cheney. He forced his thoughts away from tragic things and focused on the animate Raine.

"So, I thought, why not try something entirely new?" Raine was saying as she leaned back against the kitchen island and crunched on a pizza crust. "I was bloody sick of the London business scene, to say nothing of the social scene. The 80s are going too wild over there, just like my coke-sniffing wanker of an ex-boyfriend. So, like my adventurous uncle before me I decided to emigrate to the colonies and seek my fortune."

"We're still 'the colonies' to you?" Deliverance asked in amusement.

"You always will be," Wilde said. "It's a Brit thing."

"Even for a newly minted, naturalized citizen?" Quint asked his partner, grinning. Just that year the Union Jackers and their circle of friends had stood proudly and watch Wilde take his oath as a new American citizen. Of course, he retained his British citizenship, too.

"Especially." Wilde looked at his niece. "Are you planning to light here in the Old Pueblo or is this just a stopping-over point on your voyage of discovery?"

"I thought I'd like to stick around for a while and see how compatible I am with the desert, check out the bits and bobs."

"Then you'll stay with us," Victor said. "We've got a spare bedroom and plenty of space."

"Brilliant," she exclaimed. "You saved me the trouble of groveling."

"And Sinclairs can grovel with the best of them," Wilde added. He threw a sly look at Deliverance. "Think we can whip up a temp job for her at the office? She is, after all, a brilliant, magnificent computer master." He winked at Raine, who was theatrically preening.

"I think we can come up with something," Deliverance said. "Are you very familiar with the IBM personal computers and the Apple III's?"

"My forte," Raine replied.

"Great. My previous assistant had trouble interpreting the technology of a number two pencil. We can start you tomorrow. I'll give you the lay of the land, then we can spend a few hours tooling around Tucson to get you familiar with the street layout. You can drive, can't you?"

"Quite admirably, but as you Yanks would say, on the wrong side of the road." She helped herself to another glass of the Shiraz that Quint had broken out.

"Then we may need a few American driving lessons for you, too." Deliverance smiled at Quint. "This is going to be fun."

Quint looked at Victor and said, "I'm getting nervous. Two gorgeous, brainy, alpha females at the firm? We don't stand a chance."

"You got that right." Victor laughed.

The front doorbell rang and a distant voice—Aislinn's— screamed, "I'll get it!"

"The hell you will," Quint yelled back. "Stay in your room." He rose and grimaced at a curious Raine. "Last time she answered the door she brought in a decapitated head."

"What?" Raine exclaimed as her jaw dropped.

"Long story," Wilde said as Quint left the kitchen.

Quint returned in a few moments followed by Constantine Black Wolf.

Deliverance smiled at their new guest and said, "Constantine, would you like a glass of wine?"

Constantine shook his head. "No, thanks, Deliverance. I'm not staying. I was just in the neighborhood and thought I'd stop by to tell you all about what my brother, sister, and I decided." Before he went on he cocked his head and stared at the luscious redhead who was sipping wine and half-smiling at him as she none-too-subtly appraised him. "Sorry it took so long," he added absently as he initiated his own covert appraisal of the young woman. Six-feet-tall in barely one-inch boot heels; dark auburn hair that swung loosely past her shoulders; eyes that would have made Elizabeth Taylor sob and beat her chest in abject jealousy; and a mildly freckled oval face with a strong, straight nose and full red lips. She was wearing tighter-than-tight Gloria Vanderbilt designer jeans on long legs that stretched from Tucson to Baja, and a spandex, three-quarters-sleeve-length, sea-blue v-neck shirt that showed off her impressive breasts to their best advantage. A silver Celtic knot hung down her cleavage from a thin silver chain. She had matching Celtic knots in her delicate ears.

"I'm sorry, too," Wilde said. "I'm remiss in introducing you to my niece, Raine."

"Your niece?"

"Oh, yes. Raine, this is a friend of ours, Constantine Black Wolf."

"Ah, yes," she said mildly. "I believe you've mentioned him a few times." She stuck out her hand and smiled brightly. "Pleased to meet you, Constantine." Her steel-trap mind took in his salient points in a few seconds: late-twenties, slightly taller than she, café-au-lait complexion, thick, silky black hair maybe just a tad too long, and shockingly saturated green eyes in which a woman could be lost forever. Tall, dark, and handsome—oh, yeah.

He barely hesitated a second before he took her hand; it was long-fingered, soft, and warm. His deep green eyes met her sparkling violet ones, and for the first time in a very long time he felt an unexpected sexual rush like boiling lava running through every single vein.

"On second thought, I think I'll have that glass of wine," he said. He took the Shiraz from Deliverance's hand and took a deep sip. "Okay," he said slowly. "The bottom line is that we've decided that we're not going to approach … him. We plan on living our lives with the parents we've got. And that … 'retainer' from … him—feel free to keep it. However, if he does survive the next couple of months, we'd prefer that you don't enlighten him. Fair enough?"

"Fair enough," Quint said.

"Good," Constantine said. Then he addressed Raine. "Are you here for a visit?"

"Somewhat," she said. "I'm here indefinitely while I … find myself. I'll be working with Uncle Wilde and the gang for a bit. I've a degree in computer technology, you see. Cambridge."

Constantine's eyebrows arched. "I attended a Social Anthropology seminar there about a year ago. Lovely campus and very focused, intelligent students. I was especially impressed by the analysis on Ernest Gellner's pioneering in the study of nationalism and ethnic identity movements."

"Dr. Smythe-Dane? I remember his seminars from my time there. Very charismatic. I didn't solely take computer courses but diversified. I've even taken a couple of Anthropology and Psychology courses, and 16th Century English Literature." She smiled broadly. "I can recite virtually all of Shakespeare's sonnets."

"Smart. It's better to be academically well-rounded." He paused, unaware that the Union Jackers were watching the interaction with undisguised amusement. He went on. "Are you interested in auditing any college courses here? I can give you a tour of Saguaro Western and introduce you to some department heads."

"That sounds like a right fine plan. Are you available Friday?"

"I can be. Let's do that." He felt ridiculously lightheaded.

Raine turned to Deliverance. "May I be released from duties on Friday?"

"You may," Deliverance said, fighting back a grin.

"Why is it everyone asks Deliverance for permission and none of us?" Wilde grumbled.

"You seriously have to ask that?" Quint retorted.

"Really," Victor sighed.

Constantine was oblivious to their banter as he kept his eyes fixed on Raine's face. Without a thought he said, "Would you like to go out to dinner tomorrow night? I know a good Mexican place called Mariposa Linda's."

"Ah—the pretty butterfly. I'd love to. I expect you can pick me up at the office at, what, say five?"

"Five is … fine. Well," he said slowly as he regained some of his equilibrium, "I'd better get going. I'm supposed to have dinner tonight with my brother and his … life mate."

"That would be Cress and Gray, correct?" she said.

"I guess your uncle has updated you on our little circle. Yes. You can meet them Friday at the college. Cress's a professor of Criminology there. Gray's the Anthropology department head." He paused. "Well, until tomorrow. Gentlemen, Deliverance. Thank you for the wine."

"I'll see you out," Quint said and with fast nods all the way around he led Constantine through the kitchen and saw him to the front door.

Just before he arrived back at the kitchen he heard Raine say, "A right fit bloke. I say, Uncle—is there a chemist anywhere near here? I'd like to pick up a packet of French letters."

Quint heard Wilde choking on his wine as he entered; Victor was pounding his back and Deliverance was bent over laughing.

"What did I miss?" Quint asked.

Deliverance wiped her eyes and exchanged a wide grin with Raine. "She's got a hankering for a chimichanga, and we're not talking Combination C."

CHAPTER EIGHT

Western films were a staple of the 1910s, 1920s, 1930s, and 1940s; amongst the first if not the very first cinematic western was 1903's *The Great Train Robbery*, which, oddly, was actually shot in Milltown, New Jersey. For the most part they were filmed on the back lots of Hollywood studios. That's not to say that some movies didn't film on location, but the extent of that depended on the studio, the film itself, the budget, and the actors; i.e., whether or not they were "stars" whose cinematic efforts required the utmost reality and quality.

In 1939 William Holden and Jean Arthur were contracted by Columbia Studios to film *Arizona*, a standard black-and-white effort with an all-too-familiar plot and a huge $2,000,000 budget; adjusted for inflation, that production cost would be $14.3 million dollars in 1983. In one month and ten days a slew of energetic workers erected fifty buildings, and Old Tucson Studios was born. Billed as "The screen's mightiest spectacle of love and adventure!" the film wasn't a major hit; the *New York Times* wrote: "What Phoebe [Arthur] needs, obviously, is a strong man around - not exactly William Holden... [He is not] sufficiently far from knee-pants to seem credible as protective knight in armor." No, the film was forgettable, but the newly created old-west town certainly was not.

Over the following four decades a slew of western and non-western movies and television shows were filmed entirely or partially at Old Tucson, including *The Bells of St. Mary's, Broken Arrow, 3:10 to Yuma, Rio Bravo, Gunfight at the OK Corral, Monte Walsh, Rio Lobo, Joe Kidd, Death Wish, The Life and Times of Judge Roy Bean, The Man Who Loved Cat Dancing, Tom Horn,* and *The Cannonball Run*. With the films being made at the studio Tucson was happily inundated with Hollywood luminaries such as John Wayne, Lee Marvin, Steve McQueen, Paul Newman, Charles Bronson, Angie Dickinson, Ricky Nelson, Walter Brennan, and Burt Reynolds.

In addition to the cinematic efforts and influx of associated monies, Old Tucson brought in swarms of tourists who marveled at the realistic building façades, cheap souvenirs, and staged gunfights and stunts. Rare was it that a kid visited and went away without a tinny "sheriff's badge" with "Old Tucson" and/or his name etched on it. Tee-shirts and sepia-toned postcards with images of noble Native Americans were popular, as were fresh fudge made onsite and tiny cacti in ceramic pots to take home to boast to one's family and friends about the trip of a lifetime. Snacks and satisfying hot fare could be purchased, and one could delightfully quench his or her thirst with prickly pear lemonade.

By 1983 Old Tucson was a natural stopping-over point for snowbirds and other tourists and was always packed on weekends. It was reached easily from Tucson proper on virtually the same route necessary to take to reach the Arizona-Sonora Desert Museum and Saguaro National Monument West; simply turn left at the intersection of Kinney Road and Gates Pass instead of right, and within a thousand feet you were pulling into the spacious parking lot.

The desert land surrounding Old Tucson was expansive on both sides of South Kinney, which merged into a single two-lane road south about a mile. The Tucson Mountains in the west were visible from every angle. The desert surrounding the town seemed endless and boringly mundane in its never-ending swaths of sand, scrub brush, and cacti. However, to two bored teenagers from the Bronx it offered an exciting diversion from their mundane lives as a sophomore and junior in Stuyvesant High School, and especially from their nauseatingly oppressive schedule of sights and attractions being foisted on them by their dreary parents and their drearier three younger siblings. While Lillian and Adam Falk ushered their three youngest around the enticing sights of the attraction, fourteen-year-old Dawn and fifteen-year-old Dale carefully slipped away and jogged out of the park to explore the surrounding desert arena. Throwing covert, guilty looks behind them, they headed south on Kinney until they came to the point where the north and south separated roads merged into one and rolled off south as far as the eye could see. Right at the merge point on the west side of the road was a triangular cement inlet where cars could park or at which they could make a U-turn. At the end of the inlet was a small set of railings with an opening, and they swished past it out to the open, sandy land dotted with skinny, medium-tall saguaro cacti, brutal-looking crucifixion thorn bushes, prickly pear, jumping cholla, and ocotillo; the distant Tucson Mountains rose up against the clear horizon like a magnificent geological guard to the impressive landscape.

They followed a depressed, wide path that might have been a dry wash awaiting the monsoon rainfall and a gush of whirling water down its length. They learned from one of the guides in the attraction that washes could be dry as a bone one second, and then a dangerous battering of water and debris the next, with no warning; quite a few people had met their fates in a dry wash. Today, however, as November edged its way towards the last month of the year, the path truly was dry as they crackled twigs under their sneakers and took snapshots of the various cacti and a few skittering reptiles. Dale swore he'd seen a rattler under a bush, but his wiser sister refused to let him check it out.

Around a hundred feet down the wide path seemed to stop, although they could see past it to a very narrow path aimed north and south. Dawn argued that they should return to Old Tucson the same way they came but her brother dug in his stubborn heels. Groaning and calling him an idiot she began following him off the wide path towards a thick copse of buckhorn cholla. They made it to within five feet of the copse, then Dale stopped dead in his tracks; his sister crashed into him and called him a stupid moron and started to move around him. Then she, too, stopped dead in her tracks, and in perfect synchronicity they started shrieking and bolted back towards the road where they ran like the devil was chasing them back to the attraction and into their parents' annoyed arms. They babbled out what they had seen, and fifteen minutes later in the distance the wail of a police siren disturbed the beautiful peace of the Sonoran Desert.

Detective partners Forest Baxter and Yale Cornell watched as the unmarked police car driven by Detective Reichardt Belzer pulled up in the Kinney Road inlet. Baxter could see that Munch had a very sour expression on his face as his jaw moved under his inexorable gum-chewing. Belzer and Munch exited the car and walked over to their associates and shook hands. Munch spit out his wad of gum, much to Cornell's disgust. A fastidious man who wore three-piece business suits no matter how hot the summers might get, Cornell found Munch to be a little too "rustic" for his tastes. Still, he respected the man's professional instincts and generally managed to endure him.

"We pulled this lovely scene about an hour ago," Baxter said as he began walking down the wide dry wash. The men walked the hundred feet single file, and Belzer could see that his favorite forensics team, led by Pete Murphy, was already in action processing the scene.

"Whatcha got, Kreskin?" Belzer asked Pete as they stood about three feet away from the body.

Without looking up Pete touched his hand to his head and scrunched up his face. "I sense … a male victim, possibly between age three and ninety-three, possibly dead, although without a head I'd be making a lot of educated guesses."

"Cute," Munch growled as he shoved another stick of gum into his mouth. "Time of death?"

"Not too ripe or eaten. Maybe twenty-four hours. Maybe not."

"Wallet? ID?"

"Nope. Just this." He handed Munch a plastic evidence bag containing a playing card, a jack. "Could be a gambler."

"Any trace of the head?"

"Not so far," Pete said as he concentrated on using his pliers to pull out a tiny snake wriggling around in the savaged neck. "Critters got some of this guy but not too bad. I'll know more when he gets to the M.E.'s." He held up the undulating reptile. "Baby rattler. Cutie pie." He stuck it in a jar.

"That's why we dragged you here," Baxter said to Belzer. "Missing head, just like the one you're working. Although the ragged edges of the neck could indicate that a coyote or wolf ripped it off and carried it away. They don't usually do that, but I wouldn't rule anything out yet."

"Totally different victim, though," Belzer said as his eyes took in every possible aspect of the body and the surrounding area. He nodded towards the body. "A man this time, and an older one— look at the foot." He pointed to the bare foot, whose shoe lay two feet away with chew marks. "Bunion and rough side and heel. Looks much older on first glance, and our lady seems to be in her twenties."

"Maybe," Cornell said. He arched his eyebrows and asked

Belzer, "Gonna call your pal Quint to see if he's gotten any more deliveries?"

"I think he would have contacted us by now if he did, but I'll call him anyway. Need anything else from us?"

"Nope. Just wanted to share the joy."

"Then we're off." He nodded to Munch who followed him carefully through the brush and back to their car. They sat quietly in the car for a moment before Belzer said, "Any sense that we've got the same killer besides the missing head?"

"Christ, I hope not. Had my fill of serial killers."

"Could be a coincidence. The head could have been carried off."

"Sure."

"Okay, let's head over to Union Jack and spill our guts." He started the car and made a smooth turn onto Kinney north, then headed east on Gates Pass. At Munch's annoying, insistent urging, he pulled into a Chinese place off Silverbell and ordered greasy, fattening takeout that they finished entirely before they nudged the car up to Swan. Munch promised to make it up to him on Thursday at the Munch holiday dinner, to which Belzer was invited.

Constantine was having trouble concentrating today on his outline for his lecture on Mayan cultural practices. He had been having more than a little trouble concentrating lately, and he was well aware that it was due to his unexpected romantic life. He thought he was satisfied with his work and his family before she dropped into his life like an F5 tornado. He wasn't looking for romance or sex, but there it was, in spades. At times he felt like he was being swept up in a raging tsunami with no control over his mind, heart, or body. What surprised him the most was that he was surrendering to that tsunami without so much as a weak protest. In the three weeks since he had met Raine they had hit the sheets nearly every night.

She was an uninhibited lover, much as Cheyenne had been, but the difference was that while Cheyenne had expected to be pleased, Raine was hell-bent on pleasing him.

And she wasn't simply a stunningly sexual creature, but as intelligent as he was. Her computer skills were exemplary, and he had even let her rearrange his course files into ones more easily searched and accessed in his IBM PC. They had had an all-night discussion in bed on the anthropological aspects of Stonehenge, and she made several key points that he'd never considered before. When he showed her around campus and introduced her to Cress and Gray, she charmed them, and he somehow intuited that that charm was sincere and there was nothing artificial about her. Cress confided later that if had been straight, he would have snatched her away from his brother without a thought. Constantine hadn't yet had the chance to introduce her to Phaedra, Moon Wolf, and their kids, but he'd hoped that would take place during Thanksgiving dinner in two days. Not likely though—she wanted to spend her first holiday in the states with her uncle and his "family." She said she could come over after dinner for a drink and to meet the Begays.

A sharp knock at the door roused him from his thoughts and he smiled as Cress walked in and parked himself in his brother's guest chair.

"I see you're gathering wool again, big brother," Cress said. "The usual spinner?"

"Ha-ha," Constantine replied but not without amusement.

"Not criticizing. Just happy that you seemed to have found someone. It's about time."

"Maybe. But I guess ..."

"Guess what?"

"Guess I'm still waiting for a shoe to drop. It makes me nervous to be too happy."

"You really are hopeless," Cress sighed. "Just enjoy what you have and stop looking for hidden meanings or warning signs. Promise?"

"Yeah, yeah—I promise."

"Good. Gray and I are going to the movies tonight. Some new holiday film called *A Christmas Story*. You and Raine want to come?"

"Think I'll pass. I'm finishing up the final semester test, then Raine and I are going out for a fast dinner at The Happy Spartan."

"Going back to your place afterwards?" Cress's eyes twinkled.

"Maybe."

"Maybe. Right. When are the two of you going to move in together?"

"Whoa, little brother. That's moving too fast. One step at a time, okay? How's Boomer?"

"Prancing around acting like a proud dad to Sugarlips' litter. I knew I should have gotten her spayed right away after we adopted her. Oh, well. The pug pups are beyond adorable. We're giving one to Gray's mom and dad. They've been bereft since Saffron died two years ago and it's well past time they had a new fur child to spoil. Persa's getting one, too, and I promised one to Bliss's kid. We're keeping the fourth one, a little brownie we've dubbed Pugsley Doright. And ... there is the fifth, a sad little boy of the most beautiful ebony color that could use a good home ..."

"No dogs for me, please."

"Fine. We'll keep him until we can find a good home, or ... we'll just keep him."

"Thank you."

"That your course outline for next semester?" Cress didn't wait for an answer before he picked up the outline for a class called Inuits: Stark Landscape, Inspired Beliefs. He waved the paper at his brother. "You planning on going there to study sometime? It's chilly."

"Maybe someday. You all packed?" Cress, Gray, Victor, and Wilde were scheduled to fly off to Australia the day after Thanksgiving for a four-week vacation-cum-work trip to the land Down Under. They were scheduled to return on December 23rd in time for Christmas.

"We are. Of course, we still have to find somewhere or someone to take care of the dogs while we're gone."

"Can't Phaedra or the Kingstons take them?"

"It's not a good idea to take the whole new litter and parents up north for a long trip. I suppose Phaedra could take them, although she's busy as hell in her gallery and with the two kids. And she is pregnant." He paused and batted his eyes.

"Oh, no," Constantine said. "Oh, no."

"I suppose worst comes to worst we could euthanize them and start our pet family all over again in the new year."

"I hate you."

"I know."

"I don't really like dogs."

"I know."

"You will so incredibly owe me for this one."

"I always pay my debts."

"Fine, fine. I'll move into your house and take care of the smelly little ratbags since it would be disastrous for my townhouse."

"I've already cleaned the guest room and put on fresh new linens. The refrigerator is fully stocked, and I bought a couple new bottles of wine that your lady friend might like to try."

"Those flat-faced beasts aren't the only ratbags in the family."

Cress laughed. There was another knock at the door, and it opened to reveal a student who was working in the mailroom.

"Delivery, Dr. Black Wolf," the kid said. He placed the box on Constantine's desk and left without another word.

"Hmm," Constantine said. "I didn't order anything." He noted the bookstore address label. "Oh, wait—yes, I ordered those two new Stephen King books, *Christine* and *Pet Sematary*. *Phantoms* by Dean Koontz, too. Stocking up for the Christmas break. You can borrow them when you get back." He slit open the masking tape and flipped the box lids back. He looked down inside the box and kept looking down.

Cress frowned. He got up and walked around the desk to stare down at his brother's books. He did a double-take, then spoke casually.

"Don't you just hate it when someone mistakenly sends a head instead of hardback?"

CHAPTER NINE

It was a perfect day. Thanksgiving dawned to a mild 70°F with a nearly cloudless blue sky and the prevailing easterly winds blowing gently at a very pleasant five-to-seven miles per hour.

Moon Wolf extracted the twenty-five-pound turkey from the oven and noted with satisfaction that it was perfectly brown. Fifteen more minutes and the clan would be ready to eat. He tasted the cornbread-bacon stuffing—perfect. He smiled over at Phaedra, who was boiling potatoes to mash and putting the last touches on sweet potatoes that they'd pop into the lower rack of the oven. The gravy was simmering on the stove along with the baby carrots; the five pies—two pecan, one pumpkin, one apple, and one blueberry—were resting on the counter, awaiting the final moments of the holiday meal. Their guests had brought additional dishes to share: Constantine had made jambalaya, and Mariko Kingston had made a traditional Japanese New Year's dish, osechi ryori. Moon Wolf had prepared a Navajo recipe for baked venison and a soup made of cornmeal, wild celery, and wild onion. This was very much a multi-ethnic culinary celebration.

A gallon of unspiked eggnog was chilling in the refrigerator; there would be Jamaican rum for those who wished to doctor it up. Apple cider, wine, and iced tea would round out the drink menu. Phaedra had purchased a special bottle of expensive Dom Pérignon: today was also Moon Wolf's fortieth birthday. Phaedra promised her husband a very special birthday celebration that night when their guests left. He could barely contain his anticipation.

Moon Wolf heard the rustlings of their guests in the formal dining room. He knew that Mariko and Grayson were setting the table while the younger guests relaxed on the various sofas in the family room. He heard a sharp giggle from Persa and thought that she was being cuddled by Constantine. Another giggle proved that Wolfie was being pampered by his Uncle Cress. Moon Wolf never failed to wonder about the good luck he had to find his woman and become absorbed into her close-knit family. In his mid-thirties he had been struggling to endure a very solitary life after his Vietnam service, his wife's infidelity, and the contentious divorce that drained him of what little funds he had and what little faith he'd had in human nature.

74

Meeting Phaedra changed all that. Despite the devastating loss of the man she loved, Luke Wheeler, and getting through life as a single mother, she was still vibrant and upbeat, and as beautiful a woman inside and out as he had ever seen. They had fallen in love almost immediately, and within a month had gone into business together (he made and sold beautiful silver jewelry in her art gallery), moved in together, and married. Five years later they were as solid a couple as one could find, and he couldn't imagine living out his life without her and the kids. He was eager to assume parental duties to their third child, which would be born in February. They hadn't selected a name yet, but were bandying about French, Greek, and Navajo names. He was hoping for another boy.

Phaedra popped the sweet potatoes into the oven after Moon Wolf stuck the turkey back in. She wrapped her arms around his waist and kissed him sweetly. He held her close for a long moment before she sighed and said they needed to bring the fixin's into the dining room. They picked up the cornbread she'd baked that morning and a pitcher of iced tea and went in. Mariko and her husband had set the table for nine perfectly and had lit the candles at each end of the large rectangular table. She'd even set up the highchair for Wolfie. She made a comment to Phaedra that she just loved the new china and flatware; Phaedra laughed and said they'd come from Goldwater's especially for this occasion, and so had the expensive lace tablecloth garnished with handmade hummingbirds.

Just after 2:30 PM all nine celebrants were gathered around the table. They couldn't eat any earlier because the men made it clear that they wanted to watch the Detroit Lions-Pittsburgh Steelers football game that started at 10:30 AM MST at Michigan's Pontiac Silverdome. Gray and his father, Grayson, were Steelers' fans; the rest were cheering on the Lions. There were small friendly wagers on the outcome and stats, and both Kingstons lost their money and face as the Lions crucified the Steelers with a 45-to-3 win. Gary Anderson had made a 38-yard field goal in the second quarter, his team's only scoring points. Under the onslaught of players like Billy Sims and Ulysses Norris the Lions had steamrolled their opponents to a very embarrassing loss. Gray lost ten bucks to Cress, and Grayson shelled out a twenty to a triumphant Moon Wolf. They all agreed that

Pennsylvania teams weren't having a successful year—the Baltimore Orioles had beaten the Philadelphia Phillies four games to one to win the World Series in October.

Phaedra offered a short Catholic prayer, and Moon Wolf one from the Navajo culture. Then they all began to dig in and a rousing, cacophonous conversation flowed happily and smoothly through the warm house. Everyone was trying to steer away from the elephant in the room, Constantine's delivery of a human head. He had made a few brief statements about it shortly before they sat down to satisfy some curiosity: yes, the police were investigating and had interrogated the mailroom personnel; yes, it seemed to be the head of the body discovered near Old Tucson; no, they weren't certain if it had any relation to the headless corpse found in Sabino Canyon; yes, he had discussed the matter with the police and the Union Jackers and would probably be interviewed and re-interviewed yet again; and yes, the Australia trip was definitely on for his brother and friends.

"It was a devastating film to watch," Mariko said quietly as she scooped the chunky mashed potatoes onto her plate next to her baked sweet potato and sprinkled a generous helping of paprika on them. She was speaking of a TV movie that had been shown four days earlier, *The Day After*, about a full-scale nuclear war between the United States and the Soviet Union. The film was horrifically realistic and had been watched by one hundred million people riveted to their television sets.

"Maybe people need to be devastated," Phaedra said, "so nothing like that can truly happen again." She was thinking of how Mariko, a Japanese citizen at the time Hiroshima and Nagasaki were bombed, had lived through the horror of atomic bombs and a shell-shocked, conquered country that needed to be rebuilt. It was during the War Crimes Trials in Japan that she had met Lieutenant Grayson Grant Kingston III; they had fallen in love and defied cultures and expectations to have a child and marry, although not in that order. Gray was their only child, the blending of two races as denoted by his first and middle names: Grayson Akihiko. Ironically enough, he had been born on August 6, 1947, the second anniversary of the bombing of Hiroshima.

"I agree," Cress said. "People need to remember history in order not to repeat it."

"That theory doesn't seem to be working very well," Constantine opined as he cut off a drumstick. "Witness Vietnam, Pol Pot, Jonestown, the Beirut barracks bombing in October that killed 241 U.S. servicemen. Less than a month ago we had a Cold War scare with Able Archer 83 when the Soviets misinterpreted a simple NATO exercise."

"We'll always be in jeopardy because we're human, and humans make mistakes, misinterpretations, have emotions and hatreds. We can decrease some, eliminate others, but our world will always be at war with itself in some way," Grayson said. He turned and smiled at his wife. "All we can do to mitigate the negative aspects of civilization is love." He gently kissed Mariko's cheek. He had loved that woman for thirty-seven years and would until the day he died.

"Let's talk about a lighter subject," Grayson said. He turned to Constantine. "I hear you're taking care of the pugs while Cress and Gray are Down Under."

"I was relentlessly bullied into it," Constantine said.

"Should we worry about our puppy being drop-kicked?" Mariko asked. From photos she had selected the littlest female that she and her husband promptly named Tiger Lily.

"I promise not to exact any mayhem on the miserable little beasts," Constantine replied.

"Well, that gives me a warm and fuzzy feeling," Cress said as he piled a heap of Moon Wolf's special venison onto his plate. He had already finished half a turkey breast. He addressed Mariko. "I'm trying to get him to adopt the baby, who we've temporarily named Blackjack."

"Not a chance," his brother retorted.

"Do you know if your girlfriend likes dogs? That might be an in with her," Gray offered.

"I have no idea. I'm already in with her." He groaned almost inaudibly, thinking about the double entendre he'd made.

"Don't you think you should find out?"

"I'll think about it."

"She is coming over later to meet the clan and have a drink, right?" Moon Wolf asked.

"She'll be here around three or four. I believe they ate early so they could watch the other football game. She's not sanguine about our version of football being a real sport."

"Can't wait to meet her and give her the true skinny on my big brotherrrrr," Phaedra singsonged as she grinned and dug into her jambalaya.

Deliverance had basically banished her husband, children, and friends from her kitchen despite the excess amount of food and preparation. As modern a woman as one could find, she still stuck to traditions of the culture in which she'd been brought up and considered the kitchen solely her domicile. The one person she did allow to help her was her mother, Charity, who with Deliverance's father, Nicolae, had flown out to stay with the Quintanas for a week. They had visited once before and stayed in the casita, but since Belzer was bunking down there Quint went up to the Foothills Mall to a great furniture shop where he'd picked up their living room set. His wife had given him the task of picking out a brand-new bedroom set. She said she trusted his judgment; that made him very nervous about making a fashion faux pas, so he covertly dragged Raine into the fray and she accompanied him to the store. A half hour later he signed the papers for a cherry-wood bedroom set with a four-poster bed, two nightstands, a mirrored chest, and an armoire, to be delivered the next day. When the delivery came he watched his wife's face with a mild sense of dread, but was relieved when she smiled, said, "You done good," and directed the movers where to put the set in their unused spare room. She confessed to him afterwards that the set perfectly reflected the style of old New England, and her parents would love it. She put the handmade patchwork quilt that her mother had sewn and sent for her last birthday on the bed.

Charity checked the baked potatoes and made sure the chive and onion sour cream was mixed to her version of perfect consistency. She and her daughter chattered the whole time they were preparing the meal, and Charity was so happy that her daughter, who'd had problematic teenage years, was now happy, healthy, a loving wife and mother, a smashing businesswoman, and was on her way to a college degree. Her only regret was that Deliverance and her family were thousands of miles away, but they stayed in as close touch as possible. The Quintanas had visited the Blaskós three times, and not a week went by without Deliverance calling her mother.

"Did you glaze the ham?" Deliverance asked as she mashed the sweet potatoes, scraped them into a glass dish, and put on a thick layer of miniature marshmallows for the baking.

"You really have to ask that? Who taught you to cook?" Charity said.

"Sorry. You know I get crazy during major-meal holidays."

"Well, don't," Charity replied amiably as she stirred the pan-drippings gravy. She threw a cautious glance over at her daughter. "I have an interesting news tidbit."

"Do tell," Deliverance said as she opened the oven and put the sweet potato dish on the bottom rack.

"Dear old Winston is continuing to have a streak of bad luck."

"A thick streak?"

"Very much so."

"Good. Well—dish." Deliverance had put her rich, right-side-of-the-tracks ex-boyfriend way out of her mind years earlier. She was fifteen when he seduced her, and sixteen when she gave birth to his stillborn son, whom she had named David John Dane. Shortly thereafter when her father was beaten by thugs and her parents were threatened if she didn't leave town, she left her hometown of Salem and snowballed towards the series of life events that brought her to Tucson and to the life she had today.

"A double-header," Charity said. "His wife divorced him a few months ago and the next day married one of his fellow firm lawyers. Heard she got a whopper of a settlement—took him to the cleaners. She's pregnant, too. The cherry on the cake is that the new husband's father founded the law firm and he fired Winnie right after the divorce was final. I hear tell he's pretty much blackballed in Boston and is sending out his less-than stellar résumé to firms in Montana and North Dakota."

"Couldn't happen to a nicer guy. Hope he likes minus-zero wind chill factors and his balls freeze."

Charity narrowed her eyes. "They say he never really recovered emotionally from that unsolved kidnapping and beating he received, oh, right around the time you were married and flew off on your honeymoon."

"Darn shame." Deliverance gathered her long hair into a frothy ponytail and brushed her bangs away from her face.

"You wouldn't know anything about that, though, would you?"

"I believe it was the day I got married and then flew off to England," she said, deflecting a real answer. "So very sad, though." She knew her mother didn't believe her and silently championed what may have been a creative retribution for the pain he had caused their family. It was best if Charity had no idea that, yes, the Union Jackers were responsible for that revenge. It was Quint's wedding gift to her. She washed her hands and turned to Charity. "Time to get the food on the table before the wild beasts start massing." She cut a few choice pieces off the bird then yelled, "Quint," and a moment later her husband popped in. "Get the turkey on the serving plate and take it in, please." She tossed the turkey strips equally to the two hungry dogs sitting patiently at her feet.

"Yes, ma'am," he said.

Charity smiled to herself at the sight of the tall, dark, handsome Hispanic male toeing the line with the tiny woman who apparently ruled the roost. She noted that Quint had shaved his full, short beard off into a devilish moustache and goatee, but his ebony hair was still shoulder-length and layered. She thought that he looked like the young carny worker she had fallen in love with thirty years earlier. By the look of her grandson the boy was going to grow up looking a hell of a lot like his father except for the stunning blue eyes that came from her branch of the family.

Deliverance yelled again and Wilde and Victor came running, and a few moments later, just a tad after noon, all the food was on the table. Charity gave a Wiccan blessing and had barely gotten the last syllable out when the beasts fell on the food and started jockeying for the best cuts of turkey and ham. Deliverance shook her head and commented, "It's like watching dinner hour on the Serengeti."

Wilde, not knowing when to hold back an argument, taunted Deliverance about the "so-called 'football' game" they planned on watching after dinner. They'd had this argument many times over the years, when she had said that it was called football "because they friggin' *kick* it!" He was equally as adamant that soccer was true "football." Raine chimed in and took her uncle's side and, surprisingly, so did Nicolae, a Romanian for whom soccer was the best game of athletes on the planet. He stridently boasted that his birth country had been one of the four national European teams (Yugoslavia, France, and Belgium were the other three) that had taken part in the very first FIFA (Fédération Internationale de Football Association) World Cup in 1930. He admitted that they had lost that year and every other year for which they qualified, but Romanians were a determined people and the win was guaranteed sometime in the future.

Wilde commented mildly that England had won in 1966. He got a savage glare from his partner's father. To mollify the fierce old man, he also made a point to say the United States had placed only once, and that was also in 1930 in third place. Quint said it didn't matter—that wasn't really football and so any stats on it were pointless. He stopped eating long enough to change the albums on the stereo, and a moment later Ronnie Milsap started singing about a *Stranger in My House*. The rest of the group just groaned at the country-western album, but Quint grinned, sat down, and dumped a pile of sweet potatoes on his plate. Ah, if they only knew that the next album would be T.G. Sheppard. He loved to croon *Only One You* to his wife in intimate moments ("There's only one Eiffel Tower, One finest hour, One New York town, One 5th Avenue, There's only one Mona Lisa, One Leaning Tower Of Pisa, One Paris and there's only one you."). Sickeningly sweet, he knew, but he just worshipped his woman.

Victor rerouted the growingly contentious argument by commenting on the upcoming football game between the Dallas Cowboys and the St. Louis Cardinals at Texas Stadium. A southerner, he said that he had to put his money on Dallas and on what he thought would be the game's MVP, Tony Dorsett. Quint had a bet on Dallas, too, but Wilde and Raine, united in their arrogance about the faux-football game, placed bets on the Cardinals just to be persnickety and annoy the colonials. Deliverance and her parents opted out of the fray.

The diners segued away from sports and hit a variety of other subjects, including the entire heads' delivery situation. Raine's ears perked up when Quint told them about the investigation into the head.

Constantine had told her a few tidbits, but not too much. She was going to prod him about it later today when she visited his family. Quint mentioned that although the police department couldn't hire him to accompany Belzer to L.A. the first week of December, he was going on his own dime since he had a vested interest in the delivery of heads, and why he had been chosen as a recipient, and certainly why Constantine had been.

During the grabbing and chomping and jockeying for the best cuts of meat—and pretty much finishing off the spiked eggnog (except the kids)—the group talked about current events.

The United States invaded the island of Grenada, north of Venezuela, in October. The United Nations General Assembly nearly unanimously condemned the act as "a flagrant violation of international law." Quint was in total agreement, saying that they'd had no reason to go into a sovereign foreign country any more than they did Vietnam. He worried about the fate of young men in the future if the U.S. continued to stick its nose into global matters that were none of its business. Look what happened, he said, in Beirut—nearly three hundred American servicemen killed. He didn't want his son being put in that kind of harm's way.

Touchy subject though it was, the AIDS situation was brought up. It was gaining momentum, and many more cases had occurred, more deaths, and more scientific research. The United States Public Health Service had revised their blood donation guidelines to exclude so-called "high-risk groups" from donating blood or plasma; just the previous year a baby contracted the disease from a blood transfusion. It was bandied about that the disease was a "gay" disease, and many sanctimonious idiots were declaring that it was a just punishment from God for the evil behavior of sinful men. Deaths were occurring in countries such as Brazil, Colombia, Canada, and Australia. No one truly knew the parameters of how the disease was transmitted, and the lack of knowledge bred uncertainty and fear.

Wilde was silent on the matter. He was lost in thought about his 1978 encounter with Adam Manzone's young associate, Bandit. Bandit had been a skinny, gap-toothed, somewhat promiscuous but sweet kid whom Wilde had met when he and Deliverance traveled up to San Francisco to retrieve Quint from jail and his drifting life there after he'd resigned from the Tucson police force and left town. The night before Quint was released Wilde had spent an exhilarating evening and night with Bandit, and had some of the most inventive, satisfying sex he'd ever experienced. It was a one-night stand, and they never saw one another again. Adam had called Wilde in November of 1981 to say that Bandit had died from that new "cancer;" Adam had his friend cremated and Bandit's urn rested in the Manzone home. At least, Wilde thought, he and Victor weren't at risk for catching the disease since they had been a faithful, committed couple for the past five years. Still, he mourned the sad young life of a good man whose behavior had led to his death and to the grief of his friends.

Victor turned the conversation to a topic less depressing. He was thrilled that President Reagan had signed a bill creating a federal holiday in honor of Dr. Martin Luther King, Jr. Starting in 1986 the third Monday of every January would honor the late civil rights leader. He was less than thrilled at some of the resentment and blowback about the action, but, he said, prejudice was far from an archaic concept even as the world moved closer to the twenty-first century. He was not so well-disposed about the Reverend Jesse Jackson throwing his hat into the presidential candidacy ring for the 1984 election. He admired some of Jackson's efforts, but not enough to dissipate his doubts about him. He wondered aloud whether had King lived might he have been a viable candidate, and he hoped to live long enough to see the first black president. He agreed with Quint that Reagan—for better or worse—was a lock for a second term.

Wilde and Victor carried out the depleted meal plates and Nicolae brought in the pies. Within five minutes the two pumpkin pies were decimated, and Quint was working on the Dutch apple pie along with his kids. He kept eyeing the clock until his wife blew out a hard breath and told him to "go put on the friggin' TV." Like a herd of wildebeests, the men swarmed into the great room and parked themselves on the couches. They could hear Deliverance, Charity, and Raine banging dishes and pans around in the kitchen but basically ignored the none-too-subtle hints that perhaps they should have helped to clean up.

Quint tuned the TV set to NBC and turned the antenna box

knob slowly, moving the large roof antenna around until the picture was crystal-clear. His twins were parked to either side of him and he held Vikki on his lap. The game started on time and there were whistles and catcalls when the Dallas Cowboys Cheerleaders ran onto the field. Raine came in and sat next to Wilde, but Deliverance and Charity remained in the kitchen washing dishes and having an intimate mother-daughter conversation.

Raine hung in for the first quarter of the football game, where both the Cardinals and the Cowboys scored seven points. She stayed through part of the second quarter until Tony Dorsett rushed for five yards off a Rafael Septién kick, bringing the Cowboys' score up to fourteen. She had lost interest by that point and bid everyone goodbye and headed off to the Begay house. She told Wilde to hold her winnings on the Dallas game for her return, smirking at Victor and Quint. She was confident in her bet, but when she did return after a long night with her boyfriend, she had to shell out fifty bucks—the Cowboys had kicked the Cardinals' asses, 35 to 17, but not so badly as the Lions had creamed the Steelers.

He lowered the military-grade day/night binoculars as Raine got in Wilde's car and drove off. He picked through the ridiculously large number of fast-food bags in his front seat until he found the half-eaten hamburger. It was cold, but he didn't care; it was sustenance— of a sort. He was parked a good half mile away from the house and had a clear view of the houses and properties. He flipped open his notepad and scribbled down, "Raine left 2:47, carrying what looked like a bottle of wine."

He choked down the rest of the hamburger and slurped down the remaining warm Coke, his sad version of a Thanksgiving dinner. He had been sitting in his car, his butt slowly numbing, for two hours. He was pretty sure that the group inside would be there for the rest of the day. He raised the binoculars one more time for a few minutes, frowned at a slight movement out near the casita, then stored them in their case.

He was tired; it was time to go home. He had plans to make.

Very important plans.

CHAPTER TEN

Quint smiled over at Belzer from the payphone at the corner of Hollywood Boulevard and Sycamore Street. He flashed a thumb's-up. "Eighty-four seconds," he said proudly before finishing off his conversation with his wife. He hung up and had a big grin on his face. "Imagine that—less than a minute and a half for my daughter to solve a Rubik's Cube."

"Smart kid," Belzer agreed as he scanned the four corners with a practiced cop's eye. The streets were bustling with people and cars, and buildings and lamp poles were decorated with festive Christmas lights and ribbons and faux pine trees. They had parked about a hundred feet down Sycamore and walked back to the corner so Quint could call his wife. Deliverance was pretty much the only one holding down the fort, what with Wilde and Victor in Australia and Quint in L.A. with Belzer. Shayne Bulkeley, Fox Newberry, and Raine Sinclair were also in the office, with Shayne finishing up a missing person's case; Fox studying for a Criminology exam he was taking at Saguaro Western; and Raine madly reconfiguring the firm's computers and files to state-of-the-art technology that would probably have made Donna Pallone green with jealousy. As the Christmas season progressed the firm was at a well-deserved lull, which suited Quint just fine. He and his partners had agreed to shut down for a solid week starting the Friday before Christmas to January 2nd. Quint was looking forward to giving his wife and kids his full 24/7 attention. He laughed to himself—if anyone had told him six years ago that he'd be a domesticated husband and father, he would have thought they were crazy.

But right now, in the first week of December, he had accompanied Belzer to L.A. to dig into the old Black Dahlia case and see how it might relate to their first dead body, which Munch irreverently called "Little Miss Bisected Headless." Quint knew that Adam Manzone had spent time in the City of Angels and had begun his private investigations career there, and that his partner, Lee Jernigan (who was semi-retired, but probably never would be fully—he loved his work), still worked that end of their mutual business. He called Adam and got Jernigan's address and telephone number and called to make an appointment for this Monday at 10 AM. He didn't apprise the man of what he wanted, just that Adam had recommended him.

The eight-story, grey stone building had the entry door on the south side of Hollywood. As they approached the door Quint noticed that the building number was 701; based on the other addresses around the building it should have been in the 7,000s. Nevertheless, he went in, followed by Belzer, and checked the occupants' board near the elevator. Jernigan was located on the second floor, so they opted for the stairs. An ornate wooden door with frosted glass displayed, "Jernigan, Manzone, & Associates, Private Investigations, Lee E. Jernigan, Founder." Quint knocked, and a cheerful, booming voice told him to come in.

Jernigan's office was a far cry from the Union Jack digs; it reflected a long-time, tradition-bound occupant who didn't need flash or excess space to do his job. He had an old table by the window, on which sat a Mr. Coffee contraption as well as a tiny microwave; next to the table was a twenty-four-inch-tall mini-fridge. Jernigan's desk was scuffed and battered and had to be at least forty years old. He did have two relatively new guest chairs that were comfortable.

Jernigan stood up and walked around his desk, pumping both of their hands effusively. "Welcome, welcome. Sit," he said. "Coffee?"

"That'd be great," Belzer said as he sat down.

"Me, too, thanks," Quint said as he slipped his leather satchel off his shoulder and put it on the floor. He studied the man who was pouring aromatic French roast into three "I Love L.A." mugs. Two hundred pounds or so padding a five-foot-six-inch, late-fifties frame, Jernigan had a round, eager dark face, liquid-brown puppy eyes, and very short salt-and-pepper hair rimming the sides of a nearly bald head. On the phone Norah had broken in and said Lee was adorable—she was right on the mark. Lee put the steaming mugs down in front of his guests and reseated himself. He took a sip then smiled at the two men.

"Any problem finding the place?" Lee asked.

"Not so much," Belzer answered. "But the building number seemed off."

"Off?"

"Adam gave us a 7015 address but—"

"Those little shits," Lee said, exasperated. "One or more of the numbers missing?"

"Yeah, the five," Belzer said.

"The rotten kids around here occasionally steal numbers off the buildings just to be the entitled little assholes they are. I think my building is one of their favorite targets. Oh, well, I'll call the building manager and get it fixed. Jeez. So, who's who, as if I couldn't guess?"

"Michael Quintana."

"Reichardt Belzer."

"So, Adam tells me you wanted to explore some old case here that might have bearing on one you're working back in Tucson. He didn't mention any specifics," Lee said.

"We didn't actually get into it with him," Belzer replied. He opened his wallet and flashed his police badge. "Just so you know we're on the level. Mr. Quintana, here, is one of your disreputable ilk."

"Detective Charm means that I'm a P.I., too." He scowled at Belzer. "And he was joking about disreputable."

Lee laughed. "I've been called far worse. Maybe you could summarize your case and then get into what you want to explore here."

"Right," Belzer nodded. "We've had two murders close together in Tucson, and the first one seems to mimic a famous case from 1947. A woman, her body bisected, her legs spread, her—"

"The Black Dahlia," Lee interjected in an excited voice. "One of the most famous unsolved cases in our city's illustrious history. Was your victim a young woman with black hair, too?"

"Yes, and like the original Black Dahlia, her hair was dyed that from a dark chestnut. Unlike the old case, her head was removed. The cops still haven't identified her. Unlike the Dahlia, her finger was severed and sent along with the head."

"Did they find it?"

"You could say that," Quint drawled. "The killer boxed it up and left it on my doorstep."

"Jeez Louise!"

"Quint seems to attract the bizarre," Belzer said.

"I would say so," Lee said, "after what I read about the old ax murder case in your hometown. You think someone's targeting you?"

"Could be. I doubt that the killer randomly selected my house as his dropping off point. Besides our involvement in the ax murders case my partners and I have been involved in quite a few high-profile cases in the past five years." He decided to hold back the details on the second murder for a while. He wanted to focus on the first. "Look, we've done some reading on the case, a couple of books and old newspaper articles." He withdrew one of the books from his satchel and handed it to Lee. "This one is interesting because it has a huge chapter dedicated to newspaper articles written during the first week and over the next few years. I was particularly drawn to the articles by Aggie Underwood and Gregory Garrison." Lee's head snapped up and he stared at Quint. "What?" Quint said.

"It's just been a long time since I've heard Gregory's name," he said quietly. He leaned back in his chair and stared into his coffee cup. "He was a friend. A good friend."

"Is he still here in L.A.?" Belzer asked. "Do you think he might have additional articles or notes on the case?"

"In a manner of speaking," Lee said. He could see the confusion on their faces. "Gregory is here. He's buried next to his first wife, Amelia, in the Forest Lawn Cemetery."

"He died? I'm sorry," Quint said.

"He was murdered in 1969," Lee stated flatly.

"My God," Belzer said. "Did they catch the guy?"

"No, the bastard is still walking the earth causing havoc." He blew out a taut breath. "You didn't mention Gregory's name to Adam, did you?"

"No, why?"

Lee half-smiled. "Because as I mentioned Gregory is buried next to his first wife. His second is alive and well." He paused for effect. "Norah Maguire, Adam's wife."

"Holy shit," Quint said in a low voice.

Lee fiddled with a pencil, trying to decide if he wanted to elaborate further. He decided to take a chance. "Confidential, okay?"

"I will only tell my wife. My life would be in dire jeopardy if she found out I was keeping a secret," Quint said in all seriousness.

"I'm divorced, and I wouldn't tell my ex a secret if I had to save her life," Belzer said. "I've got a partner but I'm happy to keep him in the dark."

"Okay. Gregory was murdered by … James Danziger."

"Are you *shitting* me?" Belzer exclaimed as he looked into Quint's equally stunned eyes.

"I shit you not. But hold onto your seats. James Danziger is Norah Maguire's biological father."

"Her biological father murdered her husband?" Quint asked in shocked disbelief.

"Tip of the iceberg," Lee confirmed. "No one would ever be able to prove his involvement, and Gregory's death was ruled an accident due to a fire he caused in his office when he was drinking. He and Norah were divorcing and having custody issues, and the consensus was that he'd been carelessly drowning his sorrows. Norah had documents that were suspicious but could never be used to have him arrested let alone convicted. I really shouldn't get into any more of those details, so right now can we refocus on the Dahlia murder?"

"I need another cup of coffee," Belzer said. "You wouldn't happen to have—"

Before Belzer could finish his request, Lee pulled a bottle of single-malt scotch out of his bottom drawer. When Belzer refilled his mug and Quint's, Lee poured a generous helping of the alcohol into all three of their cups. The three men silently sipped for a long moment before Lee began with the basic facts of the murder, the missing days between the last time Elizabeth Short was seen alive and the moment she was discovered naked and mutilated in a vacant lot on a cold winter's day. He poured a little more scotch into his empty coffee cup.

"It didn't take long for the FBI to identify her through fingerprints taken after an underage-drinking arrest. Just like me, she was born in Boston in 1924, the middle of five girls. Her family lost everything in the Stock Market Crash of '29. Supposedly her distraught father committed suicide by throwing himself into the Charles River. The mom moved the family to Medford and began working as a bookkeeper. Betty—as she was known— had bronchitis and asthma and started spending part of her life down in Florida with family friends. She dropped out of high school in her sophomore year.

"Dead Daddy made his Lazarus-like skill known when he wrote to them in 1942 apologizing for faking his death. A hell of a lot more forgiving than I'd be, Betty moved to California to live with her reanimated old man. It didn't work out, and less than a month later she moved out and began a series of menial jobs and relationships with men until she wound up in 1943 in Santa Barbara and got busted for underage drinking. She was shipped home to her mother, but that didn't last, either, and she hightailed it back to Florida. Supposedly she got engaged to an Army Air Force major, who was killed in an airplane crash weeks before the Japanese surrendered. In mid-1946 she scuttled on back to Los Angeles, where she spent the last six months of her life."

"Wasn't she an actress of some sort?" Belzer asked.

"That was the rumor, but no one's ever turned up evidence of any acting jobs she may have had. Like thousands of actress wannabes, she wanted to be a film star. Like all but maybe one percent of those women, dreams were all she had. That, and apparently a lifestyle conga-lining down to eventual doom.

"On January 9, 1947, she came back from a San Diego tryst with a married man and had made plans to meet a visiting sister at the Biltmore Hotel. A few people saw her there, and one saw her on a lobby phone. After that, the next time anyone except the killer saw her was in that vacant lot. Everyone agreed that she had been deliberately posed in her death stance. There was no ID on her and it took a bit—but not too long—to identify her.

"The newspapers had a field day. That Aggie Underwood of the *Herald-Express*, Will Fowler of the *L.A. Times*, and Gregory, who was working for the *L.A. Star Herald*, were just a few of the newshounds that were writing the initial stories and investigating leads. You probably got all of those stories in your book." Lee cocked his head thoughtfully. "You know," he said slowly, "Gregory wrote one last article three years after the fact, but it was never published."

"Why not?" Quint asked.

Lee's lip curled. "Gregory was a crackerjack reporter before, during, and after World War II. He thought he'd found a long-term home on the *L.A. Star Herald.* He and Amelia were hoping to start a family. Then, at the end of 1949, the paper was sold, renamed, and Gregory was fired. Care to guess who bought the paper and kicked him to the curb?"

"James Danziger?"

"Give that man a stuffed panda! Yup, and it was the second time—Danziger had owned a small Brooklyn paper back in the early forties and fired him from that, too. There was bad blood between them."

"Danziger must have been furious when Garrison married his daughter."

"You might say that, but at the time of their marriage neither Gregory nor Norah knew of her birthright. He had started the *Voice of Angels* newspaper, and after his death Norah took that over along with her magazine. When she did put all the puzzle pieces together she fled L.A. and relocated up to San Francisco. Danziger became obsessed with her, and he's living up there now, trying to bring her into his fold. That's a long, twisting story best left for another time. But I digress," Lee said. He rose. "Sort of. Danziger never published that last article. Both me and our friend, George Henry—he's Norah's main lawyer—tried to find ground to get his job back or a settlement but we were unsuccessful. Gregory gave me a copy of his draft article to put in the official file."

"Do you still have it?" Belzer asked.

"I have everything," Lee said. "Give me a minute." With that he went into his back storage room. He was in there for a good fifteen minutes, during which time Quint made another pot of coffee and Belzer added two fingers of scotch to his newly replenished cup. They heard the sound of a Xerox copier.

"Got it," Lee said as he returned and sat down. He handed the pages to Quint. "I don't know if this will help fill in any blanks. I mean, the books and articles pretty much covered the whole tragedy. The cops brought in, what, a hundred and fifty or so people to interrogate, but no one was every identified or arrested. There have been theories about the crime and the perpetrator over the past forty years, but it's still an unsolved case."

"Let me ask you a question," Quint said as he pulled his eyes away from article, which he had skimmed. He and Belzer would read it more thoroughly in their hotel room tonight.

"Shoot."

"Do you think the killer could still be alive and recreating this crime?"

"I don't see why not," Lee said promptly. "If he was in his twenties or thirties, sure, he could very well be a middle-aged killer roaming the southwest and depositing decapitated heads on the doorsteps of unsuspecting P.I.s." He squinted at his two guests. "Okay, spill—has there been another such killing?"

"No, not at all," Belzer said. "But …"

"But?"

"We have a second murder, but it's a man in his forties who wasn't mutilated or naked, and he was shot. He's been identified as one Richard DeLage, a technology salesman from Savannah who was making the rounds of various cities to discuss personal computers and training. In Tucson he was hitting the various colleges and hospitals, and even the police stations to try to drum up interest. Divorced, no kids, kind of a cipher in the business world, just struggling to make a buck. People who knew him say he was kind of creepy, with weird eyes and a secretive manner. No witnesses so far, and no clues except a playing card. We checked out the various underground poker games, but no luck there."

"Is there something that makes you think the two murders are related?"

"Well, yes," Quint reluctantly admitted. He sighed. "The other body was decapitated, too, and the head delivered to someone in my social circle. A friend, and someone who was also involved in the ax murders case."

"Oh, wow," Lee exclaimed. "Forgive my eagerness, but this sounds like a really interesting case. Anything else I can do to help?"

"Are any of the other old reporters around?"

"Well, Aggie's health went downhill, and she left the *Herald-Express* and moved to Colorado. I don't think she'd be well enough to interview. Will Fowler's, what, fiftyish now and still around. But I doubt he'd be any help." Lee grinned savagely. "You could ask

Danziger about any of his old reporters. But I doubt he'd even deign to talk to you."

"I've met him—he's a peach," Quint said mildly.

"You have? When?"

"He came to my office last September looking for information on the late Willow Cheney. A real arrogant, entitled prick."

"You've managed to nail down his good points," Lee laughed. "Anything else I can help with?"

"I don't think so. We've got a few names from the old police force to root around on. Lee, this has been really helpful," Quint said. "Can I ask one more favor?"

"Sure. Name it."

"I'd like to get my wife something special for Christmas. Any shopping recommendations? Please bear in mind that I'm fairly clueless on women's stuff."

"He's fairly clueless in general," Belzer put in, enjoying the frown his friend threw his way.

"Sure, sure. Well, the place to shop if you're looking for hoity-toity is Rodeo Drive. It's a Mecca of overindulgence spread out over a lot of streets like Wilshire, Rodeo, Sunset, and Santa Monica. Tons of stores, but, hey, something new opened up just this year on Rodeo Drive, somewhere around the 300-400 block. It's like a 70,000-square-foot shopping mall with dozens of stores. It's called the 'Rodeo Collection.' If you can't find something for your lady there, you won't find it anywhere. Be prepared to pay premium prices. If I saved real hard I could probably get Alice—that's my wife—a keychain. Maybe." He picked up a framed photo of himself, a petite Asian woman, and three beautiful young Amerasian women.

They all laughed and Belzer and Quint rose. Belzer asked a very important question. "Got any good hamburger joints around here?"

"Do you like hot dogs?"

"I could live on 'em."

"Then head over to Tail o' the Pup. It's on La Cienega and Beverly boulevards, maybe four miles southwest of here. Best dogs outside of Coney Island."

"Then that's where we're headed," Quint said. He scribbled

down the name and number of their hotel in case Lee thought of anything else while they were still in L.A., where they planned to stay for another few days. The men shook hands and exchanged business cards, and then Quint and Belzer walked downstairs and out into the mild California air.

"Great guy," Belzer said. "He makes people like you seem so wanting."

"Nice. And I was going to spring for your lunch, but now—forget it. Pay your own way or starve."

"I'm on an expense account."

"Figures. Well, let's eat and then go back to the Roosevelt and really read this article. Can you believe the whole Danziger-Norah connection?"

"I gave up looking for sense and reasonability working with you a long time ago. Okay—feed me."

Quint laughed, and they walked to his much-loved 1972 Cougar, and pulled away from the curb towards their high-class eatery.

They stopped at Rodeo Connection; Quint managed to afford the ubiquitous keychain, and a small pair of silver fairy earrings.

CHAPTER ELEVEN

Deliverance Dane
Anthropology of the Ancient Greeks 231
December 12, 1983
Professor C. Black Wolf

Subject: Greek Sculpture and Its Relation to Anthropological Development

The beginnings of large-scale Greek sculpture date back to the 7th century, B.C. Prior to that period sculptural images were done on a small scale, principally in wood or terra cotta, and were exclusively used as temple images. Despite, however, the introduction of large-scale sculpture, the creation of small wood, bronze, and terra cotta images remained popular throughout Greek history for personal, as well as religious, uses.

The emphasis on this paper is on the larger works of sculpture: the materials and techniques used to create them, their subject matter and uses, the historical background of the phase selected (there were four phases: Archaic, Classical, 4th Century, and Hellenistic), and the artists who produced them. This paper will explore the Hellenistic phase.

One may question why the focus is on large-scale sculpture when there are so many other aspects of art which could be considered. G.M.A. Richter, in his book "A Handbook of Greek Art," answers this question quite simply: "... for in the larger sculptures one can trace in greater detail than in any other medium the development of Greek plastic art through its various phases."

Greek sculpture fell into five categories: architectural sculpture, cult images, grave monuments, commemorative statues, and ornamental sculpture. The first and second types were by far the most prominent, and used mainly as religious temple decorations in the form of sculpture, friezes, and pedimental groups. Grave monuments were in demand by private parties and were placed either in private burial grounds or public cemeteries. Commemorative statues honoring distinguished men such as victorious athletes and statesmen were set up in public places for all to see. The ornamental sculpture had no religious or social value, but was used simply as decorative artwork.

There were two basic areas of sculptural subject matter: mythology—gods, goddesses, heroes, and experiences; and daily life—athletes, warriors, common people, etc. Generally, though, early sculpture emphasized the gods conceived in human form, an ideal human form without blemish, encompassing perfection. The later periods of sculpture, i.e., 4th Century and Hellenistic, shifted away from idealized deities and portrayed common people, from athletes to drunken women to playing children to old men.

Greece had an abundance of marble, and so the majority of sculptures were carved from that substance. Limestone, bronze, wood, gold, and ivory (e.g., Phidias's Athena Parthenos) were also used. Sculptures were often carved from more than one piece of stone (e.g., the Aphrodite of Melos), mainly due to the problem in transporting large blocks of stone from the quarries to the artist's workshop. Bronze statues were created by riveting bronze sheets over a wooden core, prior to the introduction of casting (solid casting for statuettes, hollow casting for large statues). All stone sculptures were painted to some degree, and accessories of inlaid gems, ivory, and metal were added to present a more lifelike creation.

Hellenistic sculpture originated with the conquests of Philip and Alexander of Macedon, which had greatly expanded the boundaries of the Greek world. By the time of Alexander's death in 323 B.C. the Greek empire was united for the first time since the days when the magnificent Mycenaean civilization had dominated the Greek world. The empire stretched to Egypt in the south, southern Russia in the north, and to the Indus in the east (Rome and Carthage still prevented Greek domination in the west). After Alexander died, however, this mighty empire split and declined, and Greece lost the power, influence, and wealth it had once possessed. The intense expansion of Greece's boundaries, plus its decline, brought about profound changes in the arts, especially sculpture, all in the direction of increased realism.

There was no central focus in the way of subject matter, as had been the case with previous periods' concern with gods, heroes, and idealized mortals. The different themes for Hellenistic sculpture *did include these subjects, but also emphasized daily themes and trivia such as ugliness, deformity, drunkenness (e.g., Drunken Old Woman, c. 3rd century), obscenity, death, infancy, etc.—subjects little dealt with before. Portraying gods in the nude remained the norm, and nudity for female works became quite common. The sculptors' skill in rendering realistic drapery was extremely polished, and the drapery was commonly used to express moods, as in the Nike (Victory) of Samothrace (c. 200), with its swirling, transparent, clinging drapery. This winged Victory, who stood on the prow of a ship with the wind blowing and swirling her drapery backwards was the embodiment of triumph in victory. Every contour of her body, every natural fold of drapery, is vividly portrayed with an infusion of awesome vitality and life. It is undoubtedly one of the most impressive and important of all Greek sculptures.*

The development of realism in sculpture was not limited to the sphere of Athens. Different sculptural schools sprang up, the three most notable ones in Alexandria, with which the sfumato style is associated (smooth planal transitions, delicate, serene expressions); the Pergamon, with which a lively, emotional sculpture—and often close-knit groups—is associated; and the Greek mainland, with which the so-called traditional style is associated. These various styles were by no means limited to the places with which they are associated, but through the travelings of the sculptors they were spread throughout the Hellenistic world.

In 146 B.C. Greece became a Roman province, and the sculpture of the Greek world was transferred chiefly to Rome. The sculptures created there, however, were best classified as Greek sculpture under Roman rule. The contributions of the Greeks permeate civilization even today, and Greek sculpture—beautiful, individualistic, idealistic, unmistakable—is one of the most important chapters in the totality of their anthropological origins and development.

Grade: B+

Comments: *This is a very good prologue to a difficult and lengthy subject. Although you hit some high points you need to drill down further into the other three categories if only to mention their characteristics briefly. I'd like to see that and am assigning you that task as your next essay, for the spring semester of the course you've selected, Anthropological Art & Cultural Consequences, due in one month. Good job.   C. Black Wolf*

Deliverance frowned; a B+. That was a decent grade, but she hoped to achieve at least an A-. Still, Constantine had made some valid points, and a few more when they discussed the term paper in his office. She had to admit that he was tough but fair, and she was learning a lot in his class. She had finished the semester's final test that morning at the college and was hopeful of snagging an A- as an overall grade. And, she was glad that there was a school break until the second week of January. Holidays were hectic at the best of times, and right now she was a bit overwhelmed with holding down the Union Jack fort, being a wife and mother, and preparing for Christmas Day (only six days away) with the tree (which, thankfully, Quint had cut down and brought home himself) and the dinner menu. She wished her parents could join them, but at least Charity and Nicolae had come out for Thanksgiving. She was sad for her husband that both of his parents were deceased. He'd had no siblings, and the only family he did have in Tucson—an uncle, aunt, and female cousin—were murdered over five years ago. Her husband had a lot of baggage, but he was usually successful at storing it away in a closet of the soul and focusing on the many positive things he did have. She, too, had her own closet, tightly locked.

At least some of her tasks were mitigated by Raine, who had basically taken over the computer system in their office and upgraded it to sterling efficiency. Deliverance really liked Raine, who was a hard worker, smart as hell (and she knew it), beautiful, and genuinely kind to the kids. She spent a lot of nights bunking down in Cress's home where Constantine was house- and dog-sitting until his brother came home. Wonder of wonders, she had also convinced him to adopt the last of the puglets, little Blackjack, who had stuck to Constantine like glue and simply adored the grumpy young man. Constantine refused to admit that he liked the puppy but spent many evenings in Cress's easy chair or guest bedroom watching TV and petting the snoring dog. Deliverance had a few qualms about Raine, however, since when she touched the younger woman's hand she sensed turmoil and secrets. She needed to tell that to Wilde and let him see if he wanted to broach the subject with his niece.

The vacationing quartet had been scheduled to return to Tucson on December 23rd, so when Quint opened his front door to a sharp knock on Monday evening, the 19th, he was thrilled to see that their partners—Victor and Wilde—had come home four days early. The four of them spent a long evening laughing and talking about the trip and pulling out dozens of Australia-centric gifts for the Quintanas and the kids. Alex had to be physically restrained from running out to the back yard to play with his boomerang. At midnight the two exhausted travelers went to their own house and fell on their bed fully dressed; they slept for nearly twelve hours. They awoke to find the twins leaning against the bed, elbows on the mattress, patiently waiting for them to wake up. The twins ran screaming from their bedroom back to their own house. Wilde and Victor dragged themselves out of bed, showered, shaved, and donned jeans and casual shirts before heading over to the Quintana house for lunch.

The smells of roasted pork and potatoes and green-chili cornbread saturated the bright kitchen. Quint was sitting at the table monitoring his kinetic children. He grinned at his bleary-eyed friends as they seated themselves. Deliverance filled their plates with huge slices of pork and potatoes and filled their glasses with orange juice.

"Glad to be home?" she asked.

"You have no idea," Wilde said as he drank down the entire glass. "Bloody fantastic trip, but it's marvelous to sleep in our own bed."

"Didja really miss us?" Aislinn said.

"Every second of every day, ma petite," Victor said as he shoveled a huge forkful of potatoes into his mouth.

The telephone rang, and Deliverance got up to answer it. She listened for a moment then called Quint over.

"Hello? Lee, hi. Everything okay with you? What? No, we haven't watched the news this morning." Quint was silent as Lee's excited voice could be heard by the diners. Deliverance walked over to him with concern on her face when she saw the shock on his. He held up a finger and kept listening to Lee Jernigan's stream of consciousness. "Jesus. That's ... unbelievable. Look, I'll check out the news on TV and in the papers and call you back later today. Hey, thanks for calling me. Right. Later." He hung up, then said to the twins, "Take your plates into the living room and eat there. Take Vikki with you."

"Aww," Alex began when his mother cut him off. "Now, Alex, if you don't want the boomerang to become fireplace kindling."

Alex scrambled off his chair just as Wilde lifted Vikki from her highchair. The twins balanced their plates in one hand while each took one of Vikki's hands and nearly pulled her out of the kitchen.

"What is it?" Wilde asked as Quint turned on the small TV on the counter and moved the rabbit ears around.

"What channel is the noon news on?" Quint asked his wife.

"Channel four."

He tuned the TV to the channel and saw that the noon anchors were giving a report on the Christmas pageant at a local high school. "Where's the *Sentinel*?" he asked. Deliverance handed him the still rolled-up paper that they'd been too busy to read that morning. Quint pulled off the rubber band and scanned the front page; there it was. Just as he was about to show his partners the front-page headline the TV anchors rolled into the story. They watched the TV. The female anchor looked appropriately somber.

"And here's a shocking story coming out of San Francisco this morning. James Danziger, the wealthy owner and publisher of the prominent Los Angeles newspaper, the *L.A. Daily Record*, was shot to death in the city late last night. Details are still coming in, but inside law enforcement sources say that he was shot by his own daughter, Sarah Danziger, who apparently is in custody in the hospital as she sustained life-threatening injuries herself. Danziger was a remarkable entrepreneur who made his fortune in manufacturing before he purchased the newspaper in 1949 and turned it into a media force with which to be reckoned. He—"

Quint turned off the TV and showed the *Sentinel* story that occupied a quarter of the front page with the headline "Newspaper Publisher Shot and Killed;" a small headshot of Danziger was placed next to the text.

"Jesus," Victor said, turning to Deliverance. "You were right—he didn't make it to the new year."

"Who is this Lee guy?" Wilde asked.

"Didn't have the chance to update you last night on my trip to L.A. with Belzer." Quint shot off a few summarized sentences of their visit to Lee. "I'll show you Garrison's last article later at the office."

"Did Lee give you any more details than this?" Victor said as he put the newspaper down.

"Oh, yeah," Quint breathed. "Like I said, Norah Maguire is Danziger's secret daughter. She was involved in the whole shooting mess, too. She's in the hospital with her own injuries."

"What happened?" Deliverance asked.

"Apparently—and this is coming from Adam and their lawyer, George Henry—Sarah broke into the Manzone house and kidnapped Cara, one of their twins. Norah knew where she was going and went to the house and confronted Sarah. They had a massive battle and Sarah was about to kill Norah when Danziger showed up and shot Sarah. Unfortunately, Sarah wasn't dead, and while Danziger was tending to Norah's injuries Sarah shot him."

"The little girl okay?" Victor asked.

"She's fine, drugged apparently, and … Sarah used a knife to slice across her throat, but it wasn't deep or life-threatening."

"Oh, my God," Deliverance said. In a split second her entire body was drenched in ice and she was thrown back in time to a small house outside of Tombstone where crazy killer Cheyenne had held her and her babies prisoner and threatened to shoot the babies. She shook herself out of still-vivid, painful memories. "Do you think the C's know?"

"Maybe," Quint said. "Even so, I think we need to call them now and tell them just in case they don't." He dialed Constantine's office number and the anthropology professor picked up. He spoke low and for only a brief time. Constantine didn't know, and he was rattled. He promised to call Quint back after he talked to his brother and sister, since Quint said he had more details that the C's needed to know.

Quint hung up the phone and sat down hard in his chair. He shook his head. "End of an era, of sorts," he said.

"Or the beginning of one," Victor replied. "Norah's heritage is bound to come out, and the C's will know that they have one psycho sister and one decent one."

"It's up to them how they want to proceed," Wilde said. "But we should tell them about Norah right away."

"Agreed," Deliverance said as she pushed her pork around the plate. "Call him back and set up a meeting for later today. I don't think we should wait." She was empathetic about the C's and the turmoil they had gone through and might still go through, but foremost on her mind was the fact that they didn't have to give the $100,000 back to Danziger. Okay, so she was sometimes financially and socially rapacious and possibly without a fully functioning conscience, but someone had to deal with the drudge details of running a successful business.

CHAPTER TWELVE

The South Rim of the Grand Canyon presents a wide swath of temperatures during the year. Seven thousand feet above sea level, the wind exacerbates the cold air in January, which routinely dips below freezing at night, but can hit the fifties during a sunny day. Hikers far down in the canyon walking along the Colorado River often encounter temperatures as high as 120°F in the dead of summer.

Regardless of the temperatures or the seasons, hundreds of thousands of tourists visit annually, driving or making their way through other transportation to the lonely location high up in Arizona to view rocks, canyons, and colors unparalleled virtually in any natural wonder across the globe. A Mecca of geologic color and erosion, the Grand Canyon, 277 miles long with a depth of over 6,000 feet and widths ranging up to 18 miles, developed over seventy million years as part of the Colorado Plateau. Proterozoic and Paleozoic strata ripple across the immense walls of the canyon through a semi-arid climate. Geologic exposures range from the Vishnu Schist, created over a period of two billion years, to the Kaibab Limestone on the rim, a mere 230 million years old. Volcanic activity also occurred during a youthful 300,000 to 3 million years ago, adding to the erosion that produced a miraculous site that enthralls visitor from all continents, except Antarctica.

The first native Americans known to populate the Grand Canyon area were the Ancestral Puebloans, also known as the Anasazi. Archeologists still debate the period of occupation, but many hold to a general timeframe of the 13th century B.C. Over the next seven hundred years the Cohonina culture followed the Puebloans, and they were the ancestors of peoples who live there today—the Yuman, the Havasupai, the Hualapai, the Sinagua, and the Paiutes. Somewhere around the 11th century A.D. the Navajo— also known in their own language as the Diné—made their entrance and reside in the area still today along with the Hopi.

The ever-conquering Spanish made their entrance into the area under orders from the infamous Francisco Vázquez de Coronado, who sent his soldiers on a quest to the South Rim to search for the Seven Cities of Cibola. Although in awe of the stunning view and geology, the Spanish did not find Cibola, and didn't return for over two hundred years. In 1776 two Spanish priests, Fathers Francisco Atanasio Domínguez and Silvestre Vélez de Escalante, traversed the North Rim to find a route to Santa Fe. Over the next hundred years a growing swarm of European travelers explored the region and made their mark, including Major John Wesley Powell, who led the first group down into the canyon, and for whom the immense Lake Powell was named.

Rough Rider President Theodore Roosevelt visited the canyon in 1903. He was profoundly impressed, and in 1906 established the Grand Canyon Game Reserve. Two years later he designated the preserve as a U.S. National Monument. In 1919 President Woodrow Wilson signed a Congress-driven act to reclassify it as a U.S. National Park.

The pristine nature of the park was changed in 1963 with the building of the Glen Canyon Dam. Conservationists lobbied for acts—such as a man-initiated flood—to restore the lost aspects of the ecosystem, but as of 1984 the lobbying was still unsuccessful.

Lodges, businesses, and cultural exhibits sprang up over the years to entice and cater to the volume of tourists and scientists that visited the Grand Canyon for leisure, photography, or research. Famous points of interest or exploration include the El Tovar Hotel built on the South Rim in 1905; log-and-stone Bright Angel Lodge, built in 1935; the Desert View Watchtower, built in 1932; the Grand Canyon Railway Depot completed in 1910; architect Mary Jane Colter's Hopi Lodge built in 1905 and Lookout Studio built in 1910; and Verkamp's Curios, built in 1905. Both the Mohave Desert and the Sonoran Desert contribute to the voluminous types of flora that cover the canyon from surrounding areas and top to bottom. Along the Colorado River corridor ninety species of mammals roam wild and free, including twenty-two species of bats.

The intrinsic beauty of the canyon was marred at times over the years with missing hikers, missing persons, fall injuries and deaths, drownings, and other such tragedies associated with a large, wild expanse of nature. The worst event occurred in 1956 which was at the time the country's largest aviation disaster. A TWA Lockheed Super Constellation and a United Airlines Douglas DC-7 took off from LAX around the same time heading east, and ninety minutes into their mutual flights they collided over the canyon. The wreckage fell into the confluence of the Colorado and Little Colorado Rivers; all one hundred twenty-eight people aboard both planes were killed. The disaster resulted in new airspace rules and did nothing to deter visitors on the ground and in the air.

Tourism slows considerably in the winter months, but some hardy visitors ignore the often-frigid weather and make their bucket-list pilgrimage to the South Rim, as many did today. Shivering under jeans, boots, sweaters, parkas, knit caps and backpacks, at least a dozen young couples milled about taking last shots before heading down to Flagstaff or other less inhospitable points south. Three couples were hitchhiking down, and luckily all three couples were picked up by kind motorists that had warm hearts and warmer cars.

Jerry Madison and Joanna Danbury were in love. They hailed from Eden, North Carolina, which was just over the northern border with Virginia. High school sweethearts, they had both grown up in the foster-care system but managed to transcend the turbulence of their youth and graduate with high marks. With no money to fund college, and no success at gaining scholarships, they decided that when they'd graduate they'd spend a year or two traveling the country. They'd had an old beater car that only made it to the South Carolina border before it collapsed, and then they used the tried-and-true method of hitchhiking to accomplish their goals.

They stayed fairly low across the country, avoiding the cold mid-west and northern states, and spending the next seven months hitting Georgia, Mississippi, Alabama, Louisiana, Texas, and New Mexico. They stopped in Selma and walked across the bridge that Martin Luther King, Jr., had crossed in 1963. They popped down into New Orleans for gumbo and po' boys then headed over to the spot in Louisiana where Bonnie and Clyde had met their fate in a hail of bullets by Frank Hamer and his posse. They swung upwards to Dallas, where they found the gold office building that was shown in the opening shots of the *Dallas* TV series, and they were giddy with excitement when they reached the Southfork ranch. Jerry insisted that they visit New Mexico's Carlsbad Caverns and Roswell, where they debated the existence of extraterrestrial life (both thought that only a moron wouldn't believe that there was life out there). They headed north to Santa Fe, and then traversed the I-40 to Flagstaff where they swung north on Route 180; destination, the South Rim of the Grand Canyon.

The temperatures during the mid-January night dipped below freezing, and they spent a few bucks for a cheap motel room about twenty miles away. The next day they hitchhiked up to Grand Canyon Village, and spent the day snapping photographs and enjoying the cold but magnificent views of the natural wonder. They ate a skimpy lunch, bought a couple of very cheap souvenirs, then decided at 4 PM to head back down to Flagstaff since the sun would go down in an hour or so and they didn't want to try their luck in the dark. Their plan was to get down to Phoenix, root around there for a few days, then head on the I-10 into Los Angeles for a week or two before heading up to San Francisco and eventually Seattle.

They had to walk around three miles down the 180 and were passed by dozens of cars before a black Jeep Grand Cherokee pulled to the side of the road and waited for them to run up. Jerry slid into the back seat while Joana happily occupied the shotgun seat. The inside of the car was warm and toasty; the cassette deck was playing some soft instrumental song that was unknown to them but soothing.

"Thanks, man," Jerry said as he buckled in. "Thought we were gonna freeze to death out there."

"No problem," the man said as he cast a glance out of the side window and pulled back onto the 180. The eastern sky was nearly dark and there was a stream of cars heading away from the Canyon down to Flagstaff. "Where are you heading?" he asked.

"Phoenix and then L.A.," Joanna said as she unzipped her cozy parka and pulled off her knit cap. "How far down are you going?" She took off her leather gloves to reveal long, smooth fingers with soft pink nail polish.

"You're in luck," the man said. "Phoenix. Tucson, actually, but I'm going to spend the night in Phoenix since it's too long a trip to make in one day." He looked into the back seat and smiled at Jerry. "What's your name?"

"Jerry, and she's Joanna. How about you?"

The man turned back to stare at the rushing road and the stream of red tail-lights in front of him. He smiled slightly.

"Chase. Chase Hunter."

South Houghton Road a few miles past the Pima County Fairgrounds was a magnificently desolate panorama of road and land in the southeast of Tucson. Around six miles south of the I-10 cutoff and two miles north of Sahuarita Road, the flat desert rolled lazily in all four directions for miles, with the southbound stretch of the road aiming towards the Santa Rita Mountains. Traffic in both directions was light, and minimal at best during the early morning hours.

On this cold winter morning everyone's speech was accompanied by white puffs of breath that hung in the air before dissolving into nothingness. Sunrise was at 7:25 AM—still a half hour away—and the sun was just about to peek over the Rincon Mountains; the western horizon was still in the dark azure throes of night. The dusting of snow on the tips of the mountain ranges gave the blueing sky a thread of distinction between the sky and the upper points of the peaks.

Detectives Keene Swansey and Mike Welsh were standing beside the west edge of the road, bundled up in warm, fleece-lined coats and Stetsons. Both wore leather gloves and boots under their jeans. Welsh was sucking on the stub of a cigarette. He blew out a last puff of Marlboro smoke then tossed the butt to the ground and stamped on it. He looked over at his partner, who was studying the scene with a deep frown on his long, lined face.

"What are you thinking—drug-related?" Welsh asked, absently swishing away a long lock of hair that constantly fell across his right eye. In his mid-thirties, he still dressed and coiffed like a disco dancer from the seventies. His somewhat affectionate nickname back at the station was Travolta.

"Too soon to tell," Swansey said absently as he studied the bodies of the young man and woman lying just past the road edge on the sandy earth, partially hidden under an immense crucifixion thorn bush.

The bodies were separated by three feet, and nearly perpendicular to one another. The girl was lying on her back, her legs pointed straight out towards the asphalt. The boy was also lying on his back, with his left leg extended and his right bent under the left. They were dressed in what would be summer garb, both in light shirts, the girl in shorts, and the boy in faded Levi jeans. He was wearing a red tee-shirt with a Coors logo on the front. He wore minimal accouterments, a twist-band wristwatch and a gold ring with a small star sapphire in it. He was tall, but just a shade under six feet, with medium-length brown hair.

The girl was wearing a white muslin blouse and denim cut-off shorts. Her feet were encased in hot-pink wedged sandals that looked a size too big. She had on three sterling silver rings of Mexican or Native American design. One had a small turquoise stone in it with an odd mix of design, maybe Egyptian and standard Native American. Like her fellow corpse, she, too, had brown hair.

The girl might have been pretty, and the boy might have been handsome, but there was no way to tell since whoever had killed them had burned their facial features off with acid; ditto the fingertips.

"Waddya got, Pete?" Swansey asked the forensics expert.

Pete Murphy stood from his crouched position and faced the two detectives. "Both were killed by three gunshots, same pattern— one shot to the throat, one to the chest, and one to the back."

"Any thoughts on the caliber?"

"Big one, most likely a .357 or a .44. No way to tell if the girl was raped until we get her back to the lab and do a rape kit. Need to do blood tests. Both were well-groomed. No signs of needle marks. I'm guessing this isn't drug-related."

"Teeth?" Welsh asked tersely.

"Yup, they've got teeth."

"Big yucks—enough teeth for dental identification?"

"I would say so. Nothing remarkable about their teeth. Standard filled cavities, no crowns, none missing. That might be the only way to identify them since using their faces or fingerprints are out of the question. Looks like they were killed elsewhere and dumped here, but no footprints around. We'll know more when we get the full autopsy results. Okay to pack it up and take them out of here?"

"Yeah, do it," Welsh said. He looked at Swansey. "Think

we can get any more out of the guy who found them?" He nodded towards a middle-aged man who was sitting in a police car and crying. The man had been driving up to Tucson from his home on East Sahuarita Road to a residential construction site where he was a carpenter. He had an early start time, and the road was virtually empty when his headlights lit up the two bodies by the roadside. He stopped to check them out, freaked, and got back into his car, tearing up Houghton until he came to the fairgrounds where he bolted from the car and used a phone booth to call the police.

"We got his statement. We'll let him go and tell him to keep his mouth shut about this."

Welsh sighed, half in frustration at the upcoming investigation, and half in relief that the two bodies still had their heads. Even so, he'd confer with Baxter, Cornell, Belzer, and Munch on their cases just to make sure there was no perceivable connections.

"All right," Welsh said. "We need to start contacting law enforcement across the country—starting here, in Arizona—about any missing persons. Wish they had faces we could put in the papers to see if anyone can identify them. I'm thinkin' maybe they're hitchhikers."

"Why do you say that?"

"Look at the guy's soles—really worn down like he was doing a lot of walking."

"Know what's weird?" Swansey said.

"What?"

"Their clothes. Definitely not in sync with what our weather here requires. The uniforms searched the nearby area for a half mile on all sides and found no discarded or bloody clothes. Wonder why?"

"Well, Pete said they weren't killed here, so maybe whoever dumped them kept their warm clothes or destroyed them. Easy to believe that they were wearing these duds inside a warm house."

"I guess. Still odd. You'd think the killer would have taken the wrist watch and rings, though. He could have pawned them for a few bucks. You know what else is odd? Their clothes. Outside of them being inappropriate for the weather, don't they seem a bit ill-fitted? His jeans—faded, but maybe a size too big for him. And her shirt is slipped over one shoulder like it's a little big, too. Same with the sandals."

"Maybe they lost weight and couldn't afford new clothes."

"Maybe. Anyway, we'll wait for the autopsy and forensics reports. Let's head back to the station and start investigating. Belzer's probably in by now so we'll hit him up first."

Welsh grinned. "He still living in Quint's back yard?"

Swansey laughed. "Pretty sure. And I expect he fits right in with that bizarre group anyway."

CHAPTER THIRTEEN

There it was again, the soft metallic clang of the garbage can, the sound of the lid scraping against the barrel as it was being opened. Victor had heard it a few times in the past month, and Belzer had as well; both thought it was a raccoon searching for food. Victor thought raccoons were cool animals, but they could become rabid and vicious, and the presence of one on a regular basis was concerning because of the Dane-Quintana kids.

Victor looked over at Wilde, who was sleeping and lightly snoring. He carefully slipped out of bed and gently pulled open the drawer of his nightstand. He withdrew his .38 revolver, affixed a silencer to it, and padded very quietly out of the room. He didn't need a light—he could traverse his house in pitch dark. He moved through the house like a wraith until he came to the sliding doors to the back patio. He paused and listened; there was the almost inaudible scraping again. He eased the sliding door open an inch at a time, making virtually no noise. Fifteen inches later he moved outside, holding the gun up in the air with both hands as he edged his way towards the side of the house where the garbage can rested.

He half-crouched at the corner of the house, then suddenly flipped on the light switch and whirled around the corner to point the gun at the offending creature that was illuminated by the floodlights.

He stopped dead in his tracks, as did the rummager. They stared at one another for a long second before the intruder bolted from the can and started scampering off north over the desert. Victor was tall with impressively long legs but even so had a hell of a time catching up with his prey. Forty yards away he tackled the scavenger, who began screaming and clawing and kicking at him like some wild, feral animal that was fighting for its life.

"Stop it! Stop it!" Victor demanded at the top of his voice as he sought to pin strong arms and prevent the loss of his eyes from the ragged nails. Out of the corner of his eye he saw that lights went on in his house and Quint's, and he struggled to his feet and carried the angry, writhing body back towards Quint's back door. He had just made it to the door when Quint came out holding his own gun, with

Deliverance right behind him holding a machete. He heard rather than saw Wilde running up from the side.

"What is it?" Quint exclaimed as he tried to make out the wriggling bundle Victor was carrying.

"I think it's female, but I'm not quite sure," Victor wheezed. He moved past Quint into the kitchen, followed by his partners. He struggled over to the table and plunked his prey down into a chair. "Don't even think about moving," he said ominously, looking down at a strange pair of furious eyes glaring back at him.

"What the hell?" Wilde said as he took in the bizarre scene.

"Our raccoon," Victor replied.

"Is it … a girl or a boy?" Wilde said.

"Your guess is as good as mine," Victor said. "I'm thinking girl."

The four Union Jackers contemplated their "guest." Victor had guessed correctly—their momentary captive was a girl. By her size she appeared to be five or six years old, but her features were obscured by the grime covering her face. Her hair seemed to be brown, but it was greasy and matted, and currently covered with plant branches and sand from her battle with Victor. She was wearing filthy, torn jeans, a couple of ragged tee-shirts, and very worn sneakers.

But the most striking thing about her was the peculiar, bright, roiling eyes that emanated from her dirty face like brilliant lasers. She had heterochromia iridis, a condition where the irises were different colors; in her case, one eye was dark green, and one was dark blue. Her stare was eerie, a bit disconcerting, and anyone could tell that her small body was as tightly wound as a Swiss watch.

"Care to tell us your name, sweetheart?" Wilde asked

"Fuck you," the child spat out.

"Well, we know she came from a classy environment," Wilde said, half annoyed and half amused. "Could be a goddamn Kennedy."

"Let's try this again," Deliverance said. She knelt in front of the girl, who was clutching the edges of her chair and kicking the leg of the chair with her foot. "We aren't going to hurt you. We want to help you, and we can't do that unless we know who you are. So, please, what is your name?"

"Fuck you."

"Maybe that's her name," Quint opined. "So, Fuck You—where did you come from? Where are your parents?"

All four partners replied simultaneously with the girl, "Fuck you."

"All right," Quint sighed. "We'll call 9-1-1 and have someone come and pick her up. Child Protective Services can deal with her."

"She needs a bath first," Deliverance said as she rose.

"Good luck with that," Wilde said.

"If I can bathe Pyewacket without being eviscerated, I can bathe a child." Deliverance stuck her hand out. "Come on, Fuck You. Off we go."

A split second later the child bolted from the chair and thrust her way past the adults, reaching the back door just as Quint grabbed her from behind and lifted her off the ground, kicking and struggling.

"Follow me," Deliverance said as she led the way out of the kitchen with her husband right at her heels, carrying the angry, obstinate child.

When they were gone Wilde said, "I would pay to watch that bathing effort. That kid has no idea who she's up against."

Victor laughed. "Want to hang around or go back to bed?"

"Bed," Wilde said. "I've gotta get up and drive to Phoenix in the morning for the Schieler case. Got a lead on the forger that made Schieler's phony passport and driver's license. I may have to stay a few days. Wish you could come."

"You know, I think I can. I'm chasing down that missing teenager from Oro Valley, but one of the leads is up in Mesa and another one is in Apache Junction, where the family hails from. Her parents are frantic, and the cops aren't any help. So, bed then a long road trip it is." They went out the back door, turning off the patio lights before making their way back to their house. Victor stuffed all the scattered trash back into the garbage can. He noted that it seemed like the only thing scavenged from the can was the leftover food they'd disposed of in the last few days. *The kid was starving,* he thought sadly.

Wilde would have been satisfied with the experience no matter what he'd paid to watch the bathing of the unwilling child. Quint stood outside of the closed bathroom door, leaning against the wall, arms folded, as he bit back laughter at the sounds going on inside, including the very creative, high-pitched swearing that most truck drivers didn't emit even after a dozen beers. Yelling, thuds, crashing, and splashing were sounds that mashed together to present an effort that was frustrating on both the bather and the bathee. Deliverance had ordered him to find some of Aislinn's clothes to put on the child, and he had pulled out a pair of jeans and a tee-shirt that said, "Stonehenge Rocks!" Naturally Aislinn and Alex had awakened when he was sifting through their closet, and they heard the noises coming from the guest bathroom. Quint made it clear that they were not to get out of bed and just go back to sleep. He knew they wouldn't, but they also knew better than to leave their room.

The bathroom noise stopped for a moment and the door opened. Deliverance stuck her hand out and Quint gave her the clothes. The door slammed shut, and he heard a few more protests and struggles before the door opened again and Deliverance came out holding the little girl's hand tightly. Quint was amazed at the transformation.

The face under the grime wasn't just pretty, it was beautiful, with clear, soft skin and eyebrows shaped in an upward wing. Her hair was shoulder length and a glossy, reddish, chestnut-brown; Deliverance had parted it in the middle. Her ragged nails were now clipped short and even.

Deliverance smiled. "See? Fuck You is a very pretty little girl despite her unusual name and method of introduction." She batted her eyes at the girl, who scowled back at her but seemed a little calmer. Quint thought that the restrained mood was just an act and that the kid could return to her violent ways at the drop of a pin. Deliverance went on. "It's so late now. Why don't we let her stay the night and call in the morning?"

"Seriously?" Quint said. "We need to call them now. You need to rein in your maternal instincts and accept that we've done all we can, and the professionals need to take over."

"Please?"

"Deliverance …" Quint saw the stubborn look on his wife's face and sighed. He'd get no rest with her picking at him all night if he didn't agree. "Where would she sleep? Not with our kids and leaving her alone in any room will just allow her to try to escape, and probably succeed."

"I know," Deliverance sighed. "Look. I'll sleep with her in the guest room with the door and window locked. Best I can think of."

"You know, if she does get away, we're screwed with the cops."

"I know."

Quint harrumphed and bent down to eye level with the recalcitrant child. "Okay, you have two choices. One, stay with us and behave. Two, head off to Child Protective Services with complete strangers that will stick you in some available foster home for the night. Your choice."

The girl glared at him. He could see that she was thinking of all her options. Pretty, and smart. After a long minute she gave a tiny incline of her head, accepting his first proposal.

"Are you ready to tell us your real name?" he asked.

"No," she said flatly.

"Fine. One warning though—if you try to hurt my wife or kids in any way I'll tie you up with duct tape, throw you in the trunk of my car, and drive you to CPS myself. Got it?" She mumbled something inarticulate. "I'll need the answer in comprehensible English."

"Yes!" she shouted.

"Good," he said. "Del, I'll sleep in the twins' room with Vikki. Scream if you need anything."

His wife kissed his cheek and led the girl off to the guest room. Quint heard the door lock and the security chain being put in place. He went into Vikki's room and picked her up, then went into the twins' room where he placed her down by her sister and got into bed with Alex. He fell asleep after fifteen minutes, wondering about the odd child.

Quint awoke at seven to an empty room. His children were gone, but he could hear their sounds in the kitchen. He slipped on his jeans and padded down the hallway to a normal domestic sight. His kids and the new one were seated around the table devouring pancakes. He noted that the little girl had poured a half a carafe of syrup on her pancakes and was spooning up the excess. Her glass of orange juice was drained, and Deliverance was standing over her pouring another one. Cork was lying on the floor at her feet; Cocoa was sitting next to Alex with his head on the boy's leg. Pyewacket was crouched on the counter glaring and hissing.

"Smells good," Quint said casually as he walked over to his wife and kissed the top of her head.

"I have a special meat plate for you," she replied and walked over to the stove, picked up the plate, and handed it to him. "Voilà."

He grinned down at the fat- and cholesterol-ridden plate of bacon, sausages, and ham resting in a mound next to an equally huge mound of buttered home fries. "I love you," he said.

"Back atcha, Macho Man. Sit. Eat."

Quint sat, noting that the little girl was watching him carefully, and seemed a little tense. He wondered if she'd been abused and abandoned. Hopefully, CPS could find out who she was and either reunite her with her family or find her good foster one. He smiled across the table at his wife.

"Make that call yet, honey?" he asked.

"Not yet. After breakfast." She looked at the child. "Want some home fries?"

The little girl nodded vigorously, and Deliverance accommodated her.

"You know, we can't keep calling you, well, you know what," Deliverance said.

"You know what what?" Aislinn piped up.

"Never mind," her father said sternly. He addressed his wife. "I'm sure CPS will figure out her name soon enough." He decided to change the subject. "Wilde and Victor take off?"

"Yup, on their way north. Victor said they might be gone a few days checking out various leads on their cases. He said to be on the lookout for any other raccoons."

"I think we've caught the culprit," Quint said. He'd made it through half his plate when he pushed back his chair. "Tupperware this up and I'll take it into work after I drop off the kid."

"I can take her later," his wife offered blandly.

"I can take her now," Quint said pointedly. "You can drop off the kids at school and Vikki at Elena's."

"All right," Deliverance said dejectedly. She smiled at the girl. "Finish up, sweetheart. Hubby needs to take you to …" She wasn't sure how to put it.

Without a word the little girl finished her orange juice and stood up. She glared at Quint defiantly, narrowing her unusual eyes.

Quint stood and put out his hand. "Let's go."

She ignored his hand and tromped out of the kitchen in front of him as Deliverance handed him the remainder of his breakfast and called softly, "Goodbye, sweetheart," after the departing stranger who had tugged at her heart.

Quint picked up the plastic bag full of the child's original filthy garments and tossed it into the back seat. He buckled the child into the front seat and took off for CPS down on South Alvernon Way. He held the girl's hand tightly as they entered the chaos of the building. It took several frustrated tries to flag down someone who would listen to him, but finally a harried older woman sat down nervously and took his statement. Munch had once discussed CPS with him regarding a case of three abandoned, abused children that had obviously migrated north from Mexico. Munch said the CPS staff tried hard, but they were underpaid, overworked, and understaffed, and sometimes kids slipped through the cracks despite the best of intentions.

Miss ("Not Ms., thank you.") Sue Gumkowski thanked him and said they'd be in touch for any further details. He rose and gazed down at the little girl who was avoiding looking at him. He told her goodbye and impulsively touched her hair lightly; she was silent and unmoving. He felt a blanket of sadness and guilt cloak him as he left the building and told himself she was going to be okay.

He headed off to the office where his wife waited for him and grilled him on everything said and done. She was quiet for the rest of the morning; the office was quiet with Victor and Wilde gone, and Shayne downtown rifling through adoption records for a young woman who wanted to track down her biological parents. Raine was in her office downstairs engrossed in her computer tracking documents and leads into the two headless corpses that had invaded the Union Jack world. He knew she was more than just mildly engaged since she was dating the man who had received one of the heads. When he checked up on her progress she casually mentioned that she was going to move in with Constantine over the weekend. No, she hadn't told her over-protective uncle yet, but she would when he came back. She asked Quint his honest opinion of Constantine. He said she could do a lot worse and he couldn't do any better.

The next day the Quintanas were having dinner when there was a knock at the front door. That noise had made Quint nervous ever since the first head turned up on his doorstep. He opened the door to find an old woman and two young boys, all black. He thought he recognized the kids, then remembered that Victor had a framed photo of them on his desk at work—they were his late brother Shaun's grandsons, André's boys. These boys were a few years older, and unlike the smiles they had in the photo, both of their young faces were solemn bordering on blank.

"Please, come in," he said. "Deliverance," he called out and she appeared immediately, making it obvious that she'd been close by waiting, also nervously.

"Thank you," the woman said. "I'm Sabine Renard, Victor's mother."

"It's a pleasure to meet you," Deliverance said evenly, hiding her resentment over the mother's treatment of her "sinful" gay son.

"Merci. This is Beckett," she said, indicating the older boy, "and Bechet."

"Welcome," Quint said. He knew that Beckett was thirteen and the younger boy was ten. "I'm sorry to tell you but Victor is away on business for a couple of days. But please come in and sit down. Del, some tea, please?" She took off and shooed the kids back into the kitchen from their viewing point at the living room archway.

"Victor didn't tell us you were coming," Quint said as they all sat down on the couches.

"He doesn't know," Mrs. Renard said. "I called him but got the answering machine saying he was out of town for a few days. Mr. Quintana—"

"Quint, please."

"Mr. Quintana, let me be succinct. I am here to deliver these children to their uncle for his duty to raise them."

"What?"

"Let me be specific. My grandson, André, and his wife were killed two days ago in an automobile accident in Baton Rouge."

"Oh, my God," Deliverance said as she carried in a tray of tea. "Oh, we're so very sorry."

"Thank you. Chrysanthe's parents died years ago, and a sister she has up in Baltimore is not interested in taking the boys. She is rather a godless person that would prefer fast drink and unsuitable men to familial duties. My husband and I are nearly eighty, and we can't assume the responsibility of raising them. That leaves Victor. As much as we disapprove of the lifestyle he has chosen—"

"He didn't 'choose' it, Mrs. Renard," Quint said coolly. "He was born that way, and if you are a true Christian as you intimate, then God makes no mistakes and your son is who he is. And he's one damn fine man."

"I respect your opinion, Mr. Quintana, although I don't necessarily share it. Nevertheless, they are here, and unfortunately Victor is their only close relative. I have one suitcase each for them in the rental car, and my husband and I will send the remainder of their possessions when we have the chance. Now, may I impose upon you to house them until their granduncle returns?"

"You're not going to stay?" Deliverance asked.

"No. I have a flight out tomorrow morning. The funeral is the next day. I'll remain in the airport until my flight leaves. Now, could you please get the suitcases while I say goodbye?"

"Um," Quint said as he fought back his distaste for the cold, unaffectionate way she was treating her great-grandsons, "I can. Del, can you get the guest room ready?"

"Yeah," she said icily as she glared at the old woman who was ignoring her.

Quint left to get the suitcases. Mrs. Renard told the boys to behave, hold to their Christian values, and not be corrupted by sinful outside influences. Then she gave Deliverance a curt nod and left the house just as Quint was returning. She shut the door loudly behind her and drove off.

Deliverance said to her husband, "I think that bitch should consider having that stick-of-no-compassion that's stuck up her ass surgically removed by a half-in-the-bag proctologist."

"Del," he admonished loudly nodding towards the two boys.

Deliverance blushed and looked sheepish. "I'm sorry, kids. Sometimes my mouth outruns my brains. Are you hungry?" She got no response. "Well, what say we go to your room and unpack. Your uncle will be home tomorrow. You must be exhausted from the trip. I'll bring you up some sandwiches. Come on." The boys followed her wordlessly and Quint followed them, depositing their suitcases inside the bedroom. He closed the door gently and went back to the kitchen where his children were anxiously waiting to bombard him with questions.

"Who are they?"

"Are they going to live here?"

"Do we have to give up our room?"

"What's a proctologist?"

"That's my new word! That's my new word!"

"Can we play with them?"

"Are—"

"Enough! Cease and desist," Quint finally managed to get out. "We'll talk about it tomorrow."

"Are they gonna live with Uncle Victor and Uncle Wilde?" Alex asked.

"We'll see," his father said wearily. "Finish up your dinner and put the plates in the dishwasher. Then go do your homework. I expect baths and vigorous teeth-brushing."

"Will you read us a story?" Aislinn asked.

"Yes, one. Pick out a book and I'll be up at eight. Now." The twins practically licked their plates clean and did as they were told. Quint finished cleaning off Vikki, her high chair, and the food on the floor, then took her into the master bathroom and bathed her and fastened on her Sesame Street jammies. He put her down and walked past the guest room. He could hear his wife speaking softly to the boys and occasionally getting an equally soft answer. At least they weren't spending the whole evening mute. *Poor kids*, he thought.

Book read, showers taken, lights out, and the Quintana family were nestled in their beds.

Somewhere around 2 AM Quint awoke to relieve himself. He thought he heard a noise at the other end of the house. He carefully extracted his gun and made sure the safety was on. He tiptoed towards the kitchen where he saw the refrigerator door was open and someone was rustling about inside it. Then the door closed, and he came face to face with Fuck You, who was holding a chicken drumstick and a small bottle of apple juice.

"Break out of foster care?" Quint asked casually. She nodded. "Shoot anyone?" She shook her head. "Finish eating then sleep on the couch. We'll talk over breakfast. Pancakes?" She nodded again. "Sleep well, little one." He went to the linen closet and pulled out a sheet, blanket, and pillow, and made up the couch for his young guest. He went back to his bedroom and carefully slipped under the covers next to his wife. He laced his hands behind his head and grinned at the still ceiling fan.

Wilde and Victor banged on the front door at eight the next morning and came in yelling that they were home. Deliverance yelled back to come in for breakfast and they happily complied, having left Phoenix just before 5:30 AM.

They stopped dead at the archway into the kitchen and stared. Two adults and six children, all stuffing themselves with scrambled eggs, ham, bacon, potatoes, French toast, pancakes, and orange juice. Victor did a double-take when he recognized his grandnephews.

"Welcome to our Vortex of Chaos," Quint said affably as he snagged another strip of bacon.

Aislinn slid off her chair and ran up to Victor, grinning ear to ear.

"I've got a new word, Uncle Victor. Proctologist."

CHAPTER FOURTEEN

Moon Wolf Begay was a happy man. He had a wife and children he loved beyond words, a large family that although chaotic was interesting and supportive, and a profession that he'd enjoyed for nearly twenty years. He was a respected and well-known silversmith, and his jewelry designs were creative and well-made, and adorned women and men from one coast to the other.

When he had met his wife, Phaedra, in late 1978, he was a content man, but not a happy one. He had survived Vietnam and a devastating divorce. He went into the jewelry-making business with his cousin, Blue Feather, down in Tubac, and although the business was decent, it barely provided the compensation necessary to enjoy some of the luxury items of life. That, and he was frustrated and bored; his cousin was a talented artist, but haphazard in his commitment to work. Blue Feather would often go away suddenly on fishing and hunting jaunts, leaving Moon Wolf to hold the store together. Moon Wolf was ready for a change, and one day that change walked into his store in the form of a tall, dark, beautiful woman that reinvigorated his heart and soul. Within a month he had left his business and moved to Tucson to join her art gallery as a silversmith; moved into her house; proposed to her; married her; and adopted her baby daughter, Persa, whose father had been murdered before the little girl was even born.

In the past five years their family had grown by one child, and another was expected next month. He had a life partner who supported him and worked as hard as he did, and their mutual gallery of art and jewelry had grown by leaps and bounds; it was even highlighted in *Southwest Galleries* magazine, and the article resulted in additional business and recognition.

As he ran through the list of commission orders for his squash blossom sets, he was missing his wife. She had gone to her obstetrician for a routine checkup. Her brother, Cress, had driven her since Moon Wolf had an appointment with a prospective client that was talking about highlighting his new line of coral jewelry in a major retailer in Beverly Hills. The client had been enthusiastic, and they were just at the beginning of their honeymoon phase of feeling each other out. The man had left with a promise to call him by Friday with a confirmation of their tentative agreement.

Phaedra and Cress were expected at the store within the hour. Until then, he had the company of his other brother-in-law, Constantine. Their first meeting all those years ago was anything but auspicious, but over time they had developed a mutual respect and a form of love which both refused to acknowledge outright.

Moon Wolf glanced over at Constantine, who was studying a new acrylic painting by one of Moon Wolf's cousins, Red Hawk Begay. He walked over and stood beside him.

"You like?" Moon Wolf asked.

"I like. He captured the beauty of the Grand Canyon perfectly. Spectacular colors." Constantine looked askance at his brother-in-law. "How much?"

"Red Hawk uses special, secret ingredients in the paint that he doctors himself from the base product to get those colors."

"How much?"

"He uses paint brushes made of cedar wood and coyote tail fur."

"How much?"

"You have a one-track mind," Moon Wolf sighed loudly. "He wants a grand for it, but I can knock that down to eight hundred."

"Seven fifty, tax included, and you've got a deal." Without waiting for an answer Constantine removed the painting from the wall and carried it over to the register.

"I wouldn't do this for anyone else," Moon Wolf groused as he walked behind the register and started writing up a sales slip. He threw Constantine an owlish glance. "This a special gift for someone? A pretty British someone?"

"Maybe. You know, I like Indian art, too. I've got two other originals on my walls, a Redbird and a Mullan."

"Good choices. Redbird does the Kiowa proud. My favorite is Hiatt. She does stunningly simplistic, smooth lines and pastels. We have a signed print of *Time of Tranquility* in our bedroom."

"Yeah, I've seen it. Beautiful." He thought, *Just like Raine.* He had naturally been leery of entering a serious relationship after the disaster that was his first one, but it didn't take long for him to lose most of the unease and accept that maybe, just maybe he had found "the one." She seemed to return his feelings, and he was almost ready to tell her that he loved her. Something held him back. Hell, Cheyenne held him back. That period of his life and its aftermath shredded his sense of judgment, and it took years to rebuild his self-image and sense of security, but he was there, or almost there. Maybe he would have reached the finish line of life-rebuilding if he confessed his love. She hadn't said those three little words yet, but he sensed that she felt them. She, too, seemed to be holding back. She had confessed that she had come out of a bad relationship when she hit the colonial shores. He hadn't pressed her for details, and she hadn't provided any. Perhaps they'd discuss it when she was settled into his condo. He was nervous as hell about cohabitation, but strangely exhilarated. He hoped she loved the painting, his housewarming offering.

Moon Wolf's response was cut off when the front door opened, and two men walked in. He knew they were cops right away. He wondered which one of his seventeen cousins had gotten into trouble this time.

"Can I help you, gentlemen?" he asked politely.

The taller man flashed his badge. "Detective Mike Welsh, Tucson homicide. This is my partner, Keene Swansey."

"Homicide?" Constantine snapped. He had always been leery of cops.

Welsh ignored him. "Are you Moon Wolf Begay?"

"I am," Moon Wolf said evenly. He felt the hairs at the back of his neck stand at attention.

"We'd like to ask you a few questions about a case we're working on."

"Which one?" Constantine asked.

Welsh arched his eyebrows. "And you are?"

"This is my brother-in-law, Constantine Black Wolf."

"We'd like to talk to you privately, Mr. Begay," Swansey said.

"Anything you say to me you can say in front of him," Moon Wolf said coolly. "There are no secrets in our family."

"There used to be though, huh?" Swansey replied.

"What do you storm troopers want?" Constantine said coldly, pissed at the not-so-subtle jab.

Welsh pulled a plastic evidence bag out of his pocket and held it up to Moon Wolf. "Recognize this?"

"Can I hold it for a closer look?"

Welsh took the silver turquoise and coral ring out of the bag and handed it to Moon Wolf.

Moon Wolf studied the ring from every angle and nodded. "This is my work. Why?" He handed the ring back to Welsh.

"Because we found this ring at the scene of a murder," Swansey said flatly, keeping a close eye on how the artist reacted to the news. He could see the surprise and shock, but some people were good actors and it could be a false face.

"Look, I don't—"

"Shut up," Constantine said. He said icily to Welsh, "He's not saying another word without a lawyer." He met Moon Wolf's stunned gaze. "Not. Another. Word." He turned back to Welsh. "If you want to interview him then you can wait until we come downtown with a lawyer."

Welsh nodded. "Two hours." He handed Constantine his business card with the station address. He nodded again at Moon Wolf. "Make sure it's a good lawyer." He tossed off a fast two-fingered salute and followed Swansey out of the store.

"Pricks," Constantine muttered as he pulled out his wallet and rifled through it for a business card. He found what he was looking for and started dialing.

"Who are you calling?" Moon Wolf asked as he came back from putting the "Closed" sign on the front door.

Constantine didn't answer but spoke into the receiver a few seconds later. "Deliverance? Put me through to Quint, please." A moment later, "Quint? We need a lawyer. How's that rebel mouthpiece set for time right now? No, not me, my brother-in-law. Well, two cops stormed in here and basically accused him of being part of a murder case they're working on. Mike Welsh and somebody Swansey. You do? Okay. They want Moon Wolf down at the station in two hours. We're at the store but can be at your office in fifteen minutes. Great. See you then." He hung up and told Moon Wolf to write a note to Phaedra saying they'd be out for a few hours and not to worry.

They made the Union Jack office in twelve minutes, and all

four partners, Fox Newberry, and Raine were waiting for them in the Crucifixion Thorn conference room. Deliverance placed a steaming cup of herbal tea in front of Moon Wolf as Constantine began the detailed explanation of what had happened.

"So, I told them he wouldn't answer any questions without a lawyer. And here we are," Constantine finished. He felt Raine's soft hand squeeze his thigh under the table. The simple physical contact soothed him.

"You did the right thing," Victor said. "Even an innocent person should be careful with the cops." He grinned knowingly at Constantine. "You don't trust them at all, do you?"

"Never did trust cops," Constantine replied honestly. As a man of color growing up in the fifties and sixties south, he knew about police corruption and racial bigotry.

"Do you trust us?" Wilde asked. "We do have two ex-coppers here."

"The key word being 'ex.' Moving away from the dark side of the Force begs redemption."

"Good thing for you we saw the light," Quint said. He turned to Fox. "What do you think? I checked with an old buddy who told me Welsh and Swansey were working the double Doe cases." He looked at Moon Wolf. "When a body isn't identified it's usually labeled John Doe or Jane Doe. Sometimes they name it differently to relate it to the actual crime. My headless body is Dahlia Doe, and the two that Welsh is working on are Houghton Doe and Houghtina Doe. It may seem cavalier, but it's actually an attempt to humanize the victims."

Fox said, "I'd like to know why they're placing an emphasis on the ring. So Moon Wolf made it—big, fat, hairy deal. He's made thousands of rings and pendants and earrings, and it's not unreasonable to think that the Doe victim had one of his pieces. There's got to be something more to the ring. I guess we'll find out in thirty minutes."

"I'll check through my records and see if I can find the purchase receipt," Moon Wolf said. "I don't remember selling that particular piece, but it could have been sold by Phaedra or one of our employees. On the other hand, even if we nail down who bought it that doesn't mean he or she had it at the time of the murders. It could have been resold, lost, or hocked."

Shayne stuck her head into the conference room and said, "Mr. Begay, your wife and brother-in-law are on their way here. She called looking for you and I guess I wasn't vague enough. She said they'll be here in twenty minutes." She ducked back out.

"We can't wait for her," Quint said. "You're due at the station in twenty minutes. Deliverance will stay here and let them know what's going on. Okay, gang—time to marshal our forces and head down en masse."

"All of you?" Moon Wolf asked.

"Union Jackers travel in packs like wolves," Deliverance replied. "Easier to bring down our prey that way."

Fifteen minutes later two cars pulled up in the police visitor lot and everyone piled out. Quint led them into the station and asked the desk sergeant to tell them that Moon Wolf Begay and his entourage were here. The desk sergeant knew Quint from his time on the job, resented him for throwing in the towel when his partner, Luke Wheeler, was murdered, and so took his time notifying Detective Welsh.

Welsh and Swansey came over and shook hands with Quint and just nodded to everyone else. Quint introduced Fox and Welsh asked him and Moon Wolf to follow them to an interview room. When Constantine tried to join them, he was rudely dismissed. Quint pulled him over to a seat and made him sit down. Moments later, Phaedra and Cress bolted through the door, followed by Deliverance. Everyone sat and waited and talked quietly amongst themselves.

Fox was frustrated in the interview. The two detectives had been playing bad cop-worse cop for the past ninety minutes. Moon Wolf had been answering the same questions repeatedly and keeping silent the few times that Fox told him to.

"Look," Fox said in exasperation. "He's told you everything you've asked multiple times. Unless you have something new, either arrest him or let him go. Well?"

Welsh took the ring out of the plastic bag and pretended to study it. Then after a few minutes he pulled a magnifying glass out of his jacket pocket and pushed it and the ring across the table to Moon Wolf.

"Why don't you check out the inscription you put on the inside?" Welsh suggested mildly.

"Fine," Moon Wolf snapped. He held the ring close to his face and adjusted the magnifying glass where he could read the engraving. He frowned. There were two long numbers that were so tiny he could barely read them. "Three two point … zero one two three … one zero."

"And the other one?" Welsh said.

"Where is this going?" Fox snapped. Welsh ignored him and repeated his question to Moon Wolf.

"Negative one one zero point … I think that's … seven seven … three nine one one." He put the magnifying glass down. "I never engraved this with anything except my trademark, TMB." He always used his Navajo name initials instead of their English translation; in his native language he was called Tł'éé'honaa'éí Mą'iitsoh Begay.

"So, detectives, what's your interest in those numbers?" Fox asked. "Is it some kind of weird date?"

"No," Welsh said casually as he rubbed his thumb and index finger absently against the ring. He looked directly at Moon Wolf and smiled. "It's longitude and latitude. Care to guess where that location point winds up?"

"Enlighten me," Moon Wolf said coldly.

"It's the exact point where we found our Does. Got it? Your ring was engraved with the location of the body drop. Care to say anything to that?"

"He has nothing more to say," Fox broke in. "So, like I said before, either arrest him or let him go. What's the menu special of the day, gentlemen?"

Welsh smiled brightly. "He can go—for now." He looked directly at Moon Wolf. "Don't leave town." Just as Moon Wolf and Fox were rising he said, "Wait."

"What now?" Fox grumbled.

Swansey tossed an eight-by-ten color photograph in front of Moon Wolf. "Recognize him?"

Moon Wolf stared down at the shot of the head belonging

to one Richard DeLage that had been delivered to Constantine. He shook his head. "Never saw him before."

"This one?" Swansey showed him the gruesome shot of Dahlia Doe's decapitated head, gruesome with its left eye gouged out.

"No," Moon Wolf stated flatly, his stomach churning.

"Okay," Welsh said mildly. "Thanks for your time."

After they left the interview room Welsh turned to Swansey and said, "It's him. I just feel it in my bones."

"What are we going to do?"

"Nail the Indian fucker."

When Moon Wolf appeared, Phaedra ran into his arms and held him tightly. Cress patted him on the back; Constantine was standing rigid and obviously furious that someone was messing with his family.

"Let's go back to the office and we'll update everyone on what's going on," Fox said. When they all got back to Union Jack Investigations they crowded into the Saguaro Conference Room and talked past six o'clock. Phaedra made a short call to get the babysitter to stay later, and so did Deliverance, who got the feeling number six was on the verge of quitting.

When Fox finished his summary and the rousing discussion petered out, everyone was quiet.

Quint leaned back in his chair and stroked his goatee. He looked around the table, and then at Moon Wolf. "Someone's trying to frame you."

Wilde nodded. "Yeah, but why?"

"And who?" Victor said quietly.

"That's what we're going to find out," Quint said. "It can't be a coincidence that I got one murder victim's head, Constantine got another, and now Moon Wolf is being dragged into a third murder victim, or victims. And what do we all have in common?"

"The ax murders," Wilde replied. "But Cheyenne is dead, and I can't think of any person who would be upset about that enough to try to wreak havoc on people associated with her."

"And it's not like the killer or killers are recreating her crimes, either. No axes were used, and the last two crimes have no connection to the Dahlia case. It's weird," Cress said.

"No connection that we know of," Victor said. "This requires a deep dive into all three crimes." He snapped his fingers at Quint. "Think your FBI buddy Richard Ballard might be able to help?"

"Good idea," Quint said. "I'll call him in the morning. I'll nudge Belzer about getting the files on the victims. Meanwhile, I suggest you all go home and get a good night's rest. We'll meet back here at nine and plan our strategy."

Everyone stood and Phaedra hugged Quint tightly. "Thank you, my friend," she whispered. She had once asked him to find Luke's killer. He did that, nearly losing his wife and children in the bargain. She didn't doubt that he was going to sink his teeth into this situation with any less ferocity and determination.

After the C's left Wilde stretched his stiff body and yawned. He turned to Victor. "Time to get home to the kids. We'll pick up a pizza on the way."

"Oui," Victor replied. He half anticipated, half dreaded going home. The two boys had utterly disrupted their routine, and everyone was trying to come to a new normal. He was happy that Wilde seemed amenable to becoming a second surrogate father to two sullen, emotionally damaged boys, but he wasn't sure that either of them knew what they were going to be in for in the long run.

Quint and Deliverance arrived home to find that number six had left the children alone and had left a note quitting. She shook her head and wondered how they were going to find number seven.

"Alex, Aislinn, Vikki, other kid—we're home," she called. The twins and their sister came running and threw themselves on their parents. She kissed their heads and hugged them, then asked, "Where is—"

"She locked herself in the closet two hours ago," Aislinn said. "She called number six (Aislinn had forgotten the woman's name and called her the same name as her mother did) a bunch of nasty names and threw jello on her."

"Okay," Quint said. "That explains the flight and resignation. Should we extract her from the closet?"

"She'll migrate back into the real world when she smells dinner," Deliverance said as she walked towards the kitchen. "Mac and cheese, guys," she said to her cheering son and daughters, who were smart, adorable, and impish enough to drive six babysitters running for the hills (although number five's reason for flight might have been the decapitated head on the kitchen floor). Deliverance could only imagine what they did this time since she didn't think name-calling and jello were the only reasons for number six's departure.

Quint sat down hard and breathed in and out deeply. The first thing he and his wife needed to do was decide on a name to call their new foster child. Fuck You was not an option. He had started a list of names to offer the little girl and he took it out of his wallet. He stared at the list. Catherine. Antoinette. Lorreen. Tyger. Liberty. Storm. Bridget. Abigail. Reilly. Valentina.

She was still withholding her name and any clues to her origin and family. CPS had temporarily named her Mary. Two days after Quint returned her to CPS after her "breakout" he found her that evening sitting on the back-patio deck in a wrought-iron chair, sipping apple juice and finishing off a family-sized bag of sour cream and onion potato chips. He figured out that she had entered the house using the doggie door. He squatted down next to her, prepared to issue a gentle lecture, when he saw her left cheek. There was a large purple bruise, and her lower lip was split. He hissed and stood abruptly.

"Who did that?" he asked in a low, tempered voice.

She shrugged her thin shoulders and crunched on a potato chip as she stared out towards the mountains.

He called his wife who nearly exploded when she saw the bruise. She dragged the little girl upstairs, bathed her, fed her leftover beef stew, and put her to bed. The next day she took the child back to CPS and shrieked the riot act to Miss Gumkowski, who babbled under the onslaught and said that there was a dearth of foster homes to place the girl in. After an hour the harried woman agreed to push through a foster parent application, and let Deliverance take her home, just to escape the wrath of Quint's wife.

Deliverance called him at the office and told him the denouement of the encounter. She half expected some resistance, but Quint said that was a smart decision and she should stay home with the kid all day to get her settled. Deliverance drove to J.C. Penney and spent two hours buying new clothes and shoes, and incidentals like a toothbrush and hairbrush. She asked the little girl if she was ready to speak her name; the answer was a terse shake of the head.

The twins and Vikki were confused about the new resident in their home, but Mom said she was staying so … she was staying. They helped ready the guest bedroom as a permanent one.

So little Fuck You-slash-Mary joined the Dane-Quintana household.

Quint looked at his list. Tomorrow, he'd sit down with his new foster daughter and make her choose a name. Personally, he liked Liberty (from his favorite John Wayne movie), but upon reflection he realized that Storm would be a more appropriate name. However, it would be her choice. He wanted to give her some sense of control over her own life.

Someday, he hoped, she would feel secure enough to tell them what her name was, who she was, and where she came from. A thread of strange fear rushed through him; if she was identified, she'd be taken away, and he and his wife were getting a little too attached to the odd but weirdly endearing mystery girl with the unusual eyes.

CHAPTER FIFTEEN

The FBI building in Phoenix, Arizona, was in the northern part of the city right on the southeast corner of Deer Valley Road and North 7ᵗʰ Street. An impressive structure, it announced its prominence with a huge American flag unfurling against the wind in the front of the building. Five stories of flawless grey and rose granite, it housed around one hundred agents plus support personnel.

The presence of the FBI in Phoenix had started far more modestly shortly after the end of World War I. It went through a series of personnel as well as brief and elongated closures; it finally reopened permanently in 1939. During World War II and the subsequent "Cold War" the Phoenix FBI was mainly concerned with national and local security issues, but a significant portion of its focus in the late fifties was the growing problem of organized crime. Many other varieties of crimes were addressed by the growing personnel and technology, including forays into extortion, kidnapping, gang activity, fugitive retrieval, and bank robbery. In the early eighties, however, the focus was much less on these violent criminal activities than white-collar crimes such as embezzlement and fraud. As a hands-across-the border connection, the Phoenix FBI was also helping to train Mexican police officers in better law enforcement techniques.

The Phoenix office handled cases across the state, including Tucson, which was too small a metropolis to have a fully-staffed office of its own. The drive up from the Old Pueblo was brief, however, so there was no issue when Richard Ballard told the Union Jackers that he'd be happy to meet with them at the Phoenix office. He was permanently located in San Francisco, but he was doing some interview-technique training, and would be there for two weeks.

Wilde decided that he would make the journey, and his partners agreed. On a whim he decided to invite Criminology professors Cress LaChoisi and Malachi Dillinger. Gray Kingston tagged along, planning to have dinner with Cress and his parents before they returned to Tucson the next morning. They left at dawn and made it to Phoenix before 9 AM, stopping for breakfast at an IHOP off the I-10 just short of Guadalupe.

They took the I-17 cutoff north and got off at the exit closest to Deer Valley Road. Heading east they passed a small airfield, Deer Valley Airport. Originating as a tiny, single-runway airfield in 1960, the airport had expanded to a large terminal out of which the FAA directed small aircraft with its group of nearly thirty air traffic controllers. The police department occupied a huge hanger which housed their helicopter operations.

Wilde turned into the FBI site around 10 AM and parked in a visitor slot. His three companions followed him into the building lobby where he identified himself and said that SSA Richard Ballard was expecting them. They all showed their IDs and signed in for Visitor badges, and after ten minutes Ballard appeared smiling and shook everyone's hands. They followed him up to his temporary office on the second floor. An efficient secretary brought in hot black coffee, and the five men settled down around a large round desk to talk after introductions were made. Ballard told them he was waiting for a new computer search update that the FBI had expanded across the full country. He hoped it would be ready by now, but they'd had some technical issues and it was taking longer than expected.

Wilde noticed the five-by-seven framed print resting next to Ballard's briefcase. "Your family?" he asked, admiring the beautiful dark woman in a hijab and the equally dark, handsome little boy grinning between his parents. The child took after his mother a great deal, but Ballard's strong facial features and bearing were evident in the youthful cheeks and posture.

Ballard smiled affectionately as he picked up the frame. "My wife, Noor, and our son, Rōnin. He's five. Noor was pregnant when I first met Quint and Luke Wheeler, and Quint was single and childless."

"Not quite the case now." Wilde laughed. "He's a happily married man with three … maybe four rugrats. Long story."

"Then he certainly has his hands full. Now, to the purpose of our meeting. Quint updated me on some of the details of these multiple murders that seem completely unrelated. Perhaps you can fill in some of the details, so please start at the beginning when head number one appeared on his doorstep."

Wilde spent the next half hour relaying every detail of all

three murders, and the precarious position in which Moon Wolf Begay was finding himself.

"So," Wilde ended, "we have three crimes that seem totally unrelated, and yet somehow seem to be peripherally targeting members of our social group that was involved in the ax murders from five years ago."

Ballard did a double take and looked at Cress. "Oh—she was your sister. I should have made the name connection after you introduced yourself."

Cress smiled tightly. "I don't advertise our relationship, but neither do I deny it. It's just part of my life." He paused. "I loved her once."

"I understand. Have you encountered anything strange yet, Cress? Phone calls? Letters? The sense of someone following you?"

"No, and I've been pretty alert since Constantine got the second victim's head delivered to his office."

"We've put extra deadbolt locks on our house and college offices," Gray said. "And alarms on our cars." A sudden chilliness washed over him as he flashed back to the parking garage where Cheyenne had smashed a steel rod over his head three times, sending him into a four-month coma. He didn't mention the two 9mm guns that he and Cress had in their house.

"Sadly, that's understandable. It's becoming a more violent world every year," Ballard said. "All right. So there seems to be no discernible connection. Yet there must be besides the social relationships between all of you. What can you tell me about the second victim, the one that's been identified—Richard DeLage?"

Wilde said, "He seems to be somewhat of a nonentity. A computer salesman from Savannah. No wife or kids. His friends and neighbors and a few coworkers said he was efficient but kept to himself. His wallet was missing but he was recognized by someone from Savannah who saw his photo in the paper. The only unusual thing they found on him was a playing card."

"One card?" Ballard asked.

"A jack of diamonds." Wilde extracted an eight-by-ten shot of the card next to a ruler for perspective.

"Hmm," Ballard said. "The card seems … odd."

"It's just a regular deck card, right?"

"Not sure about that." Ballard took a ruler out of his briefcase and placed it against the photo. He marked down the number of inches against his ruler since the ruler in the shot didn't represent real life. He measured the top of the card and did some mathematical calculations. He looked at his audience. "Do you know the dimensions of a poker deck card?"

"Not offhand," Wilde said.

"Well, I can tell you. We broke up a gambling ring in Glendale a couple of months ago, and after reading the file I'm pretty familiar with every nuance of a regular card deck. The standard card size is two-point-five by three-point-five inches. This one isn't. Based on my calculations, it's two-point-two-five by three-point-five inches."

"What does that mean?" Malachi asked eagerly. He was taking notes. He was thrilled to be in the presence of a real G-Man and couldn't wait to start strategizing how to incorporate his new-found knowledge into his curricula.

"It means that this card is from a bridge deck. So, if your man had a card from a gambling opportunity, he was playing bridge and not poker. Not sure if that helps, but it might provide a lead."

Wilde nodded. "We'll tell the detectives when we get back."

"I'm curious about the first head," Ballard mused. "You say it had one eye gouged out."

"That's right," Wilde said. "The left one. The M.E. said it was done postmortem."

"I wonder why the eye was gouged out, and why only one— why not both?"

"Perhaps the killer was angry and did it impulsively," Malachi said.

"Was the eyelid damaged?"

"No," Wilde said thoughtfully. "It looks like the eye was, well, carefully enucleated. Do you think that was done for some reason other than rage?"

"Could be," Ballard replied. "One supposition is that the killer removed the eye to keep as a trophy. Another possibility is that he did it to help mask the identity of the victim. But then, he left the other eye. Odd. She still hasn't been identified, has she?"

"No, and that's frustrating. The killer also sent her finger, but there were no fingerprint matches."

"So, it appears that he wanted her to be identified. So why remove the eye? That's bizarre. Also, if he was trying to recreate the Black Dahlia case, why cut off her head?"

"Maybe because he couldn't send the whole body to Quint?" Malachi said.

"Makes sense. I wonder why Quint was the first recipient of this targeted approach?"

"Do you think some of the rest of us will get a … gift?" Cress asked.

"I would say that whoever is doing this is enjoying himself and doesn't plan to stop. The problematic fact is that there seems to be no victimology pattern, so trying to predict the next victim—and there most certainly will be a next victim—is virtually impossible. What's more concerning is the possibility that he'll escalate his game and start directly targeting some of you."

"You mean make one of us the victim?" Gray asked quietly.

"I'd say he's already started on that by framing Moon Wolf. He hasn't been arrested yet, though, right?"

"Not yet," Cress said tightly. "But somehow it leaked out that the police were interviewing him, and he and Phaedra have had reporters banging on the doors at home and at work, and they've lost several commissions from long-time clients. One revoltingly aggressive reporter from the *Sentinel*, Laurel Bollmeier, actually managed to slip into their house while we were watching the Superbowl." He grinned. "Was Moon Wolf pissed, and especially since he had just lost a $50 bet to Constantine. The L.A. Raiders decimated the Washington Redskins. Bollmeier was just as bad during the ax murders, and got her comeuppance when Deliverance threw a cherry slushie all over her."

"I would have paid to have seen that." Malachi laughed. "Bliss gave me the blow-by-blow description that Del told her, but seeing it in person—priceless."

"It does sound amusing," Ballard said, grinning. He refocused. "The third and fourth victims—any ID yet?"

"None," Wilde said.

"Any suspicion that the killer took trophies off of them?"

"Well, no body parts," Wilde replied. "The very odd thing was that they were dressed in warm-weather clothes not appropriate for the climate." He took out a dozen photos of the victims and crime scene—courtesy of Belzer—and handed them to Ballard.

Ballard studied each one silently for a long time while his guests watched his facial expressions carefully. After about ten minutes he finally offered, "Hmm."

"Hmm?" Cress said.

Ballard handed one shot to Cress and asked, "Do you notice anything about the sneakers?"

Wilde and Malachi craned their necks to study what seemed to be an innocuous close-up shot of the male victim's footwear.

"Okay," Wilde said. "I'm clueless." He flashed a scowl at Malachi. "No smart remarks, please."

"Wilde, I noticed that you're wearing athletic shoes. Can I ask you to untie them and take them off? Please put them on the desk."

"Um, okay ..." Wilde said, then untied both of his shoes and placed them on a piece of paper on the desk.

Ballard turned one shoe around so that one was facing away from Wilde and one was facing him. "Now, please tie the shoes like you normally would."

"I think Victor ties his shoes in the morning," Malachi said.

"Nice," Wilde groused as he complied with Ballard's request. "Okay. Shoes tied. Now what?"

"Do you notice anything different between them?"

"They look the same to me," Gray said.

"Me, too," Cress agreed. "Malachi?"

"Ditto."

"So, do you see anything different?" Wilde asked Ballard.

"I do," Ballard said. "Look closely at the knot and follow the laces to their untied starting point. When you tied the shoe aimed away from you, you used the normal technique where you took the right lace, looped it, and looped the left lace over it. That's the normal way for a right-handed person to tie a shoe. Now, you did the exact same thing for the shoe aimed towards you, but the 'right' lace was actually the left one. Gently pull the left-side lace in the second shoe until it comes away." Wilde did as he was asked. "See? The 'right' loop you used to start the tying is actually the left loop if the shoe was facing away from you. The outcome is the same for a left-handed person if the precise process was followed."

"What does that mean?" Gray asked, intrigued.

"It means that whoever tied your victim's shoes tied them facing him. It sure wasn't the victim."

"The killer redressed them," Malachi exclaimed.

"And redressed them to very specific garments," Ballard said. "His trophy may be some of the clothes that the victims originally wore. The question is—why did he redress them? We had certain parameters looking for similar cases, and so far we haven't come up with anything but we're still searching. I'll call you specifically if we find anything relevant, okay?"

"That'd be brilliant," Wilde said. He sat up straight and cocked his head. "If an eyeball is fully enucleated, is there any way to tell what color the iris was? Some biological test?"

"I don't believe so," Ballard said curiously. "Why? According to the file the remaining eye was blue."

"True," Wilde said. "It's just—I just had a thought. Remember I told you that Quint sort of had four kids?"

"Yes. I thought it an odd choice of words."

"Well, Quint and Deliverance have three natural children— the twins, Alex and Aislinn, and younger daughter, Vikki. Their sort-of fourth kid is a foster child they just took on. My partner, Victor, caught her late one night rummaging around in our garbage can. She was starving and filthy, but a feisty little shit. Quint took her to CPS to identify and place in a foster home until they could find out where she came from and who her parents were."

"Did they?"

Wilde grinned. "The next night she escaped from her temporary foster home and went back to the Quintana house. God knows how she got there. Quint took her back again."

"Let me guess—she turned up again."

"You bet, but this time with a cut lip and bruise on her face. Deliverance went mad as a bag of ferrets and took her back to CPS and reamed the social worker a new anal cavity. The outmatched woman was apparently terrified enough of our tiny, wrathful witch and agreed to fast-track her and Quint as foster parents."

"The child say anything about who she is or her past?"

"Nope. I don't think Torquemada could torture anything out of her. Tough, tough kid, maybe six or so. She still refuses to say her name, so Quint gave her a list of possible 'temporary' names, and she picked Storm."

"That's a fascinating story, but what does it have to do with our first victim?"

"Storm is a lovely little girl with very unusual eyes, one dark green and one dark blue."

"Heterochromia iridis? That's interesting. It's a rare condition, mostly inherited although some cases can be caused by illness or injury." Ballard suddenly sat up very straight. "Are we thinking that Dahlia had the same condition and the enucleation was an attempt to mask that?"

"That would limit the possibilities of identifying her," Cress said. "That condition would be very noticeable and narrow the field. Maybe he wanted her to be identified, but not too easily."

"When was the little girl, um, captured?" Ballard asked.

"Not too long ago, but months after the Dahlia was discovered." Wilde snapped his fingers. "You know what? The neighborhood had a rash of burglaries that were never solved. Nothing valuable was taken, but food was taken from refrigerators and garbage cans were knocked over. You think that Storm might be related to her and after the woman was killed Storm was on her own to survive?"

"Sounds like a viable theory," Gray said. "Anthropologically speaking, young mammals on their own find a way to survive, and often remain in the general location where their family unit was."

"According to the documents," Ballard said as he rifled through the Dahlia file, "the victim had blood type A. Do you know Storm's blood type?"

"Quint would know. He took the kid for a full health workup after she came to live with them. Mind if I use your phone?" Ballard put the phone in front of Wilde, who dialed his office number. He spoke to Deliverance and asked about Storm, then told her he'd let them know why shortly. He ended the call and said, "Blood type A."

"My God," Cress breathed. "We may have solved one part of the puzzle." He leaned forward and asked Ballard, "Can you add that eye condition to your search criteria?"

"Consider it done," Ballard said scribbling down a few notes. "Can I get a photo of Storm?"

"We'll Federal Express you one when we get home," Wilde said. "And meanwhile we have some new leads to go on back home, too, with the bridge card and the redressing. If it turns out that Storm and Dahlia were related, and the victim can be identified through her heterochromia iridis, that gives us even more to go on." Wilde noticed a sad look on Malachi's face. "What?" he asked his friend.

"I was just thinking that if Storm could be identified through these new possibilities, it might mean she has relatives elsewhere that would want to take custody of her. That would devastate Deliverance. Quint, too."

"We'll cross that bridge when we come to it," Wilde said. "Besides, you're underestimating the ferocity of the lady if you think she won't fight tooth and nail if that comes to be."

"Wouldn't want to stand between Deliverance and something she wants," Malachi said. He thought the same thing about his wife, Bliss, and their daughter, Angel.

Someone knocked at the office door and a young woman came in and handed Ballard a thin ream of green-bar paper and whispered something to him. He nodded and thanked her, and she left.

Ballard rifled through the wide pages and checked a few names that were marked with a red felt pen. "We had the search for similar crimes to victims three and four expanded. Liberty—who's a probationary agent, and smart as hell—scanned it and picked out a few interesting possibilities. She noted one in particular and has requested that the police in the associated area fax us a photograph."

"Those fax machines are going to be the wave of the future," Malachi said. "They transmit documents and photos in the blink of an eye. We have one at Saguaro Western, an Exxon Quip, and I got to use it twice getting research material from an associate in Princeton."

"They're invaluable," Ballard nodded. He indicated the green-bar sheet with a big red star next to it. "This is a case from Sumter County, South Carolina, August 1976. A man and a woman were found shot to death on a secluded dirt road off the I-91. Three bullets in each victim, one in the back, one in the throat, and—"

"And one in the chest," Wilde finished. "My God—the same number and location of wounds to our Does. What were their names?"

"To this day they are unidentified. They were named Jock Doe and Jane Doe in the reports."

"The cops catch the guy?" Cress asked.

Ballard shook his head. "The crime is still unsolved. Theories include that they might have been hijacked by hitchhikers. Items that the investigators found in their belongings seem to indicate that they'd be traveling to various areas of the country. The only clue to their identities was the ring the man was wearing—it had the initials 'JPF' engraved inside. The woman's rings had no engraving."

"What kind of rings?" Wilde asked quietly.

"Um, let's see. Three rings, a silver and turquoise ring—oh, a coral stone, too—a silver ring with an oblong black stone that had blue chips in it, and a cheap silver band with red, white, and blue stones in it. She was wearing pink sandals and he had on sneakers." He looked at Wilde. "That sound familiar?"

"Very."

Another knock at the door and agent Liberty Adams entered and handed Ballard the photo that was faxed by the South Carolina police. She left, and Ballard was silent for a long moment as he compared that photo and the one from the Tucson Does that Belzer had managed to sneak from Welsh's case file. He arched his eyebrows and wordlessly put the two photos in front of his guests.

Wilde, Malachi, Cress, and Gray stared down at the two shots, struck mute. The images were nearly the same, down to the clothes the victims were wearing and the positions of their bodies.

"Looks like you've either got the same killer who reproduced a crime of nearly eight years ago, or a very canny, meticulous copycat," Ballard said. "Since your Black Dahlia case is pretty damn close to the one in 1947, you may have two cunning copycats, or one. I don't know which option scares me more."

"Jesus," Gray breathed. "What about the DeLage killing? Think that may be a copycat of some other murder, too?"

"I wouldn't bet against it," Ballard said. "Tucson hasn't asked us for assistance on that case since they identified the victim but let me do some unofficial research and see what I can come up with." He grinned widely. "You gentlemen have certainly enlivened my day. It may seem ghoulish, but, well, it's damn exciting."

"Easy for you to say," Cress replied breezily. "You don't have to worry about opening your front door and finding a decapitated head or other body part."

Ballard smiled. "You're right. What say I get a copy of this fax, and you can take it and the green-bar readout back to Tucson and see what you can do with them? Are you heading back to Tucson today?"

"No, we're spending the night," Gray said. "My parents live in Carefree and Cress and I are planning dinner with them and we'll spend the night there. Mal and Wilde will hole up in a motel and we'll be on the road in the morning." He looked at Wilde. "You know, there's a small hotel in Cave Creek, right next to Carefree. It's called the Tumbleweed Hotel. We can call to see if they have an opening, and then all four of us can have dinner with the folks. There's a cool western place called the Buffalo Chip Saloon that serves a mean pulled-pork sandwich."

"Works for me," Malachi said.

Ballard rose, and his guests followed suit. They shook hands and made their goodbyes, then the Tucson contingent walked to the lobby. Wilde called Information and got the hotel's number, and luckily there were a few twin rooms left. They made the reservation and headed east on Deer Valley until they came to Cave Creek Road. Around thirteen miles up, they passed Cave Creek's "Frontier Town" and checked into the hotel. They drove to the Kingstons' home where they were welcomed by Gray's parents and a yapping little pug named Tiger Lily. Mariko made them sandwiches out on the back patio. The six loquacious people enjoyed a long conversation and discussed the things that the group had learned from the FBI.

At six they went to the Buffalo Chip Saloon and stuffed themselves with "real" American food. Gray brought home a doggie bag of pulled pork for the doggie. Mariko and Grayson had driven their own car, and Cress and Gray went home with them. Wilde and Malachi bunked out at the Tumbleweed and watched a rerun of *Simon*

& Simon; Wilde grumbled that he wished it was that easy and quick to solve a case.

At 7 AM after a filling breakfast at the Kingstons', the four Tucsonians piled into Wilde's car and headed down the I-10, anxious to impart their new knowledge and tasks to their partners and friends. Everyone thought it could a reinvigoration of the efforts to solve the three crimes and hopefully exonerate Moon Wolf from any suspicion.

CHAPTER SIXTEEN

"Pearl Lewis," Quint murmured as he studied the report that Belzer had handed him a few moments before. Thanks to the FBI's expanded search for a woman with mismatched eyes, Dahlia Doe had finally been identified. The Union Jack partners were crowded around the circular table in the Crucifixion Thorn conference room with Belzer and Munch.

Victor picked up the small photograph of the woman and nodded. "Ah, oui, looks just like her except with a left eye. Too bad the photo's in black and white. Can't see the mismatched eye color this way." He looked at Belzer. "The doctor confirm it?"

"Yup. Ah," he said as he scanned his notes from the telephone conversation, "Dr. Allyn Gold said that he'd treated her since she was a kid and can verify that she had heterochromia iridis. He said one eye was blue and one was brown."

"Not green?" Quint asked, leaning forward. Storm had one green eye and one blue eye.

"Nope, he was pretty specific. I spoke with the Hartford cops and they gave me the lowdown on her."

"Let's hear it," Deliverance said.

"Pearl no-middle-initial Lewis, born February 4, 1963, in Hartford Hospital, to an unwed mother, Ashley Lewis. Father unknown. No siblings. The mother lived on Washington Street in a one-bedroom apartment near some record store called the Belmont. Ashley spent a lot of time across the street at a gin mill called Trio's, and she appeared to be either a working girl with cheap rates or simply very loose with her morals. Somewhere in mid-1962 she got knocked up, probably by a customer, and kept working the bar until she got too big. Then she took a minimum wage job at the drugstore on the corner and worked there up until the day she gave birth.

"With no savings and no man, she went on welfare and moved to a housing project called Charter Oak Terrace. Let's see—that project was maybe twenty years old. It was built in the early forties to house defense workers and their families, but by the sixties it was just low-income housing. It was divided into four sections, alphabetically named 'A' thru 'D.' The Lewises resided in the 'B' section, number

29, a four-room duplex. The houses in the project were serviceable brick structures, nothing fancy."

"Were there specific demographics to the sections?" Victor asked.

"Not officially, according to the detective I spoke to, but it appeared that blacks were segregated by mutual understanding to the 'D' section, which was separated from the others by the Hog River."

"Surprise, surprise," Victor said flatly.

"Right, not at all. Anyway, Ashley didn't work but apparently carried on her sexual money-making ways until the mid-seventies, when—and this is sad—she was found beaten to death one morning in the undeveloped piece of land across the street from her apartment. No one ever found out who killed her, and since she had no known relatives, little Pearl was put into foster care. From there she bounced between eight foster homes until she turned eighteen when she was thrown out of the last one to make her own way in the world. She barely made it out of Bulkeley High School. College was certainly no option. She managed to talk her way into enrolling at the beauty school downtown and learned to cut, curl, and color hair. Supposedly, she was very talented at that. Since she was naturally chestnut-brown, she probably dyed her own hair black."

"Did she go missing from Hartford?" Wilde asked.

"Maybe. Apparently, the day after she turned twenty she bought herself a bus ticket to Los Angeles, boarded a Greyhound, and that was the last time anyone ever saw her—except her killer, of course. She was friendly with another beautician in Hartford, one Carolyn Walton, and she promised to keep in touch. It was Carolyn that reported her as missing in July."

"And before you ask the key questions," Munch interjected, "not only was it confirmed that she never got pregnant in Hartford, but the M.E. took a closer look at her skeleton when we considered that Storm might be her kid."

"Her skeleton?" Victor asked, curious.

"That's right," Munch said. "Let me read his findings." Munch flipped through a few pages before he came to the second postmortem. "Here it is. 'With one exception, a woman's bones aren't changed during or after pregnancy. Pubic bone separation occurs to allow passage of the baby through the vaginal canal, and the ligaments that attach to the bone can become torn. Subsequently, the remodeling of the bone can leave grooves on the inside surface. These are called parturition pits and show that a woman has given birth.' So, the M.E. confirms that Dahlia—I mean Pearl—didn't have these grooves and so didn't give birth."

"So, Storm can't be her daughter," Quint said quietly. He didn't know whether to be relieved or disconcerted that a clue to the child's origins was a dead end.

"That doesn't mean they aren't related," Wilde said. "What if they were half-sisters? The same father? And maybe Pearl found out who he was and was traveling west to find him. I mean, they do have the same blood type."

"Yeah, but," Munch said as he flipped a page, "the M.E. said that blood type A is the second most common blood type in the country, after type O." He flipped another page and frowned. "This is kinda interesting. The doc says that there's been some experimentation with something called DNA going on over in England."

"What's DNA?" Wilde asked.

"Um, it says here it's short for … deoxy … um, deoxyribo … nucleic acid. I don't know. It's supposed to provide some kinda biological fingerprint that's unique to a person. It can be used to see if people are related, or if they were at a crime scene, that sort of thing. Doc said it's gonna be a long time before it's refined and can be useful as a forensics tool, but it's on its way. No good for us, though."

"So, we're back at square one as far as Storm goes," Wilde said.

"But at least we know who the first victim is. And we have her history up to about six months before she was left on our doorstep," Deliverance said. "Maybe that can narrow the investigation."

Belzer nodded. "We're going to track her from that Greyhound trip to see where she got off and when. The bus's path was down the I-95 and then the I-10 west. I'm sure a lot of people will remember an unusual-looking young woman."

"She could have gotten off right here in Tucson," Wilde said.

Munch nodded. "Already got a detective down at the bus station checkin' that out." He stood up; Belzer followed suit. "We'll let you know. Meanwhile, you can rest a little easier that you've still got the kid for now."

Quint shrugged. "She grows on you. Kind of like kudzu."

Everyone laughed, and Deliverance showed the two detectives out.

Victor said, "We've got an appointment at a car repair shop. Be gone a coupla hours."

Quint asked, "Engine problems?" Victor and Wilde had come into work after him and his wife.

"I wish," Wilde said angrily. He took a deep breath. "Victor and I were at Los Niños Perdidos last night for a few hours. We were watching the Lakers beat out the Spurs. Kareem is something else. Anyway, when we left we saw a couple other guys standing by their cars and swearing up a storm. When we got to our car we saw why—some sodding wanker spray painted 'faggots die' and 'queers burn in Hell' all over the cars outside the bar."

"Jesus Christ," Quint swore. "Neanderthals. I'll bet they consider themselves God-fearing Christians."

"No doubt," Victor agreed. "Any way, we've got to get my car repainted. I sloshed some paint on it to cover the nasty words. Didn't want the kids to see that or drive through town blazing out our private life."

"I'm sorry you had to go through that shit," Quint said.

"Me, too," Wilde said. "You'd think that much of that bigotry and ugliness would have dissipated by now, but, no, we've still got a long way to go even fifteen years after Stonewall."

Quint looked pensive, then froze for a moment. "Let me check something." He dialed Cress's office number and asked him if anything unpleasant had happened. He listened for a moment, then said thanks and he'd get back to him. His jaw tightened as he faced his partners.

"Gray's car was spray-painted, too, at the college."

"That's not a coincidence," Victor said, frowning. "You think our possible serial killer is stepping up his game?"

"Could be. We need to look into this. I'll visit Cress and get the details, and why don't you two head over to the bar after you leave Victor's car off?"

"Yeah, we'll do that," Wilde said. "Oh—what about the Rodriguez case? We were supposed to meet with him about the vandalism at his business."

"I've got the file," Quint said. "I'll send Shayne."

"Thanks," Victor said. "See you later." He and Wilde left just as Deliverance was returning.

She could tell by her husband's face that something was up. "What?" she snapped.

Quint explained to her what had happened. He could tell by her eyes that she was furious. She loved Victor and Wilde as though they were her own brothers. Then her face changed into something commensurate with alarm.

It was Quint's turn to say, "What?"

"If someone is out there determined to wreak havoc with us, then I doubt that the kids are off limits. We need to figure something out to make sure our kids and the Renard boys are safe. And let Phaedra and Moon Wolf know that they need to take extra measures, too."

"You're right. Number seven's nice enough, but I don't think she has the moxey to fight off a killer." Their seventh nanny was a sweet older woman, a hundred pounds soaking wet at best.

"We could get a Doberman."

"Do you really think a Doberman would survive a battle of ferocity with Aislinn? You saw her stoning that rattlesnake out back to death while she was yelling, 'Die! Die, serpent of evil.'"

Deliverance laughed. "Valid point. At any rate, I want the whole house alarmed and have a panic button installed. You know, since Belzer is moving into his own apartment next week we could dig under the casita and build a panic room. You know, a bunker. Think about it."

"I will. Want to come with me to talk to Cress and Gray?"

"Yes. Then we'll pick up all the kids and take them home. I don't think Victor will mind having his kids extracted from school a little early." Beckett and Bechet were having trouble adjusting to their new home and life, and Deliverance knew that Wilde and Victor were stressed out trying to build their new normal. Bechet was coming out of his shell a little bit, but Beckett was proving to be the very stereotype of an angst-ridden teenager.

Victor had left the boys with Wilde as he flew back to New Orleans the day after he returned home and found his "deposited" grandnephews. He missed the funeral but went to his parents' home and had a royal blowout with them over his life, their attitude, and the way they had simply thrown the boys away without giving them time to grieve and adjust. Until that moment Victor had still held out hope that his parents would come around and accept his sexuality; that hope was shattered when his father made an icy remark that he hoped Wilde, Victor's "partner in sin," had restrained himself during Victor's absence from molesting the children. Victor picked up one of his mother's precious Waterford vases and hurled it across the living room, shattering it into dozens of pieces and leaving a large hole in the wall. He told them to send the boys' possessions, and that he would never darken their door again. Then he walked out of the house in which he had grown up, for what he knew would be the last time.

When Victor returned he had a long sit-down session with Beckett and Bechet and assured them that their great-grandparents loved them but were unable to care for them. Their maternal grandmother, Shaun's ex-wife, had died of emphysema two years earlier. He loved them, too, and he swore on the grave of their late father that he would do everything in his power to make their lives happy. The boys were still aloof and showing no sign of melting into the grief they needed. Victor was eternally grateful to Wilde, who during his two-day absence had movers put Victor's piano in one of their spare rooms and changed the music room into a spacious bedroom for the boys. He had ordered a twin bedroom set and with Deliverance's assistance made the room into something very homey for two young men.

Wilde had also ferreted out the best Catholic schools, including one only two miles from their house. Victor enrolled the boys in the school, and they settled into a semblance of family life as all four adjusted. The boys hadn't been overtly unkind to Wilde, but so far, they had brushed off his attempts to reach out to them. They were only slightly less frosty with Victor. The boys were, however, reacting a tad more positively to their next-door neighbors. The Dane-Quintana children were much younger, but more mature than most children their ages, and playtime was frequently active and affectionate. Bechet and Aislinn were especially competitive with one another, although she still beat out the older child with Rubik's Cube. Victor planned on enrolling the boys in the same karate class as the twins when school let out in May. Beckett said that he wanted to learn how to shoot; Victor told him he'd teach him when the boy turned sixteen. As much as the twenty-by-thirty-inch poster of *Sudden Impact* hung up above Beckett's bed unnerved him, he also thought it was a hopeful sign that a bit of teenage normalcy was seeping in.

As much as the Renard boys were settling in, so was the newly christened Storm Dane-Quintana. Since she had no last name, Quint and Deliverance registered her in the twins' school under their names. Since her exact birth date was also unknown, they assumed she was about the twins' age, and gave her the temporary birth date of March 15, 1978, two days' difference from the twins' birth date. She was generally quiet in the kindergarten class, but the teacher told them that she showed distinct signs of above-average intelligence. She hadn't made any friends, though, but shadowed Alex and Aislinn around the class and at recess. She was quiet at home, too, but she seemed to always be watching Quint and Deliverance, and surprisingly volunteered to help around the house. She seemed to enjoy playing with Alex at the Ouija Board, and Aislinn was teaching her tarot. Cork attached himself to her and followed her everywhere, her own personal canine guard that even slept at the foot of her bed.

Vikki also attached herself to her new foster sister, and one morning Deliverance had even found Storm sleeping next to Vikki in her bed, her arm around her protectively. She stood over them watching them sleep peacefully. She knew she was starting to fall in love with the mystery child, and also knew that the girl could be taken away at any time. It was too soon in Storm's tenancy with the family to start thinking about adoption, but Deliverance had had Fox explore the ins and outs of their situation to find out if and when that might be possible. She knew it was only a matter of time before her biological children and her foster daughter would be indistinguishable in the nooks and crannies of her heart.

So far, the CPS case worker for Storm, Miss Gumkowski, had made two home visits and was satisfied that the child was being properly cared for. The fact that she hadn't run away was a definite plus. Fox told her that there were two types of termination of "parental" rights, one voluntary and one involuntary. Adoption could not take place unless parental rights were terminated, although in Storm's situation the matter was far more complex since no one knew who she was or where she had come from. Nevertheless, Fox said, there were several reasons for which a parental right could be involuntarily terminated, including but not limited to:

- repetitive physical, sexual, or emotional abuse or neglect
- parent/s with mental diseases that prevented them from taking appropriate care of the child and putting the child in danger
- failure to support the child either financially or with physical visits
- abandonment of the child
- felony convictions committed by the custodial parent

Regardless, the state was expected to make a supreme effort to find a child's family, determine that exigent circumstances existed to permanently remove the child from its nuclear family, or determine mitigating factors that would provide a path for eventual reintegration into the family. Adoption was approved only if all necessary factors to declare parental termination existed, and the adoption was not official until the termination was.

Fox said that the potential for adopting Storm was complex and could be lengthy, but there was the strong possibility that someday Quint and Deliverance could become her legal, custodial parents. Deliverance silently held onto that hope.

The Dane-Quintanas drove over to Saguaro Western College and went up to Gray's office. They had expected him to be there, but his administrative assistant said that he was called home on an emergency and that Cress LaChoisi went with him. They drove over to the professors' home, not too far from theirs, and saw Cress's car parked haphazardly in the driveway. An older woman was standing by the front door looking tearful and frightened. Quint had seen her once before when he visited the house; she was the next-door neighbor who would walk the dogs every other day when the men were at work.

Quint didn't bother knocking but let himself and Deliverance in. Right away they could hear keening coming from the kitchen. When they walked in they saw Gray sitting on the floor, sobbing and rocking and cradling the dead body of recent pug mother Sugarlips, whose head was lolling to the side, neck broken, tongue hanging out. Cress was curled up on the floor cuddling dead Boomer, moaning and sobbing his heart out. Quint noticed the two nylon cords dangling from the pot rack above the island, and he knew that the dogs must have been hanged.

Deliverance sobbed and dropped down next to Gray and held him in her arms while he cried; Quint squatted down next to Cress and put a comforting hand on his shoulder. They let their friends sob out their grief for a few minutes before Quint gently removed Boomer from Cress's arms and helped the young man to stand. He went into the living room and wrapped Boomer in a soft blue afghan, and a moment later Deliverance followed him in and wrapped Sugarlips very gently in another afghan. Her face was streaked with tears and she threw herself into her husband's arms and cried.

After a few minutes they went back into the kitchen where Cress and Gray were holding one another, still crying. Gray managed to compose himself and summarized: Mrs. DeSisto called him at work and told him to come home right away. When they got there, she was trembling and crying and couldn't even speak, just pointing to the house. They went into the kitchen and found the dogs hanging dead over the island.

Deliverance suddenly asked, "Where's Pugsley?"

Both men froze then started running through the house calling the puppy's name, and in less than a minute the puppy squirmed out from under the family room sofa and ran to his daddies yipping and wagging his curly tail. Cress picked him up and hugged him so hard he squealed.

Deliverance turned to Quint and said, "I told you he'd come after the children."

"We need to end this guy," Quint replied in a very low, deadly tone.

"Yeah," his wife replied equally quietly. "We sure as hell do."

CHAPTER SEVENTEEN

The Pima Air & Space Museum was located on Valencia Road, adjacent to the Davis-Monthan Air Force Base. The base was commissioned in 1925 as the Davis-Monthan Landing Field, named after two World War I pilots, lieutenants Samuel Davis and Oscar Monthan, both natives of Tucson. Charles Lindbergh flew The Spirit of St. Louis into the base in 1927 to dedicate it. Customers of the air base included Amelia Earhart and Jimmy Doolittle; the latter was the first military customer of the air field which was then the largest municipal airport in the country.

The museum had its beginnings forty years later when the commander of the Military Aircraft Storage and Disposition Center (MASDC) collaborated with the Tucson chapter of the Air Force Association to establish a place where visitors could visit to learn about the history of aircraft and see genuine airplanes that were used in both commercial and military. A search for the best location ensured, and finally a 320-acre plot of Federal (BLM) land near Davis-Monthan was purchased for $800. Thirty acres for the museum proper itself was selected, and over the next few years the buildings and site were readied, and the acquisition of aircraft was well underway.

The first major acquisition of a significantly historical aircraft was, surprisingly, international, when the Republic of India provided a rare bomber, the Consolidated B-24 Liberator. General Jimmy Doolittle was one of the luminaries on hand to welcome the plane when it touched down. A World War II barracks building was moved from the Air Force base to house smaller exhibits, but for several years the growing number of planes on display rested outdoors in a fenced-in area.

The Museum opened to the public on May 8, 1976, as part of the country's Bicentennial celebration. By 1982 the first hangar had been built and attracted many more visitors who preferred to visit indoors, particularly in the hot summers. They also enjoyed a small gift shop and an upgraded Admissions Center.

Acquisitions of airplanes from every walk of life continued and exceeded the capacity of the museum to contain them outside or indoors. Rather than turn away historical memories of man's entrée into the skies, a site close by was designated as "the Boneyard," and hundreds of planes sat on the desert ground for tours that originated from the museum proper. Also known as the "Graveyard of Planes" the areas was overseen by the 309th Aerospace Maintenance and Regeneration Group (AMARG); this was widely acknowledged as the largest airplane storage and preservation facility in the world.

The museum was crowded, the very height of the snowbird season. He kept his eyes and ears alert as he encountered geriatric folks from Illinois and Indiana, couples from L.A, Austin, and Las Cruces, and families with kinetic children from a half dozen states near and far. The most annoying family had four kids, and all of them, plus the parents, had that grating New York accent. He couldn't stand them and was eternally grateful that he had never married nor had children. He thought angrily that people had to have a license to get married and a lawyer to get divorced, but there was no vetting of or license for people to cast their generally useless offspring on the world. Then world would be better off, he thought, if there were many more vasectomies or tubal ligations.

He forced himself to concentrate on enjoying the museum. He had always loved aircraft and had once had dreams to fly for the Air Force. Early in the timeline of the Vietnam War he had tried to join the Air Force but was rejected for vague reasons of emotional instability. He was determined, though, to enter the war and make his mark as a patriotic citizen. So, after grueling basic training that he managed to scrape through, he was shipped to Vietnam in 1964 with other Army recruits and assigned as a medic. The involvement of the United States in Vietnam at that time was negligible, with only 16,500 U.S. troops sent in country. Even so, between U.S. troops and South Vietnamese troops, he was busy enough fixing injuries and learning every nuance of the human body. Most of his fellow soldiers hated being there and wanted nothing more than to go home. But when his time was up, he requested another tour of duty and was granted it. By the end of 1965 the U.S. presence had increased to over two hundred thousand. Initially the public had approved of LBJ's escalation, but by the beginning of 1966 support was giving way to protest, and morale amongst the soldiers was declining; desertion rates were increasing, and many drafted young men back home were taking up residence in Canada.

He found the exacerbated activity, violence, and deaths and injuries oddly exhilarating, and he was ever more thrilled to be in the fray. He rarely partook of the unexpected "perks" of being an American soldier, but he didn't completely eschew prostitutes and weed. He just kept his indulgence to a minimum because he was more focused on his work and learning the ins and outs of his craft.

He volunteered for a third tour of duty, but it was cut short after a month when he was questioned about the dissection of an eighteen-year-old prostitute that he was known to have last frequented. There was no proof that he had strangled the girl and then bisected her thorax, removed her head, boiled her liver and spleen, and fried her uterus and heart. Still, his commander decided to send him home, and he was given an honorable discharge; no one wanted a scandal, especially with the newspapers hounding the Washington politicians and military for their policies towards the war.

Before he was shipped stateside he was spending a last night drinking with his buddies in a Da Nang dive. Another group of rowdies came in and were engrossed in their own enjoyable evening as the beer flowed and the delectable Vietnamese appetizers were gobbled up. One of his buddies called over and said that "Doc" was going home and they should raise a toast to him. The group came over, bought a round of drinks, and pounded him on the back.

That was the first time that he ever laid eyes on Michael Quintana. They barely exchanged a word, and he knew that Quintana had no memory of him when next they met. No, "Doc" was unmemorable. For the most part he was unmemorable to most people, and he distinguished himself through his work but obviously not through his personality. That certainly served him well in his latest endeavor, the series of supposedly unrelated murders in Tucson.

He needed to give himself a catchy name after his first kill, the weird-eyed bitch he'd swept away from the bus station without anyone noticing. After he'd strangled her, defaced her, gouged out her brown eye, and bisected her body at the waist, he decided on a name. After all, he planned on many more murders. Serial killers had such cool names, he thought—the Axewoman of Tucson, the Axeman of

New Orleans, Son of Sam, the Hillside Strangler, Zebra, Zodiac, the Green River Killer, Jack the Ripper. Catchy, those.

The Surrogate Scourge. Surrogate, since he was substituting himself for the perpetrator of those old similar crimes, and Scourge because that's what he was, what he enjoyed being. When the annals of crime placed his name in their ranks, he would be proud that he'd named himself something so … erotic. So … very special. Not a nonentity. Not someone taken totally for granted.

He was delighted and at the same time pissed that the police, the FBI, and the private investigators hadn't yet understood the relationship between the victims. Two of the victims had been identified finally, but their so-called "link" had yet to be uncovered. He'd had no grudge against the victims; they were simply tools to achieve his goal of ultimate notoriety. Of course, that goal also included incorporating the people who had solved the Axewoman case and had attained the glory, respect, and accolades. Tormenting them was just the cherry on top of the sundae. He had a list, and so far, he had managed to make many of them pay for their sins, but he still had a few to go, and then start all over again until the end game. He wasn't stupid enough to believe that he wouldn't be caught, but if he was, then he was going down swinging, and not going down alone.

He was disheartened that Moon Wolf Begay had been cleared of suspicion regarding the Double Does. The M.E. had determined the TOD (time of death) to be 3 AM to 5 AM on January 16th, although due to the cold weather the period could have expanded twenty-four hours either way. Unfortunately for him, Begay had been down in Tubac between January 14th through the 17th on a silver-buying-cum-family-visit jaunt. Too many people had seen him there during that period, so he was ruled out as a primary suspect. It had been suggested that he could have killed them then frozen the bodies for any period of time, but the M.E. found no cellular crystallization or bursting in the body. Begay was demoted from suspect to person of interest. His business had lost revenue, but he and his family had enjoyed true happiness when his wife gave birth to their second son, Soaring Hawk Dionysus Begay. Perhaps they were too happy …

Even so, he felt he had outdone himself by breaking into the LaChoisi-Kingston house and murdering their dogs. Unlike his dispatching of the four human victims, he did feel a twinge of guilt at killing the dogs. They had come up to him swatting him with their little legs, drooling, and begging for affection. He had responded by climbing up on the island, fastening the strong nylon cords into nooses, and then breaking each dog's neck swiftly (so they wouldn't suffer by hanging), then stringing them up to present a lovely picture of horror when their "parents" returned home. He hadn't known there was a puppy running around until after the crime had been reported. If he'd known, he might have chosen to let it live.

He walked around the beautiful exhibits of planes, stroking them reverently. He had nothing but appreciation for technology of any kind and having been in a war zone himself he appreciated even more the talent it too to build, fly, and maintain them.

Yes, technology was beautiful, but it was also becoming dangerous as progress was made in computers, machinery, and even forensics. Identification procedures unthinkable decades earlier were taking baby steps towards solid identifications that would traduce the best efforts of defense attorneys. This made it hard for the average criminal to accomplish his goals, and even made artists like himself engaged in very complex feats to prevent detection. Still, he was damned smart and so far, had evaded detection, even back during the ax murders' era. Yes, he had dipped his meddling ways into that investigation albeit in a minor way. He grinned; they were so clueless.

As he wended his way through the exhibits he was thoughtful about his next steps. So far, he had been subtle; well, in a peculiar sort of way. What he needed—wanted—was to make a definitive statement, one hell of a big splash in the realm of pain and horror.

Bliss Báthory sat close by her husband as she studied the files that Quint had given him regarding the latest updates on corpse number two, Richard DeLage. The FBI's hint that the victim might have been a bridge player turned out to be exactly on the money. DeLage was a crackerjack player back in Savannah and had attended a few games in Tucson before his demise. The detectives working his case, Cornell and Baxter, had run down most of the other card players who confirmed his presence at their games but had no further information about his personal life before or after he sat down at the table. Each of the men had been cleared as suspects.

"This is so frustrating," Malachi sighed. "It's like … it's like the answer is poking my brain cells but not hard enough to knock something loose."

"Well, honey, I'm sure those little spearchuckers are going to rev up their efforts soon enough. No one has a better grasp on crime than you do, even the police." Bliss gathered her long unruly curls into a ponytail.

"I wish that were true. Well, perhaps I can outthink those detective baboons who grilled me about Moon Wolf when they first suspected him. Swansey would need a recipe to boil water, and Welsh was too stubborn to admit that he might be wrong about his primary suspect."

"You could have been a little more restrained in your contempt when they were here questioning you," Bliss said with a touch of admonition. "Calling him a mental midget with penis envy was far from classy."

"I calls 'em as I sees 'em. Good manners aren't all they're cracked up to be."

"Good manners are a compliment you pay to the intelligent and a rebuke you administer to the stupid. Also, good manners aren't about the other person. They're about you being the kind of person you want to be. They're not something someone else earns, they're something you do because of who you are. Do you want to be an asshole by being rude?"

"On occasion."

"You deserve to be turned into a toad," Bliss grumbled.

"Better than a platypus."

"You wish. Are you going to put this stuff down in time to make dinner with Del and her family?"

"Yes, ma'am. I just want to go over a few more things. And I have to grade Del's paper on the Lizzie Borden murders. She's doing exceptionally well in class and has assumed leadership of the group I assigned her to. She's got two more papers on, ironically enough, the Black Dahlia case, and the Lady of the Dunes mystery. Wish I could convince her to switch majors from Psychology to Criminology."

"Um, she may be teetering on the fence about that. Don't give up hope. Okay, I'm going home to get Angel ready and I'll see you there is a couple of hours, right?"

"Right." They stood, he kissed her, and Bliss sauntered off.

Malachi sat down and frowned. He scratched his head and chanted in his mind, *It's there, it's there, it's there.* He blew out a taught breath and glanced down at Deliverance's paper on Lizzie Borden. She had been succinct and had captured the facts with interesting grammar and syntax even when some aspects were dry. He was glad his friend had gone back to school and was working her way to a degree.

He read through Deliverance's paper, making a few red marks for typos and inaccurate tenses and punctuation. He put an "A-" on the cover sheet and smiled. He'd give her the paper at dinner tonight. He scanned the next section of the course which included the infamous Black Dahlia case. Suddenly, as though a thunderbolt had crashed out the sky and struck him directly mid-brain, he froze and gasped. He grabbed his curriculum in his hands and stared down at the course title: Unsolved Murders, Unknown Killers. Why the hell hadn't he realized it before? There was a connection between the murders in Tucson: The Black Dahlia case had been unsolved. The Sumter County double Doe murders had been unsolved. So far, the bridge player murder was unsolved.

Malachi tore open his bottom drawer and rifled through a half dozen folders until he found the one he wanted. When he was developing his course, he had accumulated a ton of information on unsolved murders not only across the country but internationally. He had cherry-picked the dozen that his students would study and dissect in this first iteration of the course, but they were just a few out of a long list. If his course was successful, he planned on using the remainder of his material to concoct another curriculum with new cases.

Malachi read through his list carefully. He made it to page three and stopped short, inhaling deeply and holding his breath. There it was.

Joseph Bowne Elwell, born February 24, 1883 in Cranford, New Jersey. Died, June 11, 1920. Learning the new card game called bridge in a young men's club at the local church near the turn of the century, he became fascinated with the game and dedicated the rest of his life to learning it, writing about it, and teaching it to a generation of bridge players. Through marriage he was related to the Roosevelts and was a bridge partner of a Vanderbilt, who recommended him to affluent students; Elwell became wealthy enough to own a house in Palm Beach and take on a sideline as a womanizer.

His socially and financially elevated life ended one dark morning when, in his locked house, he was shot to death with a .45 bullet to the head. The notoriety of the crime generated both newspaper and literary efforts, and it was said that S.S. Van Dine's 1926 novel, *The Benson Murder Case* had its roots in the crime (and also introduced the literary world to bon vivant intellectual Philo Vance). Malachi adored the black-and-white films of the 1930s and 1940s and had seen the 1930 film *The Benson Murder Case*, three times. He thought that William Powell did a fantastic job of portraying the character from the book, and blonde bombshell Natalie Moorhead was gorgeous.

The real murder was never solved. Like the Black Dahlia case, the Sumter Does, Lizzie Borden, and many others, the killer escaped justice.

That was the link: the murders of today, mimicking those of the past, were unsolved. And if that were the case, and the pattern of a very diabolical killer, then there were a shocking number of possibilities from which to choose, and no way to determine which old unsolved case might next be replicated. Malachi suddenly said, "Oh, fuck," and ripped through a few more pages and there it was: the Sumter Double Doe murders.

Malachi gathered all his reference material and stuffed it into his briefcase, then rushed out of his office, throwing back a command to his secretary to cancel his 3 PM class. He drove with breakneck stepped out of the garage over to the Union Jack offices where he took up two parking spaces and stormed into the lobby, wheezing. Without so much as a hello he swept past the receptionist (a U of A student who worked part-time at the firm) and took the stairs two at a time until he burst into the reception/office area where Deliverance worked. She looked up in surprise when he appeared, then without asking him what he was doing there she beckoned him to follow her downstairs and she led him into the Devil Cholla Conference Room; Wilde was using the Crucifixion Thorn Conference Room with new associate Turner Jackson for a client meeting regarding industrial espionage, and Victor and Shayne were huddled in the Saguaro Conference Room with a pair of grieving parents whose teenage daughter had run away from home a week earlier. The girl's clothes had been found, stained with blood, but there was no trace of her living or dead. Based on a few points of the case, Victor was almost convinced that the pretty teenager might have met up with white slavers and possibly been taken down to Mexico.

She sat him down and poured a glass of water, then went to get her husband. Quint was working on the dog murders case. He had promised Cress and Gray that he'd do everything to find the bastard that killed their pugs. The two men were still grieving and would be for a long time. Unable to have children of their own, their dogs were their "kids" and they loved them passionately. They hadn't let Pugsley out of their sight, and even took him into work. Moon Wolf's cousin Julio Banderas had created a beautiful ceramic urn with Navajo designs on it, and the cremains of the two dogs rested on the mantle of the LaChoisi-Kingston great room fireplace.

Quint and Deliverance came in and Malachi let loose a nonstop stream-of-consciousness explanation of what he found and suspected. When he finished Quint called Belzer and told him to come over now. Malachi repeated his findings to Belzer, who sat back in his chair and whistled. Yes, they had made the connection between the new cases and two of the old ones, but that list of Malachi's—which by no means was complete—made it very clear that their killer—and now they all believed it was one killer—had a bucket full of unsolved cases which he could re-create.

By this time Victor and Wilde had finished with their meetings and Quint summarized what had gone on. Belzer said that he was going to gather all the detectives on the cases and discuss this with them. He asked Deliverance to make a copy of Malachi's reference material and she did (without her usual ten-cents-per-page charge). He told them that he'd call them tomorrow, then left.

Malachi said he'd see them soon for dinner and left. Quint

invited Victor and Wilde to join them with the boys, and Wilde was happy to accept. His cooking efforts weren't going over well with Beckett and Bechet, who actually spit out his delectable toad in the hole (sausages in Yorkshire pudding) and bubble and squeak (a miasma of vegetables and eggs). Victor said it probably wasn't a good idea yet to introduce them to spotted dick (a pudding made from suet and dried fruit).

When Quint and Deliverance got home they found the kitchen in disarray. The twins and Storm were attempting to cook scrambled eggs, which were smeared over the stove, the stove's backdrop, and a good part of the kitchen floor. Storm silently handed Quint a short note from number seven. She'd resigned and left a forwarding address for her last paycheck. He asked Storm what she did, and she just shrugged and said she didn't realize that number seven was afraid of king snakes and tarantulas. She pointed to the floor by the window, where a three-foot decapitated snake lay, Cork and Cocoa sniffing it curiously. A squashed-flat huge tarantula corpse was nearby, side-by-side with a grimy baseball bat.

Deliverance sighed. She didn't hold out much of a chance for number eight, whoever the poor woman might be.

CHAPTER EIGHTEEN

Tucker Taylor Townsend was nervous. A lean six-footer with sandy-blond hair, bright blue eyes, a chin cleft, a smile that would melt the heart of Ebenezer Scrooge, and a build like an athlete, he gave the impression of power and strength. Although he did possess those characteristics, he was also riddled with insecurity and anxiety as he moved from state to state, city to city, hoping to find a place in which he could feel comfortable and call home. His impressive physicality belied his sensitive nature.

Tucker was a Vermont native, having been born in and grown up in White River Junction, an unincorporated village within the town of Hartford, Vermont, just off the I-91 interstate. His was a tiny community with around two thousand permanent residents. White River Junction had two well-known aspects to its generally unremarkable history: one, in 1920 famous Hollywood director D.W. Griffith had filmed a silent romantic drama there, *Way Down East*, starring Lillian Gish and Richard Barthelmess. Part of the movie was filmed on the ice flows of the Connecticut and White Rivers; Gish's character, Anna Moore, barely escaped death by going over a waterfall, saved by her true love, David Bartlett. The film was critically received and became the fourth largest-grossing movie in the history of silent films.

The Townsend family was rooted in White River Junction for five generations back. They were Catholic, religious, hard workers, and community leaders. Tucker's mother took great pride in her work as a secretary in the White River Junction VA Medical Center, the second well-known aspect of the tiny hamlet. His father was a Korean War veteran, and went into construction and, eventually, politics as a member of the town council in Hartford, which by 1980 was a bustling town of nearly eight thousand people. Tucker's father was a staid, typical New England man who relished fishing and hunting, and believed women had their place in the world but never, never in some professions such as the military or law enforcement. He tried to instill these tenets in the lives of his four children of whom, unfortunately, only one was male.

Growing up in the town was a cloistered experience,

predictable and uncomplicated. There wasn't that much to do although the fresh, clean air and lush lawns and forests did provide plenty of room and opportunity for kids to play football, kickball, baseball, and Red Rover. Vermont wasn't called "the Green Mountain State" for nothing. Even so, if one wanted some sort of different cultural or emotional experience, it was necessary to drive a good forty miles or more to find one. Forty miles down the I-91 was Putney, Vermont, where the much-loved "theme park" called Santa's Land allowed kids and adults to interact with real deer and enjoy Christmas revelry. Opened in 1957, it was a go-to place for residents of Vermont, Massachusetts, and New Hampshire.

Ten miles down from Santa's Land was the city of Brattleboro, which offered many more chances for culture, shopping, and education. Bennington College, forty miles west of Brattleboro, was a private, nonsectarian liberal arts college that had a good reputation and a rural location on 440 acres; it was a hop, skip, and a jump from the Mohawk Trail in the northwest corner of Massachusetts. Originally a women's college, it went coed in 1969, and Tucker matriculated there in 1977. He took a very broad liberal arts curriculum, unsure of who and what he wanted to be. His father found that path distasteful and urged his son to at least join the armed forces when he graduated to develop a more "manly" point of view and do something "useful."

Tucker took his father's insistent advice and joined the Marines. No one could have been prouder than Taylor Townsend when Tucker got onto the bus that would take him down south to Parris Island for his basic training; no one could have been more humiliated when Tucker washed out before basic training was over. Taylor told his son not to return home until he could prove he was a man. When Tucker finally broke down and admitted to his parents that he was bisexual, Taylor disowned him and said to never, ever return to the state of Vermont let alone White River Junction.

Over the next three years Tucker roamed the country, gradually moving west. He tried a number of jobs, failing at many; the ones he excelled at he lost when people became aware of his sexuality. In between paid employment, he bulked up with decent nutrition and weight training, and learned how to shoot handguns and rifles. He considered getting contact lenses, but he liked the way he looked in eyeglasses—studious and intelligent, although some people might call him geeky. He devoured fiction and nonfiction books from the libraries he visited. He splurged a few precious bucks on a Sony Walkman and a half dozen cassettes—his musical preference was classic rock from the British Invasion period, and he worshipped at the altar of Motown. He adored children, who were innocent, natural, and didn't care about social conventions, expectations, and rejection. They were the blank slates on which the tapestry of the future was written, and they deserved care and respect.

Tucker longed for a home and some acceptance. He kept mostly to himself because that was the only time he could be himself without donning a mask which traditional people would accept. He dated both women and men but found no permanent satisfaction from any of his brief relationships. He managed a stay of four months in Santa Fe and found out that he relished the landscape and culture of the southwest, to say nothing of the delectable Mexican dishes (enchiladas were virtually unknown in Vermont). He worked at a car repair garage and enjoyed the work that wasn't challenging but useful. One of the garage owners put the moves on him, he rejected the man unequivocally, and he was fired with the suggestion that he leave town. Reluctantly he headed west on the I-40, stopping in Flagstaff for a few days, then headed down to Phoenix for a couple of weeks. Dissatisfied with the big-sprawling city, he headed south to Tucson.

He immediately fell in love with the more laid-back metropolis, the magnificent mountain ranges, the warm climate, and the army of saguaro cacti that dotted the land like ever-ready soldiers of nature. He stayed at the YMCA as he searched for a job. The unemployment office was rife with other job-seekers, and although he went out on a few interviews, nothing clicked.

One evening in a bar where he didn't have to pretend to be someone else, he overheard two men intimately discussing a friend's nanny situation, and how a potential "number eight" hadn't even lasted through the interview. On an impulse he walked over and introduced himself. He learned their names were Wilde Sinclair and Victor Renard, partners in a private investigations firm. He spent a couple of enjoyable hours talking to them, giving them a summary of his background, mentioning that he planned to leave the city next week and was headed to Texas. Victor said that route wouldn't lead him to Texas, but to Trouble with a capital "T." They took down the number of the YMCA, and they went their separate ways around midnight.

Late the next day Tucker got a telephone call at the Y, and Victor said that he might have a job interview for him. Tucker could barely control his excitement. He took down the address, and on Monday morning he arrived at a beautiful residential neighborhood, pulling his jalopy up in front of a large Santa Fe-style house. He took a deep breath, smoothed back his hair, adjusted his gold wire-rim eyeglasses, smoothed the cheap jacket and tie he'd bought at K-Mart, and rang the doorbell. A moment later the door opened, and he looked down at the petite woman with the swirling mass of long blonde hair and fierce amber eyes. Before either one of them could speak a small female voice from another room yelled, "Did someone leave another head on the doorstep?"

"Zip it, Snickerdoodle," Deliverance yelled back. She flashed a tight smile at her guest. "Sorry about that. My daughter, Aislinn. She has an odd sense of humor. Please come in."

Tucker followed her inside to a large great room decorated perfectly in southwest furniture and art, with a large hand-woven Navajo rug acting as the Saltillo tile floor's centerpiece. There was a beehive fireplace in the center of one of the walls and sliding glass doors out to the patio and back yard. He could see a couple of large dogs lounging on the brick deck; a large, mean-looking black cat was sitting on the top of the sofa on which his prospective employer was seated. Despite the cat's glare and low hissing, Tucker felt immediately at home in the warm house.

"Victor tells me you're from New England," Deliverance said, picking up a notepad and flipping it open to the first page.

"Yes, ma'am," Tucker said. "Vermont. Um, do I detect a Boston accent?"

"Salem. Where did you go to college?"

"Bennington, ma'am."

Deliverance scribbled down a note, then asked, "Degree and course of study?"

"Um, liberal arts. I took all sorts of courses. English, Math, History, Biology. But my Bachelor's degree was in English Literature."

"G.P.A.?"

"3.1." He watched as she scribbled furiously. He was getting more nervous by the second at her intensity and attention to detail. He wondered what she was writing. He noted that she had a pitcher of iced tea on the table between them. "May I have a glass?"

She nodded and as he poured she asked, "Military service?"

He took a deep draught. "Attempted. I joined the Marines but …"

"But …"

"But washed out during basic training." He rushed on. "It was humiliating for me and my family."

"Why?"

"Why? Because I failed at something important. Something with meaning."

"There's nothing wrong with failing, only with not trying. And 'meaning' comes in all shapes and colors."

"My father didn't see it that way." He paused. Out of the corner of his eye he saw four small children peeking around the wall from the next room. "Ma'am, maybe I can help you make a decision without wasting any more of your time."

"Do tell."

"I'm … sort of … bisexual."

"And?"

"And? Well, that's why my family disowned me and why I keep losing jobs and moving from city to city." He took a deep breath as she wrote down several sentences and made stars next to them.

"What kinds of jobs?"

Tucker blew out a hard breath. "Mechanic. I can fix a car engine real good. Landscaper. Pet sitter. Did a three-month job working the docks in Savannah. Cashier in Kroger's."

"Do you know CPR?"

"Yes, ma'am. I'm pretty good with other first-aid, too."

"Can you shoot a handgun?"

"Huh? Well … yes. I taught myself and I'm a dead shot. My father taught me how to shoot a rifle when I was a kid."

"Ever take care of children?"

Tucker nodded. "I babysat when I was growing up. Love kids. They're so ..."

"Nonjudgmental?"

"Exactly. They're open minded. Any prejudices or hate they learn *is* learned, nurture versus nature." He nodded towards the peeking children. "They yours?"

"Yes. Did Victor tell you anything about me?"

"He said he had a friend who needed help with her children and possibly his. Other than that, no."

"I'm more than a friend to Wilde and Victor—I'm their business partner in Union Jack Investigations along with my husband, Quint. We've been a team for six years. Look, let me bottom-line this for you. I'm a psychic and a Wiccan—witch, if you prefer. Quint is an ex-detective from here. Victor is an ex-homicide cop from New Orleans, and Wilde has always been a P.I. both back in Merry Old England and here in the colonies for the last fifteen years. We all came together by our involvement in a rather infamous serial killer case in 1977 and 1978. Ever hear of the Axewoman of Tucson?"

"Jesus, yes, but I don't know the details or made any name connections. Oh my God—that's ... that's ... exciting."

"That's one word for it when an ax-wielding maniac is holding you and your babies hostage. Anyway, what my husband and I are looking for is a combination nanny-bodyguard."

"A nanny-bodyguard? For your kids? Why?"

"Let me continue to be frank. I've had seven nannies. Each of them quit for a few common reasons, not the least of which is my children's apparent taste for tormenting people with their antics. Number five quit after she came in one morning and saw us all standing around a decapitated head that was delivered to our front doorstep. Another head was delivered to a friend of ours. Another friend was framed for murder but luckily, he was cleared. And two more friends had their home broken into and their dogs murdered. Someone seems to be targeting our group and my husband and I want to take better precautions. Hence, the desire to hire a male nanny that is strong, capable, and won't hesitate to shoot if the need arises. He would live out back in our casita and take care of two other kids as well, if need be.

"Victor lives next door with Wilde and he has thirteen-year-old and ten-year-old grandnephews that have been uprooted from their home after their parents' deaths and are still learning to cope with a new way of life. They were also indoctrinated by their parents and great-grandparents to view Victor's lifestyle as sinful. One of my daughters is a foster child who appeared out of nowhere and doesn't even have a name except for the one we gave her. This job is not, therefore, without chaos or risk, both from without and within. It pays $300 per week, including two weeks' paid vacation. Residence in the casita is free—we pay the overall utilities—but it must be kept sparkling clean. Expect spot checks. No drugs, no smoking, guns kept locked up in a wall safe. Put our kids in harm's way in any manner and we'll end you. Overnight guests are permissible as long as they don't interfere with your duties. Are you still interested in the job?"

Tucker just stared at Deliverance in utter disbelief before he broke out into a huge grin. "Yes, ma'am. I sure as hell am."

"Let me hold your hands," Deliverance demanded, holding out hers. Tucker placed his hands gently on hers, palm to palm, and waited. Deliverance closed her eyes and breathed in and out evenly, softly. She removed her hands after a few minutes and opened her eyes.

"What did you feel?" Tucker asked quietly.

"I felt a good man with demons," she said. "That doesn't disqualify you, since we all have demons." She sat up straight. "We'll have to do a thorough background check on you, and Quint will take you to a gun range to verify your shooting ability. Meanwhile, let's get you acquainted with the little demons who would be your primary charges."

Deliverance didn't need to call her wolf pack in; they ran over to the couch as if on cue and cuddled around their mother. "Introduce yourselves," she said. "Politely," she added as an afterthought.

"I'm Aislinn Maximiliana Luisa Dane-Quintana. You may call me Aislinn or Princess. Only Mommy and Daddy get to call me Snickerdoodle." She extended her hand very formally.

Tucker shook her hand and said he was pleased to meet her.

"I'm Alex."

Tucker said, "That's a much shorter name than your sister's. Don't you have any others? A nickname?"

"I do, but we're not familiar enough with one another. I may tell you the other names when I learn to trust you." Alex didn't extend his hand but looked at Tucker balefully. He sniffed.

"I think that's fair," Tucker said.

"His nickname is Scamp," Aislinn said, flashing a triumphant smirk at her brother.

"I'm gonna kick your ass," Alex replied, scowling.

"Alejandro Carlos Wilde Dane-Quintana," Deliverance exclaimed. "You're going to get *your* ass kicked if you talk like that." Alex crossed his arms tightly, sat back, and scowled menacingly at his sister.

Tucker smiled at the little blonde girl. "And your name would be?"

"Vikki."

"Just Vikki?"

"Charity Victoria Erzsébet. Um, Dane-Quintana."

"Erzsébet is unusual."

"It's Auntie Bliss's real name. She's a witch, too."

"I see." He smiled at Storm. "And your name, young lady?"

"Storm. I don't have any other names right now. Do you like my eyes?" Her gaze was challenging.

"You have beautiful eyes," Tucker said sincerely. "They say that eyes are the windows to the soul, and if that's the case, I'd say you have a very special soul."

"What's bisexual?" Her mismatched eyes bored into his with a mixture of consistent challenge and derision.

Deliverance quickly interrupted. "That's not important now, Storm. We'll save that explanation for later."

"When?"

"When you're sixteen. Now, do you kids have any questions for Tucker before he leaves?"

"What's bisexual?" Aislinn asked innocently.

"Warning you," Deliverance said ominously.

"Is it something bad?" Alex asked. "Is he going to be arrested?"

"No, but it's not relevant right now. That means stop asking or I'll bring out the nail-studded leather belt."

"Do you like tarantulas?" Aislinn asked very seriously.

"I do not. I don't like spiders at all."

"Bad piece of information," Deliverance said under her breath. The young man had already given her kids leverage for torment.

"Can you play baseball?" Alex asked.

"I can. I love to play. I can teach you some really neat throws."

"What about soccer?"

"Maybe we can learn together."

"Do you like Trivial Pursuit?" Storm asked.

"I haven't played it much, but I'd love to get a game going. There's so much you can learn from the subjects, as well as how to play games intelligently and honorably. Which topics do you like?"

"History," Storm said.

"Geography," Aislinn said.

"Science and Nature," Alex said. "Vikki's too young to play."

"Oh, I don't know about that. Perhaps we can get her feet wet when we play."

"I don't like wet feet," Vikki said loudly. "'Cept when we go swimming. Do you like to swim? I like ducks."

"I sure do," Tucker said. "And I love ducks." He was getting more excited about taking care of these four bright, intelligent kids.

"All right, wolf pack. Off you go so Tucker and I can finish up." Deliverance pointed towards the kitchen and her brood scampered off like a hoard of vandals. "They're challenging," she said. "We haven't ruled exorcism out just yet."

"Good. I like a challenge."

"Fine. Be at this address tomorrow at 9 AM sharp." She handed him a scrap of paper with the Union Jack address on it. "My husband, Victor, and Wilde will interrogate you and perform the background check, then Quint will take you to the gun range. If you pass muster with my guys, then you can move in Friday and start working Monday. We're having a barbecue Saturday and you can see my kids and Victor's in their natural element. It won't be pretty." She stood, and he followed suit.

"Mrs. Quintana, thank you," he said sincerely as he shook her hand.

"It's Ms. Dane, but you can call me Deliverance." She saw him to the door and gave him one piece of advice. "Tucker, I think you live too much in the past. You can only experience one moment—the present one. The past and the future have no reality, so why attempt to spend time there? Just keep moving forward." She didn't miss the look of wonder and gratitude on his face.

After she closed the door she called her husband at the office.

"Quint, I think we've got a nanny-bodyguard." She listened for a second then laughed. "Right—winner, winner, chicken dinner!"

CHAPTER NINETEEN

The explosion roared past one hundred thirty decibels, rupturing eardrums and shattering windows within five hundred yards of the epicenter. The car lifted off the ground as the pound of C4 ignited and was torn apart in a ball of fire and fury, splitting into four equal pieces and thousands of smaller pieces of metal, glass, and human body parts. Shrapnel embedded into walls and the few unlucky people close enough to the blast suffered its inevitable collateral effects; one woman lost an eye as well as the hearing in both ears.

Chunks of concrete flew in every direction, pieces as small as a marble and as large as a microwave oven. Once the roar of the initial blast had settled down the air was rent with screams and sobs and stunned terrified voices. Moments later the wail of police sirens, fire trucks, and ambulances ripped through the dusty air as the first responders desperately swerved through traffic to reach the blast site. Ten minutes later the media trucks rolled up and reporters and cameramen began their typical news dance of horror mixed with a thin veneer of compassion.

Ambulances began loading up the wounded as the fire was quickly extinguished and the inevitable process of interviewing witnesses began. The car was too badly demolished to identify who had been inside; body parts—ripped, torn, shredded, and burned beyond recognition—were being carefully photographed and gathered.

The investigation had begun.

Reichardt Belzer loathed Laurel Bollmeier. The woman was a thorn in the side of every decent law enforcement official, particularly him and Munch. A diligent newspaper reporter on the *Old Pueblo Sentinel* she dug and annoyed and bothered and criticized during the ax murders investigation six years earlier. He had the feeling that someone besides her patrolman husband, Don, was feeding her tidbits during the case and she had stupidly published some in her paper. Not that they had hurt the ultimate resolution, but she had let out certain facts that might have warned the perpetrator about their progress. He grinned when he thought of her one comeuppance when she made the grievous error of bothering Deliverance and for her trouble had a 32-ounce cherry slushie thrown all over her crisp white business suit.

Laurel had snagged a couple of scoops during the case, and after the dust settled she was one of the many so-called "authors" who wrote a book about the case, incorporating a mix of facts, suppositions, innuendo, and salaciousness. *Killer Across Time* was generally panned by the critics, and after only a small book-signing in Tucson's premier bookstore the book was quickly relegated to the bargain bin and Laurel's fifteen minutes of fame were over. She returned to her *Sentinel* job and was seeking another sensational crime to try for literary immortality that hadn't happened the first time. She and all the other "authors" were frustrated that they couldn't get an interview with any of the participants in the crime. Only one interview had been granted, and that was to Norah Maguire's magazine *Seraphim*. Norah's editor and writer Bruce Peterson had come to Tucson for the interview and had written an article that took up the entire space of the magazine's December 1978, issue; the issue had sold out in less than an hour.

Even so, Belzer didn't dismiss any written reports of the old crimes and had just finished rereading Laurel's book to see if it would jog any memories or ideas as to who the new serial killer might be. Obviously, he was targeting the people involved in the old case, and obviously he was defining and actioning his own pattern, which seemed to be recreating unsolved murders of the past. One aspect of the pattern that differed from the ax murders was that he was not recreating the new crimes in chronological order. Cheyenne LaChoisi had had a list of dates for each of her crimes, recreating the exact dates that the old Axeman of New Orleans had chosen for his murders. This new killer had chosen murders that linearly occurred in 1947, 1920, and 1976. The number of years between the first two murders was twenty-seven years; the number of years between the second and third murders was fifty-six.

Belzer also read the curriculum for Malachi's current criminology course, where only the Black Dahlia case was listed.

The second, third, and fourth Tucson murder victims were not in the curriculum but were on Malachi's long list of researched unsolved cases from which he'd chosen his twelve current cases. If somehow the killer was using this list or a similar one, then there were dozens and dozens of cases for which to create a new murder. Since there was no chronological pattern, there was also no way to predict which case might be copycatted. Munch was over at the college now interviewing a wide swath of people who might have had access to Malachi's list and hence might be potential suspects. So far Munch was coming up empty, but he was plugging away.

Munch suggested a possibility that Belzer didn't want to consider but had to during his investigation—that perhaps one of the circle of investigators and friends was the killer and might have even "attacked" himself to throw off suspicion. Neither Munch nor Belzer had imparted this theory to the other two sets of investigating detectives but went about quietly checking out alibis and actions of the Union Jackers, the C's, and their peripheral family circle. So far, they'd been able to keep most of their subjects of investigation—including the unsolved list—away from the press, and Belzer hoped to hell that if there was a department leak that no critical information might sift out and corrupt an eventual arrest and conviction. Loopy Laurel, as he called her, had been bugging all six detectives for information, and so far, all six had been tightlipped. She had tried to contact the Union Jackers, but from a distance—she didn't want another suit ruined. Besides the one that fell into disrepair from Deliverance's slushie, Phaedra Black Wolf Begay had smashed an extra cheesy-greasy slice of pizza on her mauve silk blouse when she snuck into their house during Superbowl.

Belzer made a spreadsheet of facts, priorities, and ratings. A little more than a year ago a new computer software product had burst upon the market from Lotus Development Corporation. An integrated spreadsheet, graphics, and database package, it was considered state-of-the art. The company had projected sales reaching one million dollars for its first year; by the end of 1983 the sales had reached fifty-three million. When Belzer broke down and bought an IMB PC for his home office (an alcove in his small but functional new apartment), Raine Sinclair had hustled over to his place and installed a lot of software on the machine that would serve to bring his investigative talents into the current decade rather than the 1950s. She was patient teaching him the basics as well as a few advanced tricks, and he was grudgingly accepting of his new techniques. It wasn't too long ago that he had deeply mistrusted technology and would scowl when he came upon green-bar computer printouts. Now, he had a PC, a dot-matrix printer, floppy disks, and a better attitude. Still, he had already destroyed one keyboard with his fists when the computer didn't respond quickly enough. He'd had to shell out money to buy a new one.

He had meticulously and very slowly entered Malachi's list of research into the columns of the spreadsheet. Then he went about rearranging the data to what he considered likely "next" potential subjects. It was a guessing game since the killer hadn't seemed to follow any pattern other than recreating unsolved cases from the past. He studied the first top-priority cases. His priority rating system was a one through a five, with a one indicating the highest likelihood.

Belzer had designated crimes revolving around water as the lowest priority, given the desert location; however, he didn't totally discount them since Tucson and its surroundings certainly did have rivers, streams, and ponds. His second-lowest designation was for crimes that occurred in public with or without witnesses. He discounted crimes committed in other countries. He made crimes committed with a gun or knife the highest priority since those were instruments used in the first four victims. He decided to list crimes committed during the twentieth century before going back any further. He refilled his coffee cup and studied his initial list of ten. The names were divided between ratings of one and two, two being applied since those killings were multiple murders by the same serial killer; their killer had chosen virtually singular murders to recreate, different types of victims, and different manners.

MURDER METHOD/ CRIME TYPE	LOCATION	DATE	VICTIM(S)	PRIO
Single Murder, Machete	St. Augustine, Florida	1974	Athalia Ponsell Lindsley	1
Single Murder, Stabbed	Holland, Michigan	1969	Betsy Aardsma	1
Single Murder, Stabbed, Beaten	Kenilworth, Illinois	1966	Valerie Percy	1
Single Murder, Shot	Mississippi	1962	Paul Guihard	1
Single Murder, Shotgun Blast	Mayes County, Oklahoma	1952	Jack Burris	1
Single Murder, Beaten, Strangled, Knife Wounds, Dismemberment*	Wyoming County, Pennsylvania	1938	Margaret Martin	1
Single Murder, Stabbed	Washington, D.C.	1954	Alma Preinkert	1
Single Murder, Stabbed, Burned	New Orleans, Louisiana	1964	Mary S. Sherman	1
Zodiac Killer	Northern California	1968-1969	David Arthur Faraday Betty Lou Jensen Michael Renault Mageau Darlene Elizabeth Ferrin Bryan Calvin Hartnell Cecelia Ann Shepard Paul Lee Stine Others suspected only	2
Santa Rosa Hitchhiker Murders	Santa Rosa Sonoma County	1972-1973	Maureen Sterling Yvonne Weber Kim Wendy Allen Lori Lee Kursa Carolyn Nadine Davis Theresa Diane Smith Walsh Unidentified Woman Others suspected only	2

Looking at the matrix he was frustrated; regardless of his care and thought going into rating the various unsolved crimes, there was absolutely no way to predict who the killer would strike next, if there would be a strike, or if the killer stuck to the "unsolved" pattern.

He drained his cup of coffee and sighed. He was tired, but he still had a lot to do. And, he still had to go to Penney's and buy three birthday gifts for Quint's twins and the ubiquitous Storm. The twins' actual sixth birthday was yesterday, March 13th, and Storm's "assigned" birthday was tomorrow, March 15th. Due to the unusual nature of the three children, their parents decided to keep them home from school today, Wednesday, and celebrate the birthdays jointly in a back-yard party. It was scheduled for 1 PM, and he was invited along with all the Union Jackers to the celebration. Even Munch agreed to come, without very much arm-twisting. Belzer was warned by Deliverance that her kids didn't toe the norm when it came to toys—Aislinn had decapitated her last Barbie doll; Storm had disemboweled a cute stuffed Care Bear; and Alex had buried his G.I. Joe action figures somewhere in the back yard under an indiscernible patch of sand. Deliverance also warned him not to bring one of "those damned weird, ugly Cabbage Patch freaky dolls" into the house.

Belzer was going to have to beg a saleslady in the toy section for help. He checked his watch and it was 11:30 AM. He'd have plenty of time to hit the El Con Mall and ferret out a few good gifts. He shut down his computer, checked his wallet for cash, then jaunted down the stairs to his car. It was a gorgeous day, bright, warm, and sunny. He was looking forward to a piece of cake from the Yvette's Old Pueblo Dream bakery. He rolled down the driver's window and turned on the ignition.

Munch finished a ridiculously huge hot pastrami sandwich. He tried in vain to wipe off the grease and mustard stains from his shirt, but to no avail. He knew he should have listened to his wife and started eating better, maybe a regular hamburger and a salad. A salad—right, Aloysius Munch was going to chow down on rabbit food. He wasn't that bulky around the middle, and he was given a relatively clean bill of health during his last mandated physical. He was going to be in tip-top shape when he stood and applauded and whistled in May when his son walked across the stage to get his high school diploma.

His was a late lunch since he had been at Saguaro Western College all morning interviewing more than a dozen people. He had a full hour session with Malachi Dillinger to discuss his research into unsolved crimes. He found the guy smart and engaging, and eager to help. Malachi's witchy ball and chain had come in for a few minutes and gave Munch the evil eye, as he called it. He wondered if she really had something against him of if she was scowling simply on principle. She was even weirder than Quint's wife. Actually, Deliverance wasn't too bad. She had even extended an invitation for this afternoon's birthday party and told him not to worry about bringing gifts—her kids would be overrun with toys and games from everyone else. Very few people invited Munch to their familial celebrations. He was a little leery but touched.

He and Belzer had discussed the list and agreed that it was unlikely that they could predict the next murder and victim—if there was one. So far, this killer (and Munch wasn't totally convinced that it wasn't more than one killer) had no real pattern and seemed pernicious in his selections and murder methods. He had enucleated Dahlia Doe's eye yet sent along a finger to aid in identification.

He had traversed all the college's buildings to talk to various academic and support personnel, and a few students. He had to be circumspect since the department didn't want any more leaks. They had been excoriated in the newspapers when it was proven that Moon Wolf Begay was not a suspect and had a solid alibi. Even so, leaking his identity after his interrogation had resulted in economic and social downturns for the innocent man. Some people still whispered that he was the killer of those two unidentified young people found by the side of the road. Munch blamed that bozo, Mike Welsh, for jumping to conclusions without a thorough investigation. He was glad that guy or his dumb partner, Keene Swansey, weren't working with him. Belzer was his foil in many ways, but they worked well together, and Munch didn't want any other partner.

Munch tossed away the paper plate and Coke cup and left the college cafeteria. He bought a last-minute jelly donut for dessert. His next stop was Begay's art gallery. He had a few questions for him and his wife and hoped they wouldn't toss him out on his ear. They had a right to be pissed about and suspicious of police officers.

Munch trudged across campus, chomping on his jelly donut and envying the students that were rushing to class or just enjoying a stroll on the green campus. He wasn't sure he could remember ever being that young, that naïve, that full of promise. He was thrilled that Aloysius, Jr., would be joining their ranks in six short months.

He entered the underground parking garage and walked to his car, his beloved banana-yellow 1980 Cadillac El Dorado coupe. He unlocked the car door and shrugged out of his suit jacket, tossing it on the front seat. He settled in, slid his seat up closer to the dashboard, and turned on the engine.

"Tucker," Deliverance yelled out the sliding door, "we need a half gallon of chocolate ice cream. Damn Quint ate the other one and Alex only likes chocolate."

Tucker was putting the last decorations on the big table that held the cake, gifts, plates, and utensils. He looked over to her. "Want me to head up to Alpha Beta and pick one up?"

"Yes, please. Get a half gallon of orange sherbet, too. And an extra can of whipped cream. And chocolate shots. I think that's it." She ducked back inside and yelled at Alex, who was nibbling on one of the cupcakes she had just frosted. "Dead meat, Scamp," she growled.

Tucker shooed Aislinn and Vikki into the house, with Storm trailing. The Dane-Quintana girls bolted from the kitchen screeching as they chased their brother to his bedroom and started shouting insults at him and pounding on his closed door.

"Okay," Tucker said as he grabbed the keys to Deliverance's station wagon. "Be back soon."

"Can I go with you?" Storm asked.

"May I go with you?" Deliverance corrected.

"May I go with you?" Storm repeated dutifully.

"What's the word of the day, kiddo?" Deliverance asked.

"Vaquero," Storm said. "V-A-Q-U-E-R-O." She had learned the word when the family attended the annual La Fiesta de los Vaqueros on Feb. 22nd. Quint had even bought her a mini-sombrero.

She had loved the rodeo and especially the women riders like Kelly Tierney of South Dakota, who was barrel racing. She didn't verbalize it, but she wanted to learn to ride more than anything. When she thought of that dream and others, she felt sick to her stomach with fear that someday she'd be taken away from this home and this family.

"Good girl. You may go with Tucker."

"Thank you ... um," Storm said, hesitating at the end. She wasn't sure what to call Deliverance or Quint and tried to avoid sentences that necessitated a title or endearment.

"Off we go, Wild Child," Tucker said as he ushered the girl out of the front door. He buckled her into the front passenger seat then got into the driver's side.

He smiled at Storm and patted her on the head, then turned on the ignition.

Cress LaChoisi patted Pugsley's head. The dog slobbered all over his beloved master's hand and butted his round head into Cress's side. He was due at the groomer's for a bath, brushing, and nail trim. Gray had taken him last time, so Cress volunteered to take the critter this time since he had no afternoon classes. Afterwards he would treat the little guy to a vanilla ice cream cone from Dairy Queen, and then a trip to Puppies Be Us to pick up some new treats and a chew toy.

Pugsley had enjoyed the morning lying in a soft bed at Cress's feet during his classes and while Cress was grading papers and developing a curriculum of his two summer courses. Neither Cress nor Gray had let the puppy out of their sight since the horror that took the pup's parents. They both knew it would be a long time before they felt comfortable enough to give the dog some private leeway or entrust him to anyone. Poor Mrs. DeSisto sobbed and apologized profusely that she just couldn't take him for walks as she did Boomer and Sugarlips. Cress understood completely.

"Okay, baby boy—time to go get beautiful," Cress said. He urged Pugsley into the back seat and fastened his seat belt. He looked out the front windshield of the car and saw Detective Munch getting into his own car in the college parking garage. He'd had a talk with Munch earlier in the day. A decent guy, but with rough edges. Still, there was that compassionate human being that leaked out at the most unexpected times. Even so, for some reason, Cress preferred the taciturn, often sepulchral Belzer. He leaned down and kissed Pugsley's head, then put the key into the ignition.

Phaedra decided to close the gallery early. She knew she had gone back to work too soon, but she felt that with Soaring Hawk five weeks old, she could spare some time to get out of the house and back into her regular routine. She didn't count on how a brisk return into the working world could drain her physical and emotional energy. Mrs. Peshlakai lived two houses down and was a godsend in watching the kids. Persa was in kindergarten during the morning, but Black Wolf was still homebound. He'd start nursery school in the fall. Moon Wolf was away for three days on a visit to the reservation to scout out some new sculpture and oil artists. He hated being away from her so soon after their son was born, but their business had taken a hit after he was investigated as a "person of interest" in the double homicide, and when stories appeared in the newspapers and through word of mouth, some people judged him as guilty until proven innocent. Even after he was cleared, some lost clients still stayed away, and some people chose to ignore the facts and think the worst.

Mrs. Peshlakai told her not to hurry back—she'd be happy to take care of the boys until their mother returned. The old lady was a distant cousin of Blue Feather Begay on his mother's side, and she had been a dream to have around. Phaedra had left home at 8 AM and opened the gallery at nine. There were a few customers, and a couple of looky-loos who peered through the front windows to see if they could catch a glimpse of maybe a murderer.

She had also been visited by that abominable reporter, Laurel Bollmeier, who was "just in the neighborhood" and was hoping for a quote on her family's situation. Phaedra was usually unfailingly polite and calm, but she told the woman to get out of her store before she called the police and pressed trespassing charges. She also mentioned that their lawyer was chomping at the bit for litigation and would be happy to satisfy his lust with a lawsuit that would strip Bollmeier and her husband of their life savings and their house. Laurel backed out of the store carefully, then turned and ran like hell to her car.

Phaedra sent her assistant home early, processed a couple of mail-order transactions in the administrative room, then locked the front door, put the "Closed" sign in the window, and left through the rear exit where their parking lot was located. She slid behind the wheel, leaned back, closed her eyes, and sighed. She loved her life and her family, and she loved her Stingray. She grinned as she strapped on her seatbelt and thought of her husband. He had caught a ride with a friend to the reservation, but she had called him and told him she'd pick him up and they could drive back with the top down and the wind in their hair. When his long, black hair was wind-tossed, Moon Wolf looked like a god, her god.

She turned the key.

Raine sat in the front seat of her car studying the newspapers from back home in England. Her parents and brothers regularly sent letters and clippings, assuring her that all was well, and she should enjoy her new life, and when was she coming home to visit? She loved reading the stories and studying the pictures in the *Brighton and Hove Independent, Brighton and Hove Leader,* and *Argus.* She used to love reading the *Brighton Herald*, but that age-old newspaper was absorbed by another in 1971 after 165 years in print. She especially enjoyed seeing the spelling that differentiated England from the United States, often adding a "U;" for example, harbour versus harbor, colour versus color, and honour versus honor. It had taken her a while to figure out the American words that meant the same as English words but were vastly different. She just didn't understand why Americans called a boot a trunk and a bonnet a hood. And so many American pronunciations were like nails on a chalkboard to her decidedly English ears. She couldn't believe that *they* thought that *she* had an accent.

Still, she was fast growing to love her new country; surprisingly, she thought the desert quite beautiful. Coming from a wet land often fraught with clouds, rain, and wind-whipped gales from the surrounding seas, she didn't expect to appreciate let alone like a dry, hot climate parsed with so much sand and weird flora and fauna. Maybe, she thought, she was acclimating to the city and its mountains and deserts due to her affection for her uncle, her enjoyable work at Union Jack Investigations, and her growing love for the ubiquitous Constantine Black Wolf.

She hadn't planned on falling in love. Her last experience with that was a disaster. When she saw Constantine she fell into lust, certainly not love. But as they grew closer she found the strata of his mind, heart, and soul peeling back like the layers of an onion, each revealing a deeper man, a good man. She knew that he had had a bad experience years earlier, and she learned quickly enough that he had been the lover of the Axewoman of Tucson, who fell to a bullet along with their unborn child. Constantine had told her that Cress was his biological brother since they learned that they'd both been adopted, along with Phaedra and Cheyenne; however, it was determined that Cheyenne—although presented as Cress's twin—had been born of different biological parents. No one except those in their close circle of friends and family knew that Cress, Constantine, and Phaedra were true siblings, triplets given up for adoption by their unknown biological mother.

Still, she thought there was something else besides simply that, and she longed to know his innermost secrets. She wouldn't push though. He deserved his secrets and telling them on his own timeline. Or not. She had secrets, too. Dark secrets.

Since she had moved into his townhouse they had had only one real argument, and that was over whose primary responsibility it was to take care of their pug puppy, Blackjack. She said it was his dog. He said she had bullied him into taking it. They both adored the little ebony pug, and finally agreed to a schedule of feeding, walking, and cleaning up. He pretended to be annoyed when she lifted the dog onto their bed and he snuggled between them.

She finished the letter from her brother, Roger, refolded it, and slipped it back into the envelope. She hadn't written her family a letter for a month now, and thought it was well overdue. She kept abreast of the technology advances and was excited about the avenues made into electronic mail, or, as it was shortened, email. She looked forward to a time when she could sit at a computer, write a letter, and send it off only to appear in her family's computer moments later. She had explored the possibility of attending a course or two at Stanford to become acquainted with the upcoming and proposed technologies. She would have to be gone from September through December, and she was of two minds about it.

Yes, she wanted to increase her knowledge and professional viability, but no, she didn't want to leave her uncle and friends. She had to decide soon if she wanted to apply for auditing the classes.

Raine stored the letters into her briefcase and checked her watch. She had plenty of time to make it to the Dane-Quintanas' birthday celebration. She liked the kids a lot, especially the mysterious and somewhat reserved Storm. She felt for the child, but at least the little girl was in a good home until her future could be resolved. Right now, it was Raine's future that was occupying her thoughts as she sighed deeply, stuck her key in the ignition, and turned it gently to the right.

The smoke was clearing but the cacophony of sirens and screaming and yelling and car doors opening and slamming as the media descended onto the explosion site had just begun. Laurel Bollmeier stood at the forefront of the crowd of cameramen and reporters, her lips parted in shock as she watched the chaos at the death scene.

It was going to make a hell of a story as part of the tale of the swath of recent Tucson murders. She already had a title for a new book—*Epicenter of Horror.*

It was only a matter of time before they called her to appear on the *Today* show to talk about her *New York Times* bestseller.

CHAPTER TWENTY

March 18, 1984, Tucson, Arizona

Sunday dawned into a beautiful cloudless, warm sunny day. The temperatures were predicted to reach a high of 72°F, in line with the usual monthly average for this time of year. The vast majority of residents and tourists were going about their business, enjoying the peace and tranquility of a church service, or tooling around the many sights and cultural events the city had to offer.

Three funerals were taking place that day, but only two were attended by a small group of grieving family and friends; the third was becoming less of a reverent occasion than a chance for raucous media personnel and ghoulish looky-loos to stir up a circus that smashed the concept of common decency and compassion into dust.

The East Lawn Palms Cemetery on Grant Road had a history going back to the late 1940s. It was a sprawling burial site served by its own mortuary and resting under a sprawling view of the magnificent Santa Catalina Mountains. The expanse of green lawn was enhanced by mature trees and beautiful sculptures of angels and saints. There was an inside space where cremains could be safely entombed. A great many of the headstones were flat, but there were many aboveground markers carefully chosen and engraved by the families and loved ones of the interred. It was a peaceful place to rest for eternity, peaceful at least for the deceased although perhaps not for all the grieving survivors.

Although the mortuary provided a small chapel in which mourners could gather, the service for this deceased took place at a well-known religious site that was filled to capacity with people who loved or respected the deceased; no blood-sucking reporters allowed. Buff bodyguards had been hired to keep the riffraff out, and they were successful, allowing the mourners the privacy and respect due them.

The religious service was beautiful and reverent, and a half dozen people spoke eulogies for their lost friend. Sobs broke the solemnity of the occasion, as they should have. The hearse and limousines that led the procession up to East Speedway then north on Rosemont and east on Grant until they reached the cemetery. Cars and crowds were already there since the location had been leaked, and cameras started snapping to catch shots of the mahogany coffin, and the people spilling out of the limos and other cars. The significant police presence made most of them stay behind the rope barriers, but a few soulless newshounds managed to sneak under and had to be dragged back to their perches.

The burial service began as a large group of black-clad mourners gathered around the coffin to inter the shattered remains of a friend and a very good person.

The self-proclaimed Surrogate Scourge watched the goings on with a barely restrained smile tugging at the edges of his thin lips. He wanted to shout to the world that it was he who had precipitated this orgy of grief and callousness, but of course he could not and had to enjoy his remarkable intelligence and planning silently, at least for now. He was of two minds on the ultimate end of his "scourge"—to select a final victim someday and fade away, never arrested, never even identified; or go down in a blaze of glory that people would be talking about for decades to come.

He thought about the cruel letter that Cheyenne LaChoisi had sent to Quint after she murdered his family. In it, she quoted poet Robert Frost: "*But I have promises to keep, And miles to go before I sleep, And miles to go before I sleep.*"

He, too, had many more miles to go before he could rest forever, either in corporeal being, or in legend.

He carefully extracted a small camera from inside his jacket and snapped a few pictures of the coffin, the mourners, and the obnoxious, salivating audience that would never understand just how wanting in character they were, and how very far beneath him they were in cunning and intelligence.

He flashed an involuntary smile, then quickly rearranged his face into appropriate solemnity.

The Stalker watched the burial from a farther distance, as oblivious to the Scourge as he was to the Stalker. He had a similar disposition to retribution, but on a far less grander scale. Right now, his intensity was focused on one person, but that could change. He was quite aware that his pernicious vacillations between love and hatred—and blame—could change in the blink of an eye.

Sometimes he would stand in front of his bathroom mirror and watch his reflection, marveling at the tsunami of emotions that rippled across his face like the waves crashing relentlessly against the shore. He loved the sea, always had, and felt akin to its roiling power. Those idiot doctors that had declared him schizophrenic had no true measure of his self, and his capacity for rational thought and action. They said that he had lost touch with reality, but they didn't understand that his reality was a living, breathing, palpable thing that superseded their stupid academic and medical suppositions.

He had plans—great plans—and no one was going to stop him. He had the resources, the skill, and most importantly the will to accomplish his goals.

After all, he was here, wasn't he? He grinned and raised the binoculars again, homing in on that one person who would soon feel his wrath as the hand of God.

The Retaliator had no knowledge of the other two men, and was the farthest from the burial site, barely able to stand up straight and see the mourners gathered around the grave. Still, he could get a glimpse of the object of his obsession, a silhouette, really. Still, there was that face, that presence, that creature that deserved all the plagues of Hell.

He squinted, focusing on the aggressive reporter that was being held back by police guards. He recognized her from the newspaper and the book she'd written. She would be a good source of information if he could approach her the right way and gain her trust and confidence.

Unknowingly, she could be an assistant to the punishment that was way overdue.

He slipped away from the burial, got into his car a half mile away from the cemetery, and drove off to his hideaway.

He needed to sleep, to dream. He relished those nights of REM, yet also dreaded them because sometimes the dreams descended into nightmares.

He knew about nightmares.

He planned to create one.

BOOK TWO

"The arid country! I look out over the sagebrush plain, panting and parched, and sense its long thirst for the rain.... Does its soul stifle when the hot winds blow and the burning sands beat down? Is its throat cracked and aching in the alkali heat? Does it know a yearning as deep as death for the sound of a purling stream?"

Muriel Strode (1875–1964), "A Soul's Faring: XXVII"

Bell Rock, Sedona, Arizona

CHAPTER ONE

July 23, 1943, Ipswich, England

Sixty miles northeast of London, the small town of Ipswich has the distinction of being the oldest continually inhabited town in England, originating back in the Saxon period. The etymology of its nomenclature came from its original inhabitants, and in its early inception it was known as Gyppewicus or Yppswyche. Located on the River Orwell, it was an important port used by the Romans to transfer soldiers and goods to towns farther into the west of the country. Its location and importance enticed settlement by European residents such as Frisian potters from the Netherlands. The town had its share of famous residents, including painter Thomas Gainsborough, Nathaniel Ward, and Lord and Lady Nelson. It also begat a namesake in the United States when John Winthrop the Younger founded the Massachusetts town of Ipswich north of Boston in 1630. That town was famous for its clams and celebrated the shellfish with its annual Chowderfest.

However, the English town had its share of notoriety and bad times. During the reign of Queen Bloody Mary, the group known as the Ipswich Martyrs were burned at the stake for their Protestant beliefs. In World War I the town was bombed by the German zeppelins, but the greatest architectural and human damage took place in World War II when the Germans bombed the town into devastation; dozens of civilians died in those bombings, and the critical docks were nearly obliterated. The population was obsessed with survival.

But not Earle B. Kensington, Jr. He thrived in the chaos, because the chaos masked his illicit smuggling of goods across the North Sea section between the English coast and Amsterdam, as well as his obsessive drive to become a budding killer. Tonight, in the darkness in a farm area outside of Ipswich, he was burying his second victim, a sweet fourteen-year-old schoolgirl named Elizabeth Harding. So that she could spend eternity without feeling too alone, he was burying her next to thirteen-year-old Euclid Burnham, whom he had strangled two years earlier.

The ground was moist from the week of hard rain that had

fallen. His efforts were sheltered not only by the dark but by the immense copse of oak trees hiding his work from any prying eyes. Not that there were any—most people were hiding in their homes with the lights out or dimmed to prevent the bastard Germans from bombing them.

Kensington struggled with the mounds of dirt he was building from his digging efforts. At twenty-one he was a strong young man, his bulk and muscles derived from hard work on his father's old farm in Rushmere St Andrew and then on the docks when the farm went bankrupt; avaricious entrepreneurs sized the farmhouse and barns and kicked the Kensington family out on the streets. That was in 1937, before the war. His mother's relatives took her and the younger kids in, but he was left to survive with his angry father on the streets of Ipswich. What made the situation even more precarious was that his old man was schizophrenic and had been since his early twenties. The word meant, literally, a splitting of the mind, and Kensington, Sr., certainly fit that bill. There were several differentiated types of the mental illness, but he fell into the spectrum category of paranoid schizophrenia. He became delusional, and spent hours trying to think of ways to protect himself from the outside forces that were "out to get him."

Year after year he became depressed on most days and manic on others, his grasp on reality easing inch by inch until three years after he and his son were discarded by the rest of the family; then, after muttering to himself, hearing voices, wandering day in night in a confused state, he ended his life by jumping off the quay in the dead of night. His body was pulled from the water the next day and he was buried in the local cemetery without a headstone. Earle went to his mother for shelter. She refused to take him back into the family and he couldn't truly blame her since he was already exhibiting signs of the mental disease himself.

Six months later he burned down their house, killing his mother and his sister, Adelaide.

By then the war had started and the German Blitz of 1940 was in full swing. London seemed to be taking the brunt of the onslaught, but smaller towns around the country weren't immune to the Nazis' efforts to spread devastation and terror. Mentally deteriorating but possessed of a fearless cunning far beyond his years, Earle began his criminal activities in earnest, and hooked up with a gang of smugglers who saw the war as a means of financial advancement. The young thugs he worked with didn't care about his mental illness and they used it to its best result. Within a year, by mid-1941, he was gaining a reputation for smarts and utter ruthlessness, and even his tough associates began to fear him. He preened at the mention of his nickname, the Enforcer.

He smoked, he drank, he got into fights where he beat men into bloody pulps, and he partook of the desperation of young whores who would shag him for a shilling or a hot meal; few women survived those encounters without notable bruises. One evening after an excessive amount of ale and cheap whiskey, he decided to take revenge on the men who had booted him and his family from their home. He knew their names, of course, and pinpointed the ones who would be his targets. But not, however, direct targets—he figured that the taking of innocent, loved lives would be crueler. And Earle did cruel in a most exemplary fashion.

So, he stalked them and planned, and one night during a round of the Blitz he climbed in the first-floor bedroom window of barrister Josiah Burnham's young daughter, Euclid, smashed her over the head, carried her out the window, and took her to a secluded place where he woke her up, gagged her, and raped her for an hour before he strangled her to death. He thought about leaving her violated body on the family doorstep, but he decided to let them grieve and wonder for the rest of their lives where their sweet only child might be and might have endured. As an ironic last action, he took her to the old Kensington farm and buried her six feet deep in the most secluded, unused area by a stone fence. He was meticulous in his self-protection, and when he was finished no one would ever suspect that the ravaged body of an innocent child lay beneath the earth. He finished his effort by grinning widely and showering the hidden grave with a stream of hot urine.

He could barely conceal his joy at the investigation and the interviews with her devastated parents. The thrill, the rush of victory ran through his veins like molten lava, and he knew this would just be the beginning. And now, two years later, he had successfully abducted, raped, strangled, and was burying the youngest child of banker Geoffrey Harding. He muttered to himself during the entire digging process, inarticulate words and babbling that sounded so much like that of his late, doomed father. When he was done he covered the grave with fresh sod that would meld into the grass there and forever hide the last resting place of two young, innocent victims of his misplaced rage.

There were others who might be appropriate targets for his confusion and rage, but he had recently run afoul of the constabulary and was thinking of moving away from Ipswich to another part of the country where he could make his mark and start fresh. London was a definite possibility; Birmingham, perhaps. Still, he liked being near the water and decided against those cities and any inland enclaves. He wanted to continue with his smuggling, so he chose Dover, the land of the famous White Cliffs. Dover was far closer to the French mainland than Ipswich was to Amsterdam, so there was the potential for bigger loads and bigger profits. His theory proved to be true, and by the time that the war ended in Europe in May 1945, he was a well-to-do criminal.

He decided to reinvent himself yet again. He decided to become "respectable." He was a callow twenty-four and had a lifetime to do so. During a slow, cunning courtship he beguiled a young lady of modest means but impeccable social mores. He was a handsome man, tall, slender, with thick, silky blond hair and sparkling blue eyes. She was plain and twenty-nine, and was besotted with the young man who inexplicably courted her. She didn't see behind the façade of normalcy or the madness that was growing day by day. They married in 1947, and nine months later she gave birth to their first child, a girl he demanded to be named Adelaide. She thought it was sweet that he named his firstborn after his late sister. She had no way of knowing that the original Adelaide was her husband's first victim.

By the time that baby Adelaide was six months old, she had learned what a monster she had married, and lived in fear every single day even as she bore him three more children, the last born in 1951 just before his reality snapped and he beat a man to death with a hammer in a bar fight. Convicted of murder, he was sent to prison.

One month later, he was found hanging in his cell; the investigation was closed quickly as a suicide, but there were rumors that several of the guards had hastened his untimely demise along. She refused to claim his body, took her four young children away, and changed her name. Luckily, few years later, she met a very good man, married him, and had the husband and family that she deserved. He even adopted her children and gave them a surname of which they could be proud. They moved to the small market town of Bury St Edmunds where her new husband worked as the manager of a large sugar factory.

The children adjusted, grew, and thrived as their mother prayed every day that the madness of their biological father would never visit their lives.

Her prayers weren't answered.

Detective Constable Graeme Garrick stood over the grave that had been discovered that first day of July 1981, watching as the meticulous forensic techs gently brushed away dirt and debris from the skeletal remains of what he knew in his bones was the body of twelve-year-old Bury St Edmunds schoolgirl Maisie Harrington. She had been missing for three months and was only discovered by chance when an old fisherman decided to get away from his nagging wife and take his pole and a good book down to the stream (he had been chomping at the bit to dive into Ellis Peter's latest Cadfael novel, *One Corpse Too Many*). Maisie was buried a good twenty feet away under an oak tree; a skeletal toe was sticking up out of the dirt which was clearly disturbed by some wild animal.

Garrick didn't look forward to notifying Maisie's distraught parents, but at the very least they'd have the closure of a funeral and a burial where they could visit the grave of their youngest daughter. So far, the Nicolas Brockwell family wouldn't have that closure; their sixteen-year-old daughter, Davina, was still missing after six months.

He called to the forensic tech. "I say, any idea as to manner of death?"

The head tech shook his head. "Can't be sure. There's a deep fissure on the left side of the skull. Could be that. We'll know when

Doc Hugh examines her." He handed something small to Garrick. "This was on her wrist."

Garrick examined the small beaded bracelet with the six letters that spelled Maisie's name. He knew that her mother had made that for her last birthday. "Is there a matching necklace 'round her neck?" Maisie's mother had made the matching pieces out of seashells she carved herself.

"None."

Garrick dropped the bracelet into a plastic bag and walked off to his partner, Detective Constable Britt Welker.

"I want this whole area explored in grid fashion for a full quarter mile. The bastard buried Maisie here, he might have buried Davina close by, too."

"Right," Welker said. "You don't think we've got another Yorkshire Ripper on our hands, do you?"

"Bugger, I hope not," Garrick said. Peter Sutcliffe, AKA "the Yorkshire Ripper," had cut a swath of vicious murders of young women from 1975 through 1980, taking thirteen lives and attempting to add seven more to that total. He had been caught just in January of this year, with his trial scheduled for May. His legal team planned on pleading him not guilty on grounds of diminished responsibility after a diagnosis of paranoid schizophrenia. He was disclaiming responsibility for his actions, stating that he was only the instrument of God's will. The jury didn't fall for the so-called defense, and after two weeks of trial he was found guilty and sentenced to twenty concurrent life sentences.

Welker nodded, unconvinced, then walked off to coordinate the search. Garrick gave a few instructions to the other policemen standing around the gravesite, then he got into his car and drove off. He drove into town and passed the Angel Hotel, where he glanced at the welcoming plaque on front: "Charles Dickens Stayed Here." Despite the beautiful quaintness of the town and the love its people had for it, Bury St Edmunds wasn't exactly a hotspot of tourism regardless of where Dickens made his bed. And Garrick, for one, liked it that way. The town was built in 1080 by an abbot and originally called Beodericsworth, but in modern times despite its impressive full name the residents simply called it Bury. There were dark periods to its evolution (such as the massacre of fifty-seven Jews in 1190, and the subsequent expulsion of others of that religion), but also historical ones that imbued the populace with a sense of pride: supposedly the Magna Carta had its origins there when the English barons met in the Abbey Church and swore that they would force King John to accept the precursor to the Magna Carta, the Charter of Liberties.

He passed St. Mary's Church where he and his wife worshipped on Sundays and headed towards a residential section close by the River Linnet and not too far from the police station. He pulled up in front of the Harringtons' house and reluctantly dragged himself out of the car and up to the front door. Both Mr. and Mrs. Harrington opened the door and looked at him expectantly. Their faces crumpled at the telling look on his, and when he withdrew the bracelet in the plastic bag Mrs. Harrington let loose a totally inhuman wail of grief and despair and collapsed on the front stoop. Garrick had called in for backup and one of the women officers arrived in time to help Mr. Harrington get his wife into the house where her wails echoed through the house and into the neighborhood like the howls of a demented banshee.

Garrick stayed for an hour and made it clear that the remains had yet to be officially identified, but, yes, he believed the body was that of their daughter. He described the tattered remnants of the clothing that the body was wearing—a forest-green corduroy jumper and a frilly white blouse—and Mr. Harrington, through chokes and sobs, confirmed that they matched the clothing that Maisie was wearing the day she disappeared. Garrick caught a glance at the framed photo of Maisie taken on her tenth birthday; it showed a brown-haired, blue-eyed girl with dimples smiling brightly, a slight gap in her front upper teeth. She could have been anyone's daughter. She could have been Garrick's daughter, Gloriana, had that little girl survived the leukemia that took her three days after her fifth birthday.

Garrick left the grieving parents in the care of the woman officer and drove back to the gravesite. It was getting dark. He could see a dozen officers making a grid search pattern. He noted that the forensic techs had finished their excavation of Maisie's body and the remains had been loaded into the coroner's van. Just as the van drove away there was a loud call from a hundred feet north of him and Welker, and the two constables ran over to a secluded copse of elm trees.

One of their associates, who was tightly holding the leash of a cadaver dog, was pointing to a slight mound of dirt that didn't seem particularly natural. Garrick told the nearby tech to start moving the dirt away very, very carefully. A cluster of men stood around anxiously in a semi-circle as young Billy Hopkins carefully used his hand trowel and brush to uncover what lay beneath of damp soil. After ten minutes of meticulous work, he leaned back on his heels and stared along with everyone else at the white skeleton hand that revealed yet another tragedy that warm summer night.

An hour later the remains of Davina Brockwell were being gently brushed by respectful technicians under the glare of floodlights as the crickets chirped and the leaves rustled softly under the auspices of the mild nighttime breeze. The soft sounds of a beautiful evening were interrupted by the crying from the police officers and forensic technicians.

Garrick stood far away from prying eyes as the tears ran down his face and he dreaded the task of notifying yet another set of parents that their lives were just destroyed. Dawn was breaking as the techs finished their initial excavation and the full-frontal skeleton decorated with shreds of decomposed flesh stared with eyeless sockets up at the cloudy sky that was threatening to spill a torrent of its own tears onto the land and the sad souls beneath it.

Garrick attended both funerals and was assigned to the task force investigating the disappearances and murders. Those were the only two; then, it seemed that either the killer had died, moved away, or simply stopped for whatever reason. After six months the task force was disbanded, and the case had only Garrick and Welker assigned to the investigation part-time. Six months later that assignment was deemed a cold case and they went about their busy business of catching other criminals in their hometown.

The people of Bury St Edmunds breathed a sigh of relief and went about their lives. Garrick worked the case even after it went cold. He made lists of suspects and covertly checked people out. His cozy den in the cottage he shared with his wife, Patricia, had all the photos and wall art removed; in their place he stuck photos and newspaper articles and lists on the wall with tacks. His battered old desk had a new computer on it where he logged his progress and notes. His wife gave up cleaning the room, where her husband spent hours every day and many nights going over and over the crimes. She had to badger him into taking their basset hound for a daily walk. She had to drag him to church services where he had a permanent scowl on his face in his growing disillusionment in a merciful God.

He never forgot the sights of those decomposed girls resting in the hard, unforgiving ground on the outskirts of a lovely English village.

And he would never stop searching for the monster that had destroyed two innocent lives, and the peace and tranquility of a once beautiful place to live.

Never.

CHAPTER TWO

Alaska Packard Davidson was Iris Flynn's hero. Her name and accomplishments were virtually buried in history, but she had served as a very important footnote in the annals of law enforcement—she was the very first female FBI agent.

Born a few years after the end of the Civil War in Warren, Ohio, she had very little formal education. Not much was known or documented about her personal life, but it was specified in the census that she was married twice and gave birth to one daughter. She also had a significant tie to the growth of transportation in the United States: Her brothers, James and William, founded the Packard luxury automobile manufacturing company in 1899, which was later absorbed by Studebaker after nearly sixty years of independent operation.

At the advanced age of fifty-four in 1922, she was hired by Director William Burns to work at the Bureau of Investigation as a special investigator in New York. The Mann Act of 1910 (also known as the White-Slave Traffic Act) was a federal law designed to address the felony of transporting across state lines "any woman or girl for the purpose of prostitution or debauchery, or for any other immoral purpose." It was thought that a woman agent might have additional insight into the crime, its victims, and its consequences, and Alaska was assigned to help investigate not particularly "rough" crimes since she was considered "a refined lady."

Alaska was assigned to the Washington, D.C. office at the rate of $7 per day. In addition to cases related to the Mann Act she also participated in other investigations and was a productive agent until 1924 when the face of the Bureau changed—J. Edgar Hoover became the director after the Teapot Dome Scandal. Hoover was already gaining a reputation as a tyrant and had a vision for what would become the Federal Bureau of Investigation. That vision did not include female agents, and when Alaska's supervisor stated that he had no work for a female agent, Hoover asked for and received her resignation. Two other female agents, Jessie B. Duckstein and Lenore Houston, failed to survive the new regime, and by 1929 the FBI was returned to a men-only boy's club. It remained that way until Hoover's death in 1972. Alaska died at the age of sixty-six in 1934.

In 1972 the FBI started to come out of its dark period, and the very gradual hiring of female agents began. That year saw the investiture of two female agents, Susan Roley Malone and Joanne Pierce, an action that was highly publicized in the news. Despite their qualifications and hard work, they routinely encountered hostility from fellow agents. They both knew—as did the young women coming after them in the next ten years—that it would be an uphill battle.

Iris understood that on an intellectual level when she graduated the University of Pennsylvania with a Bachelor's degree in Criminology and Georgetown Law School with a Juris Prudence degree. She was at the top of her class in both universities, and the day after she graduated Georgetown in 1981 she applied to the FBI, where her father had been an agent for twenty-nine years. He wasn't enthusiastic about her choice but supported her; her mother, a little less so. Her brother was a detective in Baltimore and was very much not in favor of her career choice, but she knew what she wanted, and she wanted to be an FBI Special Agent. That was all she ever wanted to be.

Training at Quantico was tough; there was a lot of pushback and hazing, but also some unexpected acceptance and kindnesses. She made the grade and her entire family—including her dour brother, Andy—was in the audience clapping as she received her credentials. With no seniority or track record, she was assigned to the other side of the planet (as she called it) and wound up in the Seattle field office. After two years and a distinguished service record, she applied for and was transferred to Phoenix. She relished the heat and had always hated the winters back home.

She thrived in Phoenix. Her long blonde hair was streaked gold with the excessive sun, and after hours she enjoyed all the outdoor activities available to her—hiking up Camelback Mountain and Squaw Peak, riding a dirt bike and practicing her rifle skills out in the desert, photographing the unusual cacti, trees, and desert creatures, and taking an occasional ride down the Salt River in a tube. She rarely dated, having set her sights on career advancement and putting her personal life a definite second in her rarified suite of priorities. Her longest romantic involvement was three weeks, and that ended when he found out that he was sleeping with a cop—and he was a cop himself. Her most nurturing relationship was with her cat, Juju, who as a kitten she had found starving in a garbage can. The orange tabby worshipped her and followed her everywhere in the condo she rented.

At twenty-eight she was happy and satisfied with her life and was already planning her eventual ascent into the highest echelons of the FBI. She hoped to be able to transfer to the home office in D.C. by the age of thirty. She had set the goal of forty-five for being the Deputy Director and at fifty, the Director of the FBI. She was ambitious, and never apologized for that mindset. Her unapologetic ambitions put off a lot of people, including some of her superiors, all men. That, and her openly deprecating opinion of getting married and having children. Uh-uh, nope—not going to happen.

Unfortunately, her immediate plans in June for a quick weekend jaunt down to Cancun were derailed by her new immediate supervisor, Steve Shaeffer. A very short, dumpy, supercilious version of a man, Shaeffer was one of those agents that was transferred frequently with no definitive reason, although after a brief tenure people understood why. An excellent sycophant, he tried to follow higher-ups from post to post, praying that he wouldn't be fired for his vacuous uselessness and that he'd land at some spot where he could execute his not-so-subtle tyranny and cluelessness. Somehow, he wound up in Phoenix, replacing a great boss who for medical reasons had to take an early retirement.

Shaeffer seemed to home in on Iris from day one, and nothing she did met his expectations. Then, during a staff meeting of his group three weeks in, she finally lost her temper and dressed him down in front of her associates, who later applauded her for saying what they were all thinking. She received a reprimand in her file, but no further action since her retired father had been a respected force in the Bureau, and Shaeffer's supervisor, Nick Lisbon, held her in high esteem. Still, Shaeffer assigned her piddling tasks, and then the one that blew her Cancun weekend to shreds.

And that was how she was stuck indefinitely in Tucson

assisting other FBI agents and city law enforcement on investigating the car bomb that had killed one of their own, Detective Aloysius Munch. She rented a long-term room in one of the less expensive motels on the east side and was assigned to be third-string to two other agents who legitimately had higher seniority and experience with that type of crime. They were decent men, and some of her anger dissipated under their consideration and respect. After three months the crime was still unsolved, and her first task was to re-interview all the primary professional and personal associates of the murdered police officer. The other agents were assisting the police in investigating the arrests and convictions in which Munch played a part to see if anyone stood out as an avenger for wrongs done to him or her by a good cop.

She had spent several days interviewing Munch's fellow police officers, including his partner, Reichardt Belzer. Captain Rupert Ferdinand, forensic tech Pete Murphy, and Munch's other associates were forthcoming and eager to help; Belzer was taciturn, crabby, and dismissive, but she sensed that his aloofness wasn't directed at her as either a woman or an FBI agent, but because he was deeply grieving the loss of his partner and best friend of fourteen years. He basically brushed her off the first two times she tried to engage him, and she was frustrated. She knew that he spent a lot of time with his friends in Union Jack Investigations, who were intimately involved in the series of murders that had culminated with Munch's death. The official line was that the police hadn't found a motive or suspect yet, but internally everyone thought that his murder had to do with the happenings around his circle of friends and the four murders that seemed to be committed by the same perpetrator.

It was mid-week and Iris was bound and determined to corral Belzer and get him to sit down for an in-depth interview. One of the detectives said he mentioned going over to the Quintana house to talk about something, and he gave her the address. Michael Quintana was the next person on her interview list anyway, so perhaps she could kill two birds with one stone. She pulled out her Tucson map and studied the best way to get there, and soon she found her classic 1964 blue Mustang headed east then north. She went too far on Tanque Verde and had to backtrack up to Sabino Canyon Road.

She found the Quintana house and noted the relative isolation of the home, surrounded by several acres of desert and next to another Santa Fe-style home that she knew belonged to two other potential interviewees, Wilde Sinclair and Victor Renard. If Belzer and Quintana weren't around, she'd hightail it over to the P.I. firm and maybe snag more than one name on her list.

There were no cars in either driveway, but both houses had three-car garages and Belzer's could have been stored in a cool garage instead of boiling out in the hot sun. It was close to ninety-five today, and she found herself drinking a gallon of water already. She couldn't complain though—any heat was better than shoveling snow in zero-degree wind chill factor back home.

She parked by the driveway and walked up the front path to the carved wooden double-door. She pressed the button and could hear the echo from inside the house. She tried again, but no one opened up. She knocked hard, then after a moment of waiting she decided to go around back and see if anyone was there. She reached the back gate, which was locked. She knew that at that point she should have abandoned her search, but she was annoyed and climbed over the stucco fence, dropping down four feet near the side of the house. She moved swiftly and silently towards the back. She spied a large casita that seemed empty. Out of habit she withdrew her holstered gun and walked to the rear sliding doors to try to see inside.

Iris was directly in front of the door looking into the kitchen when she froze solid at the touch of what she knew was a gun barrel at the back of her neck.

A cold, hard voice told her, "Don't move and raise the gun slowly so I can take it. Hands up. One false move and I'll take you out."

Iris slowly raised her gun and a man's hand took it carefully from her grip. The barrel of his gun was pulled away from her head. She was still frozen in place when he said, "Turn around slowly." She did as she was told with her hands up and came face to face with a tall man standing back a good five feet, aiming a 9mm Luger directly at her chest.

"Who are you and what are you doing snooping around here?"

Tucker asked flatly, his eyes never leaving her face and his gun never wavering.

She held her palms outward and said slowly, "My name is Iris Flynn and I'm an FBI agent. I'm going to reach into my fanny pack and take out my creds."

"Don't try anything," he warned.

"I won't." Iris unzipped the pack and carefully extracted her creds, opening them for Tucker to see her photo and the FBI image clearly.

Tucker nodded towards the wrought-iron patio table. "Toss them over there." She did as he asked, and he moved sideways to the table. He picked up the creds and studied them while keeping his eye and a gun on her. He slowly lowered the gun and tossed the creds back to her.

She stored them in the pack and asked coolly, "May I have my gun back?"

He handed her the service pistol as he backed away another few feet.

"I should throw your ass in jail for that little trick," Iris said, scowling to hide her embarrassment at being caught off guard.

"You're trespassing, and I have a permit for this gun."

"Who the hell are you, anyway?" she demanded.

"Me?" Tucker grinned. "I'm the nanny."

Iris stared at him in disbelief until he turned and whistled loudly. Four young children and one older boy piled out of the casita along with two large dogs.

Tucker thumbed towards them. "My darling charges. Care to meet them inside and have some iced tea?"

Iris nodded, mute. The pack of children rushed past her into the house, and Tucker bowed and swept his arm wide to usher her in. She found herself in a beautiful, spacious kitchen that was tastefully decorated in southwest-style colors, tiles, and art. The kids surrounded the kitchen island where a round cinnamon cake with banana icing appeared to have been cooling off. Tucker pulled out a handful of paper plates and plastic forks and began carefully cutting the cake into equal slices and placing them on the plates.

"Storm," Tucker said, "please get a glass of iced tea for Miss Flynn."

"It's Special Agent Flynn," Iris retorted.

"What kind of an agent?" Alex asked.

"She's a federal agent," Tucker said as he placed the last slice of cake on his own plate.

"One of those hoity-toity cops that Daddy told us about?" Aislinn asked.

"Yup."

"Here's your iced tea," Storm said as she handed Iris a glass.

"Thank you," Iris said, trying to avoid staring at the girl's unusual eyes. She was thirsty as hell and took a long draught of the cold liquid before choking and spitting something out onto the floor. She bent over and picked it up. It was a dead, wet cricket. All the children were giggling.

"Storm," Tucker admonished. "What have I told you about feeding insects to guests?"

"They're protein, Number Eight," Storm said mock politely.

"They're *bugs*, Number Four," he replied curtly. He sighed theatrically and shook his head. "Let me get you a bugless glass," he said to Iris.

"I'll pass. So—shall you introduce me to your charges? And is Number Eight your real name?"

"Tucker," he said. "Tucker Townsend. Number Eight is a long story." He reached into the fridge and withdrew an unopened bottle of water and handed it to her. "These are the Dane-Quintana children, or, as I prefer to think of them, the spawn of Hell and the bane of my pathetic existence. That's Aislinn, Alex, Vikki, and Storm. This young man is Bechet Renard, Victor's grandnephew. Unfortunately, we don't have the elegant presence of his older brother, Beckett, to complete the spawn circle. I believe he's stewing in his teenage angst somewhere."

"Haven't we all," Iris said as she scrutinized the water bottle then twisted off the cap and took a long, safe drink. She noticed the smirk on Storm's face. She put the bottle down, and slowly twisted the cap back on as she took in Tucker's salient points.

Mid-twenties (a few years younger than she); tall, at least

six-foot-two; athletic build; glossy, layered golden blond hair; sparkling blue eyes identical to her own; a killer smile; and an unexpected combination of toughness and gentleness. This was no type of nanny she'd ever encountered. She was quite aware that he was appraising her, too, and she wasn't sure if she liked that.

"I'm here because I was hoping to find either Detective Belzer or Mr. Quintana. Is it a safe assumption that neither is currently in residence?"

"She sure talks funny," Alex said as he fiddled with the crumbs of cake on his plate.

"Daddy said the fibbies are full of themselves," Aislinn added. "They think they're hot shit."

"Aislinn," Tucker exclaimed in shock. "That's no way to treat a guest."

"Mommy said we should always be honest," the little girl replied primly.

"There's a time for honesty and time to be circumspect," Tucker said sternly. "And that, little lady, is your word of the day. Go look it up in a dictionary." He had barely gotten the last word out when Aislinn fled the kitchen, running towards the library. She left a piece of her cake on her plate, which Storm quickly gobbled up. Tucker had noticed her propensity for scarfing down every visible morsel on anyone's leftover plate. Quint had told him that she had been "captured" while scavenging for food in Victor's garbage can, and even after months of living with a normal family (he used air quotes around "normal") she still seemed afraid to not eat when she had the chance. Tucker was determined to draw her out as much as he could, but it was slow going.

"Can I assume you're here on the bombing case?" Tucker asked.

"That's right. I was assigned to re-interview all the principles surrounding the murder." She glanced at the children, who were looking at her with rapt eyes. "Can we discuss this privately?"

"We know all about it," Alex said dismissively. "Someone killed Uncle Munch. And left us a head."

Tucker shook his head ruefully. "It's no use trying to keep

them away from the facts. These imps are too smart for their own good."

"Circumspect," Aislinn declared as she came back into the kitchen. "C-i-r-c-u-m-s-p-e-c-t. It means to consider all circumstances and consequences."

Iris cocked her head and studied the girl. She was stunning, and as smart as a whip. She reminded Iris a little of herself when she was a know-it-all, annoying, pissant little kid. "Do they all have a special word of the day?"

"They do," Tucker said. "Although today I haven't assigned the rest. Guess I'll have to come up with something to beat Aislinn's word."

"May I?" Iris asked. When Tucker nodded, she turned to Alex. "Prosecution. Miss Vikki, yours is … lawyer. And you, Stormy Eyes—your word is distinctive."

"What's my word?" Bechet asked. He was leaning forward with anticipation.

"Well, you're a big boy, so maybe something a little harder. Let's try … malfeasance. And Aislinn, how about a second word for you—gentrification." Iris barely finished the last syllable when the pack tore off yelling, heading back to the library.

"Nicely done," Tucker said admiringly.

"We hot-shit fibbies have our moments," she replied, smiling for the first time. Tucker noticed that she had perfect teeth. "Do you have any idea where Belzer is right now?"

"If he isn't at the Union Jack offices then he's probably either roaming the streets looking for clues or holed up in a bar somewhere drowning his sorrows."

"I wouldn't think that his superiors would allow him to participate in the case since Munch was his friend and partner."

"They aren't, but Detective Belzer seems to be operating on his own set of rules to find the killer."

"And his people know that?"

Tucker hesitated. "It's a source of contention. From what Quint told me Belzer is as much on the razor's edge of being suspended much as Quint was when his partner was killed. Well, that was when

Quint quit the force and became a member of the P.I. firm that Wilde founded. He understands the obsession."

"I'm sure he does." She paused. "I read a summary of that old case. Fascinating. I'd like to read more details. Aren't there a few books out on the crimes?"

"Lots. Every hack writer tried to jump on the serial killer bandwagon and make a buck off people's misery. One of the reporters here in Tucson wrote a book, too. Laurel Bollmeier. I read it. Half-assed effort that went nowhere. I think she's going to write another one on these latest crimes."

"Hmm. Maybe I'll interview her, too." She pulled a small spiral notebook out of her fanny pack and flipped through a few pages. "That explosion also injured several people, including a Crescent LaChoisi, who was in a car in that garage not too far from the one that exploded. Injuries included a dozen pieces of shrapnel and a bad concussion. He was in the hospital for a few days and his dog—name, Pugsley—was at the vet's for a week." She scowled at a few notes on the next page. "Someone broke into his house and hanged his two dogs. Bastard," she breathed angrily. She was a cat person, but she revered all animals. How anyone could hurt an innocent, helpless creature was beyond her understanding. "He's on my list of interviewees along with his family members and professional associates. Quite a swarm of interesting people involved in the old case and this one." She flipped the notebook closed and stood. "Well, I'd better get over to the P.I. offices and see if I can get at least one or two of my interviews done today."

"Wait," Tucker said suddenly. "Give me a moment." With that he left the kitchen. She waited patiently, the two dogs sitting at her feet, demanding affection. She petted them and thought that dogs weren't really that bad. Tucker came back, followed by the arguing children. He shushed them and said to Iris, "I called Deliverance, and she agreed to have you over for dinner to discuss the case. That way you'll have a whole rowdy bunch of interviewees to interrogate. Six o'clock good for you?"

"Um, that would be great. Thanks. So … what are we having for dinner?"

"The best shepherd's pie west of Salem's Pot o' Gold Saloon. Chili cornbread, too, polenta, and sangrias."

"Sounds enticing. I'll be here."

"Dress casual," Tucker said. "None of that pantsuit stuff you're wearing. We're a jeans group here."

"I'll remember that."

Tucker told the kids to stay put as he walked Iris to the front door. She turned to him with a sardonic grin.

"Do I run the risk of being shot when I knock on the front door?"

"I'll refrain, but my employers are another matter. I'll try to rein them in."

"What kind of wine do they drink?"

"Anything with alcohol in it. The field is wide open."

"Makes it easier on me."

"I aim to please."

"The perfect nanny."

"Top line on my résumé. What's yours?"

"Takes no shit from nannies. See you at six." With that she walked down to the sidewalk without turning around although she desperately wanted to. Had she given in to her instinct, she would have seen Tucker Taylor Townsend grinning from ear to ear.

CHAPTER THREE

Quint relaxed in his office with the morning paper, taking time for peace and quiet before the weekly staff meeting. He scanned the front page, noting the small article about the progress of the bombing investigation; no real progress had been made and the article specified an editorial in the issue for the publisher's opinions on the lack of progress.

The 1984 Olympics in Los Angeles were scheduled for opening ceremonies on July 28th, less than a month away. Just like the games four years earlier, the event was already marred by controversy since the Soviet Union and a dozen other eastern-bloc countries had decided to boycott it. That action was clearly in retaliation for the United States' boycott of the 1980 Moscow Olympics in response to the Soviet Union's invasion of Afghanistan. The Moscow games were boycotted by sixty-six invited countries, including Canada and China, but the Soviets held the U.S. responsible.

Barely two weeks away, the Democratic National Convention was scheduled to take place between July 16th and July 19th in the San Francisco Moscone Center. The occasion was just a formality, since Walter Mondale was already designated through primary elections and caucuses as the man to run against President Ronald Reagan, who was attempting a second election. Arizona was a die-hard Republican state, so the clear majority of citizens were hoping that Reagan would whip the liberal's butt. The Republican National Convention was scheduled for August 20th through the 23rd in Dallas's Kay Bailey Hutchison Convention Center. The one major difference in this presidential election was that a designated Vice-Presidential running mate was a woman: If Mondale won, then Geraldine Ferraro would become the first woman Vice President. A lot of people still rooted in the dark ages weren't too thrilled at that prospect.

June had been an eventful month across the globe, not just in the United States, but that country was naturally at the top of the Monthly Review section of the *Old Pueblo Sentinel*. Publisher Santiano Bronson devoted a half page at the back of the paper to summarize the various newsworthy occurrences of the month. He designed and wrote the items himself, barring even his top reporters like Laurel Bollmeier and Judie Sutphin from contributing. Besides the Olympics and convention summaries, he listed the best or most notorious of June 1984.

Ronald Reagan had visited his ancestral home in Ireland. Bruce Springsteen released his seventh album, *Born in the U.S.A.*, to wide-spread critical acclaim and financial success. Prince released his sixth album, *Purple Rain*, which ran to the top of the charts like a freight train. Cyndi Lauper was riding high with *Time After Time*, and Deniece Williams dominated the airwaves with *Let's Hear It For The Boy* from the movie *Footloose*.

Two Hollywood blockbusters were released, *Ghostbusters* and *Gremlins* (Quint had been badgered into buying four stuffed Gizmo dolls for his brood; okay, he admitted, they were cute). People were looking forward to the premiere of *Revenge of the Nerds* in August, a film that had been partially shot in Tucson. A few other films of notes marked June as their release dates, including the third *Star Trek* movie (*The Search for Spock*), *Once Upon a Time in America*, *The Karate Kid*, *Rhinestone* (with Stallone as a singing, bedazzled Dolly Parton love interest), and the totally pointless *Cannonball Run II*.

The town of Barneveld, Wisconsin, was nearly destroyed by an F5 tornado that claimed nine lives and saw $25,000,000 in damage. On June 18th, Paul McCartney's forty-second birthday, Denver radio host Alan Berg was shot to death in front of his home by the white nationalist group The Order. A jubilant France celebrated their Euro 84 European Football Championship victory by beating Spain 2-0. The Boston Celtics beat the Los Angeles Lakers in the NBA Finals to snag their fifteenth NBA Championship.

And as Tucson grew yet another high-end resort was being constructed and would open in December, the Loews Ventana Canyon Resort on the northeast side of town. It was only a matter of time before other developers followed suit and built new monuments to growing tourism, but venerable resorts like the Westward Dream, the Hacienda del Sol, and the Arizona Inn could never have their history or ambiance replaced.

Quint refolded the newspaper and drained the last cold dregs of his coffee. He checked the wall clock; five minutes to nine. This would be the first staff meeting with their new associate and he wanted to set a good example. Besides, Deliverance would tear him a new one if he was late; she ran the office like a fine Swiss watch. His status as husband meant nothing to the little martinet.

Quint left his office and met Wilde in the hallway walking to the Saguaro Conference Room. Wilde handed him a cup of fresh coffee and winked. They entered together and found everyone else seated, two large boxes of donuts and one of bagels spread out across the table, an item or two from a chosen box in front of each of the gathered crew. He grinned as he took his seat and found two giant bear claws waiting for him. His lovely little martinet.

"Okay, ladies and gentlemen," Wilde began from his seat at the head of the table. "We have a busy day so let's get going. But before we start let's officially welcome our newest member of the Union Jack crew, Reichardt Belzer."

Belzer looked distinctly uncomfortable as his new associates clapped and welcomed him. A private man, he'd never liked the glare of publicity or laudatory acknowledgment, but he knew they all meant well. And he was damned lucky to be able to transition to a new but familiar environment among friends.

He'd gone, as Quint casually remarked, batshit crazy after Munch was murdered, blown to bits. As Quint had done when Luke Wheeler was murdered, he tried to insert himself into the investigation—which was being led by detectives Forest Baxter and Yale Cornell—and refused to be pushed out. Captain Ferdinand endured the contentious disrespect for a short while, but finally he suspended Belzer for two weeks. All that did was to give Belzer free rein to spend nearly twenty-four hours a day pursuing unofficial leads. Both deliberately and accidentally he stepped on a lot of toes, and Ferdinand dragged him into his office and told him that either he stood back and let the other detectives and the FBI do their jobs, risk being fired, or take retirement since he'd been on the job for thirty years. It was a no-brainer—he retired (and with full pension thanks to Quint's digging around during his divorce; a few salacious photos and illicit activities on his ex-wife's part and she agreed to a minimal settlement). Upon learning of the situation Quint offered him a part-time job at Union Jack where he'd have great resources and support and could ease into a new chapter of his professional life.

"Um, thanks everyone," Belzer said. "I really … I really like being here. Even though most of you are too damn young."

"I resemble that remark," twenty-seven-year-old Shayne Bulkeley said.

"You and me both," Deliverance remarked. "Well, at least we have a few old fogies to balance out beauty and youth."

Victor narrowed his eyes. "I assume you're speaking of my ancient presence."

"You, Wilde, and Fox, and Quint is certainly moving into decrepit middle age."

"Hey," Quint objected. "I just turned thirty-nine."

"Ancient," Thayer Burton said mildly. She was thirty-two, but in fantastic physical shape from her years in the Army and her three-year tenure in the San Francisco police department. A lithe, athletic woman of five-foot-nine, she had her auburn hair cut into a perpetual pixie style, and her hazel eyes sparkled with mischief and a hint of viciously sarcastic wit. She had hooked up with Union Jack after she left the force for personal reasons and decided to move to the southwest. An ex-detective she knew, Trenton Grant, told her about Quint and company, and she contacted him when she hit Arizona. She meshed right away with the partners and thrived in the desert city and climate.

"Practically relics from before the pyramids were built," agreed Turner Jackson, a twenty-five-year-old ex-college-football-player with a stocky build and a black buzzcut. His grey eyes were light and eerie, but when he smiled his dimples belied his tough exterior. His body was heavily muscled from his daily weight workouts and jogging regimen. A native Arizonan, he'd never left the state, his only divergence from his hometown of Tucson the four years he spent studying pre-med at ASU in Tempe. He was madly in love with Shayne Bulkeley, who was a delicate but determined woman who was working her way through the U of A law school. So far, there was no indication that she returned his feelings, but he never gave up hope.

"And now that we've finished insulting all the senior members of the firm, let's run through our statuses so that you young whippersnappers can get your butts in gear and earn your weekly pay," Victor said. "Thayer? The Jalava case?"

"Right." Thayer nodded. She flipped through a notebook. "Wilhelmina Siljander Jalava, born in 1902 in Oulu, Finland, brought to the States in 1904 and grew up in Fitzwilliam, New Hampshire. Married Johannes Jalava in 1924 and produced three children, Oskar, Olga, and Josefina. Widowed in 1961 and was enjoying the later years of her life with her kids and grandkids when she met a younger man named Henry Farmer. Henry apparently swept her off her feet and to the dismay and objections of her family she married him in 1964. They honeymooned on the ship *Queen of Bermuda* as it went to and from Hamilton, Bermuda and New York, and then they settled into her lakeside home in Fitzwilliam.

"By all accounts it was an unhappy marriage and he took her for every penny. There was an unsubstantiated incident where he clocked her in the face, bloodying her nose and breaking her glasses. He pretty much drove her to an early grave in 1974, and then did everything he could to snatch her house and fifty-two prime acres for himself when it should have gone to her children. They fought the good fight for years until Henry died, but then his fourth ex-wife, Ellen, tried to get her claws on the property and that's where we are today, trying to find proof that Wilhelmina wanted her property to go to her descendants and that some of the documents assigning Henry part of the inheritance were forged."

"If the property and claims are in New Hampshire, why are we handling it?" Fox asked.

"Because I got a call from an old friend of the family up in Jaffrey who knew the Jalavas and had doubts about the lawyer and investigator they were using."

"You're from New Hampshire?" Shayne asked as she bit into the last buttermilk bar.

"Guilty as charged," Thayer replied, "My dad was born in Jaffrey and spent most of his adult life working at the Inn at East Hill Farm in Troy. I worked there in the summers before I went to Dartmouth and then into the Army. I wound up in the Presidio Army base in Frisco and when I decided not to reenlist I joined the police force there. I left after three years and the rest is history. Anyway,

Mr. Richards knew I'd joined a P.I. firm and called me with his concerns. Wilde said I could take the job on. I called the Jalavas and they agreed to pay my way back and fund me for three weeks to see what I could uncover. I leave Friday and fly into Hartford where I'll pick up a rental car and drive up through Massachusetts to my family home and meet with Mr. Richards."

"Weekend plans?" Victor asked amiably.

"Hiking up Mount Monadnock, eating roast beef, popovers, and corn fritters at the Black Lantern Restaurant, shopping at the new Colony Mill Marketplace, and stuffing my face with pancakes from Parker's Maple Barn."

"Sounds like a plan," Deliverance said. "My dad took me to that restaurant once when I was a kid. Never forgot the taste of those fritters."

"You definitely make a mouthwatering fritter yourself," Quint said.

"Maybe I'll just have to make you some tonight."

"Bring me back some dark maple syrup," Deliverance said to Thayer.

"Okay, then," Wilde said. "Next—Turner?"

Turner sighed and shrugged. "Nothing as monumentally important as Thayer's case, but I have a solid lead on the set of thirty mint-condition silver Peace dollars from 1921 that our client, Mr. Carlton, 'desperately needs' to complete his collection. They may be up in Scottsdale, according to my source. Besides our usual hourly rates, the client has offered a ten-percent bonus of the cost of the coins. He's one of those obsessive coin collectors that would spend anything to acquire a piece. I'm driving up there tomorrow."

"Any excuse to eat at Carlos O'Brien's." Quint laughed.

"No comment," Turner replied as visions of Lunch Special A rippled across his culinary senses.

"Shayne?" Wilde said. "Update on the Hickey girl?"

"Tracked the missing girl up through North Carolina. Her last known location was Asheville where she registered in a cheap motel under her real name, Yvonne Lee Hickey. Considering that she's a country music fanatic I'm pretty sure she hugged the east coast to throw anyone off and she's really headed to Nashville to make her mark as the next Lynn Anderson or Barbara Mandrell."

"Only a lonely heart knows," Quint said.

Deliverance groaned; would her husband never give up his affection for the country wailers? Well, she supposed that some of them might be better than Michael Jackson. Alex would disagree with that; he danced to *Billie Jean* all the time.

"I notified the Nashville police to be on the lookout for a slip of a girl carrying a battered old guitar and sporting immense blonde hair. If I don't hear back by Wednesday I got the parents' permission to fly there and scour the streets."

"Good job," Wilde said. "Raine?"

Raine quickly swallowed the masticated lump of onion bagel in her mouth and took a sip of coffee. "I've correlated a number of crime reports from across the country and courtesy of FBI Agent Ballard and I'm writing an analysis program to prioritize likely candidates for the next potential target." She smiled at Belzer. "That matrix you created was excellent and I've used that and your analytic thought process to drive my program. I should be finished coding by Wednesday and run the first simulations Thursday, and then we'll apply it to real-life data and see what pops up."

"Have you figured out any error ratios?" Deliverance asked.

"I won't be able to do that until my first few test runs with control data. I've been in contact with Donna Pallone up in San Francisco for guidance on the algorithms and she's agreed to come down here if I need her to review my code and results. Or, I could fly up there. I've always wanted to see the city."

"You could take Constantine with you and make it a work-personal experience," Wilde said. "I hear that driving across the Golden Gate Bridge up to Napa is a spectacular journey, and you deserve a little bit of me-time after all the hours you've put in."

"I'll ask him. Thanks, Uncle Wilde."

"Okay, youngsters," Wilde said. "You can depart for your exciting assignments while the partners take care of a few indoctrination tasks with Mr. Belzer."

"So, what should we call you?" Turner asked Belzer. "Reichardt? Belzer? Mr. Belzer? Old fella?"

"The first or last one will get you shot in the ass," Belzer growled. "Belzer's fine."

"Yikes," Shayne whispered loudly to her three teammates and Fox as they walked out of the conference room. "Those geezers are testy, aren't they?" She shut the door and the people in the room could hear good-natured laughing as the "youngsters" walked to their own offices on the first floor.

"Who was it that said youth is wasted on the young?" Victor asked.

"George Bernard Shaw," Wilde answered. "One of the few things an Irishman's said that makes sense."

"Watch it, Brit Boy—I'm half-Irish, remember?" Quint said.

"The bad points are canceled out by your hot-blooded Hispanic side, partner," Wilde replied seriously.

"I'll remember that half-assed save next time you ask me to do something around your house." He looked at Belzer, who was studying the professional interaction between his new associates. Some of his initial wariness was wearing off as he began to feel more at home in the presence of friends who cared about him and about the late Aloysius Munch. "Belzer, you'll be on the Munch case nearly full time, but you need to contribute to the firm with other assignments."

"Understood," Belzer said. "Got one for me?"

"Not at the moment, but I'd like you to sit down with that FBI agent, Flynn, and dig deep into what she's got and what you can provide her. I know you've talked with her a bit but from what Tucker tells me it was like pulling teeth."

"Tucker? What does he have to do with it?"

"Our nanny seems to have developed a friendship with the lady," Deliverance said. "And she's a pretty decent fibbie, much like Ballard. Not so stick-up-the-ass and willing to consider theories. We had a nice discussion with her when she came over for dinner, and she's come over a couple of other times, too. She even accompanied Tucker and the kids on an outing to Reid Park Zoo."

"Huh," Belzer grunted. "Does she know he's light on his feet?"

"You're a Neanderthal, Belzer—you know that?" Victor said.

"No offense," he said quickly. "Just making an observation."

"Well, our observation is that they're simply becoming friends. Anything else and I'm sure they'll handle it," Wilde said.

"Okay, okay," Belzer sighed. "I got her phone number and I'll give her call today."

"Don't try to hit on her," Quint warned half-seriously.

"Are you kidding me?" Belzer said. "She's just a baby and I'm—what did the whippersnappers say?—a geezer. Not to worry." He stood and stretched. "If that's it, I'd better go and call our lady G-Man. Or should I call her a G-Woman?"

"I'd be careful about showing your antiquated opinions since she has a gun and apparently doesn't take shit from anyone. I called Ballard and asked for his thoughts on her and he said she was one of the best agents he's seen. A dead shot, so behave."

"Will do," Belzer said. He left without another word just as the telephone rang.

"Yeah?" Deliverance said as she answered the phone. She had set up her "executive assistant" phone to ring the conference room if a call came in. She listened for a few moments, frowned, then handed the receiver to Victor.

Victor listened to the agitated voice at the other end, took a deep breath, and sighed. "Yes, ma'am, I'll be there shortly. Thanks for calling." He hung up. He looked at his partners and shook his head ruefully. "The boys' school. Beckett's spending the summer there making up for two failing courses during the regular semester. Seems there was an incident and they want me to pick him up."

"Uh-oh," Deliverance said. "Is he okay?"

"Right now he is, but I can't guarantee that state of being when I get him home. Gotta go. Be back as soon as I can."

"Want me to go with you?" Wilde asked.

Victor shook his head. "Better I deal with this alone for now. Later." He left the room quickly.

"Are things getting any better?" Quint asked.

"Better's a relative term," Wilde said evenly.

"The kids aren't giving you any shit, are they?" Quint asked.

"Not as much as they did in the beginning. Man, their great-grandparents and parents did a bloody fine job on their heads with all the talk about sin and evil. They were pretty sullen and uncommunicative in the beginning, and at least Bechet has come around—mostly. But, Beckett is the proverbial angry teenager. Victor gets the brunt of that."

"Yeah, Tucker mentioned his attitude and resentment of authority."

"I hope this dissipates eventually because, well, it's starting to affect our relationship. I mean me and Victor."

"Parenting is not easy," Quint said. "Del and I have our issues with our kids, too. Aislinn is becoming a little too aggressive towards her siblings, Alex is getting quite a lip on him, and don't even get me started on Storm."

"I thought she was getting better?"

"She is, but it's slow going. She still tries to hoard food and occasionally we find her curled up sleeping in her closet. Sometimes she'll go a day without speaking. She and Aislinn have gotten into arguments over stupid things, and I think on her part it's insecurity and on Aislinn's part it's jealousy. We've intervened a few times but generally let them work it out. Last week we made an appointment with a child psychologist and she's going to see her once a week."

"Nothing yet on her background?"

"Nope, still a mystery. But there's still hope." Quint glanced over at his wife. "We were talking with her case worker about possible adoption. Still a lot of administrative hoops to jump through." He smiled ruefully. "She's a pain in the ass sometimes, but we've kind of grown attached to her."

"And she's a bit on the weird side, enough to fit in with our crew," Deliverance added.

"A 'bit on the weird side?'" Quint said with eyebrows arched as high as they could go. "That's like saying Linda Blair had a slight tick in her neck during that head-turning scene in *The Exorcist*. Every time she does something outside of the box I feel like throwing Holy Water at her and chanting 'the power of Christ compels you.'"

"That's scary. Well, I need to finish up some paperwork while I wait for Victor's call. Knock if you need anything," Wilde said, then left the room.

"You know," Quint began, "we minimized the situation, but

I'm starting to get more than a little concerned about Storm. I found something under one of our bushes this morning that unnerved me."

"What?"

"A half dozen decapitated rattlers, their tails cut off. Pretty sure it was Storm's efforts."

"Then we need to talk to her. Tonight, after dinner. I'll have Tucker take the other kids out to a movie and tell Storm we want to spend some alone time with her. I'll have him take Bechet, too, so Victor and Wilde can have a heart-to-heart with Beckett."

Quint shook his head. "And you want more kids?"

"Yup. One or two, depending on what happens with Storm. I think you could use another son."

"Swell. Another boy that's obsessed with the Ouija board and tarot cards."

"But he plays the piano damn fine."

"That's true. Hey—maybe we should insist that all of the kids learn an instrument."

"No drum sets," Deliverance replied ominously. "No tubas, no harpsichords, no trumpets."

"Make a list and we'll see what's left."

"Your wish is my command, Macho Man," she replied as she flounced off to her own office.

Quint thought he knew exactly where he could get a hell of a drum set. He grinned.

CHAPTER FOUR

The Superior Court of California in San Francisco was spread out over several locations in the city, differentiating between juvenile and adult adjudications as well as other separations of criminal and civil cases. The criminal courtroom was packed that day as it usually was during the various proceedings surrounding the prosecution of Sarah Noelle Danziger for the murder of her father, James Danziger, as well as Rikhart Loeb, Joanna Carr, Frances Soto, and Dean Landis (of whose murder she vehemently claimed she was innocent). She was also charged with the kidnapping of three-year-old Cara Manzone; the attempted murder of George Henry and Norah Maguire; the aggravated assault of Mindy Stanavige; and arson, burglary, and vandalism for her assault on the Norah's father's bookstore, the Troll Cave. Connecticut wanted to try her for the murder of Celeste Maguire, her and Norah's mother, and the district attorneys in San Francisco and Hartford were jockeying for position in that case.[5]

Today Sarah's lawyer, Ryan Cutler—who at one time had been her fiancé—was making a motion to have the charge of murdering Dean Landis dismissed. He had made similar motions before regarding each of the alleged victims and each time the presiding judge rejected them. Since the crimes were committed six months ago and earlier, one would think that some of the notoriety and interest would have died down, but the opposite was the case. Sarah and her lawyer seemed bent on extending the length of the prosecution, and those in the know believed that it wouldn't be until early- or mid-1985 until the legal matters were resolved. That was, of course, before all the inevitable appeals' processes were initiated.

Constantine, Cress, and Phaedra were seated in the back of the courtroom in three of the precious public spaces allowed. They probably wouldn't have stood a chance of getting in except that Norah Maguire, as a favor to Quint, secured them. Quint told Norah that his friends were in the city to spend a few days relaxing while Raine Sinclair was conferring with Donna Pallone on the coding and testing of her projection matrix. Norah didn't give a real thought to

---

[5] Please see the novels *Voices of Angels* and *Out of the Ash* for the background and resolution of Sarah's crimes.

the oddity of the three attendees, but was happy to agree to Quint's request, especially since he and his circle had given Norah the only interview after the Axewoman of Tucson murders went down. Norah assumed that the C's were simply interested in a notorious case—who wouldn't be?

Phaedra was seated between her brothers, antsy and queasy. This would be the first time that any of them had seen their paternal siblings in person, and that was a whole different ball of wax than seeing their images in the newspapers. Phaedra thought it was ironic that now that Norah Maguire had been revealed to be James Danziger's daughter she had inherited and was running his newspaper, the *L.A. Daily Record*. She was torn, because part of her thought she and her brothers might be better off never revealing their biological connection, but her other half craved the possibility of gaining a new, loving sibling and her family. She knew that Norah was married and had three children, Phaedra's nephew and nieces. She'd like to know them. Would Norah like to be an aunt to her sons and daughter? Those thoughts tormented her, especially now that it would be only moments away before she'd see her sisters in the flesh.

Cress twisted a little in his seat; his hip was still hurting from the four-inch shard of shrapnel that had ripped through his side on a downward angle and embedded itself in the flesh and bone. He knew he was damn lucky to have suffered few collateral damages from the explosion that tore apart Munch's car a mere sixty feet away. He had been slammed against the driver's door as the reverberations of the explosion tore through the garage, and he'd lost consciousness for a minute or two before he awakened to a chaotic scene of dust, fire, and devastation of the surrounding concrete and cars on level two. He was aware of something warm and sticky running down his face into his eyes, and his right hip felt like it was on fire. The front of his shirt was shredded, and he was vaguely aware of streaks of red slashing horizontally and vertically across his chest, as well as the wide swath of flesh burn caused by the straining of the seat belt. He couldn't hear; the world was totally silent for him although he didn't really register that fact until after he shoved himself into a sitting position and screamed for Pugsley. He felt the boulder on his chest lift off as he heard strong whimpering from the rear of the car and a moment latter a bloodied, shaking, terrified but very much living pug stuck his head between the front bucket seats and whined at his master.

Cress's memory faded in and out and he was only cognizant of a lot of snapshots of the remainder of that day. People staring into the car with looks of horror on their faces. Someone pulling his door open and trying to stem the blood from his scalp wound while another tried to unfasten the safety belt. Screaming. Sirens. EMTs. Someone taking Pugsley out of the car gently and holding him in his arms. Being strapped into an ambulance and a mad ride to the hospital. Awakening to find Gray by his bed holding his hand and telling him that their dog was okay. Falling asleep and then reawakening to his life mate, brother, and sister standing beside his bed. Doctors and nurses coming in and out of his room checking his vitals and speaking to him, telling him that he'd been in surgery to remove the hip shrapnel and that his hearing would return (that's what his brother told him afterwards since for the first few days he still couldn't hear). And Quint visiting and telling him that the car bomb had claimed Detective Munch's life, and that several other people suffered minor injuries, except for one woman, Professor Calabrese, who had lost an eye and had both of her eardrums shattered.

Cress was released from the hospital after three days and Gray immediately drove him to the vet's to see Pugsley. The dog was ecstatic at Cress's appearance. The vet said that the pug's ribs were bruised and there were a few minor cuts and bruises, and that he wanted to keep him for a few more days. After a week Pugsley returned home. Cress was on pain medication for two weeks and had physical therapy for a month afterwards for his hip injury. He felt decent now, although his hip twinged every so often; the doctors said that would most likely dissipate as time went by. He couldn't return to his classroom duties for the remainder of the semester, and Malachi managed to convince him to take the summer off and "just breathe," especially since this was the second time that he had cheated death. He decided to use that time to work on his curricula for the next year. When Constantine told him that Raine had to go up to San Francisco to confer with technology master Donna Pallone, he found out that there was going to be another courtroom motion in the Danziger case, and that would be an opportune time to see in person the daughters that his biological father had raised in whole (Sarah) and in heart (Norah). Constantine was going to go with Raine and spend a couple of days in Napa with his girlfriend. Since the brothers decided to go, Phaedra decided that all three of them should take the opportunity to see the Danziger twins.

Constantine pretended to be blasé about attending the court session, but inside he was sweating a long-held emotional tie to the past, and he needed to put some questions to rest. Raine still had no idea that the C's were Danzigers, and that his affair with Cheyenne was unknowing incest. He wasn't ready to share that yet. He was eternally grateful to Quint's crew, Belzer, and Munch for keeping those secrets out of the official record; the lives of the C's and their families were upended enough with the known facts. Still, Raine was perceptive, and he sensed that she knew he was keeping a secret even though he had opened up to her more than he had to any woman, Cheyenne included. Hell, they were living together, and for Constantine, at least, it felt so right. He sensed that she felt the same way, but he also sensed that she, too, was keeping secrets. Normally, his tense manner and aggressiveness would try to impose upon her and dig the secret out, but he had changed—wanted to continue changing for the better—so he decided that whatever she needed to tell him she would in her own time. Until then, he was content—happy, even—being in love and sharing a life with an unusual and special woman.

There was a buzz suddenly and the C's turned their heads and saw Norah Maguire come into the courtroom with her husband and an older man. People buzzed as she and her companions looked neither right nor left, passing the C's and taking their places in the front row behind the prosecution, a man and woman team that appeared middle-aged and radiated competence and determination. There was a fortyish man at the defense table, no doubt the ex-fiancé lawyer, and a young woman assistant who looked barely old enough to have graduated law school.

Phaedra thought that her sister looked beautiful, regal, poised, classy. She was dressed conservatively in a navy-blue pantsuit with minimal shoulder pads, a pale-blue silk blouse, and a single white pearl on a neck chain that matched the pearl studs in her delicate ears. Her dark brown hair was wrapped tightly into a back twist, held in place by a pearl comb. She wore a spectacular diamond ring, and pale pink lipstick. She was tall, even without the high-heeled black pumps. Her husband was tall, handsome, and dressed in a black suit with a coral shirt and umber tie. His hair touched the shirt neck; it wasn't as long as Quint's, but it showed an irreverent side to the fortyish man. The older man had grey hair and wore a simple brown suit. Norah sat between the men, staring straight ahead even as her husband whispered something in her ear. Phaedra had caught a glimpse of Norah's brilliant hazel eyes—so like her own—and knew without any declarations or genetic tests that this woman and she shared a bloodline.

Then the judge appeared, and the audience stood as he seated himself high up on his platform and nodded to the bailiff. The defense lawyers stood, and a few seconds later Sarah Danziger was brought into the courtroom in a wheelchair. She was wearing sunglasses. Her washed-out blonde hair was brushed simply and hung to her shoulders. She wore a simple white short-sleeved dress down to her ankles. Her stance was rigid, her head stiff, her demeanor unfathomable behind those glasses. Phaedra knew that this sister hadn't survived her murderous efforts without consequences besides arrest; Norah Maguire had smashed her spine with a steel rod, placing her forever in that wheelchair, and somehow her eyes had been damaged by turpentine from the painting supplies in the fateful attic where James Danziger met his doom. Phaedra involuntarily shivered for some unknown reason when she looked at this sister. She suddenly knew that she wanted nothing to do with her, especially since she'd already had one demented, murderous sibling.

Unconsciously the C's held hands tightly while the proceedings started. Ryan Cutler presented his motion with hour-long details before the prosecution rebutted. The judge said he'd render an opinion by the next morning, but from his attitude, questions, and remarks, most of the people watching assumed that he'd reject that motion, too. Court was adjourned, and the brief proceeding was over. Cress got up and pulled his sister into the aisle as people began moving out. She was still holding Constantine's hand and the three of them walked into the hall which was crowded with audience members, lawyers, and media. A moment later Norah, Adam, and George Henry came out and Adam angrily fended the TV and newspaper reporters away from his wife. They came within a foot of the C's when Norah stopped suddenly, turned, stared at them, then smiled.

"The Black Wolf twins and friend, I believe?" She stuck her hand out and Phaedra impulsively took it. She thought that Norah had a warm, welcoming touch.

"Yes," Phaedra said. "Thank you for making it possible to watch this and letting Raine confer with Donna on her program."

"You're welcome. I'm sorry I can't offer you any more attention right now. I have a meeting with the *Record's* lawyers that I'd like to put off but can't. Perhaps we can break bread another time if you're up here or I have a chance to visit your city. I'm very grateful for the exclusive you gave me on your ... experience. I hope you are all doing well?"

"We are, thank you," Constantine said tensely. "We appreciate your time, but we, too, have another commitment. We wish you the best in getting this whole thing behind you." He paused for a brief second. "It takes time. A lot of time, but with family and friends ... life goes on."

"But we do want to offer our condolences for the death of your father," Cress rushed on. "We'll let you get out of here now. I think I see some intrepid reporters massing for an attack."

Norah glanced over his shoulder and saw the usual contingent of Fourth Estaters waiting. "The vultures do enjoy picking at the bones of your life when something this salacious enters their tunnel vision."

"You were very respectful and decent with your *Seraphim* issue. We appreciate that," Cress said.

"I promised I would be," Norah said, smiling sadly.

"Unfortunately, that's the trouble with far too many people today—their word isn't their bond and honor gives way to expediency and selfishness," Constantine said.

"Too true," Norah replied.

"Well, we all must be going," Cress said. "Good luck and take care."

He shook Norah's hand as did the other two C's before they

hurried out of the building and into the breezy summer air. Phaedra shivered and pulled her knitted shawl closer around her shoulders. "What's that Mark Twain was supposed to have said about the weather?"

"The coldest winter I ever spent was a summer in San Francisco," Cress said. "Although it's disputed that he actually came up with that or just repeated it."

Constantine checked his watch. "It's almost one. Want to get some lunch? Raine said she wouldn't be free until four or five."

"I'm starving," Cress nodded.

"Good," Constantine said. "Are we up for Italian or something else?"

"Something else," Phaedra said.

"Didn't Wilde mention a Chinese place that he heard about from his old friend, some kid he met while he and Deliverance were up here dragging Quint back from his lost weekend?"

"I think it was a lost three months or so, but, yeah, he did," Cress said. He pointed to a phone both across the street from the courthouse. "Let me give him a call and find out where it is. You two head over to the car."

Ten minutes later Cress opened the car's back door and slid in. "Okay," he said. "I got the address." He handed the slip of paper to his brother with the name of the restaurant and the directions to Kearny Street, and ten minutes later they found a spot a half block away then entered the aromatic Mandarin Delight. A tiny, scowling Asian woman growled at them to follow her and she led them to a small table behind a large, unruly fern. She smacked down three laminated menus and said she'd be back.

Cress looked at his siblings. "Wilde said that his friend said that this place has great food, but the owner/hostess is a terrifying little shit that makes Deliverance look sweet and prim."

"That's … frightening," Constantine said just as the woman returned, held up an order pad, and demanded—not asked for—their orders.

"Busy. Not have all day," she snapped. "What you have?"

"What do you recommend?" Phaedra asked.

"All good. Not your mommy. Choose."

"Is this jade chicken spicy?" Phaedra asked.

"It chicken. You want—yes or no."

"Um, okay, I'll have an order of that with white rice and two shrimp rolls. An iced tea, please."

"You?" the hostess snapped at Constantine.

"I'll have a beer, and the fish eggplant, diced bean curd, and fried rice. Spicy, if possible."

"You get how he makes it. You?" she said brusquely to Cress.

"The green onion pancakes and jade chicken. A Coke, lots of ice. Thank you."

The woman harrumphed and whipped the menus out of her customers' hands and scuttled off.

"Wow," Cress said grinning. "I'd pay to see a matchup with her and Deliverance."

"You and me both, brother," Phaedra said. "Well. Let's talk about it. What are we going to do about Norah? She seems like such a nice person."

"Doesn't mean she'd welcome new siblings into the family," Constantine said. "Or that we should. Look, we don't care about the money or we would have hit up dear old Dad when we learned his identity. As I see it, we have a lot more to lose than gain by revealing ourselves."

"Lose?" Cress asked.

"Think of the notoriety we have now because of our late crazy sister. Multiply that ten-fold if the world learns that we're part of the Danziger clan and have yet another psycho sibling. We'd have a nonstop parade of vultures like Laurel Bollmeier beating down our doors. You can kiss off any privacy we might have. Phaedra—you really want to subject your kids to waiting reporters and cameras at their schools and when their nanny takes them for a walk? Do you want our parents to have to draw their shades every day to escape scrutiny by our hometown newspeople?"

Phaedra shook her head. "No, I don't."

"And Cress—you want people digging into your private life and making judgments about who you are as a person and as an academic?"

"Not especially," Cress said.

"And let's not forget about the peripheral people in our lives like Gray and Moon Wolf." He frowned. "Do they know?"

"Of course my husband knows. We have no secrets," Phaedra said.

"Ditto with Gray," Cress said. He narrowed his eyes at his brother. "You haven't told Raine the full truth yet, have you?"

"No," Constantine replied curtly, then refocused. "And then there's also the disruption of Norah's life and world. She seems like an accepting person who might welcome us and might be inclined to share her substantial inheritance. But maybe not. Maybe she has life plans that are built around financial and familial linchpins that would be out the window with two new brothers and a sister. She's also undergoing a life of notoriety with the happenings and revelations of the last six months."

"You're right," Cress said slowly. "I hadn't given all that consideration to the matter. There are positive aspects of revealing ourselves, but a lot of negatives." He glanced over his brother's shoulder. "Uh-oh—Rambolina's back with our food. Stay cool."

Their grumbling hostess slammed their plates down hard and handed out their drinks. As she was huffing off Cress said, "Miss? There's no ice in my Coke."

She narrowed her eyes and replied, "Life full of disappointments. Get over it."

Cress's jaw dropped as Constantine chuckled and cut into his fish eggplant. He took a bite and smiled. "It's delicious."

"All I asked for was some ice," Cress muttered as he took a sip of his Coke. At least it was ice cold.

"Life full of disappointments. Get over it," Phaedra said as she cut into her jade chicken.

The siblings ate silently for a while, enjoying the excellent food while they considered their discussion. They had agreed before coming to San Francisco that whatever decision they made had to be unanimous; if not, then they'd have to keep considering the options back home. It was obvious which side Constantine was on. Phaedra, the earth mother, was on the fence but leaning towards revealing their connection to Norah. Cress had kept his opinions to himself, close to the vest.

They were just about done with their meals and talking quietly about their situation when Rambolina appeared as though by magic. "You want dessert?" she snapped.

"Uh … what do you have?" Cress asked nervously.

She whipped out a small menu from her belt and handed it to them. She was tapping her foot as her customers scanned the small list of offerings.

Constantine looked up at her and handed the menu back. "Three orders of the pan-fried water chestnut cake, and three cups of coffee."

Their hostess shook her head and as she walked away muttering, "No imagination. Tourists. Ugh."

"We're never coming here again," Constantine said irritably.

"Oh, I don't know," Phaedra said, grinning. "It's kind of exciting to eat a meal never knowing if you're going to wind up at the end of a samurai sword."

"That's Japan, not China," Constantine said.

"Well, whatever the Chinese use to slay their customers. Oh boy—here come the shōgun."

A moment later they were enjoying their dessert and coffee without much conversation. When Constantine finished his cake, he looked at his siblings and said, "Let's vote. I vote for keeping our identities a secret." He looked at his brother. "Cress?"

Cress sighed deeply. "I was on the fence before, but I have to agree with you, for all the reasons you stated. Norah Maguire seems like a lovely person I'd be proud to have in our family, but the downsides are too convincing."

"She's still a member of the family, just a … secret one."

"We have so many secrets," Phaedra said softly. "It's a struggle enough to deal with them now and in the future without adding to the burden. With a little reluctance and doubt, I agree with you boys. Let's keep our siblinghood a set of three. The future? Who knows? I think we should keep the option open."

"Good, agreed," Constantine said brusquely. He froze for a second as Rambolina strutted over and handed him the bill and three fortune cookies. "Come back soon," she tossed over her shoulder as she waved and sauntered off.

"Yeah, when it can be scientifically ascertained that Hell has frozen over," Constantine muttered as he pulled out his wallet and threw a few bills on the table, inclusive of a generous tip. He broke open his fortune cookie and read the saying. "Darkness haunts your love life. What the hell kind of prediction is that?"

Phaedra opened hers and smiled. "A surprise is on its way. I guess that could be good or bad, but I'll take it as a positive omen."

Cress cracked his cookie in half and unrolled the slip of paper. "Life full of disappointments. Get over it." He looked at his siblings. "I don't ever want to come here again."

CHAPTER FIVE

The monsoon season in Arizona typically occurs between mid-June through late September, with the most voracious thunder, lightning, and rain storms taking place in mid-July and mid-August. Arizona averages around thirteen inches of rain per year, and the monsoon accounts for approximately half of that. Stunning bolts of jagged lightning light up the skies with unparalleled brilliance, and thunder often resembles the booming of cannons. The rain can batter the earth like the output of a fire hose, and often turns roads, rivers, and washes into swollen expressions of cascading, dangerous water. Flash floods destroy animal and plant life, as well as the few humans unlucky enough to be caught in their fury.

The word "monsoon" is derived from an Arabic word, "mausin," which means wind shift. The event itself is caused by warm air that creates low pressure zones that draw moisture from bodies of water, usually the ocean. Arizona winds are usually westerly and with the other weather conditions result in bursts of heavy rainfall from roiling grey and black clouds that resemble an impressionist painter's interpretation of the vast horizon.

Tucson in August of 1984 was experiencing its familiar storm bursts, which filled the washes with brutally rushing water and debris. People smart enough not to tempt fate kept well away from the water and its banks, but there were always those who were intrepid or stupid enough to get too close.

Brothers Tommy and Danny Clark were a mixture of both. Pantano Wash, which cut through Tucson northwest to southeast, originated at the Tanque Verde Creek at the north end and ran to the far south of the city to Cienega Creek Preserve. The wash split off into two arms around two miles east of South Houghton Road on Drexel. Drexel Road itself stopped around six hundred feet from the splitoff, and it was not recommended to traverse that short section without four-wheel drive; most people who hiked to the area parked at the end of Drexel and walked. A few homes dotted the area in the 11,000 block, and the Clarks lived in one of those homes with their parents and three younger brothers.

It was a Saturday and Friday's deluge had ended around 3

AM, so the ground was still wet, and the wash was still threatening to overrun its banks. Their parents had warned them not to go near the water but being mature ten- and eleven-year-olds they promised then quickly broke that promise and headed off to the western leg of the wash through a wide, rough desert patch rimmed by cacti, trees, rocks, and sand. The sand was disrupted all over by tire tracks from dirt bikes that had been there days before the storm. The boys walked over to a copse of green trees by the bank and sat down beside the rushing water which had pushed layers of sand up along the banks to form small dunes. There were a few large scrub bushes in the wash, surviving as they had for many years from the excess water and pressure.

The boys threw rocks into the water and across to the other bank, bored, but preferring the experience to staying home and playing with their annoying kid brothers. Tommy caught a small gecko and examined it before letting the tiny creature scuttle away to the underbrush.

"What's that?" Danny asked as he stood up and squinted at one of the large bushes in the wash, about twenty feet down from where they were sitting.

Tommy got up and shielded his eyes from the early morning sun. "Dunno. Something white. Hey—maybe it's a deer or something. Maybe we can get some antlers. Come on." With that he strode past his brother and walked along the edge of the bank until he came with five feet of the object. He still couldn't clearly what it was since only a portion was visible from his angle. He looked at Danny. "I'm gonna wade in and see."

"Don't be an idiot," Danny said. "That water's going pretty fast. And if Dad ever finds out you got washed away I'm toast."

"Oh, for Christ's sake," Tommy growled. "The water ain't more than five or six inches deep here. It couldn't wash away a gecko. I'm going."

"Be careful."

"No shit, Sherlock." Tommy removed his shoes and rolled up his pants leg and began carefully wading through the shallow, quick-running water. It was only a few feet to the bush, so he made it in a minute. He stared down at the object, then whirled around screaming, tearing past his brother without bothering to take his shoes. Danny was hot on his tail as Tommy continued screaming until he got to their house and collapsed, wheezing, into his mother Carol's arms. He choked out what he had seen, and a moment later Carol was dialing 9-1-1.

"Waddya got, Pete?" Detective Yale Cornell asked as he stood impatiently watching the forensic tech examine the body that had been photographed in its bush before being carried to shore for a preliminary examination.

Pete Murphy was squatting over the corpse as he carefully used a pencil to push back the lips for a cursory tooth examination. He hmm'd a few annoying times before rising and facing Cornell and his partner, Baxter.

"A woman, obviously, maybe on the down side of thirty. Hard to tell with the decomp."

"How long you think she's been dead?"

"Won't be able to tell till she gets autopsied, but from the condition of her flesh and the insect activity, I might guess one or two weeks."

"Manner of death?" Baxter asked tightly.

"The autopsy will verify, but it's a tossup between either the blunt force trauma that caved in the left side of her head, or the strangulation that nearly decapitated her. She had some decent dental work, but it looks like several teeth were extracted postmortem since there's no blood around the roots. However, that could be because she was face down in water for a while."

"Long time in the water?" Cornell asked.

"Don't think so. She was barely bloated, and her frontal skin wasn't badly puckered."

"What about the arm?" Baxter asked. "The fingers?"

"Well, I doubt the forearm and hand came off by themselves, ditto the tips of her right-hand fingers. Looks like a ragged severance, but—"

"But the autopsy will tell us more. Yeah, Murph, we got it. Anything else?"

"She's got long red hair, but I noticed dark roots coming out. Her toenail polish is pretty chipped, but it looks like it was pink. Five-foot-seven, maybe a hundred thirty pounds. "Don't quote me on this, but I'm guessing the arm, fingers, and teeth were taken to prevent identification. Maybe she had a tattoo or some digital irregularity. Maybe those missing teeth had some sort of dental work that could be easily identifiable. Just a thought."

"What kind of jeans were under her head?"

"Does it matter?" Pete asked.

"Every detail matters. Well?" Cornell snapped irritably.

"Wrangler jeans, not brand new but not old, either. Anything else right now?"

"Nope. Let's load her up and deliver her to the medical examiner. I want a full report pronto," Cornell said.

"As opposed to him holding it back just to annoy you?" Pete said.

"Right now, the only thing annoying me is you. Next time I'm gonna ask for Ben Deuel." He walked off, followed by Baxter, not noticing the glower that Murphy was throwing at his back.

Cornell noted the uniforms that were holding back the press. He saw too many familiar faces and knew that they were wondering the same thing he was—was this crime one of the serial "unsolved" reproductions, or just a regular old murder? He slid behind the wheel of his car as Baxter rode shotgun.

"Where are we going?" Baxter asked.

"We're heading over to Saguaro Western to talk with Malachi Dillinger. We can peruse the list we have of unsolved crimes, but he knows the nitty gritty of each one better than we do."

"Think it's our guy?"

"I think it is, but I'm not making any definitive judgments without further investigation."

"Hey—look over there. Don Bollmeier's rotten half."

"Does that surprise you? She's like one of those insects that burrows into the skin and torments you with nonstop itching."

"You could accidentally run her over."

Cornell laughed. "Don't tempt me," he said as he pulled away quickly and did come within four feet of the intrepid reporter.

Malachi settled himself into Quint's guest chair, barely able to contain his excitement although he attempted to temper it since it concerned another murder. He had an enthralled audience, and he confessed to himself that he loved that.

Quint was behind his desk with Deliverance sitting on an edge with her shapely legs crossed. Victor was on one side of Malachi and Wilde on the other. Belzer was standing at the closed door, leaning back against it with his arms folded.

"So, like I confirmed to the detectives that most definitely mimicked an old crime from July 1974. The cops called it 'the Lady of the Dunes' since the woman was found in the Race Point Dunes in Provincetown, Massachusetts. This new victim down in Pantano Wash mirrors the state of the 1974 body extremely well."

"And, of course the 1974 victim's killer was never caught," Victor said.

"No, not only that, but she was never identified. She was buried in October. There were a lot of theories about who she might have been or who might have killed her. Some said she was a gangster's moll, and the name Whitey Bulger was tossed around. There were a couple of missing women who might have been her, but they were ruled out. It's been ten years and I think the case is considered ice cold. Cornell said he was going to call the Provincetown police and see what facts or suppositions he could dig up. They did a clay facial reconstruction in 1979, and even exhumed her body in 1980 to see if they could develop any more clues, but so far, no luck. You know, when they buried her they buried her without the head, which they kept for forensic developments."

"Lovely," Wilde said. "One last indignity to the poor woman's life."

"So, does this give us any clues to go on, to solve the other cases and Munch's death?" Victor said. "The FBI making any headway in the bombing?"

"They'll never admit that," Deliverance said, "but Tucker's friend, Iris, doesn't seem especially sanguine at this point after five months. They haven't managed to trace the C4."

"Speaking of Tucker," Malachi said, "would you guys and he be amenable to having Angel over for the weekend after next? I wanted to surprise Bliss with a mini-vacation up to Sedona. She's been working her butt off this summer and she needs a break before the fall semester starts, and I want to force the issue."

"Hell, no—bring the kid over. She'll have a ball with our pack, and I think she has a mad crush on Alex, anyway," Deliverance said. She narrowed her eyes at her friend. "I sense there's another reason you want to take her away. 'Fess up."

Malachi grinned ear to ear, and blushed. "Okay, it's a sort of celebration. My witchy wife ... has another little supernatural bun in the oven."

"Oh, my God!" Deliverance yelled and ran over to Malachi and hugged him. "Congratulations."

"Yeah, man, fantastic," Quint said, standing and leaning over his desk to shake Malachi's hand. He noticed the longing look on his wife's face. "Uh-uh, no—don't even think about it. Four's a full house for now."

"I didn't say anything," Deliverance said mildly and totally unconvincingly.

"It's written all over your evil face," Quint replied.

"Bear in mind that that evil face can make you sleep on the couch for the next week or bunk in with Tucker."

"He's a pretty good cook," Quint mused. "Does a hell of a pot roast. But—for the sake of conjugal harmony, I'll keep my opinions to myself on the subject matter." He looked at Malachi. "Anything else?"

"Nope, that's it." Malachi checked his watch. "Oops—gotta get home and take Angel to her ballet lessons. Del—you gonna pick her up Saturday and take the brood to their karate lessons?"

"Nine sharp, bucko. Give Bliss my love."

Malachi smiled and said, "Call me if you have any questions. Later, guys." With that Malachi scooted out of the office.

Quint hit the speed dial to Raine's office. "Raine? Come to my office, please. Thanks." He noticed Victor looking distracted. "You okay?"

"Oui, certainement," Victor said. He noticed Wilde giving him the arched-eyebrow skeptical look. "Perhaps not so much."

"The kids?" Quint asked, already knowing the answer.

"Mainly Beckett," Wilde confirmed. "Bechet is still struggling against his better instincts, but he's coming around."

"What's the angst-ridden teenager's problem now?" Deliverance asked.

"Same as always. Not happy that he's here. Not willing to cut me and Wilde any slack on our lifestyle. Stubborn and arrogant when he was at school. Determined to be his own person regardless who he offends. Pas de sens du respect véritable." Victor tended to lapse into his ethnic language when he was angry or frustrated, so everyone knew that he was close to bursting at the seams.

Deliverance tried to lighten the mood. "At least his side hair is growing back." That day that the Catholic school called Victor to come pick Becket up Victor had been appalled that sometime between leaving the house and arriving at school Becket had managed to get his hair cut into a Mr. T mohawk style—and get his ear pierced. He went on to call his nun teachers "Fool!" for an hour before he was dragged to Mother Superior's office and an urgent call was put into his uncle.

"Oui." Victor nodded sadly. "I'm not entirely sure where to go from here, other than banning the kids from watching *The A-Team*."

"You need to have a come to Jesus talk with the kid," Quint said. He glanced at his wife and said pointedly, "Just like we need to have a talk with Storm." He looked at his partners. "She was fighting at the last karate class and has been sullen lately. I mean, more so than usual."

"No luck on the background front?" Wilde asked.

"None," Deliverance said. "Hubby and I have been seriously discussing adoption. We have another appointment with *Miss* Gumkowski Wednesday to go over the steps."

"Maybe that's what she needs," Victor said just as Raine knocked and entered. "A real sense of security and identity that she doesn't have right now."

"You're probably right," Quint agreed. "Raine, let's update you on what just transpired, and then you can give us your take on it." With that Quint summarized Malachi's visit and news as Raine held onto every word like glue. When he finished he said, "So, your hypothesis was right."

Raine nodded. "Looks like it. When I came up with the matrix based on the coded parameters the logical possibilities appeared at the top, but I had a nagging feeling that this killer is insidious enough to break any pattern of reasonable victim selection and go outside the box. In this case, reproducing a crime that took place near water, which in our matrix would have appeared much lower in the list."

"So, basically—matrix, logic, or not—there's no way we can truly predict the next move in his murderous chess game," Belzer said. "Right now, he's got all the checkmate moves."

"Not all of them," Victor said. "He diverged from pattern when he murdered Munch. He upped his game to show us how smart he is. That narcissistic need to tangibly prove he's the smartest and best at what he does—that could prove to be his downfall. And, he stupidly chose a victim that would make the murder very personal for all of law enforcement."

"But meanwhile we sit here waiting for the next victim— besides that poor woman near the wash," Belzer said tightly. "Where do we go from here?"

"We keep doing what we've been doing," Quint replied. "We have leads and ideas, so we follow them. Raine, I'd like you to sit down with Agent Flynn and brainstorm about her efforts and your matrix. Do it as soon as you can, please."

"Righto," Raine said. "Unless you need me for anything else, I'll call her now."

"Go ahead," Wilde said, and Raine departed. He grinned. "She's getting to be quite a brilliant asset, eh?"

"Yeah, for a Brit," Quint said.

"Behave yourself, or I'll start invoicing you again."

"Works both ways, dude. I figure it was about $50 in labor for putting that TV antenna up on your roof. Let's see, there was also the landscaping, planting that lemon tree—shall I go on?"

"You've made your bloody point," Wilde grumbled.

"Aw," Deliverance said. "And I was just getting a banjo riff in my head—Dueling Invoices."

Victor grinned, feeling genuinely at ease for a moment. He wished there were more of those moments lately. He had an idea.

"I'm going to take off for a while. See you at home, Brit Boy." He left quickly, to his partners' surprise.

"He okay?" Deliverance asked Wilde.

"It's a day by day thing. You know, once I was sorry I couldn't have children, and didn't really miss them although I had yours to practice on. But with the boys living with us, well, I'm not sure I was ever cut out to be a parent." He hesitated. "And even after six years, I'm not entirely sure I'm cut out to be a semi-married man."

"Nobody's 'cut out' to be married," Quint said. "It's not an accomplishment, it's a journey that unfolds day by day until the death-do-you-part thing."

"He's right," Deliverance said. "Lifelong commitment is not what many think it is. It's not breakfast and coffee together every morning. It's not a clean home and a homemade meal every day. It's not cuddling in bed together until both of you peacefully fall asleep. It's actually someone who steals all the covers and snores. It's slammed doors, a few harsh words, fights, and the silent treatment. It's children, pets, family, and everything that comes with them. It is, despite all those things, the one thing you look forward to day in and day out.

"It's coming home every day to the same person that you know loves and cares about you. It's laughing about the times you accidentally did something stupid. It's about cheap, easy meals late at night after a crazy day. It's when you have an emotional breakdown, and your love lays with you, holds you, and tells you everything is going to be okay ... and you believe them. Living with the person you love is not perfect or easy, but it's amazing, comforting and the best thing you'll ever experience. It isn't always easy, but the rewards far outweigh the problems."

"You have to take the good with the bad, and make your peace with it, or admit you can't and let go. Personally, I think you'd be a sodding wanker to let go of Victor even with the spawn of Hell living with you," Quint added.

"Maybe you should recommit to one another with a ceremony of some sort," Deliverance said. She snapped her fingers. "Hey— what about a handfasting? That's symbolic."

Wilde cocked his head thoughtfully. "Maybe. Let me think

on it and talk to Victor. Meanwhile," he said with a snarky curl of his lip, "I can buy a little good will with Bechet. Or, adopt a little good will."

"Huh?" Quint asked.

"The kid loves your dogs and I get the distinct impression that he'd love a mutt of his own."

"What about Victor?"

"Tosh—Victor brought two kids into our home—I can bring one needy puppy. Think I'll head over to the pound. I haven't forgotten that Fox and I have a meeting with that probate lawyer at two."

"Good luck with the mutt," Quint said. "Can't wait to meet it tonight."

"We'll pop over after dinner." Wilde bounced off with a smile on his face.

Deliverance shook her head. "He has no idea what havoc a puppy is going to wreak on their carpets and other furniture items, especially if it's going through its teething phase. That's how I lost that Leon Uris book."

"Cork did well with that—barely anything left except half the cover."

"He's as ravenous as his daddy."

"I prefer nonfiction, but in a pinch ..."

"Do you think we should get a special pet for Storm?"

Quint looked at her suspiciously. "What did you have in mind?"

"A hamster. Small, but cuddly."

"Or, as Pyewacket would meow, lunch." He narrowed his dark brown eyes at her. "You're serious, aren't you?"

"I think it would give her a sense of being one of the gang and also teach her some personal responsibility. It's a hamster, Quint—not a rhinoceros."

"Fine. We'll ask her. If she's okay with it, we can go to the pet store on Campbell. But under no friggin' circumstances on this planet or any other one in our solar system will we be getting a breeding pair. Got it?"

"Got it, Macho Man. Now get back to that report on the Morales embezzlement. I want to send out the invoice by end of day.

Chop, chop—I have a business to run and a Psychology paper to turn out." She strode out of the room and Quint sighed and sat back in his chair. Neither he, nor Wilde, nor Victor were ever going to let her know just how much they depended on her in every way.

Four kids, he thought. Wouldn't be so much of a difference with five, not really …

CHAPTER SIX

Deliverance Dane
Psychology 202
August 22, 1984
Professor M. Greengrass

Subject: Telepathy, Clairvoyance, and Precognition

Telepathy: a. Literally, the word "telepathy" is derived from the Greek and translates as "distant feeling."
            b. The communication of impressions of any kind from one mind to another, independently of the recognized channels of sense.
Clairvoyance: The ability to perceive future events.
Precognition: Previous knowledge or cognition.

Although clairvoyance and telepathy have common denominators, such as the fact that they are both connected by extraordinary perception by the mind, they do differ. Clairvoyance, in simple terms, is the perception of events that will occur, the perception being exercised only by the individual without any sensory or extrasensory assistance. Telepathy, on the other hand, is a method of perception that employs more than one individual. It is a combination of intertwining mental perception between two or more people and is often referred to as "mind-reading."

Skepticism and objection have always confronted the question of the authenticity of extrasensory perception, commonly referred to as ESP. Many objections stem from the belief that experimenters are not always as objective when testing subjects as they should be. It is supposed that all this investigation in this research might be stopping at some strategic moment—say, after some high scores have been made and just before a series of low scores might be made. The most frequent objection is on the basis that high scores on ESP tests are merely due to a run of luck and coincidence and should not be attributed to some unseen and indisputably proven psychic powers. There is always the possibility of fraud on the part of the experimenter, as there is also the proposed possibility of the subject *concocting some sort of "system" in order to defraud a legitimate experimenter and audience.*

The key word is "experimentally." By observing results of tests on precognition, it is necessary to take into account that the results are acquired under artificial conditions. Therefore, any understanding of perception and its connection with the nervous system could not be complete because any spontaneous reactions that might occur outside of the testing could be diminished due to certain conditions and stresses imposed on the subject. It can therefore be implied that experimental testing does not always determine accurate results because of the surrounding stresses encountered by the subject.

> *Grade: B*
> *Comments: Decent, could use some more work.   Greengrass*

"It doesn't seem like anything I turn in gets me a grade higher that 'B' with this guy," Deliverance said to Bliss as she slouched in her friend's office chair, a sour look on her face. She took a sip out of her Pepsi can and frowned. "And he doesn't give me any direction on his comments, or when I query him. 'Could use some more work.' Can that be any less helpful?"

"Greengrass is an asshole," Bliss said as she finished the last of her egg salad sandwich. The two women were having lunch in Bliss's office, enjoying a rare moment of peace in their bustling lives. "Last year he failed two students who were acknowledged as bright, hard-driving, and methodical by all of their other professors. My take is that he doesn't like women. He has gone far beyond the zenith of awesome stupidity with some of his opinions and actions. Just between us, I think the governing board isn't going to renew his contract next year. I personally think he's pants-crapping insane."

"I'm not going to play the devil's advocate on that point." Deliverance laughed then went serious at the pale look on Bliss's face. "Are you okay?"

"Oh …" Bliss muttered as she jumped up and bolted through her office door into the hallway and over to the Ladies' Room ten feet away. She burst through the door and barely made it to a stall before she vomited out her lunch and the remnants of her breakfast into the toilet bowl. She heaved for a long minute, feeling her friend behind her holding her hair back. She dry-heaved for a few more seconds before getting up on wobbly legs and flushing the toilet. They backed out of the stall and Bliss washed her hands and rinsed out her mouth, then washed her flushed face. Deliverance handed her a paper towel.

Bliss smiled weakly. "I knew that egg salad sandwich was a bad mistake."

"Go back to your office. I'll go down to the caf and get you some ginger ale. That always settled me down when I was pregnant." Deliverance left the restroom and Bliss went back to her office, where she wrapped up the rest of her lunch and chucked it into the trash can. Ten minutes later Deliverance came back with two cans of ginger ale. She popped one's top and handed the can to Bliss, who drank deeply.

"Better?" Deliverance asked.

"Better. Thanks. You know, I realize that you wanted to go for a degree in Psychology, but come on, Del—you have a real knack for crime investigation. Malachi thinks you should switch your major. Hell, he gave you an 'A' in his spring course, and he told me you were spot-on with your facts and research. Make psychology your minor—you get the best of both worlds."

Deliverance sighed. "I'm starting to think that *you're* psychic. That's exactly what I was thinking. I talked it over with Quint, and he feels the same way but left the decision up to me."

Bliss whooped and clapped her hands. "Fabulous, sister! Come over to our place soon and you and my darling husband can map out a plan. I'm so happy!"

"Then you'll be even more ecstatic at this tidbit—I'm going for my P.I. license. I figure that after being part of our team for six years I've done enough investigating to qualify me. I meet all the basic requirements, and even though it's recommended that I have an Associate's degree or a Bachelor's degree in criminal justice, it isn't a hard and fast rule. I'd have to be an apprentice with a licensed private investigation agency—which I certainly qualify as—and then apply for a Private Investigator Employee Registration Certificate under the sponsorship of the agency. I filled out the paperwork and I have an interview with the licensing board next week. Wilde and Victor don't know—I planned on telling them tomorrow—but Quint does. He supports me all the way."

"Who'da ever thunk you could tame that wild Spanish stallion like you have?"

"It was an uphill battle." She grinned. "The spurs and bullwhip helped. Mind if I touch your belly? I want to get a reading on the newest bank robber."

"Go for it."

Deliverance walked around Bliss's desk and placed her hand gently on Bliss's bump. She smiled slightly, closed her eyes, then nodded. "Want to know the sex?"

"Well … yes—yes, I do!"

"Angelique will be big sister to a healthy little … brother. Congrats."

"Oh," Bliss said happily, "Malachi will be so happy. I know he doesn't care if it's another girl, but secretly I think he wants a son." She straightened up and preened. "He may even be amenable to naming the kid Barnabas."

"Abso-friggin'-lutely perfect," Deliverance exclaimed. Angelique Lara Dillinger was named after the beautiful witch in the old TV series *Dark Shadows*; Barnabas Collins was the resident vampire and her nemesis. "You know," she said coyly, "I've been thinking that Quint could use another son to carry on the stallion line."

"Isn't Alex fitting the bill? He's pretty good at baseball and soccer from what I've seen."

"Tucker's been working with him on both. But, he has a sensitive soul and seems more attuned to his musical talent and his keen sense of the supernatural. Remember when he was in Mal's office playing with the Ouija board? He wrote down 'd-a-h-l' shortly before we learned that our head woman was a reproduction of the Black Dahlia. I've seen other inklings of ability since then. I've been spending more one-on-one time with him to glean the extent of his potential."

"Any sign from the girls?"

"None. I think if I've passed on the Dane abilities it's to Alex."

"That's cool. Natch, there's no sign of that in Storm since she's not your blood child. How's she doing? Any improvement?"

"Some. She's still too quiet and has her quirks, but she's really taken to her new pet hamster she named, oddly enough, Napoleon. As a matter of fact, Quint is home now spending time with her. Tucker took the other kids to the Pima Air Museum. Hubby wants to draw her out some more and thought she could use the individual attention."

"Let's hope that helps. She's such a pretty little girl. She deserves to be happy."

"Don't we all? Life doesn't always work out that way, though." Deliverance thought of baby David, the child she had borne and lost when she was sixteen. David would have been a teenager now. She felt a strong pain in her heart at the absence of her firstborn, at the absence of what could have been.

"They're nocturnal," Quint said as he sat on the couch watching Storm hold Napoleon, who was bound and determined to curl up and sleep on his mistress's lap. "They sleep in the day and play at night."

"Then how can I play with him?" Storm asked. "I'm supposed to sleep at night."

"There should be an overlap, and you can take him out during the day sometimes, but not always. He needs his sleep, too." Quint studied the child's intense face as she absently petted the soft, grey creature. He was surprised at her next words.

"I did that," Storm said very softly.

"Where?" Quint asked, equally gently.

"In … in … the forest. Near a stream. I think." She leaned over and kissed Napoleon's head.

"Near here?"

"I don't know." She looked up at Quint with surprisingly vulnerable eyes. "Can I tell you a secret?"

"You can tell me anything, sweetheart."

Storm wriggled over to him, touching his side with hers. She looked down at the hamster, and when she turned her eyes to him he saw that they were rimmed with tears. Impulsively, he put his arms around her and held her tightly.

"It's okay, baby. You can tell me."

Storm cuddled close to him and reached up as far as she could and whispered, "I couldn't tell you my name. I couldn't."

"Why?"

"I don't know my name," she sobbed, the waterworks bursting forth like Niagara Falls. "I don't know who I am."

Quint held her tightly, noting that Napoleon had awakened and escaped from his mistress's grip. He shushed her and murmured soothing words until she stopped shaking and crying enough to look up at him.

"I … I woke up near a bunch of trees. My head hurt so bad. It was bleeding. No one was around. I yelled but no one came. I was so scared! And cold. I found a big bush and got under it and cried and I fell asleep. It was dark when I woke up. I couldn't see no lights. I don't know how long I was there. I didn't know where I was. I … I started walking. I was so hungry."

"Such a brave girl," Quint murmured, kissing the top of her head. "Una chica tan valiente."

She snuggled closer to him and went on. "I saw a house somewhere. I was gonna knock on the door, but they were having a huge fight inside and I was scared. I found their garbage can and got some food. A chicken bone and some potatoes. I slept in their tool shed for two days before I … left and kept going. I don't … I don't know how long."

"Why didn't you go to another house?"

"I was scared after all that yelling. A lotta people had barking dogs, not quiet ones like Cork and Cocoa. I didn't know what to do."

"Do you remember your parents? Your mom?"

Storm shook her head. She spoke almost inaudibly, choking back another flood of tears. "I don't remember anything before I woke up."

"So, you kept scavenging until you got captured by Victor?"

Storm nodded her head against Quint's side.

"Did you tell any of this to your therapist?"

"No," she said almost inaudibly. "I don't trust her. She's … cold."

"She is, kinda. Let's see if we can't find you a nicer person."

"I want to … be someone."

"You are someone, honey. Someone special. That's obvious."

She looked up at him with heart-rending, pleading eyes. "I don't want to go away."

"What makes you think you're going to go away?"

"That's what the social worker says. She says that someday you'll need me to go away."

Quint fumed. "She's an idiot. We don't want you to go away. We've done everything we can to try to find out who you are and see if you have family, but so far, we haven't found out anything." He paused. Deliverance would want to be here for this next part of the discussion, but now was the time and he didn't want to lose an important moment that could define the rest of Storm's life. "I have to ask you something important, Storm."

"Okay." She sniffled and rubbed her nose.

"Deliverance and I have been talking, and we thought that if we can't find your family—if there is any—we'd like to make you a permanent part of ours."

"You mean, adopt me?" she said hopefully.

"Exactly. You seem to get along well with our other kids."

"Aislinn and I fight sometimes but I like her. She kicked the ass of that mean kid that made fun of my eyes in karate class and tripped me." She smiled wanly. "I love Vikki. Alex's okay, even though he's a boy."

"Boys are tough, especially for little girls. But from what I've seen you can pretty much handle anything." He noticed the wistful look on her face. "What?"

She spoke hesitatingly. "Do I have to wait till you can adopt me, or can I call you … Daddy?" Her voice had trailed off into a mixture of hope and dread.

Quint hugged her tightly. "You can call me Daddy right now, and you can call your new mom, Mommy."

"Will I be your real daughter?"

"Baby, just as much as Aislinn and Vikki. You know, they

were gifts Mommy and I gave to one another. We didn't have any say in how they looked or acted. But we *choose you* to be our daughter. In all the children in the world … we choose *you*. Your destiny is to be our daughter."

Storm jumped up on the couch and threw her arms around Quint's neck. "Daddy," she yelled.

"Works for me," Quint said, grinning. "What say we have a special dinner out tonight to celebrate?"

"Chocolate cake?" Storm asked eagerly.

"They aren't any real celebrations without chocolate cake."

"Yay!" Storm yelled brightly and hugged her new daddy with every ounce of her forty-five-pound might. Quint could tell by the look on her face that some great weight had sloughed off her shoulders. He felt at that moment that she was going to be all right. They were all going to be all right. He hugged his new daughter tightly and silently promised her that he'd never let anything bad happen to her again.

When Deliverance came home a half hour later she found Storm and Quint on their hands and knees, searching under the couches and behind plants. She stood over them scowling, arms akimbo, as they looked up at her guiltily.

"The rat got away, didn't it?" she asked evenly.

"Well …" Quint acknowledged, "sort of."

"Sort of? And you, young lady—what were you doing when the beast scurried away?"

Storm jumped up and stood directly in front of Deliverance. "I was telling Daddy about waking up."

Deliverance looked at her now-standing husband. "Daddy?"

"Yeah," he said, quite satisfied with himself.

Storm tugged at Deliverance's sleeve. "He said I could call you Mommy."

"He did, did he?"

"Yup."

"Then you damn well better. No half measures in this house." She bent down and kissed Storm on the forehead. "Now let's find that rotten little beast before it chews through any wires."

After fifteen more minutes of searching Deliverance emitted

an ah-hah and pulled Napoleon out from under one of the couch cushions and handed him to Storm. The girl cuddled the annoyed rodent then ran to her bedroom to put him back in his cage.

Quint slipped his arm around his wife's waist. "You know what this means, don't you? We've got to come up with two middle names to balance her out."

"We'll decide one together, but her last middle name is already a given."

"And?"

"Grace, after my grandmother. Storm something Grace Dane-Quintana."

"Sounds like a plan, Witchy Woman." He drew his wife to him, kissed her, and thought that he had a plan for just the two of them when they returned home tonight from their celebration.

CHAPTER SEVEN

The Bum Steer was yet another of the many iconic restaurants in Tucson. Opened in 1974 at 1910 North Stone Avenue, it was a hulking building that resembled a giant barn tall enough to house a T-Rex. Red boards with white stripes, with two stories and a special higher section bearing the name of the eatery, it rose above that section of the avenue, drawing in the eye, and drawing in a devoted clientele as well as new tourists and other customers. It wasn't simply a restaurant that served typical southwestern fare, burgers of many varieties (including a peanut butter option), and famous barbecued ribs, it was also a de facto museum of eclectic décor that made for enjoyable lunches and dinners. A real small airplane hung from its rafters, as well as a cornucopia of posters, tools, and other items hanging from the ceiling and on the walls. Kids begged their parents to take them there to eat, and although it was a family delight during the day, at night it became an over-21-only nightclub.

As August was coming to a close the restaurant wasn't particularly busy at noon, so Iris and Raine had their choice of tables. They chose one in a quiet, private corner, ordered, and sipped strong black coffee as they relaxed and enjoyed the camaraderie. They had met five times before and each found a kindred soul in the other.

"Another dust-up at the Phelps-Dodge mine," Iris sighed as she refolded the morning's *Sentinel*. She hadn't paid much attention to the goings-on in the Tucson area before she was sent down for what was becoming a very indefinite period, but the longer she stayed the more interest she took in the people, places, and events. Tucson definitely had a few points over Phoenix, not the least of which were the many wonderful places to eat and eat some more. Of course, there were issues as in any city, and since July of the previous year one of the ongoing ones was the strike at the copper mine in Morenci. The struggle between the company and twelve unions was as bitter as they come, and there had been intermittent violence on both sides. The company had lost a staggering $64 million in 1983, and it needed to cut back on labor costs.

The unions underestimated the determination of the company and paid the price when they were unsuccessful in resolving the strike and going back to work. The air was constantly rent with screams of, "Scab! Scab! Scab!" at non-union workers that were hired to replace the strikers. Now, thirteen months later, the face of the town had significantly changed, with many people moving away to find other jobs. Homes were abandoned, and the parks where children had once happily played were empty of the carefree, joyous laughter. The community of the miners and their families had never been engaged in true economic comfort, but now it looked, sadly, like a ghost town of lost souls.

"Striking's an ugly business," Raine replied as she blew on her coffee. "They're having a barmy time of it back home. The coal miners started striking in March with a walkout at Cortonwood Colliery. Maggie Thatcher and her gang are trying to come to some agreement with the unions, but so far neither side is giving. This doesn't bode well for the miners or the people depending on coal energy. I think the unions are trying to force the issue like they did in '72, thinking that causing an energy shortage will gain them victory."

"Does anyone actually win in one of those kinds of strikes?"

"I think not, but that's from the perspective of a middle-class girl who never went hungry or had worn-out shoes."

Iris nodded. "I hear that. Here comes the food."

A tall, handsome young Hispanic man with a long, black ponytail sauntered over to them with a heart-melting smile on his face and deposited the food in front of them. He smiled and told them he'd be back to check on them to see if they needed anything. He let his winsome gaze linger on Iris's face before he walked off.

Raine laughed. "The señor is hot for you. All you'd have to do is crook your finger and one hot night of lust and eroticism awaits you."

"Thanks," Iris said breezily as she lifted her immense cheeseburger towards her salivating lips, "but I'm not interested." She bit into the burger and a hot line of grease rippled down her chin. She wiped it away as she chewed. She closed her eyes and moaned. "Oh, that's so good."

Raine laughed and took a bite of her bacon cheeseburger and followed that with a bunch of hot French fries draped in ketchup and salt. "Not too bad," she admitted. "Next time I'll try the onion rings."

She gave Iris a baleful look. "So, does your lack of interest in Señor Gorgeous mean you have a boyfriend back in Phoenix?"

"No, not really. I was seeing someone, but it fizzled out. He didn't like a girlfriend who carried a gun."

"Some men are intimidated by powerful, talented women. I know that for a fact."

"He was a cop."

"Ouch. You'd think he'd be more open-minded."

"Yeah, right. They're the worst. I fought with my own father and brother about joining the FBI, and Dad's a retired FBI agent himself. Brother's a detective."

"Any other reason you're hesitant about picking up a new guy?" Raine asked mildly as she swirled her straw around in her iced tea. "Hmm?"

"What do you mean?" Iris replied just as mildly.

"I've seen you with Tucker."

"Tucker's just a friend. That's all."

"Right."

"Besides, he's … gay."

"He's not gay—he's bisexual. He swings both ways."

"Well, I don't. And I'd be crazy to try to land a guy who might dump me for another guy, doncha think? Anyway, I think he's dating someone of the male persuasion." There was an unmistakably sad tinge to her voice.

"You're crazy about him." Raine smirked as she finished off her fries. "Admit it."

There was a significant pause before Iris said, "I take the Fifth. I refuse to admit that he's cute, and funny, and charming, and loves kids, and can shoot like Annie Oakley, and can make a pot roast, roasted potatoes, and pumpkin pie that would make Julia Child dissolve into sobbing angst in her kitchen."

Raine smacked her hand down on the table. "I knew it," she exclaimed. She began crooning quietly, "Tucker and Iris, sittin' in a tree, k-i-s-s-i-n-g."

"I thought you were a nice person at first, but you're just another rotten, evil limey Brit, just like your uncle."

"It's genetic. I expect to pass the trait down to my own ankle biters someday."

"Thanks for the warning. I'll leave the country well before then. I understand Antarctica needs colonization. You might want to consider being one of the penguin people."

"I don't think my boyfriend would like the cold weather."

"The right fit bloke is utterly besotted with you—he'll go wherever you go. Do you want him to? I mean, is it that serious? Are you thinking of marrying him?"

"Yes. Yes. I don't know."

"Easier path to citizenship if you marry a U.S. citizen."

"I'm not sure I'd want to be a citizen of a country that's on its way to re-electing an actor whose co-star was a chimp to the presidency and whose wife consults an astrologist—with apologies to Deliverance."

"There's really only one thing to consider other than Bonzo Boy—do you love him?"

Raine was quiet for a very long minute while she absently sipped the last watery dregs of her iced tea. She sat back and made eye contact with Iris. "Yes. I love him."

"Have you told him?"

"No. It's … complicated. Let's change the subject. After all, we came here to discuss the murders. You know, Wilde told me that the cops are calling him by a nickname—the Beguiler."

"Like the Clint Eastwood movie?"

"No, that was *The Beguiled*. They mean that the word 'beguile' means to lead by deception, and since he's replicating unsolved murders with no other discernible pattern he's trying to deceive the investigators into following false or misleading clues. Well, that and the fact that's someone in the station thought it was a cool name. Victor is furious—he hates validating these sorts of perps by designating them in some salacious, catchy fashion."

"I wonder what he thinks of himself," Iris mused.

"I imagine he's all puffed up with narcissistic pride, especially since we have no clues to the wanker's identity or to his method of selecting victims."

"You know what I've been considering?" Iris said slowly as she glanced around to make sure no one was listening. "What if the killer is a cop?" she whispered.

Raine straightened in her chair and stared at Iris. "Oh, my God—I've been thinking the same thing. It makes sense. I mean, whoever is doing this obviously knows police procedure and how to leave no trace of himself."

"And I wouldn't be surprised if he was the one who's leaked tidbits to the press." Iris snapped her fingers. "Weren't there a lot of leaks in the ax murders case, too?"

"That's what Wilde said. Of course, the cops and our intrepid Union Jackers tried to pry the leaker out of the reporters like Laurel Bollmeier, but they bullshitted about protecting their sources, blah, blah, blah. First Amendment my arse."

"Well, there has to be some protection. If not, we wouldn't have found out about the Pentagon Papers and Watergate. Same goes for lawyers."

"Don't get me started on barristers," Raine said flatly. "Sodding wankers of the lowest order. Worse than pond scum."

"Don't hold back—how do you really feel?" Iris laughed. She saw that Señor Gorgeous was coming over with the bill. He handed it to her, his fingers just barely touching hers. She smiled and thanked him and handed him her Master Charge. She winked at Raine. "My treat this time. You can get the check next time."

"Uh-oh—where are we going next time?"

"The Platinum Room at the Westward Dream."

"You bloody git. Fine. Two can play at this game. But right now, where are we headed?"

"Back to the police station. I want to root around and see if I can uncover anything on the leak. If that doesn't pan out, we'll hit up the two most avaricious reporters on the *Sentinel*, Laurel what's-her-name and that other gal, Judie ..."

"Sutphin."

"Right, her. Didn't she try to sneak into your offices last week?"

"Yeah, for the second time. But this time karma bit her in the arse—she set off the new alarm and twisted her ankle trying to get away. Wilde told her he'd press charges if she came within a hundred feet of them, and he filed a restraining order. He's got one against Bollmeier, too."

"How should we play this with them?" Iris asked as she scribbled her name on the bill and added a ten-percent tip, then scratched it out and made it fifteen percent. "Good Brit, bad fibbie?"

"I like that. It's accurate."

"You know, I can initiate an FBI file on you. And call someone I know in the IRS."

"That would be a misuse of power as well as friendship, and just when I was getting used to that nasal east-coast accent."

"You should talk about accents."

Raine affected a stereotypical version of a cockney accent. "Oy, mate. I ain't got no idea 'tall what you mean."

Iris cringed. "That's even more painful than listening to someone from New Jersey."

Raine started to say something else when Iris held up a hand and said, "Stop, please. No more. If you stop, I'll let you take me to a cheaper place. I'll bet you haven't been to The Good Earth on Broadway, have you? Tucker told me it's got fantastic pastries and an out-of-this-world beef stroganoff."

"And that infamous tree-sitting Tucker makes yet another appearance in your mind."

"Enough! Let's head over to the station and I can make an arrogant fibbie demand to get a list of the task forces from the ax murders case and the recent ones. Let's see if there are any matchups between personnel and investigate their backgrounds first."

"Brilliant. Lead on, arrogant fibbie."

The women got into Iris's car and drove over to the police station where Belzer and Quint once worked and waited an annoying twenty minutes before Captain Ferdinand let them into his office. He didn't like the feds, but he had to admit that this one was a decent cop and she showed the necessary amount of respect and deference to the local police. He couldn't say the same for her two male associates who acted like bulldozers rather than comrades in arms. He hesitated a few moments before agreeing to provide the list of names, then called his secretary and gave her the task of copying them. Ten minutes later she came in and handed the lists to Ferdinand. He scanned them, then handed them off to Iris.

"I'm not sure exactly what you're looking for, but if you have any questions you can contact me anytime. It's not only to help resolve these current cases, but if we can identify the leak then I want to kick his ass out and prosecute him if at all possible. Bad cops don't deserve anything more," Ferdinand said.

Iris rose, followed by Raine. "You'll be the first to know, Captain, if we find anything. It behooves all law enforcement agencies to squash cops that don't honor their vows." She shook his hand, thanked him again, then she and Raine left the station.

"Are we off to track down the reporters?" Raine asked as Iris shifted into Drive.

"Let's pend that until tomorrow. I want to focus on the lists." She peered into traffic and pulled away from the curb, angling through streets that would take her northeast. Raine recognized the direction.

"We're headed to my office?"

"Nope."

"Quint's house?"

"Not quite." Iris threw her a smile and said, "Tucker made some of his famous banana bread last night and I believe there's still some left. We can nestle into his casita, nosh, and do our work in privacy."

"Isn't he there?"

"He might be if he didn't take the kids out, but if he's not I learned to pick a lock before I was six." Iris grinned. "They're probably at the Foothills Mall picking out new bedroom furniture. Now that Storm is going to be a genuine Dane-Quintana, Deliverance decided to let her and Aislinn share a room and move Alex into his own room. Makes sense anyway since the twins are getting older and should have their boy-girl privacy."

"It's so nice that the kid's settling in and learning about being in a normal home." Raine laughed. "I misspoke, since that family is anything but normal. Same goes for Uncle Wilde, Victor, and the boys."

Iris made good time and pulled into the Quintanas' driveway shortly before two. She noted that Tucker's car was there, too, and she felt that silly twinge of pleasure when she knew she'd be seeing him. She was insane—if ever there was a hopeless relationship, this was it.

Iris knocked on the casita door and a few seconds later Tucker opened it, surprise on his face. Seconds later a gaggle of Dane-Quintanas surrounded him, as well as Bechet and his new beagle puppy, Beignet. Beckett was in chess class.

"Tucker, sorry. I didn't think you'd be home and Raine and I wanted a private place to do some brainstorming," Iris said.

"No problem," Tucker said. "We're just playing a game of Trivial Pursuit, and we can move it to the main house, unless you'd be more comfortable there?"

"We're in the middle of the geography category," Aislinn said. She was holding her stuffed Gizmo under her arm as though it were the Holy Grail.

"I'm winning," Alex said, preening.

"You're not winning," Storm scoffed. "You blew that last answer about Africa."

"Did not."

"Did so."

"Did not."

"Okay, my aggressive little trivia warriors. The game's still in progress so no one's won just yet." Tucker smiled at Iris. "Back door's open, so why don't you ladies head over there and make yourselves comfortable in the great room? Help yourself to drinks from the fridge, and I'll bring over some banana bread." He narrowed his eyes at Iris. "That *is* why you came here, right?"

"Pleading the Fifth," Iris replied blithely then dragged Raine off towards the house.

The women settled cross-legged on the floor on opposite sides of a large coffee table made of saguaro skeletons. The table was resting on a beautiful red and orange Navajo hand-woven rug, five-feet by six-feet. They had snagged Cokes from the fridge, and just as they'd settled down with notepads and lists, Tucker came in and placed a huge slice of his banana bread in front of each woman.

"My secret ingredients are to use real, cut-up bananas in the batter, a dash of banana schnapps, and substitute brown sugar for white. Enjoy," he said as he went back to his casita.

Raine took a bite and sighed. "I'd marry that man if only for his cooking skills."

"Don't start. Okay, here's what we need to do. Let's make up a matrix of team members on each task force and see who crosses over."

They perused the lists and began sketching a rough matrix of names and assignments. That took a solid two hours before they were satisfied with their preliminary results.

TASK FORCE	MEMBER	POSITION	COMMENTS
Ax Murders, 1977-78	Michael Quintana	Task Force Leader	Replaced after LW's death
	Luke Wheeler	Secondary	Murdered before case resolved
	Reichardt Belzer	Task Force Leader	Quintana Replacement
	Aloysius Munch	Secondary	Wheeler Replacement
	Jefferson Washington	Detective	
	Madison Ward	Detective	
	Russ Babcock	Research Analyst	
	Judd Saxon	Computer Technician	
Black Dahlia 1983	Reichardt Belzer	Lead Detective	Retired before case resolved
	Aloysius Munch	Secondary	Murdered before case resolved
	Yale Cornell	Lead Detective	Belzer Replacement
	Forest Baxter	Secondary	Munch Replacement
			Consolidated 7/22/84 into a single Task Force
Bridge Player 1983	Yale Cornell	Lead Detective	Consolidated 7/22/84 into a single Task Force
	Forest Baxter	Secondary	
	Chester Cromwell	Detective	
Hitchhikers 1984	Mike Welsh	Lead Detective	Consolidated 7/22/84 into a single Task Force
	Keene Swansey	Secondary	

Lady of the Dunes 1984	Yale Cornell	Lead Detective	Consolidated 7/22/84 into a single Task Force
	Forest Baxter	Secondary	
=============	=============	=============	================
CONSOLIDATED BEGUILER TASK FORCE	Yale Cornell	Lead Detective	
	Forest Baxter	Secondary	
	Mike Welsh	Detective	
	Keene Swansey	Detective	
	Chester Cromwell	Detective	
	Jefferson Washington	Detective	
	Madison Ward	Detective	
	Russ Babcock	Research Analyst	
	Judd Saxon	Computer Technician	
Aloysius Munch 1984	Merritt Erdoni	Lead Detective	Remains separate task force
	Whitney Oakwood	Secondary	
	Edgar Macht	Detective	
	Morgan Talcott	Detective	
	John Hudson	Detective	
	Russ Babcock	Research Analyst	
	Judd Saxon	Computer Technician	
	Arnold Bonner	FBI Agent	Lead
	Sidney Price	FBI Agent	Secondary
	Iris Flynn	FBI Agent	Tertiary

"Notice anything about the matrix that sticks out?" Raine asked.

"Yeah, sure—I'm the only woman. Surprise, surprise. And that may change any day now," Iris said icily. She met Raine's curious

263

eyes. "My asshole of a boss in Phoenix has been making noises about calling me back and replacing me with someone else."

"Someone with a penis?"

"Give that girl a cupie doll. He is 'dissatisfied with your results.' And Bonner and Price don't exactly have my back. Well, at least they aren't doing anything to screw me. That's something."

"I'd miss you, girlfriend," Raine said sincerely. "Outside of Deliverance and Phaedra you're kind of my only female friend."

"Half ditto—you and Deliverance are my only girlfriends. I'd miss you."

"And?"

"And what?"

"And who else would you miss?"

"Let it go, limey Brit. We're going to put that matter to bed. I have to take this to my associates and see where they want to go from here. I imagine we'll divvy up the list and start doing more in-depth background checks on the men, especially financials—maybe they have deposits in their bank accounts that correspond with the leaks that appeared in the news."

"Let's swing by the office and make a copy for me so I can sit down with the partners and see what they think. Maybe they can come up with an idea to legitimately keep you around a little longer, at least until you work up the nerve to ask Tucker out on a date."

Iris swung her arms and chanted, "Warning! Warning! Danger, Will Robinson!"

"I have no bloody idea what that means."

"You Brits are so TV deprived." Iris shook her head then rose from the floor and looked at her empty bread plate ruefully. "I've got to get that recipe from Tuck." She gathered the papers and stuffed them into her briefcase, then left the house by the front door with Raine singsonging, "Tucker and Iris, sittin' in a tree, k-i-s-s-i-n-g." She let out a yelp as Iris elbowed her in the ribs.

CHAPTER EIGHT

The Mexican Independence Day celebration for 1984 was the usual glorious experience of fun, food, costumes, and good will. Most of the favorite restaurants were burgeoning with reservations, and any walk-ins would likely be disappointed or wait two hours for a table. Since it was a Sunday more people were out and about during the day partaking of various celebrations and opportunities. Laurel Bollmeier's husband, Don, was out with some of his police buddies at the Mountain Golf Course at Ventana Canyon. Opened just this year, it was a popular course for both residents and tourists, and on a brilliant September Sunday was packed to the gills. Don's brother-in-law was one of the pros there and managed to squeeze his group of four in after a state senator from New Mexico and before a CEO of one of the major hospitals.

Don promised to be home by four at the latest, and he and Laurel had reservations at Mariposa Linda's for 6:30 PM. He had suggested that they join Mike Beckham and his fiancée, but Laurel wanted her husband to herself if only for one uninterrupted evening. With his work and hers, personal time had become all too brief and precious these days. She admitted that most of their lack of together time was her fault—she was immersed in not only her reporting duties but in writing her new manuscript. She was nearly forty thousand words into the book and still there seemed to be no end to the tale in sight. Her worst fear was that whoever was doing these killings wouldn't be identified or prosecuted, and she wouldn't have a definitive end to her book. Readers didn't like that. She had learned from her mistakes with her ax murders book and knew that this one would be so much better.

She had finished the draft of the latest chapter this morning, but even so didn't have time to take a breather. Her boss at the *Old Pueblo Sentinel*, Santiano Bronson, had finally let her pry his egomaniacal fingers off the monthly summary page and agreed to let her produce September's list of happenings. She was thrilled at the opportunity and swore to him that she'd uphold his quality and standards. As she left his office she swore to herself that she'd do a hell of a lot better than he ever could. She went into the kitchen of their small house on the west side and poured herself a huge glass of iced tea. She brought it back to her desk, took a drink, then picked up her handwritten notes and scanned the list of events she had targeted for the summary.

In early September in Miliperra, a suburb of Sydney, Australia two vicious motorcycle gangs, the Banditos and the Comancheros, engaged in a brutal massacre at the Viking Tavern that left seven people dead and twenty-seven wounded on Father's Day. Laurel knew that Bronson rarely included any international news, but she thought this would tantalize the public since the gang names were far more reminiscent of the southwest than of the country Down Under. A few days after the melee the state of Western Australia became the last state to abolish capital punishment.

The Space Shuttle *Discovery* landed safely at Edwards Air Force base in California on its maiden voyage. A new version of the syndicated TV game show, *Jeopardy!,* premiered with Canadian Alex Trebek as the host. Retired Air Force Colonel Joseph William Kittinger II, a Vietnam war hero and former prisoner of war, became the first person to traverse the Atlantic Ocean solo in a gas balloon. The movie *A Soldier's Story* premiered on September 14th to critical acclaim and Oscar buzz (this was on the list of films that Laurel and Don wanted to see). The Red Hot Chili Peppers' debut album was still burning up the charts. *MTV* was growing its viewers by leaps and bounds, and Michael Jackson was still a mainstay on the channel as he dazzled the world with *Billie Jean, Beat It,* and *Thriller.* The workers at Phelps-Dodge were on the verge of voting to decertify the unions; it was projected that if the vote were successful, thirty-five locals would be decertified in Arizona, Texas, and New Mexico. Even so, it was rumored that the strike might extend another year.

Laurel put the finishing touches on the summary draft. She couldn't finish it for another two weeks, but she had a solid foundation to dazzle Bronson and the reading public with her acumen.

The grandfather clock in the living room dinged 2 PM. Don wouldn't be home for at least another two hours, so she could relax until then. She relaxed for about five minutes before she groaned and went back to her manuscript. She began proofreading her latest chapter, the meat of which she had gotten from her source in the police department. It was dynamite, and she ached to reveal the information in a newspaper article instead of waiting. But, he said that it was a theory only and nothing definitive had been proved. It would be a hell of a scoop when she could report it, and she was damned determined that it would indeed be her scoop. As she red-penned changes on the hardcopy pages the phone rang. She thought it might be Don, so she rushed over breathlessly and answered.

It wasn't Don, but it was her source who whispered that he had another delicious tidbit for her investigation, and one that could accelerate her article on the latest theory. Laurel eagerly asked what it was, but he said he wanted to talk with her face-to-face and this meeting had to be absolutely, positively confidential. She agreed to meet him at their usual secluded place, which they had used since he'd first contacted her after the Bridge Player murder. She fluffed her short, pixie-cut hair, dabbed on some lipstick, threw her tote bag over her shoulder, and left the house. She headed a few blocks south to Ina Road, then turned right and headed west, far past the I-10 interchange for a little more than three miles where that road ended in the foothills of the Tucson Mountains. It was secluded out there, and a little eerie with the dearth of houses and people, but it was mid-day and she felt safe enough.

She waited impatiently in her car with the windows closed and the air conditioner turned on high. She had her radio tuned to the rock station and enjoyed the sounds of oldies like *Born to be Wild* and *Sympathy for the Devil*. She loved the Stones. Hell, she had even been at Woodstock—where she had lost her virginity—although that was a fact that few people including her close friends knew. Don knew, and he thought it was "far out" as he seemed particularly thrilled that he had a unique wife. Christ, she loved Don. Maybe it was time to start thinking about having a kid, even though she was pushing forty and he was fifty-one. He'd be a great father, even if she was only a mediocre mother.

She turned down the radio when she heard a car engine and breathed a sigh of relief when she recognized her source's black Jeep Grand Cherokee. She shut off the car and got out as he pulled up behind her and waved.

Laurel leaned back against her car and waited for him to walk up to her. She flashed a quick smile as she took her notepad and pen out of her tote. She tried not to appear too eager, but her excitement radiated from every pore of her compact, slender body.

"Hi," she beamed as he came up next to her and leaned against her car. He was dressed more casually than she'd ever seen him, in jeans and a worn blood-red tee-shirt that said "Tucson – Home of the Axewoman" and had an image of a blood-dripping ax under the words. She was surprised that he—or anyone, for that matter—would wear something as tasteless. She knew they'd been selling that shirt and others during the aftermath of the 1977-78 murders, but she hadn't see one in over five years. She wondered why he was wearing thin leather gloves in this heat.

"I enjoyed your last article on the Lady of the Dunes murder," he said by opening. "You made some very key points on the cops' lack of progress."

"Well, they haven't made much, have they? Other than finally realizing that so-called pattern of replicating old unsolved crimes."

"The Beguiler is cunning."

"Beguiler?"

"That's what they're calling him now. It's catchy. It's a much better name than the Surrogate Scourge. Has that Hollywood aura about it. At any rate, you came here to hear about the latest theory, right?"

"Oh, absolutely. I can't tell you how thrilled I was when you first contacted me during the old case and gave me those wonderful hints and facts. I was even happier when you contacted me after the Bridge Player murder and agreed to meet with me. Before that we only talked over the phone and I never knew your identity. I'm so glad you agreed to meet during this case." *Surrogate Scourge?* she thought. She hadn't heard that name from him or anyone else.

"It's completely my pleasure. I hope that my part will be included in your next book since you omitted me from your last one."

"I don't … understand? I didn't know who you were back then."

"But you knew all the details of the cases, all the personnel that worked on them, and you only acknowledged the major detectives. None of us—what do they call it in the movie business? The supporting players."

"Well, I'm … sorry about the omission. It certainly won't happen this time, I assure you."

"Have you documented me anywhere? Your research files? I wouldn't want my part in your efforts known until the bitter end."

Laurel tapped her head. "No, it's all kept right in here. I promised total anonymity and I always keep my promises. I do that with all my sources. Nobody can root them out. Now—what was that tidbit you wanted to tell me?"

"Ah, yes. The newest theory. Well, it shouldn't come as much of a surprise to someone as erudite as you, but our law enforcement inner circle theorizes that the killer is a cop. And there's absolutely no doubt that the Beguiler also blew poor Detective Munch into oblivion."

"I knew it!" Laurel exclaimed pumping her fist into the air. "I knew it! I was going to discuss that with my publisher and see if someone on the task force could confirm it. It makes so much sense."

"Indeed it does. Someone on the inside would know the goings on, the plans, the evidence, the reports, everything. Someone on the inside would know how to commit a crime without leaving evidence. Virtually anyone on the force. Even … me." He smiled; it never reached his eyes.

Laurel straightened involuntarily. There was something in his voice … She met his eyes; they were fathomless and colder than ice.

And she knew.

Before Laurel could yell out or move he whipped out a blackjack and clocked her hard on the left temple. She went down without a sound and lay at his feet. He cast a glance around and was satisfied that there wasn't anyone within a mile or more. This was a desolate section of the foothills, which was why he had chosen it. Someday civilization would wreak havoc on the quiet, secluded section of land with homes and people, but right now it was the perfect place to meet, the perfect place to initiate another crime. He bound and gagged the unconscious woman and stuffed her in the back floor of his car, tossing a grimy old blanket over her. He knew she'd be out for a solid hour if not longer. He pulled an old bicycle he'd found in a junkyard out of the back of the Cherokee and jammed it into Laurel's trunk, then got into her car, made a U-turn, and drove back on Ina for a mile until he stopped at an empty stretch of road and land. He took her car keys, then got on the bicycle and pedaled back to his waiting car and victim. He stored the bicycle in the back and made a U-turn and headed back on Ina far past the I-10 interchange. He pulled into the Foothills Mall to a secluded section of parking close by the landscaping trees and left the bike propped up against a tree. He drove home, parked in the garage, then pulled Laurel out of the car. She was still unconscious, blood from her scalp wound staining her face and blouse.

He had plans, meticulous plans, and he needed time to complete them. He tied her to a pile of cinderblocks then popped open a Bud from the mini-fridge. He drank the whole can, then pulled over a few pieces of lumber to the workspace and began sawing and hammering.

"I like celebrating the holiday this way better," Deliverance said as she turned a few hamburgers over on the backyard grill. "A nice meal at home, Tejano and jazz albums on the stereo, margaritas in the pitcher—life doesn't get much better."

"Oh, I wouldn't say that," Quint said as he watched his kids trying to bust apart a papier-mâché donkey piñata filled with chocolates and hard candies. Right now, Alex had the bat and was swinging wildly as his sisters screamed at him and tried to keep out of his way. So far Storm had come the closest to whacking the hell out of the candy-laden beast, but none of them were tall enough to make it easy.

"The donkey's history if Bechet gets the bat," Victor said languidly from his position on a lounge chair. He was sprawled out wearing shorts, a tee-shirt ("New Orleans Saints!"), and his favorite Birkenstock sandals while he sipped a frozen strawberry margarita that Wilde had just whipped up. He was especially mellow today since both Bechet and Beckett were behaving themselves. Beckett was playing chess with Tucker as Bechet anxiously jumped back and forth waiting his turn at bat. He thought that some of their stress and anger had dissipated when he decided not to re-enroll them in their Catholic school and enrolled them into the nearby public school where the Dane-Quintana children were getting an education in both academics and socialization. He was not thrilled when Beckett came home two weeks earlier sporting a new Voodoo symbol tattoo on his upper left arm, but he let it slide. He needed to choose his battles if he was to win the war.

"I hope so," Wilde said from the lounge chair next to him. "I'm in dire need of sweets." He was wearing denim cutoffs and a Ralph Lauren polo shirt; his feet were bare. His skin was getting alarmingly pink from the sun; as a "fish-belly white limey Brit" (Quint's assessment) he tended to burn quickly.

"The sopapillas are coming soon enough," Deliverance said as she flipped the burgers onto a plate and set it down on the serving table next to the hotdogs and tamales. She filled a plate with a hamburger, hotdog, tamale, and blueberry muffin. "I'm taking this out to Officer Orbach." She poured a tall glass of iced tea. "If he's stuck out front watching the house he might as well have some good food. Be right back." She carried the plate and glass around the house to the front.

Quint carefully placed a cut-up chicken on the grill and turned up the heat. "It was decent of Cornell to have a uniform guard the house on the anniversary of our head delivery."

"Can't believe it's been a year," Wilde mused. "So much has happened. We've got three new kids and a grown niece in the family, we're embroiled in the middle of another baffling case, we've lost one cop friend, and another is bunking down in the smallest associate room in the office while he obsesses on his quest for vengeance."

"Don't forget our nanny-bodyguard and his not-quite-a-girlfriend. There's an unusual relationship if I've ever seen one." Quint laughed.

"Are you in the pool?" Victor asked. "I don't mean that one—" He pointed at the sparkling swimming pool that was awaiting the children when they beat the donkey into submission. "—I mean the one Wilde and I've started about when Tucker and Iris will figure out that they're weirdly meant for one another. Fifty bucks to enter."

Quint pulled two twenties and a ten out of his wallet and said, "Halloween."

Victor pocketed the money. "Might take longer since Iris was called back to Phoenix and she's battling to come back down here. I've taken Thanksgiving."

Wilde raised his hand. "Pearl Harbor Day." He glanced over at Tucker and Beckett. "I say, the kid's really taken to the game."

"Thank God," Victor sighed. "The first real sign of normalcy. At least he's speaking in full sentences instead of grunts and growls nowadays. You know, we were thinking of taking the boys back to New Orleans for Christmas to see their great-grandparents and visit their parents' graves. I'd like to see Shaun's, too. I haven't been there since the funeral."

Wilde took a sip of his margarita before he said, "Maybe it's good idea that I don't go with you. Might make things more palatable for your parents. Anyway, I'm overdue for a visit back in the Motherland. Perhaps I can convince Raine to come with me. She could bring Constantine."

Victor frowned. "I don't like the idea of negating our relationship by excluding you."

"Let's be practical," Wilde said quietly. "Your parents will never accept me. Period. Forcing the issue will only make it pointlessly harder on everyone. Besides, my parents are dying for me to come home. Look, we'll talk about this later. Today is a day for celebration, not introspection." He saw Deliverance coming back around the house and called out, "When am I getting my sopapillas?"

"When are you getting off your ass to make them?" Deliverance responded tartly. "No? Then stop being the stereotypical whinging pom and they'll be here when they'll be here." She clapped her hands loudly. "Alex! Give Bechet a chance. You and the girls aren't making any progress."

Alex muttered something under his breath but held out the bat to Bechet, who grinned at Storm and said, "Watch this." He pulled a blindfold over his eyes, then began swinging as his friends yelled and tried to distract him. Three swings and the piñata burst open and it rained candy. The kids began scrambling to load up on as much as they could carry. Alex went over to where Tucker and Beckett were playing chess and plunked a handful down in front of each. Then he put his hand on Tucker's shoulder and grinned. His grin faded, and he pulled his hand away and walked off. Deliverance noticed the brief incident. She was certain that Alex had felt something when he touched Tucker's shoulder. Yes, he had inherited her powers. She was sure of that now.

Quint yelled at the kids to come and eat, and for the next hour they chowed down on the best mix of Mexican and regular-old-American food. Beckett pleaded with Quint to change the jazz album to Michael Jackson, and despite minor groans from the adults, the strains of *Thriller* rent the late afternoon air. After they'd eaten and chomped at the bit for thirty minutes, Deliverance okayed the swimming and the six kids and Tucker jumped into the pool and began splashing around. Deliverance smiled warmly as she watched Tucker carefully showing Vikki how to swim with her little ducky tube around her waist. She noted that Aislinn was swimming back and forth like a fish. Storm and Bechet were throwing a blowup ball back and forth; there was a look of adoration on Bechet's face and Deliverance realized that he had a crush on the younger girl. Why hadn't she picked up on that before? She needed to exercise her abilities more or they might go dormant like Aunt Hope's.

Deliverance went into the kitchen to make a fresh batch of sopapillas for her family. The men brought in the plates and dishes and while Wilde washed them Victor dried. Beckett ambled in and moved to the island and plunked down on one of the stools. He watched her cooking preparations and after a few minutes slid off the stool and offered to help. She smiled and told him to sift the flour twice while she prepared the spices. She sensed that he wanted to speak but let him take his time. She waved her hand at Quint and he followed his partners back outside where Victor was stripping off his shirt, kicking off his sandals, and yelling, "Cannonball!" seconds before he jumped into the water and drenched the kids in a tidal wave of chlorination.

"Anything you want to discuss, honey?" Deliverance asked the teenager as she took the sifted flour and emptied it into the bowl with the baking powder, sugar, salt, vegetable shortening, and a touch of ginger. She began smoothly, slowly stirring the mixture as she waited for a response. She studied him, thinking he was a handsome boy with deep-set dark brown eyes. His nose was wider than Victor's and looked like the one she had seen in Shaun's picture. His sienna skin was flawless, like his brother's; they were destined to be very attractive men in the not too distant future.

"Do you ... do you think my Uncle Victor is a good man?" the boy asked hesitatingly as he began grinding the fresh cinnamon sticks.

Deliverance stopped stirring and met his eyes. "Your Uncle Victor is one of the finest men I've ever known. I trust him with my children's lives, and they are the most precious things in the universe to me." She cocked her head. "You've know him your whole life and you've lived with him for many months. Is there something that would make you believe otherwise?"

Beckett looked pained and ran his hand over his stubbly scalp hair that was finally growing back after his impromptu mohawk. He seemed unsure and nervous. He rushed on, though. "Grand-Mère said that he lives a sinful lifestyle. It's an abomination for a man to lay with another man."

"Look," an exasperated Deliverance blew out hard. "That's why I don't approve of organized religions. They jam all these ridiculous sins and evils down the throats of gullible people to keep them in line. And you do know that all these so-called sins were not developed by some big guy up in the clouds, but by ignorant, intolerant men thousands of years ago, men who thought women were little more than cattle and had slaves. You think those beliefs are all right?"

"No, of course not."

"Then let me make it clear—a decent human being is defined by love, compassion, affection, and respect for other human beings. That being the case, your uncle is an exemplary human being and you're lucky to be living with him."

"I guess," Beckett said thoughtfully. "His ... friend, Wilde, has been really nice to me and my brother."

"And I'm sure you didn't make that easy," Deliverance said tartly. She was satisfied that he dropped his eyes and had an ashamed look on his face.

"No, ma'am," he acknowledged.

"Wilde Sinclair, by the way, is your uncle's life mate, not

his 'friend.' And I trust him every bit as much with my kids as I do Victor."

"I wanted to go home to New Orleans so bad," Beckett confessed.

"No, really? Never would've guessed. How do you feel now?"

"I … kinda want to stay. Bechet, too." A wide smile split Beckett's handsome face. "He's got a crush on Storm, you know."

"I do now." She noticed that the smile faded as quickly as it had come. "What?"

"Grand-Mère called the other day. She said … maybe it was time we came home to live with her. She said she and Grand-Père feel really good and think they can raise us better now."

Deliverance gritted her teeth. "Did you explain to her that you *are* home now?"

Beckett hung his head. "She's kind of … intimidating."

So am I, Deliverance thought. She put a hand on Beckett's arm and squeezed gently. "You need to tell this to your uncle so he can deal with it. It's too much for a young man like yourself to handle it on his own. Okay? You'll talk to him?"

"Yes, ma'am," Beckett sighed. She was right—it was time for him to man up. He was a freshman in high school and would be fourteen in another two months. He wasn't a kid any more. Why in God's sacred name did he ever get his hair cut? That at least would grow back, but the damned tattoo …

"Good," Deliverance said as she turned on the gas under the large frying pan full of corn oil. As soon as the oil was hot enough she'd drop batter into it and fresh, hot sopapillas would be ready for the clan to nosh on when they sat around the family room and put the VHS tape in the player to watch *Pete's Dragon*. Alex loved that movie.

The movie was nearly at an end when the phone rang around nine-thirty, and Quint got up to answer it. He spoke softly and listened, then hung up the receiver slowly. Deliverance looked over at her husband and saw the solemnity on his face. She moved Vikki off her lap and walked over to him. He pulled her off to a private alcove.

"What's wrong?" she asked.

"That was Belzer. He got a call from Don Bollmeier—you know, Laurel's husband?"

"Yeah? What does the queen of yellow journalism want now? I'd be happy to slushie her again."

"She's missing," Quint replied flatly. "She was supposed to be at home at four so they could get ready to go out to a restaurant for dinner. She wasn't there when he came home. No note, nothing. He waited, called around to their friends and the newspaper, and he hasn't been able to find her. He called in a missing person report, but the cops can't act officially on it for forty-eight hours. He called Belzer to see if he'd heard from her, or if maybe one of us had."

"Oh, my God," she said softly. "You don't think ..."

"Yeah," Quint said tersely. "I do."

CHAPTER NINE

Iris Flynn stood five feet back from Laurel Bollmeier's car, which had been noticed three days after her disappearance. Although whoever kidnapped her had left it in plain sight, it was still on a desolate road, and even people who might have been driving that way would only have seen a car by the side of the road, with no damage and no reason to think it was part of a crime scene. The forensic teams from both the Tucson police department and the FBI were scrutinizing every centimeter of the car inside and out. They hadn't found any blood or any fingerprints that didn't match Laurel's or Don's, but her purse and sunglasses were nowhere in sight. Based on the evidence and known facts about the kind of person Laurel was, the missing-person classification had been switched to kidnapped. Hence, the involvement of the FBI. Since the federal agents were already there working the Munch murder, Iris's sourpuss supervisor had grudgingly sent her back to Tucson to assist their double investigation. She was lucky that Bonner and Price gave her a lot more leeway in helping with Laurel's abduction since they considered the bombing a higher priority; they didn't say that out loud, but Iris sensed their priorities. In this case, it had helped her get back to a place where she felt at home and enjoyed the people. She even brought her cat with her this time, and Tucker agreed to keep it in his casita.

The crime scene tape was circled around the car and adjoining desert with a twenty-foot radius, and the Tucson forensics team was moving its way west on Ina searching for any evidence or clues. They knew that the road ended about a mile away, so they had a limited range to search unless they found signs of a struggle or dump site where the road ended. If not, Laurel might be deeper into the foothills, or she might not. From what Iris knew about her as a reporter and writer—with her ambush tactics and tactless questions—she didn't care much for the woman, but Laurel was still a human being who didn't deserve to die or be brutalized. Iris tried to push away the torments Laurel's abductor might be inflicting on her. Iris had to focus and be objective in her investigation.

She glanced over at Don Bollmeier, who was standing far behind the tape. As the victim's husband he wasn't allowed to participate in the investigation, but all his associates had empathy for what he was going through, and they allowed him to visit the crime scene while they worked. She had never seen him before, but she doubted that the man had ever looked as devastated and terrified as he did now; his face was unnaturally pale and drawn, his eyes watery, his hair unwashed and lank as he watched his friends inspecting the scene and quietly speaking to one another. She knew she'd have to interview him even though he'd been interviewed several times already, but she decided to postpone that unpleasant task until tomorrow or the next day. She'd already spoken with the FBI team and given them the phone number where she'd be staying, and they promised to call her with a report in the next few hours. She hugged herself as a cold shiver passed over her body. It was hot today, close to ninety, so she didn't know why she'd suddenly felt cold.

She shrugged it off and went back to her car, then drove east on Ina, which turned into Skyline then Sunrise. She stayed on Sunrise all the way to Kolb, and then shortly she turned into Snyder and made it to the Quintana house and parked behind Tucker's car. He had offered her the pullout couch for her duration in the city, and she had happily agreed. Not, she was careful to explain to a smirking Deliverance, because she wanted proximity to Tucker, but because it was a cheaper and more comfortable alternative to a long-term motel. That was her story, and she was sticking to it.

When she entered the casita the strong aroma of bubbling beef stew assaulted her olfactory senses, and she sighed; much better to eat home-cooking than the fast-food junk she usually noshed on when she was traveling. Juju meowed loudly and jumped down from the easy chair and into her arms. She cuddled and purred to him, then tossed him down and moved to the kitchenette where Tucker was smiling and stirring his stew.

Iris sniffed. "Smells like heaven." She ignored the sight of his tight, low-cut jeans that highlighted the muscles in his long legs.

"Closest thing," Tucker agreed.

"Where did you learn to cook?"

"My mom taught me some basics, Deliverance showed me a few things, and the rest I picked up with experimentation, some of which produced spectacular failures."

"A man of many talents, my gun-toting nanny."

"Anyone that would be a nanny for you would require gun proficiency." He took a sample of the stew, then held the spoon out for her. She took a taste, closed her eyes, and um'd. "If you want to assist, you can set the table for four."

"Four?" she asked as she opened the cabinet.

"I invited Raine and Constantine over. I thought you'd enjoy breaking bread with a good friend."

"Excellent," she said as she pulled the utensils out of the top drawer. She set the table. "I think I'll change. This suit is too damn hot."

"Shorts and a tee-shirt are de rigueur for the evening."

She laughed and went into his bedroom to change. She pulled out a pair of jeans, gave that a second thought, then pulled on a short-short pair of denim cutoffs and a tank top. Tucker was mixing a batter for jalapeño corn muffins when she came back out. He arched his eyebrows and whistled.

"Not bad, fibbie," he said casually. Suddenly he felt this weird tingle in his nether regions and he moved closer to the counter so it wouldn't be obvious. What the hell was wrong with him? He was dating a cool guy that made him feel comfortable. He didn't need this complication. Maybe having her stay with him wasn't the smartest idea in the world. Still, he felt more than comfortable in her presence and he really didn't want her to leave. He nodded towards the couch. "Why don't you watch TV while I finish? I told them to be over at six."

"Is Quint home yet?"

"Yeah, he and the missus blew in about thirty minutes ago."

She checked her watch. "I think I'll head over to the main house. I have some questions for them. I'll be back before our guests arrive. Ciao." Before he could respond she bopped out of the casita and headed to the back patio. Deliverance was in the kitchen and waved her in.

"Any progress, G-Woman?" Deliverance asked as she swatted Vikki's hand away from the biscuit batter bowl.

"Not much," Iris confessed as she hopped up on a counter stool. "The forensics units are still processing the car and the scene. I wanted to ask your husband about his thoughts on Bollmeier's alleged abduction."

"Alleged?"

"There's no definitive proof that she didn't leave on her own, although I admit that's a very slim possibility."

"From what I've heard," Quint said as he came into the kitchen dragging Alex behind him, "the Bollmeiers had a very close relationship. Doubtful that she'd leave him and certainly not without a word or a note."

"You think the Beguiler is behind this?"

"Absolutely. And I think that he's a cop and that he may have been her leak source on these cases and the old ax murders' one. Of course, that narrows it down to a lot of people, and there's the also slim possibility that the killer's not a cop but someone peripheral to law enforcement."

"If he was her source and enjoyed leaking facts to the public via Bollmeier, then why would he kidnap or kill her?"

"Any number of reasons. He might have felt that he was becoming too visible in some way and wanted to stem the flow of information to protect his identity. Maybe she pissed him off somehow. Maybe he woke up needing to kill. With someone this cunning and deliberate, there are millions of things that could have set him off. A dust mote, for example."

Iris sighed and began peeling a banana. "Do you have any suspects at this point? Some intuition?" She looked at Deliverance. "Do you sense anything that might help?"

Deliverance shook her head. "There weren't any homes to feel like there were in the old cases. The only thing I've physically touched was the box holding Pearl Lewis's head, and I got nothing from that. I did hold her finger, but, again, nothing."

"We know the cops are doing their best and everyone's highly motivated to solve these crimes, but we're taking a part in the investigation, too, although it's not something sanctioned by the department, or those pesky fibbies," Quint said.

"Ha-ha," Iris said.

Quint went on. "We're splitting up to do some intense background investigations on the victims to see if there could be any possible link. First thing Monday I'm headed off to Hartford to dig into Pearl's past, Shayne's headed off to Savannah with Fox to root around in DeLage's, Victor's on his way to South Carolina to investigate that double hitchhiker murder back in '76, and Wilde and Raine are on their way up north to see if they can backtrack any hitchhiking on the part of our two unidentified teenagers. The cops found a couple of items that might indicate their presence up the I-17 near Sedona or the Grand Canyon."

"Like what?"

"A pack of matches and a postcard. Nothing definite, but at least it's a clue."

"What about the Lady of the Dunes, part two?"

"Since I'll be in New England, I'll move on to that and Deliverance will join me."

"My parents will come down from Salem so we can have dinner at Durgin Park," Deliverance said. "They'd love to meet their new granddaughter, but we're leaving all the kids here with Tucker moving into the house to look after them."

Iris hmm'd. "So, let me summarize what's touched your circle of family and friends. You got a head. Constantine got a head. Moon Wolf was nearly framed for murder. Cress and Gray's pugs were murdered. Munch was killed, and now Bollmeier is missing. Anyone in your family circle that hadn't been directly touched?"

"Victor and Wilde haven't been hit … yet," Quint said. "We've taken extra precautions in both our houses and offices by installing state-of-the-art security systems and cameras." He grinned. "And of course, we hired a gun-toting nanny to look after our kids. How's it feel bunking in with him?"

"You have a comfy pullout couch," Iris replied blandly.

Deliverance reached over and grasped Iris's hands. Then she held them for a few seconds before grinning. "Can I give you some advice?"

"Do I have a choice?"

"Not really," Quint confirmed. "No one ever does."

His wife continued. "I firmly believe in grabbing for the golden ring. I jumped this lug's bones before he knew what hit him. He didn't stand a chance."

"What's jumping bones mean?" Alex asked. "Daddy's a slug?"

"No, sweetheart, lug. Not slug. Mommy will explain the jumping part when you're sixteen. Take your sister into the family room and play. Where are your other sisters?"

"Up in their room playing with my Ouija board. Can't you get them one of their own? My planchette always feels funny when Storm uses it."

"I'll think about it," his mother said. "Now, your word for the day is—"

"De rigueur," Iris interjected.

"That," Deliverance said, nodding. "Tell your sisters that their words are etiquette and decorum. Let them fight over who gets what."

"Okay, Mommy," Alex replied as he grabbed his sister's hand and virtually dragged her out of the kitchen.

"So, as I was saying," Deliverance continued, "you need to take the bull by the horn—so to speak—throw him down on the bed and have your way with him. Just *go* for it!"

"He's dating someone," Iris said. "Some guy named Kenny. He said they've been going out for three weeks." There was no mistaking the disappointment in her voice.

"So? It's not like they're living together. Right now, you are, in a manner of speaking."

"I'm not about to break up a relationship for my own selfish purposes."

Deliverance sighed theatrically. "Let me impart a few wise words from one of our esteemed Founding Fathers, Thomas Paine. 'The harder the conflict, the more glorious the triumph. What we obtain too cheap, we esteem too lightly; it is dearness only that gives everything its value.' Chew on that one for a while, fibbie. And just remember this—most people on their deathbed don't regret the things they've done so much as the things they haven't done." She noted the astonished look on Quint's face. "What? I'm pulling A's in my English and History courses. You didn't marry a pea brain."

"I'm well aware of that," Quint said. "It's simply that when I think I can't be any more impressed by or proud of you, another beautiful day rolls around." Deliverance melted into his arms and they completely forgot about Iris as they kissed as deeply as they ever had.

That's what I want, Iris thought. *That kind of marriage.* She sighed and nibbled on a corn chip.

When Deliverance finished exercising her husband's tonsils she smiled sheepishly at Iris and asked, "Do you and Tucker want to come over for dinner? We have plenty."

"Thanks, Deliverance, but he's cooking up a beef stew and invited Raine and Constantine over."

"That's good. When you finish and if you feel the need for an after-dinner glass of Merlot, head on over."

"I'll think about it," Iris said as she rose. "Well, I should get back and help finish dinner prep. Thanks for the banana." She smiled and left as Deliverance and Quint arched their eyebrows at one another.

"Don't even think about interfering," Quint said. "Let them figure it out."

Deliverance held up her hands. "No problem. Unless they take too long and really need a nudge."

"You just want a gun-totin' FBI agent living in the backyard, too."

Deliverance just smiled.

It was five-thirty when Iris and Tucker finished readying the food and chilling the wine, so they had a half hour before their guests were to turn up. They sat together on the couch with Juju between them and talked about the Bollmeier case until a sharp knock jolted them out of their intense conversation. Tucker opened the door and found Raine and Constantine there with a bottle of Cabernet Sauvignon and a box of Yvette beignets.

The four friends sat down to a luscious meal and scintillating conversation. Constantine waxed enthusiastic about his plans for Christmas vacation when he'd go to New Orleans and visit his parents, whom he hadn't seen in two years. Phaedra might come with her husband and kids, but it depended on their business situation; they were still rebuilding clientele from the disastrous aftereffects of Moon Wolf having been under suspicion for murder. Cress was also considering a trip back home to see his parents. Constantine cast a sly look at Raine and said she might consider accompanying him on the trip if the one to England didn't materialize. She flashed him a noncommittal smile.

Constantine also excitedly imparted that on spring break he had plans to attend a conference of anthropologists in Mexico City with Gray Kingston to discuss new theories about the origins and cultures of the Aztecs, Incas, and Mayans. He was practically bursting with pride as he told them that the galley proofs of his first nonfiction book, *White Captive, Indian Heart,* were ready for his final proofreading, and by mid-October the book would be on the shelves. That revelation led to a lot of whooping and congratulations, and a kiss on the cheek from his girlfriend.

"Of course, we'll all want signed copies of your literary masterpiece," Iris said.

"Done," Constantine agreed as he broke apart his second beignet.

"Are you planning a new book anytime soon?" Tucker asked.

Constantine took a sip of his iced tea. "Well, I have been considering an outline for a book on adoption across cultures. You know, its benefits, pitfalls, reasons, the path of an adoptee throughout life, and how it impacts subsequent generations. After all, since I'm adopted I have an insider's view."

Raine looked at him curiously. "I thought you wanted to keep that part of your life private?" She took a paper napkin and gently wiped away the powdered sugar moustache over his top lip.

"My personal part I do, but there's a lot to explore in the general anthropological aspect. Anyway, enough about me. Tucker? What's new in your exiting world of nannyhood?"

Tucker stretched and took a deep breath. "Well, I had to pick up Alex from school yesterday. Seems he was reading his tarot cards and told one of the other kids that she was doomed. Aislinn broke a kid's ruler and stomped on her homework, and Storm stared down a teenager who was tormenting her about her eye color. Apparently, she didn't say a word but made him nervous as hell."

"She makes me nervous sometimes," Raine confessed. "It's not just those eyes, but the way she uses them to stare at you. And have you seen her shuffle a card deck? Like she was a Vegas dealer. Wonder where she got that talent?"

"No idea," Tucker said. "Maybe if we ever find out something about her background we'll understand. Until then, just don't play poker with her or—God forbid—ask her to play her new drum set. You should have seen the look of death Deliverance gave Quint when he brought that home along with a clarinet for Aislinn and a tambourine for Vikki. I'm terrified that they may turn out to be another Partridge family. Come on, get happy!"

Raine laughed and rose. "Well, Voodoo Man, time for us to get going. I've got an early workday at the office." She smiled at Tucker and Iris. "Wilde assigned me two new cases to work on outside of the 'big one.' I must admit, I rather like investigative work almost as much as I do technology. And since they're coming together ever so nicely these days, I get the best of both worlds."

Constantine put his arm around her waist. "I'm a lucky man—or so she tells me three times a day."

Tucker and Iris saw them out, then Iris began doing the dishes. Tucker frowned. "I can do those. You just sit and rest."

"I'm not tired. I just feel like doing something normal instead of chasing a serial killer. Here—dry this." She handed him a plate and he complied. They were silent for the next ten minutes as they washed and dried and put the plates and utensils away. It was a comforting, familiar silence. Iris turned on the TV at eight and they watched the premiere of a new "family" series, *Highway to Heaven*. Tucker thought it was quaint; Iris gagged and said she'd rather be watching *The Fall Guy*. They spent the aftermath arguing about who was "cuter," Lee Majors or Michael Landon. They agreed to a draw when *Dynasty* came on, then argued throughout the show about the women's outrageous fashions, Iris stating categorically that she'd slit her own throat before she'd ever wear shoulder pads the size of honeydew melons.

Iris had an early meeting with her FBI associates, so Tucker turned off the TV and made up the couch. He had offered to sleep there so she could have the bed, but she adamantly refused; the pullout was fine. He awkwardly kissed her cheek and mumbled good night, then set the security system and went to his bedroom. Iris stripped and slipped under the covers and breathed evenly in the darkness as she stared up at the ceiling fan whirring above her. Juju nestled in closely to his mistress and curled up into a ball.

It is dearness only that gives everything its value.

And just remember this—most people on their deathbed don't regret the things they've done so much as the things they haven't done.

Deliverance was right about that one. Iris threw off her covers and padded naked quietly to Tucker's bedroom door. She leaned in and listened; nothing. He was probably asleep. Or maybe he was staring up at his own fan wondering about her. She was torn about what to do, then she took a deep breath, and gently opened the door. She could see him lying on the bed, his face illuminated by the moonlight streaming in through the window. His eyes were open. He watched her without a word as she moved like a wraith towards his bed, gently lifted the blanket, and slid next to him.

There were no words exchanged, not for several hours, not for the time it took to give in to their unspoken feelings. They fell asleep in one another's arms for a couple of hours before they awoke and gave in yet again.

Iris bounced out of bed before Tucker the next morning at 6 AM and let a hot deluge of shower water soothe her muscles and soul. She grinned as Tucker came in with her and cuddled her from behind, and with scalding water and Dove soap and soft, inarticulate moans they consummated their newfound relationship once more.

Deliverance looked out the kitchen window as Iris left the casita and fairly bounced to her car. Quint came up behind his wife and watched Iris take off.

Deliverance turned around and grinned knowingly as she said, "That woman just got laid well and proper."

"About time," Quint agreed laconically.

"Yup," Deliverance said. "About time."

The Stalker put down his binoculars after he watched Iris drive off and then a half hour later watched the Quintanas drive off with their three oldest kids. That left the weirdo nanny alone with the littlest one. He didn't underestimate Tucker's firearms' proficiency, but the Stalker had righteousness, determination, and time on his side, not to mention an excess of charm. He stored the binoculars in the glove compartment, checked his hair in the rearview mirror, and got out of the car.

He walked up to the casita door and knocked. A moment later, Tucker opened the door, a surprised look on his face.

"Kenny. What are you doing here?" Tucker smiled, but it was a little strained after the night he spent with Iris. He grabbed for some straw of etiquette. "Do you … would you like some breakfast? I was about to make pancakes for Vikki."

Kenny grinned widely. His eyes sparkled as he contemplated the cute little three-year-old in her highchair. "I'd love some pancakes."

Tucker shushed Juju, who was hissing at the unexpected guest.

CHAPTER TEN

Hartford, Connecticut was the capital of the state and located mid-state along the Connecticut River. The city was named after a town in England, and the state was an anglicized version of an Algonquin word, quinnehtukqut, meaning "beside the long tidal river." The area was originally inhabited by the Algonquin Federation, which was comprised of the Native American tribes Algonquins, Podunks, Poquonocks, Massacoes, Tunxis, Wangunks, and the Saukiogs. The Dutch were the first Europeans to explore the area and in 1623 they established a trading post they named Fort Hoop (Hoop meant "House of Hope") near the current Charter Oak section by the Park River. Years later a Pequot chief sold a larger section off to the Dutch for a small amount, and the area is still known today as Dutch Point, and the street called Huyshope Avenue points back to the original etymology.

The British never let an opportunity to colonize a fertile area pass them by, and by 1637 they started arriving in droves with their leaders, Puritan pastors Thomas Hooker and Samuel Stone. In 1639 Hooker's document, the Fundamental Orders of Connecticut, was ratified and allowed the English settlers to self-govern rather than being under the thumb of the Massachusetts Bay Colony. Originally called Newtown, the settlement was rechristened Hartford in honor of Samuel Stone's hometown of Hertford, England.

Hartford grew by leaps and bounds as the decades passed, achieving success in trading and other economic ventures. The population grew, as did the wealth and prominence of the town. Hartford had its share of notoriety, however, and went down in the history books as having the first execution in the thirteen colonies for a witch on May 26,1647. A woman named Alice Young was accused, tried, and hanged. Very few details other than her name and unsubstantiated facts about her marriage and children are known, and it has been debated as to whether her name was Alice or Alse.

As Quint drove down the I-91 from Bradley International Airport in Windsor he wasn't especially impressed by the city and its small skyscrapers, but at least, he thought, it beat the hell out of Chicago. He had visited the Windy City during the ax murders case, where he had met a man named Trent Plaine and inadvertently sent him on a course towards killing the woman he blamed for his wife's and daughter's deaths, Willow Cheney. Quint had hated Chicago and most aspects of Boston, his mother's hometown, but he thought Hartford was a nice, small city that would be a decent place in which to grow up. He remembered that Adam Manzone had told him over their dinner that day he was released from police custody that Adam and Norah had both grown up in Hartford and would always hold a special feeling in their hearts for the city that had spawned their lives and love.

Quint had at least two or three people and places to check out regarding Pearl Lewis's life and disappearance. He wanted to talk to the friend who'd reported her missing, as well as any social workers or teachers that might remember something about her life that would help in solving her murder. On his address list he had the Hartford City Hall, Bulkeley High School, and the beauty shop that Pearl and Carolyn Walton had worked at when they graduated beauty school, The Comely Curl on Franklin Avenue. According to his list the beauty shop was two blocks north of a place that Adam had lauded as the perfect place to eat a decent Italian offering, Franklin Grinder. Quint was starving and feeding his growling stomach took priority over any interview.

Parking was a real problem on Franklin Avenue, and he couldn't find a spot. He turned into Brown Street, a residential neighborhood, and breathed a sigh of relief when he saw an opening on the south side. He parked and walked a half block to Franklin, then tempted fate by crossing the street at rush hour. He survived, then joined a long line of people waiting. The line went fast, and after fifteen minutes he was paying for a giant meatball grinder dripping with sauce, peppers, and melted mozzarella. He carried the grinder and a can of Coke back to his car and sat in it eating the delectable feast. He checked his watch and frowned; it was four-thirty, and he hoped that the beauty shop was still open. He gobbled down the last of his grinder, then walked quickly down Franklin until he came to The Comely Curl. He blew out a deep breath when he saw several women cutting hair and yammering about who knew what. He could never figure out beauty salons and the need of women to patronize them. Deliverance did her own hair.

The doorbell jangled as he came in and every head in the salon stared at him. He felt as out of place as any normal man would in such an environment. One of the cutters walked over to him and said, "Help you, honey?" Her smile was genuinely warm.

"Yes, please. I'm looking for Carolyn Walton," Quint said.

"What you want with Carolyn?" a tall, slender, young black woman asked with a tinge of belligerency. She had a milk chocolate complexion, huge brown eyes, and high cheekbones that seemed to indicate some Native American heritage back a generation or two. Her glossy black hair was pulled back tightly into a chignon.

Quint took out his P.I. credentials and showed them to both women. "I'm here investigating the murder of Pearl Lewis. I just want to ask her a few questions."

The black woman harrumphed and twisted another lock of her customer's hair into a prickly roller. "That's me." She bent over her sixty-something customer and said, "Honey, let these set for a few minutes while I talk to this guy."

"Um-um," the old lady said, winking at her. "He cute, ain't he? Ask if he's married."

"He wearing a ring, silly. Now just be good and let it set. I'll be back soon enough." With that Carolyn beckoned to Quint to follow her into the back room. She pointed at a cracked vinyl chair near the hair dye supplies. "Sit there."

Quint complied and waited as she seated herself and lit up a Salem.

"Now," she said after a couple of deep drags, "what you want to know? I told the Hartford cops everything I knew. The stupid FBI, too." She narrowed her eyes. "They weren't too polite."

"I'm sorry to hear that. Everyone should be treated with respect and dignity."

She snorted. "You doan know much about our cops, do ya? Where you from? Lemme see that badge thing again."

Quint pulled out his creds and handed them to her. She studied them as though she were expecting a test, then handed them back.

"You from Arizona?"

"Yep. Born and bred, although my mom was from Boston."

"A Boston Mexican? Ain't that weird."

"She was Irish. Look, ma'am, I know you're busy, so maybe I can get to my questions and let you get back to your job?"

"Ask away." She took another pull of tobacco, breathed the smoke out, and coughed. She waved her hand at him.

"Thank you. You went to high school with Miss Lewis?"

"Last two years. I went to Weaver before that, but we moved to Dutch Point in the south end for my old man's job. Got stuck in Bulkeley, me and my sister and cousins. Too many white people there. Too many damn Italians."

Quint ignored the ethnic jab. "Were you and Pearl good friends? Did you hang out?"

Carolyn shrugged. "She had them weirdo eyes and that turned off a lot of people. Kids made fun of her all the time and she got into a few scrapes. We said hi in the hallways and met up at some Bulldog football games."

"Bulldog?"

"Them's the name of Bulkeley's sports teams, except the swim team."

"Let me guess—the Bullfrogs?"

Carolyn had stubbed out her cigarette and clapped her hands. She began singing, "We are the bulldogs, the mighty, mighty bulldogs, everywhere we go, people wanna know who we are, so we tell them, we are the bulldogs, the mighty, mighty bulldogs ..." She stopped and smiled sadly. "Kinda miss those days."

"We all do," Quint said, genuinely sympathetically. "So, you also went to beauty school with her?"

"Yeah, that was unexpected. She used to bad-mouth Hartford all the time and I figured that as soon as she grabbed her diploma she'd blow town. But she did the course and was really good at coloring and styling hair. Almost as good as me." Carolyn puffed up in her seat. "You know, you'd look really cool with a copper streak in your hair. Maybe a couple. I'm reasonable and could do you soon's I finish Miss Jackson out there."

"I'd need to think about that and consider my wife's reaction. Although, when she and I met she had shocking pink hair and looked like a reject from Woodstock."

"There ya go. She'd probably love it. Well, think about it anyway. I'm here all week."

"I will. Now, did Pearl give any indication why she left the salon and the city? Man trouble?"

Carolyn laughed. "Anything but, handsome. Pearl was a lesbian. Didn't have no truck with the male species. Huh. You know, think I forgot to tell the cops that, but it didn't seem to matter. I know she had a few dates around here, but I never heard no names."

"I'll let them know," Quint said. Now that was an interesting fact, and maybe added a twist to her case. "Do you know—was she ever pregnant?" He trusted the M.E. but it never hurt to check.

"Hell, no, unless she carried and bore something the size of a troll."

"Anything else you can tell me about her?"

Carolyn pursed her lips and shook her head. "Not really. I mean, she was pretty, and smart—maybe not book-learnin' smart, but street smart. I think if she'd've stuck with it, someday she'd probably have owned her own salon. I plan on doing just that."

"Carolyn," Quint said sincerely, "I don't doubt for a minute that you will." He stood and stuck out his hand. She took it hesitatingly and they shook. "Thank you for your time and the info."

"You gonna think about those hair streaks?"

A wide grin split his face. "Actually, I am. I'm supposed to meet up with my lady in Boston, and I wouldn't mind seeing the shock on her face. I'll be here two more days before I leave. How's about you put me down for some streaking Wednesday morning, around nine?"

She smiled. "I'll do that, Mr. Quintana."

"Quint."

"Quint. Lemme see you out." She led him back into the salon where Miss Jackson was pouting about the delay. Quint handed her his business card and left. Carolyn tapped the card against her palm and smiled. That man was going to be one spectacular dude when he walked out of the salon Wednesday morning.

Quint decided to find a hotel and chill for the rest of the day. He'd had an eight-hour flight with the connection layover to change planes in Atlanta, and he was drained by the drive to Hartford and the search for the grinder place and beauty salon. He had a list of three viable hotels and decided to take a room downtown in the Hotel Garde on Asylum Street. The seven-story brick building was small and tasteful, and he was lucky enough to snag one of the two rooms available. His fifth-floor room overlooked High Street, and he was relieved that the shower had steaming hot water and great pressure. He bathed, shaved, then turned on the small TV and let it run as background noise as he studied his maps and lists. Adam had mentioned a couple of Italian restaurants, and he called the front desk to check on the location of Ficara's. The eatery was back on Franklin not too far from Carolyn's salon. The front desk concierge told him to order the lasagna.

He drove back south and parked in the nearly full lot at six-thirty, and he was greeted by an older woman with a strong accent. She led him into a spacious dining room that was bright and filled with happy diners. He ordered the lasagna and garlic bread, and a carafe of wine. After twenty minutes he stared in disbelief at the huge brick of lasagna that the waitress brought, and although the size was intimidating he finished every bit of it, and three large slices of heavily buttered and seasoned garlic bread. He paid and left a fifteen-percent tip.

Quint parked back at the hotel then decided to take a walk downtown. He hiked up the wide cement stairs to Constitution Plaza where he had a lovely view of the river and the skyline of East Hartford. He stopped at Brentano's bookstore and rifled through their paperback section, picking up the Joe McGinness book, *Fatal Vision*, on the true-crime murderer Jeffrey MacDonald. The hardback was out the year before, and the current news story about the book, the killer, and the author was the lawsuit that MacDonald filed against McGinness. MacDonald contended that he was sandbagged by the author who actually believed him guilty but strung him along for more facts and tidbits that would produce a bestseller. Quint picked up a second book by crime writer Ann Rule, *The Want-Ad Killer*. He had been enthralled by her first crime book on infamous serial killer Ted Bundy, *The Stranger Beside Me*.

He read a few chapters of the Rule book before falling asleep fully dressed. He slept eight solid hours, awakening at 6 AM. He showered again and put on fresh clothes, watched a little TV, and ached to call his wife but it was three hours earlier back home. He took a refreshing walk around Bushnell Park and found a little breakfast hole-in-the-wall where he had a surprisingly satisfying meal of scrambled eggs and sausages.

He knew that the high school was opening by now as the teachers and administrators prepared for the onslaught of students that would tramp into class, most wishing to be anywhere else. He'd never felt that way, relishing every moment he spent in school learning and better comprehending the world. After he'd mustered out of the Army and had his bizarre experience with the Manson clan, he spent six years getting a degree in History from the U of A and he was proud of that accomplishment. And the word proud was totally inadequate to describe his feelings for his wife, who had struggled against teenage odds and tribulations to not only build a great life with him, their children, and their partners but was more than halfway to her own college degree. She had switched from Psychology to Criminology and he was thrilled.

He opened the front door of the large blond-brick high school building and met a teacher right at the door. She took him to the administrative office where the vice principal inspected his credentials and agreed to let him review Pearl Lewis's records. The VP stressed that the cops and FBI had already talked to several teachers and the guidance counselor about Pearl's experience at the school, and he could only spare two teachers' time to talk to him, Pearl's guidance counselor and her mathematics teacher.

Quint read through Pearl's records, especially the handwritten notes by her teachers. All the notes indicated that she was smart, clever, and perhaps a little too introverted. She trusted too much and put up with a lot of crap from her classmates about her eyes and her background in foster care. The guidance counselor and math teacher said pretty much the same and shed no light on the subject at hand. Both were surprised when Quint mentioned her sexuality; neither had had any indication of that. He thanked them and left after making a lot of his own notes. He thought the school excursion was a bust.

He headed west on New Britain Avenue until he turned right on Newfield. He passed the dark, filthy Park River as he drove into

Charter Oak Terrace a half mile away. He pulled up in front of the second brick complex on the street and checked the number—176 Newfield Avenue. He studied his notes that Belzer had given him, noting that Pearl's old address was B-29, not 176. He assumed that the public housing community had simply had a change of address designations. He got out of the car and dodged a couple of kids tearing down the street sidewalk on scooters, and he took the three steps up to the sidewalk that led to 176. He knocked on the door; no answer. He knocked again, then decided that no one was home and turned to leave. The door to the next-door duplex opened and a frightened-looking Hispanic woman peered out and babbled in Spanish that they weren't home and wouldn't be for a few more days.

Quint replied to her in Spanish and that seemed to put her at ease. He asked if she'd known Pearl Lewis, but she shook her head and said she'd only moved there six months ago. He thanked her and left. He was exasperated at the little he'd turned up in his visit, but at least he knew a few more things about Pearl's character, and maybe that would help in some way.

He drove to downtown Hartford and found a parking space whose meter swallowed up his loose change. He went into City Hall and asked around for the social worker section, and he was directed to the second floor. The overworked middle-aged woman sitting at a desk covered with folders and documents had no time for him, but when he explained that he was investigating a murder she relented and pulled Pearl's folder from an old file cabinet in a storage room. The information was skimpy and added nothing to his search. He asked about her case worker, and the harried woman said that she's retired a year earlier and was living in Boca Raton. Quint thanked her and left.

He decided to take the rest of the day off since there were no more names on his list. He had his briefcase full of documents with him, so he drove back to the hotel, parked, and walked over to the Old Burying Ground cemetery on Main Street next to the First Church of Christ, where a few people were sitting on the grass eating late lunches and enjoying the oasis of calm in the middle of a big city. He sat under a big tree and began re-reading his material. Nothing jumped out at him, and after an hour he gave up. He meandered around the graves, admiring the ancient stones from the 17th century, many of which were badly worn and degraded from hundreds of years of weather and touching. He found a few where the carvings were readable, like the one that designated the grave of M Abigail Talcott, the wife of Captain John Talcott, who died at the very advanced age of eighty on February 14, 1784. The last time he and Deliverance visited her parents they went through a similar ancient cemetery in Salem, reading each stone, and wondering about the lives that had ended their human journey there. They always stopped for a moment of silence at David John's grave in the newer cemetery.

He hit the Honiss Oyster House for dinner and enjoyed a seafood meal that would rival any in Boston. He called home and spoke to his wife and kids. Deliverance said she was all packed and her flight would take off for Logan Airport at 5 AM. She had a two-hour layover in JFK and would land in Boston around two-thirty. They signed off and he fell asleep after he packed.

Wednesday morning, he had a casual breakfast at the hotel dining room, then at 8:45 AM headed over to the beauty shop. Carolyn was waiting for him with a sly smile on her face; that unnerved him a little. She shoved him down into one of the chairs and whipped out a large bib. He told her not to go crazy, just a few streaks. She um-hmm'd as she ran her fingers through his thick hair, massaged his scalp, and studied him critically. She told him his hair was lovely but just a tad too long. She asked him if he liked Don Johnson. He replied that he had no idea who that was. She told him not to worry, because soon he'd be as stylish as a handsome vice cop on the new smash TV show that had premiered a few days earlier, *Miami Vice*. He became nervous at that point but gave her the go-ahead to "do your worst."

Ninety minutes later when she let him look in the mirror, he gulped. He had shorter, layered hair that had a half dozen copper streaks in it. It was a shock, but he thought, well, it would grow back, and he could wash the copper out if anyone gave him shit about it. At least she hadn't mangled or colored his goatee. He told her it was fantastic and that she was truly an artist; Carolyn preened happily and was even happier when he gave her a twenty-dollar tip. He left the salon whistling, then bought a huge veal parmesan grinder and a quart of Coke and took off for I-91 north.

He pulled onto the Massachusetts Turnpike north of Springfield, which took him all the way to Boston. He knew that the Blaskós would be picking up their daughter, so he took Route 1 west of the Boston area and cut over to Salem, where he drove to the Blaskós' house. He saw that Nicolae's station wagon was parked, so he knew that his wife was within hugging distance.

He knocked on the side door and didn't wait for an answer before opening it. Like many people in this day and age, locking one's doors wasn't widespread in small towns and communities. He called out when he came in, and less than five seconds later four small, kinetic kids screamed, "Daddy! Surprise!" at the top of their lungs and lunged at him, knocking him down and inundating him with their hugs and kisses. When he managed to move their wriggling bodies off him and look up, he saw his wife standing over him with a scowl on her face. She was tapping her foot.

"Why does the father of my children look like Sonny Crockett?" she asked.

He didn't really have a good answer but wondered if every woman in the world knew who the hell this Sonny Crockett was.

CHAPTER ELEVEN

It had rained the day before Fox and Shayne arrived in Savannah, warm, gentle showers that left the river town moist and dewy the next morning. The temperature was projected to rise to 85°F with no clouds, and the sun would turn the cool early morning into a sultry, humid afternoon. They'd arrived at the Savannah/Hilton Head International Airport at 2 PM, rented a car, and drove to the new East Bay Inn on Bay Street. Just two blocks from the river and easy walking distance to the city's Historic District, the inn was perfect as a base to not only accomplish their research mission but to find a few extra hours to explore the city's amazing variety of restaurants and fabulous architecture. It was a little pricey due to its brand new renovated interior and exterior; the building was originally constructed in 1852, and saw many enterprises within its elegant brick walls, including a steam bakery, consul offices, a lodge meeting hall, and—its tenancy the lengthiest in the building's history—the Columbia Drug Company. In 1963 the building was left vacant, and it stayed that way until 1983 when it was purchased and turned into the inn.

Deliverance had originally booked a different hotel, but an unexpected cancellation and perfect timing allowed her to reserve their double-queen room on the second floor. Neither Fox nor Shayne had any issue sharing a room, and when they dragged their suitcases upstairs they were thrilled at the luxurious décor and the two large beds covered with handmade comforters.

Both Union Jackers were starved and strolled into the riverfront business area to find a good place to eat. They were inundated with options, but suddenly Fox grinned and pointed, and pulled Shayne into a small bistro that overlooked the river; the Southern Biscuit tantalized prospective customers with its signs promising "Good ole downhome _SOUTHERN_ cookin'!" Shayne was skeptical, having been born and raised in Barnstable on Cape Cod, but she was adventurous and willing to try (almost) anything.

The bistro was full, and they had to wait ten minutes before a table was cleared and they were seated. While they waited Shayne took in every nuance of the décor, which could best be described as love of the Confederacy. There was a big Confederate flag hanging on one wall, and framed prints of Robert E. Lee and Jefferson Davis beside it. A large, yellow metal rectangle with a curled rattlesnake and the declaration "Don't Tread on Me" hung over the entryway to the kitchen. Several black-and-white framed old photos of Confederate troops and battle images lined the other walls, surrounding a "The South Will Rise Again!" plaque. Shayne wondered if she'd be shot if anyone found out that she was a damned Yankee from New England.

Fox saw the look on her face and smiled. When they were seated he said, "Worried that they'll shoot you when they hear your accent?"

"I don't have an accent," she sniffed. "You do. So, this is the kind of world and cuisine you grew up with?"

"Yup. A good ole southern boy lovin' good ole southern food. Ever had grits?"

"The pleasure's never been mine."

"Let me order for you. I guarantee a stomach full of wonderful." He saw the skeptical look on her face. "I promise."

"Okay," she said, drawing out the word to make sure he understood that if his promise wasn't true she'd make him pay dearly.

A sassy young waitress came over with water glasses and a menu and came back a few minutes later to take the order. He gave her a double order for grits, collard greens, cornbread, fried chicken, and pecan pie for desert, two coffees. He added an over-easy egg to his order. He ordered sweet iced tea while they waited, and the waitress smiled brightly, said, "Y'all got it, mistuh!" and sashayed off.

"Did she just sashay?" Shayne asked.

"I believe she did. So, while we're waiting, how about we talk of fun things instead of the case?"

"Like what?"

"Like, why did a Yankee gal wind up in the desert southwest?"

"I like mean snakes, giant spiders, and enchiladas."

"None back on the Cape?"

"Not like we have out there."

"What was it like growing up back east?"

"Fun. Barnstable was a neat little town, and we had lots of beaches for swimming, sunning, and whale watching. The winters were brutal, but summers—ah, they were sweet. And we were close to Boston, so we had the best that a thriving metropolis had to offer, especially with food and historical sights."

"Sounds like a place you wouldn't want to leave."

"Part of me will always think of that as home, but the other part, well ... I wanted something different, something ... adventurous. My brother went to Harvard and now he's working at a hoity-toity New York law firm as their go-to contracts guy. I went to Brown, but even though I had pretty good grades they weren't good enough to get me into their law school or Harvard. I did a year at the University of Connecticut's law school, but I was itchy and unsatisfied, so I decided to make as big a change as I could."

"Hence, far west. Not California?"

She made a face and shook her head. "I applied to ASU in Tempe and got rejected, so I moved to Tucson, got a job as a paralegal while I went to the U of A—which thought I was a worthwhile law student—then heard about an opening in our firm. I kind of liked the idea of being an apprentice P.I., and the partners gave me the opportunity to keep going to law school, so here I am. Now—what the hell's a southern boy doing in a desert city?"

Fox deflected her question for the moment as their happy waitress came over with their food. He thanked her, and she flounced off.

The two diners seasoned their food with a generous amount of salt and pepper, and Shayne watched in horror as Fox dumped his grits over the over-easy egg and began mashing them together until there was a runny yellow mix of grits and egg all over the small plate.

"That's disgusting," Shayne said.

"That's real southern eatin', girl," he replied as he grinned at her and dumped a huge spoonful of eggy grits into his mouth.

She made another face and said, "At least the fried chicken's superb." She was noshing on a drumstick that was greasy and crispy, the chicken tender. She smeared a heaping of butter on a generous cornbread slice and closed her eyes in culinary satisfaction. "Okay, you've saved yourself from my wrath. The food's wonderful."

"Told you so," Fox said with a smirk as he scraped the last of his eggy grits off the plate. He started in on the collard greens.

"So," Shayne said as she finished the drumstick and started in on the chicken thigh, "you went to Yale, right? And why, oh *why* would a boy from Charleston head up to enemy territory for an education? Didn't you consider places like Duke or Tulane?"

"Sure, but we didn't have much money and Yale was the only one that offered a full merit scholarship. And, hey, I was only sixteen when I entered Yale, so it was scary."

"They make fun of you a lot?"

"You think? Yeah, the accent didn't help. But I was lucky in that my freshman year overlapped with another guy's senior year in law school. I was taking criminology courses, and he was offering tutor services, and that's how we got together. His name's Barnaby Lucas. Great guy and smart as hell. He was instrumental in helping me get through my first year. When he graduated he headed west and wound up in San Francisco. He's a top lawyer there and works for both the Prescott family and the Maguire family. Quint's friend, Adam Manzone, as you know, is married to writer and publisher Norah Maguire."

"Did you keep in touch?"

"On and off over the years. When I wrote to tell him that I was moving west, he suggested that I contact Union Jack since he knew they were looking for an in-house lawyer. Barnaby helped them after the ax murders, when Deliverance had killed the Axewoman, Cheyenne LaChoisi, and got Quint and Wilde off on minor offenses that were related."

"He sounds like a great guy."

"The best."

"So, why didn't you come back to Charleston to practice law?" Shayne saw a shadow pass over his face.

"I did, for a while. It just … didn't work out. Here's our pie," he said as the waitress plopped two huge slices down in front of them along with their coffee and removed their empty plates.

Shayne took a bite and smiled; the pie was remarkable. She sipped her coffee. "Okay, Rebel Boy—spill. Why did you really leave? If it's confidential, I can keep secrets. I never told anyone that Abigail Boucher boinked Eddie Redfern at the senior prom."

Fox gazed out the front window and chewed. Shayne was a

great associate and person, and he could always use a friend's ear. He cocked his head and studied her before saying, "My name is kind of anglicized, or made to sound that way from its original ethnicity."

"Eskimo? Antarctican?"

"No, German. I was born Fauk Neubauer on May 15, 1946 in New York. My parents migrated there after the war from Frankfurt. My father changed our name when I was a year old and moved us south to start fresh. Fritz Neubauer became Fred Newberry and Elfrieda became Ellen."

"Why did he change your names?"

"To obscure our German ancestry. The war was still fresh in everyone's minds and Americans weren't terribly thrilled with people of that descent. Also …"

"Also?"

He took a deep breath. "Also, my father was in the German army fighting the Allies. Ex-Nazis were even more despised than regular people. He was just a … soldier, but people tend to think all Germans were murderous bastards that crucified Jews. You know what's funny? Papa also had to conceal his religion from his own people."

"Jewish?"

"To our very kosher bones. And although we kept our religion pretty secret when we got there, the south wasn't overly tolerant of anyone who wasn't a Southern Baptist or some other Bible Belt-approved religion. We didn't disabuse anyone of the notion that we were Christian, and that's always been a point of personal shame for me, denying part of who I am. But the south in those years wasn't so kind to those of the Hebrew persuasion. I got a lot of shit at school when people ferreted out my true nature."

"Like what?"

"You know how some northerners think southerners are simpletons, and they use nicknames like Goober to put them down?"

"Yeah?"

"Well, my nickname at school was Jewber."

"That's disgusting," Shayne said, scowling.

"Tip of the iceberg, my friend."

"Do the partners know?"

"Absolutely. I wouldn't keep something hidden that could come back to bite me in the ass someday down the road. I'd already had that lovely experience." He signaled the waitress for another cup of coffee. He knew Shayne would interrogate him about that, so he confessed. "I fell in love when I was thirty, with a young lady from a classy background. Her father was a judge. We never discussed religion until after I'd proposed, and she accepted. I wanted to be honest with her."

"What happened?"

"It was a romantic evening. I took her for a carriage ride through Charleston and we sat by the waterfront and held hands. I got down on one knee—ever the southern gentleman—and she said yes even after I told her I was Jewish. Then she went home and told her parents. The next day a messenger returned the engagement ring with a brief note from her rescinding her acceptance. The messenger gave me a verbal admonition by her father to leave town and never darken the door of her or any purebred southern lady again. He said there would be dire consequences if I failed to heed his warning.

"I tried to contact her several times but no luck. Then one night the sheriff stopped me for speeding and a DUI—I hadn't done either—and I spent a night in jail. It was made clear to me that if I were prosecuted and found guilty I'd wind up in jail and my law license would be yanked. There was no doubt in my mind that this would happen, so I closed my practice and started drifting west. I worked a few ad hoc cases in Dallas and Oklahoma City, then a few in Phoenix. That was when I contacted Barnaby and he sent me to Tucson. Best thing that ever happened to me. I get to work with a great group of people on exciting cases, and I have a few separate clients that need my services. I'm a lucky man."

Shayne reached over and took his hand. "We're lucky." She straightened and finished her coffee. "You ready?"

"I am," he replied as he stood, looked over the bill, and pulled a ten spot out of his wallet to cover the meal and a tip. They walked outside to the bright sun and sat down on a concrete bench by the water. They watched the boats and cargo ships plugging lazily up and down the river, and the tourists that were enjoying a visit to the city.

"You know," Fox said, "Savannah is considered the most

haunted city in the south. Over the course of its history there was a mashup of bloody battles, disease, fire, monstrous slavery, and mysterious murders like Savannah antiques dealer Jim Williams' struggle to avoid prison for the 1981 slaying of Danny Lewis Hansford, a supposed male prostitute. Then you've got the 1959 murders of three sisters in the city's Calhoun Square. There be spirits scuttling about the entire city. They have evening ghost tours to tantalize gullible tourists and true supernatural aficionados."

"Deliverance would kill to take those tours. Any chance we can take one tonight?"

"I don't see why not. We're scheduled to meet that bridge club guy in about an hour at five. His address is just a few blocks away. Plenty of time before to shop for souvenirs and afterwards to take the tour. Tomorrow we have a busy day, but today we can do fun stuff."

Shayne looped her arm through Fox's. "It's a good thing I packed light, so I have plenty of room to bring home lots of tchotchkes. Lead on."

They walked up the steep stairs to the main thoroughfare and began browsing shops where Shayne went crazy buying gifts for the Dane-Quintana and Renard kids, and for her friends. She found a great book on haunted Savannah for Deliverance, as well as a Voodoo doll and a special candle that was used to help summon spirits. Fox just stood back and let her have fun, and then they walked a few blocks to the bridge club and met with two of Richard Delage's former card-playing buddies.

It was all Shayne could do not to react when she met them—one was a dead ringer for Boss Hogg, and the other looked like Clark Gable, if Clark Gable had lived to be eighty. They spent two hours discussing the dead man. The two players confirmed the basic facts that DeLage was a computer programmer turned salesman and was hawking personal computers and training lessons to high schools and colleges in the area before he began meandering across the country to do the same. They said he was essentially a lonely guy, and his marriage hadn't lasted three years; however, he and his ex-wife were on genial terms. He seemed to glom onto anyone who showed him a smile or a kind word, and perhaps he was too easily led.

Boss Hogg (whose real name was Bryan Broughton) and

Clark Gable (whose real name was Howard Barnard) said that DeLage was a decent bridge player but nothing too special. Since bridge was a game requiring four players, he was generally friendly with his group and with any new players. He occasionally played double dummy bridge with only a single partner and two hands of dummy cards. He often found himself in that type of game when he met someone agreeable in a bar. They noted that most of the bridge club played games with a standard deck (excluding the Jokers), but for some reason he liked to play games with a special bridge deck that had the same types and numbers of cards, but whose cards were slightly different in size. Boss Hogg thought that DeLage tended to bid erratically, annoying his partner. He said that when DeLage began playing he'd bid first before he learned the plays, which turned off most players.

Clark Gable said that the last time they'd seen DeLage he was packing up his car and was heading west on the I-10 after he hit the Florida connection at the I-95. Fox knew that although the police had explored the dead man's life in Savannah they hadn't hit any of the towns on that route and picked up the trail when he'd arrived in Tucson. He had seen police reports to that effect and knew that they didn't include any of the details he and Shayne had learned about his impatience and the habit of meeting "dummy" players in bars. Fox told them that they were going to interview his ex-wife the next day, and then the small computer company for whom DeLage had worked as a salesman.

Fox and Shayne left their meeting satisfied with what they'd learned. The sun was going down, so they walked to one of the tour kiosks on the riverfront and bought two tickets for a haunted tour that began at 8 PM. They walked back to the inn, dropped off Shayne's bags of souvenirs, and rested for a while. At 7:30 PM they headed back to the riverfront where they waited with fifteen other people for their walking tour. Their sepulchral guide joined them two minutes late and led the group throughout Savannah, hitting "haunted" houses and locations. The tour was fun and lasted two hours. He suggested that if anyone wanted to see a remarkable cemetery that was famous for its headstones, they should head over to the Bonaventure Cemetery. He handed out slips of paper with the address and driving instructions.

The humidity of the day had filtered off to a cool, breezy night, and the city and river were awash with lights and life. They snagged a couple of giant blueberry muffins and espressos and ate them on a cement bench, then headed back to the inn, took turns showering, and went to sleep. Fox couldn't help noticing that his companion had washed, dried, and brushed her glorious mane of long, blonde hair, and that in her sleeping clothes—a tight tee-shirt and shorts—her legs were tanned, slender, and as long as a hot summer night. He ran his fingers through his nondescript brown hair, knowing that he had always come up short in the looks department. His features were symmetrical and pleasant, but no one would ever think of him as remarkable. It took a while for him to fall asleep thinking about those sparkling green eyes.

They hit the Southern Biscuit for breakfast and once again Fox disgusted Shayne with his gooey mixture of egg and grits. She had bacon, scrambled eggs and two biscuits with gravy and said it was a shame he couldn't eat the bacon or any pork. He replied that he kept to most Jewish dietary constraints, but he discounted sweet and sour pork as being among the food he shouldn't have. He never told his parents but thought they might be okay with that.

The mist over the river had dissipated by the time they finished breakfast, and they sat on their favorite bench sipping coffee and watching the boats pass by. Both were raised near water, and both missed that living in the desert. Around nine they headed off to meet with their murdered victim's ex-wife. She was obviously well off; they pulled up in front of a large, gorgeous mansion off Savannah's Calhoun Square. The square, two blocks northeast of Forsyth Park, was laid out in 1851 and named after John C. Calhoun, who was a South Carolina senator and a two-time vice president. The Wesley Monumental United Methodist Church, a Gothic-style house of worship, towered over the square.

The former Mrs. Richard DeLage lived in a white colonial, three stories, with a full front wraparound porch complete with hanging plants and an oak rocking chair. The house would have been perfectly attuned to the antebellum world of the south. The gentile lady that met them at the door could have been a neighbor of Scarlet O'Hara. Perfectly coiffed silver hair, perfectly applied makeup, an elegant designer suit, and an unmistakable aura of breeding and class defined a woman who was certain of herself and her place in a rarified world.

Allison Bouchard DeLage welcomed them in with a genuine smile, and they found themselves in a luxurious sitting room with expensive tea poured into silver cups. A gracious host, Miss Allison (as her uniformed maid called her when she brought in the tea service) answered all their questions but gave little new information about her ex-husband. She confessed that it was an impulse marriage and they were socially and intellectually unsuited, but he was a decent man that had never belittled her or cheated on her. Their divorce was amicable, and despite a prenup she had given him a separation settlement of $20,000. She hadn't seen him for nearly a year. She had retrieved his body and at her own expense buried him in the Bouchard family plots.

An hour later they bid her goodbye and she wished them luck, saying if there was anything she could do to help—including funding—she'd be happy to do so.

Fox and Shayne hit a couple more friends of the dead man at the small computer company but got no more facts than they already had. In the late afternoon they took the car and found the Bonaventure Cemetery where they spent an hour meandering around the beautiful, park-like atmosphere and took pictures of some of the stunning monuments. They got back to Savannah after five, found a crab shack on the river, and chowed down on shrimp, cod, onion rings, and mint juleps. Back at the inn Shayne showered while Fox wrote up his notes in an organized fashion and called the airline to check on their flight out the next day. When Shayne came back into the room her skin was glowing from the shower, her hair a river of gold cascading down her back. She turned on the TV, sat cross-legged on her bed, and watched her favorite show while Fox ensconced himself in the bathroom.

He took a cold, cold shower and thought sadly that he was just plain fercockt.

CHAPTER TWELVE

"You know, we've hit, like, twenty tourist shops in Sedona alone," Raine said as she drained her vanilla milkshake. They were sitting on an ornate wooden bench in a cleverly designed little shopping area called Tlaquepaque as they took a break from pounding the main streets of the small town in northern Arizona.

Wilde couldn't mistake his niece's tone for anything other than disappointment and frustration. He couldn't blame her; they'd been on the road north for two days stopping at likely places that a hitchhiking pair might visit. The journey was a hunch anyway since there was no definitive proof that the two unidentified teenagers were hitchhikers; that assumption was based on the original crime back in South Carolina. And even if they were hitchhikers, there was no definitive path they might have taken—they might have been traveling east to west or west to east rather than north to south. Still, the matchbook and postcard made their excursion north a reasonable selection.

"I know," Wilde sighed as he took the last two bites of his hamburger. "Still, that's what we came up here to do. We'll bunk down at a motel tonight and head up to the Grand Canyon tomorrow." He glanced at her with a knowing smile. "You miss Constantine, don't you?"

"Maybe," she replied vaguely.

"No maybe about it, bird. You're crazy about the guy."

"Maybe."

"Have you told him, or are you waiting for the Four Horsemen of the Apocalypse to come riding in before you confess your feelings?"

"It's not that simple."

"Yeah, sweetie—it is."

Raine stared out at the bubbling fountain in the middle of the small plaza before she answered. "If I told him I loved him I'd have to tell him all about my past, and I'm not ready to do that."

"Revealing the one does not necessitate revealing the other. Has he told you that he loves you?"

"Yes."

Wilde was a little hesitant to bring up the secret that only a few people knew. "Has he ... told you anything about his relationship with Cheyenne?"

Raine ducked her head and flashed a smile. "Yes, Uncle—he came clean. He told me that Cheyenne was his blood sister."

Wilde blew out a relieved breath. "That's good. Only our little circle knows about that. The general story is that Cheyenne and Cress were adopted at the same time but came from different biological parents, and that's why Cress is his true brother. No one outside of our cloistered little group knows that Willow Cheney was their mother and James Danziger was their father. You know, he was tormented by all those revelations for years. It changed the intrinsic man inside of him. You brought him out of his shell, and I think he's helped to bring you out of yours. He won't care about your secrets."

"I care." She suddenly straightened and looked him in the eye. "Do any of our coworkers or friends know?"

"Just Victor. No one else. They wouldn't care, you know." He saw the look on her face. "But it's up to you. I urge you to enlighten him."

"Someday." She checked her watch. "It's four-thirty. Maybe we should find that motel and make plans for tomorrow?"

"Works for me," he said as he rose and chucked his fast-food bag and wrappers into a trash can. He opened his Sedona town map and scanned it for motels. He decided to try the Poco Diablo Resort, which Bliss and Malachi raved about from their visit seven years earlier. He didn't hold out much hope for a vacancy, but since it was late September and school was back in session, the area was divested of many families. He was thrilled to learn there were several rooms open; less thrilled at the price for a night's stay. Raine bullied him into taking a double-queen room with a magnificent view of the red rocks, and he gave in. They settled in, then drove into Sedona proper to take some time to browse the art galleries and tourist shops they'd only stopped at briefly. Raine found a hand-carved coiled rattlesnake made of cottonwood that she just had to have, and Wilde found an African-looking copper mask that he thought Victor would love. Raine named her snake Sam.

They ate dinner at a barbecue place on the way back to the resort. Both were enamored of the pork ribs and bought an extra order to nosh on during their trip to the Grand Canyon. At the resort they turned on the TV and Wilde watched the news while Raine showered. Then, he took his turn. He found her on the phone with Constantine when he came out of the bathroom and felt sad that she hadn't yet told her man her secrets. It was clear from her demeanor and voice that she loved him.

She hung up as he jumped on his bed. "You know what?" he said. "I actually miss the boys."

"No!" She laughed. "After all those complaints?"

"Hey—it's not easy being a father out of the blue of living beings with needs and angst and attitude. If Victor didn't attend to our yard all the cacti and flowers would be dead under my care. I could kill a rock."

"Yeah, you definitely have a black thumb."

"I resemble that remark!"

"Resemble all you want—it's true. Okay, enough uncle abuse. We should leave around seven tomorrow morning and head up the 89 till we get to Cameron then bear west on 64. That'll take us right to the South Rim. We can stop at an IHOP in Flagstaff for breakfast." She took a deep breath and slid down to a reclining position on her bed. "You can watch TV. I'm going to sleep." She turned off her bed stand light and snuggled under the covers. "'Night, Unk."

"Good night, sweetie." Wilde turned the volume down and watched the end of an episode his favorite light-hearted drama, *Remington Steele*. He wished to hell he could be as urbane and elegant as Pierce Brosnan. Raine was snoring lightly when the show ended, and he turned off the TV and the light. He fell asleep in a few minutes.

They stopped in Flagstaff the next morning and splurged on pancakes, bacon, eggs, and waffles, and two huge glasses of orange juice. They caught the 89 north and in a couple of hours parked at the El Tovar Lodge on the South Rim. They desperately needed coffee so they went to the lodge's restaurant and satisfied their craving. When they finished they asked various staff personnel whether they had encountered the young man and woman. Wilde only had a photo of a facial recreation since the killer had badly damaged their faces with acid. No one remembered seeing them or encountering anything unusual—other than normal Grand Canyon odd people and behaviors.

They hit the various shops around the rim, as well as tourists that were swarming about. In one shop they found an exact match for the postcard that the dead teenagers had in their backpacks. They bought several and asked the salesgirl if these were only sold here; no, she said, those postcards were sold all over Arizona.

Raine noted that a lot of the tourists looked like backpackers. She accosted a few and asked them how they'd gotten there and how they'd travel once they left. Everyone was friendly (the British accent might have helped), and most of them said that they'd hitchhiked to the Canyon and planned on leaving the same way, walking down the main road and then sticking their thumbs out.

They finished their tasks around five and headed south the same way they came. They stopped at the Poco Diablo, which fortunately had two rooms left. They had dinner at the same barbecue place (they'd finished their takeout ribs earlier in the day), then went back to the resort and collapsed in exhaustion from the day. They were on the road at 7 AM the next day and after gassing up the tank they drove straight through to Tucson.

Wilde dropped Raine off at Constantine's place and drove home. He knocked on Quint's door and a happy Tucker drew him in and said the boys would be almost as thrilled to have him home as Tucker was. Even though he didn't have to take care of the four Dane-Quintana children (who were with their parents in Salem), the Renard kids had worn him out.

The boys were in the living room, Beckett in front of a chess board where he had been trouncing Tucker, and Bechet playing with his beagle puppy in front of the TV. They looked up and saw Wilde, and before they could hide their impulsive smiles, Wilde sensed genuine pleasure that he was home. His jaw literally dropped when Bechet said, "Nous sommes heureux que vous êtes à la maison Oncle Wilde." Happy he was home? Uncle Wilde? He let Beckett finish his chess game, then took the kids to their own home just as Iris came in the front door. Wilde winked at Tucker knowingly; the nanny blushed.

Victor flew into Charlotte, North Carolina on American Airlines. His reserved car was waiting for him at the Hertz counter, and since he hadn't checked a bag he was quickly on his way out of the airport with his route marked on the map that the Hertz lady had given him. Victor couldn't put his finger on the precise aspects that made him feel at home, but being in the south, where he had grown up (albeit slightly more southerly in New Orleans), he had a very satisfied, peaceful feeling.

The Sumter County road on which the unidentified young man and woman were found murdered in 1976 was close to one hundred miles from the airport. He took the 77 south, passing Fort Mill, Rock Hill, Richburg and Ridegway before he angled east on the 20. He pulled over about five miles from the site into a small eatery where he was ecstatic to find "real" southern food. He ate a piece of fried chicken and some grits. He had the name and number of a State Police contact, a Sergeant Ron Hutchinson, who agreed to meet him in thirty minutes at the site. Victor ordered a piece of pecan pie and nearly moaned out loud at the taste. He drove down to Locklair Road off the S.C. 341 (Lynches River Road); Sergeant Hutchinson was already waiting for him.

Victor's guard was up the moment the policeman stepped out of his car. If there was ever a physical representation of a good ole southern boy, Hutchinson was it. Tall, pot-bellied, ruddy-faced, the man looked like something out of *Smokey and the Bandit*—and not in a good way. He drew himself up and strode over to the cop, extending his hand. Hutchinson took it right away and pumped a solid and genuine hello to a visitor to his neck of the woods. He smiled, showing a gold front tooth.

"Welcome to South Carolina," Hutchinson said. "First time here?" He pronounced "here" like "hee-yah."

"No," Victor said. "I've been to Savannah a couple of times, and Columbia once. It's a beautiful state."

"You from the south?" Hutchinson asked, squinting. "That ain't no Yankee accent."

"Born and bred in New Orleans."

Hutchinson laughed. "I just love that city! Ain't nothin' like the food and Mardi Gras. Been there a half dozen times. Me and the missus plan on going next February, then take a steamboat cruise up the Mississippi."

"You'll love that," Victor said. "Do you know the background as to why I'm visiting?"

Hutchinson nodded. "My boss briefed me on the murders out there in coyote country." He stuck his arm in his car and pulled out a thick folder that he handed to Victor. "Y'all can keep that."

"Thanks," Victor said, rifling through the papers and photos. "Can you summarize for me?"

"Sure," Hutchinson said affably. Victor mentally chastised himself for the stereotypical negative thoughts he'd had about this man. Never judge a book …

Hutchinson walked over to a spot by the road and pointed. "This's where we found 'em. Young boy and girl. They didn't have no ID on them, and when we sent out the descriptions, photos, dental x-rays, and fingerprints, nothing came back. They were both white but 'cause they were dead weren't no way to detect any accents. They had the same kind of clothes and haircuts that most young people did back then."

"I see they were named Jock and Jane Doe. Why Jock?"

"Some guy we interviewed said he'd met them and Jock Doe told him he and the girl were from Canada, and that his old man was a doctor. From that we started calling him Jacques, and I guess it mutated into Jock. Other than that, no clues. We found stuff in their belongings that made it seem like they were traveling around the company."

"What'd the M.E. say?"

"Same as your folks, each shot three times. We thought the boy was maybe twenty or so, but the M.E. said his dentition showed that he coulda been upwards of late twenties, thirty. He had an appendectomy scar and some scars on his back. M.E. thought he might've played sports. He was olive-complected, just like the girl. She might be anywhere from twenty to twenty-five. No way of telling for sure."

"Was she raped?"

"No sign of that."

"Any sign she may have given birth?"

"Nope."

"What about the positioning of the bodies? Do you think they were deliberately posed that way?"

"Didn't seem so. Looks like they fell that way when they were shot. Were your two posed?"

"Apparently, since the crime mimicked yours down to the bodies' positions and the clothes. Our guy wiped out their faces with acid. He burned off the fingerprints, too. But that might not have given us anything to go on if they were never arrested or fingerprinted."

"Your guy seems pretty thorough."

"He's a meticulous son of a bitch. You got any thoughts on who might have done this crime?"

"One theory's that they were jacked and whoever took their car killed them. After the information on the crime was released some guy up in Nebraska said he'd done some repair work on a car that may have had Oregon or Washington plates, and their descriptions matched the car's owners. Nothing ever came of that lead."

"So, the case is cold?"

"Cold as a polar bear's ass," Hutchinson confirmed. "Don't suppose your guy and our guy is the same killer?" He stuck a toothpick in his mouth and began to chew.

"A very remote possibility, but I think not. Our guy—whom we've been calling the Beguiler, much to my distaste—seems bent on recreating old crimes. Look, this isn't for general knowledge, but some of us think it may be a cop."

Hutchinson's eyes opened wide and he whistled. "That's fucked."

"But not unrealistic to surmise. He has intimate knowledge of the old crimes and is very adept at not leaving any evidence or clues. I'm hoping it's not the case, but I've run across enough dirty cops in my career to be skeptical."

"Were you a cop?"

"Ah, oui, twenty years, a lieutenant in the NOPD Homicide division after I got out of uniform."

Hutchinson shook his head "What's a good ole southern boy doin' in the godforsaken pit of Hell with all them snakes and Injuns?"

"It's a long story, but basically I was investigating my brother's murder and I became close to a group of investigators. After that was solved along with the ax murders, I decided to retire from the NOPD and stay."

"Real sorry about your brother. Lost mine to a drunk driver when he was eighteen. Ain't something you ever get over."

"No, it's not. Is there anything else you can tell me about your crime?"

"I reckon you got all the facts. Maybe you can spot something in the folder. Y'all can call me anytime you need details or want to bounce something off me. Here," Hutchinson said as he took the folder and scribbled down two phone numbers. "That's one's my station and the other's my home number."

"Merci," Victor said. He pulled out a business card and handed it to Hutchinson. "You can call me anytime, too. My home number's on the back. Listen. You've been really helpful to me. Can I repay you with a good down-home-cooking dinner?"

"I'd sure love that. The wife and the kids are visitin' her parents to give me some quiet time. I gotta do some studying for an upcoming convention. Ever' year we hold a regional get-together to discuss unusual cases and forensic measures. Gets all kind of attendees, not just from our state. Lasts a coupla days, and this one starts tomorrow. Gonna have to drive up to Columbia, but it's a good session and always nice to meet up with old friends and associates."

"Wish I could be there, but I've got to get back to Tucson. Got a couple of grandnephews I'm raising. My brother's grandsons. Their parents were killed in a car accident earlier this year and they're still adjusting."

"Man, that's tough. Hope they turn out okay. Hey—I know a special little place where you're just gonna die for the food they got, so follow me." Hutchinson ambled off to his car and Victor followed suit.

They drove to a small restaurant called the Rebel's Roost, whose parking lot was full. Victor understood why when he gnawed on another resplendent piece of fried chicken and the best mashed potatoes he'd ever had. He and Hutchinson enjoyed easy conversation that veered away from the crimes at hand and ranged from the food they were devouring to the upcoming presidential election to the state of race relations across the country. Victor gave him a synopsis of what had transpired with the Axewoman of Tucson case, and how this new case had frightening "assaults" on his partners and friends.

Hutchinson was surprisingly liberal in his views and Victor finally understood why when his new friend pulled out his wallet and showed Victor a shot of him and his family—his wife was a sweet-looking black woman and their three smiling kids were beautiful mixed-bloods. Hutchinson laughed at Victor's facial expression and commented exactly what Victor had been thinking—never judge a book by its cover.

Victor spent the night in Charlotte and flew home the next morning. He was happily surprised when Wilde and the boys were waiting for him at the airport. All three looked happy to see him, and he was delighted that both Bechet and Beckett were chatty on the drive home; Beckett bent his ear about the new chess club at school, and Bechet told him that he'd taught Beignet two new tricks. Wilde didn't go into his excursion up north; that would be saved for when they had some privacy.

They arrived home to find that Deliverance had made them a nice lunch and left it in their refrigerator. Her note said to enjoy and come over tonight for dinner when they could discuss everyone's progress. She, Quint, and their children had arrived home late the night before and she was staying home while he was at the office attending to firm business.

The Renard clan ate and talked, then the boys ran off to do their homework while Victor and Wilde talked intimately. They were both looking forward to that night when everyone would be in bed, and they could indulge in a real welcome-home.

The Stalker watched the arrival home through his binoculars. He tapped his left index finger repeatedly on the steering wheel of his car as he clenched and unclenched his jaw. He was not thrilled to have limited access to knowing what was going on in the two households. He had insidiously wormed his way into Tucker's life after he had followed him for weeks to determine his schedule. He had orchestrated their meeting at Los Niños Perdidos; the next night they went out on their first date to see a movie, *Red Dawn*. He whispered in Tucker's ear that he adored Patrick Swayze. When he said that, he squeezed Tucker's leg.

The Stalker wanted to take it slow since he knew that anticipation could breed more desire. He was good at manipulation. Very good. He wasn't gay, but he could simulate that kind of desire and by their third date Tucker and he fell into bed. He didn't care for the sex, but it was no big deal. He called himself Kenny Barron, and he was certain that he could deepen Tucker's interest in him by his faked interest in Tucker's job and the family and friends he had.

He hadn't counted on Tucker's interest in a woman, a woman who happened to be an FBI agent. He pretended to be blasé about the breakup, but inside he was seething, seething so much that his flesh ached.

He added Tucker's and Iris's names to his list, where his main target was at the top, written in blood-red ink.

CHAPTER THIRTEEN

"Thanks for making the time for this sit-down parlay," Wilde said to the large group gathered in the Union Jack Saguaro Conference Room. The already large table had been expanded by a wide insert, and it was covered with papers, photos, and enough lunch food to feed the proverbial army.

"Anything for free food," Detective Forest Baxter said as he helped himself to a dish full of chips and salsa and popped open a can of Pepsi. He noticed Quint's arched eyebrows. "What? You never accepted a free donut?"

"When I was a detective I had the self-respect to hold out for cheeseburgers," Quint jabbed as he dumped a large spoon of German potato salad on his plate then speared two mini beef chimis. Deliverance had the Mexican food catered in from Mariposa Linda's but made the sides and desserts herself. Quint liked the food from the restaurant, but over the years his wife had applied herself to learning the cooking of his ethnicity and produced remarkable results that could have come from the kitchen of an award-winning cocinero from Guadalajara. He was sad that she had learned on her own and that his late Tia Max hadn't had the opportunity to teach her; that chance had been obliterated when the Axewoman of Tucson murdered her, his uncle, Tio Carlos, and his cousin, Luisa.

When all the plates were filled and the drinking glasses full of water, Pepsi, orange juice, and other beverages, the crew began discussing the progress and suppositions on the Beguiler killings and the abduction of Laurel Bollmeier. Wilde sat at the head of the table with Deliverance on the other end; Quint, Victor, Fox, Shayne, and Iris sat on one side facing detectives Yale Cornell and Forest Baxter, who were seated next to Belzer and Raine. Thayer and Turner were out in the field chasing down leads on their case, an art theft at a major gallery that reeked of an inside job. With a ten-percent recovery fee the firm stood to make a lot of money if the two T's could unravel the theft.

Cornell was slicing his spinach-cheese enchilada as he began. "So, that was a good idea you had, Victor, about checking Laurel's car again for something very specific. Forensics did a great job searching

318

for evidence or at least trace of someone else besides her and Don. They found nothing. The dirt and sand on the driver's floor matched what was in the area, and if she had gotten out and then in the car she would have tracked that in. No evidence that someone else did."

"The Beguiler has been meticulous," Victor said, "but even the most thorough criminal is bound to make some mistake."

"What are you talking about?" Iris asked as she cut into her pollo fundido drenched in extra jalapeño-cream cheese sauce.

Cornell explained. "Victor suggested that we check the length that the driver's seat was pushed back. When Pete Murphy measured it was clear that whoever sat in the seat last had to be at least five-foot-ten tall. Laurel was five-three."

"Then someone else drove it to the abandonment place and forgot to pull the seat back into a Laurel position," Shayne said.

"Exactly. That gives us at least one clue to the nut's physicality. Forensics is going over the car centimeter by centimeter again."

"And a man that big wouldn't have much trouble overpowering a pint-sized reporter," Wilde said.

"How's Don doing?" Quint asked. He all too vividly remembered the sickening horror in the pit of his stomach when his wife and kids were in the hands of a murderous madwoman.

Baxter shook his head sadly. "He's a mess, barely holding it together. He loves that woman, heart and soul. Christ—he told me they were thinking of having a kid."

"Has he been trying to insert himself into the investigation?" Quint asked.

"Did you?" Baxter asked with a slight touch of humor. "We like to pretend we're all professionals but the truth in that supposition's superseded by our humanity."

"True. So, no ransom note, nothing?"

"Nope."

"She's dead, isn't she?" Deliverance asked quietly.

"It's unlikely that anything else's the case," Cornell said. "But there's always hope."

"Did Malachi have any unsolved kidnappings in his research that might correspond with Laurel's?"

"He had a few kidnappings on his list," Deliverance said as

she studied her sheet. "1935, a Welsh journalist named Gareth Jones was kidnapped and murdered in China. No arrests, but a strong suspect was Soviet agents who killed him in retaliation for a story he did on the Ukraine famine in 1932-1933. 1970, Italy. Journalist Mauro de Mauro was kidnapped and murdered although his body has never been found. All bets are on a mafia hit. 1979, the U.S. Ambassador to Afghanistan, Adolph Dubs, was kidnapped by militants who put a bullet through his head. Again, the Soviets were prime suspects, but no one was ever arrested." She put the list down. "That's about it for unsolved kidnappings."

"I don't think this has anything to do with his pattern. I think this was a random act of his for personal reasons. Maybe she was getting too close to identifying him. Maybe her articles pissed him off somehow. Maybe he just felt whimsical and decided to throw in a red herring. We won't know the reason until we catch him," Cornell opined. He took a huge bite of his beef taco and washed it down with ginger ale.

"Iris," Wilde said. "Any updates on the bombing?"

She shook her head. "No, nothing. They've determined that the C4 was military-grade, but so far investigation hasn't uncovered any missing C4 from any military stockpiles. As you know the explosion was triggered when the ignition turned on. That trigger is one of the two most common, the other one being a pressure switch under the driver's seat, where once someone sits or gets up—boom." She threw Belzer an apologetic glance. "Sorry."

"Quint," Wilde said, "what'd you learn from Hartford? Our clique knows the facts, but our compatriots here don't."

Quint nodded. "I met with Pearl's friend, Carolyn. Lovely young woman."

"She responsible for the new look?" Baxter laughed, referring to the Don Johnson haircut and the copper streaks.

Quint narrowed his eyes. "Nothing wrong with a little fashion change."

"At least he didn't come home wearing a pastel shirt and loafers with no socks," Deliverance said.

"So, as I was about to say before being excoriated by you mavens of fashion," Quint said, "Carolyn went over the same things with me that she did with the police and FBI. Pearl had a pretty unhappy childhood and took a lot of shit about her eyes." He paused and scowled. "Our Storm goes through the same stuff. Kids can be cruel little bastards. Anyway, Carolyn said she was street-smart, and she gave me one little tidbit that the cops and fibbies didn't uncover— Pearl was a lesbian."

"That's a twist," Belzer said thoughtfully. "So, she wouldn't be led astray by a guy, or necessarily trust one."

"Very likely," Victor said. "Although she probably hid her sexual preference to fend off any social repercussions. I can understand that. Anything else, partner?"

Quint grinned. "Franklin Grinder has the best grinders on the planet."

Wilde harrumphed. "I beg to differ. New York City has the best grinders and every other kind of food on the planet."

"We'll put that to a test someday," Deliverance said, "but right now let's focus on non-digestible concerns. I need everyone's brain cells to link arms and sing kumbaya in harmony." She scowled menacingly at Wilde. "Don't. Even. Think. About. It."

"No, ma'am," Wilde replied. "I guess we can discuss our journey up to canyon country." He flipped the postcard he'd bought onto the table. "Identical to the kids' postcard, but the saleslady said they're sold all over the state, not just at the Canyon. Same thing with the matches."

Raine picked up. "The country up north is dazzling, and a lot of people explore through the time-honored method of hitchhiking. We talked to a few kids that were traveling doppelgangers for our victims, and they said they'd walk as much as they could, but especially when leaving the Canyon would hitchhike down the main road south. We showed the facial mockups to them, other tourists, and people who worked at the various stores from Sedona to the Canyon, but no one recognized them."

"Anything else?" Belzer asked as he scribbled down a few notes.

"At the risk of setting off Deliverance's ire," Raine said, "We found the best barbecue place in Sedona. And Bliss was right about the Poco Diablo—superb accommodations."

To head off any further discussions of food and lodging, Victor plunged in. "I had a nice chat with a State Trooper down in the Palmetto State. Ron Hutchinson, a good ole boy who really is a good ole boy. He took me to the site of the 1976 murder scene and we went over the facts. I took a few photos, too. He confirmed that Jock and Jane Doe didn't seem posed and fell where they were shot. No sign that the girl was raped. They have no leads. It's a dead end."

Wilde sighed. "Lovely. Anything else you'd care to impart to our audience?"

"Well, at the risk of seeming like a competitive sort of guy, I must say that the Rebel's Roost has the best fried chicken—"

"—on the planet," Baxter finished. "You people are obsessed with food."

"Huh. This from someone whose gobbled down two enchiladas, three tacos, a pile of Spanish rice, and frijoles," Quint accused.

"I didn't say there was anything wrong with that," Baxter replied mildly as he cast a glance at his plate; it was scraped clean. He eyed the sopapillas but wasn't sure if he'd get his hand slapped if he reached for one. He was getting a slight pot belly and his wife was after him to diet. She'd freak out if she knew what he'd eaten for lunch. No reason to enlighten her. He decided the best defense was an offense, so he asked Fox, "What did you and Shayne come up with in Savannah?"

Fox took a deep breath and glanced at Shayne. "Look, let me just get this out of the way first, okay? The Southern Biscuit on the riverfront had the best grits and biscuits with gravy—"

"—on the planet," everyone else in the conference room said in unison. Baxter shook his head.

"Okay," Fox said, "now that that's out of the way, we'll enlighten you about our excursion. Shayne—you're up."

"Ah," she said, "we met with his ex-wife, a few work associates, and a couple members of a bridge club. The ex-wife was the epitome of a southern lady. We got tea from a silver service, poured by a uniformed maid. Miss Allison—"

"Is that like Miss Scarlet?" Victor asked with a very slight edge to his voice. He'd bet a year's salary that the maid was black.

"Precisely. Miss Allison was very gracious and forthcoming. She admitted that their marriage happened on impulse and they really had nothing in common. They lasted three years, then apparently had a very amicable divorce wherein she gave him a $20,000 settlement. She even paid to have his body returned to Savannah and interred in her family plot. She offered us any help we might need to uncover his killer, including funding."

"Sounds like she still had feelings for him," Deliverance said.

"Maybe, but I think most of her actions were based on a lady's interpretation of class and duty. Not that there's anything wrong with that. She did do right by him."

"What about the work associates?" Belzer asked as he poured himself another glass of ginger ale. He was four weeks on the wagon and desperate for a real drink, but he knew that to find his friend's killer he had to straighten up and act like a man—a sober man.

"Virtually nothing helpful from them. They said he was adequate, but no superstar salesman," Shayne said.

"But we got a few tidbits from the bridge players," Fox said. "Boss Hogg—"

"Boss Hogg?" Quint said. He was all too familiar with the character; his kids loved *The Dukes of Hazzard.*

"You'd have to see it to believe it," Shayne laughed. "The other one we call Clark Gable."

"So," Fox continued, "Boss Hogg told us that DeLage liked to play with a special bridge deck rather than normal card decks, and that he seemed lonely and would glom on to people to have company."

"Sad," Iris said.

Fox nodded. "It is. Now, they also gave us a tidbit that didn't seem to be in any of the police reports we've perused. Did you ever hear of dummy bridge?"

"Is that something a Republican would play?" Quint asked.

"Sweetheart," Deliverance said, "that's not nice. I'm sure there are some wonderful Repubs out there just lovin' the common man and desperate to do great things for the country." The sarcasm dripped from her voice like the ship-eating acid from the movie *Alien.* She held up her hand. "Sorry. I'm from Massachusetts. We're die-hard Democrats. Fox, please continue." She folded her hands in front of her and smiled.

"Thank you. Anyway, dummy bridge uses two partners instead of four, and the absent two are dealt dummy hands, as though they were present. DeLage apparently would pick up a partner in bars and play that type of bridge."

"So, he might have engaged in that style of play with a single person here rather than three," Wilde said. "That would potentially isolate him with the killer if they met in a bar, then went someplace private to play a game." He addressed Cornell. "Has your task force hit bars to show his photo around?"

Cornell blew out a breath. "Only a couple around his motel area. Two bartenders recognized him but said he just stopped in for a drink and didn't leave with anyone. I reckon we'd better send the team out in an expanded search area."

"I'll send Welsh and Swansey out with Chet Cromwell to scour the bars between the motel and the I-10."

"Really? Swansey?" Quint said.

"We're stuck with him," Cornell sighed. "Welsh isn't so bad, but I'll never understand how Swansey could have ever made detective."

"Maybe it has something to do with being married to a sheriff's deputy's daughter?" Belzer said. He couldn't stand Swansey. "I can say this now since I'm retired—he's the stupidest creature on the planet."

"You've obviously never met his father-in-law," Cornell offered. "If you ever listened to his political and social views you'd come to the quick conclusion that he needs a cork shoved up his butt to keep what's left of his brains from flowing out. Apparently, he takes a triple dose of verbal Ex-Lax every day. It seems to be genetic. The deputy's old man's a grouchy old accordion-playing hoarder with a penchant for loud polka music and peeing out the back door every morning."

"Great," Deliverance said. "Keep him out of our efforts. I don't suffer fools gladly."

Cornell squinted at her. "Any chance you could turn him into a spider?"

"Why?"

"So I could step on him."

Deliverance grinned at her husband. "I really like this guy."

"What about me?" Baxter groused.

"I'm working on it. Check back with me in a week or two. So, what's the plan?" Deliverance asked.

"We're doing all we can to investigate the Munch murder and the other cases. We still have no clues to the identity of the Lady of the Dunes even though we've sent her photo, fingerprints, and description to law enforcement around the country. No fingerprint matches and about a dozen leads that didn't pan out," Cornell said.

"I took a half day down in Boston to ask a few questions about the original case," Quint said, "but no go. Didn't learn anything new."

"Okay, we have a few new avenues to pursue with what your team has discovered." Cornell noticed the looks passing between the Union Jackers. "What?"

"The possibility that the killer is a cop. We've come to the conclusion that that's a likely scenario. Have you?" Quint said.

"It's a possibility," Cornell said noncommittally. "That's something we're all hoping isn't the case, but it's a viable path to check out." He caught Quint's steady gaze. "I expect that you've been investigating that?"

"Yeah," Wilde confirmed. "We have, starting with background checks on all of the members of your task force and moving beyond that into other cops."

"I don't much care for that tactic," Baxter said.

"Neither do I," Cornell agreed, "but it's a reasonable avenue of research. Found out anything yet?" He raised a challenging eyebrow.

"Good news," Victor said. "You two came out pretty clean in our background checks."

"*Pretty* clean?" Cornell said.

"Well," Quint drawled out, "there's the little matter of illegal poker games and sports betting, but we decided that was acceptable."

Cornell and Baxter looked at one another. Baxter shrugged; he was a heavy Vegas bettor but never to the extent of losing money he couldn't afford. Cornell had a weekly poker game with a few other cops and one sketchy old friend that may have been playing on the wrong side of the tracks and with money that wasn't especially acquired legally.

"Of course, we're checking others out. There seem to be a few odd aspects to Swansey's life, but nothing that would make us think he could be the killer."

"Certainly not his brainpower," Wilde added.

"Unless he's a very good actor," Iris said. "Did you find out yet who the leak was who gave Laurel her tips?"

"No," Cornell said, blowing out a frustrated breath. "We searched her house, her computer, her documents and found nothing to indicate who she might have been conversing with."

"I'm not totally surprised at that," Victor said. "She probably kept the person's contacts and notes in her head so no one could get ahold of them and trump her efforts."

"We did find a draft of her manuscript for her next book on all these crimes, but she never mentioned any tipster in the text. She did mark down a few possible footnotes but left them blank."

"All right, then," Quint said. "I guess we continue our efforts and hope for the best." He got up and stretched and everyone followed suit; it had been a long afternoon.

Just as Cornell and Baxter were about to leave Cornell turned around and smirked at the Union Jackers and their friends. "You know," he began slowly, "we've been doing a little investigating on our own—on your crew."

"We know we're not above suspicion either," Victor said in amusement. "Find out any interesting facts?"

"A few," Baxter said. "Like you've been taking your older nephew to the gun range to teach him how to shoot. From what I hear, the kid's getting to be a dead shot." He looked over at Iris. "There seems to be more motivating you to stay in our fair city than investigating murder cases." He arched his eyebrows at Raine. "You, ditto. How's the exciting world of anthropology these days?"

"Exciting," Raine said spiritedly.

"And you, Quint. You've been waffling about building a ramada for Victor and Wilde here with only your own three efforts or hiring a few day workers to get the job done. Workers, I might add, that aren't necessarily here legally."

"I see no reason to not give a needed job to a few decent men and paying and feeding them exceptionally well while they're on our properties," Quint replied.

Cornell held his hands up. "Just sayin'. We're compiling a list of facts on all of you, too. Hope you don't have any deep, dark secrets that we might uncover." He turned and left with Baxter following, missing the looks of concern on several faces.

Suddenly Raine said, "I have to get home. Sorry. It's important. I'll be in early tomorrow." With that she rushed out of the office to the surprise of her friends.

"I have to check in with our team about what's transpired," Iris said. "I'll catch you guys later. Tell Tucker I'll be home around six." With that, she left, too.

"Ah, to be young and in love," Victor said. He winked at Wilde and thought that love at an advanced age was pretty darn good, too.

Raine burst into Constantine's office, much to his surprise. He was with a student discussing an essay. Raine stared at the student and said flatly, "Leave." The kid had no illusions about her tone and he scrambled out of the chair and fled the office.

Constantine stood and looked at his girlfriend curiously. This was definitely out of character. He waited.

Raine drew herself up, locked her bright violet eyes with his emerald ones, and said, "I love you. Constantine Dionysus Makris Black Wolf, I fuckin' love you." Then she threw herself into his arms.

The Stalker had sat outside of the Union Jack building, across the street in the Alpha Beta parking lot. He finished off a Big Mac and large fries while he watched the building, and watched the people come and go. When the cops left he shifted in his seat and pulled out his binoculars. He had been watching the Quintana house since 7 AM, and when Quint and his wife left he carefully followed them the short distance to their office. After he parked he saw all the other meeting attendees drive in, and it wasn't for another two hours that they began leaving.

When Raine left he waited a few minutes, wondering if anyone else was going to leave. When the fibbie came out and drove away, he started his car and headed north to Sunrise, where he turned left just as Raine had. He parked outside of Constantine's condo and waited.

Less than an hour later the man in question drove up and he and Raine got out of the car. They seemed to be in a hurry to get into the home.

He took out his list and made a note. Next to it he drew a fat star. He drove off.

He didn't notice the other car that had pulled up a few spaces away, the same car that had been a couple of aisles away in the Alpha Beta parking lot.

The car with another man with binoculars and a keen, electric sense of watching … watching.

CHAPTER FOURTEEN

Tucker's culinary expertise was in full flourish Friday night. He had the whole weekend off since his employers were taking the kids (AKA, "the Wild Bunch") overnight to Phoenix to explore the Botanical Gardens and the zoo and visit the old west town of Rawhide. Victor and Wilde were in sole charge of their boys as well, leaving Tucker free rein to dazzle Iris with his kitchen skills. He prepared a meal of Dover sole and wild rice, with glazed baby carrots, grilled asparagus, and crème brûlée for dessert. He had perfected the perfect prickly pear margarita, and the blender and special hand-blown glasses awaited their luscious liquid. Iris had to work that day, so he was left alone to micromanage preparations. He had prepared a special surprise in the bathroom. He hoped he'd bought enough candles.

Iris managed to get home by six, as exhausted as she usually was but grateful that the week was over. She gave him a quick peck on the lips before diving into the bedroom and changing into shorts and a tank-top. He was making final tweaks on dinner as she came into the kitchen asking if she could help. He shooed her out and told her to put on some albums. A few moments later the magnificent sounds of Simon and Garfunkel's album *Parsley, Sage, Rosemary and Thyme* set the mood for a lovely evening.

Iris flashed a gentle smile at him. "What's your favorite song on the album?"

"Tough one," Tucker replied. "Have to be a second-place tie between *Flowers Never Bend with the Rainfall* and *Poem on the Underground Wall.*"

"First place?"

"*Patterns,* hands down. When I first heard that shivers ran up my spine. You?"

"Ditto. Quite wonderful sitar solo."

Tucker had already set the table and poured two glasses of wine. She argued that she wanted to help but he demanded that she sit and be served "like a queen." She groaned and parked herself in her chair and watched silently as he brought all the food to the table, then sat down himself and asked her for her plate. She complied, and

Tucker filled it with every dish he had prepared. He filled his own plate and studied her expressive face as she cut into the sole. He could tell she was genuinely pleased.

Easy conversation flowed as they ate and one after another the Simon and Garfunkel albums finished then dropped another on the turntable and began a new song. Both steered away from the murders and investigations; Iris had promised that this evening would be for pleasant things that were soothing to the soul and not disruptive. His special margaritas mellowed her even more.

When they finished Tucker loaded the plates and utensils into the dishwasher while Iris took her last margarita into the living room and collapsed on the couch. He saw that she was setting up a chess game in front of the now-roaring fire. He wondered if that was her way of foreplay. He was game. Tucker joined her at the board, sitting cross-legged on the floor as he studied Iris's first move. It took him a few minutes to respond, but when he did he was rewarded with an appreciative look from his companion, who required more than just a few minutes to get her Queen out of danger. The game lasted nearly an hour, with Iris winning as she usually did. Tucker raised his glass to Iris in acknowledgment of her growing tactical prowess.

Iris rose and stretched, and Tucker took it as a sign that she was tired of the game, so he put the board and pieces away. A new album dropped down and seconds later the beautiful sounds of *Chances Are* wafted through the air in Johnny Mathis's inimitable voice. Tucker held out his arms and Iris melted into them. They danced to the song without speaking, holding close. When the song finished he reluctantly let her go and shut off the record player.

He turned to Iris, who was standing by the back doors and admiring the bright blanket of stars that were sparkling over the mountains and desert. The moon was vivid and streamed its light down on the desert floor to illuminate the flora and occasional animal that scurried across the sand and rocks. Iris could see a plethora of constellations glittering in the sky, and she sensed Tucker's close presence. She pointed out several easily identifiable constellations, like Orion, Canis Major, Cygnus, Aries, and Cassiopeia.

"Tired, my love? Tense?" Tucker asked softly as he massaged

Iris's neck and shoulders gently and pressed his knuckles into the small of her back.

"A little," Iris admitted, as her body started to loosen up and be soothed under Tucker's tactile ministrations.

"Give me a few moments, FBI lady, and I promise to relieve some of your physical discomfort. I will ... pleasure you, Special Agent Flynn," he ended softly. Iris caught her breath as she nodded wordlessly and let her eyes follow Tucker as he moved like a wraith towards the bedroom. Iris closed up the house and set the security system, but her mind was on the man so very close to her and she could barely concentrate. She finished just as the soft, familiar voice called to her. "Iris?"

Iris walked slowly towards the bedroom, the professional side of her urging caution, but the human side of her wanting to sprint and be there in a second. They had mated a number of times, but always, it seemed, in a hurry and with a dash of trepidation.

She entered the bedroom and her lips parted in wonder. The dozens of flickering candles that Tucker had set on the window ledge, niches, furniture and floor took her aback—how could he done that so fast? All different sizes and colors and some with aromas, they cast strange and sensuous shadows on the walls and ceiling as the flames danced and swirled from their burning wicks. She noted that there were similar flickerings coming from the entry to the bathroom, but before she could move towards it Tucker entered the bedroom from the arch.

You take my breath away, Iris thought as the naked young nanny stood before her, a few yards away, his eyes locked on Iris's face. She took in the tall, perfectly proportioned body, and the skin darkened by outdoor labors and burnished by a healthy sheen resulting from his good diet and regular exercise. He had let his near-shoulder-length layered hair fall loose, and the bangs and side hair fell softly around his face, framing the high cheekbones and stunning blue eyes. He'd removed his gold wire-rim eyeglasses.

He stood casually, arms crossed, leaning with one shoulder against the bathroom doorjamb, with just the slightest touch of haughtiness. Iris found that enticing on this occasion, rather than annoying. Tucker deliberately waited a few long seconds before walking towards Iris. He opened his lips slightly, sensuously, and let his own eyes roam over Iris's face as he swiftly pulled her tank top over her head, exposing her firm, full breasts. He slid his hands under the sides of her shorts and seconds later she was standing naked before him, nothing between them except pure sexuality and desire.

Iris took Tucker's face in her hands and murmured softly, "Pleasure me, nanny," hoping that the tone would belay any misinterpretations that Tucker would have about the words themselves. It was on the tip of her tongue to abandon all sanity and tell Tucker how she really felt, but before she could get the words out Tucker forcefully crushed his lips against Iris's own and thrust his probing tongue into her mouth. Iris returned his passion and for several long moments they were both locked in a passionate embrace of bodies and arms and hands and lips and mouths. Iris couldn't stand it any longer and broke away so that she could pull Tucker down on the bed.

Tucker resisted, which surprised Iris. Tucker shook his head and grasped Iris's right hand tightly in his own and started pulling her towards the bathroom. Iris allowed herself to be led and when they entered the bathing area she saw that Tucker had lit dozens more candles and that a steaming bath of scented, bluish oiled water was awaiting her. Tucker motioned her to get into the bath. Iris slid into the soothing water and rested her head back against the rear edge of the tub. She closed her eyes and enjoyed the sensations that the water and the previous sensuous passion had melted throughout her entire body. She turned her head and opened her eyes to see Tucker standing over her, holding something that glinted in the candlelight. She recognized his sleek, sharp, old-style shaving razor when Tucker knelt beside the tub and placed a small dish of creamy shaving soap on the edge. He met Iris's eyes knowingly and smiled enigmatically.

"Worried, my pretty fibbie? I can understand a cop's concern to see her beguiling nanny-bodyguard standing over her with a sharp instrument in hand."

"Not worried, just curious," Iris replied, trying to appear unconcerned and casual as she wondered about the words that had just matched her exact thoughts. She leaned back against the tub.

"Nothing to be curious about, my lovely one. I simply want to pleasure your body from head to toe tonight, and the act of drawing a razor across one's slender, tanned legs can be as sensual as consummated sex under the proper circumstances." He cocked his head to one side, his eyes never leaving Iris's, and said, "Lie back and try to relax your legs."

Tucker used his left hand to raise Iris's right leg. He gently lathered the leg. Iris tensed perceptibly as she felt the edge of the razor lightly touch her calf. Tucker drew it upwards in a deft, gentle motion, then repeated the process until Iris's leg was clean and smooth from ankle to groin. He lathered Iris's left leg and shaved it, too. Iris closed her eyes about halfway through the swipes up her left thigh and pushed her fears aside to enjoy what were soothing, sensual actions. If anything was to build between them, it had to start with trust. Affection and love weren't enough; the man was still very much an enigma to her, and she didn't trust herself to wholly surrender.

When he finished, Tucker put the razor down on the sink along with the soap and cupped some bath water and rinsed Iris's face with it. Iris opened her eyes. Tucker nodded his head. "Move forward." Iris looked at him. "Move forward," Tucker repeated firmly, lightly putting his hand behind Iris's back and urging her forward to the front of the tub. Iris slid towards the front and Tucker stepped into the tub and slid down, leaning his back against the tub and pulling Iris back to rest against him. He held Iris's body firmly between his strong thighs. He picked up the special oiled soap he had bought from a new-age vendor earlier in the week and began running it in circular motions along Iris's breasts and belly, and up along her arms and down along her legs. Iris was leaning back against him, eyes closed, enjoying the quiet intimacy as Tucker's hands and fingers washed and massaged and aroused her. Tucker's tongue and lips caressed, nibbled on, and gently bit her shoulders and neck and face. She was almost certain that she had moaned several times when it became too difficult to hide the pleasure.

The erotic bathing went on for nearly an hour. Iris came close to climax several times when Tucker's hands took slow pains to massage her genitals and the nipples on her breasts. Tucker always stopped short of bringing her to that climax, as though teasing her with things to come as he ran light fingers back and forth across Iris's shoulders and nipples. Iris didn't mind, however, since the point to which she was brought was already far past anything she had ever experienced at any man's hands. True, she had climaxed innumerable times during their sexual consummations when he had penetrated her, and when Tucker had satisfied her orally, but this was another matter altogether.

Gradually Iris realized that Tucker had decreased his movements and this portion of their evening was winding down. Tucker pushed her lightly forward with his upper body, and Iris moved. Tucker rose from the tub and reached for a large, plush towel. Iris stepped out of the tub, dripping, as Tucker knelt and began to towel her dry from the feet up. When he finished he dried himself and tossed the wet towel over the tub. Tucker followed Iris out of the bathroom. They left the candles burning. Tucker stopped at the entrance to the bedroom and poured a draught of brandy for Iris, who swallowed it quickly and made a negative motion with her hand when Tucker offered more. Tucker hesitated a moment, then put down the decanter as Iris reached out for him.

Iris was more than ready for the next step and pulled Tucker down on the bed eagerly. The young man laughed and maneuvered his body so that he could push Iris backwards and loom over her. Iris lay back, waiting quietly. Tucker looked down at her for a moment as he sat back on Iris's legs. Then he smiled and leaned over Iris and started to kiss her lightly on her lips and face and throat, working his way down and increasing the intensity of his oral exertions as he reached her chest and stomach, and descended further to where he knew Iris wanted him to be. But he stopped just short of performing the oral sex that Iris wanted and instead rose up and sat back on Iris's legs. He smiled, then reached down to the nightstand and retrieved a small jar with a viscous liquid inside. At Iris's inquisitive look he said silkily, "Damiana oil. A very sought-after, effective tactile aphrodisiac that comes from Texas, Mexico, and the Caribbean. It's a known aphrodisiac since ancient times. The Aztecs had a particular affection for it. Lie back."

Iris complied, and Tucker deftly opened the jar and thrust his fingers into the liquid, which he rubbed all over his hands. Tucker reached down and pushed his thumbs into the high insides of Iris's thighs, then drew them down hard and slowly for the full length of her thighs as his slick palms caressed the tops of Iris's legs. Iris arched her back involuntarily at the fiery sensations rippling through her legs and lower body. Only years of training and emotional restraint prevented her from screaming out at the exquisitely painful pleasure that Tucker's hands were providing. She had never known that this portion of her anatomy was so sensitive and wondered vaguely how Tucker had discovered this erogenous zone. She didn't care, as long as he kept doing what he was doing.

Tucker rubbed his thumbs and fingers up and down Iris's thighs until she gasped for him to stop. He smiled in the flickering light and let his hands rest unmoving and lightly on Iris's legs, enjoying the power he had over the woman as he watched her closed eyes flutter as she regained her normal breathing and licked her dry lips. It seemed that experimenting with his own body to find sensitive and erotic places had paid off.

Tucker bent over Iris and restarted his oral exertions on her stomach, licking and nipping and teasing. He moved downward and let his lips and tongue and teeth provide her with what he hoped would be an unparalleled experience in oral genital stimulation. As Tucker performed his deft movements Iris could no longer suppress her groans, and her lover was gratified to know that he had succeeded in bringing Iris at least to her emotional knees. Iris reached down and grasped Tucker's hair, forcibly holding him down as though to prevent him from stopping what he had started.

He let his mouth massage Iris for at least five long minutes, stopping when he thought she was too close to climax, then starting again with even more fervor. He stopped and started several times until he felt Iris clutching his hair too tightly with her reflexive response to the physical sensations. He finished his exertions almost violently until Iris yelled out and arched her back and climaxed and fell back panting on the bed, gradually releasing Tucker's hair and head from her grasp. Tucker sat back on Iris's legs, gasping as both took a long while to regain their even breathing and composure. Tucker opened his eyes to meet Iris's own. His lips felt dry and he slowly licked them before speaking.

"Again, FBI lady?" he asked softly as the tips of his fingernails stroked Iris's inner thighs.

"Yes. God, yes," Iris answered feverishly as Tucker immediately started to perform the same actions again. It took a few minutes longer this time for Iris to climax, but when she did she felt as though her head and chest had exploded, and at that point if Tucker had taken the razor and run it across her throat she wouldn't have even cared. She would have had all that a woman could ask for before that moment of death.

After the second time, Tucker stretched his body out alongside Iris's on the bed and she grasped his face. The two lover-combatants were locked in a long and passionate bout of kissing and touching and unintelligible murmurs and sounds until Iris was sufficiently aroused. Even in the throes of her passion she thought of their safety and comfort and reached for the small packet of condoms on the bed stand. She was careful, unlike their first time "bareback." Both had been tested for sexually-transmitted diseases; the tests were negative, including the test for the HIV virus. It was generally considered a "gay disease," but Iris thought that was misdirection and that everyone should be careful regardless of feelings and desires. She took double safety measures by being on the pill.

She quickly sheathed him a split second before Tucker plunged into her and they began a marathon engagement of erotic acts punctuated by moaning and thrusting and raking of fingernails until they exploded in ultimate pleasure and collapsed beside one another wheezing and gasping for air.

Neither moved for what seemed a long time until Iris regained her senses. She stroked Tucker's back with her cheeks and lips and tongue. She forced him onto his back and mounted him. She welcomed in his erection and began a rhythmic bucking until she screamed and collapsed on top of him. Tucker didn't try to move Iris's weight off him but instead let the woman enjoy herself and come to the end of this coupling in her own time and way. After a while, Iris groaned and withdrew and fell on her back next to Tucker, gasping for a few moments before she reluctantly left the bed to wash. When she returned Tucker was lying on his side, his arms wrapped around the pillow, his eyes lightly closed as he waited for his bedmate to return. Iris slid into bed beside him and wrapped herself around Tucker, and they fell asleep for an hour, contented and relaxed and spent.

Iris awoke first, still tightly wrapped around her mate. Her movements startled Tucker, who was awake and alert. He disengaged himself from Iris and rolled over on his other side lazily, smiling and yawning at the same time as his lady took in his face and movements. They watched each other for a few minutes until Iris leaned closer and kissed him gently and affectionately, then turned to lie on her back as Tucker raised himself up on his elbow and looked at her almost curiously. He let his fingers run lightly across Iris's stomach as Iris closed her eyes and smiled slightly.

"What are your thoughts, lovey?" Tucker inquired softly, as his hand continued caressing Iris's breasts, playfully teasing an erect nipple.

"I'm thinking … this is an unexpected development in my life," she whispered softly.

"Because of my confused sexuality?" he asked lightly.

She sighed and shook her head. "No, because I had my life path all mapped out, and this wasn't even a rest stop on that highway. I had it all planned. I made it to the top of my classes in the University of Pennsylvania and Georgetown. Hell, I got my law degree in two and a half years instead of three. I figured a few years in Phoenix before I finagled a transfer to D.C., and then by forty-five a Deputy Director and by fifty a full Director."

"Doesn't leave much time for a personal life," Tucker murmured.

"That didn't bother me. Getting married and having kids just wasn't anywhere near the top of my life goals. I don't know why I feel that way. Having a family was never important to me. I never gave it much thought. Not sure that's changed." She paused. "I'm not sure I want it to."

"So where does that leave us?" Tucker said quietly.

"I have no idea," she confessed. She stroked his cheek with the backs of her fingers. "I love what we've become, but to be honest I don't know what the future holds."

"You could always consult Deliverance and her crystal ball," he said lightly.

"She actually has a crystal ball?"

"Yup. Lots of other witchy stuff, too. But she's like Glinda—a good witch."

"I wouldn't argue that point. I adore her."

"Then … is it because I've had relationships with men?"

"I've made my peace with that. It's not an issue. You're not the issue—I am."

"What do you want?"

"If I knew that we wouldn't be having this discussion." She flung her legs over the edge of the mattress and without another word padded into the kitchen where she picked up the brandy decanter and filled her snifter before walking over to the sliding glass doors that led to the back yard. Tucker watched her from the bedroom arch. He could sense her turmoil. He wondered if she could sense his. He had secrets. He wondered what her secrets might be. He came up behind her and wrapped his arms around her. She leaned back against him. They were comfortable with one another, neither really knowing why, but content that they had reached that step on their relationship ladder.

The living room was dark as they stood there staring out at the darkness, the only illumination the moon and the vast blanket of stars that twinkled like Christmas lights in the sky. It was darker in Tucson at night than other cities and towns because of the Kitt Peak National Observatory, which was located on the Quinlan Mountains fifty-four miles west-southwest of Tucson on the Tohono O'odham Nation. A critical astronomical observatory, it required dimmed lights in Tucson to prevent glare that would skew its activity searching the night sky and analyzing the cosmos.

Tucker told her that one weekend his parents had taken him and his siblings down to New York City to see the Planetarium, and he'd found it fascinating, and considered becoming an astronomer. He said his father didn't think that was a worthwhile profession, and soon enough his enthusiasm flagged. Iris confessed that she'd had childhood aspirations of becoming either an archeologist or a veterinarian, but the FBI was her true calling.

He was silent, thinking he could never compete with her aspirations, and those aspirations were a barrier to anything they might build together. Life in his parents' generation was so different. Life had a slower pace back in the day. Traditional. Structured. Back then it was like enjoying fine wine, not slamming down a shot of adrenaline. But this was the world they had, and everyone had to adjust.

He had a fleeting thought of Kenny, his short-term ex-lover, who was whimsical and carefree, and accepted Tucker just as he was, with no demands, no judgments. He wondered what Kenny was doing tonight, if he was with someone else or alone in a bar. Kenny had called him a few times just to talk, and they'd met twice for coffee and chat after they'd broken up. He sensed that Kenny would be amenable to a one-night stand, but he wasn't. When he was with someone, he was monogamous, and that wasn't too hard to be with Iris. He was so damned confused as he nuzzled her body and soon drew her back to the bedroom.

The Stalker sipped his cold coffee from his vantage point away from the houses on Fire Water Lane. He knew his main target wasn't anywhere in the proximity, but he was drawn to the place, even in the cool, dark night. He was restless, and he felt a need to at least watch the casita where his seduced ex-boyfriend was bunking down with the FBI bitch. Kenny had called and met with Tucker, but the inadvertent information flow had dwindled. He'd have to use his own resources to continue surveillance and eventually action his retribution.

And he had made so many options of how to do that. None of them involved mercy. He had no mercy. He was ruthless, and every cell in his body ached to finish his journey. The hairs on his arms and the back of his neck stood constantly at attention as he considered the endgame. He hadn't given much thought to what might come afterwards. That was one of his problems, the inability to see long-term consequences. He operated on raw nerves, on instinct. That had served him well until the target had traduced his path, destroyed his freedom. He flexed and unflexed his fingers as his hands shook. He—

The Retaliator whipped open the passenger door to Kenny's car and plunked himself down in the seat. He had a silver automatic gun in his hand, pointing it at Kenny's side. He smiled; his eyes were cold.

"We need to talk, buddy boy," he said as he jammed the gun into Kenny's side. "Drive."

CHAPTER FIFTEEN

"I've checked. There are no monsters under your bed, Storm," Deliverance said as she rose to her knees after checking under her daughters' beds twice for the monster with the glowing eyes. "Yours either, Aislinn." She stood and studied the two young girls huddling under their covers, both frightened. That was odd since both girls were generally fearless.

"We heard something outside," Aislinn said.

"What did it sound like?" Quint asked as he sat on her bed and stroked her hair.

"Like low whistling, Daddy."

"And then we saw a tiny red glow, but it went away fast," Storm said. "We thought it came into our room."

"I'll go outside and check," Quint said. "I'll make sure there are no monsters out there, too." He rose and left the bedroom, encountering Alex and Vikki in the hallway holding hands and staring up at him. He nodded towards their sisters' bedroom and they ran in while he got his gun and slid the back doors open to check the perimeter of the house. He circumnavigated the entire house, stopping and listening for any sounds that shouldn't be there, and searching for any sign of a glowing, red eye. Nothing, except the normal sounds of the night creatures. A pack of coyotes was screaming in the distance, and there were soft rustlings of lizards scampering about the sand and shrubs. The lights were off in the casita and Wilde's and Victor's house; after all, it was 1 AM. He stood by the road and scanned for cars or people; none.

Quint went back into the house and padded to his daughters' bedroom only to find it empty. He heard giggling and had a feeling he knew where everyone was. Upon entering his bedroom, he saw his wife and four kids snuggling on the king-sized bed, inundating their mother with pint-sized affection. He had a feeling no one was going to get much sleep tonight. Alex scooted closer to Vikki giving Quint enough room to fit into the bed even though he was precariously positioned damn close to the edge of the mattress.

"All's well outside. No monsters," he said as he hugged Alex and patted Vikki on the head. He smiled at his youngest daughter, who was growing up too fast. At three, she had started nursery school, and in two years she'd be in kindergarten.

"I'm still scared," Aislinn pouted.

"There's no reason to be, Snickerdoodle," her mother said. "We'll always be here to protect you."

"Did you ever get scared of monsters, Mommy?" Storm asked.

"Oh, I've been scared lots of times," Deliverance replied, involuntarily shivering at the memory of nearly losing her baby twins to a madwoman. She squeezed her daughters. "Want to hear a story about one time I was really, really scared?" The response was a resounding, "Yes!" from the four little ones. She looked over at Quint.

"I want to hear, too," he said, knowing she'd never tell them— yet—about their near brush with death when the twins were seven months old.

"Okay," Deliverance said. "It was January 1974. I was a dumb eighteen-year-old kid. I was spending a couple of months up in the Catskills in a small trailer with a couple friends of mine."

"Why on earth would you head up to the Catskills in the dead of winter?" Quint asked.

"Did I mention that I was eighteen and dumb?"

"Okay, I'll give you a pass on that."

"Thank you. So, my friends had to work late, and I was in the trailer by myself. We had this pathetic old TV antenna, but we managed some decent reception. I was knitting when a *Movie of the Week* came on. ABC did a weekly series of those movies, and most of them were pretty good."

"You were knitting?" Quint asked skeptically. He had never seen her anywhere near a skein of yarn.

"It's a dark part of my past. Better off that you never saw any of the results. So, this was a horror movie about this werewolf creature killing people in California. It was called *Scream of the Wolf* and it was freakin' scary. Here I was in a dark trailer by myself with no one else around watching people getting slashed in fog-filled forests."

"Why didn't you put on the lights?" Storm asked, enthralled. She loved monster movies and scary things. *Gremlins* was her

341

favorite film, and right now she was clutching her stuffed Gizmo as she huddled close to her mother and sister. Suddenly a wave of terror engulfed her as she flashed back to waking up in the forest with a crushing headache and no memory. Her heart began beating wildly.

"Because she was a dumb eighteen-year-old, dork," Alex said crossly. He sighed theatrically; sisters were so annoying.

"Alex, behave yourself," Quint warned.

"What did you do, Mommy?" Vikki asked.

"Well at first I sat there watching and getting more and more frightened. And then after a really scary part, I jumped up and ran to the tiny kitchen."

"Did you cook something?" Aislinn asked. "Wheatena?"

"No, sweetie—I got a butcher knife out of the drawer and jumped back on the couch. I spent the rest of the movie clutching that knife and praying that my friends would come through the door and not the Wolfman."

"Did they come back?"

"Yes, and I still had the knife in my hand. They laughed at me and I tried to make a joke out of it. But, I was really, really scared even though it was a fantasy threat. What I'm trying to say is that even though there may not be monsters in the darkness, your feelings are as true as if there were."

"Are there monsters in the darkness, Daddy?" Vikki asked.

Quint and Deliverance locked eyes over their children's heads. She nodded slightly.

"Yes, baby, there are," he said, "but that's why moms and dads are put on this earth—to protect you. And you can't live your life looking under the bed each night. You have to have faith that the monsters will be turned away from this house before they can ever get in the door."

"And they're also put on this earth to snuggle with their kids in bed and go to sleep," Deliverance said as she turned off her bed lamp. "Everyone cuddle up, and let's close our eyes."

Quint turned off his lamp and the six Dane-Quintanas found their comfortable sleeping positions in the big bed that could hold a full measure of family love. The silence lasted two minutes.

"Mommy," Aislinn said drowsily, "can I get a tattoo? You have one."

"No, you may not," her father answered flatly.

"Just a little one, Daddy. I want a hummingbird and Storm wants a sword."

"A sword?" Deliverance said.

"Regardless of the image, none of you are getting tattoos until you're eighteen," their father said firmly.

"Why?" Alex demanded. He wanted a dragon wings tattoo like his mother.

"Because the world as we know it would fold in on itself like a dark star," Deliverance said. "Do you want to be responsible for destroying the world?"

"No," Aislinn said sadly.

"Then go to sleep. We'll have this discussion in another twelve years."

There was a little muttering, but the kids settled down and within ten minutes everyone was asleep except Storm, who was lying still and staring up at the ceiling, fearing the darkness, fearing the monsters that might be locked in her head.

The next day Quint and Deliverance headed into the office while Tucker got the kids ready for school. He was scheduled to come into the office and do some research in the afternoon when he finished some household chores.

Raine and Wilde were in her office huddled over a notepad and talking quietly. They looked up when Quint knocked then came in.

"What's so intriguing?" Quint said.

Wilde straightened. "We think someone may be watching your house," he said.

"And you're of that opinion because?"

"Couple of things," Wilde said as he sat in Raine's guest chair and crossed his legs. "Both of us have seen a parked car a distance away that seemed just to be waiting."

"Same car?"

Raine sighed. "Actually, no. It was dark out and too far to really make out the color or model. It was only two times, but I guess we're just leery."

"What else?" Quint said.

"Victor and I found a few dead snakes in our back property. Not natural deaths—they were cut into pieces."

Quint blew out a deep breath. "Might have been Storm. Remember, she killed a bunch and stuck them under that bush."

Wilde shook his head. "She didn't confess to that when you confronted her, did she?"

"No, she denied it even when we pressed. We assumed she was just too scared of admitting that kind of violence and being sent away."

"I don't think she did it," Raine said. "I honestly don't think she would have denied it if you'd confronted her. I've spent some time with her and she's a smart little thing, but I don't believe she's duplicitous."

"What else?"

"I've found a number of broken branches that look like someone broke them skulking around. I'm pretty good at validating covert spying like that. There were also a few footprints."

"Did you make a cast?"

Wilde shook his head. "I planned to but a day later it rained and washed them out. Still, it had to be a man's shoe, maybe size ten. I know—that doesn't narrow it down. You know, it could be nothing, just some kids or hikers cutting across the properties, but I'd rather be safe than sorry."

"Agreed. I think we need to upgrade our security system. We have a motion sensor front and back, but its range is limited. We need to install one with a longer range. You, too."

"Yeah, that's what I was thinking," Wilde said. He waved a note. "Got the name and number of a high-end security firm in Phoenix that I'll call shortly. Pay them to come down and beef everything up. We've got alarms and all that, but I was thinking we should put in cameras front and back just as an extra precaution."

"Good," Quint said. He checked his watch. "I've got to make a call. Less than a month away to our fifth anniversary and I thought I'd take my little witch up to Sedona for a long weekend."

"Are you daft, man?" Wilde said grinning. "That's All

Hallow's Eve. A very important holiday for the Wiccans. Won't Bliss be holding a coven meeting?"

"Look, I go through that every friggin' year. This year Bliss can find a substitute thirteenth coven member for the celebration. My wife and I are going to have a special few days for ourselves. No Wiccans, no limey Brits, no Cajuns, no kids, no crime scenes, blood, or guts. The traditional gift for that anniversary is wood, and I went through Phaedra to commission one of her Yacqui artists to carve cottonwood images of the Horned God and Moon Goddess. I need to pick them up today, but right now I've gotta make a reservation at the Poco Diablo."

"It's fabulous," Raine said. "Make sure you get a room facing the mountains. I'll write down the name and address of that barbecue place."

Deliverance poked her head into the office. "Quint, call for you from Cornell. Sounds urgent."

"Oh, Christ—I hope there aren't any bodies popping up. Can you transfer it in here and get Victor, please?"

Victor and Deliverance joined them in a few minutes. Raine answered the call and put it on speaker.

"Hey, Cornell. What's up?" Quint asked.

"Quint, hey. I'm on my way to a crime scene in south Tucson. Looks like there are several bodies and right now we don't know if it could be related to our cases. I thought I'd let you know if one of you wants to join me and offer your astounding insight."

"Astounding? Flattery will get you everywhere," Wilde said.

"That's what I thought," Cornell said with a noticeable touch of amusement in his deep voice. He rattled off the location. "See you there?"

"Victor and I will join you," Wilde said. "Takes about a half hour to get there."

"See you," Cornel signed off.

"Okay," Wilde said as he nodded to his partner. "We'll call you as soon as we know anything." He and Victor headed out.

"Well," Quint said, "we can't make any judgments until we know who and how, but in preparation, we need to immerse ourselves in Malachi's unsolved list to refamiliarize ourselves with the crimes and details. Let's convene in Crucifixion Thorn. I'll get the list."

"I know that Malachi is investigating other possible unsolved crimes that he didn't have on his original list," Raine said, "so why don't I head over to Saguaro Western and have a talk with him? You can call me there when you have any details from Cornell."

"Good idea," Deliverance said. "At the risk of appearing like an executive assistant, I'll make a fresh pot of coffee." Deliverance had gotten her provisional private investigator's license a month earlier and still hadn't stopped flaunting it in everyone's faces. All the partners and associates had name plaques on their desks with just their names emblazoned in gold. Hers said, "Deliverance Dane-Quintana, P.I." She said if it was good enough for Magnum, it was good enough for her.

"Later, mates," Raine said as she left the office.

Traffic was heavy, and it took Raine twenty-five minutes to pull into the college garage. It was only ten-thirty and there were just a few students pulling in and parking. She checked her briefcase by habit, then got out of the car and locked the door.

That was the last thing she remembered before the sap crashed across the back of her skull and she dropped to the ground unconscious. Two men quickly carried her off a few yards where they'd parked their car—left running—and stuffed her and her briefcase in the trunk. They screeched off, nearly running over a young coed who had to jump to get out of their way.

The Stalker smiled as he drove. Target acquired.

Raine moaned, her voice muted by the gag in her mouth, her sight negated by a tight blindfold. Her head was wracked with excruciating pain. Her back ached. She forced herself to focus and realized that her hands and feet were bound, and she was lying on something hard; a floor. At least she was still clothed.

Wherever she was it was cool, and she heard distant sounds—birds and crickets. No indications of people or cars. She was in a house of some sort. Suddenly, her whole body clenched—she wasn't alone. She could hear light, even breathing. A second later her assumption was validated—a savage boot kicked her in the hip, sending her tumbling over on her stomach. Another kick and she was on her back again.

With stunning ferocity and power, a strong hand wrapped itself with her long hair and dragged her upright. Hot, fetid breath blasted her face just before a stunning blow sent her crashing back to the floor. She immediately rolled over and over trying to get away from the man, but he grabbed her hair again and dragged her across the floor. She screamed behind her gag and kicked her legs and twisted her torso trying to free herself. A sickening, fathomless fear gripped every cell in her body as she tried to keep her stomach away from the blistering attack.

Oh, baby, baby, baby, she wailed in her head as her bladder let loose a hot stream of urine. She hadn't told Constantine yet that she was carrying his son or daughter and she prayed that she'd live to tell him and that their baby would be all right. Then the heavy silence of the room was broken.

"I told you I'd bloody come for you someday, bitch," a sibilant voice hissed, every word, every tone saturated by animosity and madness.

She recognized the voice and the madness. She screamed and screamed behind the gag, knowing that Constantine's baby and its mother were doomed.

CHAPTER SIXTEEN

"No, Quint. She hasn't arrived yet," Malachi Dillinger said into the phone. Bliss was sitting on his desk, legs crossed, swinging one salaciously. "When was she supposed to get here?" He listened as his brows drew together. "That's three hours ago. Look. Maybe she went to see her boyfriend first and got entangled. I'll check with him and call you back."

Malachi hung up the phone and looked at his wife, whose come-hither look had changed to one of concern.

"What's wrong?" she asked.

Malachi leaned back in his chair. "Raine was coming over here to go over my updated list of unsolved cases. She should have been here three hours ago." Without another word he dialed Constantine's number and asked him to come to his office. Constantine arrived quickly and looked at his friends.

"What's up?" he asked.

"Has Raine been in to see you today?" Bliss asked.

"Here? At the college? No, why?"

Bliss and Malachi looked at one another. They both got a feeling of dread at the same time.

"When did you last see her?" Malachi asked.

"This morning when she left for work. What's this all about?" Constantine asked tersely.

"Um, Raine was headed over here to discuss my list."

"And?"

"And that was three hours ago. She hasn't turned up. I thought she might be with you."

Constantine stiffened and narrowed his eyes. "Did you call Union Jack?"

"They called me and asked if she was here. That was just before I called you."

"Look," Bliss said. "Let's check the parking garage and see if her car's here." She'd barely gotten the last word out when Constantine whirled around and headed into the hallway. The Dillingers followed him to the stairs which he was pounding down like a gazelle fleeing a hungry lion. He burst out of the building and ran towards the garage with Bliss and Malachi hot on his heels. He pushed open the heavy door and entered the ground level.

The three professors split up and walked aisle by aisle on the first level looking for Raine's car. They found nothing, then took the stairs to the second level and split up again. After a few minutes Bliss yelled out, "Over here."

Malachi and Constantine came running to where Bliss was standing next to Raine's car. She was staring inside but saw nothing out of the ordinary. She tried the driver's door; it was locked. They circled it and looked for anything out of place but saw nothing. Then, Malachi knelt and looked under the car. He reached under and stood up with a set of car keys in his hand. He handed them to Constantine.

"These hers?" Malachi asked.

Constantine nodded. He walked to the back of the car and stood trembling for just a few seconds before he took a deep breath and opened the trunk. He exhaled loudly—no body, no blood.

Malachi patted him on the back and said, "We need to call Quint back."

"He took her," Constantine whispered. "The Beguiler."

"We don't know that, honey," Bliss said soothingly. Even to her ears the denial rang false.

"Let's go and call him now," Malachi said as he gently urged Constantine towards the exit.

A half hour later they were standing in the same spot along with all the Union Jack partners and Belzer. Victor was snapping photos from every angle as they waited for detectives Cornell and Baxter.

"He must have come up behind her and coldcocked her," Quint said. He suddenly realized that this section of the garage had just been renovated—it was where Munch met his doom and Cress and other innocents were injured. He wondered if the kidnapper had chosen this area specifically or if it was just the luck of the draw that Raine had parked here.

"No trace of blood, though," Deliverance said. "That's promising." She put a comforting hand on Wilde's arm. "We have to assume the best and act on that."

Wilde pulled away from her, his face a mask of anguish and

fury. "The fucker's decapitated two people, butchered three others, and kidnapped Laurel Bollmeier. There's no reason to think that any measure of mercy is on his bloody dinner menu," he spat out. He suddenly caught the pain on Constantine's face and relented. "But, you're right. We can act, and we can hope."

Cornell pulled up in his unmarked car and got out with Baxter trailing him. He shook Quint's hand tautly. "The forensics team is on their way. We're keeping this off the airwaves and under wraps for the time being. We still don't know if this was foul play or not." He caught the furious looks on Wilde's and Constantine's faces. "Look. Right now, there really is no evidence that she went anywhere except of her own accord. She's an adult, and we can't classify her as a missing person for twenty-four hours. Nevertheless, we're going to act on that assumption right now."

"What can we do to help?" Victor asked.

"I assume you brought photos of Raine, right?"

"Right," Quint acknowledged. "You want us to start canvassing?"

"Yes, right away. Split up between the buildings and the quadrangle. I—"

"Is everything okay here?" A young pair of college students was standing about twenty feet away, each holding four or five books in their arms. They looked nervous.

"Yeah, everything's fine," Cornell said. "Who are you?" He flashed his badge.

"Um, I'm Serene Galloway and this is Sam Restin. He's my boyfriend. Did that car get damaged?"

"What do you mean?" Baxter snapped.

"Well, I … I just mean that some guy sped outa here a few hours ago and nearly hit me. Son of a bitch swerved and just kept going. I think he was coming from this level or the third deck," Serene said.

"Could you see who was in the car?" Wilde said anxiously. "Was it a woman?"

"Um, I don't … I don't think so. I didn't really get a good look. I just saw someone behind the wheel."

"Anyone in the passenger side?" Victor asked.

"I ... I don't know."

"Can you describe the car?" Cornell asked.

"Maybe. I think it was dark blue. Maybe black?"

"Two-door? Four-door?"

"I don't know," Serene said. She was ready to break down under the questioning from all these strange people standing around the car.

"It's okay, honey," Deliverance said, taking her hand. "Just take a deep breath and think, and then you can answer a few more questions."

"Why don't you go with Detective Baxter here and give him a preliminary statement. That would be very helpful," Cornell said gently. Baxter could be gruff—like the late detective Munch—but he had a calming effect on witnesses and was known to elicit details that no one else could. He nodded to Baxter who politely asked the two students to join him by the stairwell.

"Okay," Quint said. "Deliverance and I will take building one. Wilde, you and Victor take building two. Belzer, three."

"Bliss and I will take the quadrangle and the caf area," Malachi said as Quint handed him a photo of Raine.

"Where do you want me?" Constantine asked tightly.

"You come with us," Deliverance said. She addressed Malachi. "Call our crew and get them all out here. Don't elaborate—just make it clear they're to be here immediately. And call Tucker and have him pull all the kids out of school and have them stay with him at our place. Tell him to bring his gun."

Just as the Union Jackers broke off to canvas Pete Murphy and his forensics team rolled in and parked. By that time a dozen students had gathered twenty feet away and were watching the scene closely. Murphy walked over to Cornell.

"What's the deal?" Murphy said.

Cornell answered tensely. "Possible—probable—kidnapping by the Beguiler. This time it's closer to home—Raine Sinclair, Wilde's niece. This is her car and she's been missing for four hours." He handed the car keys to Murphy. "I know you're the best, Pete, and I need this car and area analyzed centimeter by centimeter." He noticed the distant look on Murphy's face. "You okay?" Cornell asked.

"Yeah, fine," Murphy replied. "I'm just surprised that the Beguiler would kidnap a second woman. Not his style."

"His 'style' is insanity, so this fits right in," Cornell said. "After you finish here have the car towed to the impound lot and bring a second team in to re-do the forensics."

"Excuse me?" Murphy said, surprised. "I hope you're not doubting our capabilities." There was an unmistakable resentment in his tone.

"Not in a million years," Cornell said firmly. "I just want everything done to perfection. Call me paranoid, but we're really nowhere with the investigation and this may lead to a clue about who and what our perp is."

"Got it," Murphy said as he signaled his team of two to come over. He gave them their assignments and the three of them began scouring the car and nearby area for any evidence. Cornell and Baxter corralled the students and began showing them Raine's photo and asking if anyone had seen her.

Phaedra smiled at her customer after giving the "Noo Yawk" woman her change and the lady left happily carrying her gift box of an intricate squash blossom necklace and earrings set, a virtual masterpiece that Moon Wolf had created only a week earlier. Her husband had been working nonstop to create an enticing new line of jewelry that he hoped would bring more new and old customers back into the gallery. A few old customers had returned, ashamed that they had abandoned their favorite silver artist after his brief brush with notoriety when he was a suspect in the hitchhikers' murder. The uptick in his renewed and growing popularity was helped by an article in the *Southwest Galleries* magazine, which bumped up the typical number of photos, giving Moon Wolf a featured three-page spread.

"Got to admit," Cress said as he finished the last vestiges of a Reuben, "that was one fine necklace. Inspired that you used rhodochrosite instead of turquoise."

"Pink's a popular color," Moon Wolf said as he crunched on a potato chip. "That white lady will be the star in her next garden party."

"Great," Cress groused. "Now I'll have that Ricky Nelson tune stuck in my head all day."

Phaedra crooned, "Yoko brought a walrus ..." She stopped and laughed at the look on her brother's face.

The front door jangled as Gray came in. Before walking any farther, he turned the Open sign to Closed and locked the door. There was no mistaking the tense look on his face.

"What's wrong?" Cress asked right away. He knew his life partner's body language all too well. He immediately jumped to conclusions. "Is it Pugsley? Is he all right?"

Gray waved his hand. "He's fine. This is something different. Constantine blew into my office a short while ago, barely keeping it together." He took a deep breath. "It looks like Raine was abducted."

"Oh, God, no," Phaedra exclaimed. "Is he sure?"

Gray summarized what his brother-in-law had told him. His audience's faces drained of color and Phaedra's eyes were brimming with tears. She was shaking her head and clutching her husband whose arms were wrapped around her. Moon Wolf's jaw was set hard and his eyes were fiery.

"So, he's helping in the campus search," Gray said. "He doesn't want any of us involved but did want us to know what was happening in case we need to take precautions." He'd barely gotten out the last sentence when Moon Wolf was on the phone calling his cousin Yellow Coyote, who was more or less the black sheep of the Begay family (there were quite a few on the vast spectrum of grey). He sold drugs and used strong-arm tactics for his "collection" activities, but he was devoted to family. Moon Wolf told him to head over to their house and watch the children. Yes, he could bring a few "friends," and Moon Wolf would explain everything when they got home. He told Yellow Coyote to pack a couple of bags for each child—they were going on a trip. Then he hung up.

"We're going on a trip?" Phaedra asked.

"Yeah," Moon Wolf said flatly. "We're going east to visit your parents for a few weeks, maybe more."

"What about our business?"

"Fuck the business. This is about protecting our family, and I want you and our kids as far away from this insanity as possible."

"But my brother—"

"I love your brother too—even though he sure as hell doesn't make it easy—but this is our kids' safety, and nothing comes before that. *Nothing.*"

Phaedra nodded sadly and looked at Cress.

"He's right," Cress said. "Big Brother will understand. I'm staying, and I'll keep you up to date on any developments. Who knows? It could … it could turn out fine." No one outwardly agreed with him. No one believed that.

The rest of the day was a flurry activity with everyone rushing about either trying to solve the apparent kidnapping of Raine Sinclair or making arrangements to get out the vortex of danger that had engulfed the large circle of family and friends.

While Phaedra was arranging for her college student intern to keep the gallery open on a part-time basis and pay the bills from the business account, Moon Wolf was making a travel agent's life horrible by standing in her office and demanding that she make flight reservations to the New Orleans airport that very day. The harried woman was practically quaking when she finally put down the phone and babbled that she'd gotten seats for the family on an Eastern flight out of Tucson at 9 PM, connecting in Dallas after a two-hour layover, then in Miami after an hour's layover, arriving in New Orleans at eight in the morning. Moon Wolf fished out his Master Charge and the woman printed out his tickets and breathed a deep sigh of relief when he left her office.

His wife was on her way home and he met her there, managing to crack a smile when he saw his long-haired, long-bearded, leather-clad, heavily tattooed cousin, Yellow Coyote, and a couple of his Hell's Angel-looking friends spread out in the living room with the kids. One of them was playing with Persa and seemed to be on the losing end of a game of checkers. There were six small suitcases packed with children's clothing and toys. Phaedra had arrived home twenty minutes earlier and had managed to pack three suitcases for herself and her husband. At 7 PM the Begays and their temporary "bodyguards" made the trip to Tucson International Airport and at eight-thirty boarded the flight. Phaedra had called her parents and the Makrises would pick them up at their final destination. Yellow Coyote headed north to drop off their dog at Cress's home.

It was inevitable that the crime would leak out, given the number of law enforcement people milling about the campus and the number of people who were interviewed. *Old Pueblo Sentinel* reporter Judie Sutphin took a page out of Laurel Bollmeier's professional tactics' portfolio and tried to shove her way past the crime scene tape in the garage while sticking a microphone from her cassette recorder in Detective Cornell's face. When that didn't work she rushed off when she spied Quint and Deliverance standing in the quadrangle talking to a couple of professors. She was a little hesitant about approaching Deliverance—she knew the story about Laurel's white suit and Deliverance's red cherry slushie—but she had a job to do and a ruined outfit was little enough to pay for a quote or even better, a scoop. Fortunately, Deliverance was cupless, but Quint's furious face made Judie back off in hopes of keeping her chaotic life for a few minutes longer. She might have ignored her concern except that professor Constantine Black Wolf's face was set in stone and with a look that absolutely made her body shiver.

Wilde and Victor scoured the campus to no avail, then went up to Malachi's office where Wilde broke down and sobbed in abject fear. He loved his niece. He had held her in his arms when she was an hour old and had watched her grow and thrive and endure hell and bounce back from the abyss only to be snatched once again into its depths. His body felt as frigid as an Alaskan glacier; his soul was screaming. Victor tried to comfort his life mate, but he knew that there was every probability that the monster who had taken Raine had no intention of letting her live. That wasn't the Beguiler's style.

Victor managed to calm Wilde down enough to still his trembling. Wilde stuttered that he needed to call his family back in England and let them know what was going on before they saw anything about it in the news. Victor held Wilde's hand after he talked to his father, who was devastated at the turn of events. Davey said he'd talk to the rest of the family and that someone would be on the first plane to "the colonies."

Daylight turned to night and by that time it was out in the open that another woman closely associated with the unsolved murders' case had been abducted. Reporter Judie Sutphin had blazed like lightning on her computer keyboard and whipped out a scoop that *Sentinel* publisher Santiano Bronson splashed across a special evening edition of his newspaper: *The Beguiler Strikes Again!* The rumors and then that edition prompted yet another onslaught of salivating media people against the investigators and the academics who had been targeted in the current suite of murders as well as the ones from six years ago.

Cress and Gray wanted Constantine to move in with them for the duration, but he decided to impose himself on the Dane-Quintana family so that he'd be in the middle of any news that might arise. Deliverance moved Alex into Vikki's room and gave Constantine the boy's room. Since they had installed bunk beds in Alex's room for when he'd have a friend over for a sleepover, they had Tucker move in as well rather than having the family separated. It was a crowded household but a safer one in everyone's minds. Iris had been sent back to Phoenix the week before, so she wasn't a factor.

No one except the children slept the first night; the same with the second night. The minutes crawled by like hours, bringing with each one the sickening certainty that Raine was no longer amongst the living. Raine's father, Wilde's brother Danny, had arrived and bunked in with Wilde and Victor. Victor kept his boys home from school the first day, then stayed in his car watching the school the next day, unwilling to allow anything or anyone to slip by him and get to the kids.

On the fourth day the media still hadn't subsided and massed when Detectives Cornell and Baxter pulled up in front of the Dane-Quintana house. They shoved past "those fuckin' parasites" (as Baxter called them) and entered the crowded house. Baxter was wearing a sly grin—he had "accidentally" stepped hard on Judie Sutphin's foot as he elbowed past her.

"Pricks," Baxter grumbled as Quint slammed the door shut. The detectives followed him into the kitchen where the vertical blinds were drawn to keep out the prying eyes circling the property. Tucker and the kids were nowhere in sight, but Cornell could hear them in the other side of the house. All the adults were spread out in the kitchen, bleary-eyed, sipping coffee and forcing themselves to eat snippets of leftover food. Cornell noticed Wilde's brother, a man close to fifty who looked very much like him, a tall redhead with dark blue eyes that may once have been sparkling but were now dull. Danny's face was drawn and stubbled with an unshaved red and silver beard.

"Anything?" Constantine asked anxiously.

"Yes and no," Cornell said. "We haven't found any trace of Raine or her abductor, but we have heard from the Beguiler."

"What!" was the simultaneous exclamation from nearly everyone. They all began talking at once, but Cornell held up a hand and withdrew a note from his jacket. "This is a copy of what was delivered to the station today." He handed it to Quint and everyone crowded around him to read the note that was very carefully typed (clearly on a regular typewriter and not printed on a dot-matrix printer), succinct, and to the point.

My Dear Adversaries,

Although it is not my style to publicize my efforts—as spectacular as they are—I must correct what it clearly your inaccurate assumption of this latest development. I will state now and for the record that I had nothing to do with the abduction of Raine Sinclair. Period. Were her situation the results of my efforts I would gladly take credit, but such is not the case. You will have to look elsewhere for your answers.

But stay tuned, my friends—I am not done yet. No, not by a long shot …

Warmest Wishes,
The Beguiler (I say—I do love that nickname!) ☺

"This could be just some sick distraction from one of the vast number of ghouls out there, trying to sandbag the investigation," Belzer said. "We've seen that before."

"True," Cornell agreed. "But the note didn't arrive alone." He took a plastic evidence bag out of his pocket and held it up. "Laurel Bollmeier's watch."

"Then he could be telling the truth," Victor said quietly.

"Yes," Deliverance said in an equally hushed tone. "But that means—"

"—that we've got another psycho out there," Quint finished.

The kitchen went silent as all absorbed the horror of that implication.

CHAPTER SEVENTEEN

Quint and Wilde had pulled the round patio wrought iron table inside, which was now taking up a large space in the kitchen dining area. It was set up for the six kids while the regular table and breakfast bar were set up for the eight adults. Deliverance had taken a modicum of pity on the media camped outside in hopes of a photo or soundbite and had baked a couple of trays of brownies. They descended on her like a plague of locusts when she took them out, and she regretted not taking Tucker's suggestion that she add a packet of Ex-Lax to the mix before she baked.

When she got back Quint was making another pot of coffee and Tucker was mixing corn muffin batter. Everyone had glum expressions and the chatter was at a minimum. Deliverance knew she'd have to take the reins of conversation if they were to make any progress; so far, the police and FBI were making none. She shooed the children into the living room after they'd finished eating.

"Look, people," she began. "If it's true that the Beguiler isn't responsible—and I'm kind of thinking he isn't—then we need to figure out who this psycho is and what he wants. I mean, why Raine? Was she an object of opportunity or was she the actual target?" She looked at Wilde. "Does she have any enemies?"

"Of course she doesn't," Constantine answered angrily. "You know her. That woman's a decent person. Who could want to hurt her?" His tone demanded no dissension. Then he noticed a look that passed between Wilde and Danny. "What?" he barked, his last nerves unraveling.

"Wilde?" Quint said. "Look. We all have secrets, things in our past that we'd prefer to keep hidden. But if there's anything in Raine's life that might have some bearing on this situation, we have to know."

"I don't … I don't think it has anything to do with this but you're right—let's talk about it." He turned to his brother. "Danny? You okay with this?"

Danny Sinclair's jaw hardened, but he shook his head in resignation. "Tell them."

Deliverance handed Wilde a cup of fresh coffee and he took a sip before beginning.

"You remember when we were celebrating Raine's 21st birthday back in Brighton, right after your wedding?" Quint and Deliverance nodded. "She'd come down from Cambridge for the occasion."

"We all had ale and fish and chips at The Druid's Head," Deliverance said. "You know, she seemed pretty happy, but every so often there was a look of ... I don't know—sadness on her face."

Wilde nodded. "She was going through something. Let me go back to the beginning. In Raine's second year she met an older grad student, a guy who was smart, handsome, and charming. He was studying medicine, and it wasn't long before she was head over heels for the guy. His name was Earle, but he called himself Barry. Said Earle made him sound too much of a nob. He treated her like a queen and by the time she'd started her third year they'd moved in together in a small studio apartment close to campus. They visited the family twice and everyone seemed to like him."

"I never fully trusted him," Danny said quietly. "I wish I'd listened to my instincts."

"What didn't you like about him?" Victor asked.

"He was too perfect. There was this ... cloyingness about him. I made the mistake of pushing my suspicions away until it was too late."

"I wasn't around at the time, so I'd never met him." Wilde said. "I never even saw a picture of him until it was all over. So, after they moved in together he began to change. He got possessive and controlling, and I know they fought a lot." He paused, a look of guilt pasted across his drawn face. "I should have ... I should have investigated him. Done a background check. Something." He looked at his brother compassionately. "Danny, I think you should fill in the rest."

Danny nodded. "When Raine called or came home for a visit she seemed different, and she tried to blow off any suspicion that things might not be well with them. But I knew things weren't right. I knew. I finally got her to admit that he'd been verbally and physically abusive and that she'd decided to break it off."

"He hit her?" Constantine asked icily. His hands trembled at the thought of the woman he loved being subjected to physical abuse.

"Twice," Danny confirmed, "but it was just before she came down that the second occurrence took place. After she went home from that birthday party she packed her stuff and moved out. I gave her the money for a small flat and she moved in there a few nights later. He called her at least twenty times a day until she had her phone shut off. He turned up at her classes until she finally called security and they threw him off campus. By that time, he'd stopped going to his own classes and made his life's work the bloody stalking of my daughter."

"Jesus," Quint breathed.

"Then after a few weeks he simply stopped. No calls, no visits, no sightings. Raine finally could breathe and move forward with her life. She hadn't started dating again and said she didn't even want to, but she went to a few events with her girlfriends and began living life normally. She was a semester shy when it happened."

"He came back," Quint stated.

"With a vengeance," Danny replied in barely a whisper. "I'll never forget the night her mum and I got the call from the police in Cambridge. The hospital there was two hundred kilometers away and we made it in three hours. When we got to the Intensive Care Unit and identified ourselves to the doctors and police, they let us in. We could barely recognize her," Danny sobbed, breaking down in his brother's arms. Deliverance encircled his back with her arms and let the man sob himself out before he could continue. Constantine didn't know yet what happened, but he was crying, too.

Danny managed to calm down and drank a glass of water that Victor handed him. He nodded, then went on.

"She was sleeping after midnight when he broke into her flat. He beat her savagely and he … he … raped her. He nearly killed her before someone in a neighboring flat heard the commotion and called the police. He fled, they found her barely breathing, and they rushed her to the hospital. She was in a coma for two days before she regained consciousness and could speak. The police put out a bulletin and a day later he was apprehended near the Scottish border at Newcastle-upon-Tyne. Put up a hell of a fight and injured two policemen.

"Raine was in the hospital for a month. Her jaw was broken

and wired shut, her left wrist was broken, and she had eight broken ribs. Her face was unrecognizable for the first week and we were afraid that she would lose her right eye. Thankfully, she recovered enough for us to take her home. But it wasn't over." Danny was breathing heavily at that point.

"This Barry asshole was in jail, though, right?" Belzer asked.

"Yeah, he was," Danny said.

"What happened?" Constantine asked, hanging on every word, planning in his head how he was going to find that guy someday and tear him apart.

Danny took a deep breath. "Raine became pregnant from the rape."

"Oh, shit," Quint said, shaking his head.

"Yeah," Wilde agreed. "Oh, shit."

"She had barely recovered and then that comes along. She made the only decision she could, and we all supported her."

"She had an abortion," Deliverance surmised.

"Fortunately, the UK's Abortion Act of 1967 was in effect, and we had two family doctors sign a statement that read that the termination of her pregnancy was necessary to prevent grave permanent injury to her mental health. She was eight weeks gone when the operation was performed. She spent the first eight months of 1982 getting her physical and mental strength back, then went on to her last semester in Cambridge and got her degree."

"What about the bastard that raped her?" Tucker asked.

"A scum-sucking piece of shyte barrister dug up a lot of incidents from his past that you'd think would put the nails in his coffin, like assaults against two other girls he stalked while a teenager and at least a dozen incidents of vandalism and arson. Raine's testimony in court was heart-wrenching, especially when the barrister tried to turn things around and put her on trial. But she was strong and faced him down in court. Never prouder of my girl. The shyte got the dolts on the jury to find him not guilty by reason of insanity and he was committed to a hospital for the criminally insane.

"Meanwhile, although Raine recovered physically from her ordeal she was still having a devil of a time coping with it emotionally. She began seeing a therapist, who eventually suggested that perhaps a radical change of environment might assist in her healing. She considered France and Australia but decided to stop in on her favorite uncle and his Yank friends for a few weeks." Danny managed a sort of smile. "So much for a few weeks."

"The first thing we need to do is make sure that Barry is still incarcerated in the looney bin, so we can rule him out. Anyone else similar in her past?" Quint said.

Wilde shook his head. "No one." He glanced over at the kitchen clock. "It's nine-thirty here, so that means it's four-thirty back home. I'll call Mum and have her find the number for that looney bin." Wilde left the house for his own where he closeted himself in his den and rang up his mother.

While he was gone Quint dived into the possibilities if Barry was the abductor or if it was someone else. In either case, where would he take her?

Wilde came back twenty minutes later, his face as white as a sheet. "The fucking morons on the hospital board gave him a furlough in January to attend his mother's funeral. He didn't come back. And even though they have a warrant out for him somehow notifying the family slipped through the cracks."

Danny nearly exploded. "That bastard's on the loose? My *God*!"

"Mum said the coppers said that there was no indication that he left the country. At least his passport wasn't used."

"Getting a phony passport and ID is a piece of cake," Victor said.

"So, this guy's a definite possibility," Deliverance added. She handed Tucker the pitcher of orange juice to put in the fridge.

"Yeah," Wilde said bitterly. "Earle Baron Kensington is definitely on our radar." A loud crash followed his pronouncement and all eyes turned on Tucker, who had dropped the glass pitcher on the floor as he stood rigid, his jaw open in stunned disbelief.

"Tuck—whatever's wrong?" Deliverance asked as she rushed to get a roll of paper towels.

"Earle Baron Kensington?" Tucker choked out. "Oh, my God …"

"What? What is it?" Quint demanded.

Tucker stared at Wilde intently. "What … what does he look like?"

"Tall, six-three maybe, blond hair, blue eyes—what?"

"Kenny Barron," Tucker whispered in shock. His eyes were wild. "The guy … the guy I was seeing before Iris."

"Baron Kensington. Kenny Barron. Mon dieu," Victor exclaimed.

Wilde grabbed Tucker by the upper arms. "Tucker—think! Did he ever give you the impression he was interested in Raine?"

Tucker shook his head. "No, never. I mean, he was interested in me and my life. I never talked about Raine or anyone else in depth. I wanted to keep those details private." He tensed. "Once in a while his speech changed just enough to make me think he was from or had lived in another country, but usually that gaff came and went in seconds. When I mentioned it, he said he'd spent his teenage years in Australia and had picked up an accent there. I thought it was … charming."

"He must have been stalking Raine and wormed his way into her world on the sidelines by inserting himself into Tucker's life," Quint said. "Tucker—did you ever go to his place?"

Tucker shook his head. "No. He said he had a roommate, so we usually met here or someplace else private." Tucker brightened. "But I know his address. I saw it on his driver's license one time when he paid for drinks." He rattled off the address on a side street off Broadway.

Quint pointed to his wife. "Del, call Cornell and give him the twenty. Tell him he needs a search warrant. We're headed there now."

As Deliverance dialed, the rest of the men—except Tucker—poured out of the house and into two cars that screeched off towards their destination.

The apartment complex was on a busy side street, the building three stories of weathered brick. Quint, Wilde, Victor, and Belzer drew their weapons with an unarmed Danny and Constantine bringing up the rear as they quietly climbed the staircase. They reached apartment 2B and fanned out around the door. Quint knocked and said hello. No response, and he tried again.

"We should wait for Cornell," Belzer said.

"Screw that," Constantine said, then shoved Quint away from the door and kicked it in. He entered and over his head Quint said to Victor, "He'd make a good P.I."

The apartment was a studio, one large room with a tiny kitchenette and a single window on one side. A closet-sized bathroom was off to one side, the general layout unremarkable.

What was remarkable—stunning, even—was the décor.

Every single wall was covered with candid photos of Raine and quite a few of the people in her life both in Tucson and back in England. There were newspaper articles plastered on the wall as well. Dozens of the photos were slashed and sections of her face blacked out, especially her eyes. Several shots of Raine had knives stabbed into them, piercing the walls and sticking straight out. On the west side the photos surrounded an open space of wall on which was written in red paint, "DIE BITCH DIE!!!!" In the middle of a particularly full wall of hate Victor saw two photos and an article that had nothing to do with Raine. He stared at the photos of two young girls, the names Maisie Harrington and Davina Brockwell scratched in ink on their bottom edges. The article mentioned that there were no clues or arrests forthcoming in the murders of the two girls. The newspaper was the *Bury St Edmunds Bee*, dated August 2, 1981.

There was a small table shoved up against one wall. Resting on it were knives, a blowtorch, and a jar of acid. Victor picked up a piece of paper and showed it to Quint.

"Looks like Raine isn't the only one on his hit list." The notepaper listed, in order, Raine, Wilde, Victor, Constantine, Tucker, and Iris. Next to each name was drawn a skull and crossbones.

Another small table was made up to look like an altar, with half-burnt candles and an eight-by-ten photo of Raine on which rested a pile of red hair, a knife thrust so deeply into the hair, photo, and table that half the blade was hidden.

Wilde lightly touched the hair and turned to his friends. "Did I mention he cut all her hair off in the attack? It never turned up."

Constantine touched the hair lightly, his face absolutely expressionless. For the first time in years he felt that frightening beginning of a migraine, but he vowed he wouldn't black out—the life of the woman he loved was at stake.

CHAPTER EIGHTEEN

"There's no discussion, here, Flynn," SSA Steve Shaeffer boomed out loud enough for other people in the FBI Phoenix office to hear him through his closed office door. There was a soundproofed window looking out on the bullpen, and other agents were trying not to be too obvious when they managed a glance at the two people arguing inside.

"You don't get to choose where you go—your superiors do." He was standing behind his desk, and he leaned forward and slapped his hands down, glaring at Iris with as much menace as the little man could muster. "So, get your ass packed and get on that flight tomorrow for Cheyenne." His thin lips curled in derision and satisfaction. "You'll have plenty of time to pick up some parkas for the upcoming winter. Adios." He sat down and proceeded to ignore the furious woman that was standing in front of his desk.

Iris stared down at her immediate superior in utter disbelief. He had just given her a barely-meets-requirements performance evaluation and told her that he was transferring her to the Wyoming field office—now. Besides the location, the so-called indefinite assignment couldn't have come at a worse time, when Raine Sinclair, her best friend, had been kidnapped. Tucker had called her that morning to update her on the person they believed had abducted Raine and the reasons why. Iris's heart bled for Raine's painful past, and her first impulse was to drive down to Tucson and help in the search. She had requested a leave of absence from Shaeffer. He had responded with the bad evaluation and the papers transferring her to the middle of nowhere. She could fight both, of course, but she'd have to do it from Cheyenne if she wanted to keep her job.

She turned slowly and walked to the door. She opened it.

Four hours later Tucker opened the front door of the house to find Iris Flynn standing there with her cat in her arms and a duffel bag in her hand. She came inside and threw her arms around him and kissed him for all she was worth.

Tucker pulled back afterwards, surprised but ecstatic. "What are you doing here?" he asked, completely unaware that the four

Dane-Quintana children were gathered around him, staring up at the two people who had kissed like they were in a movie.

"I had to make a choice," she replied. "It was either keep my career and wind up in a cold, wintry, wild-west town dating men with cowboy boots, sheepskin coats, and chewin' tobaccy in their ruddy cheeks, or come down here and be with the people I care about—and find my best friend. Best friend outside of you, of course."

"What about your job? They let you come here?"

"Pretty sure after I threw a chair through my boss's office window and told him to shove his orders up his fat, hairy, dwarf-like, mentally deficient ass that my career has pretty much run its course."

"You didn't!" Tucker exclaimed.

"I did. And after he stormed out to head up to the big boss's office, every damn person in that bullpen stood up and applauded."

"Right on, Iris," Storm yelled and stuck up her hand for a resounding high five. Storm looked disparagingly at Alex. "I *told* you she'd come back to find Raine." Alex stuck his tongue out at her. Juju was in his arms purring.

"I've got all I need for a few days in my bag," Iris said. "Should I take it to the casita?"

Tucker shook his head. "No, we're all cloistered in the main house for the duration. I'm bunking in with Alex, so I guess that means you'll have to make do with the couch for a while."

"I'm good with that."

"You can sleep in our room," Aislinn said. "Me and Storm can share my bed and you can have hers."

"You're giving away my bed?" Storm huffed.

"Zip it, Wild Child," Aislinn sniffed. "She's our friend."

"Yeah, okay, I guess," Storm said semi-sullenly.

"Have you been given your words for the day?" Iris asked. They all shook their heads no. "Okay. Aislinn—behavioral. Alex—habeas corpus. Vikki—court. And Storm—dissociation." Alex dropped the cat and they all ran off to the library to flip through the well-worn dictionary.

Iris put her hand on Tucker's shoulder. "You gave me the summary, but I want the whole story, no details left out. Any fresh coffee?"

"Fresh coffee and newly baked lemon poppyseed muffins." He led her into the kitchen and they sat down over their snack while Tucker filled her in on every gruesome detail. He showed her photos of Kenny's apartment and she was blown away by the dark obsession that came through from every image. She took a deep breath when he told her that both of their names were on his kill list.

"I imagine that the partners and the cops have grilled you about any conversations you had with Kenny?" she asked.

"Grilled to charcoal perfection. I'm your basic Vermont briquet."

"Well, I'm going to grill you, too. So, make a fresh pot of French Roast and let's get down to brass tacks." While he complied, she went into the living room to get her notebook. They sat for two hours as he relayed everything he could think of regarding his relationship with Kenny—rather, Earle Baron Kensington. There were very few details that he had forgotten, but a word or two extra came out under her incisive urging.

"So," Iris said, pen poised, "he was interested in the old ax murders but didn't unduly focus on them?"

Tucker nodded. "Right. I suggested that if he wanted to know more factual details he could read any of the books or newspaper articles put out afterwards. But I don't know if he ever pursued that. It's not like they had anything to do with Raine."

"Did he ever borrow any of the books on those events from this house or the casita?"

Tucker shook his head. "I have a couple that Deliverance gave me to brush up on the family's history, but they never left my house."

"Let's go look at them, just for the hell of it," Iris said, rising.

Tucker whistled loudly, and the four kids came barreling into the kitchen. "Road trip, guys," he said. "Off to the casita." A disappointed, simultaneous "Aw!" erupted but Tucker shushed them and led the way. He settled them down on the living room floor with a game of Trivial Pursuit, then pulled out the three books he had on the Axewoman of Tucson. He watched as Iris flipped through them, hmm-ing at certain places, ignoring some of the boring sections.

"This writer, Cruz Garcia, seems to have the best style."

She scowled. "Laurel Bollmeier seems to mistake purple prose for legitimate writing."

"Once the novelty and interest wore off she didn't sell many books," Tucker said as he took *Killer Across Time* from Iris and absently flipped through it. He stared at the full-page color photo of Cheyenne LaChoisi. He couldn't reconcile the stunning young woman with the monster that had rained terror on an innocent city and a dozen victims. He thought about Cress and how she had almost killed her own brother when she kidnapped him and imprisoned him in that root cellar in a small cabin up in Summerhaven. While Iris was perusing the last book, he flipped to the section where Cress was found by Wilde and Gray. He froze suddenly; Iris noticed.

"What?" she demanded, her nerves on edge.

He showed her the page. "All the yellow highlighting on the cabin and where it was. I never mark up my books, and I'm sure this wasn't yellowed out when I first read it."

Iris read through a few pages that described the cabin, what it was like inside and outside, and that it was difficult to reach. She looked up at Tucker. "Whatever happened to the cabin?"

Tucker replied, "Deliverance said the dentist that owned it couldn't sell or rent it anymore, and the only visitors were ghoulish looky-loos that were excited about visiting a real crime scene. I guess after the flurry of interest it's just abandoned now. Probably's fallen into disrepair."

Iris was still and thoughtful. She spoke slowly. "I wonder why the pages were marked?" She cocked her head at him. "I'm going up there." She held the book and started walking to the door when Tucker stopped her.

"You're not going alone," he said firmly.

"You can't leave the kids."

"I don't plan to. Just wait." He sat down on the couch and dialed Constantine's number and told him to come over immediately—they may have a lead. Constantine said he'd be there in ten minutes. Then Tucker made another call and spoke low and urgently to the man at the other end of the line. Finally, he relaxed and said, "Thank you, thank you, *thank* you!" He hung up and grinned at Iris. "Fifteen minutes and you can take off. Constantine will go with you."

"According to the notes in that book on the topographical map, the most direct way is through back roads that need a four-wheel drive. The Catalina Highway is cleaner but longer."

"Don't worry about that," Tucker said as he dialed Information. At her curious look he said, "I'm going to call the Sheriff's department to get someone out there asap." He connected with the Sheriff's office as Iris quickly changed into heavy jeans, an FBI sweatshirt, and hiking boots. She had just finished tying the left one when Constantine burst through the door. His face and eyes were wild and desperate. Iris jumped up and hugged him and blurted out what they were doing and why. She still had her government-issued gun and clamped it on her belt.

"We'll take my car," Constantine said.

"No need for that," Tucker drawled just as the sound of whirring helicopter blades grew closer and closer. Iris stared at him. He smiled. "Before the infamous Kenny I dated a helicopter pilot who does tours of the desert and mountains. He owes me a favor and I called it in." He swept his arm wide and Constantine and Iris ran out the back sliding doors to the astounding sight of a small helicopter landing in the Quintanas' back yard, blowing up a wild sandstorm of dirt and dust. The pilot set down and madly waved to them to get in.

Just before Iris pulled the door closed she leaned down to Tucker and whispered, "I love you." Seconds later the chopper ascended and headed northeast.

Tucker ran back to the casita and started calling Quint, Wilde, and everyone else. Ten minutes later Wilde and Victor careened into their street and flew out of the car and Tucker told them what was going on.

The cabin that had once held Cress LaChoisi as well as the corpses of two unlucky hikers had fallen into considerable disrepair over the years, but it still had its roof and four walls. The window glass had been shattered long ago, but the openings were boarded up tightly, and if anyone went inside they would see that the wall and windows were soundproofed with bubble wrap. There were signs all about the property warning off trespassers; a few were deliberately destroyed but several were still in good shape. The path that had once led from FR 10 at the edge of Summerhaven to the cabin was extremely overgrown, as were most of the forest bushes and flora that dotted the once pretty lot. Now, in October, there were fewer hikers and visitors in the Summerhaven area, but it was still warm enough to draw quite a few people. Virtually all of them walked past the beginning of the path since the story associated with the cabin had long been divested of general interest.

Inside the cabin was a rickety old metal bed, upon which Raine Sinclair was bound and gagged, naked. Her captor had removed her blindfold since he wanted her to see him, every inch of him as he affected his revenge on the woman that had sent him to the madhouse. He enjoyed the irony of keeping her prisoner in the same place where her uncle had helped free Cheyenne LaChoisi's victim, knowing that it was very unlikely that whoever was looking for her would consider the location a viable possibility. If they did, well, he'd have to finish up fast and scoot away into another new life. He had several phony passports and IDs, and money his mother had stashed in her closet before her death.

He was absent for the moment, having decided to travel back to his apartment and pick up the rest of his personal belongings before he concluded his mission. He'd left his car up in Summerhaven. He stroked her hot, damp thighs and murmured in her ear that he'd be back soon, and they could "make love" again. He had raped her three times since he brought her to the cabin. He kissed her swollen cheek and left the cabin.

As she had before when he had left for a short time she desperately twisted her wrist bonds, but they were plastic—not cloth—and they seemed unbreakable as they dug into her flesh and smeared her hands and forearms with blood. At least her badly swollen eyes had gone down so she could actually see.

Every inch of her body ached from his fists and feet, but at least she had managed to protect her stomach in the initial onslaught. She was sickened by the violent rapes, terrified that they'd cause a miscarriage, but so far, she felt none of what she thought would be the symptoms of that. His physical and emotional assaults were meant to break her down, but Barry had underestimated her will to live and fight back. She was determined not to die, not to give him the benefit of hearing her beg for her life. She was backpedaling a little on that last vow since she had two lives to think about, not just hers. If she didn't live, her baby wouldn't live.

She was covered with sweat, urine, and feces, and not a small amount of dried blood. Her stomach was growling from hunger, but she wouldn't try to indicate that to him. She wanted to keep the gag in her mouth so that he wouldn't ram his penis into it as he had tried before she screamed bloody murder and he gagged her to shut her up. She didn't trust herself to not bite him, which she knew would be tantamount to signing her death warrant.

She closed her eyes and forced herself to breathe as evenly as she could. She concentrated on something pleasant, the last time she was in bed with Constantine. His touch. His scent. His voice. His caressing hands. After the horror of Cambridge was over she thought she'd never let herself be vulnerable to any man ever again, and then Constantine came along with his own demons, his gruffness, his soft, gooey center (as Phaedra once ruminated). She knew he'd be devastated if she died, especially if he learned his baby had died along with her. History repeating itself, she thought. She didn't think that a second go-round of that horror would allow him to ever recover, to ever love again.

She twisted her wrists and ankles but without any success. She wondered when he'd be back. Perhaps she should try to work the gag off and scream for all she was worth. Dying wasn't the worst thing that could happen at this point. She moved her tongue and lips but had no luck. Then she heard a noise and froze. Someone was pounding towards the cabin, running hard. Her heart began to beat just as hard. The door burst open and—

Earle Baron Kensington stood in the doorway, wheezing, his face a mask of fury. She tensed for a split second, then accepted the inevitable—she was about to die. Her body felt light, as though it were floating. She heard an odd, distant noise like a hum but before she could focus Barry stood over her, a newspaper crushed in his hand. He held it up—the *Old Pueblo Sentinel*, with his picture and name on the front page, the headline stating that he was wanted for questioning in the Raine Sinclair abduction case.

"Looks like your bloody, fucking friends have uncovered

me, bitch," he snarled. "Guess I won't have much more time to finish teaching you your lesson." He whirled around, looking wildly for something. He strode over to his tools table where he kept the pliers he'd used to pinch her breasts and pull some of her groin hair out. Her long, red hair was scattered about the floor. He had cut it all off as he had years earlier, leaving her with bare fuzz on her scalp. Somewhere in the back of her mind it registered that the hum was growing louder. Was that other faint sound a siren?

He picked up a jar of acid. He turned towards her and grinned. "They'll have to use dental records to identify you since your face won't be of much help. I had planned on peeling it off with a paring knife, but I won't have the time." He noticed that she was trying to say something, so he pulled out her gag as he stood over her with his hand on the jar cover. "Any last words?" he asked sarcastically.

"Yes," she gasped. If she was going down now, she'd be going down with one last thrust of courage. She curled her swollen lips and spat out, "You're a fucking coward! Your mother should have aborted you like I did your rotten bastard. You're a piece of shyte and worth less than cesspool slime. You and the man I love are as different as pig slop and caviar. Your family jewels are paste, just like your soul. The worst mistake I ever made was to think of you as a decent human being. You're worthless. A cipher. *Nothing.*"

Barry's face was engorged with blood that made him look like he was wearing a vermillion mask. His eyes were popped out and his mouth was involuntarily moving like a gulping fish. Without warning he screamed at the top of his lungs and threw the acid jar against the wall, then jumped on Raine and began choking her.

The pain was excruciating as Raine's eyes rolled back in her head and she struggled to breathe. She was choking and gasping as his fingers tightened around her throat like a vise. Just when she thought she was done his hands fell away as someone pulled him off her and the two men tumbled to the floor. She opened her eyes and saw Iris's face above her and felt a knife cutting through the plastic ties. Iris pulled her up into a sitting position then turned around where she was momentarily numbed by the furious hand-to-hand fighting going on in the middle of the floor.

Constantine was on top of a prone Barry smashing his fist

like a jackhammer over and over again into Barry's jaw and face and skull. Blood was gushing from a smashed-flat nose and Barry's left eye had popped out of its socket and was hanging halfway down his cheek; his jaw was broken. Iris raised her gun and screamed at them to stop. She screamed again, and Constantine seemed to come back to reality from his furious vengeance against the man who had brutalized Raine. His fist was raised in the air, and he hesitated for a split second, enough time for the madman under him to draw back a leg and kick Constantine off him. Barry let out a roar of fury at the same time that he pulled a butcher knife from his belt and raised it to stab Constantine.

The small cabin was rocked with a loud retort as Iris fired her gun and hit Barry in the left shoulder. He was blown back a foot and stared at her in a mixture of hatred and disbelief, but instead of giving up he tried to stand upright and throw himself on her. The second bullet tore through his heart and he collapsed on the cabin floor, dead.

Constantine scrambled off the floor and rushed to Raine's side. He held her in his arms while she sobbed and kept saying his name over and over again. Iris handed him a blanket and he wrapped Raine in it then picked her up in his arms and tore out of the cabin. Iris stood over the dead man, relieved that he had tried to kill her, thus justifying the shooting. She smiled as she realized that she would have shot him dead anyway and made sure it looked like a justified shoot. Raine and Constantine would have backed her up. She acknowledged sadly that perhaps she didn't have the temperament to be an FBI agent. Oddly enough, that didn't bother her.

She swayed gently as the police siren wailed close by and the helicopter took off for the closest trauma hospital.

CHAPTER NINETEEN

The hospital room was dim and quiet except for the sounds of the machines hooked up to Raine to monitor her bodily functions. She was sleeping quietly and was in better shape than the myriad of bruises on her body would indicate. Her mother had arrived the night before and Mamie had gently shaved her head instead of leaving the uneven strands and stubble, crying at each sweep of the razor when she encountered another purple bruise on Raine's skull. Still, the doctors said that Raine was in serious but stable condition, and there was little doubt that she'd heal from all the physical torments; the psychological long-term effects were another matter and would require intensive therapy. She had slept for the first twelve hours but then awoke and was coherent, and even evinced a slight touch of humor when she compared herself to Kojak. Although the doctors and nurses tried valiantly to keep visitors out, her family and friends were constantly going in and out of the room. Her father and Constantine had slept by her bedside for the first night, and afterwards she was never in the room alone; someone was always on "Raine watch."

Currently, Iris was on watch, sitting beside the bed and quietly reading a novel while her best friend snoozed and occasionally snored. There was a police guard outside the door to keep any slimy media people away; Judie "Fuck Common Decency" Sutphin had tried to sneak in but was summarily tossed out of the hospital on her ear. Constantine would spell Iris in a half hour, and it was all anyone could do to keep him out of the room. Cress had physically removed him late the night before and forced him to sleep in his guest room.

Iris put down the book and studied her friend's face. The bruises would heal and there was no structural damage or brain trauma past a mild concussion; three teeth had been knocked out, but new ones could be implanted. Obviously, the fiend that had assaulted her wanted her conscious for his methodical torments. Raine had managed a few descriptive sentences but waved away any in-depth discussion until she felt better. Iris knew that Raine had been beaten and raped, but the details were confined to the doctors and her father, mother, and uncle. However, the doctors had told Raine something that seemed to put her in a peaceful, relieved state of mind; Iris wondered what that was.

Raine mumbled in her sleep and tried to turn on her side, but Iris gently prevented that and Raine was still for a moment or two before her eyelids fluttered and she found herself staring into the smiling face of her best friend. She weakly raised her hand and Iris took it and kissed the palm.

"Nice to have you back amongst the living, girlfriend," Iris said as she pressed the button to raise the bed into a sitting position.

"Good to be here," Raine sighed. "Didn't think that was going to happen." She twisted her head to look around. "Mum here?"

"Your dad took her home to sleep. They'll be back first thing in the morning, but your boyfriend will be here soon."

A strange look passed over Raine's face at the mention of Constantine.

"What?" Iris asked.

"I just wish he didn't have to see me in this shape. Must have been horrifying for him."

"Sweetie, just like everyone else the only thing that matters is that you're alive. Everything else will fall into place. I guarantee it." Iris glanced up to see Constantine standing at the door. She nearly burst out laughing when she saw his brand new 'do—he had completely shaved his head, obviously to be simpatico with his bald girlfriend. She had to admit—with the clean scalp and the goatee he was growing, he looked rather devilishly handsome. She rose and kissed Raine on the forehead then said, "I'll be back tomorrow."

Constantine walked over to the bed, leaned down, and kissed Raine gently on her bruised lips. He held both of her hands in his as he carefully perched on the bed and gazed down on her, drinking in her living face. She saw that his face was drawn and there were bags under his eyes that denoted too little sleep. She reached up a shaking hand and brushed his cheek with her fingers.

"You saved me," she said softly.

Constantine forced a smile. "It was a joint effort. But—I confess—if I had to swoop in and carry off my lady fair there's no better way than in a red helicopter with the logo *Old Pueblo Chopper Tours.*" His smile faded suddenly. "I was so scared I was going to lose you," he whispered.

"Ditto," she said as her eyes suddenly brimmed with tears. Her lower lip was trembling when she said, "Nice shave job, Voodoo Man. You look like that guy from *Live and Let Die.*"

"Thought you'd like it," he said as he swept his hand across his skull and got off the bed. "Look—I wanted to do this in a different location and atmosphere, but maybe this is the perfect place." He drew himself up straight, then reached into his jacket pocket and withdrew a black ring box. He dropped down on one knee while she watched him with her mouth open.

He grinned at her. "Best I can do under the circumstances." He opened the ring box to show her an elaborate white-gold diamond ring with a center round stone of two carats surrounded by a cluster of pavé-set tiny black diamonds. "Raine Keaira Sinclair, will you do me the greatest honor by becoming my wife?"

Raine just stared at the ring in his hand, then looked up at him and saw the absolute love and honesty in his face. She burst into tears and nodded before saying, "I sure as hell will, you bloody git."

Constantine slipped the ring on her left hand and they put their arms around one another and kissed, sealing a deal that was a foregone conclusion.

When they broke apart Raine smiled as brightly as a thousand-watt bulb and said to her fiancé, "I have something to tell you."

Constantine looked down as she placed her hand gently over her stomach, then back at her face. She nodded.

"You are?" he said in awe.

"I am."

Wilde dropped his brother and sister-in-law off at the hospital and stayed for a few minutes to hug his niece. There was no mistaking the happiness on Raine's and Constantine's faces when they announced their engagement. Arabella shrieked and threw herself on her future son-in-law, and there were handshakes all around. Arabella's second shriek was twice as loud and ecstatic when Raine told them she was pregnant. Wilde left the family and drove back to the Union Jack offices, smiling for the first time in a week.

The lot was full; all the partners and associates were in residence. As he walked up to the front door he noticed a rental car and wondered if they had a new client. The new receptionist, Harrison Lowell, told him an older gentleman had come in a half hour earlier and Quint had come down to take him upstairs. Wilde headed up and found Deliverance in the upper reception area studying a few black-and-white photos. She looked up and smiled.

"How's Raine?" she asked.

"Better," Wilde said. "Her mum and dad are there with Constantine … her fiancé."

Deliverance whooped and jumped up and down. "Thank God she has something wonderful to focus on."

"Well, that's not the only thing they'll both be focusing on," Wilde said slyly, drawing the revelation out.

Deliverance scowled. "Spill, limey Brit."

He took her arm. "I'll 'spill,' Witchy Woman, when everyone else is gathered. I say—where are they? Do we have a new client?"

She shook her head. "A visitor, yes, but not a client. C'mon— follow me." She gathered up the photos and a folder and led him into the Devil Cholla Conference Room, the only clean one since the other two had been used 24/7 during the kidnapping situation and there were plates and leftover food and trash everywhere.

When Wilde entered the Devil Cholla Conference Room he found Victor, Quint, Cornell, and an older, tall gentleman that his impeccable radar had determined was another Brit. The man was in his fifties, at least six-two, with receding grey hair and wearing a dapper three-piece suit. Besides his ethnicity the man gave off the unmistakable aura of law enforcement. He took a few steps towards Wilde and extended his hand. Wilde noted that he had a very strong shake.

"I say—you must be Wilde Sinclair. Terribly glad to meet you. I'm Detective Constable Graeme Garrick. Bury St Edmunds."

Wilde nodded. "I recognize your name from that article in the *Bee*."

Cornell enlightened Wilde. "When we found those photos

and articles about the kidnapping-murders in England I called Detective Constable Garrick and updated him on our situation and the prospective kidnapper. He researched Kensington as a possible suspect in the murders of Maisie and Davina."

"Right," Garrick said. "Straightaway I found the missing links to our unsolved cases. My team found that Kensington attended Cambridge and after we showed his photo around a few business owners in Bury recognized him. Given his history with Miss Sinclair and additional crimes going back years he seemed like a very viable candidate for our kidnapper. We found quite a few interesting facts as we searched back in his family's history."

"And this pretty much sealed the deal," Cornell said as he took two small plastic evidence bags out of his pocket. They had been retrieved from "Kenny's" apartment, hidden under a loose floorboard. One bag contained a child's necklace with dice-shaped shell beads that spelled out M-A-I-S-I-E; the other contained a small cross necklace with a broken chain.

"Those belonged to the murdered children," Garrick said. "They were wearing them when they went missing."

"How sad," Deliverance said.

"Indeed," Garrick agreed. "But at least their parents will have some sort of closure and know that their daughters' killer isn't roaming the earth taking other innocent lives."

"Brilliant," Wilde exclaimed. "So, what's this about his family?"

"Apparently, Earle Baron Kensington II, his father, was as barmy as anyone who'd ever been confined to Bedlam. There were rumors as well as facts about his life as a youth, none of them good. He pretended to clean up his act after the war, married, and spawned four children, our Earle III being the youngest. Long story short, Earle II died in a prison cell and his wife moved away, changed her name, and married a decent man. Everyone's reminisces indicate that she was good woman and three of her children grew as upright citizens. Not Earle III. He eschewed his adoptive name and went back to his birth name. You've got the lay of the land from the happenstances with your niece and the trial. Now that we've filled in the blanks with his efforts of the last few years we can continue to backtrack and see if there are any other victims back home or here. I must say, I am eternally grateful that he didn't add that young woman to his list of dead bodies and that he never lived to have some sodding prat of a barrister try to mitigate his crimes."

"Dead is good," Victor agreed.

"I don't suppose that young woman who put two bullets in him is on the premises? I'd very much like to shake her hand," Garrick said.

Quint shook his head. "Nope, sorry. She's back at our place with our … nanny. When are you flying back to Heathrow?"

"Day after tomorrow. Detective Cornell, here, has promised me some time to get a few facts down later today, and tomorrow, well—I'm in the bloody colonies so I might as well see a bit of your snake-infested homeland while I have the chance."

"Well, then, you can meet Iris tonight at dinner. Seven?" Deliverance asked.

"That's right proper of you, madam. I'd be honored."

"Excellent. Then we'll treat you to the best foods the southwest has to offer. I'll write down directions. I'm sure you have a map but if you run into any trouble just call our home number," Deliverance said as she began scribbling down the directions from the office to the house.

Cornell spent a few minutes talking about the media coverage before he ushered Garrick out of the office. Deliverance immediately jumped from foot to foot as she grinned at Wilde. "Tell 'em."

"Raine's doing much better," Wilde said. "Her mum and dad are with her and—"

"She and Constantine are engaged," Deliverance shouted.

"That's fantastic," Victor exclaimed.

"Awesome," Quint added.

"You said there was something else?" Deliverance said to Wilde, her eyes narrowed as she dared him to hold out for any second longer.

"Oh, that," Wilde said as he slapped his forehead. "Yes, well, it seems that, um, in the not too distant future I'm going to become a granduncle." He was grinning ear to ear.

Deliverance shrieked, "She's pregnant! Oh, my God!"

For the first time in a long time the Union Jack partners were all genuinely happy and peaceful, if only for a brief time. They all knew that reality would come washing back over them.

There was still a deadly enemy out there ...

CHAPTER TWENTY

October 29, 1984, Tucson, Arizona

Pete Murphy was working late in the forensics lab. One of his newer junior techs was also burning the midnight oil but was doing so very quietly and without intruding on Pete's efforts and thoughts. Pete liked to work nights when it was peaceful and without too many prying eyes looking over his shoulder. His situation had gotten more intolerable ever since Ben Deuel had been giving dominion over the forensics department. That promotion should have been Pete's. He had seniority as well as talent, and he was devastated when he was passed over. Politics, it had to be all about politics.

He glanced down at the latest edition of the *Old Pueblo Sentinel* with the story of Raine Sinclair's rescue and the statement that this crime had nothing to do with the series of crimes perpetrated by the Beguiler. That being the case, after the flurry of activity around the kidnapping some of the interest had fallen off. Too many people had a short time span of concentration on even salacious topics; even interest in the Beguiler's crimes had waned a bit since there was no further crimes during the past couple of months.

Pete zipped up the last of the evidence items from Earle Baron Kensington III's apartment and logged it. The necklaces from those two murdered English girls went back to the UK with that constable from the small town where the crimes had taken place. Pete imagined that the kidnapper's family would be inundated with media and law enforcement interest as the investigation proceeded and soon concluded. He waved absently to the tech as he left the lab and headed home.

He popped open a can of Bud when he got home, drank it down, then popped open another. It had been a long day. His head was throbbing, and the booze didn't help. After he heated and ate a sorry Swanson's TV dinner he went down into the basement. Basements were relatively uncommon in Arizona, but he'd specifically looked for such a feature when he was house-shopping. This basement was dank and not entirely finished, but it reminded him of his family home in Mobile, Alabama. He'd pounded in some drywall and sloshed a coat of beige paint on the walls to provide some semblance of hominess.

Against one wall was a four-tier length of ten-foot-long, six-inch-wide lumber, the four pieces set between cinderblocks to produce a poor man's bookcase. On the makeshift shelves rested all sorts of books, but over fifty percent of them had to do with true crime across the ages. There was a special section for the books and magazines written about the ax murders in Tucson in 1977 and 1978.

His blood boiled whenever he contemplated that section from his reclining chair near the bookcase. He had been the forensics lead on all of Cheyenne LaChoisi's victims, and his stellar work was acknowledged by the police chief. Still, he was passed over for promotion. His name appeared on all the requisite internal documents related to his analysis, but he hadn't been mentioned in any of the media conferences or in any of the books. He had slyly fed tips to a few of the more influential newspaper and TV reporters under the guise of "a reliable police source," hoping to maneuver his way into some semblance of visible acknowledgement. After the denouement of that case and the plethora of books and articles, he had faded back into his relatively obscure job of analyzing boring crime scenes. All of them paled in comparison to Cheyenne's crimes and the electric excitement associated with the hunt.

As the years passed he became more and more dissatisfied with his life and possibilities. He watched as the detectives associated with the case were given commendations, and Michael Quintana and his weird crew established a thriving, very visible private investigations firm.

He seethed, but only showed the world his happy, compassionate face. He hated the nickname "Kreskin," which he felt was a subtle put-down of his role in evidence gathering.

But what really sent him over the edge was the promotion of Ben Deuel to head of the forensics lab. Deuel had less talent, experience, and seniority, and Pete wound up working for him instead of the other way around.

Pete decided that the only way he could topple Deuel as well as pay back those miserable people who had used his talents and then gave him no credit was to produce another suite of crimes that would send the city's population to the edge of fear as had the crimes of years earlier. Pete was utterly meticulous in his actions, and he had intimate knowledge of how to analyze a crime as well as perpetrate one that left no clues.

But what kind of crimes? He didn't want to reproduce those committed by the madwoman from New Orleans. He had been taking Entomology courses at Saguaro Western to increase his analytic skills in determining time of death by insect activity. That brought him into the various halls of the college where he was privy to academic conversations and curricula. He had heard the husband and wife team of Bliss Báthory and Malachi Dillinger discussing his prospective course on unsolved crimes. Pete was intrigued, and one night stayed late and broke into Malachi's office and rifled through his desk drawers and computer; locks proved no challenge at all, and dumb Dillinger hadn't bothered to shut down his computer. Pete found the long list of crimes that Malachi had developed. He printed out a copy, took it home, and spent two weeks making a plan, one he knew would test his own mettle as well as theirs.

After all—he was the Beguiler, and he held all their fates in his hands.

BOOK THREE

"Have you heard
The voices
Whispering on the desert winds
Which fall
From midnight peaks
And crags.
They whisper, 'Silence,'
Whisper, 'Stay.'
They whisper... 'Peace.'"

J.A. Christensen, "Desert Murmurs," in
Arizona Highways, October 1978

Montezuma Castle, Camp Verde, Arizona

CHAPTER ONE

July 4, 1966, Da Nang, South Vietnam

July was the hottest and wettest month in both South and North Vietnam. Although the temperatures never reached the heights of places like Arizona or Death Valley, California, the humidity was shockingly high and even 90°F felt worse than 110°F in the desert southwest. Besides the uncomfortable weather the American troops sequestered in country to fight a war that fewer and fewer were finding acceptable were subjected to animosity, harsh living conditions, bad food, and living in a world that seemed a galaxy away from where they had grown up.

Many of the troops salved their sore existences by concentrating on hearth and home, on families, wives, children, the future, the hope of getting out of their hellhole in a single piece. Others took the edge off with drugs and alcohol and easing their sexual frustrations with the soothing ministrations of whores and sometimes "wives" that made a semblance of home for them, at least until they received their orders to go home.

The ramshackle, tiny house deep in a decrepit alley in the poorest section of Da Nang was sweltering. A tiny, rusty fan had long since broken, and the only ventilation was by the rare breeze that wafted in the cracked window on the second floor. The floorboards creaked mercilessly as Anh Dung Nguyen padded across them, bent over, collapsed in on himself as he tried to avert his eyes from the tiny bed shoved up against the north wall and the lump of flesh resting on it in a bloody pool. Shame passed over his numb mind as he thought that his given name meant strength and heroism; nothing could be further from the truth. His father should have named him nhát gan—coward. He would always think of himself in that way from this night forward.

Anh Dung was a poor man who made a pathetic living fishing and doing odd jobs. He had long since fallen into further disrepute when he began acting as a middle man for his countrymen drug runners and the American troops that needed something which could take the edge off their assignment to this inhospitable country. He had started out simply by transferring marijuana between the drug runners and the troops, but to make more đồngs he added heroin and opium to what he called his gói niềm vui—packets of joy. He felt no compunction about providing the Americans with drugs; after all, they were invaders to his country and they brought with them more death and destruction than even the northern Communists had. He had a secret alliance to the Viet Cong, but never breathed a word of that outside of his own home and amongst his like-minded friends.

He had to make a living. He was forty-four years old but looked and felt at least ten years older. His wife, Ngoc, had given him nine children. He wouldn't consider what she had done as "blessings;" eight of the children were damnable females, and his singular son was weak in both body and mind. Three of the girls could be considered pretty, but the others were plain and not very bright, especially the middle daughter, Dao. Ngoc had named her newborn baby "Peach Blossom," which was a Tet flower. She hoped her daughter would live up to the beauty of her name, but Ngoc's hopes fell through as the child grew into a dull, undeniably ugly child that was soon shunted aside in favor of her less unappealing siblings. Dao could do simple things like laundry, but her cooking was atrocious, and she often wound up on the wrong end of her father's open hand. Anh Dung wished so many times that she was dead or simply vanished into the night. His wishes were never answered.

Then, as the war between North and South Vietnam began to hit its stride and American troops began pouring into the country, Anh Dung devised a plan to add to the family's coffers. Ngoc adamantly refuse to go along with his idea, so he beat her until she was a sobbing, defeated creature huddled on the kitchen floor nodding her head and saying yes, yes, yes. He didn't especially like beating his wife, but she should never disagree with him or try to act out of place in his house.

Dao was sixteen and her sister, Lan, was seventeen. Both were virgins. Neither girl was even remotely pretty, but their father knew that many men wouldn't care and only wanted sexual release regardless of the age of the female; some men preferred the very young ones, and Anh Dung was counting on that. He shoved away the slightest inklings of shame at his actions, focusing on the fact that he had to provide for his large family in any way possible. And he would give the girls a few đồngs so that they felt valued and weren't working for absolutely nothing.

He took his daughters to Madame Hoa Đẹp, the premiere brothel owner in the city, and after some very contentious negotiations she bought the girls' lives and bodies for 1,890 đồngs per month (the USD equivalent of $10), with 1,512 đồngs going to her and 378 đồngs to Anh Dung. He had hoped for more but understood that the girls' youth was negatively mitigated by their plain faces and thin, petite bone structures. The girls sobbed and begged their father to not leave them, but he took an advance on the first month's pay, shrugged them off, yelled at them, then left. He stopped in a neighborhood bar on the way home and got stinking drunk.

Madame Hoa Đẹp had her minions bathe the girls, cut their ragged hair, and apply creative facial makeup. She made it clear that if either of them gave her one iota of trouble, she would kill them. They believed the woman they both came to think of as the Dragon Lady. That night, Lan's services were sold to a middle-aged Vietnamese aristocrat, and Da'o's thin, innocent young body was sold to a gruff American soldier with sergeant stripes on his shirt. She cried the entire time and begged him to stop, but he didn't. He let Madame Hoa Đẹp know that her newest girl was not cooperative; Madame Hoa Đẹp refunded his money and told him he could come back for a "freebie" the next night. Then she dragged Da'o to her parlor and beat her bloody. The next night she sold the girl's services to two Army buddies; Da'o whimpered and cried softly as the men used her but gave them no resistance. When she saw her sister Lan two weeks later, both girls had the same shell-shocked, defeated look on their faces. One week later, Lan was gone and Da'o never saw her again.

Da'o's life was a daily whirlwind of sex, brutality, and hopelessness. She learned to cope by shutting down her mind and going to a secret place where she was as light as air, as free as a bird. Some of the men weren't horrible, although the case could be made that anyone who used a teenager sexually could never be considered a good man. But some hurt her less, and some were strangely kind. One man stood out as her first year of captivity ended, a young Army medic that other girls and a few soldiers called "Doc."

He was a young man in his early twenties. Some of the girls thought he was nice-looking, but the physical differences between Asians and Caucasians was so vast that she couldn't comprehend what did and didn't constitute handsomeness in an American male. The black ones were even harder to fathom. Occasionally he brought her trinkets or a giant meat sandwich that she wolfed down with wonder and passion. He asked her questions about her family but told her virtually nothing about his except that he was born in some exotic place called Alabama; she could barely pronounce the place and he'd laugh at her when she tried. He was finishing up his second tour of duty in South Vietnam and was hoping for a third. He said he enjoyed his work and the location and people and felt that he could ease the pain and stress with his efforts. She asked him in broken English why he didn't want to go home. He just gave her an enigmatic smile.

By the time she turned eighteen she had been a seasoned prostitute for two years and had accepted her life and fate. She dreamed some day of getting married and having children, but few men wanted a well-used whore for a wife. Still, it wasn't outside the realm of possibility. She even wondered if some American G.I. might want to take her home. She would be such a good wife. In hesitant, soft terms she offered her hope to Doc, who didn't encourage her but didn't discourage her, either.

And then he offered her an option that was the next best thing. He offered Madame Hoa Đẹp 10,000 đồngs for Da`o, and since the girl was pretty worn out and bringing in less đồngs on the open market, Madame Hoa Đẹp agreed to the purchase. Doc took the girl and her tiny bag of possessions home to her family and made a deal with her father to visit her whenever he liked, and she would be exclusive to him. Anh Dung heartily agreed, especially when Doc mentioned the $10 per month in American money that he would hand over to Anh Dung.

Doc came to the Nguyen home once per week except for the month that he was out of Da Nang with his unit in the battle areas shortly after his third tour of duty began. When Doc returned to Da Nang he immediately visited the Nguyen family and was greeted with enthusiasm. He noticed that Ngoc and Da`o were slightly less effusive in their greetings, but he didn't give it much thought. In bed that night he told Dảo about his work in the battlefield, how he had helped save lives and even had to amputate a soldier's arm. He was unusually aggressive sexually, and she was unusually passive. He wondered about her attitude but didn't give it much thought. He gave her 100 đồngs and told her he'd be back soon.

Doc came back three days later, and Anh Dung pulled him aside for an uncomfortable conversation. Doc's face drained of color even as it hardened into glacial ice when Anh Dung told him that Dảo was pregnant with Doc's child—he swore on his life that Doc was the father and no other man had touched Dảo. Doc was silent, breathing rhythmically in and out for a few minutes before he forced a smile and said that there was no problem—he'd handle it. Doc didn't show the slightest reaction when Anh Dung hesitatingly hinted that it wouldn't be a good thing if Doc's superiors learned of the pregnancy in his teenage daughter; at the look in Doc's eyes Anh Dung backpedaled and said he was just concerned for Doc's reputation—he meant no disrespect. Doc thanked him and handed him 500 đồngs.

Dảo was surprisingly pampered by her mother and father in the next few weeks. She thought they saw her as the mother of their eighth grandchild; they saw her as a means of extracting money from the silly American. They had visions of Doc returning home to America with a full Vietnamese family in tow; they'd be living in a land whose streets were paved with gold. He visited Dảo twice a week for three weeks. They always used the tiny bedroom she shared with five of her siblings, who were kicked out while the American did his business.

Anh Dung didn't quite understand the holiday that the Americans called Independence Day, or the Fourth of July. He vaguely understood that it had to do with kicking the British out of America, much the same as the French had been kicked out of Vietnam. He did know that the troops liked to have special food and drink and carouse in bars and with prostitutes. Doc had told him that he'd come to see Dảo on Monday, July 3rd, and stay until Wednesday, July 5th. He expected complete privacy since he had something special planned for him and Dảo. Anh Dung wasn't happy about having to relocate the entire family for two nights, but Doc sweetened the situation with 2,000 đồngs. Anh Dung, his wife, and their remaining six children (two daughters were married and living with their husbands) left their house at 2 PM just before Doc arrived. They would stay with Anh Dung's brother, who would be the joyous recipient of 200 đồngs.

Da'o was antsy in anticipation of her lover's arrival. She had bathed and tried to make herself pretty, even though she knew that was a losing battle. She hoped that the child she was carrying would be a boy with looks far better than hers. She worried that he would look too American. She had seen Amerasian children and although they were beautiful they were spit upon by true Vietnamese children and adults alike. Her only hope—her baby's only hope—was to go to Doc's country where life would be good. She prayed that he would feel the same way. She would be such a very, very good wife. She was getting taller and filling out, and surely she could pass for her early twenties with just a few more months of growing fuller breasts and artfully applied cosmetics.

Doc brought a large cloth sack with him, and the first thing he withdrew was her favorite American pastry—a raspberry jelly donut. He watched approvingly as she gobbled it down, a wide, happy grin splitting her plain face enough to make it seem almost pretty. Almost.

When she finished the donut, he took her hand and led her up the rickety, narrow stairs to the second floor and the familiar tiny bedroom. He undressed her gently and scooped her up, laying her on the bed as he drank in the small, fragile body with the almost indiscernible bump on her belly. He stroked her belly, then stripped and climbed on top of her and made passionate love to her as she sobbed in joy at his touch and knew—just *knew*—that he wanted her forever.

When he climaxed and collapsed on her she smiled and stroked his damp hair. It was hot in the room, and they were both covered with a sheen of glistening sweat. For the first time, she felt like a woman and not a girl. She was barely aware of his hand movements as he touched her wrists and bound them to the headboard. Her eyes snapped open, and she saw an odd look on his face. He put his fingers to her lips and shook his head.

Then suddenly he thrust a gag into her mouth and tied it

tightly. She automatically writhed and tried to free her hands, but the bonds were too tight. She opened her eyes wide and there was no mistaking the fear in them as Doc sat back on her legs and stroked her belly. He jumped off the bed and tied her ankles to the footboard. He didn't say a word, not a word, even as he withdrew several medical instruments from his bag; they glittered even under the dim lamplight. Da`o whimpered behind her gag and peed herself.

At 3 PM he strangled her into near unconsciousness; at 3:15 PM he did it again, careful not to crush her larynx.

At 4 PM he aborted her fetus, laying the mass of dead cells on her belly.

At 4:15 PM he strangled her a third time, this time breaking her neck and ending her short, sad life. Afterwards, he was hungry and whipped out the food he'd brought with him. He had acquired a craving for banh xeo, a crispy crepe stuffed with pork, shrimp, and bean sprouts, and it was one of his favorite in-country meals. He'd also brought a large container of cao lau, a pork noodle dish with wonton crackers. He stuffed himself, relishing the delectable foods even as he stared at the corpse on the bed. He had already ceased seeing her as a human being, so the bloody remains didn't really bother him.

He hmm'd over his instruments, selecting a large, strong scalpel which he used to draw a deep line down her chest from neck to groin. There was little blood; she had been dead for over an hour and the blood settled in her lower regions. He cut back her chest flaps, exposing her rib cage and her lower internal organs. He reached into his bag for a hammer and a sharp, thick metal stake, and it took several minutes and strong battering to crack her chest cavity. He pulled back the ribs he broke, exposing her heart. He had studied the internal workings of the human body and spied the liver and spleen right away. He used the scalpel to remove them and place them on the sagging, bloody mattress. Then he cut away her uterus and fallopian tubes and removed her heart. His movements were swift and sure; he had acquired quite a repertoire of dissection abilities during his two-plus tours as a medic. He had honed those skills in dark nights and darker days on dead or dying Viet Cong on whom he came across during his forays with the troops in the fields. He was almost caught twice, but his luck held.

He stood over Da̓o's ravaged body, studying his work as though in an academic class. He was almost satisfied—but not quite.

He packed up his instruments a few hours later and left the house in the dark of night. He got back to barracks and took a cold shower, then slipped into bed and slept like a baby.

The next evening Anh Dung came home early, alone, to see if he could bring his family back a little earlier. He was having arguments with his brother, who wanted his family out of his own crowded household. Anh Dung found the house abnormally quiet. There was an odd smell coming from the kitchen area, so he followed his nose, entering the kitchen where he saw a battered metal pot on the stove; the odd smell was emanating from the pot. He stared down into the murky, broth-like water and saw two large slabs of meat that he couldn't really recognize—or that his mind wouldn't let him recognize. There was a pan on the second burner, a pan that contained two blackened blobs of … something.

He listened and heard nothing. He quietly and slowly mounted the stairs and very, very gently pushed open the bedroom door where he expected to find his daughter and the American in bed. He stared at the thing on the bed, and the head on the dresser. He dropped to his knees and let out a howl that had no relation to anything human. He moaned and rocked and swayed and moaned.

An hour passed, and then another hour before he dragged himself off the floor and began silently removing all traces of his dead, mutilated daughter before her mother could ever see the denouement of the horrific mistake he had made. He cleaned for hours, scrubbing the floors and turning the mattress over. He tossed out the boiled and fried meat into the street where they were gobbled up by wild dogs.

Anh Dung suffered the indecision of whether or not to go to the Americans and tell them what one of their people did. He knew about retribution, and that no one cared about poor, ignorant people. He told his wife that their daughter had run away into the jungle. She didn't believe him, but she didn't question him, either.

He finally mustered enough courage to walk to the American

barracks and speak to a captain. He poured out his story. The captain thanked him and said he'd investigate it. Anh Dung didn't believe him.

One week later Anh Dung's house was burned to the ground. Thankfully, no one was killed but his wife was badly burned. A week after that he learned that Doc had been sent home to America. The day after he learned that, he took his family north and joined the Viet Cong.

That same day in Mobile, Alabama, Peter Patrick Murphy, newly discharged, joined the Mobile police force as a forensics technician. Over the years he made his way west, moving to Tucson, Arizona, in 1975.

He came to really, really love his work.

CHAPTER TWO

The Christmas season in southern Arizona was both recognizable and unusual. Northern Arizona was a different matter, with its snow and cold, and the forests that were reminiscent of those climates and landscapes enjoyed by people from places like the Northeast and Midwest. The "feel" of Christmas in the state's north was a far different experience than the one in the south.

The exterior of the holiday was both beautiful and a little unnerving to those who had migrated to Tucson from areas north and east. Live Christmas trees were sold in fenced-off lots or chopped down by hardy souls who cherished that old-fashioned method of providing the family tree. Artificial trees were also popular and were often indistinguishable from the real thing; the days of aluminum silver trees and color wheels were long gone. Artificial trees dotted the landscape in front of businesses and houses along with brightly colored strung lights; manger scenes and Santas with reindeer decorated lawns and brought a seasonal feel to the neighborhoods when darkness fell.

Perhaps the most unusual method of celebrating the holiday was the lights wrapped around the trees and cacti that defined the southwest city. Small to giant saguaros, palo verde trees, prickly pear cacti, and other flora were alit with red, green, blue, and white lights that made the evenings wonderlands of beauty for children and adults alike. Although snow was rare except for the mountain peaks the December air had a definite nip and one could easily feel that they were back east awaiting a sleigh full of toys while sipping on a hot toddy and nibbling on homemade cookies.

Deliverance's parents had always made the holiday special, with a real tree heavily decorated with glass bulbs, candy canes, strung popcorn, multi-colored lights, and silver tinsel. She had missed that after she fled Salem and for the years in between before she had settled down with her husband and new twins. They were too young, of course, to appreciate the Christmas tree and presents, but as they aged and Vikki joined the family the holiday grew in importance and magnificence. She made Quint go out into the forest and cut down their own tree. Her mother had sent her several boxes of family ornaments, and she acquired special new ones each year. She began making clay ornaments with her children as they grew, and this year was no exception. The difference was that there was a new child in the family and this would be Storm's first Christmas with the family. For that reason alone, Deliverance wanted to make the holiday extra special. Besides having a huge tree, she badgered Quint into stringing lights around the outline of the house as well as the two tall saguaro cacti in their back yard that now glowed neon-blue in the night.

The Dane-Quintanas debated whether to go back east for the holiday, but after the last year and all its trials they simply wanted to nest in their home and revel in the intimate aspects of family. Charity and Nicolae said they understood and said they'd call on Christmas day; meanwhile, they sent boxes of toys for the kids and special gifts for the parents.

Victor took the boys back to New Orleans to visit their great-grandparents although he planned on remaining at a hotel while they visited. He'd sworn he'd never enter their house again and nothing had changed his mind, certainly not after a contentious phone call between them. Wilde had considered heading back to Hove for the holiday with Raine, but that was before her kidnapping and rescue. She was still physically recuperating from her ordeal as well as dealing with her pregnancy, and she decided to remain in Tucson with Constantine. Phaedra and her family were still in New Orleans with her parents and they decided to stay until the start of the new year. Moon Wolf was enjoying the different culture and had started on a new jewelry line whose roots lay back in Africa and Greece. Phaedra had discovered a fantastic new black artist that painted stunning portraits that harkened back to the days of slavery and related to the Voodoo and Santeria religions. Since Cress and Gray were staying in Tucson as well—with a long weekend visit by Gray's parents—Raine and Constantine would celebrate with them. Wilde accompanied Victor and the boys back east for a week's visit.

That visit was cut short after three days and the Renard family returned to Tucson a few days before Christmas. Victor was at first tight-lipped about the reason but finally admitted to Quint that his parents told him they decided to seek legal custody of

Beckett and Bechet. Victor said he was going into battle to keep his grandnephews. He retained Fox Newberry, who would be assisted by law student Shayne and possibly Iris Flynn. Wilde ran out the morning after they'd gotten home and bought a tree and boxes of new ornaments and garlands.

Judie Sutphin had written an in-depth story on the rescue of Raine Sinclair and Iris was the heroine of her article. Iris made sure that Judie referred to her as "ex-FBI Special Agent Iris Flynn;" Iris didn't want her former employer to get the credit for the rescue. The same day that Judie's article was published in the *Sentinel* Iris was contacted by Steve Shaeffer's superior, who was unusually conciliatory about the situation that had caused her to quit. He offered Iris her job back with no letter of reprimand in her file, and no transfer to the wilds of nowhere. He said she could be permanently stationed in Tucson rather than Phoenix if that was her desire. He also mentioned that Shaeffer was being transferred to North Dakota. She thanked him politely but said she was content with her decision. He persisted, and she conceded that she'd think about it. An hour later her father called her and read her the riot act about being a team player and not being stupid enough to throw her career away and humiliate him in the process. She hung up on him.

Quint now had two dead shots living in his back yard. He offered Iris a job at the Union Jack firm until she could decide what she wanted to do with her life. She accepted and split her time between work and studying to take the Arizona bar. Tucker suggested that she go home for the holidays to try to repair her family relationships, but she was reluctant until he said he'd go with her. They flew out to D.C. four days before Christmas. After a rousing argument with her father and brother Iris changed their return flights to December 24th and they headed back to Tucson where both realized that they felt very much at home.

Deliverance was inundated with holiday preparations but was on the cusp of having it all pulled together by Christmas Eve. She planned a hearty ham dinner and then the opening of one gift per child after she read them *A Visit from St. Nicholas.* She was upset when Quint told her he had to go out for a short while before the reading and that it couldn't be helped. He told her to make sure they had hot toddies for when he returned. There was no snow, of course, but the night air was chilly and crisp. She and the children were sitting around the floor of the family room as they enjoyed the tree when Quint came home. He pulled his wife off the floor and said he had a special gift for her. At that moment Charity and Nicolae came in and Deliverance threw herself into her parents' arms. The children jumped around and hugged their grandparents while Deliverance wrapped her arms around her husband and told him that she loved him. He told her she'd have to prove it after the kids went to bed. She did.

Christmas day was a rollicking event for the family, with tons of gifts opened and wrapping paper scattered all over the floor. The kids were up at 5 AM and the adults not much after. Around noon Victor, Wilde, and the boys came over for their gifts, and the extended family sat down at 2 PM for an exemplary dinner that was made by Deliverance, Wilde, and Charity. The conversation was generally easy, but one hot topic was the December 22nd shooting of four black youths on a New York subway in the Bronx by a man the media called "the Subway Vigilante." They'd tried to rob him; he shot all four of them. The media exploited the incident and depending on the viewpoint he was either considered a monster or a hero. The identity of the man was still unknown, but the incident had ignited a country-wide debate on self-defense, gun control, and race relations. Victor was especially concerned with his grandnephews growing up as young black men in a country that still had polarizing views on racial equality.

There were no football games on that day, but Quint had recorded the Thanksgiving game between the New England Patriots and the Green Bay Packers, who cleaned the Patriots' clock 28-17; it was obvious to all concerned that the Pats wouldn't be playing in Super Bowl XIX in January. Everyone already knew who won, but they had promised to watch the game together on Christmas. Tucker and Iris came over and while she watched the game with the guys he played a couple of chess games with Beckett, who was fast becoming a chess master. Belzer came over for the game. He had spent Christmas day with the late Detective Munch's widow and children as they tried to navigate the blackness and sorrow of their first Christmas without their husband and father. Belzer had spent a good deal of time over the many months since Munch's murder with Pamela and Munch's son, helping them to navigate their grief and the new normal of their lives.

Raine and Constantine came over at seven for eggnog, and everyone was relieved to see how much she had physically improved after her ordeal. Her hair was starting to grow back, but it seemed that Constantine liked his shaved look and planned on keeping the Kojak style for the foreseeable future. She was proudly sporting her healthy baby bump and said that she and her fiancé were discussing names, but they didn't want to jinx it by revealing their preferences. Constantine said that Phaedra and her family would be coming home the first week of January now that the immediate danger was over. Raine told her overjoyed friends that she and Constantine had settled on a wedding date, June 22, 1985. The baby was due in May, and she wanted to be able to wear a wedding gown without "looking like an overfed hippopotamus." Iris was going to be her maid of honor, and Cress the best man.

No one mentioned the fact that the Beguiler was still at large.

As in the previous year the Union Jack offices were shut down until after January 1st so everyone could have family time. This time the Union Jackers and their friends met at Wilde's house to watch the Cotton Bowl where the Boston College Eagles decimated the Houston Cougars 45-28. Heisman Trophy winner Doug Flutie rolled the Eagles to a three-touchdown lead by the end of the first half. There were two minutes left in the game when someone knocked on Wilde's door and he crabbily jumped off the couch to answer it. After all these years in "the colonies" he had finally gotten used to the Yanks' version of "football" and enjoyed watching the games. They'd never replace soccer, though—real football.

The hair on the back of his neck stood on end when he saw Detective Yale Cornell and his partner, Baxter, standing on the front stoop. He could tell by the looks on their faces that it wasn't going to be a pleasant visit. The men looked tired and haggard, and like they'd slept in their suits.

"Come in," Wilde said, and they entered. "Did he strike again?"

"'Fraid so," Cornell said.

"Hang on," Wilde said. "Let me get my partners." He nodded towards a set of open French doors on the west wall. "Go in there." He walked into the family room and asked Victor, Deliverance, and Quint to come with him. When they were all in the room Wilde shut and locked the French doors. He addressed Cornell. "Bring it on."

Cornell handed Wilde a photo of a teenage girl with brown hair, freckles, and a thousand-watt smile. The photo looked like it came from a high school yearbook. "Christine Cummings, twenty. A Biology student at Saguaro Western."

"She dead or missing?" Victor asked as he studied the photo.

"Dead," Baxter said flatly.

"How?" Quint asked.

"Ice pick," Cornell said.

"C'est différent," Victor murmured.

"What precisely happened?" Deliverance asked. "Where did you find her?"

"In the St. Lawrence O'Toole Church in southeast Tucson. The priest, Father Cyril, unlocked the church at 5 AM and found her."

"A church?" Victor gasped. "She was murdered in a church?" The vestiges of his youthful adherence to Catholicism sent pricks of horror across his soul.

Cornell nodded. "Based on the crime scene and blood it looks as if the deed was done there and not elsewhere and the body moved. The ice pick was sticking out of the back of her head but there were also signs of strangulation." Cornell's jaw went rigid. "That wasn't all. The bastard sexually assaulted her with an object."

"A cross?" Deliverance asked softly.

Cornell shook his head. "A twelve-inch-long white altar candle. He left it inside her and left one between her breasts."

"The sick fuck," Wilde hissed.

"Did you check Malachi's list?" Quint asked.

Baxter nodded wearily. "It's on the list, and we called him to verify his agreement on the crime." He pulled out his notebook and flipped it open to the first page. "October 13, 1974 up in Stanford, California. A newlywed of two months, nineteen-year-old Arlis Kay Perry, was killed the same way in the Stanford Memorial Church on the campus. Her husband Bruce was a suspect, but semen left by the perp ruled him out. Ditto the church security guard that found the body. The case is still unsolved. Stanford offered a $10,000 reward for information on the murder, but no one took the bait or was willing to talk. Malachi said he'd dig around into the crime and see if he could come up with any more details."

"Was this Christine married, too?" Quint asked.

"No, not so far as we can tell. At least she wasn't wearing a ring and there was no indentation on that finger. She still had her purse and we went to the studio apartment listed on her driver's license where I picked up this photo. I sent Chet up to the college to get into the student files and find out her stats and next of kin. The president of the college wasn't too happy about opening up on a holiday, but I don't give a shit and told him so."

"Anything else that differentiates this crime from the others?" Victor asked.

"Funny you should mention that," Cornell said. "We're keeping this back from the public. There was etching on the vagina candle. Seems our Beguiler has left us another communication."

"What did it say?" Quint asked.

"Happy New Year."

CHAPTER THREE

"You know, I'll probably get fired for letting you do this," Cornell said to Quint and Wilde as he unceremoniously dropped a large evidence box on the table in the Saguaro Conference Room. The box was marked "Houghton Does" and contained all the gathered forensic evidence and reports associated with the young man and woman hitchhikers that the Beguiler claimed as his third and fourth victims.

"Nah," Quint opined as he removed the box lid after snapping on a thin pair of latex gloves. "If we turn up anything that helps solve the case you'll get the lion's share of the credit. You can be the hero of Judie Sutphin's next article and claim your own fifteen minutes of fame. Anyway, it's not like you're leaving this alone with us. You'll be watching us like a hawk as we rifle through."

"And Baxter will be watching your other halves when they rifle through the Cummings and DeLage boxes in the other room. Or, at least Deliverance. Where's Victor anyway?"

Wilde's jaw tightened. "He's down at the courthouse with Fox. There's a preliminary hearing about custody of our boys. The Renards are back in New Orleans but they sent their shark of a lawyer out here to rile things up." He noted the querulous look on Cornell's face. "Victor's parents are suing for full custody of the boys."

"I thought they dumped them out here?"

"They did but apparently had second thoughts. Unfortunately, there was no legal custody agreement so everything's up in the air. I'm pretty sure the boys want to stay out here, but they're kids and can be swayed by people they've been close to all their lives." Wilde shook his head. "I'd never have thought it when they first arrived, but I've kind of gotten used to being an uncle to them. They're not as bad as I'd originally thought."

"I want that documented in writing." Quint grinned. "That way I'll have the proof next time you rant and rave about teenage angst."

"I would just take the Fifth," Wilde replied as he withdrew one of the dead man's sneakers from the box. He studied the laces. "That was a great catch by Agent Ballard about the shoes showing the kids were redressed."

"It shows that the perp isn't infallible," Quint added. "He made a mistake, and I'm betting that we can find other mistakes that will give us some clue to his identity." He glanced at Cornell. "Did you get an updated profile from the FBI based on his latest kill?" Cornell nodded but Quint held up a hand. "Hang on." He hit the speed dial to Iris's office and asked her to join them. He grinned. "She's not an agent any more but I'll bet she has some insight into the guy based on her experience."

"Sure she'll talk to us?" Cornell said. "After all, she's a hero and probably doesn't want to mix with regular folks."

"That's why we ex-fibbies have such a problem with you local cops," Iris said as she walked into the room in tight jeans and a tighter spandex top. "Your sucky attitude." She stuck her left hand out to Cornell. "You may kiss my ring."

"Blimey," Wilde exclaimed. "That's some rock." He grabbed her hand and stared at the stunning engagement ring which had a two-carat square diamond with a smaller round diamond abutting each side. The gallery was yellow gold in a leaf pattern. "When did this happen?"

She smiled. "I proposed to Tucker last weekend. But, of course, I made him buy the ring." She arched one delicate eyebrow at Quint. "He's going to need a raise. His savings account has been blown all to hell, not that I feel one whit of guilt about that."

Quint smiled widely. "I'll speak to my better half about that. I suppose you want to expand the casita?"

"Well, since you're expanding the back of your house anyway for two new rooms, it would be logical to do both projects at the same time." Quint and Deliverance had decided to upgrade their house by another thousand square feet to accommodate a new bedroom as well as a second den/playroom.

"Quite logical," Quint agreed. He refocused on less pleasant matters. "Cornell has an updated profile that your old company did on the Beguiler."

Cornell opened his briefcase and extracted a thick folder. He pulled out a ten-page document and handed it to Wilde. He pulled out a second copy and gave it to Iris. The three Union Jackers took a few minutes to scan through the high points.

"So," Wilde began, "your brainiacs at Quantico still consider him a sexual sadist, someone who gains sexual pleasure at the torture, pain, suffering, and humiliation of others. I'm not sure I agree with that."

"Neither do all the experts," Iris replied as she flipped through pages two and three. "They feel that based on the deaths and conditions of the victims that he may be a simple sadist."

"What the hell's a simple sadist?" Cornell demanded. "Isn't that kind of a ridiculous assessment?"

"You need to remember, Cornell, that these assumptions and designations are psychological in nature. The regular sadist—for want of a better term—has no sexual component to his actions and simply enjoys inflicting pain in complete disregard for the victim's feelings or physical discomfort. A sexual sadist gets an erotic physical rush from inflicting pain, and generally completes his actions by not only death but mutilation," Iris said. "He gets a hard-on both during and after the deaths of his victims."

"So why is there a divergence in opinion from the experts?"

"Probably because the victims show different end results," Quint surmised. "DeLage and the hitchhikers seem to have been simply shot, with no indication of torture or abuse. Dahlia Doe was mutilated, according to the coroner, after she was dead. As to what happened to her specifically before death they can't say because of the disarticulation and the decomposition of her body. Munch's death was as quick as it was brutal. Cummings definitely had a sexual element to her death what with the candle used to violate her vaginally."

"Laurel?" Iris asked. "Where does she fit in?"

"We may never know," Wilde said. "There's no doubt in my mind that she's dead but for some reason the Beguiler doesn't want her body found." He flipped through the document until the end. "Huh. He's characterized as narcissistic, arrogant, and psychotic. Tell me something I don't bloody know."

"That could be his undoing," Cornell said. "He's too full of himself, too full of hubris. Look—he sent us a message about Raine's abduction, and then inscribed the Cummings candle. He likes the attention."

"So nothing new, or nothing that will actually help us find

him," Quint said, the exasperation heavy in his voice. He had been rummaging around in the evidence box but put everything back. He shook his head. "Nothing here. I'm betting Del hasn't found anything either. Maybe she'll get some sensory impressions." He grinned at Cornell. "I know you don't believe, but she's been on the money too many times for it to be luck or coincidence."

Cornell put his hands up. "At this point I'm willing to have a séance to help solve this. She, uh … doesn't do that kind of thing, does she?"

"She's a psychic, not a medium," Wilde sighed. "Psychics receive information from the energy of persons, places, or things. They can see or feel things that have happened or will happen. A medium may have psychic abilities but is differentiated by being able to directly communicate with spirits." The uninformed were so … uninformed. He changed the subject. "Have you finished your background checks on everyone?"

Cornell nodded. "Nothing untoward on my team or the detectives that worked on the ax murders. Everyone's got something small they'd prefer not to publicize, but nothing that would indicate either a leak or a madman."

"Maybe we should extend our search," Wilde said thoughtfully.

"How so?" Iris asked.

"Well, besides our Union Jackers and our social circle, we've explored the detectives and analysts associated with the old and new crimes. But there have to be many other people who've touched the cases on the peripheral."

"That's a lot of people," Cornell said. "You got the uniforms that answered the initial calls, the forensic techs, the lab assistants, just to name a few."

"You got a better idea?" Quint asked.

"Not a damn one," Cornell confessed. "Okay. I can get started making a list for each crime scene and see what we come up with, but it's gonna take some time."

"Can I make a suggestion?" Iris asked. "Play this close to the vest and keep the tasks confined just to you and your lead detectives. If someone on the peripheral is involved, we don't want to give it away."

"Good idea," Wilde acknowledged. At that moment Deliverance came into the room shaking her head.

"Didn't get much from the DeLage and Cummings boxes," she said, "but I did get an odd feeling when I touched the candle and the bridge card. Something … familiar, but not terribly strong." She went silent and Quint thought that she had something else to say but wanted to hold it until they were alone.

"Okay," Cornell said. "I guess Baxter and I will head back to the station and start on our little research project. Let me know if you think of anything else." He picked up the box and left the room.

Quint looked at his wife. "Okay—give."

She shrugged. "It's just odd. I don't think I mentioned that when that head was delivered to us and we were all dealing with the cops coming in that I got this weird … electric feeling up my spine. It lasted a second and then disappeared, but it was definitely there."

"It probably had to do with the head," Wilde said. "Did you get that same feeling when you were examining the evidence just now?"

She shook her head. "It wasn't the same sharp sensation, more like a dull throb on the edge of my consciousness. Nothing … specific."

"Did you sense evil?" Wilde asked, remembering her impressions during the ax murders case when they had walked through the house of the first victims, the Catalanas.

"What do you feel?" Wilde asked quietly from behind her.

"Evil," she stated flatly. "Anger. Confusion."

"Whose? Mrs. Catalana's?"

Deliverance shook her head, her pink locks and braids swirling around her head and shoulders. "No, the killer. His evil just … just … saturates this room."

"I sensed purpose and determination, but it seemed nondirectional, a little unfocused, almost as though he were making things up in the moment."

"Which doesn't make sense," Quint said. "According to the FBI's profile he's what they call an organized killer. Very definitive, high IQ, leaves little evidence and a controlled crime scene, not sloppy at all. Likes to play games. He's definitely focused."

"I can't explain it," she said. "It's almost … it's almost as though I'm getting mixed signals from multiple people, not just a singular killer."

"Are you thinking he has a partner?" Wilde asked.

"No," she replied slowly. "It's as though there are two separate paths that have somehow converged."

"That's a little nebulous, but we'll keep it as a distant option," Wilde said.

"Do you think he'll continue to send the cops communications?" Iris asked thoughtfully. "He seems to want us to know what he's done and not done. He was working in the shadows but now it seems—"

"As though he wants publicity, as though he's tired of being unknown and he wants at least part of his story told," Quint reflected. "That could be his undoing."

"Let's hope," Wilde said just as Victor and Fox came into the conference room. Wilde saw the tense look on his life partner's face. "Should I even ask how it went?"

"Not well and with an unexpected twist," Fox said as he dropped down into a chair.

"Victor?" Wilde said quietly. "What happened?"

"My parents' fucking lawyer threw us a curveball," Victor said coldly. His anger was virtually emanating from his entire body. He looked ready to spit nails. "Ce morceau de merde. He said my parents were seeking custody because they'd received a tip that … that …" He could barely speak.

"What?" Wilde asked desperately.

Fox interjected. "Someone contacted the Renards secretly and said that the boys had been … molested."

"What?" Wilde, Quint, and Deliverance exclaimed simultaneously.

"By whom?" Quint said.

"By Wilde," Victor said softly.

"What? What?" Wilde gasped. "You know that's not—"

"Of course it's not true," Victor breathed. "That's not something you even have to deny."

"Where does that leave us?" Quint asked tightly.

"The judge ordered the boys to be removed from the house and put in Child Protective Services while the matter is investigated,"

Fox said. "The police will have to interview Victor and Wilde as well as you two and anyone else who might have perspective on this. They'll interview the boys, too."

"What about this so-called 'tip?' What was it and who sent it?" Deliverance demanded.

Fox pulled a Xerox copy of a typed letter from his briefcase. "This was sent anonymously from Tucson to the Renards shortly before Christmas. It's unsigned, of course. I demanded that the original letter and envelope be dusted for prints and the other lawyer grudgingly agreed."

Wilde stared down at the letter that stated that he had been observed being "handsy" with Bechet on multiple occasions and that he had put his hands on both boys in "an inappropriate manner" when Victor wasn't around. The letter urged the Renards to "save the innocent boys" and get them out of that "terrible situation."

Wilde dropped the letter on the table and slumped in his chair. He looked devastated. He looked up at Victor. "I'd blow my own brains out before I'd hurt either of those kids in any way."

Victor dropped into the chair beside him and put a strong hand on Wilde's shoulder. "Don't you think I know that?" He touched his forehead to Wilde's and closed his eyes.

Fox picked up the letter and handed it to Iris, who scanned it and frowned. He said, "We'll fight this tooth and nail, but we have to follow the law and procedures to get the boys back. Shayne is downtown filing papers to see if we can get the kids put into a chosen foster home until we resolve this. Quint and Deliverance aren't an option because of their personal and business relationships. Shayne might be an option and we're pushing for that." He noticed the odd look on Iris's face. "What's wrong, fibbie?"

She showed Fox the letter and pointed a long red fingernail to several words. "Check out the t's. They're ever so slightly higher than the other letters. Just barely, but you can see it."

Quint and Deliverance squinted at the individual words. "That's right," Quint said. "It could point to a very specific typewriter if we can pin down the anonymous person that sent this."

"But that's not all," Iris said slowly, then bolted from the room. She came back three minutes later holding another Xerox copy.

She handed it to Quint. He saw that it was a copy of the note that the Beguiler had sent denying culpability in Raine's kidnapping. "Look at the t's in this letter."

"They're the same," Deliverance said. She looked at Victor with her lips curled in disgust. "The Beguiler sent the letter to the Renards. The fucker went after you guys in a demented but creative way."

Fox took the two copies and compared them, nodding. "I believe you, but this won't stop the procedures in motion. However, it may speed up a resolution. I'm taking these down to the police station and courthouse and see what I can accelerate. I'll make a copy for Cornell. With this we may be able to get the original letter and see if there's anything besides fingerprints or postage stamps that can tell us something about the sender." He looked apologetically at Victor and Wilde. "I can't stop CPS from assuming custody of the boys, but at least this is a light at the end of the tunnel. I'll call you as soon as I can." With that Fox rushed out of the room.

"I want this son of a bitch dead," Wilde said in a low, frightening voice. "What he's putting us and our kids through … I want that wanker *dead.*"

"Oui," Victor agreed. "Moi aussi." His jaw hardened. "I know the letter is damning, but I will never forgive my parents for believing the worst about us, for damaging our reputations without even asking if it were true. Mon dieu—I'm their *son.*"

Deliverance put a gentle hand on Victor's arm. "There's time for healing after this is all over and done. Don't rule out anything just yet." She could see that he wasn't being swayed, but it was too soon for that.

Wilde rose and was staring out the picture window at the Catalina Mountains, a blank look on his handsome face. "Where are you, you bloody bastard? Your time is counting down."

Her hands were shaking badly as he stood over her, looming like the wrath of Hell, her very own personal Torquemada. The lighting was bad, and her watery eyes could barely make out the notes on the paper as she typed furiously on the computer keyboard. She swayed slightly as she tried to steady herself and type the stream of consciousness words that were pouring out of his thin-lipped mouth.

She typed by rote, vaguely unaware of the content of the words, performing her duty only as it related to her survival. She ignored the savage rumbling in her empty stomach. He fed her once per day—maybe—and she wasn't certain when the last time was that she had choked down the bland Cream of Wheat. Time—it had no meaning for her. She couldn't intuit seconds let alone hours or days. She had no concept of what day or week or month it was, how long she had been held prisoner as she was forced to work on his life story, his manifesto, his psychotic ramblings. She tried not to think about what would transpire when he considered her efforts complete. She couldn't let herself think about that.

So, Laurel Bollmeier just shut off her emotions and typed as the Beguiler stood over her, her fate in his demented hands.

CHAPTER FOUR

Raine had been going crazy staying at home and not working. She understood that her body and mind needed to heal, but her forays outside of the house to the grocery store and her twice-a-week therapist didn't suit her natural social needs. Constantine had been a doll, patient and compassionate, and obviously so in love with her. He held her each night in his arms, gently rubbing her growing belly as they both looked forward to being parents.

They hadn't made love since her rescue, and that worried her. She had been raped, but she understood on every level that those events had nothing to do with sex and everything to do with power and control. She was concerned that perhaps Constantine thought she might be "damaged goods," but those thoughts evaporated in days. She realized that he was just terrified of hurting her with an aggressive intimate act. She realized that she needed to take the lead in reestablishing their intimacy, and she planned on doing just that tonight; after all, it was Valentine's Day. She had gone out the day before to Goldwater's and picked up a sheer black negligee that would entice any red-blooded man. There wasn't much she could do about her hair, but at least it had reached a half inch all over her head and had come back an even brighter auburn. She kind of liked the short style—so much easier to take care of. Of course, Constantine had it even better with his shaved pate.

Raine planned a nice intimate dinner at home, but that was a problem since her cooking skills were on the level of a preschooler. She thought about ordering a catered meal from one of the high-end restaurants in Tucson, but Iris had pooh-poohed that idea and told her that Tucker would prepare an exquisite meal and she'd bring it over. Raine had depended on Iris for so much emotional support over the last few months, and their friendship had deepened into something solid and comfortable, and that each knew would last a lifetime.

She sat on the couch cuddling Blackjack. The little black pug followed her everywhere and although technically he was Constantine's dog, there was no doubt where his loyalty and affection lay. A brisk knock on the door announced Iris's arrival after three and

411

Raine opened the door to find her best friend standing there with a half dozen paper bags nestled around her feet.

"How did you get all of these bags here in one fell swoop?" Raine asked as she grabbed a few and backed into the condo.

"We ex-FBI agents are tough," Iris replied as she dumped two bags on the kitchen counter and began pulling Tupperware and other dishes out of them. She smiled at Raine. "Tucker outdid himself this morning. We have beef bourguignon, roasted baby potatoes and glazed carrots, grilled asparagus, and a southwest version of jambalaya. Tucker made fresh garlic-cheese biscuit dough that you can pop into the oven ten minutes before you eat. It's a secret recipe that he won't even share with me. For dessert we have a strawberry-banana cheesecake and raspberry tarts. Oh—I also picked up some fresh beignets at Yvette's, and a special espresso blend that's taking the coffee-lovin' world by storm."

"That sounds beyond marvelous," Raine said. "I can't believe that Tucker whipped this all up on his own. I know you're about as competent in the kitchen as I am."

Iris nodded. "So true, although I do excel at takeout. You know, this is just the tip of the iceberg. Tuck's taking cooking courses at the Old Pueblo Culinary Institute. Before you know it, he'll be whipping up French meals that you'd find in the finest eateries in Paris. He seems to be exploring his feminine, nesting side. Since I have a rather strong masculine side, we're a perfect match. It's weird, but it works. Oh yeah—got a bottle of sweet cider as an aperitif since you can't have alcohol."

"I'm sure Constantine would like a little wine to go with dinner, though."

"Voilà!" Iris exclaimed as she withdrew a bottle of Cabernet Sauvignon from the last bag. "The pride of the Bordeaux wine region in La France. Maybe he'll let you sniff it."

"You're a mean woman."

"I pride myself on that," Iris said as she began stocking the containers into the refrigerator. "There's hardly anything in here," she said disapprovingly. "You need to go grocery shopping. We'll head over to Smitty's Saturday since I have some stuff to pick up, too."

"Sounds like a plan. Help me set the table," Raine said. There was a large alcove off the kitchen where the couple ate their meals on a beautiful cedar-wood round table with four chairs. Constantine had found it in a custom furniture place off Speedway and bought it just before Christmas. Raine opened a cabinet drawer and extracted a plain cotton tablecloth. Iris took it out of her hands.

"Nuh-uh," Iris said as she put the tablecloth back and pulled out a lovely off-white, handmade lace tablecloth from her canvas tote bag. "Deliverance's mother made this for her two years ago and she lent it to you for the occasion." Iris flipped the tablecloth on the table and adjusted it. She smiled. "Wish I had a mother who could create things like this, but my mom was always too busy suing companies over discrimination cases. Where are your good dishes?"

"Well, we don't exactly have 'good' dishes, but the ones that aren't cracked are in that cabinet." She pointed to the west counter.

"Not to worry," Iris said as she went to the front door, opened it, and ducked out, coming back carrying a small cardboard box. "Del's loaning these to you, too. She mentioned that if you break one you die. I don't think she was serious, but …"

"Wow," Raine whistled. "You have all the bases covered. I don't suppose there's a mariachi band waiting in the wings to serenade us?"

"Sorry, but I did bring this." She pulled out a new jazz album from the china box. "I know you'd prefer the Stones or Beatles, but you need to make sure your fiancé enjoys music on his level, too."

"I'll try to endure it. Sure you have nothing by Cyndi Lauper or Boy George?"

"Don't even go there."

Raine began bouncing her head around, singing, "Karma, karma, karma, karma, karma chameleon, you come and go, you come and gooooo …"

"Okay, that's a cool song, but let's not ruin the evening by subjecting Voodoo Man to it."

"It's a deal," Raine agreed as she started placing the plates and glasses in their proper places.

Iris pulled out two silver candlesticks and said to Raine, "These are my treat. Got red candles, too. You know, it's too bad that

Voodoo Man already proposed to you in the hospital. Tonight would have been engagingly stereotypical."

"I think he chose just the right venue," Raine said softly. She straightened and looked her friend in the eye. "You know, he told me that if I wanted to move back to England and live there that he'll go with me. He said he can find a job at a university there."

"That's a pretty big sacrifice for him," Iris said. "What did you say?"

"I said I'd think about it. I've thought about going home so many times, and then I realized—wherever Constantine is *is* home."

"So … you're going to stay here?" There was no mistaking the anxiousness in Iris's voice; she obviously didn't want her friend 6,000 miles away.

"99.99% certain. That other hundredth of a percent will depend on what I feel when the baby is born."

Iris grinned. "Do you know if it's a boy or a girl?"

Raine grinned right back as she finished setting the flatware. "I do."

"Well?"

"It's a boy or a girl." She laughed at the crestfallen look on Iris's face. She leaned close and whispered in her friend's ear. "It's a girl."

Iris shrieked, and the friends hugged tightly. "Got a name picked out?"

"We do, but Constantine still doesn't know the baby's sex. But I'll tell you." Raine paused for dramatic effect. "Alexandra, after his mother."

"That's beautiful," Iris said.

Raine nodded. "Alexandra Iris Black Wolf. As long as you don't mind." She grinned at her speechless friend. "I love you, you know."

"Yeah, I'm kind of fond of you as well," Iris said as they hugged. They broke apart suddenly, each a little embarrassed by the strong emotions.

"Good," Raine said. "Then I guess you might consider being godmother?"

"I'd be honored," Iris said sincerely. "Does this mean I'm

tasked with teaching the kid hand-to-hand combat, how to shoot a handgun, and how to kick a rude date's ass?"

"That goes without saying."

"I'm fine with that. Say—what time does your better half get home?"

"5:30-ish. He has an extra hour of student sessions to go over questions on their midterm tests. Why?"

"Because," Iris said as she opened her tote bag, "I thought you might like to exercise that limey brain of yours and see what we can come up with on this data." She was holding out a few floppy disks. "Detective Cornell compiled some lists of peripheral personnel associated with all of the cases and I thought we could go over the names and see if there are any patterns. Cornell's team just finished these lists this morning and haven't done any detailed comparisons yet, but it never hurts to have other objective eyes reviewing the results."

"Great," Raine said enthusiastically. "My brain is turning to mush without any real work. I feel like I could become a Stepford wife if I don't get any intellectual stimulation. Let's take them into the den."

Iris followed her friend into the den that Raine shared with Constantine. Raine booted up her IBM PC and inserted one of the disks into the data drive. A moment later she clicked on the Excel icon and brought up the first file labeled "Dahlia Doe." Iris pulled over a chair and they both studied the spreadsheet, the names, and the comments data on each line.

"Wow," Raine said. "Sure were a lot of people involved in that case." She looked over at Iris. "You know what I don't see? Any names from non-law enforcement personnel. You know, like passersby, or even media people. I mean, there are a few official witnesses, but that's all."

"They'd spend a year trying to find the names of everyone who was within screaming distance. They have all the Union Jack people and the kids since Dahlia's head was delivered to Quint's house."

"Hmm," Raine replied absently. "Let's do this, same thing I'm sure that the cops are doing. I'll load up all the files, then merge and sort them in new columns. We'll see who overlaps in all or most of the cases. Can you get me a glass of milk, please?"

"Anything for the mother of my goddaughter," Iris said and headed off to the kitchen. When she got back there was a complex spreadsheet with a half dozen columns up on the monitor and Raine was leaning forward studying it intently. Iris handed her the glass and Raine took a long sip. "Thanks," she said as Iris reseated herself.

"What do we got?" Iris asked.

"Well, it looks like no one was involved with every crime scene. Different cops, different tech teams. So, I guess we'll just see where the best overlaps are." Raine's hands ran gracefully over the keyboard as she sorted and merged in a different pattern after she'd saved the original sheet. After a few minutes there was another sheet displayed on the screen with six more columns and textual highlights.

"Well, we have a few overlaps that meet a 40% rate or better. See here?" Raine pointed to a name in column A. "Technical analyst Hortense Garcia, who was running background checks on the victims. She did three of the victims—the hitchhikers and DeLage—but the other four—that's including Laurel's kidnapping—were done by different people. Munch's case was a joint effort between local and the FBI."

"I met her when I was doing initial interviews. Nice gal, and I'd bet my next paycheck that she's not involved. However, I wouldn't entirely rule her out as the leak."

"Okay," Raine said, "this guy—Jerry O'Brien, the driver of the coroner's van—was at three crime scenes, the hitchhikers, Cummings, and Dahlia Doe. We'll bold his name and Garcia's, too. And here's one patrolman, Mike Beckham, who was at three of the crimes scenes. He's Don Bollmeier's partner. All right. Hmm."

"Hmm?" Iris echoed.

"Yes, hmm. This guy was at five of the crimes scenes as the forensics lead. Pete Murphy. Dahlia Doe, Delage, the hitchhikers, Lady of the Dunes, and Cummings. The forensics head man, Ben Deuel, directed the Munch and Laurel efforts."

"Quint calls him Kreskin," Iris said. "He's pretty much the main guy in the forensics sector. From what I've gleaned about him he has an excellent reputation, which is interesting," she mused.

"Why?"

"Because according to Belzer, despite his talents and seniority he was passed over for promotion, which Deuel got instead. That must have pissed him off."

"It would piss me off," Raine agreed. "You talked to him, right?"

Iris nodded. "I did. Nothing jumped out during our two conversations, except that he seemed almost too eager to help. But that's not abnormal in a situation like this."

"Do you have any data on his efforts during the ax murders case?"

"Huh. I'm not sure Cornell added that into his sheets. Nothing on the disks about that?"

"Nope. Maybe we should get those lists, too." Raine glanced at the wall clock. "But not right now. My man will be home in a half hour and I need to start getting the food ready. I hate to throw you out, but ..."

"Yeah, your guilt is written all over your face," Iris said, smiling. She stood and picked up her tote. "I'll call Cornell and see if he has the data for those old murders. Also, I just have a nagging feeling that what we need is somewhere in your sheets. I'm going to start with that Pete Murphy and backtrack his life. See if there's anything in his background."

"Be careful," Raine said as they reached the door. "We don't want to go bulldozing down a wrong path at this point, and we don't want to start any career-killing rumors."

"I hear you," Iris said as she pecked Raine's cheek. "Have fun tonight."

"I will. Thank Tucker for me. I'll send him a note tomorrow."

Iris took off and Raine went into the kitchen and began putting the meals in Corningware dishes to reheat in the oven, which she turned on to medium. She preferred that over the microwave. She chilled the wine and cider then went back to her desk and fiddled around some more with the case data. She found a couple more 40%ers and added them to the checkout list, and left Iris a message on her answering machine.

At five-thirty on the dot Constantine came home and she

wafted into his arms and kissed him deeply. She smiled at the dozen red roses he was carrying. He was rarely "romantic," but when he was, any woman would fall for his charm. His sister, Phaedra, who had returned a few weeks earlier from New Orleans, said that he had a "big, fat, gooey center" that few people were privileged to see. Over the year they had been together, Raine perceived that without question.

She took the roses and told him to relax while she put them in water. She took out the Waterford vase that the Makrises had given her for Christmas, filled it with water, and clipped the rose stems down. She put it in the middle of the dining table and lit the red candles. She checked the oven, then opened the wine and poured a goblet for her fiancé and one with cider for herself. She slid onto the couch next to him and handed him the wine. They both sipped.

"Something smells good," Constantine said as he sipped. He nodded. "Excellent wine."

"I have a feast fit for a king just about ready for my valentine," Raine said lightly.

"Ah, so you sneaked out, bought the fixin's, and prepared it yourself?" He arched a knowing eyebrow.

"If I could get away with saying yes, I would," she laughed. "Our dinner is courtesy of one Tucker Townsend, chef-in-training. Iris brought everything over a while ago. She knows I can't cook any more than she can."

He nuzzled her neck. "You can do other things," he murmured.

Raine felt a thrill at the touch of his lips, and an electric sensation rolled through her entire body as she realized that she was ready-oh-so-ready. They stared into one another's eyes for a very long ten seconds, then Raine jumped up, pulling Constantine behind her as she headed for the bedroom. Blackjack whined as the door slammed in his face. He curled up beside the door and waited until his mom and dad were ready to pay attention to him.

Constantine burst out of the room an hour later when he heard the smoke detector and smelled smoke and hurried to turn off the oven that was emitting the smoke from the burned beef bourguignon and the shriveled-up baby potatoes that now looked like over-dehydrated figs. The carrots and asparagus were a total loss, too, but fortunately

Raine had left the jambalaya in a pot on the stove without turning on the burner, and the cheesecake was safe in the fridge.

"So much for our glorious Valentine's Day meal," Raine said as she waved her hand back and forth to dissipate the smoke.

"Could be worse," he said. "We could have lost the jambalaya. But I'm not sure that pot's going to satisfy our hunger, so let me order something to be delivered."

"Pizza?"

"Pizza." He checked the phone number of the fridge magnet and called in an order for a large pepperoni, then hung up. "Forty minutes."

"Hmm," she mused. "How will we pass the time until then?"

Without a word he took her hand and led her back into the bedroom, this time gracing Blackjack with the honor of curling up in his soft bed by the nightstand as his parents passed the time. Later, he was treated to a slice of pizza and a sliver of cheesecake.

Iris was looking forward to her own Valentine's Day meal that Tucker tantalized her with when he was making the food for Raine. He mentioned something about good old New England chow, but wouldn't give her any details. She didn't press him; as long as she wasn't stuck with takeout she was happy.

Iris had a special gift for him in the trunk of her car—a 20-piece set of T-Fal cookware she'd picked up at Goldwater's that morning. It might not be romantic, but he'd love it and get good use out of it. Sometimes Iris thought she was just too practical, but that aspect of her personality served her well in her job. As she drove back to the casita she ruminated on whether to accept reinstatement in the FBI. Part of her wanted that desperately, but the other part liked the atmosphere and freedom she had outside of federal service. She and her father hadn't spoken since that disastrous Christmas visit. Her mother had called her twice to urge her to apologize to her father. She said she had nothing to apologize for. Multiple stubborn Flynns in the same family did not make for easy relations.

She hadn't told them about her relationship with and engagement to Tucker. She had no doubt that her father would run an exhaustive background check on him and try to dig up any piece of dirt that he could. Tucker's bisexuality would start a conflagration in her family, much as it had in his. She and Tucker hadn't set a wedding date, but when they did, and their families were notified, all hell would break loose. She was thinking more and more about elopement. Deliverance had once mentioned thinking about elopement herself and had envisioned running off to Vegas with Quint to be married in a strip chapel by an Elvis impersonator. Maybe that wasn't so farfetched ...

She and Tucker had the entire evening to themselves. Quint and Deliverance had custody of their children and were taking them out for dinner at Mariposa Linda's. Victor and Wilde were staying in with their boys. They had finally gotten them released from foster care the week before and Fox was finishing up the necessary paperwork to grant Victor legal custody of the kids. Beckett and Bechet had been traumatized by the entire experience and were having trouble readjusting. Victor scheduled therapy sessions for them starting tomorrow. He was not on speaking terms with his parents and there was a good chance he never would be. The Renards had accepted the fact that they'd been duped about the molestation, but they hadn't apologized, just withdrawn their custody application. At least Wilde's name had been cleared, but the emotional damage still lingered.

Iris knew that other members of their work and social circles had plans for the evening. Fox and Shayne were going out on their third date, which surprised everyone. Thayer had a date with her latest boyfriend, and a dejected Turner was spending the night in a bar watching sports with other "losers." Cress and Gray were eating out at The Happy Spartan along with Phaedra and Moon Wolf. Bliss and Malachi were up in Sedona enjoying a long weekend at the Poco Diablo Resort. Bliss was due to give birth to their son Barnabas Collins Dillinger next month, and she wanted one last hurrah of freedom before she settled down as a mother of two kids.

Iris was glad that her friend, Raine, was well on the mend and there seemed to be a happy ending in the offing. She hoped that .01% chance that Raine would go back to England would fall away. She'd never had a "best friend" before, and she relished their relationship. Truth to tell, she had a very full life here in Tucson, and she had never expected that when she had first driven into the city limits. She knew she could make a go of it as a private investigator, but there was still that FBI pull. She had talked it over with Tucker, and he said he'd back her whatever her decision. Right now, she was leaning towards reinstatement, especially since she could be permanently stationed down here. It had nothing to do with her father—this was strictly for her life. And Tucker's, of course.

There was a lot they hadn't yet talked about, like the idea of children. They kind of hedged around that subject. Tucker loved kids and he was doing a fantastic job with the Dane-Quintana children, but having his own was another matter. And Iris wasn't sure she even wanted them. She made a mental note to refill her birth control pills prescription.

She pulled into the driveway and locked the car. She walked around back and noted that Quint and his workers had framed the new house extension; they would start on expanding the casita when the main house was finished. Wilde and Victor thought their place was big enough for their family of four, and there were no impending additions to that crew to necessitate expansion.

The front door was unlocked and as soon as she opened it she could smell dinner. She knew the aroma—pot roast, no doubt with gold potatoes and carrots he'd bought at the nearby farmer's market. As usual she marveled at his many talents—he could cook like Julia Child, shoot a gun like Dirty Harry, care for kids like Mary Poppins, and make love like Casanova. She had lucked out.

Tucker came into the living room drying his hands on a washcloth. He grinned at her. "Everything's ready for dinner, m'love," he said saucily as he pecked her on the lips. "All you have to do is put on a few albums and set the mood." He went back into the kitchen as she selected a few albums and set them up on the stereo spindle. She clicked on the first one and the soulful sounds of Marvin Gay saturated the warm home.

Iris went into the kitchen. "Anything I can do to help?" she asked.

"Nope, got it all in hand. You just relax. How's Raine?"

"Worshipping your god-like culinary expertise. She thanks you mightily for your efforts."

Tucker laughed. "I aim to please. Okay, the pot roast's ready.

421

Go sit down." She complied, and he brought the food to the table. She insisted on cutting up the beef and placing a pile of slices on both their plates. She dumped a heavy measure of potatoes and carrots onto their plates and covered her meal with his homemade gravy.

Their conversation was easy and nonstop. They ate by candlelight and rarely took their eyes off each other's faces. Iris cleared the plates while Tucker brought out the Dutch apple pie; they both had two slices, covered with vanilla ice cream. Then Iris went out and brought in the T-Fal, which thrilled Tucker. He shyly handed her a gift bag that contained a hand-tooled new leather holster for her service weapon.

Iris watched Tucker as he loaded the dishwasher and cleaned the dining table and kitchen counters. She suddenly felt a wild urge to do something crazy. She turned off the stereo. He noticed.

"What?" he asked.

"Marry me," she said.

"I thought that's what the diamond ring meant when you bullied me into spending my life savings buying it for you."

"Marry me now," she elaborated.

"Huh?"

"What's the name of that pilot friend of yours?"

"Uh, Josh Wyllys?"

"Right. Call him and tell him we need a ride to Vegas and I'll pay him $500."

"You want my ex-boyfriend to fly us to Vegas to get married? Are you out of your mind?"

"Obviously. Well? Chop, chop!"

Tucker blew out a hard breath and dialed his friend. When Josh gave him pushback Iris took the phone and explained her pay rate, and that it was always nice to have an FBI agent as a *friend*. He said he's pick them up in an hour.

"So, you've decided to go back to the FBI?" Tucker said laconically. He knew she would. That was why he bought her the holster.

"Looks like I'll have to if I need sway over some of the residents of this backwater desert town."

"Well … well … are we staying overnight? Should we pack a bag?"

"Nope, in and out." She giggled at the double entrendre.

He looked at her aghast. "Man," he said slowly, "you really do wear the pants in this relationship, don't you?"

"Tight designer jeans. I'll let you wear them once in a while."

"Thanks."

"Well, what are you waiting for? Change into your best jeans and western shirt and boots. I don't want the wedding photos to look horrible."

"Yes, ma'am," he said and went into their bedroom. She followed him and by the time Josh descended his chopper in the back yard as he had once before, they were dressed in casual western clothes. They boarded the chopper and buckled in, and Josh took off northwest to Sin City.

Three hours later Iris and Tucker were standing in front of an Elvis impersonator who was a dead ringer for the late singer; Josh acted as their witness. Their vows were phrases from Elvis songs and after ten minutes of kitschy ceremony that would have made the most die-hard Elvis fan groan they were pronounced Mr. and Mrs. Tucker Townsend. Just before Iris kissed her new husband she said, "I'm keeping my maiden name."

At 2 AM Tucker swept Iris up in his arms and carried her over the casita threshold. It was the manly thing to do.

CHAPTER FIVE

Judie Sutphin was putting the last touches on the *Sentinel*'s February news summary. Laurel had been assigned to take it over from Santiano Bronson, the newspaper's owner and publisher, but she had disappeared before her first summary could be published. Bronson had assigned Judie to finish the task and gave her leave to do it "You know, until we get Laurel back." It was unspoken within their organization, but no one expected Laurel to come back.

Unlike Bronson Judie decided to present a brief sentence or two on happenings around the end of the month before. That was easy—Ronald Reagan had been sworn in for his second term publicly on January 21st (privately, the day before). On January 28th a gaggle of famous singers and entertainers gathered together to record the song *We Are the World* to promote visibility and funding for charity. Judie shook her head in wonder at the photograph of the stunning array of men and women who had donated their time to the effort—Michael Jackson, Lionel Ritchie, Bob Dylan, Stevie Wonder, Cyndi Lauper, Diana Ross, Billy Joel, Huey Lewis, and Bruce Springsteen were just a few of the world-renowned artists that participated.

February was a busy month across the globe. The DEA was dealt a savage blow when one of their undercover drug enforcement officers, Kiki Camarena, was kidnapped in broad daylight and murdered by the Gallardo cartel in Mexico; his body was yet to be discovered. Rumor was that he had been unbelievably savagely tortured before his death, including enduring a power drill into his skull. Bloody savagery extended to the other side of the globe when the Provisional Irish Republican Army launched a deadly mortar attack on the Royal Ulster Constabulary, killing nine officers.

The South African government extended an offer of freedom for long-time political prisoner Nelson Mandela; he refused and remained imprisoned. CNN reporter Jeremy Levin was freed by his Lebanese captors; two days later Israel began withdrawing troops from Lebanon the same day that the Hezbollah ideology was declared in Beirut. On a happier note, heart transplant recipient William Schroeder was able to leave the hospital, and the border between Spain and Gibraltar was reopened for the first time since Francisco

Franco had closed it in 1969. The FDA was days from establishing a blood test for AIDS to screen all blood donations.

Judie added a touch of entertainment to the summary when she mentioned the January Barry Manilow concert in the McKale Center at the University of Arizona. Judie loved Manilow and had attended. Unlike the reviewer in the *Arizona Star*, who said that "Manilow was dressed mostly in black, a color well-suited to his new smoky saloon tunes ..." Judie was effusive in her praise for his sexy leather jacket, his long, fluffy mullet, and his aviator sunglasses. She nearly cried when he sang her favorite song, *Mandy*. She included two sentences about the well-respected Arizona Theatre Company, which had such excellent plays on its 1985-86 roster as *Death of a Salesman, My Fair Lady*, and *The Robber Bridegroom*.

Judie finished proofing the summary then took the floppy disk down to typesetting. She had been given Laurel's cubicle, which was much larger than hers had been, and she had made it her own with framed pictures of her dogs, a stuffed teddy bear, and a plaque commending her on a story she'd done in 1983 on the July 21st recorded temperature in Vostok Station, Antarctica, as $-89.2°C$ ($-128.6°F$). She'd compared it to the highs reached in America in Death Valley, California, which reached a stunning $134°F$ ($56.7°C$) on July 10, 1913, at Furnace Creek. These were the coldest and hottest temperatures ever recorded on Earth.

Judie decided to keep Laurel's desk, which was newer and more spacious than her own. She had removed all of Laurel's items and papers and stored them in a plastic box in the *Sentinel*'s storage room so that Don could pick them up. She replaced them with her own tools of the trade. She had just bought a new label maker and plastic tape at Radio Shack, and removed the hard shell covering the label maker. She inserted the tape and created a label with her name and "Do Not Open" on it and applied it to the bottom right desk drawer. She opened the drawer to store her new toy; the drawer was nearly full. She frowned, and there was something teasing at the edge of her brain, but it didn't quite coalesce. She shrugged off the feeling and rearranged the bottom and middle drawers to accommodate all her stuff. Then she grabbed her shoulder bag and headed off to cover a "soft" story on Lute Olsen's kids' basketball camp.

Fox and Shayne were cloistered in the Saguaro Conference Room with their three clients, who had engaged Union Jack to backtrack two young women who claimed to be their father's illegitimate children. They had come out of the woodwork after his death and the obituary in the newspaper that mentioned he had left an estate in the neighborhood of fifteen million dollars. The two brothers and their sister didn't believe their claim for a second and wanted them exposed as frauds. Shayne had mapped out a strategy for following a paper trail, and she was scheduled to drive to Santa Fe in the morning to investigate their lives there.

Quint and Wilde were confined to the Crucifixion Thorn Conference Room since Deliverance was using Devil Cholla for her meeting with Sue Gumkowski regarding the adoption process for Storm. Iris was meeting with them along with Raine who simply refused to stay out of the office any longer. The men were relieved to see that she looked great physically, and neither planned on saying it, but they thought she looked beautiful with her thick, short dark hair.

Instead, her devoted uncle mused, "You've gotten rather plump, haven't you?"

Raine arched her eyebrows at Wilde and pursed her lips. "Pregnant women tend to do that, you sodding prat," she said coolly. She turned to Iris. "It's so bloody unfair that blokes don't have the same issues we women have."

"I hear you," Iris replied. "But, then again, they have to deal with ours in one way or another. I, for one, make sure that Tucker enjoys the monthly *perks* of being married to a woman."

"And on that thought," Quint said, "we're not going to bring up again the fact that you eloped, and we weren't at the wedding, but we do want to have a celebration soon to commemorate your big life change."

"Oh, please, nothing huge and formal," Iris begged. "Really— we don't want a big deal made of this."

"How about a barbecue in our back yard?" Quint said. "Plenty of room between our properties for grilled chicken, burgers, and hot dogs. We invite our tight little circle of family and friends and toast your marriage with prickly pear margaritas."

"That works for me." Iris nodded.

"Um, should we invite your family?" Wilde asked.

Iris shook her head. "It wasn't a pretty situation when I called my parents and told them I was married. They screamed and lectured, and I hung up. My dad called back a week later and gave me the so-called lowdown on my new husband and his military and sexual history. Dad was shocked when I told him I knew all about it. He went ballistic when he brought up Tucker's current job as a nanny. Then he hung up."

"I'm assuming that Tuck's family shouldn't be on the guest list, either," Wilde said.

"Not in this lifetime," Iris said, shaking her head.

"That's too sad," Wilde said quietly. "But, at least you've got us."

"You should be trying to make her feel better, not worse," Raine jabbed.

"Silly me," Wilde jabbed back.

"All right, children," Quint said. "Let's focus on the reason we're here. Wilde? Hortense Garcia?"

"The stereotypical picture of a nice woman struggling to make it paycheck to paycheck. She's a very good analyst and researcher and has a sterling reputation. She goes to church every Sunday and is generous with the donation plate despite her bills and mortgage. No odd financial activity. Husband is a carpenter, same good reputation. They came to the States from Juarez in '72 and were naturalized in '82. Two kids." Wilde shook his head. "The facts and my gut tell me there's nothing there, especially since she's five-foot-four, so nowhere near the five-foot-ten person we're looking for."

"Good enough for me," Quint said. He flipped through a sheaf of paper. "Jerry O'Brien, the driver of the coroner's van for three of the murders. Nothing unusual about him, and he didn't come to Tucson until after the DeLage killing. That doesn't entirely rule him out, but it does place him far down on the list as far as I'm concerned. Also, he's six-foot-one."

"Agreed," Iris said. She looked at her notes. "Mike Beckham is a decorated patrolman who's Don Bollmeier's partner. Or was—Bollmeier is on an indefinite leave of absence. According to sources he's pretty much fallen apart. Poor guy. Seems like he really loved his wife."

Quint nodded. "Beckham seemed like a good guy, a little green. He and Bollmeier discovered Barbara Schindler's body and as I recall Beckham hurled his breakfast. Anyone would—that was a terrible crime scene." Quint remembered the Axewoman of Tucson's pregnant victim; the woman and her near-term baby were killed in their home and shortly thereafter the widower took his own life. "There's nothing there to indicate that he has a dark side and would take his partner's wife. Interestingly enough, there was a rumor that the inimitable Laurel Bollmeier turned up rather quickly at that crime scene on a tip from a neighbor. I'm betting it was on a tip from her husband. And I certainly wouldn't be surprised if he was the leak."

"Height?" Raine asked.

"Six-foot-two."

"Any sense that Bollmeier might be our perp? Many men have killed their own wives," Raine said.

"I doubt it. I know Bollmeier and I don't think he's the type," Quint said. "But we keep him on the list anyway and keep digging."

"And that leaves Pete Murphy," Raine said. She pulled out her prints from the ax murders data that Cornell had given them. "He was at a lot of the ax scenes and even got a commendation for his forensics work."

"I talked to a half dozen of his colleagues and they had pretty much nothing bad to say about him, even his boss, Ben Deuel," Iris said. "Although, there were hints that he was dissatisfied with recognition in general and royally pissed when Deuel was promoted over him."

"They say why that happened?" Wilde asked.

"Deuel seems technically competent and has had multiple commendations, and he's considered more of a people person that can handle media scrutiny and is more politic in his verbal interactions. Apparently, Murphy can be snippy sometimes with members of the press and even other law enforcement officials."

"Do we have any significant background on him?" Raine asked.

"Some, based on his application and background references.

But they never tell the whole story," Iris said. "You know, I have to spend a couple of days up in Phoenix signing papers and getting an orientation for my reinstatement, so I may be able to do some background research on him now that I'll be part of the FBI again," Iris said.

"Our very own fibbie," Wilde said, grinning.

"You do know, of course, that I'll have actual Bureau work to do, not just carry you Union Jackers on my broad shoulders?"

"And without those horrid shoulder pads," Raine added.

Quint redirected the conversation away from fashion. "So, what are our basic facts about Pete Murphy?"

Iris sighed. "Born on July 15, 1943, making him forty-one. Birthplace, Mobile, Alabama. Parents Maria Delaney and Ed Murphy. No siblings. Graduated high school near the middle of his class, nothing distinguishable there. Did two years of community college studying biology until he decided to enlist in the Army. Sent to Vietnam in 1964 and was there as a medic until '66 when his third tour was cut short."

"Why?" Raine asked.

Iris shrugged. "He got an honorable discharge and went home to Mobile to join the police force as a forensics technician." She flipped through a couple of pages and went on. "Never married or had children. Five-foot-eight. Brown hair, blue eyes, no distinguishing characteristics. He stayed in Mobile until 1970, then started moving west, taking forensics jobs in Dallas, Albuquerque, and Phoenix before settling in Tucson in 1975. So, he's been working here for ten years. I haven't had the chance to check with Mobile and those other cities to see what his work was like or why he moved on multiple times. I'll have to see if my new boss will let me explore those employments. It shouldn't be an issue since this all relates to the unsolved cases and Munch's murder."

"We should also see if we can find someone in the Army to discuss his tours of duty, maybe his superiors or fellow soldiers," Quint said. "Since I was lucky enough to serve in that garden spot of Asia I can take the reins on that."

"You know," Victor said as he meandered into the room, "you can tell a lot about a person from his abode and possessions."

He had just been to a parent-teacher meeting to discuss Bechet's test scores; the younger boy had a high IQ and the counselors were recommending advanced placement classes in science and math. Bechet had actually smiled broadly when they said this, and Victor hadn't seen him smile since the custody battle had raged.

"I say," Wilde said, "you aren't suggesting that we invade his privacy in a most devious and illegal manner, are you?"

Iris clapped her hands over her ears and chanted, "La, la, la, la, la, la." She went into her Sergeant Schultz mode. "I hear nothing. I see nothing. I know nothinggggg."

"Typical FBI agent," Quint muttered then quickly dodged a swat from Iris.

"I cannot condone what you are suggesting," she said, "but I'll keep my mouth shut since my husband might wind up on the unemployment line if his employers are put in the slammer."

"Mighty considerate of you," Quint said, smiling. "So, Victor—what do you have in mind?"

"Well," Victor drawled in an overexaggerated, honey-sweet southern accent, "if we can be sure of a time when Murphy's out of his house for a while then we can knock politely on the front door for admission. If that doesn't work, well, Wilde and I have some experience with jimmying a back-door lock without being seen." At Raine's curious look he added, "Willow Cheney's house in New Orleans."

"You know," Wilde said as he drummed his long fingers on the table, "we should also find out if he has any other properties in the area. A vacation cabin, maybe."

"At least we know he won't be using that cabin up in Summerhaven," Raine said mildly, trying not to remember the horror she endured there. Quint, Wilde, and Victor had made the Phoenix dentist an offer on the property, and since it was unsellable and unrentable due to its notoriety, he snapped up the low-ball offer. When the papers were signed, the men and a few friends—including Constantine, Cress, and Gray—went up there with chain saws, sledge hammers, and other tools and demolished the cabin. As a nice final touch Quint sprinkled Holy Water over the remains, and Deliverance performed a Wiccan purification ritual.

"I'll have Fox do a discreet property search on Murphy's name," Quint said. "Meanwhile, I'm going to ask Cornell to re-measure the car seat leg distance just to make sure. I'll call Belzer and see if he can finagle some information through his cop contacts about any extended absences Murphy's going to have, like a forensics convention or something." He noticed the startled look on Victor's face. "What?"

"Forensics convention," Victor repeated slowly.

"Yeah?" Wilde said.

"When I was in South Carolina, remember I met up with that state trooper Ron Hutchinson?"

"Yeah?"

"He mentioned something shortly before we parted, after he treated me to the best fried chicken on the planet."

Raine blew out an exasperated breath. "You bloody men are obsessed with your flippin' stomachs. I'm beginning to think you don't have hearts, just second stomachs thumping away, begging for food 24/7."

"What's your point, bird?" Wilde asked.

"I have no point. I just needed to get that out. Continue, Victor, please."

"So, Hutchinson mentioned that his wife and kids were out of town and he had to go home to study for a forensics convention in Columbia. He said it was a regional get-together to discuss unusual cases and forensic measures and that there were attendees from all over the country."

"Jock and Jane Doe would possibly have been a case that would be studied, you think?" Quint said.

"Maybe," Wilde said, not entirely convinced. "It's interesting, though. Malachi's research had a lot of facts and some pictures, but I don't remember seeing the shots of the original victims until after we'd equated them to our case. Think if it was discussed at the convention they would have had those?"

"Ah, oui, absolutely," Victor said. "So, what I need to do is call my new buddy Ron and see if he can get me a list of the conventions in, say, the last five years and who attended them, and confirm if the Doe case was discussed."

"Let's revisit our plan to explore Murphy's abode," Wilde said, glancing over at Iris. "Perhaps you'd like to absent yourself from this part of the discussion?"

Iris sighed. "In for a penny, in for a pound. And it's better that I know what you're doing so I can … assist in some way if you need an—what's the word I'm looking for?"

"Alibi," Raine said.

"Right." She checked her watch. "Oh, boy—I've got to get going. I promised I'd pick up groceries since Tucker's spending the day with Vikki at the zoo before he picks up the kids from school. I'm leaving for Phoenix tomorrow morning. I'll call with any updates on my background checks and you can update me on your … invasion plans. Keep my hubby company while I'm gone. He tends to sob and kvetch when I'm not in the vicinity."

"Kvetch?" Raine asked with one eyebrow arched high.

"Fox has been teaching me some Yiddish words." She winked, gathered her folders and saluted her friends, then left just as Deliverance came in and parked herself next to Raine.

"Everything go okay with *Miss* Gumkowski?" Quint asked his wife.

Deliverance smiled and nodded. "She wasn't a butthead for once. She said all their reviews of our home and finances checked out and since there's been no luck on identifying either Storm or any possible family members, they should be able to legally terminate 'parental rights' in a few months."

"And then we'll be able to adopt her."

"Righto. So, I expect we'd better start figuring out a middle name."

"Congratulations," Raine said enthusiastically. "That's a wonderful thing you're doing. She's a lucky kid."

"We consider ourselves just as lucky," Deliverance said. She squinted at Raine. "So, are you going to keep us in suspense until the birth or tell us what you're having?"

"Well, since I finally broke the news to my fiancé, I guess it wouldn't a problem to let you know we're having a girl," Raine said proudly. Her revelation was followed by shrieks and hugs, the tightest, longest one from her teary-eyed uncle. "We're calling her

Alexandra Iris—Sasha for short—and she'll be baptized at the same place we'll be married at, the Mission San Xavier del Bac. Phaedra was married there the same day that Persa was baptized."

"Fantastic," Deliverance said, literally jumping up and down. "Have you started planning the wedding?"

"Not exactly, just the venue, and Moon Wolf's cousin is arranging for an exception to made for us so we can be married there."

"Well, count on the women in your life helping with all the arrangements. You, Iris, Phaedra, and I will sit down in the next few weeks and come up with a strategy. We'll have a conference call with your mom to get her input."

"Thank you," Raine said sincerely. "I don't think I could put it all together myself."

Deliverance hugged her. "That's why you have family and friends."

"Smashing," Wilde grumbled. "Are we done with the chick stuff so we can get back to manly topics?" He managed to keep a straight face when both his partner and niece gave him the look of death.

"Yes, absolutely," Raine said blandly. "I wouldn't want to offend your rampant masculinity." Wilde knew that he was going to pay for that remark in some horrendous way.

"All right, here's the plan," Quint said. "I'll investigate Murphy's military service. Iris will do background checks on his previous employers and path west. Victor will contact his southern fried chicken buddy and get data on those forensic conventions. Raine will keep analyzing the personnel data to see if we've missed anything. Wilde, you talk to Belzer to see if there's any upcoming absences that would give us a window for, um, inviting ourselves into his house to root around. Ask Belzer to re-interview Don Bollmeier about Laurel's personal effects just to make sure we haven't missed anything."

"What do you want me to do?" Deliverance asked.

"Plan Raine's wedding," Quint said.

"You sexist pig," she replied.

"It's his best quality," Wilde said.

"You're not much better, Brit Boy." She scowled at Victor, who was grinning. "What are you laughing about? You're just as bad as your two buddies here. Men," she expelled in as exasperated a tone as they had ever heard. She muttered something under her breath, then took Raine's arm and led her out of the room to start on Quint's directive.

Quint, Wilde, and Victor held their breath until they were sure that the two women were out of earshot, then burst out laughing.

CHAPTER SIX

Belzer knocked on the front door. He listened closely but could hear no one moving about inside, and no electronic noises like the TV or radio. He was sure that Don Bollmeier was home, and he wasn't going to go away until he talked to him no matter how painful it might be for the man. He was grateful that there seemed to be no reporters hovering around the fringes of the neighborhood; one might think that that ilk had compassion, but he knew better. He thought it ironic that the husband of one of those reporters was now under scrutiny himself. Still, he couldn't help but feel compassion for the guy. He knew about lost love.

He knocked again and called out but again got no response. He decided to go out back and see if he could peer into the sliders. When he rounded the back corner of the house he saw his quarry slumped in a lawn chair on the back patio. The ground around him was littered with empty beer bottles and a pizza box; the half slice inside was crawling with ants. Don was staring straight ahead, unblinking, showing no more movement than a mannequin.

"Don?" Belzer said softly. No response. "Don? It's Reichardt Belzer." At that Don shivered and looked up.

"Jeez," Belzer said without thinking. Don Bollmeier was a bare shadow of his former self. At six-one he was always slender, but now he looked skeletal in faded jeans and a torn shirt. His cheeks were sunken; his eyes watery with dark bags under them. His once salt-and-pepper hair and goatee were now pure white. He was just over the edge of fifty, but he looked seventy-five. There was a hopelessness about him that saturated the air like burning rubber. He was holding a rosary in his left hand. His lips moved in what Belzer thought might be a greeting, but no sounds came out.

Belzer sat in the chair next to him and clasped his hand. "Don," he said quietly, "you've got to hold on. Hope isn't gone, man."

A single tear dribbled down Don's cheek and he savagely rubbed it away. "Sure, sure. Hope. Why didn't I think of that?" He pulled his hand away from Belzer's and then seemed to rouse himself with a straight back and a scowl. "You got any news for me?"

"No, I wish I had. But—"

"Then what do you want?" Don's tone had turned aggressive, which Belzer thought was both good and bad; good, because it gave him a little more liveliness and bad because the anger inside him might be counterproductive to the case investigation. Well, Belzer thought, his job was to help catch the killer and Don Bollmeier's sensitivities be damned.

"What I want," Belzer said, making his voice sound hard (he cringed inside at doing that), "is to ask you some more questions about your wife. And let me get this straight out—I don't give a shit if it angers you or hurts you. This fucker has murdered seven people—yes, probably eight—and we'll do whatever's necessary to find and stop him. So why don't you stop feeling sorry for yourself, get off your ass, make me some coffee, and we can get down to brass tacks."

Don jumped up, balled his hands into fists, and glared at the man in front of him. It took him a split second before he decided against breaking Belzer's jaw and making that coffee. Belzer followed him into the kitchen where weeks' worth of dirty dishes covered the sinks and counters. Dried splotches of ketchup stained the floor, and a fly buzzed around a half-eaten plate of shriveled French fries.

Nothing was said while Don cleaned out the Mr. Coffee carafe and filled it with water. He used extra coffee in the pot; both men liked their brew extra strong. When the coffee brewed he poured two mugs of black and carried them to the kitchen table where Belzer had cleaned a space for them.

Don took a sip then said without inflection, "What do you want to know?"

"You have the personal effects they cleaned out of Laurel's work desk?"

"Shit, I have everything. I wouldn't throw away a post-it note that woman touched. It's all I have left of her." He began sobbing.

Belzer let him cry for a minute then, hating himself, asked, "Can I see the stuff, please?"

Don swiped his sleeve across his runny nose and nodded wordlessly. He took another sip of coffee with his shaking hand, then rose and left the kitchen. Belzer began to feel a little more compassion for Laurel seeing the depths of grief that her husband was enduring.

She had to have some redeeming qualities to elicit this much love and passion in another human being.

Don brought in a medium-sized plastic box marked "Laurel's desk." He placed it gently on the table and sat down hard, staring into his coffee cup. He barely looked up as Belzer started going through the contents. Occasionally Belzer asked a question and Don answered in a monotone. After a half hour Belzer sighed and stored the box contents as they had been.

"I don't suppose they missed anything at the office?"

Don shook his head. "They were thorough, same here. I let them turn this place upside down looking for clues to her work and the police leak, but nothing. Not a fucking thing."

Belzer pursed his thin lips together. "Everyone says that Laurel kept her contacts and informants in her head. You sure she didn't write anything down?"

"Your forensics team analyzed her computer files and every paper file she had, but there was nothing. Look, I know my wife played things close to the vest, but I still have doubts about her not writing something down, just in case. I checked our safety deposit box and there was nothing there, either. I know for sure she wouldn't have shared anything with her newspaper associates—it's a cutthroat business and she was very careful not to reveal anything that someone might use to get a leg up on her."

"All right, Don," Belzer said quietly. "I won't bother you any more today, but please try to remember what I said—there's always hope. Hang on to that. I'll show myself out." Belzer left the house without looking back. He half-expected to hear a gunshot as he walked to his car and was relieved when he didn't. Still, he knew that Don had guns in the house and he wondered if he could somehow get them out.

Belzer's visit was a bust, but he had one more thing to try. He headed over to the *Old Pueblo Sentinel* offices. He'd been there a dozen times over the course of his law enforcement career, but not since last year. The newspaper's owner, Santiano Bronson, had apparently expanded the parking lot and added some premium covered spaces, an excellent perk in the hot summer heat. He pulled into a reserved covered slot and put his old police tag on the dashboard.

The receptionist announced him to Bronson who came down a moment later and pumped his hand.

"Good to see you again, Belzer. Uh, I mean—"

Belzer smiled. "I know. Don't worry about it. I wanted to ask a favor."

"Shoot."

"You still have Laurel's desk, right?" At Bronson's nod he went on. "I'd like to inspect it. I know it's been done before, but we're just re-covering all the bases."

"Well, we gave Laurel's cubicle, desk, and computer to Judie Sutphin, and she's out covering that drug bust down in Green Valley. But we have master keys to all desks and I guess she won't mind. Come with me." With that Bronson led Belzer up to the third floor and Judie's cubicle. Belzer took in the salient points—Judie was neat and minimal, and clearly loved her dogs. Bronson left for a few minutes to get the master keys, which he handed to Belzer.

"I won't hover over you while you're searching but come to my office when you're done. Listen—if you uncover anything that helps break the case—"

"You'll get first crack at a scoop," Belzer promised honestly. Law enforcement and the media—it was all about scratching one another's backs.

"Have fun," Bronson said as he walked away.

Belzer examined the exterior of the desk from all angles, including getting down on the floor and looking under it. Then he opened the middle drawer and examined the contents; Judie was a neatnik but had at least two of everything—staples, paper clips, packs of rubber bands. The desk had three drawers on each side, and he began with the top drawer on the left side. He carefully removed everything in the drawer, took it out, and studied it from every angle. He did the same with each of the left drawers, getting more disappointed as he realized that this was as fruitless as checking the box at Don's house.

He took apart the top drawer on the right, noting that it was stuffed with three staplers and two three-hole-punches. The second drawer was stuffed to the gills with pens, pencils, and markers. Belzer checked a few; apparently, Judie liked to pick up a new pen (or six) here or there, including banks, real estate offices, and four from the police station.

He locked the middle drawer and keyed open the bottom one. He pulled it out and it got stuck, and he examined it to determine why. He used his hand to move things around and finally managed to get it all the way open. He saw a label maker (which had obviously been used to label that drawer), plastic tape, rulers, a protractor (a protractor??), two cameras, and four unexposed rolls of 35mm film. He extracted all the items and removed the drawer and studied it. As he flipped it over to look at the bottom, he thought that he heard something. He shook it; there was a light noise. He put the drawer down on the floor and stared at it for a long moment, then he reopened the middle drawer. He took one of the rulers and measured the depth of the drawer—five inches. He slowly measured the depth of the drawer on the floor—four inches. He opened the top drawer and it measured the same as the middle. He didn't need to measure those on the left.

Belzer picked up the empty drawer and scrutinized it. He noticed a few scratches at the back of the drawer on the bottom, as though something had tried to pry it open. He flicked open his penknife, took a deep breath, and inserted it so that a quarter inch was under the bottom at the side. He wriggled the knife for a few seconds before he heard a tiny crack and then he shoved the knife under the false bottom and pried it out.

There it was, a one-inch deep space under the false bottom.

And there they were, handwritten notes and pieces of paper. Belzer inhaled sharply, looked around suspiciously, then stuffed all the papers into his inner pocket and wedged the false bottom back on. He placed the label maker and other items back in and locked it. He made himself look cool and calm as he entered Bronson's office, thanked him for his help, and returned the keys. No, he didn't find anything of merit.

Belzer could barely drive with his hands shaking as he rushed to the Union Jack offices and tore up to the second floor. Deliverance was filing something in a cabinet, took one look at his face, and ushered him into the Saguaro Conference Room. She got him a glass of cold water, asked him what he had, and a moment later told him to "keep your ass in that chair" as she ran out to call her partners. Iris was up in Phoenix and Raine was at a doctor appointment. Quint was at the Veteran's Administration, and Wilde and Victor were in Wilde's office looking over summer curricula for various camps that their boys might want to attend. When she called Quint, he said to go ahead with their meeting and he'd be there as soon as he could.

Belzer spread out all the papers and slips on the table as Deliverance, Wilde, and Victor picked them up and studied them. Deliverance had made photocopies of all the papers and was taking notes on common reference names or codenames. Laurel had been meticulous in keeping notes, and for every tip she'd gotten she wrote down the medium, date, times, contents of the tip, and a codename for the tipster. There were three codenames that popped up more than others—Troy, Doc, and Tex. There were no indications as to whether these people were men or women.

The contents of the notes indicated that she had received tips for the ax murders as well as the current suite. "Doc" had been the main source for both situations, but a few tips came in from Troy. Tex seemed to impart various tidbits associated with different, minor stories. They focused in on Doc and Troy, but there was nothing to indicate the people's real identities.

"Doc, Doc, Doc," Wilde murmured as he contemplated the note from January 14,1984 on the double hitchhiker case: "Cops interrogating silversmith Moon Wolf Begay, arrest possibly imminent. Doc, confirmation by Troy." Wilde looked up. "Well, at least we know that the leak definitely is in the police department. Now all we have to figure out who the hell 'Doc' and 'Troy' are."

"Well, normally, the Doc nickname would apply to a doctor," Victor said. "But there are a hell of a lot of different types of doctors out there—medical, dentist, shrinks, PhDs, the like. Doesn't narrow it down."

"And," Deliverance added, "it could be some obscure nickname that really has nothing to do with the medical profession. But it's something to go on. How about Troy? A reference to Greek mythology? Someone named Helen? Turkey?"

"Aren't there a lot of towns in the country with that name?" Belzer asked. "I mean, I've heard of Troy, Michigan. Actually, been there. And there's a ghost town named Troy right here in Arizona in Pinal County. Used to be a mining camp, but now it's a private ranch."

"I'll bet Raine can come up with a list of Troys," Deliverance said. She dialed Raine's number and left a message for her. "Now, how about Tex? Besides the obvious?"

"Well, we'll scan the personnel files and see who's from Texas and that might help narrow it down," Victor said. He arched an eyebrow. "By the way, aren't we technically obstructing justice by not turning these notes over to the cops? That's a rhetorical question, since I once was a cop."

"Yeah, but that was before you turned to the light side, Darth," Wilde replied, grinning.

"We will turn this stuff over today," Belzer said. "I'll take full responsibility for absconding with it for a period of delay, and hope that Cornell is as understanding as I was when Quint held back that letter that the Axewoman sent him." During the old ax murders case the killer had sent Quint a threatening letter after she had murdered his family, and he hadn't turned it over to the police for a while. It was Belzer who read Quint the riot act and threw him in jail for an hour, stating that Quint damned well better not withhold any information in the future, or he'd be swabbing floors in Florence Prison for six months.

"I'll bake you a pound cake with a file in it," Deliverance said breezily.

"I feel so loved," Belzer said.

They were still discussing the various notes an hour later when Quint came in carrying two pizzas.

"How did you know we were starving?" Wilde asked, eyeing the pizza boxes hungrily.

Quint gave him a funny look. "I bought these for my lunch and breakfast. So, now you want a slice, too? The shit I have to put up with after spending a gruesome half day at the VA."

"Oh, my poor darling," Deliverance commiserated as she ripped one of the pizzas from his hands and placed it on the table. "Dibs on the slice with the most cheese," she said as she left the room to get beverages.

Victor opened the box and spied the slice with the most cheese and snagged it for himself. He shrugged. "She doesn't always get her way, oui?"

"C'est vrai," Wilde conceded as he snagged the next best cheese-laden slice. He looked directly at Quint. "You aren't going to rat us out, are you?"

"Not a chance," Quint replied as he pulled apart the slice with the most pepperoni and sausage. He looked up guiltily as his wife came in with a six-pack of Coke. She stared at the three slices that were already bitten. She smiled at them evilly but didn't say a word. She took note that Belzer had appropriated a slice with very little cheese or meat on it.

In between mastication Belzer updated Quint on what he'd found. Quint listened thoughtfully without making any remarks. Belzer had nearly finished his explanation when Raine came into the room and all three of the men jumped up. She scowled at them and said, "Sit, sit. I'm not a delicate flower. Ooh—pizza. I'm starved." She plopped down next to Deliverance and grabbed a slice and a Coke. She handed Deliverance a sheet of paper.

"Luckily, I've been collecting scads of data disks and had several with geographical info on the colonies. I did a merge and sort and came up with your list of Troy towns. Can you believe that over half of the states have a town named Troy?" She took a huge bite of the pizza and groaned in pleasure. "All I had today was cottage cheese and a banana. This is so good."

Deliverance smiled as she scanned the list and began running the states off. "Wisconsin, West Virginia, Virginia, Vermont, Texas, Tennessee, South Dakota, South Carolina, Pennsylvania, Oregon, Oklahoma, Ohio, North Carolina, New York, New Hampshire, Montana, Missouri, Mississippi, Minnesota, Michigan, Maine, Louisiana, Kentucky, Kansas, Iowa, Indiana, Illinois, Idaho, California, Arkansas, Arizona, Alabama." She frowned. "Isn't Thayer from New Hampshire?"

"Think so," Quint said as he took a second slice.

Deliverance hit the preset for Thayer's phone and asked her to come in. A minute later Thayer bounced into the room and eyed the pizza. Quint nodded, and she helped herself.

"What can I do ya for?" she asked as she gulped a dripping edge of cheese.

"You're from New Hampshire, right?" Victor asked.

She nodded. "Yup, Jaffrey. Tiny town with a few good diners and not much else. Why?"

"Ever hear of a town named Troy?"

Thayer laughed. "Of course. It's just down the road from Jaffrey, ten miles at most. Remember I told you I worked summers at the Inn at East Hill Farm in Troy?"

"Right." Wilde nodded. He didn't really remember.

"What do you need to know about it?" Thayer asked.

"Are there any places or things there that are noteworthy?" Wilde asked.

"No, not really. The Inn, like I mentioned. Mt. Monadnock. The old blanket mill. It's a pretty tiny town. I'm sure there aren't even a thousand residents. You want any action you have to head northwest for about ten miles to the small city of Keene to get any decent food or shopping. Anything larger is much farther away." She noticed the looks on their faces. "What?"

"Nothing," Victor said. "Hey—take another slice and thanks for your time."

"Okaaaay ..." Thayer said, understanding that whatever there was to be discussed didn't include a junior associate. She grabbed another slice and headed out, anxious to gossip with Turner.

"Keene?" Quint said. "Keene Swansey, detective un-extraordinaire?"

"Gotta be," Belzer said. "Well, that's one nickname down, and two to go. I'll mention this to Cornell when I turn over Laurel's papers. He can verify whether Swansey is one of the leaks." He nodded to Quint. "Get anything from the VA?"

"Yes and no. They're legitimately closed-mouthed about any official records. They wouldn't confirm or deny whether Murphy has been treated for anything, and they had no information about his Vietnam service or discharge. I badgered a few doctors and vets I saw there and nearly got thrown out. But, I did find one guy who sort of remembers a Pete Murphy in Da Nang, where he lost his legs."

"We had no business being in that war," Victor growled. He

had marched against the war as well as for civil rights and had strong opinions about the U.S. presence there.

"No argument from me," Quint replied. He thought about one of his old platoon mates, Sergeant Doug Newcombe, who had survived the war but came home to a cheating wife and eventually took his own life. Quint thought about his own life after his discharge in 1967 and how he had almost been fatally tangled up with the Manson family in San Francisco.

"Anyway," Quint went on, "he said that Murphy spent two tours and part of third over there and was considered a decent soldier. He gave me a few names of platoon mates that I could try to track down, and the name of Murphy's immediate superior, a Lieutenant Wadsworth. He couldn't really add anything else."

"Did he say what Murphy did over there?" Wilde asked.

"Yeah, he said he was a medic." Quint suddenly stopped and stared down at the notes his wife had made. "Doc," he whispered.

Victor sat back hard in his chair and stared at his partner. "It's reasonable to assume that soldiers would call their medic Doc, isn't it?"

"More than reasonable," Wilde added as he shuffled some of the notes, looking for the cases that Murphy had worked. He nodded slowly. "Most of these tips Laurel wrote down correspond with the timeframes after Murphy finished the forensics reports."

"Maybe if you talk to that vet again or the names he gave you we can verify that Murphy was called Doc," Wilde said.

"And I'd like to know why his third tour was aborted," Victor added.

"And why he moved cross-country multiple times from his old hometown," Raine said. She swirled her Coke around and said slyly, "So, Uncle—perhaps you and Uncle Victor should consider jimmying a certain house lock."

"Are you suggesting we commit a criminal act?" Wilde said, eyebrow arched in mock shock.

"I'm suggesting no such thing. It was just a whimsical thought that came out of nowhere." Her facial expression belied her carefully selected words.

Wilde harrumphed. "Belzer, you get any info on upcoming things that might take him out of his house for a few hours?"

"Nothing, but I'll figure something out," Belzer said.

"Good," Quint said. "Victor—you get anything from your South Carolina buddy?"

"He's faxing over some lists to Iris up in Phoenix. The fibbies have those machines and I vote that we get one, too. It's the wave of the future."

"Agreed," Deliverance said. "We can thank the late Mr. Danziger for the funds with which to do so. I think we should also get mobile phones in our cars so we don't have to experience that non-communicative terror that Wilde went through coming down the mountain. All in favor?" Everyone raised their hands. "Good. I'll get on both of those items tomorrow."

"Meanwhile, back at the criminally inclined ranch ..." Raine said, flashing a look at her uncle.

"We need to come up with an entry plan. I'd prefer to do it at night, but that's the most likely time he'll be home," Wilde said. "Daytime's too risky. His house is in an older neighborhood with lots of homes and people."

"Wish we could get a search warrant," Victor said, "but with what we've got no judge will sign that."

"Then night it is," Quint said. He glanced over at Belzer. "We need to get him out of his house for a few hours—a day or two would be better. Maybe the guy at the VA could help—some kind of reunion or something up in Phoenix."

"That's weak," Deliverance said. "He'd be too suspicious especially if he hasn't had any contact with old buddies these past nineteen years." She paused. "We could always, um ... put him in the hospital."

"You mean physically assault him, so he'd need to stay there overnight?" Raine said incredulously. "Tantalizing, but not a good idea. Hmm ... maybe we can get him up to Phoenix to the FBI to consult on the cases. That's legitimate. Iris could probably help with that."

"That's a great idea," Victor said. "But we need to get one or two more people up there so he won't be suspicious."

"I'll call Iris and see what she can whip up," Raine said, rising. She let out a sudden, "Oomph," and everyone stood at attention, thinking she was in pain. She smiled. "I'm fine. Sasha's kicking like a world-class football player." She rubbed her stomach.

"Can I feel?" Deliverance asked eagerly. At Raine's nod, she placed her hand on the big baby bump and smiled slightly as the baby inside moved around aggressively. "Special girl," Deliverance murmured sagely. She grinned at Raine. "You're going to have your hands full."

"Uh-oh," Wilde said. "I'd worry about that."

"Shush," Deliverance admonished.

"I've got to get going," Raine said. "Constantine's taking me to The Happy Spartan for dinner and then we're going to a movie. I haven't been to one in ages."

"What are you going to see?" Victor asked. He hadn't taken the boys to a film for over a month and they were overdue. They were making noise about going to see *Ghoulies*.

"*The Purple Rose of Cairo,* the new Allen film, unless I can twist his arm and antagonize him into seeing *The Mean Season*. Kurt Russell is one right fit bloke. Call you guys later." With that Raine took off.

"Okay," Belzer sighed. "I've put it off long enough. I'm heading over to see Cornell with Laurel's papers. Hope we have enough money in petty cash for bail if he gets snippy and I wind up in the slammer."

"Poetic justice." Quint laughed.

"Up yours," Belzer said as he walked out of the room.

CHAPTER SEVEN

Pete Murphy wasn't overly thrilled with the choice of a motel in Phoenix. The Desert Land Motel was a mile away from the FBI building and stuck in the middle of several strip malls, small businesses, and fast-food places. He would have preferred something a bit more upscale, but since he and his two associates were on an expense account the Tucson PD wasn't about to pay for elegance and comfort. Still, the motel was less than two miles from a Cracker Barrel, and there at least he could get a reasonable facsimile of the type of down-home southern cooking with which he grew up. That is, if he could convince that cocksucker Ben Deuel to eat breakfast there instead of at that damn Mickey D's. They came up in one official car, and since Deuel was the head of the lab he got the last word on where he'd drive it. Josie Ross, the third member of their crew sent to the state capital to participate in a two-day brainstorming session on the Tucson murders, was easily led; she let the two men argue about where to go and when. She was just thrilled to accompany them to this important meeting and said so too many times on the drive up.

Murphy was giddy with anticipation. He could barely contain his excitement and derision when he thought that the purpose of the meeting was to identify him, the Beguiler. No one had any clue—he was far, far too smart and cunning. They'd never catch him, unless at some point he decided he wanted them to. Of course, he wanted people to know at some point, and that was why he had been holding that bitch Laurel Bollmeier hostage while he had her type his life story. Despite the flaws in her last book she was a fairly decent writer, and, really, there was no one else. English wasn't his best subject in school, although he managed decent technical reports for his job. He gritted his teeth; that was one of his doesn't-meet-expectations categories on his last review, rated, administered, and logged into the official record by his hated boss, Ben Deuel. Someday, he was going to crush that insect. He wished he could make the man one of his victims, but that was hitting too close to home. He wasn't stupid.

He was relieved that he didn't have to share a room with the prick. At least his room was spacious, clean, and airy, and faced the back parking lot instead of the street that was full of busy traffic.

They had driven up in the morning and it was after eleven, almost time for lunch. Deuel had grudgingly agreed to eat before they were to head over to the FBI building for the all-afternoon session. Murphy suggested the Cracker Barrel; Deuel had dismissed that idea and told them they'd head over to the Olive Garden.

Deuel rapped sharply on his door and yelled to come on. Murphy took his time before he left the room and got into the back seat of the Ford. Josie had claimed shotgun, and she and Deuel chatted nonstop while he drove to the restaurant. Murphy was only slightly mollified with his chicken parmesan and spaghetti, but he relaxed a little as he watched his teammates chatter mindlessly. He was so far above them.

They made the FBI with minutes to spare and were rushed through the administrative processes required to get them Visitor badges. Murphy did a double-take when he saw Iris Flynn coming towards them with a tall, distinguished-looking man beside her. She smiled at him as her companion introduced himself as Special Agent in Charge Nicholas Lisbon. They exchanged handshakes and names, then Lisbon led them to the elevator and up to the third floor where they entered a spacious conference room where another man sat waiting, sipping a cup of coffee. He rose and introduced himself as Special Agent Richard Ballard from the San Francisco office.

Murphy knew that name; it was Ballard that helped identify two of his victims and had inserted himself into the case. He wondered about Iris Flynn—according to the newspaper articles she had resigned from the FBI, and he knew she was working part-time in the Union Jack offices. This was a surprise, and one he wasn't sure he liked. She was too smart by half. He forced a smile as the agents made small talk for a few minutes before getting into the meat of the matter. Lisbon took the lead in summarizing why he wanted the sessions and said that they'd be joined by several FBI agents who had been working with the evidence. He planned on spending the first hour or two letting the Tucson contingent summarize their findings and observations. Ballard interjected and said the FBI was depending on the talent and insight of the Tucson forensics team to move the cases forward with a resolution before another victim was taken. He seemed to focus his attention on Ben Deuel but threw an occasional and somewhat unnerving glance over at Murphy. Iris focused almost entirely on Murphy. No one paid much attention to Josie.

When Lisbon finished his summary, he called his forensics team in and four more people joined them. It took them two hours to go over the Dahlia case alone, and they had barely finished the DeLage case when it was eight o'clock. Dinner had been brought in and most of the agents wanted to continue, but Deuel said they'd had too long a day. Lisbon agreed, and everyone was packed up and leaving by 8:30 PM. They agreed to start fresh at 7 AM.

Deuel drove them back to the motel and all three crashed in exhaustion. Murphy called his next-door neighbor to check on his house, but she said that all was well. He gave her the phone number of his room, took a hot shower, broke into the mini-bar, and went to bed thinking that maybe a great candidate for his next victim would be a resident of Phoenix instead of Tucson—that would throw the cops off. He needed to come up here on his own and scope out the possibilities.

He had been lucky or clever in his victim choices. Finding that Pearl Lewis coming off the bus with a bewildered look on her face and a battered suitcase led to her being selected as the first. He had simply walked up to her and asked if she needed help or directions. He could be gentle and charming when he wanted to be, and she fell for it. An hour later she was under him trussed up like a pig ready to be led to slaughter in a cheap motel in south Tucson. Two hours later she was in his trunk unconscious as he drove into a deserted section of the desert. He strangled her, then gouged out her eye, decapitated her, and left her buried in a shallow grave so he could take the time later to move her. It came to him like a bolt of lightning that he could initiate a new series of killings by dragging in his old police buddy, Michael Quintana. That's when he carefully deposited Pearl's head on the doorstep. It cracked him up when he was the one called to the scene to process the evidence.

DeLage was easy—he met the idiot in a bar and struck up a conversation that eventually led to the subject of dummy bridge. Knowing that a similar victim was on Malachi's unsolved list (which he had purloined one day when he was on campus auditing a class), victim number two presented himself quite handily.

From then on he went looking for victims, based on the list. They were easy to find, two young, dumb hitchhikers; the skanky whore who became the Lady of the Dunes—he'd had to remove her tattooed forearm to make identification more difficult, as well as remove her fingertips and a few teeth (to date they still hadn't identified her); and the teenage college student who made the mistake of simply being in the wrong place at the wrong time. Munch was another matter—Murphy wanted to make a statement and he needed something spectacular to do so, and, boy, that was spectacular. It was all he could do at the funeral to not burst out laughing as he sadly offered his condolences to the widow.

And Laurel. She was the conduit with which he issued leaks and tips, just to be bitchy and self-satisfied that he was in control. The problem was that she wasn't as appreciative as she should have been, even though he'd tipped her several key times during the Axewoman of Tucson case. She never mentioned him in her book, not even a footnote. And he wasn't sure that she'd do so in her second book on the unsolved cases. Anyway, he was bored with her, but recognized her writing talent, a talent he needed to get his full story out. He waffled between becoming known and notorious, or notorious and a historical enigma. He chose the former. Of course, when he finished his reign of terror he'd have to kill her, and perhaps write the last chapter or two himself.

He fell asleep smiling, pleased with himself, very pleased indeed.

"You do have the advantage, you know," Wilde whispered to Victor as they sat in their car two blocks away from Murphy's house. Sunset had fallen an hour earlier, and the streets were dark with only a few dim streetlights providing minimal illumination. It was unseasonably chilly for a March night, and few people were walking around.

"How's that?" Victor asked as he scanned the neighborhood with his night-vision binoculars.

"You're black," Wilde replied. "And wearing those black jeans and sweatshirt you blend into the night like a wraith.

Victor put the binoculars down and looked at his partner. "You're just realizing I'm black? What was your first clue?"

"The addiction to fried chicken—ow!" Wilde exclaimed when Victor punched him in the arm before resuming his surveillance of the Murphy house. Wilde rubbed his arm. "Bloody hell. That hurt."

"Good," Victor said as he scanned the neighborhood. "What time is it?"

Wilde checked his watch. "Nine-fifteen. Think we should go in?"

"Oui. Put your makeup on."

Wilde reached into the backpack resting on the passenger floor and took out the small jar of black face paint. He smeared some all over his face, then used a baby wipe on his hands and slipped on thin black leather gloves. "Well?" he said.

Victor studied him and sighed. "You'd've been a hit in those old minstrel shows in the deep south. Al Jolson would be sobbing in his mint julep."

"Thanks. Your effusive praise is what I live for, my African prince."

"I figured. Okay, let's go."

Wilde pulled away from the curb very slowly without turning on his headlights. He hugged the side of the road then came to a stop twenty feet away from Murphy's driveway. They looked around and no one was on the street, and quite a few homes had their lights off. Murphy didn't have a light over his front door, so his house was one of the dark ones. They moved quickly but quietly, one to each side of the house, meeting up in the back. Luckily, there was no block fence surrounding the house so entry into the back was simple.

Wilde checked for any sign of a security alarm, but there was none. The back door, like the front, had two deadbolt locks. He studied them with his small pen light, satisfied that they could be easily jimmied. Victor withdrew his B&E kit and made short work of the locks. He gently pushed open the back door, waiting for an alarm to go off; it didn't. It creaked ever so slightly as the two men entered the house and when Victor shut the door and reset the deadlocks.

They found themselves in the kitchen, which even in the minimal light seemed neat and clean. Wilde closed the blinds over the kitchen window and the back door. They didn't plan on turning on any lights, but they didn't want to arouse anyone outside with their flashlights and pens.

Wilde opened the refrigerator a crack. "Not much in here. The man likes condiments." He opened the freezer section. "Lots of TV dinners, mostly Swanson." He cast a guilty glance over at his partner. "Don't hit me again, but I love their fried chicken."

Victor sighed theatrically. "So do I. And those little apple tart thingies for dessert. Keep focused. Any heads in there?"

"Nope, unless you count the one attached to the frozen trout."

"I'll photograph it anyway," Victor said as he fiddled with the camera he'd brought. The expensive camera took excellent low-light photographs. He set the exposure and focus to manual and set it to the largest aperture. He took shots on the inside of the refrigerator, then the kitchen from every angle. "Let's move into the living room."

There was less neatness to the living room, but it was designed with minimal furniture. A sofa and lounge chair faced the console TV that looked like it had been left over from the sixties; one of the antenna on the rabbit ears was broken off. Wilde pulled the blinds on the picture window, the Victor snapped a dozen shots of the room, including looking up the chimney flue.

"Look at this," Wilde said, holding up a small framed photo. Victor looked at the shot of three soldiers in some sort of jungle; clearly, Murphy was in the middle and it had to be taken during his tour in Vietnam. "See the medical patch on his shirt?"

"Oui. Take the photo out and see if anything's written on the back."

Wilde opened the frame back and took the photo out. There were three names, a place, and a date written on the back in ink— 1965, Da Nang, Joey, Doc, Chuck.

"So, we know he's Doc," Victor murmured as he studied the young faces of the three buddies. He wondered what happened to the other two, and what they could tell him about "Doc." Wilde slipped the photo back in the frame.

"Let's check out the rest of the house," Wilde said.

They moved through the small house room by room, checking the closets and taking photographs. They carefully rifled through his clothes and drawers but came up empty. They went into the garage and were able to put on the light since there were no windows. While Victor examined the black Cherokee Wilde rummaged through the tools and storage boxes. They spent fifteen minutes in the garage then went back into the house. Wilde nearly forgot to turn off the light but remembered at the last second.

"Well, not much joy here," Wilde said, disappointed. "On the plus side, I don't hear any police sirens, so we may yet stay out of the Big House."

"Too bad it's a single story. I'd love to explore an attic."

"My parents' house has an attic and Danny and I used to love going up there to play."

"Shaun and I used our basement as a secret place to avoid our parents and play our games," Victor mused. He felt that longtime pang of missing his big brother.

"Yes, we had a basement, too. Most houses out here don't. That's what keeps the cost of housing down. Too bad Murphy doesn't have a basement we could root around in."

"Yeah," Victor replied thoughtfully. "None of the doors opened to basement stairs."

"Think we should head out?"

"You know," Victor said, "let's do one more run through the house. Pay attention to the walls—could be some hidden panels we missed. Also, let's look under the rugs for any floor safes."

"Sounds good."

The men started pulling up the scatter rugs on the various floors and found nothing except floor. Wilde took the east side of the house while Victor took the west and they inspected the walls, moving aside wall pictures and artwork.

There was a large sideboard against a hall wall. Wilde tried to move it, but it was tall and heavy, and he called Victor over. They moved the heavy piece of wooden furniture to the side, cursing as they left a scrape on the wooden floor. Wilde noticed that there were other scratches there before they'd moved it. The sideboard wound up four feet away from its place. Wilde and Victor stared at the wall.

There was the outline of a small opening, perhaps three feet tall and three feet wide. There couldn't have been more than a sixteenth of an inch space between the sides of the opening and the wall in which it was placed. Victor pointed at a small barrel slide lock near the bottom of the door. He pulled it across carefully, then pulled the door open, noting that it was hinged on the inside. All he could see was darkness.

"If there's a basement down there it's weird," Wilde said softly. He stood and began running his hands over the wall, scrutinizing the paint and drywall. "Look at this closely," he said, pointing his flashlight around the wall. At Victor's querulous look, he went on. "It almost looks like this entire wall was redone. The paint seems newer, and the consistency is smoother than that other wall, which has more texture. Like a homemade job of an amateur."

"Suddenly you're a contractor?"

"I've been watching the guys work on Quint's addition."

"You think there was another door here that was done over and hidden?" Victor's voice had taken on a hint of anticipation.

"Maybe. Ready to descend to the depths of God knows what?" Wilde flashed his light into the darkness and saw the stairs. Without waiting for an answer, he turned around and backed into the opening, moving down the stairs very slowly and carefully. The staircase was at a forty-five-degree angle but the steps were wide and solid and there was a sturdy handrail. Wilde was nearly to the bottom when Victor backed into the staircase and began his descent. By the time he reached the bottom Wilde had found and turned on the light.

"Well, it's a basement all right," Wilde mused as he scanned the underground room. He took in the key points—a double bed that had been neatly made with an extra-large southwest-design comforter that draped over the sides, a dresser with a record player on it, a filing cabinet, and a wooden chair next to a small desk with a computer and an old Royal typewriter on it; next to the computer was an empty binder. Strangely, there was also a simple toilet and a small sink in one corner of the room. There was a long, narrow glass window high on the west wall, but it had been obscured by black paint. "Huh," he said. "Looks like a mini studio apartment."

Victor walked over to a homemade bookcase of lumber and cinder blocks and checked out the books. "He's got a lot of stuff on true crime, including the Axewoman case. Son of Sam, Ted Bundy,

Manson, Jack the Ripper—he's definitely got a focus on the macabre. Here's Laurel's book, too." He glanced over at his partner. "Find anything?" He snapped off a dozen shots of the basement.

Wilde was rooting around in the desk. "Nothing. Shyte."

Victor blew out a hard breath. "Well, we tried." He glanced over at the bed. "You check under the bed? Why the hell would someone have a second bed down in a basement?"

Wilde shook his head then walked over to the bed and pulled back the edge of the comforter. "Well," he said, "he's practical."

"What do you mean?" Victor walked over to the bed and craned his neck.

"He made a built-in, under-bed storage drawer. See the wood? It's definitely not store-bought. It's not even sanded properly. Check the other side. See if it goes all the way."

Victor complied and said, "Yes, it's here. It's rough, too, and no pull knobs."

"The handles are on this side." Wilde gently juggled them. He looked up at Victor. "You think we should pull it out?"

"We came here to explore, and so far that drawer's unexplored territory, so, yes—let's pull that sucker out." He squatted down next to Wilde and grabbed hold of the second handle. "On three. One, two, *three*."

They pulled their respective handles and the drawer pulled out a few inches. A rank smell hit their olfactory senses. Whatever was in it was heavy. They pulled harder; the drawer seemed to stick then pulled out two feet. Victor fell back on the floor and scrambled backwards. His jaw dropped, and he just stared, then chanted, "Mon dieu, mon dieu, mon dieu!" over and over again.

Wilde burst out into full-body goose bumps as waves of ice rippled over his body. He backed up and desperately pulled the drawer out another foot, yelling to Victor to call the police. He sat down hard and stared, momentarily frozen, and thought back to his Shakespeare courses in university. He loved the Bard of Avon, and *The Tempest* was one of his favorite plays. In it, Ariel said something that could easily apply to what they had uncovered.

Hell is empty, and all the devils are here.

CHAPTER EIGHT

Reva Dunn had lived in her neighborhood for thirty years. She was one of the first people to buy a home there after the gentrification of the area began. She'd paid $10,250 for her house, and now it had more than tripled in price, not that she'd ever consider selling. Originally from LaGrange, Georgia, she had moved west with her husband, James, who had gotten a job at the Hughes Missile plant after he mustered out of the Army when the Korean War ended. James had asthma and his doctor recommended a hot, dry climate, so they chose Arizona and Tucson. They had two daughters, Kim and Mandy, who were now on their own as smart, professional businesswomen. James had passed away three years earlier, and although Reva had a nice pension from her late husband to rely on, she spent some of her free time cashiering for Alpha Beta. She liked people, and her job gave her the opportunity to talk and laugh and in general help make the world a better place.

She was considered the "grande dame" of her neighborhood, and enthusiastically welcomed new residents with a basket of homemade food (including her famous brandied peaches) and a bouquet of flowers. Her smile was fetching, and her snowy hair was always cut in the old Sassoon style of the late 1960s. She adored her grandsons, Randy and Devin, who visited often.

Reva also kept an eye on the homes around her street. There had been a burglary two years earlier, but crime in the area was virtually nonexistent. Still, she watched and made notes, and was vigilant. She liked to go to sleep by ten o'clock at the latest since she was an early riser and liked to take a morning walk with her chihuahua, Taco, and water her garden before the temperatures heated up too much. March wasn't bad, but she dreaded July and August when the monsoon would roll in.

She had barely fallen asleep when she was awakened by screaming police sirens and squealing tires. She flew out of bed and ran to her living room, where she pushed back the drapes and stared out at the four police cars that were clustered around her neighbor, Pete's, house. Their car lights were blaring in the dark night and a flood of uniformed cops were flying out of their cars, headed towards the front door. There was a tall man dressed in black at the door waving them in. A moment later an ambulance screeched up.

Reva was baffled. Pete lived alone, and he was up in Phoenix. Whatever the problem was, he needed to know about it, so she put on the lamp, sat down, and dialed the motel room number he'd given her shortly before. He seemed a little put out when he answered sleepily but snapped awake when she told him what was going on at his house. He thanked her curtly and hung up. Reva slipped on a robe and went outside where several other neighbors were standing around whispering and pointing. They'd all been standing around for nearly a half hour before two EMTs came out with a body on a gurney, an oxygen mask strapped to the person's face; Reva couldn't tell if it was a man or a woman, but she couldn't miss the urgency with which the EMTs were loading the gurney into the ambulance. Moments later the ambulance tore off with a police car leading it down the street at breakneck speed.

By that time two more police cars, including one unmarked, pulled up, followed by a media van from one of the Tucson TV channels. She could see two men dressed in street clothes get out of the unmarked car and run to the front door. She thought they were probably detectives since the uniforms deferred to them. The tall man in black was waiting for them at the front door then all three men disappeared inside the house. With all the lights she could see that he was black and in his fifties.

A half dozen of the uniformed officers were spreading out, heading towards the people standing around. Clearly, they were interviewing them, probably about Pete Murphy. Reva wondered what the hell was going on as one cop walked over to her and greeted her urgently but politely. He asked questions about Pete Murphy and she answered them. She told him that she was keeping an eye on his house and that she had spoken to him twice that evening, once to tell him all was well, and then when she saw the police cars pull up. Even in the dark she could see the young officer pale as she told him that she and Pete had spoken just a half hour earlier. He ran off without saying thank you and disappeared into the house. A moment later, he reappeared with one of the detectives, who strode over to her with fervency written all over his taught body.

Reva thought that this was going to be one long night …

Don Bollmeier muttered to himself angrily as he padded to the front door in bare feet, shorts, and tee-shirt. He had been up for nearly twenty-four hours and had finally managed to fall asleep fifteen minutes ago thanks to a half bottle of Jameson whiskey and two sleeping pills. He had been drinking Jameson excessively, both as a means of calming himself down and because it reminded him of their honeymoon in Ireland. They'd toured the whiskey brewery, and both fell in love with the smooth varieties of the world-famous alcohol. He flipped the light switch, unbolted the door, and swung it open, ready to give whoever was there a big piece of his mind in no uncertain terms. He was startled when he saw Belzer standing there with an anxious look on his face. Suddenly, Belzer grinned widely.

"She's alive, Don. Laurel's alive. Get dressed."

Iris Flynn, Richard Ballard, Nicholas Lisbon, and four other FBI agents broke down the door to Pete Murphy's motel room, guns out and ready. The room was empty, man and suitcase gone. Lisbon directed Special Agent Liberty Adams to go to Ben Deuel's room and bring him here. The junior agents slipped on latex gloves and began examining the room; one photographed it.

"How did the cocksucker know we were coming?" Iris growled.

"I don't know," Lisbon said. "Maybe Deuel can tell us." He noticed a disturbance outside the door and turned to see Liberty instructing another agent, who took off like a shot. She came inside.

"Ben Deuel's dead," she said flatly. Ignoring the gasps, she went on. "He didn't answer so I broke the door in. He was lying on the floor with his throat cut. The blood was fresh, and his flesh was warm—he can't be dead more than ten or fifteen minutes. I went to the next room and Josie is fine—didn't hear a thing. I told Parker to call it in and stay with Deuel's body."

"Anything missing from Deuel's room?" Ballard asked.

"I don't know," Liberty said, "but his wallet was on the dresser, rifled through, I'd say. No sign of car keys." She froze and rushed out of the room to verify that the car was gone.

"Odds are pretty damn good that he took the car," Iris said. "I'll find out the make and model from Josie." She started to walk away but Lisbon stopped her.

"I need you here with us." He called over to another agent. "Veazie, go to Josie's room and get the make of the car. The clerk downstairs should have the license plate." He looked at Iris. "Think hard, Flynn—where would he go? Back to Tucson? North? L.A.?"

She shook her head vigorously. "He'd figure we'd consider those options. And I'm betting that if he hasn't already he'll ditch that car and jack or hotwire another one. Likely he'll take other plates and put it on the new car. He knows all the tricks." Liberty came back into the room and mouthed to Iris, "The car's gone." She stood by waiting for orders.

"Yeah," Ballard agreed. "That's why he's been so successful and two steps ahead of us all the way. He knows every in and out of law enforcement and forensics and how to clean a scene. He's smart as hell, and he's been luckier than a ringer in Vegas."

"Luck always runs out," Iris said. She gritted her teeth and said to no one in particular, "And I'm gonna make sure his runs out real soon. That son of a bitch is about to throw snake eyes."

"Easy, Flynn," Ballard said mildly. "We have to be smart, too, and letting emotion into the equation gives him even more of an edge. Right now, we need to use the protocols we have—set up roadblocks, have state troopers on every major road leading out of Phoenix, and, as much as I'm reluctant to do so, immediately notify the media and get his face on every TV set in the state."

"Agreed," Lisbon said. He turned to Liberty. "Get going on all of that." She nodded and took off. Lisbon heard the wail of the ambulance siren as it closed in on the motel. He asked Iris, "Deuel got any next of kin?"

"I think Belzer said he was married but that's as much as I know. Do you want me to call the Union Jackers and update them on what's happened and find out about Deuel's family situation?"

"Yes, do that," Lisbon said. "Get one of the vacant rooms—on this floor if possible—and set up a temp command center there. Two rooms adjoining would be better."

"Will do, Boss," she said and left the room.

"She's a hell of an agent," Ballard said casually after she'd left the room. "Glad she decided to reinstate."

"That makes two of us," Lisbon said. "She's a little unpredictable, but Mensa smart and tough as nails. Her husband is a nanny?" He grinned.

"Nanny-bodyguard," Ballard corrected. "Yes, it should be an interesting marriage. Thanks for letting her station down in Tucson."

"I see her as the future linchpin down there. But don't tell her I said that. It's all I can do to keep her under some kind of control now."

"Your secret is safe with me."

Even close to midnight the lights in all the offices at the Union Jack building were on and everyone on the payroll was present. Tucker and the Dane-Quintana and Renard kids had taken over the Saguaro Conference Room with sleeping bags, pillows, and futons; Quint insisted that the youngsters be in safe reach while the Beguiler—AKA, Peter Patrick Murphy—was on the loose and the private investigators were working. The men had shoved the large table against the wall, leaving a large floor space for the kids. They had moved the largest TV in the office in, and right now it was tuned to Johnny Carson. Beckett was sitting cross-legged on the floor in front of a chessboard. He was teaching an intense Storm how to play, and she was comprehending the game too fast in his estimation, especially for a seven-year-old. The partners were running things from the Crucifixion Thorn Conference Room, and the junior associates were huddled in the Devil Cholla Conference Room.

Detective Cornell had assigned a patrol car to stay in the parking lot as extra protection. He, Baxter, Welsh, and Cromwell were running their end from the precinct. The infamous "Troy" —AKA Keene Swansey—was on paid suspension until a hearing could determine whether he'd be tossed off the force; his partner, Mike Welsh, was paired up with Chet Cromwell for the duration. Hortense Garcia—who under direct questioning admitted to being

"Tex"—was also on unpaid leave, but she was on better footing than Swansey.

Shayne brought in a fresh pot of coffee to her bosses while Fox carried in a case of bottled water. Fox had found a pizzeria that was open to midnight and had ordered a half dozen pizzas that were gobbled up as a matter of adrenaline rather than hunger. He had also just made it to the supermarket before it closed and picked up three dozen donuts, a dozen bagels, and cream cheese, plus the half gallon of orange juice that Quint demanded. Fox wisely picked up two half gallons.

Fox had also been tasked with notifying the C's and their families about the turn of events, as well as Bliss and Malachi, who were up with their cranky week-old son, Barnabas. Fox told Raine to not come in unless they called her. Thirty minutes later a very pregnant Raine turned up with her annoyed fiancé. She marched into the Crucifixion Thorn Conference Room and sat down in front of the computer, ready to do technological battle if the need arose. Deliverance tried to get her to go home, but Raine was stubborn as a mule, as Constantine stated loudly. His fiancée told him to be quiet unless he had something constructive to say and to work on his outline.

Constantine's first nonfiction book, *White Captive, Indian Heart*, had hit the retail shelves five months earlier and was lauded by anthropologists and literary figures alike. Saguaro Western College had even selected the book for their Anthropology department. He was encouraged to write another, and he had decided on a biography of New Orleans Voodoo Queen Marie Laveau with the emphasis on how her life and practices shaped the religion in the rarified environment of his hometown. He had promised the outline of *Voodoo Queen, African Icon* to his editor by April 12th. He grumbled but sat next to her, reaching for a piece of cold sausage pizza as he took his papers and red pen out of his shoulder bag.

Shortly after midnight Belzer walked in and all eyes turned to him with the same questioning look.

"She's in bad shape," Belzer said, "but the doctors are optimistic."

"Mon dieu," Victor breathed, "I thought she was ready to

expire when we first saw her. That poor woman! She looked like skin and bones."

When he and Wilde had pulled the bed drawer out all the way they were far beyond shocked at the woman lying in it, naked, hands bound behind her back, a gag and blindfold covering her face. They spoke soothingly to her before Victor took off to call an ambulance. She began whimpering as Wilde gently removed the blindfold then the gag and ever so carefully turned her over to remove her hand ties. He extracted her from the drawer. She was as light as a feather and couldn't weigh more than ninety pounds. He placed her on the bed and sat beside her holding her hands as she cried and sobbed. She managed to babble a few words, including "Don," but was too discombobulated to make any sense. She stank from body odor, urine, and feces, which smeared the bottom of the drawer where she'd been lying. Her hair was limp and matted, her cheeks sunken, her eyes unbearably terrified.

But—she was alive. Wilde could hear police sirens and then an ambulance siren as Victor backed into the basement again, followed by two uniformed officers. The young men were stunned at the sight as Wilde quickly covered her nakedness with a blanket. Victor threw out that he'd called their partners after he called 9-1-1 and Cornell directly. It was only a matter of a few more minutes, but it seemed like an eternity before two EMTs backed down into the basement and got to work stabilizing Laurel, putting an oxygen mask on her, and strapping her to a gurney they deftly maneuvered up the stairs and out into the hallway.

Wilde and Victor stayed put as the ambulance and the lead police car tore off to the hospital. Cornel and Baxter turned up shortly and Wilde and Victor told him their story. He berated them for breaking and entering, but intimated that the criminal action might be forgiven by the D.A. under the circumstances. He viewed the basement, his lip curling in disgust as Baxter called the FBI to tell them to arrest Murphy up in Phoenix. He was unaware that well-intentioned neighbor Reva Dunn had called Murphy at the motel, giving him the chance to get away before the FBI broke into his room; they had missed him by ten minutes, long enough to get Deuel to open his door and die wordlessly from a slashed throat.

Belzer had driven Don Bollmeier to the hospital where they ran up two flights of stairs to the intensive care unit. The security guard held them back from the room where Laurel was being treated by a slew of doctors and nurses. Belzer calmed Don down enough to keep him from punching out the security guard to get to his wife. They sat next to the ICU door for thirty minutes before a doctor came out and said Don could see his wife for five minutes, then she was going down to x-ray. Don fled into the room and nearly threw himself on his fragile wife, who was awake and trying to smile at him. He burst into tears and sobbed for the whole five minutes, then followed his wife and her attendant down the hall to x-ray, still sobbing.

Belzer finished telling his friends about the scene at the hospital. "She was able to speak, and—thank God—she was able to say that he hadn't raped her."

"Then why the hell did he keep her for all these months?" Quint asked harshly.

"The manuscript," Wilde replied. "There was a divider between Laurel's body and the other side of the drawer. That side had folders, papers, and a partial manuscript that I flipped through just to get the gist. It looks like he was dictating his life story to her, and she was typing it. Unfortunately, I didn't get a look at any of the other stuff before Cornel and his boys nabbed it. Hopefully, it will give evidence and clues to what he's done and what he's planning on doing." He shook his head in disgust. "There were also trophies of his kills—a jar with Pearl's eye floating in formaldehyde, fingertips from the Dunes lady, a bridge deck, and separate locks of hair they think belong to Cummings and the hitchhikers." He paused for a second. "And Detective Munch's desk nameplate."

"The fucker," Belzer hissed. He'd thought that someone at the station had put it in the personal effects box that was given to Pamela. He should have checked.

"Any word from Iris on the manhunt?" Raine asked. She was fiddling with her geographical disks and finding the most likely routes out of Phoenix that a desperate man might take. There were just too many options.

Deliverance shook her head. "Not yet, but law enforcement from every sector will be blanketing the state to find him.

Remember—he didn't just kill a lot of people, he blew up a cop and cut the throat of a police tech. They take that very personally."

Quint asked, "Did they notify Ben Deuel's family?"

Belzer nodded. "Cornell said he went personally to Deuel's house and told his wife. Susan and Ben were married for eighteen years and have two teenage boys." He remembered how devastated Munch's family was when he was murdered, and Belzer ached for the Deuel family's pain.

"Bugger, this is frustrating," Raine said. She looked up at all the eyes directed towards her. "There are so many ways he could get out of Phoenix and head towards another state. If I were him, I wouldn't take a well-traveled road but use backroads that aren't patrolled or have many people along the route." She pointed to the map of Arizona on her screen and they clustered around her. "See? For example, he could head east to 60, then get on the 77 northeast to Globe, and branch off on the 61 until he gets to an obscure crossover to New Mexico. That's just one option."

"Yeah, shyte," Wilde said, nodding. "There are too many places for him to run to to predict where he might go."

"What if he's not running?" Constantine said quietly. "What if he's holed up somewhere close by, waiting for some heat to die down before he makes a move?"

"His face will be all over TV by morning. It's not like someone won't recognize him," Quint said. "Sure, there's a chance that he could try to get some motel room in an out-of-the-way place, but that's too iffy, and he's not stupid. Crazy, but not stupid."

"What if he's already holed up somewhere?" Deliverance said.

"It's been three hours since he took off. He could be as far as Flagstaff or already into California or New Mexico. Hell—he could be close to the Mexican border," Victor opined. "We don't even know what kind of car we're looking for since he ditched Deuel's car and stole a new one. There've been no stolen car reports according to Baxter. And the state cops can't stop every car to check."

"What about family?" Constantine asked. "Married? Kids? Parents?"

"Never married, no kids," Belzer replied. "His father's dead but his mother is still living in Mobile. Cornell called the police there and they're heading to her place to interrogate her."

"I don't think he's going to drive to Alabama, but you never know," Victor said.

"He might call her to have her send money through Western Union," Raine offered.

"Possible, but I'm thinking not," Quint said.

At that moment Tucker came into the conference room and all eyes turned towards him.

"Kids okay?" Deliverance asked quickly.

"They're fine," Tucker said, eyeing the leftover pizza, "although Napoleon got out of his cage and they're chasing him around the room before he can slip out somehow or Coco eats him. Cunning little furbag. My badass wife called me and told me to let you know that she got that convention list from Victor's buddy, Big Bad Ron. There was a forensics convention in Columbia on August 12, 1982 through the 13th. Pete Murphy was one of the attendees, and the session did include the 1976 Sumpter County double murder, including dozens of photographs." Tucker gave in to his hunger pains and snagged the last piece of mushroom and onion pizza.

"Bingo," Quint said.

"Another piece of the puzzle fits," Victor said as he smeared cream cheese on an onion bagel. He addressed Belzer. "Did Cornell mention rechecking Laurel's car seat?"

Belzer slapped his forehead. "He did mention that when I talked to him this morning. Sorry. He said that Murphy's measurements were off by two inches, meaning that the person seated there could have been five-eight, not five-ten. And five-eight is Murphy's height. It could have been a simple miscalculation, but since we know that Murphy's the Beguiler we can assume that he faked the data to eliminate himself from consideration."

"I wonder what else he fudged on these cases and any others?" Wilde mused.

"Cornell said he was going to have an independent team from the FBI go over every piece of evidence and see if anything's iffy."

"Christ," Quint expelled angrily. "If Murphy's been doing any fudging on other cases, that could mean a shitstorm of lawsuits for the city and lawyers massing to have their clients' convictions overturned."

"It won't be pretty," Belzer agreed.

"Let's worry about that another time," Wilde said. "Right now, we need to help figure out where he might be and how to catch him. None of us are really safe until that wanker goes down. I'll bet he knows everything about us, every nuance of our lives that he might leverage."

"Yeah," Quint said as he stared out the window at the lights of the street and the businesses whose closed signs contrasted with their night lights. "Where is the fucker?"

It was ten-thirty when Grayson Kingston flipped on the porchlight and opened the front door. He had looked through the peephole and the man outside had flashed an official Tucson PD identification. He wondered what the guy was doing way up here in Carefree. He shivered; surely it had nothing to do with his son, Gray. He had spoken to Gray and Cress that morning and all was well.

The man smiled at him pleasantly and extended his hand. Grayson automatically took it.

"Mr. Kingston? I'm Pete Murphy from the Tucson forensics lab. May I come in for a moment? This won't take long."

"Is it my son? Is Gray all right?" Grayson asked urgently.

"Oh, he's fine. Nothing to do with him, I assure you." He peered around Kingston and saw Grayson's wife, Mariko, standing a few feet away with a small pug by her feet. Murphy inclined his head slightly and said very politely, "Good evening, Mrs. Kingston." He looked at Grayson. "May I come in?"

"Oh. Certainly. Please," Grayson said and stepped aside.

"Thank you," Murphy said as he entered the house and Grayson Kingston shut the door.

CHAPTER NINE

Iris hadn't slept in thirty hours and couldn't even try—she was too keyed up. She had dozed a couple of times for ten or fifteen minutes, but those interludes only increased her exhaustion rather than alleviating it. She admitted to herself that the hunt was addictive and that she had made the right decision by reinstating into the FBI. She still planned on taking the bar and getting her license to practice law in Arizona, but that was a fallback option, as was being a private investigator. She fit right in with the Union Jack crew, but she was all too aware that their cases would not always be as exciting as the one she was on now. The chase, the hunt, the apprehension—those fired up her blood.

She was glad that she'd be assigned permanently to Tucson. Had that not been an option, it might have impacted her new marriage. She and Tucker had never discussed him relocating to Phoenix. She knew that he loved the children and his life in Quint's back yard and had no perceivable ambition to change the comfortable parameters of his world. She was ambitious, and constantly warred with herself about wanting to drive towards the upper echelons of the FBI and a less stressful professional life that would balance a decent personal life. She suspected that she'd always be at war with herself. She hadn't quite made peace with that.

Lisbon had finally told her to get the hell out of the motel and get some sleep. She had a motel room at another place, but fellow agent Liberty Adams tossed her a set of house keys and told her to check out of the motel and bunk in at her apartment. Iris didn't argue, and an hour later she was groaning in abject pleasure as the cascade of hot water in Liberty's shower soothed her aching body. She shampooed and conditioned her long blonde hair and shaved her legs before toweling herself dry with the fluffiest terrycloth she'd ever felt. She felt a thousand percent better.

Liberty had a guest bedroom perfectly ready for an occupant. Iris slipped on a pair of shorts and a tee-shirt but decided that she needed to check out the news before getting some shuteye. She plopped down on the living room couch and turned on the TV. *General Hospital* was on, so she started channel surfing until she came to one that had local news. The pert redheaded newscaster was smiling and babbling on about a story of the snowbirds readying for their journeys home. *Good riddance*, Iris thought crossly. They might add bucks to the economy, but in general they were a pain in the ass. The woman finally ended her story, then turned it over to a handsome older man who was the perfect expression of a male anchor. Luckily, he went right into the story about Pete Murphy. Iris turned up the volume and watched the screen intently.

Murphy's face flashed on the screen as the anchor reiterated the story and the FBI manhunt. Iris had seen the photo before—it was the one in Murphy's official file. She had an eight-by-ten of that exact photo in her file. She'd stared at it for a long time, finally deciding that there were no facial characteristics that would mark him as anything other than what he had presented himself to be. Charles Manson— now *those* crazy eyes bespoke of a madman. But Murphy—no such indication. He was nondescript, and that gave him the power to make people underestimate him.

Iris finished watching the news then shut it off and went into the bedroom. She threw herself on the bed, hoping she could sleep. She was snoring in two minutes. When she woke up six hours later she found herself covered with a soft blanket and could hear noises coming from the kitchen. She dragged herself out of bed and walked into the kitchen where Liberty was making pancakes.

"Pancakes for dinner?" Iris asked, smiling.

"The best kind of comfort food," Liberty said as she flipped a pancake onto a stack beside the stove. She handed the plate to Iris and nodded towards the table. "Pure maple syrup and butter await your pleasure, Agent. Milk's in the fridge."

Iris filled two glasses, sat down, and forked three pancakes onto her plate. She smiled; thoughtful Liberty had melted the butter. She poured half the butter on her stack then a good four ounces of maple syrup. After her first bite, she though the unusual dinner tasted better than anything in the world. She had a sweet flashback to eating pancakes as a child in her grandmother's kitchen—her mother rarely cooked.

"This is so good, thank you," Iris said. "You've been very kind. Sure is nice to bunk out in a home instead of a motel room."

"I hear that," Liberty said as she replenished the syrup on her half-eaten stack. "I hate hotels. They're so impersonal. I had to spend a week in one when I was assigned here before I found this place."

"Where were you before?" Iris asked as she chewed.

"In the boonies—the Helena, Montana field office. Hated it, but you've got to pay your dues. When the Phoenix opportunity came up I jumped at it—no more damn zero-degree and below winters. I'll take one-hundred-ten-degrees summers any day."

"Amen. So—where're you from?" Iris went over to the stove and snagged two more pancakes.

"A tiny little town up in northwest Massachusetts—North Adams. Damn cold winters up in the Berkshires, too." Liberty swept back her shoulder-length sable hair. She had dimples and a cleft chin and sparkling emerald eyes that made her look like a teenager when she smiled. Iris had checked out her evaluations and saw that Liberty had scored in the top five percent of her Quantico class and never got appraisals with less than "exceeds expectations." She had graduated Brown in the top third of her class with a degree in Psychology.

"You're a long way from home," Iris said. "Miss your family?"

"Like crazy! I've got a twin brother and two sisters, all still happily rooted in our hometown. Guess I was the restless one."

"Nothing wrong with that." Iris pushed a small portion of pancake around her plate as she asked, "Ever think of transferring?"

"Always. Did you have some place in mind?"

"The FBI is beefing up its presence in Tucson and I'll be stationed down there permanently, which in my case is sort of necessary since my husband lives and works there. Tucson's a smaller city, a little cooler, but very, very nice. Interested?" She half-expected Liberty to hedge but was surprised at the immediate response.

"Yes." Liberty smiled. She raised her glass of milk, Iris did the same, they clinked glasses, and Liberty said succinctly, "Chick power."

Cress came into the house after walking Pugsley. The house was quiet, so he called out to Gray who called back from their joint office. Cress unleashed the dog who began wildly yapping and running towards his other daddy. Pugsley sniffled and chuffed as

Gray reached down to pet him. Despite his short legs Pugsley jumped up on Gray's lap and nuzzled him.

"He's getting fat," Gray said.

"He's robust, not fat," Cress said.

"He's 'robust' because you keep feeding him spaghetti when you think I'm not looking."

"Should I be feeding himself something unnatural, like real dog food?" Cress prepared homemade food for their pet, usually cut-up chicken breasts, veggies, and brown rice, or ground sirloin in place of chicken. They knew that they were spoiling the beast, but he was their 'kid' and they had no reason not to spoil him, especially after they lost his parents to such a violent act. Cress leaned over Gray's lap and smooched the dog's head. "No, you don't want Alpo, do you? Silly beast." He noticed the outline on Gray's screen. "What're you doing?"

Gray replied, "Getting my outline for the summer course on feudal Japan. It's not a subject that's usually taught and I think the students will be very engrossed."

"Did you think of getting your mom's viewpoint on the subject?" Gray's mother, Mariko, was Japanese; his father, Grayson, was an Army officer in Japan after World War II who fell in love with and eventually married her.

Gray nodded. "I have. I wanted to get the outline firmed up before I call her to see if she can spend some time talking with me. We have a long weekend coming up in the beginning of April for Easter, and I thought you and I could drive up and spend a few days with them." He rubbed Pugsley's head. "And this little fella could spend some time with his sister, Tiger Lily."

"Sure, sounds perfect. Don't forget that we're flying to New Orleans in June to spend a week with my parents." Cress had timed the vacation to ensure that he'd be back at least two weeks before his brother and Raine got married, plenty of time to get a well-fitted tux for his position as best man.

Gray smiled slyly. "I look forward to returning to the place where we fell in love."

"Bullshit," Cress said. "You just want to gorge on the food."

"Your mom makes a mean gumbo."

"I have news for you—it's my dad's gumbo, but she does make a luscious pot of jambalaya."

"I love your parents," Gray sighed, "but I do wish their son learned to cook decently."

"A Swanson's TV dinner for you tonight, grump. Come on, Pugs—let's let mean daddy finish his outline while you and I defrost a meal for his culinary displeasure." Pugsley jumped down and panted after Cress as he went into the kitchen.

After ninety minutes Gray meandered into the kitchen and grinned at the smell of stew emanating from the stove. He'd just been kidding—Cress was an excellent cook, and they shared kitchen duties.

As Cress stirred the thick mixture of beef, potatoes, and carrots he glanced over at his life partner and asked, "You thinking maybe this course could turn into another book?" Gray had published four nonfiction books of anthropology since the late seventies— *The Aztecs: A Culture of Beauty and Brutality, Toltec Spring, Tawantinsuyu: Seasons of Tradition & Change,* and just recently, *Aboriginal Sunset.*

"You know me too well," Gray replied as he sat down, and Pugsley jumped up on his lap. He addressed his next comments to the dog. "So, Puggy boy—what would you think about having a brother or sister?" He cast a sly glance over at Cress, who was staring at him. "What?" he said. "Baby Boy here needs a sibling. It's too lonely for him when we're at work. Don't you want another puppy child?"

Cress put down the ladle and turned off the stove. "Of course I do. I just thought you weren't so inclined, you know, after ..."

Gray turned serious. "Boomer and Sugarlips are gone. I'll always grieve for them, but that doesn't negate the potential for loving a new dog or two. We can go down to the pound after Easter and pick up one or two pups that need a good home. What do you say?"

Cress grinned. "I say yes. Now, set the table, please. Are you finished with your outline?"

"Yes."

"Good. Then call your mom after dinner and see what her schedule is like."

"Pushy, aren't you?" Gray said as he reached into the cabinet for the plates.

"It appears to be that Danziger blood coursing through my veins."

"Glad you've made your peace with that," Gray said quietly.

Cress shrugged. "It's part of who I am, so there's no point in denying it any more than there is the fact that my sister was a murderous psychopath. Luck of the genetic draw." He frowned involuntarily as he thought of the sister he'd grown up with—Cheyenne had given everyone the impression that she was sweet and kind when in reality she had killed even as a child before her spree in Tucson, one aspect of which was her failed murder attempt on Gray that had put him into a coma for four months.

"Speaking of murderous psychopaths, have you heard any updates on the Pete Murphy situation?" He put two huge slices of frozen garlic bread in the toaster oven.

Cress nodded. "Malachi told me that Deliverance called Bliss and told her that there were still no clues to his whereabouts. Personally, I'm hoping he makes it to the Grand Canyon and falls off." Murphy had broken into their home and murdered their two pugs by hanging them in the kitchen. Afterwards, Gray and Cress pulled down the pot rack above the island where their dogs had died and plastered over the ceiling. "Although," Cress continued, "I'd be happier if he fell into the Everglades and was torn apart by a half dozen starving gators."

"From your lips to God's ears."

"Sit. Stew's ready," Cress said as he grabbed a potholder and brought the pot over. He ladled generous helpings into his and Gray's soup bowls, then put the pot back on the stove. Gray had filled their glasses with iced tea and had toasted the buttery garlic beard to a golden brown.

"You know what I was thinking?" Cress asked as he chewed a butter-saturated piece of garlic bread.

"What?"

"It'll be seven years in September since we moved in together. I'm thinking we're a safe bet for a lifetime commitment, and maybe we should do something to commemorate that."

"What did you have in mind?" Gray heavily peppered his stew after he slipped a chunk of tender beef down to Pugsley.

"Well, the world hasn't evolved enough for us to get legally married, but I was thinking of some kind of ceremony. You know, I talked to Victor about this subject a few weeks ago and he said that he and Wilde were planning a Wiccan handfasting ceremony like the one Deliverance had with Quint. They've even chosen the date—October 31st, Halloween. That's Quint's and Deliverance's sixth anniversary, and Bliss and Malachi's seventh."

"Huh," Gray said thoughtfully as he ran a hand through his shoulder-length, glossy black hair. "Think our Christian parents would approve?"

"I hope so, but it doesn't matter in the long run. This is about us." Cress slid off his chair and knelt on the floor next to Gray. He took Gray's hand and looked him in the eyes. "Will you sort of marry me?"

"I guess I sort of will," Gray conceded just as they both rose and exchanged a heartfelt kiss. Gray nuzzled Cress's neck and murmured, "Maybe I'll call my mom tomorrow. I have other plans for tonight."

"Will I like them?"

"Je crois que tu le feras, mon bien-aimé," Gray whispered. In honor of his life partner he had learned French years earlier, and they used the language in their most intimate moments. This qualified.

"Sorekara, watashi wa anata no saizen no handan, watashi no ai o mokunin shimasu," Cress whispered back in Japanese; Mariko had been his teacher since last year and he was coming along well although he had a long way to go before he could be a true conversationalist.

Gray put his half-finished bowl of stew on the floor and Pugsley attacked it as though he hadn't eaten for a week. They ignored their dog child as Gray led the way into their bedroom.

Deliverance was restive in bed although her husband was dead asleep. She had at least been able to nap during the day, but Quint was running on adrenaline and hadn't slept more than two or three hours in the last twenty-four. Everyone was exhausted both physically and emotionally. Poor Tucker was played out taking care of five kids and a teenager and worrying about his wife. At least Quint had hired three bodyguards to lurk around their house, casita, and Wilde's house, and she felt better about that. The men were ex-Vietnam vets who were tough and ready to lay down their lives for their clients. Deliverance hoped it would never come to that. The men had already scared off a few reporters as well as some looky-loos that just seemed ghoulish in their attraction towards the homes of people involved in major crimes. One of the bodyguards had to physically remove some guy that was lurking around the back of the house. He appeared harmless, but you never knew.

She kept her eyes closed as she tried to regulate her breathing. She also thought about April 19th when she'd hit the Big 3-Oh. A month later her old man would turn forty. Both ages were young, but time ticked by. Already her oldest kids were seven. She remembered their birth like it was yesterday. As wasn't unusual her thoughts drifted to David, who would have been fourteen in June. Her firstborn hadn't even taken a breath when he was delivered, but she still loved him and mourned him and always would despite the joy she took in her three daughters and son.

Almost by coincidence she saw a shadow at the bedroom door. It was dark, but she could see that it was Alex, who was just standing there without saying a word. She wondered if he was sleepwalking. She turned on her bed lamp and studied her son. He was absolutely unmoving, his arms hanging limply at his side, the pupils in his blue eyes huge and almost hiding the stunning azure color. He was staring straight ahead as though he were in a trance.

Deliverance carefully slipped out of bed and walked over to her son. She knelt in front of him and took his hands; they were ice cold.

"Alex, honey?" she whispered softly. "You okay, baby?"

He didn't answer but slightly swayed; his unblinking gaze remained straight ahead.

"Baby?" she said gently. She put a hand on his forehead; it was hot. She heard Quint shuffling in the covers and sensed him coming towards them. A second later he squatted beside his wife and son and mimicked the forehead touch.

"Is he sleepwalking?" Quint asked.

"I don't know. Maybe. His forehead's hot but his hands are cold. They—"

Suddenly Alex raised both of his arms and cupped his mother's face with those cold hands. He looked directly into her eyes and said, "Tasukete. Tasukete."

"What the hell does tahsuketti mean?" Quint frowned.

"Not a clue," Deliverance said as she studied her son's face. "Maybe Italian?" She stroked Alex's cheek. "Honey, what does tahsuketti mean? Alex?" She could see that the slight trace of animation in his face when he spoke the word was gone and the trance-gaze was back. "Okay, sweetie—back to bed." She stood and took his hand and slowly led him back to his bedroom. He pulled his hand away and climbed into bed and snuggled under the covers. Deliverance leaned down and kissed his cheek, amazed to see that he was lightly snoring. Yes, she thought—he was sleepwalking. She closed his door except for a two-inch crack and turned to face her husband.

"Maybe we should take him to the pediatrician," she said.

"That's a good idea. Let's have all the kids checked out just to be on the safe side. Has Storm's therapist said anything unusual about her?"

"Not really, just that she thinks the kid may have an eidetic memory. I've seen hints of that myself, and I think it's what's driving her amazing ability in chess games and getting straight A's in school. Beckett hasn't beaten her in months."

Quint grinned. "I'll bet that pisses him off."

"I'm sure. He's a good kid, but he also has a very healthy ego. It's a good thing for him to fail once in a while."

"So, is it a good thing for our kids to fail once in a while?"

"Hell, no."

"Wow. No pressure there."

"Do as I say, not as I do."

"I always do as you say. I have no death wish."

"Good. I'm glad that's clear. Come on, big boy—back to bed." She took his hand and led him back to their bedroom.

Deliverance was up at five the next morning and directed her efforts to making a huge, spectacular breakfast. Tucker sauntered over at six and she put him to work on the waffle mix.

As he was mixing the batter she asked him, "Did you ever hear the word tahsuketti?"

He shook his head. "Nope. Italian?"

"I don't think so. It's not important. Alex had a tiny sleepwalking incident last night and it was something he said. I'll ask him when he comes to the table. Did Iris call yet?"

"Yup. She's bunking in with another agent. She sounds tired but kind of exhilarated. I think she likes the hunt." He paused. "I miss her."

Deliverance put a gentle hand on his arm. "At least when this is all over she'll be down here permanently with you. I know from experience that when a man and woman put their hearts and minds to it, the future is infinite." She stood on tiptoes and kissed his cheek. "Heat up the syrup and butter, please."

"Yes, ma'am."

While Deliverance was frying bacon, the twins came in shouting and wild, followed by a demure Storm holding Vikki's hand. She noticed that Alex seemed fine and didn't appear to have any residual effects from his episode the night before. She pulled a tray of corn muffins out of the oven and gingerly picked up each one and put them on a large platter, then took them to the table. She swatted away Storm's hand and scowled at her as she said, "They're hot. Give it a minute." She looked at Alex. "Sleep well, baby?"

Alex nodded without looking at her. He was keeping an eye on the muffins and his lips were moving as he dutifully counted to sixty.

"Alex," Deliverance said. "Alex." The second time got his attention and he looked at her guiltily as he picked up a warm muffin and put it on his plate.

"Yeah, Mom?" he answered as he reached for a butter knife.

"Do you remember anything after you went to bed last night?"

"Huh? Nope," he said as he slathered an enormous blob of butter on the top of his muffin.

"You didn't wake up?"

"Uh-uh."

"Okay," she replied and went about cracking a dozen eggs into a big bowl and scrambling them before pouring the mix into a large frying pan. Tucker was slicing the ham shoulder she'd baked the day before into small chunks and sticking a toothpick in each piece.

Quint came in dressed in faded jeans, cowboy boots, and a Ralph Lauren Polo shirt. He hated the shirt, and only wore it occasionally to forestall her griping. She thought he looked even more handsome than he did eight years ago when she first met him in a police interrogation room. She had jumped his bones barely twenty-four hours after that meeting.

Quint sat down next to his son and ruffled his hair. "Gotta ask you a question, Ouija Boy. Ever hear the word tahsuketti?"

"Is that a vegetable?" Aislinn asked.

"Maybe," her father answered. "Alex?"

Alex shook his head vigorously. "Nope. Sounds like a vegetable. How come?"

"It's not important," Quint said. "Eat your home fries."

"I've got an idea," Deliverance said. "I have to head over to Saguaro Western for a Criminology class and I know they have a linguistics department there. I'll ask Cress to suggest a professor that might recognize the word."

"Great," Quint said as he scrambled to get the last scoop of eggs that his children had already devoured. He scowled at Vikki as she slyly tried to grab a pile with her hand. She giggled and pulled her hand back.

Deliverance poured a large cup of coffee in a disposable cup and piled bacon, ham, eggs, and home fries on a paper plate. She grabbed a fork and took the meal out to their overnight bodyguard.

"She's such a kind person," Tucker said as he wiped goo off Vikki's face.

"Yeah," Quint said thoughtfully. Every day he was amazed by his good fortune to have her as his wife and the mother of his children. He took a swig of orange juice and looked at Tucker. "Tomorrow's Saturday and I think the old lady and I can handle the kids for a couple of days. Why don't you drive up to Phoenix and surprise your wife?"

"Really?" Tucker said excitedly. "That'd be fantastic."

"In fact, drive up this afternoon. I'll pick up the kids from school. You leave then, and you can be there before three."

"I love you, boss."

"Don't let your wife hear you say that."

"Does this have something to do with bisexual?" Storm asked.

Quint choked on his current swallow of juice and gave her the stink-eye. "Like Mom said, we'll discuss that when you're sixteen."

"Huh," Storm said as she slid off her chair and began walking her empty plate over to the dishwasher. "I already know."

Her equally enlightened siblings giggled.

CHAPTER TEN

Gray had an early morning meeting with his anthropology professors and teaching assistants. Theirs had been a busy week at the college and they voted to hold a short ("Short, Gray—right?") meeting at eight to review any issues and proposals for new courses. Gray wasn't ready to share the outline he'd concocted for his class on feudal Japan, and luckily his associates had few issues and only two proposals that he said he'd take under consideration. They were out of his office by 8:35 AM. He pulled up his schedule on his PC and saw that he had two classes to teach and three meetings to attend, ending the day at 4 PM. Not a bad day.

He glanced over at the desk clock and saw that he had a half hour before he needed to head over to Administration for his first meeting. He closed and locked his door, then sat down and dialed his parents' number. A week never went by without talking to the folks at least twice, and he was looking forward to Easter weekend.

After four rings the call was answered.

He smiled at the voice. "Hi, Mom. Ogenkidesuka?"

"I'm fine, sweetheart," Mariko said in a pleasant voice. "How are you?"

"Busy as hell, Mom. Finishing up stuff for the spring semester and working on summer classes. Say—Cress and I were thinking of coming up for the long Easter weekend. You and Dad game for two men and a pug?"

"That sounds wonderful, sweetheart. And you know you and Crescent are always welcome here, the pugster, too."

"Great. Dad there? I wanted to say hello."

"Sorry, my kyūseishu—Daddy's out in the back yard weeding the garden. He has to travel up to Flagstaff this afternoon for a client meeting, so he won't be able to call you back for a few days."

"You going with him?"

"I just might, love. You know how he is on the road with no one to give him directions—completely Fukushima'd." She laughed brightly.

Gray was silent for a few brief seconds before he shrugged off an odd feeling and said, "Okay, Mom. Have Dad call me when you guys get back. I have some exciting news to tell you both."

"I love you, sweetheart," Mariko said just before she hung up.

"Love you, too—" Mariko's phone buzzed. Gray thought that was odd—she always hung onto their calls until the very last word. He put the receiver down slowly, shrugged off his weird feeling, and gathered his papers for the meeting.

"Nicely done, Mrs. Kingston," Pete Murphy said as he lowered the gun from Grayson's temple. "Now, like I said, just behave yourselves and you'll come out of this just fine. I have nothing against either of you, and just need to hide out for a few more days." He sat down on the loveseat and picked up his glass of iced tea. Tiger Lily was sitting next to him and he stroked her soft fur.

Mariko walked over to her husband, bound and gagged in his easy chair. She removed the gag and sat in the chair next to him. She let her neutral face drop and glared at the man who had not only murdered so many people but had also invaded her home. She was nervous as she watched Murphy stroke the dog; after all, he had cruelly murdered her son's dogs. She was stunned that this monster could so easily insinuate himself into their lives.

After Grayson closed the front door when he admitted Murphy into their house, the man had whipped out a gun. He told her to tie up her husband; when she balked, he clicked back the hammer and started counting to three. Grayson told her to do as Murphy said and she reluctantly complied. She used silk cords from her craft box to bind Grayson's hands behind him (Murphy checked to make sure the knots were tight) and to bind his ankles after he sat down in his lounger. Murphy thanked her politely then proceeded to tie her hands behind her back and sit her down on the couch. He left her ungagged and her ankles free. He clicked on the remote and began channel surfing until he came to a news story about him. He grinned, sat back, and enjoyed the tale of the discovery and manhunt. Occasionally he glanced over at his hostages and loved the shocked looks on their faces. He preened.

After further channel surfing to stop at two more news stories he gently eased Mariko to her feet and told her they were going into the kitchen—he was hungry. He gagged Grayson and told him not to worry—he just needed food because it had been a helluva long day. He laughed and walked Mariko into the kitchen with his hand heavy and menacing on her shoulder.

Mariko's hands were shaking as she opened the refrigerator and took out the leftover meatloaf. She cut two big slices, covered them with gravy, and stuck them into the microwave. She removed two slices of wheat bread from the bread box. She took a large china plate from the cabinet and when the meatloaf was hot made a large, delicious sandwich out of it. She took a can of Coke out of the fridge and placed it next to the plate on the table in the kitchen alcove. He waved the gun at her and she sat down across from him. He kept the gun close to his hand while he devoured the sandwich.

"Don't worry," he said between mouthfuls. "I'm not going to hurt you. I just need a refuge for a bit while I figure things out."

"Do the right thing and give yourself up," Mariko said quietly.

"Not in this lifetime, Geisha Girl."

"You will address me by my first name or by Mrs. Kingston." Her brown almond eyes narrowed at him. She may have been four-foot-ten, slender, and sixty-two years old, but in her own way she was formidable.

Murphy smiled. "Sorry, you're right. No need for disrespect." He looked around. "Got any dessert?"

"I have dorayaki I made this morning."

"What is it?"

"Red bean pancakes wrapped around sweet Azuki bean paste."

"Get it, and get me another drink, please."

Mariko rose and walked to the fridge, all the time wondering how she and Grayson could either escape or overpower the psycho in their home. There was not a doubt in her mind that he'd kill them at the slightest provocation, and that given his history and actions there was no reason to believe that he planned on letting them live at all. She had to bide her time, and somehow manage to prevent her husband from trying anything brave or stupid.

It was after midnight and he looked out of the front window. The street was dark; the gated community had no streets lights, and the new moon was still in effect, bringing no sky light to the neighborhood. He walked Mariko out to the garage where he shoved her into her car and backed it out of the garage. He drove his stolen car inside and closed the garage door.

It was a long night as she dozed, hands bound, on the couch while her husband got no sleep from the lounge chair where he watched their captor like a hawk. She tried to meditate, to relax her mind, and inside her head she chanted over and over again, *Kami wa watashitachi o tasuketekudasai, tasuketekudasai—God help us, please help us.*

Murphy didn't sleep, egging on consciousness with adrenaline and pots of coffee. When dawn broke he shook her awake and told her she could use the bathroom. He followed her there and much to her embarrassment left the door open while she relieved herself. He made her stand with her back to him as he did the same. He ushered her into the kitchen and rummaged in her cabinets until he found a crystal flower vase. He handed it to her and said she needed to relieve her husband unless she wanted to endure the smell of urine in her neat living room. She stuck out her chin and held her head high as she walked to Grayson and motioned towards his groin and then the vase. He shook his head no vigorously, but Mariko was a practical woman. She unzipped his pants and gently removed his penis, aiming it into the vase. A long stream of urine resulted as well as a face flushed with embarrassment. She zipped him back up and put the vase down. She stared at Murphy, waiting.

"I know you both work, so around eight you'll make a call to your school saying that you're staying home to nurse your husband from a flu attack." He looked at Grayson coldly. "And you'll call your office and say that you're sick. If either one of you tries something, or says something I find suspicious, I'll start shooting out the other one's knees—for starters."

Grayson and Mariko contacted their respective jobs and did exactly as Murphy instructed. He was glad that the couple's phones all had speaker buttons on them, so he could hear the other end of the conversation. Shortly after Grayson hung up the phone rang and every nerve ending in Murphy's body snapped. He dragged Mariko over to the phone and made her answer it. The caller was her son,

Gray. He listened closely to the discussion between the two and found nothing odd about it—lucky for her.

When Mariko hung up he pushed her back down on the couch and turned on the TV. He was enjoying the hell out of the news reports, and occasionally burst out into maniacal laughter. Mariko and Grayson thought the same thing—he was deconstructing, and that didn't bode well for their survival.

"Love the assignment you gave us," Deliverance said as she perched on the edge of Cress's desk in his now-deserted classroom. The class had finished five minutes earlier and everyone rushed out to lunch or their next course. There were scowls all the way around when Cress assigned them to write an essay on the mystique of Ted Bundy, and whether a man far less handsome and erudite as he could have succeeded in attracting the same victims.

"It's something to make you think," Cress said. "Physicality often plays a role in criminal and victim behavior." His lips tightened. "Look at Cheyenne. She was a drop-dead knockout with a killer instinct. Who'd've thought?"

Deliverance put a kind hand on his arm. "No one. Stop beating yourself up about it, okay?"

He smiled wanly. "Okay. Say—you mentioned something at start of class about needing a reference?"

"Yes, right. Who's the best linguist in the college?"

"Hmm. That would be either Brendan Danova or Rudy Cary. I'd go with Brendan first. What do you need?"

"Just some insight on a word. Last night Alex was sleepwalking, and he repeated a word. He sounded—I don't know— urgent. I've never heard the word before and I'm curious if it's real and what language it is."

"What's the word?"

"Tahsuketti."

"Sounds like an Italian vegetable."

Deliverance laughed. "That's what my kids said."

"Well, Brendan or Rudy should be able to help you. They're the best." He flipped open his rolodex and wrote down their names and phone numbers and handed the post-it note to Deliverance.

"Thanks. I'll check with them. Well, gotta go. Tucker's driving up to Phoenix to surprise Iris, so Quint and I have kid duty amongst our other voluminous tasks." She smiled broadly and whipped out a few pages stapled together. "I love going to your brother's anthropology classes even though my degree won't be in that discipline. He is a really good teacher, and he gave me a great grade on this paper and made a wonderful suggestion in his comments." She handed it to Cress, who slipped on his reading glasses and perused the essay.

Deliverance Dane
Anthropology 226
March 23, 1985
Professor C. Black Wolf

Subject: Minorities in Anthropological Context

Before one can discuss the typeologizing of minorities, it is necessary to define what a "minority" is. A minority is a group of people, with a small distribution of power, who because of physical or cultural characteristics is given differential or unequal treatment. A minority person is restricted to his group and is treated not as an individual but as a member of his group. A minority has several properties:

- *Its members experience disadvantages from another social group.*
- *Its disabilities are related to special characteristics that its members share and that the majority holds in low esteem.*
- *Its members have a "consciousness of kind" which affects their behavior.*
- *Its members are usually born into the group, and endogamy is the usual practice.*

One of the most striking things about the class discussion on the four methods used to perpetuate subjective views of the Indian is the universality of obliteration, disembodiment, defamation, and disparagement. That is to say they are not limited to the Indian situation but extend to almost all minority groups in almost every society. In the United States, for example, all four of these methods were used to distort the black experience, prior to and subsequent to the blacks' emancipation. The perverse, degrading aspects of slavery—the whippings, the humiliation of the auction black, etc.—were either played down, glossed over, or totally omitted from historical accounts, and in their place were found testimonies to the "happy" lot of the slave, his contentment, his relatively good treatment at the hands of the owner.

There were, of course, some accounts of the evils of slavery (e.g., Uncle Tom's Cabin), but until recent years the reality of the black experience was, at the most, distorted greatly, and at the least, understated. Black contributions—like Indian contributions—were rather neglected, and the black man was further degraded by the white majority's refusal to acknowledge him as an actual human being (he was either subhuman animal with abominable characteristics, or an inferior human being who was made to know his place in the society of the superior white majority).

The parallels between the history of the Indian and the black man are quite vivid, with the one very painful exception that while the latter has definitely come up in white society—socially, economically, politically—the former is still very much excluded from the advantages of white culture. It is only in the last sixty years that the Indian has gained the vote; he still lacks the educational, vocational, and economic opportunities theoretically guaranteed to every willing and able American. His life is almost certain to be shorter and more difficult than that of the average white American—the Indian is, in short, in almost every way the "underdog" of the American society, a society which is supposedly the most advanced culture in the world (not advanced enough, however, to eliminate the gross injustices done to the Indians as well as to other minority groups, still including the blacks, Chicanos, etc.).

Perhaps one of the most difficult things to understand is why the Indians (and other minority groups) were and are treated in the manner previously discussed, the most incensing aspect of the treatment being the often-blatant hypocrisy of the white majority. The obvious answer is that the white majority—the colonizers, settlers, slaveowners, etc.—had its own self-interests in mind, and it would have been misguided stupidity on its part to have a deep concern (if any) for these peoples who in any way would hinder the majority's self-development. Hence, the removal of Indians from lands that should be settled by the white man; hence, the justification and maintenance of slavery in order to perpetuate the economic prosperity of the south; hence, the continued prejudice against and subjugation of those minorities which would impose on the resources desired by the less than charitable (in general) white majority.

If one considers all of these points it becomes less difficult to understand the motivation behind such historical episodes as the uprising at Wounded Knee, the seizure of Alcatraz, the sometimes less than peaceful demand for recognition made by the Indians and the other minority groups. That is the essential beginning— recognition—before society can go on to solve the problems that it has created, and that for its own good it must admit to exist.

On the other hand, some of the "stereotypical" assumptions regarding Indians, both negative and positive, originate from eyewitness accounts to this culture and actions. The Reverend Henry White in his 1843 book The Early History of New England deals with many observations of the New England Indian tribes made by early colonists during the 17th and 18th centuries. It includes viewpoints from one end of the spectrum to the other, from the concept of the good-hearted, noble savage where nothing could exceed their courtesy and friendship, their eloquent, distinguished council and their bravery in war, to the concept of the savage, vicious barbarians with respect to miserably depraved morals. There are a number of eyewitness accounts concerning the captivity of whites by Indians, including subsequent journeys into Canada where the captive whites were sold into slavery.

While there is a great deal of objective material which deals with the cultures of the different tribes—specifically concerning their clothing, ornaments, food, and shelter—and which does contribute to an accurate account of the various tribes, there is also, unfortunately, a great deal of subjective material which serves to distort the picture of the American Indian. For example, a great deal of the documented observations was made by clergymen, missionaries, and other Christian-minded individuals who judged the Indians' behavior in terms of the Christian standard; i.e., the Indians' policies, religion, and manners were directly opposed to "the Gospel's" pure doctrines and morals. These Christian observations gave a somewhat slanted view of Indian culture and values. These observations could have been significantly improved by infusing them with more objectivity and understanding on the part of the observer, and by eliminating the philosophical judgments based on one ideal standard. The subjectivity of the observers is understandable, however, given the time and circumstances of their Puritan society, and contributes to our understanding of why the Indian was treated as he was by the colonials.

Still, the concept of racism in some form goes back to the beginning of civilization, and makes the assumption of racial superiority or inferiority, that a person's race exclusively determines his behavior, value system, morality, etc. In any society the presence of "races" presupposes the presence of racism, "races" being determined by physical differences—it is how society regards these differences that makes them significant. Racism, unlike ethnocentrism, is not a universal phenomenon: culture rather than biology most usually determines superiority or inferiority. The importance of "race" as we define it today and its characteristic behavior did not appear in western society until the 18th century: prior to that mankind was divided into two religious groups, the Christians and the non-Christians.

In summary, there are five basic necessary antecedent conditions to the development of racism: contact, social visibility, ethnocentrism, competition, and unequal power.

- *Contact between two or more distinct social groups usually occurs through migration.*
- *Social visibility necessitates conspicuous features that identify them as distinct groups.*
- *Ethnocentrism tends to divide groups into "us" and "them," rating "them" in relation to "our" standards.*
- *Competition between groups for scarce resources tends to breed prejudice and resentment.*
- *Unequal power, wherein the dominant group uses its greater power to maintain its dominance over the repressed minority group, also fosters tension and resentment between groups.*

Today, however, in the 1980s, some of the aspects of building and maintaining racism and the concept of majority/minority are *crumbling, albeit slowly. Eventually—probably not in the lifetime of this generation—the country will truly be a melting pot where, as the great Martin Luther King, Jr. once said, "I have a dream that my four little children will one day live in a nation where they will not be judged by the color of their skin, but by the **content** of their **character**."*

And then the concepts of anthropology will need to be redefined yet again if not altogether put on the shelf of historical archaism and memory.

Grade: A-

Comments: A very enjoyable summary of a critical aspect of studying the causes and effects of racism and minorities. Although you hit the heart of what I required for the essay, I would have liked to have seen a summary of a few other "minority" groups. You may take on this task as extra credit. I know that you are planning on acquiring a degree in Criminology, but perhaps consider how you could expand this essay and its tenets to a Master's thesis for that discipline; i.e., melding the two studies into a single thesis that addresses how criminology and anthropology are interrelated. I am available for guidance if you need assistance in defining an outline for such and effort. This is a great start!   C. Black Wolf

"That's an excellent area to pursue," Cress said. "So many aspects of human civilization contribute to crime, its root causes and its outcomes. I'd follow his suggestion."

"I will," she said, stuffing the paper back in her shoulder bag. "Okay, see you Monday. Have a great weekend."

"You, too." When Deliverance left Cress pulled up an outline on his computer and studied the course he'd be teaching in the fall, *Psychopaths & Their (Willing?) Victims.* The outline needed a lot of work, and he still had to pick out the text books. He checked his calendar and groaned at the two classes and one long staff meeting he still had on his plate. He and Gray wouldn't get home until it was dark. He had an hour before his next class started, so he grabbed his car keys and went home to feed and walk Pugsley.

CHAPTER ELEVEN

The Beguiler Command Center at the FBI building was going on in a large room, with dozens of people coming in and out as information filtered in through the tip lines and other media. Nicholas Lisbon was in charge, and his titular second-in-command was Richard Ballard, who had extended his stay to assist. His wife, Noor, was home in San Francisco with their son, Rōnin, and wasn't happy about his extended absence, but she understood the man and his dedication to duty.

Iris Flynn was the unspoken third-level commander, and Lisbon watched in appreciation as she made decisions and issued commands with the confidence and talent of a real pro. He was amused by the clear devotion that Liberty Adams had for her female superior, and he was also pleased with her smarts and accuracy in her tasks. They'd be a formidable team down in Tucson. Part of him wished that Iris could stay in Phoenix; his interest in her was more than just professional, but he respected the institution of marriage and would never make a move.

The phone rang, and Iris grabbed it. She looked surprised and said a few words, then excused herself for a few minutes and left the room. Lisbon wondered what was going on.

Iris saw Tucker before he saw her as she walked into the lobby. She had only been away from home for a few days but suddenly she felt like a giddy teenager. She thought he was gorgeous—tall, svelte, with long blond hair, broad shoulders, and wearing form-fitting western wear. This was her man. He saw her and smiled, and she managed restraint from throwing herself in his arms. She nodded at the receptionist and took his hand and pulled him a few feet away, conscious that the receptionist and the agents milling about were waiting to see her next move.

"Come with me, Mr. Townsend," she said loudly. She turned and walked down a hallway, opening a small conference room door to see if anyone was in; it was empty. She gestured him inside, then followed, closed the door, and jumped up on him as he struggled to link his arms under her butt as she wrapped her legs around him. They kissed and kept kissing until Tucker groaned and stood her back on her feet.

489

"Good, God woman—what are you eating here? Lasagna three meals a day?" he said.

She swatted him and grinned. "I have a roommate that makes exceptional pancakes."

"A quart of syrup and a stick of butter on each stack?"

"That goes without saying. What are you doing here? Is everything okay at home? The kids okay?"

"Everyone's fine," he soothed. "Quint and Del will be handling the kids this weekend and he said I should come up and spend some time with you. I fought him on it, but in the end—here I am."

She touched his cheek. "I'm so glad you're here. It's been a nonstop whirl. We have so-called tips coming in that've put Murphy anywhere from Singapore to Guatemala. One said they saw him sucked up in an alien spaceship on a farm in Nebraska."

"I always worry about that happening, which is why I stay away from Nebraska. Say—any chance you can get away for a bite to eat? I'm starved."

Iris frowned. "I wish, but I don't think so. We're having our bi-hourly checkpoint meeting on the situation in fifteen minutes and that lasts for a while. Why don't you head over to my friend's place and rest up? You should find a takeout place nearby. I'll call you and let you know when I can get away."

"Not ideal, but I'll take it." She handed him the keys and gave him driving instructions. He kissed her on the forehead. "Go get 'em, G-Woman."

Iris walked Tucker out and waved as she left the building. She whirled around and ran back to the command center.

"Thanks for meeting with me, Dr. Danova," Deliverance said as she shook his hand. A busy man, he had made room for her in his schedule at 3 PM but told her he only had fifteen minutes to spare.

"My pleasure, Ms. Dane," he said, sitting back down at his desk. She sat in his guest chair. "Now, what can I do for you? You mentioned something about identifying the etymology of a word?"

"Yes," she said. "I don't really know how to spell it, but it sounds like tahsuketti. Is that Italian?"

He shook his head. "Not to my knowledge, and I took four

years of Italian in high school. My forte is romance languages like Italian, French, and Spanish, and I'm pretty sure it doesn't relate to any of those." He held up a finger and hit one of his presets on the phone and the speaker button. After two rings a deep baritone voice answered. "Rudy? Hi. It's Brendan. Got a question—ever hear of the word tahsuketti?"

"No, never," Rudy answered. "What language is that?"

"That's what I'm trying to find out. Okay, thanks. See you later at dinner." Danova hung up and smiled wanly at Deliverance. "Sorry, but I have no immediate answer for you. But I will research it and get back to you as soon as I can."

Deliverance rose. "Thank you, Dr. Danova. I appreciate that. Have a good rest of your day." With that she left and couldn't hide her disappointment. She didn't know why, but she thought that Alex's recital of the word was something more than sleepwalk babbling. It was just a feeling she couldn't shake. Her son was a sensitive—she was sure of that, as sure as she was that she shouldn't ignore her feelings.

She found herself walking towards the building where the Anthropology department resided. She didn't know why; it was as though she were being pulled in that direction. She walked up the stairs to Gray Kingston's office. As the head of the department he had a nice, spacious office decorated with a wall-to-wall bookcase and whose walls were hung with Native American and Japanese art prints. His window overlooked the grassy quadrangle. It was a comfortable yet professional space to address his duties.

Gray's door was open, and she peeked in. Cress was sitting in the guest chair and they were having some kind of breezy conversation. She knocked, they looked up, and Gray waved her in. She dropped down into the second chair and sighed.

"Busy day?" Cress asked.

"Just like any other. Don't let anyone tell you that having four kids is as easy as having one. Aislinn was acting up at school and I had to have Quint run over and pick the kids up early. He's at home cracking the whip and keeping them in line."

"Where's Tucker?" Gray asked as he fiddled absently with a Rubik's Cube.

"We gave him the day off and he drove up to Phoenix to surprise Iris. He'll be back late Sunday or maybe Monday morning."

"Any word on the psycho?" Cress asked.

"Just that scads of tips are coming in on the hotline and they have to check out every one. Well, maybe not the alien spaceship."

"Seriously? That might be a legitimate tip if we were in Roswell, but not here," Gray laughed. "You know, if the newlyweds need a break they could always visit my parents. They'd be glad to host them for a relaxing evening in front of the firepit. Wine, good conversation—that'll take the edge off."

"I'll call Tuck and let him know," Deliverance said. "Meanwhile, what are your plans for the evening?"

Gray and Cress looked at one another. Gray said, "Well, none. What did you have in mind?"

"Dinner and wine at our place? You can bring the dog."

"Well, since you added that caveat, I can't think of a reason why not. What time?" Cress asked.

"Dinner's at six. Come over at five-thirty so the kids can enjoy you and your beast." Deliverance got up, and the men stood. "See you then." She waved as she left the office. She was out of the building before remembering that she hadn't told Cress about her meeting with Dr. Danova. Well, she'd tell him tonight.

"Thank God," Cress said. "I did not want to cook tonight."

"Don't you mean defrost?"

"Shut up."

Tucker nearly slipped on the tiled bathroom floor scrambling out of the shower to answer the phone. He dripped across the hallway to the guest bedroom phone and grabbed the receiver.

"Hello? Iris?" he said as he sat down on the edge of the bed and used one hand to towel his hair.

"Sorry to disappoint, Tucker, but it's me," Deliverance said. "You're wet, aren't you?"

"How did you know? Never mind. Everything okay? The kids?"

"The little monsters are fine. Well, three of them are. Aislinn got suspended for two days because she let a baby king snake loose in the classroom. She sneaked it out of the biology lab. And she mooned the principal in his office."

"That's my girl," Tucker said proudly. The one thing the Dane-Quintana kids weren't was boring.

"You better not be encouraging their pranks, Mr. Townsend," Deliverance said ominously. "There are many nanny-bodyguards around that are salivating for your job."

"It's a plum assignment," Tucker laughed as he wiped the dampness from his chest and thighs. "What's up?"

"Not much. We're having Cress and Gray over for dinner, and Gray mentioned that if you and Iris have some free time this weekend you could always visit his parents up in Carefree and relax there. They're wonderful people and would welcome you with open arms. Let me give you their address and phone number." She paused for a minute while Tucker found a pen and paper, then relayed the information. "How's Iris?" she asked.

"Running herself ragged but enjoying every second of it. She's an FBI agent down to her very bone marrow. I'm so proud of her."

"I don't doubt for a second that she feels the same way about you. Okay, I've got to start dinner and decide the appropriate punishment for my firstborn daughter. Think about visiting the Kingstons and call me if you need anything. Love you. Bye."

"Love you, too," he said then hung up. He realized that that was the first time either of them had said the words. He sat on the bed in wonder. He had a real family, a family he loved and that accepted him just the way he was. He lay back on the bed and grinned up at the ceiling. The joy of life was infinite.

Cress and Gray rang the Dane-Quintana doorbell at five-fifteen, a little early but they were sure that Deliverance wouldn't mind. Gray was carrying an expensive bottle of Merlot, which brought a grin to Quint's face when he opened the door.

"Come in and bring that wine," Quint commanded. "It'll never go to waste here."

"Nor in our house." Cress laughed as he tried to restrain

Pugsley's leash; the pug had obviously smelled other dogs and was chafing to explore. "Okay if I let him free?"

"Absolutely."

Cress unleashed Pugsley who made a beeline yapping towards the kitchen; a few seconds later there was a cacophony of barking from the three dogs that were in the process of smelling one another's butts as the three men walked into the kitchen.

"Can I—may I have one, Mom?" Storm asked as she petted the pug much to his pleasure.

"We have two dogs, a hamster, and a guinea pig, so, no," she replied.

"You have a guinea pig?" Gray asked.

"Don't even go there," Quint growled as he mock-glared at a non-contrite Alex, who had found the animal one day by the roadside in front of their house and brought it inside. Neighborhood flyers produced no desperate owners, so the fat rodent became a member of the household. Alex named him Guido.

Quint put the wine in the fridge to chill and motioned to the table where a large bowl of corn chips and a quart of salsa awaited their eating pleasure. "Help yourselves."

"Can I help you with anything?" Cress asked Deliverance.

"Nope," she said. "All under control. Just relax."

"Victor and Wilde joining us?" Gray asked as he filled a plate with corn chips and dug one into the salsa bowl.

"Nope," Quint replied. "They took the boys out miniature golfing."

"Glad they're getting back to some semblance of normal," Gray said.

"Yes, finally," Quint said.

Deliverance shooed the men and kids out to the great room while she finished dinner. Quint grabbed the chips and salsa. Cress stuck around and made her let him help, so he found himself kneading rye dough to bake bread.

"Tucker normally does that," Deliverance said. "Oh—by the way, I called him and let him know where Gray's parents are in case he and Iris want to visit."

"Good," Cress said, then suddenly stopped and slapped his

head. "Damn it—I forgot. His parents are headed up to Flagstaff this weekend for some business meeting. Rats. I'll bet Gray forgot, too."

"Well, not to worry. If they call no one will answer, and if they drive up, well, it's a nice drive. Hand me that spatula and don't forget to sprinkle caraway seeds on the top before you put it in the oven. We'll eat as soon as it finishes baking."

Iris's and Liberty's olfactory senses were hit hard when they opened the apartment door—something wonderful was being prepared in the kitchen. Iris took a deep breath.

"Spaghetti and meatballs with homemade sauce. One of my hubby's best recipes," Iris said.

"You are one lucky woman," Liberty said as she shrugged out of her jacket and removed her holster.

"I keep telling her that," Tucker said as he walked into the living room drying his hands on a dish towel. "I figured you ladies would be starving, so I went shopping and made a very nice dinner. Picked up chianti, too, and cheesecake for dessert." He stuck out his hand to Liberty. "Nice to meet you. Tucker Townsend."

"Liberty Adams," she said. "It's nice to finally meet the legend."

"Oh, God," Iris groaned. "Now he'll be insufferable to live with."

Liberty and Tucker laughed. Tucker told them to sit and relax and dinner would be ready in ten minutes. The women went to the bathroom to wash their faces and gab about good men. Ten minutes later the huge bowl of spaghetti covered with tennis-ball-sized meatballs was sitting on the table and three wine glasses were filled. Tucker had lit several candles and put one of Liberty's classical music albums on the stereo.

The conversation was easy and steered far away from the manhunt. Liberty laughed her head off at Tucker's stories about the energetic Dane-Quintana kids and how his second night on the job he had thrown back his bedcovers to find a dozen spiders clustered on the sheet, courtesy of Aislinn. He knew the little girl was waiting for the next day when he'd freak out and tell her parents, but instead he killed the spiders, put on new sheets, and never said a word. That made him A-Okay with Aislinn, although it took a little longer to entice Alex into friendship. Vikki adored him from the get-go.

They finished dinner around seven and Liberty loaded the dishwasher. Tucker told Iris about possibly visiting Gray's parents, and she thought it was a beautiful evening, so maybe they should just drive up, knock on the door, and introduce themselves. If the Kingstons weren't home or were busy, at least they'd have a nice ride. She'd put down the top of her Mustang convertible, and they'd enjoy the cool breeze and leisurely landscape. He agreed, and they told Liberty where they were going. She told them to drive carefully.

About twenty minutes after they left her phone rang, and an anxious female voice identified herself as Deliverance Dane and asked to speak with Iris Flynn, asap. Liberty said she wasn't there and that she and her husband went for a ride up to Carefree to visit a friend's parents. There was a sharp intake of breath at the other end of the line, then Deliverance told her that she needed to get ahold of Iris and tell her to call home immediately. Before Liberty could respond a man came on the line and in a deep, troubled voice told her that she needed to get agents up to the Kingston home right now. It may be a false alarm, but better safe than sorry. Liberty asked what the hell this was about, and Quint summarized the situation in less than a minute. Liberty said she'd call him back, then she hung up, called Lisbon, and told him about the call. After she hung up she strapped on her holster and tore out of the apartment. She slid behind the wheel of her 1969 silver Corvette and squealed off north on Cave Creek Road.

"That was absolutely delicious, Deliverance," Gray said. He rubbed his stomach. "I'll be going to the gym twice a day for weeks to work it off."

She smiled and said, "Glad you enjoyed it. It's my mom's shepherd's pie recipe. I only make it on special occasions."

"She considers it a special occasion once a week," Quint quipped. At his wife's scowl he hastily added, "Not that we don't enjoy eating it. Yum."

"I'd love the recipe," Cress said, "so I can experiment with it, maybe put a New Orleans touch on the spices."

"I'll write it out before you go home," she said. "In return, you have to give me your dad's gumbo recipe."

"Deal," Cress said, smiling. He pushed away from the table and began picking up plates. Deliverance told Quint, Gray, and the kids to go into the great room while she and Cress cleaned up. She didn't have to tell the kids twice as they ran like a hoard of vandals out of the kitchen.

When they were gone Cress said, "How on earth do you manage holding down a full-time job and being a wife and mother to those rabble-rousers?"

She shook her head. "I have no idea. I just do it. But I confess, sometimes I want to scream. Quint's great with the kids, and Tucker is a godsend. I couldn't do it without them." She handed him a pot. "Put this on the top rack."

While Cress finished loading the dishwasher she cleaned the table and the counters. Then she took Cress's hand and walked him into the great room where the kids were sitting on the floor in a circle playing Slap Jack. Quint was in his lounger and Gray was occupying one side of the loveseat. Cress sat next to him, took his wine glass, and sipped the last few ounces of wine.

"Say," Cress said. "I meant to ask you—did you hook up with Danova or Cary?"

"Yup, but no luck. Danova said he'd research the word and get back to me, though." She threw a glance at Alex. "Sweetheart, no trying to peek at the cards."

Alex looked guilty and nodded. Storm threw down an ace, then the Jack of Diamonds.

"Slap Jack," Alex yelled, whooping—he'd gotten the last jack. He jumped up and started doing a disco dance in triumph.

The adults laughed, and Gray leaned over and raised his hand for a high five. Alex bopped over to him and smacked his hand. In a moment, the smiling adults fell into silence.

Alex froze as solid as a statue, his hand still raised without even a tremble. His eyes unfocused, and his pupils dilated. He stared straight ahead.

"Alex?" Quint said quietly as he rose and knelt beside his son. He put a hand to the boy's forehead; the child didn't move. He looked at his wife. "His forehead's hot, just like it was last night." He touched Alex's upraised hand. "It's cold." By that time Deliverance was kneeling at Alex's other side. She craned her neck to stare at his eyes, which were nearly black due to the dilated pupils.

"Hey, kids," Cress said. "Let's head into the kitchen. There's still some cheesecake left." He took Storm's hand and pulled, but the little girl frowned and stared at her brother.

"What's wrong with him?" Storm asked.

"Nothing," Deliverance snapped. "Go with Cress now." She nodded at her friend who ushered the three children out of the great room. Then she rubbed her fingers against her son's hot cheek and said, very quietly, "Tell me."

Alex slowly turned his head and locked eyes with his mother. He didn't blink. She could tell that he wasn't really seeing her but looking at something unfathomable outside the realm of natural perception. Then he spoke in a monotone.

"Tasukete. Tasukete." He paused for a second. "Taigāyuri."

"There it is again," Quint said. "We've got to find out what he's saying. It—" He stopped short at the querulous look on Gray's face. "What?" he asked his friend.

"It's Japanese," Gray said slowly. "And perfectly accented."

"Japanese?" Deliverance said. "Did he pick that up somehow from you?"

Gray shook his head. "I doubt it. I only speak it to my parents or Cress."

"Then you know what it means," Quint said.

"Of course. Tasukete means help. He's asking for help." An ice-cold rush ripped up Gray's spine. "Taigāyuri is a flower—Tiger Lily. Mom and Dad's pug."

"Oh, my God," Cress breathed as he came back into the room. "Do you think your mom was communicating with Alex?"

Gray shook his head. "I can't believe that. Sorry, Deliverance, but I'm just skeptical."

"Where are your parents?" Quint asked. "Home?"

"No. Mom said she and Dad were driving up to Flagstaff for a business meeting this weekend. I talked to her yesterday after you left my office."

"Just to humor me," Deliverance said, "can you call and see if they're home?"

Gray nodded, picked up the phone, and dialed. He let it ring eight times. He shook his head. "No answer. I'm sure they're in Flagstaff."

"Do you have the number of a neighbor or friend who can check? I don't mean to be an alarmist, but even you can see that something's up with Alex."

Gray drew his wallet out of his back pocket. "Mrs. Roberts lives across the street. I can call her." He took out a slip of paper and dialed. It rang three times before Mrs. Roberts answered. "Hi, Mrs. Roberts? It's Gray Kingston. Fine, thank you. Sure. Listen—do you know if my parents are home? I tried calling them but got no answer. Okay, I'll hang on." He put his hand over the mouthpiece. "She's checking for their cars." A moment later the woman came back on line. "I see. Okay, I appreciate your time. No, you don't need to go over. Thanks again." He hung up and said, "Mom's car is in the driveway, and she sees dim lights behind the blinds. It's kind of odd, though. Mom and Dad always park their cars in the garage."

"Okay, but don't you think it's odd that they didn't answer?" Quint asked.

"Yeah, I do." Gray looked at the paper slip again and began dialing as he told them that he was calling one of his father's law firm associates, a good golfing buddy. A few seconds later his next call answered. "Doug? Hi—it's Gray. Fine, thanks. Listen—did Dad have a business meeting up north? I see … No, no problem—just trying to reach them. Speak to you soon. Bye." He looked up. "Dad called in sick with the flu yesterday morning. There is no meeting up in Flag. What does this mean?" He snapped his fingers. "You know what else? Mom's … words were kind of peculiar when I spoke to her. She kept calling me by endearments and referred to my father as Daddy instead of Dad. We haven't called him Daddy since I was six. She called Cress Crescent, too. She mentioned being Fukushima'd—kind of a family in-joke and not something she'd normally say."

Quint and Deliverance looked at one another. "You don't think …" Quint began.

"I do," Deliverance said. She looked hard at Gray. "I know

you don't believe, but I do. I believe your mom was calling out for help and it came across Alex's mind waves. We need to get someone to go and check things out."

"Call Iris," Quint said. "I'll call Cornell." He looked at Cress. "Please use the phone in our den and get the number for the Carefree sheriff's office. We may need it."

Cress didn't hesitate to spring up and rush towards the den, Gray following.

Deliverance was still kneeling beside her son. She gently clasped his cheeks with her hands and found that the fever she'd felt before had almost completely gone. She kissed his forehead. "I love you, Alejandro. You're such a good boy."

Alex's pupil dilation had subsided about fifty percent and he seemed more animate, less in a trance. A faint smile crossed his lips. "Watashi mo anata mo daisuki, Mama," he said.

"I'm thinking he's speaking in Japanese again," Quint said in wonder.

"Our son is special. He has my gift, and lot more, I think," Deliverance said thoughtfully. She rose and grabbed the phone and dialed the number of Iris's friend. After she identified herself Quint took the receiver from her hand and spoke to the woman who answered. As they spoke Alex began chanting.

"Tasukete. Tasukete. Tasukete. Tasukete."

CHAPTER TWELVE

Cave Creek, Arizona prides itself on being a truly western town; it even has a small "Frontier Town" section with old-west-style buildings that house gift shops and a ribs restaurant, and a wigwam that sells tchotchkes that tourists find adorable. It is also known as a biker's haven, and every year hundreds of men and women on hogs convene at several locations to hobnob and enjoy the freedom of just being themselves.

The town of only a few thousand packed into thirty-seven square miles is overwhelmingly white even though Native Americans and Hispanics make up a decent percentage of the state overall. It is considered a rowdy, freewheeling place to live and visit and attracts snowbirds by the hundreds. There were several well-known residents who had made Cave Creek their home, including comedian and actor Dick Van Dyke; from 1971 through 1974 Van Dyke filmed his sitcom *The New Dick Van Dyke Show* in a studio in nearby Carefree.

Cave Creek is easy to reach—one just heads north on Cave Creek Road, which starts in north Phoenix and snakes all the way around the town to North Pima Road. Cave Creek bumps up against the town of Carefree, which considers itself rather "exclusive" with high property prices and classier residences and businesses. Carefree has many small communities, many gated to provide security and a sense of the elite. The Boulders is perhaps the most exclusive community, as anyone can tell by the gate-guarded entrance. The homes are well-spaced and elegant, and individualistic unlike the myriad of tract-home communities in Phoenix. The community looks like a Flintstone village, with, literally, boulders piled on top of boulders, some the size of small houses. The small mountain on the other side of the road is dotted with houses that wind their way all the way to the top; stacked boulders is apparently the natural design of this section of the Valley of the Sun.

The Kingstons had bought their Santa Fe-style home in The Boulders in 1970 shortly after their son graduated college. The home rested on three-quarters of an acre of natural desert land. It was three-thousand square feet inside, four bedrooms, a den, a large great room, and a modern kitchen that had been upgraded two years earlier. The backyard was fenced-in, as was the courtyard in the front. Over the years Grayson had planted a dozen barrel cactus in the front and installed a working fountain where birds frequently drank and took baths. The large palo verde tree in the courtyard housed three hummingbird feeders and a set of windchimes. The backyard had a large covered patio, a brick firepit, and a beehive fireplace, as well as a small putting green for Grayson to practice his strokes. Two immense crucifixion thorn bushes rimmed one side of the fence, and a tall, blooming ocotillo sprawled near the middle of the other. Grayson had built a beautiful Japanese garden for his wife the year after they moved in, and a koi pond under a small arched bridge provided a relaxing place for her meditation. For their thirtieth wedding anniversary in 1978 their son Gray surprised them with an above-ground redwood hot tub that his mother used nearly every night.

The home had a two-car garage that housed Mariko's candy-apple-red Ford Thunderbird and Grayson's gunmetal-grey Mercedes. They never kept their cars outside, particularly in the summer. Grayson washed both cars every weekend as part of his Saturday ritual. That was why Mrs. Roberts thought it was so peculiar that the T-Bird had been outside for two days collecting dust. Maybe she should go over and knock on the door? The people living on Staghorn Lane were a friendly lot and kept an eye out for one another's homes. It was dark out now, and a mild breeze was kicking up. She'd just finished dinner and was washing the dishes. No, she wouldn't bother them tonight, but she'd go over tomorrow morning to ostensibly "borrow" some car wash, secretly hoping that nice Grayson would volunteer to wash her car when he finished theirs. Yes, that was the plan. She finished the dishes and parked herself on the couch, dialing the local pizza parlor in Cave Creek to deliver a medium pie. That cute new series, *Detective in the House*, was coming on shortly on CBS, and then her two most seductive guilty pleasures—*Dallas* and *Falcon Crest*. Mrs. Roberts adored Friday nights and absolutely worshipped the conniving J.R. Ewing.

Iris maneuvered her car slowly up Cave Creek Road once she passed the small sheriff's office. Once she rounded the bend she saw a place that was selling acres of Mexican pots and knickknacks, and tons of ceramic geckos hanging on a rickety wooden fence. An eighth of a mile past that Tucker grinned and pointed at Frontier Town and said they needed to come up during the daytime and explore all the stores and sights. Iris said she noticed a barbecue place close by the American Legion and that they could eat lunch there.

It was still tourist season, and everything was open late as people from mostly northern states milled about enjoying the atmosphere. Iris smiled at an elderly couple who were standing in Frontier Town in front of a board with head cutouts and painted gunslinger bodies. She turned serious, wondering how she and Tucker would look and act if they made it that far in life.

Still driving slowly (since the road signs said 25 mph) she navigated around a smooth curve and began an upward swing towards Carefree and the intersection where she'd turn south on Tom Darlington Road. Iris had just made the turn when she was startled by the flashing lights coming up fast behind her. She pulled over automatically and parked, then craned her neck to see Liberty's Corvette screech up behind her and stop scant inches from her rear bumper. She and Tucker got out of their car just as Liberty did.

"Libby," Iris exclaimed. "What the hell? What's wrong?"

Liberty seemed out of breath as she turned off her flashing lights. "So glad I caught you before you got to the Kingston house," Liberty said, breathing hard.

"Why?" Tucker said tightly. His neck hairs were standing on end. He just sensed something urgent in his wife's friend.

"Your buddies Quint and Deliverance called minutes after you left," Liberty said. "They think … they think Murphy may be holing up in the Kingstons' house."

"The hell," Tucker said. "What? Why?"

"Okay," Liberty said. "This is the Monarch Notes version." Her story streamed out nonstop as she explained the Japanese words little Alex was saying in a trance-like state, and the strange non sequiturs that Gray's mother had inserted into her conversation when they last spoke. She ended with Gray's call to the neighbor and Grayson's work associate. "I called Lisbon right away but didn't wait around and tried to catch you. You know, when we get down to Tucson we should have mobile phones installed in our cars."

"Right," Iris said absently. She locked eyes with Tucker. "We can't wait for the rest of the gang. Murphy's unpredictable at this point and could turn in a second." She looked at Liberty. "I don't suppose you had the time to stop at that sheriff's office and let them know the score?"

Liberty shook her head. "All I could think of was to get to you as quickly as I could. Should I call them now? I don't have their number."

"Find it," Iris said flatly. "You know the address?" Liberty nodded. "Okay, get backup and make sure you come in quietly, no sirens or flashing lights. This guy is fucking nuts, and anything could set him off. The Kingstons may still be alive, and if so, we want to keep them that way. Tucker, you stay with Liberty."

"No fucking way," he said angrily. "I'm going with you."

"The hell you are."

"The hell I'm not. You're wasting time making an argument you're gonna lose." He scowled at her, obviously digging in his heels.

"Pain in the ass nanny," Iris muttered. She looked at Liberty. "Go!"

Liberty whirled around and tore open her car door, slid inside, and made a dangerous U-turn to get to the other side of the road where a small gas station had a couple of customers. Iris and Tucker got into their car and Iris took off. The entry to The Boulders was two miles south. As she drove Iris nodded towards the glove compartment. "Got a spare piece in there."

Tucker opened the compartment and moved stuff away from a Glock 17. "Sweet," Tucker said. He checked the magazine; fully loaded. The 9mm, short recoil–operated, locked-breech semi-automatic pistol was a top performer in reliability and safety tests; the U.S. Department of Defense was considering it for use in the States although it was already becoming a mainstay in Europe. He glanced over at his wife. "You know I can handle myself. I can back you up without blinking."

Iris kept her eyes on the road, spotting the entry to The Boulders.

"Yeah," she said. "I know that." A sudden chill starting at

the small of her back made her think that someone was walking on her grave.

"I love you," he said quietly.

"Yeah, I know that, too. Be cool," she said as she turned into the community and pulled up behind another non-resident car. The guy was talking to the guard, who was smiling and nodding.

"Get the fuck going, asshole," Iris hissed at the other driver. A few seconds later he drove off and Iris pulled up to the guard. She flashed her FBI creds. "Official business," she snapped. "There'll be other cops coming along soon so leave the gate up and keep your mouth shut." The guard looked surprised but nodded and raised the gate. "How do we get to Staghorn Lane?" she asked. The guard gave her directions and she drove off to the left quickly but carefully. The roads were narrow, hilly, and curvy, and her route took her past a golf course.

The community was dark with no streetlights and she almost missed the turn into Staghorn. She turned then stopped and backed out and parked her car twenty feet down from the street entrance. She turned to her husband.

"I don't suppose I can convince you to stay in the car?" she asked mildly as she gathered her long mane up into a high ponytail.

"It's really dark," he whispered, then pointed up in the sky, "but if you stare real hard you can see them thar pigs flying over the golf course."

"Asshole," she replied affectionately.

"I yam what I yam."

"Okay," Iris said. "We don't know the exact layout of the house and property, so we need to do some fast reconnoitering before law enforcement descends on this block."

"Think we should go to that neighbor's house and question her? It might be a good place to gather the troops."

"I don't know. Maybe. Let's see first how the house is set up and—uh-oh." She nodded towards the direction from which they'd come. Liberty's Corvette was moving slowly towards them, headlights off. She pulled up behind Iris's car and got out of hers soundlessly.

Liberty whispered to her teammate, "Called the sheriff's

deputy from the gas station. If you can believe it, he was on the other line with Quint. He said he'd call our office and see how close the other agents are. What's the plan?"

"Reconnaissance," Iris replied as she drew her service weapon. She scowled at Tucker. "Dirty Harry, here, is coming with us. He's got my Glock but will *not* use it unless instructed to do so, right?"

"A man's got to know his limitations," Tucker said in his best Clint Eastwood impression.

"No more action movies for you," Iris said, forcing away a smile. She sobered. "Okay. The Kingston house is the second one on the left. You said the neighbor lady lives diagonal across the street?" Liberty nodded. "Don't suppose Quint mentioned a spare key anywhere outside?"

"Damn it," Liberty cursed. "I didn't think to ask."

"Don't worry about it," Tucker said soothingly. "I can pick any lock from here to Burlington." His wife's eyebrows were near the top of her forehead. "What? I wasn't an angel when I was growing up. Someday I'll tell you about my adventures in shoplifting."

"Bad enough I married a governess let alone an adolescent criminal," Iris murmured. She checked her Smith & Wesson. "Libby, you go to the neighbor's house and see what intel you can get from her—if she's seen the Kingstons or anyone else, light patterns, the like. Tucker and I are going to reconnoiter the house and see if we can determine any potential entry points. Don't come over until the rest of the agents or deputies appear."

"I think I should go with you two," Liberty said, an edge of annoyance creeping into her low voice.

"That's an order," Iris stated flatly. Her tone brooked no dissension. "Go."

Liberty grudgingly nodded and moved off to the right on Staghorn crouching low and being quiet. After a few seconds Iris nodded to Tucker and they moved off left towards the Kingston house.

Quint hung up the phone after talking to the deputy in Cave Creek (whose sheriff's office serviced Carefree as well). His face was a mask of frustration. "I fuckin' hate being stuck down here when this is going on," he said angrily.

"How do you think I feel?" Gray retorted, also angry. "That murderous psycho might be holding my parents hostage."

Without warning Deliverance ran out of the house, the three perplexed men watching her flee into the back yard.

"What's that all about?" Cress asked.

"Not a clue," Quint said. "I guess we'll find out." He scowled. "Cress, call information again and get the number of the Desert Ridge Miniature Golf Park. Tell them that this is a police emergency and to find Wilde and Victor and tell them to come home. Don't give them any specifics." Cress nodded and sat down with the phone and dialed 4-1-1. He spoke softly, scribbled down a number, and dialed that.

Quint could see the roiling fear in Gray's eyes and put a strong hand on his shoulder. "It's going to be all right."

"You don't know that," Gray said.

"No, I don't, but I have faith." He glanced up just as Cress ended his golf call and Deliverance burst back into the room crushing a piece of paper in her hand. She whipped the phone out of Cress's hand and plopped down hard next to him and dialed, ignoring the curious looks.

"C'mon, c'mon, c'mon," she chanted as the phone rang. "Fuckin' finally," she spat out as the person answered on the fifth ring. "Josh? This is Deliverance Dane. Yeah, that's right—Tucker's friend. We need your helicopter. No, I'm not batshit crazy, but I'm desperate, mad as hell, pissed off, and ready to rain hell down on anyone that stands in my way. This is literally a matter of life and death. So, for $1,000 and my eternal good will—which is not inconsequential—get your pilot ass in your bird and land it in my backyard RIGHT. FUCKING. NOW. Hmm? Good. Carefree, north of Phoenix. You do? Excellent." She slammed down the receiver and smiled at the astounded men. "What? Didn't I make myself clear with him?" She pointed at Quint and Gray. "You two are going for a chopper ride. Cress and I will hold down the fort. Well?" she snapped at her husband. "Get your gun."

Iris moved as stealthily as a hunting panther to the Kingston house, her husband behind her within touching distance. She hand-signaled him that they were going to move to the side of the house

507

with the garage doors. She stopped for a brief second and wiped her hand against the red Thunderbird. She rubbed her fingers; dust. The car had been sitting outside for at least two days. She motioned Tucker to crouch and duck walk past the car to the side of the garage where she was relieved to see a door that allowed entry into the garage. That was the good part; the bad part was that it had a strong dead-bolt lock.

She whispered to Tucker, "I don't suppose your childhood burglary habits refined the ability to get past a dead-bolt?"

Tucker ran his fingers over the lock. "I had no problem with Mr. Shackett's lock in his mom and pop store, but this model just came out. It's tough. Not sure." He paused. "You know how we have an extra key to get into the casita if we get locked out? Maybe the Kingstons have the same thing."

"Could be anywhere," Iris murmured. "It's dark, and we don't have time to look."

"We need to make time," he countered. "Let's just search for five minutes. Two—two minutes, okay?"

"Yeah, fine," she said. She felt around the top of the door. "Of course not. That would be too easy." She looked around and moved farther back against the house, coming to the gate that allowed entry to the back yard. There was no padlock on it. "We caught one break," she whispered as she very, very gently lifted the latch. She stopped dead after a tiny squeak, waited a few seconds, then finished opening it. She prayed silently that the door's hinges wouldn't creak, and she let out the breath she was holding when the well-oiled gate opened noiselessly. She moved into the back; Tucker followed and closed the gate carefully so that it wouldn't latch and would allow someone else to enter without a telltale creak.

Tucker heard the slight babbling of the low waterfall at the edge of the koi pond. He could see slits of light emanating from what he assumed was the kitchen or great room at the wide patio. Iris put a finger to her lips, then made a motion to her ear. Tucker listened and nodded. He could hear very faint voices coming from inside.

Iris hugged the rear wall of the house as she crept very carefully along the length. She stopped suddenly; Tucker nearly ran into her. She leaned against the wall and pulled off her high-heeled boots. He understood; shoeless she'd make fewer sounds as she encroached on the target. He pulled off his own boots and they continued creeping against the wall.

Iris came to a window whose blinds were drawn nearly closed. Slits of light were radiating out and taking a deep breath she carefully inched her head up to try to catch a glimpse of the interior. She could make out bits and pieces of the kitchen—a refrigerator, a stove with a pot on one fired-up burner, a table with dirty dishes piled one on another. The voices had ceased, and she saw no movement, but suddenly a movement did catch her eye and she saw a man pushing an older woman in front of him towards the stove. Iris fell back away from the window and looked at Tucker.

"It's him," she rasped. "The fucker's here. Mrs. Kingston is with him. No sign of the husband."

"What do we do?" Tucker asked softly, the gun heavy in his hand.

"We need a diversion," she whispered back, then froze at a sound coming from the gate area. Automatically both she and Tucker turned and raised their guns, relaxing in a second after they recognized Liberty.

"I thought I told you to stay put," Iris said crossly as the other woman joined them.

"Write me up," Liberty replied, half serious. "The neighbor wasn't any help. She didn't say anything more than what she told Gray. She was ticked off that I disturbed her enjoyment of *Dallas*. She was eating a Hawaiian pizza. Who the hell made the culinary misstep of putting pineapple on pizza?"

"I'll put that on my list of things to investigate tomorrow," Iris snapped. Then she brightened. "Perfect. We need a diversion so we can get into the house from the back."

"Maybe we should wait for the rest of your guys to show up?" Tucker offered. "Did Mrs. Kingston look okay?"

"She did, but that could change on a dime. Liberty—go back to that woman's house and appropriate the pizza box. You're going to make a delivery."

"Um, okay," Liberty said.

"Make it loud. Well? Go," Iris exclaimed a little too loudly.

She clapped her hand over her mouth and they all froze, but apparently no one inside had heard. Liberty scurried off.

Iris and Tucker pressed themselves against the wall, their arms touching, the only sounds in the night their harsh breathing and the babbling of the waterfall. They were silent, waiting. Without warning Tucker threw out a thought.

"Ever think of having kids?" he asked.

"I honestly haven't given it much thought in the past."

"What about now?"

"I'm thinking about it." Iris craned her neck and saw that Murphy and Mariko were still in the kitchen, and she was dishing out a hot bowl of soup. "Although I'm not sure what kind of a kid would come out by breeding a cop and a nanny."

"A kid that could cook, clean, shoot, and arrest people on weekends while folding the laundry perfectly."

She turned her head and smiled at him. Even in the dark her smile could brighten his world.

Tucker was about to press further when they heard loud knocking coming at the front door. Iris tensed as Murphy grabbed Mariko by the hair and shoved her out of the kitchen, ostensibly to the living room. Iris smiled slightly as she heard Liberty call out.

"Hello? Hello?" Liberty said loudly. "Pizza delivery. Hello? Mrs. Roberts?" More knocking broke the still night air.

Iris looked at Tucker. "They're out of the kitchen. You'd better not be exaggerating when you say you can jimmy any lock."

"I didn't say any," Tucker muttered as he knelt in front of the sliding glass doors from the kitchen to the patio and pulled out his car keys, flicking open the small pen knife. He withdrew his Goldwater's credit card and carefully used the two items to jimmy the door lock. There was a soft click and he looked up at Iris then rose and very gently pushed the door open just a crack. He slipped inside, and Iris followed then moved in front of him. They could hear a man speaking and detected Liberty's voice saying that, no, she was sure she had the right address and that a Mrs. Roberts had ordered a Hawaiian pizza, as disgusting as that might be.

Iris hugged the kitchen wall as it merged with a large arch wall that seemed to lead towards the voices. At this point Murphy's voice was belligerent as he tried to get Liberty to go away. Iris had made it to the edge of the living room and she could see Murphy standing partially behind the door. His gun was in one hand and his fingers wrapped tightly through Mariko's hair as he held her behind him. Iris could see the terror on her face and wondered where her husband was.

"Look, bitch," Murphy snarled at Liberty, "we didn't order any goddamn pizza so get your skanky ass out of here. Eat the damn thing yourself." With that he slammed the door shut and was about to throw the dead-bolt when the door crashed open as Liberty turned the knob and threw herself against it. Murphy lost his hold on Mariko's hair and stumbled back but didn't fall. Mariko dropped and rolled away, scrambling behind a chair.

"FBI—freeze, fucker," Iris screamed.

Murphy was distracted only for a split second before he whipped around holding his gun up, facing Liberty, whose gun was drawn. With no warning he simply shot her. She shrieked and went down. Iris got off a round, but Murphy was fast and dropped to the floor long enough to drag Liberty up by the hair and position her as a human shield, the crook of his left arm nearly crushing her throat. Blood was pouring out of Liberty's badly damaged shoulder and her gun had dropped to the floor. Murphy kicked it away while he put the barrel of his gun up to Liberty's right temple. He moved a foot to his right, pulling his hostage along with him.

"I will blow her fucking brains out unless you back off," Murphy snarled as he jammed the barrel of the gun as hard as he could against Liberty's head.

"You're not getting out of here, Murphy," Iris said as calmly as she could. "You went to a lot of trouble to keep Laurel alive so she could write your story. Don't let the last chapter end before that story is truly finished."

Murphy flashed an evil grin. "Smart bitch, aren't you? I knew you'd be trouble from the first time I met you. Heads above the local constabulary, most definitely."

"Thanks. Ever read William Faulkner?"

"I'm a southern boy—of course. I liked *The Reivers*. McQueen was miscast in the movie. Not so well-disposed towards *Sanctuary*. Why?" Murphy tightened his arm around Liberty's throat.

"There's a quote from Faulkner that I think applies to you."

"And that is?"

"'If a story is in you, it has to come out.' There's more story in you and no one will ever know that unless you come through this storm."

"You have no idea how right you are," Murphy laughed. "You ever read Frank Herbert?"

"*Dune* is a freakin' masterpiece," Iris said with just a touch of reverence in her voice.

"Herbert said, 'There is no real ending. It's just the place where you stop the story.' Maybe my story stops here."

"It doesn't have to."

"Shoot him, Iris," Liberty cried.

"Shut up, bitch," Murphy said as he kept circling the room slowly, Tucker and Iris doing the same opposite him. Iris looked behind the chair and saw that Mariko was uninjured and crouching as small as she could make herself.

Iris kept trying to distract him with praise. Ballard had diagnosed him as narcissistic, and that emotional hubris could be the key to disarming him intellectually enough to gain an edge. She registered that her gun hand was sweating. She pressed on. "You've already written your name in the history books, Pete. But the name and a few tidbits aren't enough for the world. Look at the books written about Manson, Bundy, Son of Sam, the Axewoman of Tucson. Do you just want to be a footnote in a compilation, or do you want the intellectuals of this world to sweep those books off the shelves and let the ones about you stand alone?"

"Shoot him through me," Liberty shrieked. "Don't let him get away." By the time she said that she and Murphy were backed into the arch that led to the kitchen. Tucker thought that the odd play of lights coming from behind him and towards him cast a demonic impression on his unremarkable appearance. Murphy's unnatural, wide grin made him look as mad as a hatter, as evil as the devil himself.

Iris had both hands on her gun now, her arms straight out. She was vaguely aware of Tucker being behind her, scarcely a foot away, his own gun steady in his hand. She was also aware of the unmistakable sounds of cars arriving and doors opening. *Could they be any louder and more obvious?* she thought crossly.

Murphy backed into the kitchen, dragging a badly bleeding Liberty with him. He grinned.

"I've got to say, I've enjoyed tonight, matching wits and guts with you. Much better than those overrated Union Jack bastards and their cop buddies. You know, in another life we could have been a … what—a modern day Bonnie and Clyde? Wreaking havoc until we both went down in a hail of bullets? That would be a sweet ending, wouldn't it?"

"The whole point is you don't have to end. You have a lot of life left to say your peace."

"In prison," he said contemptuously.

"A smart lawyer can get you committed to a hospital. More freedom, more attention by appreciative professionals, more respect. That's what you want, isn't it—respect?"

"I sure as shit didn't get any from the police force or those damn writers," he spat out savagely. "Do you know how much I did on all those ax murder cases? No one in the lab had more insight, more attention to detail, better reports. But, no—people like Belzer and Munch and Quint got all the credit, all the glory. Their names were in the books—mine wasn't, not even in that bitch Bollmeier's book and when I even gave her tips about the cases. They treated me like a nonentity. They promoted that bastard Ben Deuel over me. They treated me like *dirt*."

"But you got back at them, didn't you?" Iris said calmly as her furtive eyes searched for some section of his body that she could shoot without hitting Liberty.

"Damn right I did."

"Your name will be in all the books."

"Fuckin'-A."

Iris noted that his pupils were fully dilated. There was madness in his eyes, madness that could no longer be contained under a thin veneer of sanity and humanity. He was about to blow. She had to take action. *So, so sorry Liberty,* she thought as her finger began to close on the trigger.

Iris blinked at a sudden movement from her fellow agent as Liberty pulled a switchblade from her jeans pocket, snapped it open, and plunged it into Murphy's thigh.

An inhuman scream broke the stifling air in the house as Murphy angrily smashed his gun into Liberty's head and involuntarily released her from his death grip. She fell to the floor in a heap. He had the presence of mind to get off a few shots that missed Iris and Tucker, who had dropped to the ground. He ran like hell towards the sliding doors as Iris yelled at him once again to freeze.

Murphy barreled out of the sliders and into the back yard where he made a split-second decision that if he was going down he wasn't going to do so alone. Just as he got to the lowest section of the fence where the two crucifixion thorn bushes stood guard—knowing that with his damaged leg he'd never be able to propel himself over the fence—he whirled around, and without hesitation got off three rounds; each bullet found its mark in Iris's chest before she could even squeeze her trigger once.

Even before she hit the ground his reign of madness came to an end as Tucker howled to the heavens and emptied the entire Glock magazine into Murphy's body, blasting holes in his torso, head, legs and arms, throwing him back into the bushes like a bloody rag doll. His arms were thrown out wide as blood flowed down his face where the top of his head was missing. He looked like a hellish Christ figure that had met his predestined fate. His dead face was fixed in a maniacal smile.

The loud buzzing in Tucker's ears drowned out the sounds of men and women flooding into the house, guns drawn. He was only barely aware of men calling his and Iris's names as he dropped down to his knees beside his wife's still body. A pool of bright red blood was seeping out from behind her back and spreading across the patio.

He crouched over her whispering, "C'mon, baby, c'mon," as he began CPR, pumping her chest and breathing into her mouth. Someone who said his name was Lisbon dropped down to Iris's other side to help him, but Tucker savagely pushed Lisbon's hands away and frantically tried to get her breathing again.

"C'mon, baby, c'mon, baby, c'mon, baby." He could barely see her features through his veil of tears.

Lisbon looked up at Richard Ballard, who was standing over him. Their eyes met sadly as the sound of an ambulance siren ripped through the dark night.

The only other sound was the koi pond waterfall splashing like the cascade of tears rushing down Tucker's face.

CHAPTER THIRTEEN

Twenty-four hundred miles south of Hawaii, Tahiti could legitimately be called paradise. The largest island in French Polynesia, its four hundred square miles are surrounded by the stunningly blue Southern Pacific Ocean; it is world-famous for its black sand beaches, remarkable peacefulness and beauty, and its seclusion from much of the world. Black Tahitian pearls are considered the crème de la crème of ocean jewels, sought after and cherished by kings, queens, aristocrats, and middle-class poseurs who want to seem elite; a single, perfectly round natural pearl could sell for thousands.

The northwestern portion of the island is called Tahiti Nui ("Big Tahiti") and its population and tourists are clustered around the coast, mostly near the capital town of Papeete; the internal section is nearly uninhabited. The southeastern portion of the island, Tahiti Iti ("Small Tahiti"), is virtually inaccessible except by foot or boat.

May through October is considered the high season for tourists, but some of the resorts and hotels up their prices on April 1st. April is a lovely month where the high temperatures still barely inch past 80°F, and there is an average of six days of rain. Despite being an isolated island in the ocean Tahiti also has lush rainforests, rivers, and waterfalls besides the beaches, and tourists descend on the tranquil Elysian Fields year-round.

Deliverance sighed and turned over on her back, which had been exposed to an hour of sun and tanning. She needed to do the other side. She was wearing a miniscule string bikini that left nothing of her svelte, compact figure to the imagination. She had been the object of stares from the people who passed by and saw the tattoo on her back, a winged dragon that rose from the small of her back to her shoulders. Brilliant vermillion with wings of orange and yellow fire, it was a masterpiece. The skull tattoo inching up the side of her neck was another eye-catcher.

"Oil me up, Macho Man," she murmured to her husband, who was lying beside her on his own lounge chair at the edge of the beach.

Quint wordlessly reached for the mixture of baby oil and iodine that his wife had mixed up before they hit the sand. He poured a generous helping in his hand and dripped it on his wife's stomach.

He began massaging the oil into her thorax and legs, then addressed her shoulders and arms.

"Another day or two and people will mistake you for a Hispanic chick—well, except for the golden hair," he said as he rubbed a bit of oil all along his own chest, arms, and legs.

"We'll look like Victor when we get home," she replied as she sat up and reached over for the daquiri bottle in the cooler. She took a long sip, then smiled at her husband. "This is the best birthday ever," she said seriously.

"Well, since you've hit the ancient age of thirty I thought something special was in order." Quint had suggested that they spend her thirtieth birthday up in Sedona, and she was agreeable with that. She'd had no idea that he had planned and paid for a two-week holiday in Tahiti. Bliss had talked his ear off once about how wonderful her honeymoon had been there, and he thought that his wife should be regaled with something out of the ordinary. He had arranged with Charity and Nicolae to come out to Tucson and stay with the kids for those two weeks, and they were happy to do so. He hoped fervently that she wasn't planning anything too immense for his Big 4-Oh next month.

She raised one eyelid and glared at him. "I'm still younger than you, Big Boy. And maybe you'd better start worrying that the older I get the more I might be disposed to having a boy toy on the side."

"I'll bear that in mind," Quint said as he lay back in the lounge chair. He felt the hot sun and cool breeze on his face, and for the first time in a long time felt at peace. The events of the last eighteen months were thankfully fading away in his mind and soul now that the last enemy was vanquished and, as Deliverance said, all was right with the world.

Quint closed his eyes and sighed; yeah, life was good. He smiled and hoped that his four hellions weren't driving their grandparents crazy. Tucker could help some but most of his efforts were legitimately focused on taking care of his recovering wife. Quint involuntarily squeezed his eyes tightly shut as he thought about those insane few days when the reign of the deadly Beguiler—AKA, Pete Murphy; AKA "Kreskin"—had come to an end.

Quint, Gray, and Josh Wyllys were in Josh's chopper high above the Arizona landscape as they raced at 120 mph up to Carefree from Quint's backyard. As Josh took them up he muttered something about building a heliport and installing a fuel depot in the Quintana backyard since it seemed he'd be making a lot of trips there. Quint told him he'd think about it and Josh just smiled. He pushed his chopper to its max and made excellent time on the course he'd plotted. When they hit North Scottsdale, Gray squeezed Quint's arm and whispered that they were fifteen miles from his parents' home.

As the chopper reached the Boulders area they could see a myriad of flashing red and blue lights as well as a news chopper that was hovering over the west end of the community.

"I don't know where we can land without being arrested," Josh shouted over the din of the whirring chopper blades.

"Put it down over there—the golf course," Gray shouted back. That section was a hundred yards from the Kingston home.

"I don't know—"

"Just set it down," Quint yelled. "I'll pay your bail if it comes to that."

"Fines, too?" Josh said as he dipped and headed in for a landing.

"Fines, too, damn it. Down!"

As Josh landed his bird they could see several cops running towards them with guns waving.

"I am so screwed," Josh muttered as he switched off the ignition just as his passengers bolted out of the chopper and ran helter-skelter across the moist green lawn. Two of the cops broke off after them while the third one motioned Josh to get out and put his hands up. "So screwed," he muttered again before the cop whirled him around and handcuffed him.

Gray and Quint dodged bushes and fences to get into the middle of the flashing lights. Quint automatically counted eight cars, two without official markings. *FBI*, he thought. Quint was relieved when he spotted Richard Ballard standing on the landing of the front door issuing orders. Quint yelled at him just as the two cops caught up with them and shoved him and Gray to the ground. Ballard yelled at them that it was all right and to let the men up. Gray scrambled to his feet and tore into the house.

When Quint made it to the front door he shook Ballard's hand and slipped inside. His whole body sagged with relief when he saw Gray, his father, and his mother locked in a tight embrace, all three crying. Quint turned to Ballard, and before he could speak he saw the blood on the floor. He paled.

"Who got hurt?" Quint asked, his heart pounding savagely.

"One of our agents, Liberty Adams, got shot in the shoulder. She should be at the hospital now. The wound's not life-threatening." He paused. "Iris Flynn was shot by Murphy, three to the chest."

"Sweet Jesus," Quint whispered. "Is she ..."

"She was, for a couple of minutes, but that damned nanny husband of hers kept doing CPR and screaming at her to hold on, and she started breathing. She's in very bad shape and a chopper just took off with the two of them for the nearest trauma hospital."

"Tucker okay?"

"Physically, but he's a mess with his wife all shot up."

"Murphy?"

Ballard nodded and turned, and Quint followed him out to the backyard. Quint stared at the scene of Murphy dead, spread against a huge crucifixion thorn bush in, ironically, a crucifixion pose. Ballard smiled slightly. "Never knew a nanny could shoot that well."

Quint stared at him. "Tucker killed him?"

"Emptied a whole fucking Glock magazine into the bastard's body." He pointed. "Shot the top of his head off. That is one dead Beguiler."

"Good," Quint breathed. He straightened. "The Kingstons are okay?"

"Yeah, they're fine. We're still collecting all the facts about how he got in here and what went on, but it seems that he didn't hurt either of them except to tie them up and keep them gagged much of the time. Mr. Kingston was shoved into a locked closet this morning, but Mrs. Kingston was left out so she could prepare food and, I guess, keep him company. She said he didn't rape her."

"He didn't rape Laurel Bollmeier, either."

"A considerate psycho," Lisbon said as he came up behind them. He stuck his hand out. "Nick Lisbon, Iris's boss."

"Michael Quintana, the nanny's boss." He smiled.

"That's some fella you've got there," Lisbon said. "Could use a gutsy shot like him in the FBI."

"Sorry," Quint said, not sounding sorry at all, "but he's mine until the kids graduate college. How bad is Iris?"

"As I said, three shots to the chest, so we don't know if any of the bullets hit the heart. She was breathing after the CPR but not conscious. I'll pin down the hospital they've taken her to so you can head over there if you like."

"Um, I have a helicopter but no car."

"Helicopter, huh? Nothing like a big entrance. One of my guys will drive you over."

"I need to call my wife and partners."

"I don't imagine the Kingstons will mind you using their phone. There's an extension in the den, second door to the right past the kitchen."

"Thanks. Oh, one more thing—can you not arrest my chopper pilot?"

"I imagine that can be arranged," Lisbon said, "although I can't officially condone his landing on a private golf course during a crime scene investigation."

Quint grinned then left them and headed into the living room where Gray was sitting on the couch with his parents. He looked up and flashed Quint a quick smile and head nod. Quint gave him a thumb's up and headed into the den where he dialed his home number. Deliverance picked up after one ring.

"Baby, it's all over," Quint said. "Murphy's dead and the Kingstons are all right. I know. I know. Honey—listen! Iris … Iris has been shot. She's in critical condition and they flew her to a hospital. I'm going there and when I know anything I'll call you. Yeah, Tucker's okay. Listen—he was the one who shot Murphy to death. Yeah, a lot of bullets. Another agent got shot but she'll be okay. I have to go. Tell everyone that I'll call as soon as I know anything. What? Yeah, tell Cress to drive up but *not* to speed. Do not let Raine try to drive up with or without Constantine. There's nothing any of us can do. It's all up to the doctors. Call you. Yeah, I love you, too. Hug the kids for me, will ya?" He hung up and took several deep breaths to steady himself. He felt dizzy with all the tension and action, but grateful that the chaos didn't involve his wife or kids. He all too well remembered that terrible night when he went to rescue Deliverance and the twin babies from the madwoman Cheyenne, who had abducted them. He remembered his nerve ends being on fire, the pain of the bullet that hit him, the smell of the gunfire when his wife shot Cheyenne, the way time seemed to melt into slow motion as Cheyenne dropped dead to the floor.

Quint shook himself out of his memories and jumped up and went back into the living room where Lisbon was talking to the Kingstons. He spied Quint and waved him over.

"I'm having one of mine take them to the hospital to check them out, the same hospital where Iris was taken. You can ride shotgun if you like."

"I like," Quint agreed.

Grayson Kingston put out his hand and shook Quint's. "Thank you for bringing our son up here. Best medicine possible."

"Thank my wife. She's the one that browbeat our poor pilot into flying us up." He looked at Lisbon. "Josh out of cuffs yet?"

Lisbon nodded. "He's outside being debriefed by my agents. We'll need to do the same to you and everyone else involved, but that can wait until tomorrow. What's important now is getting these folks to a doctor and seeing how Iris is doing. We'll be here all night, so if you hear something please call. I don't have to mention that talking to any reporters wouldn't make me very happy?"

"Zipped lip," Quint said. "I don't hold much truck with them anyway."

"How's the Bollmeier woman doing?"

"She'll live but it'll take a lot of medical treatment physically and mentally. Her muscle tone is practically nonexistent. She's as skinny as an Auschwitz survivor and pretty much went through hell." Quint laughed. "One good sign—when she was conscious and lucid she told her husband to get a lawyer to make sure she gets the manuscript she was typing back to her so she could finish the whole story and publish it. Don hired my guy, Fox Newberry, to handle that.

I have a feeling this second book will be better than the first, certainly from the first-person perspective. Tough lady."

"I would say so." Lisbon grinned. "There's a rumor that your wife slushied her once."

"Not a rumor—fact. But this time Del brought her roses. That doesn't mean there won't be a cherry slushie in her future if she crosses the line again. My wife has a short forgiveness span."

A young male agent walked up to Lisbon. "Ready to go, sir," he said.

Lisbon nodded. Gray helped his mother put her coat on and the three Kingstons followed the agent out of the house. Quint tossed off a fast salute to Lisbon and left, too.

Gray sat between his parents in the back seat as the agent drove swiftly, lights flashing, down Scottsdale Road. The trip seemed to take forever but it was only twenty minutes before the car pulled up in front of the ER entrance. Quint trailed the agent and the Kingstons into the reception area where he flashed his creds and told them to get a doctor, stat. Five minutes later Mariko and Grayson were led off into examining rooms and Gray sat next to Quint in the waiting area as the agent spoke quietly to the nurse on duty.

"I don't know what I'd have done if they weren't alive," Gray said quietly. He bit his lip and added, "They're everything to me."

"I know the feeling," Quint replied. He awkwardly patted Gray's hand. "But they're fine, and you've got Cress and a whole lot of family and friends to fill your life. You're blessed. We both are."

"Christ, I sure hope Tucker's just as blessed," Gray said just as the agent came over.

"I spoke to the nurse and she said that your friend Tucker is being brought down here to wait with you. Should only be a few minutes. I'll wait around, too." He turned and went over to the pay phone and began dialing.

About five minutes later a harried, bloodstained Tucker appeared. He looked around wildly until he saw Quint and Gray and rushed over to them. Quint pulled him down on the bench.

"How is she?" Gray asked.

Tucker was trembling and shook his head. "She's in surgery. They said she might be there for hours. They won't even guess at her odds." He dropped his head into his hands and mumbled, "She was dead. No pulse. I got her heart started but she was … dead for several minutes." He looked up at Quint. "Doesn't that mean brain damage?"

"I don't know," Quint said. "I think that depends on how much time she … wasn't breathing."

"Five minutes," Gray said flatly. He looked at Tucker. "That's what Cress was told when I was in the hospital. Of course, I wasn't technically dead, just in a coma, but it was something the doctors discussed with him since my heart stopped once when they were drilling burr holes in my skull and they had to defib me."

"Five minutes," Tucker murmured. "I don't think it was five minutes."

"Don't think the worst," Quint said. "Let's sit here and hope for the best, okay, Tuck?"

Tucker nodded absently then roused himself. "I should call her family. They should know."

"Yes, you should," Quint agreed. "Look—Agent Russ is off the phone. Go do it now."

Tucker nodded and jumped up. They watched as he pulled out his wallet to get the number, then dialed. He wasn't on for more than two minutes before he put the receiver down and walked back to the two men. "I spoke to her father. He screamed at me and then babbled something about flying out. Sure can't wait to meet him," Tucker said sarcastically.

"Screw him," Quint said. "Your only concern should be your wife."

They fell silent and waited for a half hour, and then the Kingstons were led out and Gray jumped up. His parents assure him that they were all right, then Grayson broke away and walked over to Tucker.

"Thank you, young man, for all you did. You and your wife were amazing. Any word on her?" Tucker shook his head. "Well, then, we'll all wait right here with you until we do get word. Gray, pull that other bench over so we can be together." Gray complied, and the five exhausted, frightened people waited.

And waited.

It was 5:35 AM when Cress blasted into the ER, spied his life partner and family and rushed over to embrace Mariko and Grayson.

"Thank God, thank God, thank God you're all right," he gushed as he hugged Mariko again. He smiled wanly at Gray, then turned to Tucker, whose face was a mask of neutrality.

"Any word?" he asked Quint.

"She's been in surgery for over five hours," Quint said as he sipped the last ounce of his cold, bitter hospital coffee. "We don't know what's going on or how long it will be. You know, Gray, maybe you should take your parents home—or to a nice hotel so you all can get some sleep. We'll call you when we know anything, I promise." He saw that Mariko was about to protest, so he added, "Mariko, you're exhausted, your husband's exhausted, and your son is exhausted. You all need to get some rest. There's a great resort not too far from here, the Camelback Inn. It's elegant and peaceful, and you simply need to be there and not here right now. Gray?"

"I agree with him, Mom. You and Dad need rest. Think Agent Russ can take us?"

"I'm sure he can," Quint said as he waved the young agent over and explained to him what they needed. Russ was happy to accommodate them as long as Quint was staying with Tucker. When Cress and the Kingstons left Tucker turned to Quint and said, "They're good people. Glad they survived."

Quint put a hand on Tucker's arm. "So will your wife. You have to believe that."

Tucker nodded absently and continued staring straight out at nothing. Out of the blue he asked, "Do you think I'd be a good father?"

Quint laughed. "Are you kidding me? The FBI wants you, but I told them you were mine until the kids get out of college. My kids are my world, and you're one of the handful of people I trust to care for them. A good father? Shit, man—the best."

At that moment Lisbon entered the ER and walked over to them. They updated him, and he sat next to them, waiting.

At 8:41 AM two doctors with blood-soaked scrubs came over to them. Tucker stood up, his heart about ready to smash through his chest. They told him that they had removed all three bullets, one of which missed her heart by three millimeters. They'd stopped the internal bleeding. She was in critical condition in the ICU and they couldn't make any accurate prognosis of her survival rate, but they said she was one tough lady and they had their best people on the case. If she did survive, she was going to need a long recovery time and dedicated care. Tucker could see her for five minutes but after that not for hours until she stabilized.

Tucker followed the doctors to his wife's ICU room.

Quint turned to Lisbon and said, "Tucker's not going to face any charges for killing Murphy, is he?"

"Christ, no," Lisbon said. "If it were up to me I'd pin a medal on his chest. Technically, Murphy was still pointing his gun in Tucker's direction after he shot Iris, so it's a clear-cut case of self-defense."

"Even after emptying a whole magazine into the bastard?"

"Instinct takes over in a situation like that and I'd be surprised if he didn't keep shooting. Between you and me, I'm glad Murphy wasn't taken alive. Some scum-sucking lawyer would take his case and we'd waste years and millions prosecuting him, not to mention putting the victims' families and everyone else through legal hell. Even if he was convicted and got the death penalty—and if ever there was a case for that, this is—he'd likely spend decades on Death Row waiting for the needle. No, it worked out for the best. Of course, that's not something I'd ever say to the media or anyone else, and I'll call you a bald-faced liar if you say I ever said it."

Quint stroked the close-cropped beard he had been sporting for the past month. "Maybe not bald-faced. Our secret, and I wholeheartedly agree with you." He cocked his head at Lisbon and said evenly, "Does she know?"

"Know what?"

"That you're sweet on her? Iris?"

"You don't know what you're talking about," Lisbon snapped. He paused, then said, "Is it that obvious?"

"Only to me. I know the signs about being sweet on someone. She doesn't know?"

"No, and she won't. She loves her husband and he's obviously insanely in love with her. I would never do anything to hurt that relationship."

Quint smiled sardonically. "That's good, because I wouldn't let you. Tucker is family as far as I'm concerned, and I always protect family. Familia lo es todo."

"Good to know," Lisbon said before falling silent.

Fifteen minutes later Tucker returned and sat down. "She's pale as death, but alive. She's still unconscious, but hopefully she'll wake up soon and we can see if she's … you know."

"Yeah," Quint said.

The three men waited another two hours, alternately gabbing, being quiet, or making phone calls. It was nearly noon when the doctor came over and said Iris was awake and talking, and Tucker could see her again.

Quint groaned in relief. He wasn't sure when he'd get home, but the first thing he'd do is kiss his damn wife like she'd never been kissed before—and that was a pretty high bar to vault over.

Iris was in that hospital for two weeks before she was able to go home to Tucson. Tucker stayed with her, at her side constantly until they walked in the door of the casita to rousing cheers from the Dane-Quintanas, Raine, and all their other friends, including much-put-upon pilot Josh Wyllys. Iris was thin and pale, but she was gaining strength every day and knew she was lucky to be alive. A few days later Deliverance's parents turned up, and she and Quint flew off to celebrate her thirtieth birthday in style.

He booked the finest accommodation in the resort, a huge hut suspended over the startlingly azure water on strong stilts. They arrived on April 14th; her birthday was on the 19th. Quint had made reservations at a very expensive restaurant for dinner, which would happen after a day at the beach, swimming, sunning, tanning, and just being together in absolute peace without any external interruptions. Of course, they called home every day to check on the family and speak to the kids. They weren't surprised that Storm had aced a math test, Aislinn had been put in detention twice for classroom pranks, and Vikki had stolen a classmate's Ding Dong and gobbled it down before her teacher could pry it out of her hands, then pulled out a canister and Silly Stringed the teacher (a prank her sister,

Aislinn, had taught her). They were surprised when Charity told them that Mariko Kingston had visited twice and had full conversations with Alex in Japanese; Charity had no idea how he could speak so eloquently in that language. She and Deliverance agreed that the mental communication between Mariko and Alex had resulted in a "core dump" of her native language into his brain.

At dinner they gorged on the finest seafood in the southern hemisphere, and Quint presented his shocked wife with a sixteen-inch necklace of knotted Tahitian pearls. She asked how much it cost. He told her not to worry, he was already scoping out second and third jobs and could swing a caddy position on weekends. The wait staff brought over a small, beautifully decorated cake; they sang happy birthday and Deliverance made a silent wish and blew out the candles.

Quint and Deliverance returned to their hut, where they stripped naked and went for a moonlight swim. Afterwards they showered, slipped desperately into bed, and made passionate love. The cool night breeze blew in their open window, and the moonlight lit up Quint's face as he slept.

Deliverance lay on her back, enjoying the breeze, the moonlight, and the closeness of her husband. She smiled up at the gently whirring ceiling fan, hoping that her wish would come true. After all, she had stopped taking her birth control pills days before they boarded that flight at LAX.

CHAPTER FOURTEEN

"She's perfect," Constantine murmured as he gazed down at his day-old baby daughter, Sasha. The eight-pound-two-ounce baby was lying on her back in the antique crib that his parents had sent them for just this occasion. She was sleeping, her heavy-lashed eyelids closed over her large green eyes, her thick, silky sable hair swirled around her head, her café-au-lait newborn skin soft and utterly unblemished.

"I'll remind you of that observation when she's a teenager," Raine said in amusement as she gazed equally lovingly at her daughter, her hand gently caressing his shoulder as they stared down at their present and their future. She felt the slightest tremor in her fiancé's body, barely there but enough for her to recognize as attuned to him as she was. "What?"

He glanced at her and smiled slightly. "Nothing. It's just … okay, I wish she had been born a day earlier or later. May 19th just makes me … queasy."

"I understand," Raine said softly as she brushed her lips against his cheek. "You know, you can consider her birth date auspicious and put a positive spin on it."

"I guess you're right," Constantine replied thoughtfully as he contemplated the amazing living, breathing human being he had helped to create. "It's just that that's the same day that the four of us were born in 1955." Constantine's biological mother, Willow Cheney, had given birth to her quadruplets—Constantine, Cheyenne, Cress, and Phaedra—on May 19, 1955. Willow had split them up into two sets of twins, one set for each pair of adoptive parents, each set with forged birth certificates; Constantine and Phaedra had been "born" on August 5, 1955 while Cress and Cheyenne had been "born" on July 22, 1955. The three C's celebrated their official birthdays on those dates specified on the certificates, although secretly for the last seven years had acknowledged their true births on May 19th. Only their adoptive parents and their close circle of friends and family knew the truth.

"Besides," Constantine said, grinning, "if she's anything like her mother I won't have a worry in the world. Anyway, she won't be dating until she's thirty, so I have time to adjust."

"Thirty, huh?"

"At least."

"You're barmy," Raine said in as derogatory a tone as any English lass had ever espoused to a clueless American mate. "She's half me so she'll be chasing right fit blokes by the time she's fifteen."

"Not going to happen."

"Drinking ale, smoking fags, hair dyed purple and nose pierced."

"When Hell's frozen ten times over."

"Swearing with such abandon that seasoned dock workers in Liverpool would keel over in shock."

"Not my little angel."

He was startled by the loud knocking on the front door. "Uh-oh—relatives. Stay strong." He left the nursery and a moment later Raine heard Cress, Gray, Phaedra, Moon Wolf, and the Begay brood split the airwaves with happy voices and laughter. Phaedra rushed into the nursery carrying baby Hawk and immediately began oohing and ahhing over her niece. A minute later the men, Persa, and Wolfie joined them and the family began babbling about Sasha's adorableness and the upcoming wedding and, oh, yes—Phaedra was pregnant again! And Cress and Gray adopted two new puppies, a dachshund named Oscar and a chihuahua named Olé.

Wilde missed the birth of his grandniece due to unexpected circumstances—his old friend in New York, Gilead Blackledge, had passed away from a heart attack at the age of eighty-three. He and his beloved wife, Charlotte, had gone out to dinner at Delmonico's to celebrate the birth of their son, Branwell's, first child. They ate a magnificent steak dinner, they drank French wine, they went home in a horse-drawn carriage, Gilead kissed his wife goodnight, and then he fell asleep forever. Davey and Mamie Sinclair flew over the pond for the funeral, which Wilde of course also attended. The Blackledges had hosted him when he first came to the United States and were true, kind friends. He owed them and grieved for the loss of a very special man. He planned on spending several days with Charlotte and his parents to ensure that she had everything she needed to go on without the man she had loved for over forty years. He could only hope that he and Victor would have that same relationship and longevity. He told Charlotte about their plans for a handfasting on Halloween and she declared that she would certainly attend.

Quint had commissioned the best contractor in Tucson to build an extension at the back of the casita to house a small gym and a second bedroom as well as a covered patio deck. He decided against adding a garage, but had the men build a decent carport for Iris's beloved Mustang convertible. He offered to purchase the gym equipment necessary for Iris's rehabilitation and future strength training, but Tucker drew the line at that and said that he'd buy the stuff; as it turned out, it was Iris's father who provided the training materials as a sort of belated wedding gift. Tucker funded the state-of-the-art security system for the casita, which had quite a workout during the first few weeks after he and Iris returned home.

Iris had been out of surgery for ten hours when her parents turned up in Phoenix after Tucker had called them. At first, he was hesitant about letting them in to see her, knowing their strained relationship, but Iris weakly said it was okay and she and her parents reconciled while machines beeped and IVs dripped and doctors and nurses came and went in the ICU and then her private recovery room. The introductions and interactions between the Flynns and Tucker were brief and strained, but grudgingly George Flynn accepted his daughter's decisions on her professional and personal lives. He wasn't happy, but surprisingly tolerant. His wife, Ellen, was less so, and she was chilly to both her daughter and new son-in-law. Tucker wondered how the hell his vibrant, loving, compassionate wife had ever sprung from her loins. She left after a day to return to Washington where she was litigating a sexual harassment case, but George Flynn stayed for four days and spent long hours talking with his headstrong daughter. He actually gave Tucker an awkward hug when Tucker dropped him off at Sky Harbor for his flight back. Tucker was under no illusions that he was unreservedly welcomed into the Flynn family, but at least they hadn't shot him.

After nearly two months of recovery and rehab Iris was nearly back to her usual top-shelf physical health. Point of fact she had recently been able to kick her husband's butt in their hand-to-hand combat training in the new gym. Three times out of four Tucker found himself flat on his back on the floor mat with his wheezing, sweaty wife standing over him with an annoyingly self-satisfied look on her beautiful face.

Just the past week she had started her new assignment in Tucson along with Liberty Adams, who had recovered quickly from her shoulder wound and was looking forward to being partners with her fellow agent. Iris was happy that Liberty got along famously with her best friend, Raine, and a little surprised when Liberty began dating one of Quint's associates, Turner Jackson; they had met when Liberty went to the Union Jack offices to meet the crew and literally ran into Turner when she was coming in the door. She jabbed at his clumsiness. He jabbed back, and that night they went out for pizza.

As expected both Iris and Tucker were inundated by the media after the showdown at the Kingstons' home. It certainly wasn't a local news story—the countrywide media appeared on everyone's doorsteps to get the story and scoops or soundbites. Everyone in the close-knit circle of those affected in Tucson and Phoenix were tightlipped although it was necessary for law enforcement to give out information and endure interviews and questions. The inimitable Laurel Bollmeier—first from her hospital bed and then from her home where husband Don was catering to her every whim—badgered the Union Jackers with pleas and attempts at pulling at their guilt and heartstrings. She was generally unsuccessful, but Deliverance did grudgingly agree to sit down with her and fill in certain aspects of the case for her literary edification. That didn't sit too well with Judie Sutphin, who had always been Laurel's rival and was digging for whatever could shoot her to the top of the newspaper reporter heap. When Santiano Bronson casually mentioned that if Laurel came back to work she'd need her old cubicle back, Judie went ballistic. Bronson told her to get over herself.

Although Iris's family had more or less come to terms with her choices and visited her in the hospital, the same couldn't be said of Tucker's family. He was now well-known as the man who ended the death reign of the Beguiler and was lauded by virtually everyone as a hero and a man of courage and action. There was simply no way that his family in Vermont could not know what had happened, and yet no one reached out to him. Quint had taken it upon himself to call Taylor Townsend, but seconds after identifying himself the man hung up on him. Even the salty Deliverance hadn't heard such curse words spewing out of a human being as when Quint slammed the receiver down. They agreed that they wouldn't tell Tucker what had transpired. Two days later Quint got a short hand-written letter from Tucker's mother asking him to tell her son that she was proud of him. Quint gave Tucker the letter. He read it and cried.

Tucker received quite a few job offers from companies ranging from personal security to private investigations and was mercilessly solicited by literary agents and people looking to make a buck off his actions and notoriety. He turned everything and everyone down flat, content to be where he was, what he was, and who he was. Iris was proud of him and protected him as best she could, as did the Union Jackers. After a month or so some of the attempts to lure him into business and media ventures tapered off, although at least a few times a week, strangers were unceremoniously hustled off the Dane-Quintana property by the security team that Quint kept on for the foreseeable future. There were a few late-night events with alarms going off and people running in the dark, but it was inevitable that they, too, would evaporate once a new media sensation hit the airwaves. There was always the sense that someone was watching and waiting but that didn't trouble most of the residents and visitors considering the circumstances—and the fact that there was a guard roaming the properties, unseen and always ready, and guns in all three residences.

Victor had been teaching his grandnephew, Beckett, how to shoot a gun for many months now, and the teenager was adept at handgun protocol. Twice a month Victor took Beckett to the gun range, and occasionally Wilde joined them although neither man was comfortable bringing eleven-year-old Bechet along—yet. Victor reluctantly promised to do so when Bechet turned fourteen. He was unaware that Beckett had been teaching his younger brother the basics on the sly. Beckett had turned a very significant emotional and familial corner after the custody scare and had allowed himself to love his uncle and Wilde, and respect them and how they were trying to raise the boys. Beckett missed New Orleans, but was enjoying his desert home, public school, and the pretty girl that had moved a few blocks away and was in his Biology class and had the biggest goddamn blue eyes he had ever seen. He was a good student and his grades improved since the fall semester began. He was toying with the idea of someday going to law school and had even begun investigating the universities in Arizona and on the west coast. Bechet had no idea what he wanted to be. He and Storm spent a lot of time together talking about their futures and whenever she mentioned an idea about school or life he fell in line. He had a mad crush on the girl despite their four-year age difference.

Storm was relatively oblivious to Bechet's crush. He was her buddy, period. After all, she was only seven and all she knew about boys was that they were usually annoying. Beckett was, and sometimes—although not always—so was her brother, Alex. Alex wasn't like most boys. He had turned a bit quiet and introverted, and seemed to prefer intellectual pursuits to the rough-and-tumble playtime of his sisters and friends. She didn't understand why everyone made such a big deal out of his new-found Japanese linguistics, but it seemed to amaze her parents. Her mother said that Alex was special in his own way, but so was she, Aislinn, and Vikki. He could play the piano and speak French, too. She was a little miffed and maybe jealous, so she applied herself to learning the violin and picking up Spanish from her father. He taught her quite a few curse words on the down low. She worshipped Quint.

She never thought of Quint and Deliverance as anything but her father and mother. She was troubled by her lack of a past and memory, but she shoved away her disquiet and told the therapist what the woman wanted to hear so that no one would send her away. She'd die if Mom and Dad sent her away. She'd *die*. She didn't tell them about the weird times that she froze and in her mind's eye saw black-and-white snapshots of hazy adults and places, words that didn't make sense, colors that were too bright and didn't mesh. She would squeeze her eyes together and think and think and try to focus on something that made sense, but nothing ever did. Her reality was the one she had now, and she'd do anything to keep it. Anything.

Aislinn got along well with her new sister, and although at first she was jealous of the attention her parents showed the strange child she understood that it had nothing to do with their love for and attention towards her. And, Storm could be fun, more fun than younger Vikki and sure as hell more fun than their brother. They shared a bedroom and would whisper together for hours at night until their father would open the bedroom door and tell them to go to sleep *now*. Still, Storm was more serious and didn't have the knack of playing the kinds of pranks that Aislinn enjoyed. Of course, at school they got her into trouble, and she had been grounded and stripped of her home privileges a few times when Mom or Dad had to extract her from the principal's office. Aislinn's teachers called her "challenging," a term that left much open for interpretation.

Even so her punishments were tempered by her excellent grades and her knack for charming people even when they didn't want to be charmed. Still, at her dad's fortieth birthday barbecue he hadn't appreciated the gift-wrapped tarantula she'd given him. It had crawled out of the box and stupid Alex had squashed it with a tennis racket. Deliverance had given her the stink-eye and Aislinn had muttered, "I'm screwed, aren't I?" which resulted in several attendees spitting out the beer they'd been drinking. She was grounded for two days for the curse word, although her mother did commend her for the proper use of "aren't" versus "ain't."

Alex kept his exasperation about his sisters to himself. He thought they were hopeless even though all three had potential. He felt certain things about them, Storm's emotional chaos, Aislinn's intellectual chaos, and Vikki's introspection. He thought his youngest sister was going to do something with animals in her life, maybe be a vet. Storm? She'd change the world. Aislinn, too, although perhaps on a less grand scale. And he? He didn't know. There was so much roiling around in his head that it exhausted him. There were the multiple languages and the electric sensations when he'd touch things or people. He couldn't coalesce what those sensations meant, just that they were "good" or "bad" or … he didn't know what. When he touched Storm, he got the sensation of fire. When he touched Aislinn, his fingertips were cold, cold as ice. Nothing when he touched Vikki; she was neutral, neither cold nor hot.

When he hugged his parents a deep, comforting warmth seeped through every cell of his body and he knew that despite his uncertainty, he was going to be all right in the long run and so were they. Contact with other people like his uncles produced a wide variety of sensations that he couldn't understand and didn't dwell on too much. His mother seemed to sense his disquiet and told him that she'd guide him, that she'd always guide him. That was his balm. His Aunt Bliss told him the story of the Balm of Gilead and sang the song to him; that comforted him, and the music always made him think of his mother. He taught himself to play the song on the piano, and sometimes little Angelique Dillinger would sit beside him and hum along.

Aunt Bliss and Uncle Malachi weren't around as much as they had been since they were overwhelmed by their work and the new baby, Barnabas. During the few times that they had brought him over to visit the baby had been cranky and crying, but Alex's mother said that he would settle down when he grew older. Deliverance said that the baby had a unique future ahead of him, and that someday he and Alex would be best friends. Much older Alex seriously doubted that, but his mom was rarely wrong. He just didn't feel it.

At least the family was settling down now that the threat to their world had been neutralized. Quint still had one bodyguard roaming the residences on a random schedule, and the children never went to school by themselves. Tucker was able to spend more time on the kids now that Iris was getting so much better. Yes, Alex thought sagely, life had returned to normal—or as normal as life could be in the unpredictable Dane-Quintana world.

The Retaliator had been watching all of them for well over a year, more than a month before he had covertly attended the Munch funeral in March 1984. He was patient and found that he truly enjoyed his invisibility and the fact that no one had any idea of his presence or purpose. Of course, the doomed Kenny-cum-Barry-cum-Earle-cum-whoever-the-fuck-he-was knew of his existence for a brief period, but that psycho whackjob had fortunately met his just desserts before he could reveal that knowledge. There was the miniscule chance that Kenny's victim, Raine Sinclair, could have some possible vague memory of two men lifting her in and out of the car trunk, but since she had been rescued six months ago and nothing had been mentioned in any news articles, he felt safe. The only mention of her was in a birth announcement from yesterday, May 19th—she had given birth to a baby girl. He couldn't have cared less if she had lived or had died as long as she didn't interfere with his plans.

He hadn't spent the entire year-plus ensconced in the desert armpit where his ultimate target lived. He had made quite a few trips back into civilization to ensure that his identity was secure and people who knew him wouldn't be too suspicious of his extended absences and lack of communication. He had an entirely new identity in Tucson, bought and paid for with a large chunk of his remaining funds. He'd rented a room under his new name, and was a quiet, unobtrusive tenant that paid on time and gave the boarding house lady no cause for concern. To her—really, to anyone—he was a nonentity.

Exactly the way he wanted it.

Exactly the way he needed it for one month and nine days, until he could exact his retribution.

Until he could retaliate.

CHAPTER FIFTEEN

Twenty-Six Days Until Retaliation

"I'm fat," Raine moaned as she twisted this way and that in front of the full-length mirror, wearing her wedding dress at the last fitting.

"You just had a baby," Iris said crossly as she squinted critically at the tight waistline of the lace and satin gown. "Of course you're fat."

Raine's jaw dropped in disbelief. "You're my best friend! You're supposed to tell me I'm not fat and I look bloody, fuckin' beautiful!"

"As you said, I'm your best friend—I won't lie to you. That's your fiancé's job." Iris relented. "You're not *that* fat. Two or three more pounds and it'll be perfect. Just starve yourself for the next week or so. Eat low-fat cottage cheese for breakfast and *no* beignets. You've got three weeks to make yourself perfectly svelte."

Raine gave a grunt and a half turn as she craned her neck and tried to see how the low-cut back looked. At least her shoulder blades weren't bony. She ran her right hand down the length of her left arm, which was encased in a snug sleeve of handmade lace that ended in a point midway across the back of her hand. The dress had been designed by an up-and-coming English designer that patterned her fashions after medieval garments; Raine looked like a queen of ancient days and would look even more so with the floor-length lace veil and the tasteful diamond tiara that her mother had provided as something "borrowed."

She sighed. "I can do cottage cheese for a week. Constantine will just have to suffer without any visits to Yvette's." She grinned slyly at her friend. "Ready to try on the maid-of-honor gown?"

"Sadly, no. I have a meeting at the office with Liberty and the team on a couple of new cases sent down from Phoenix. I promise the dress will fit to perfection when I stand by your side at the church."

"You do like the color?" Raine asked, fretting. Raine and Iris had gone back and forth between pale blue and vivid turquoise, with Deliverance inserting an opinion about dusty rose and cinnamon, and Phaedra disposed towards mint green. Raine had finally left the decision up to Iris, who refused to tell her what color she had selected, as well as the style although Iris promised that it would complement Raine's wedding gown. Both women were more than just disposed towards the potential fashion statement after Deliverance told them about her Halloween wedding in 1979 and the flamenco costume she as the bride had worn. The clique of strong-willed women had a long laugh at Deliverance's wedding album and Raine nearly fell on the floor at the eight-by-ten shot of best-men Wilde and Victor dressed as vampires.

"I expect I do since I selected the color," Iris replied tartly. "And, no, you don't get to see the color until the big day comes."

"As long as it won't conflict with the bridesmaids' gowns," Raine said. Deliverance had gotten her way with the dusty rose color for those, including the flower girl dress for Persa. She sighed deeply. "I can't wait for the whole rigmarole to be over. We're already as good as married anyway. We should have eloped to Vegas like you and Tucker did."

Iris ignored the comment; part of her wished in retrospect that she had had a normal wedding ceremony. "Cress and Gray all set to take care of Sasha while you're honeymooning in Hawaii?"

"Yes. I'm still not sure if we shouldn't have Phaedra keep the baby but she's got too many as it is."

"The boys will be fine, and they can always get Mariko to come down or run over to Deliverance for help."

"And I'm still thinking that Constantine and I should postpone our honeymoon for a while until Sasha gets older."

"What—until she's twenty-one?"

"No, but, seriously, since we're getting married and getting ready to move in the next two months we've got a full plate." Constantine had suggested buying a real house and selling the condo, and Raine had happily agreed. She was nervous about a bigger home and property and all the upkeep it would entail, but he pointed out that they needed a bigger place for a growing family and their daughter needed a big yard to play in. Phaedra had recommended her realtor and the woman had found several perfect properties in the Catalina Foothills. The home they selected and successfully bid on was located on a cute street named Good Earth Drive, and was unostentatious in its one-story, adobe-style, Santa Fe architecture. The walls and nearby landscaping were all earth tones, save the several beautiful, large bougainvilleas that dashed colors of red, purple and orange about the home and garage. There seemed to be a detached little guest house near the rear of the garage.

When they viewed the interior, they were both taken with the simplistic yet warm and comfortable design. The various room entrances seemed to all be arched, and at least the great room and the small den on the other side of the hallway had walls the color of cinnamon. The great room had a huge beehive fireplace set above a raised ledge of Saltillo tile that spread out across the full measure of the floor; there was a wall niche on each side, each holding a handmade cottonwood Navaho kachina. The ceilings were striped with heavy cylindrical wood beams. The matching couch, loveseat, and chair were of a rough material of deep reds and browns in some sort of Native American pattern. The coffee and end tables were hand-carved, one-of-a-kind juniper.

They would have loved to buy some of the owners' furniture, but the realtor said the couple was taking all the furnishings with them when they moved back to San Francisco. She whispered that it wasn't general knowledge, but the home belonged to the infamous Zack Lassiter/Prescott, whose life had been the subject of writer Norah Maguire's critically acclaimed book, *The Long Storm*. Raine and Constantine were surprised, but it didn't impact their decision to purchase. Prescott (as he was now known) accepted their first offer and he, his wife, and their three daughters were scheduled to close on July 18th and be moved out that very day.

"I just—" Raine began but was cut off by her frustrated friend.

"Enjoy the time with your new husband. You both need to get away. Your baby is healthy, happy, and has scads of family and friends to see to her every need."

"I know, but——"

"Bugger, woman—just flippin' go to Maui and enjoy yourself!"

"Fine, fine." Raine stared at her reflection in the mirror and scowled. "I'm fat."

Mike Beckham missed his partner of eight years, Don Bollmeier. Don had broken him in when they shared a patrol car and had been patient and supportive during their years as partners. They had been through a lot together—the ax murders, these latest Beguiler murders, Laurel's disappearance, Don's emotional disintegration, Mike's disastrous marriage and divorce, and the daily grunt work that a uniformed patrolman encountered on a routine basis. He'd hated it when Don took the leave of absence and Mike had been assigned a new rookie partner for the short term, but it seemed like that was becoming a long-term thing. Don was still on leave and it was very iffy as to whether he'd return to the force.

At least having a new partner seemed to be long-term. The rookie had been reassigned and now Mike was saddled with a very disgruntled Keene Swansey, who had been busted down from detective to uniform. Most cops would prefer being fired than suffering that humiliation, but Swansey had opted to take the demotion and assignment in a patrol car. Beckham was one of those cops that was happy being in uniform and had no aspirations to become a detective, and Don was one of those rare birds, too. Mike hoped that Swansey's bad attitude and resentment weren't going to become an issue. He had the niggling feeling that eventually they would if patrol today was any indication.

It was only Monday and already they had responded to five calls before noon. At 8 AM they had broken up a fight between two homeless men on Congress Street near Veinte de Agosto Park—they were arguing over a prime napping spot under a tree. Beckham calmed them down and sent both in opposite directions while Swansey leaned against their car and watched the scene in disgust.

At nine they pulled up in front of the Merciful Savior Funeral Home where someone had broken into the storage area and stolen a coffin—a very expensive stainless-steel, brushed-blue, utterly GUARANTEED WATERPROOF coffin with a silk lining (and white velvet pillow) and meticulously polished silver accents and hardware, as the angry funeral director screeched in a lilting falsetto. The coffin had been earmarked for the funeral of an important neighborhood ex-politician and now the director was on the hook to find and order an identical one before Wednesday's viewing and Saturday's burial.

He was on the verge of a nervous breakdown as Swansey finished jotting down notes and cavalierly said that there wasn't a snowball's chance in Hell of finding the coffin before the viewing. Beckham wanted to chastise his partner for the remark, but the director's voice and over-the-top reaction had grated on him, too.

The next call was a domestic dispute between two elderly lesbians, which was quickly squashed when Beckham made a point of complimenting their furniture and drapery, and politely declined the offer of chamomile tea. He agreed with them that the concept of an English Tea Time should be enforced for the middle class, yes, in all states, and got back into his patrol car with a half dozen freshly baked chocolate chip cookies.

The cookies lasted until Beckham and Swansey pulled into the Vista View Elementary School to investigate a break-in and vandalism in the boys' gym. They got more than a few names and addresses of potential teenage suspects to investigate. Their last call before they broke for lunch two blocks from the station at the Café Coyote was to take notes down on a stolen bicycle that had been modified for its disabled young owner. Beckham thought that someone had to be a real shit to steal a crippled kid's bike.

Beckham was delighted that Swansey ordered takeout instead of sitting down to lunch with him and surrounded by cops that knew his story. Detectives Chet Cromwell and Jeff Washington waved him over to their booth and he ordered his usual patty melt, extra-large fries, and a diet Pepsi. He enjoyed the meal with the two men and they talked about the Beguiler case and the Bollmeiers and the Union Jack clan. He hated leaving to pick up Swansey and complete the day's tour, but that was his job. He waved at Chet and Jeff as he walked into the sunshine of the early June day and went about his business.

"Did you see the article in the *Sentinel*'s Entertainment section?" Wilde asked Victor over a late breakfast in the latter's office. They had just come off the weekly staff meeting, and Deliverance had ordered a hearty breakfast delivered for the partners; the associates were on their own. Victor had scraped away every bit of his buttered grits and was finishing his sourdough French toast with his second cup of espresso.

"No, someone's been hogging that section of the paper," Victor replied as he wiped away a smear of butter from his upper lip and moustache and glanced down at the front page of the Sports section. There was a gruesomely chaotic photograph of the Heysel Stadium in Brussels, Belgium, where a few days earlier a riot had broken out at the European Cup final between Liverpool F.C. and Juventus; thirty-eight spectators were killed. He shook his head; no damn sporting event was worth physical anger let alone the loss of life. "Why?"

Wilde ruffled the paper and handed his partner the folded article. "Another death due to that damn AIDS. It's a growing epidemic. This time it's that former '40s cinematic heartthrob Tory Huntington. It's been an open secret that he had a long-term, not-so-secret life with our favorite beignet baker, Elliot Belmont. Supposedly they've been together for around forty years."

Victor scanned the article. Nowhere did it mention the dreaded four-letter acronym, but the implications were clear. Belmont was described as "a good friend." A good friend. What a cold, totally inaccurate description of a love and life that had existed for four decades. Victor was glad that some things had progressed since then, but still he and Wilde were generally acknowledged as just "partners" and "friends" by most people outside of their immediate circle of family and true friends. He glanced over at Wilde.

"He's being buried tomorrow at Forest Lawn next to Belmont's late partner, Henri-Georges Boulanger," Victor said. "I wonder if Belmont has the same affliction. One of them—or both—must have cheated with the wrong man or men."

"And it cost him his life," Wilde said quietly. "That's a savage consequence for a mistake of character." He paused. "You've never asked, but I've been totally faithful to you since that first night we gave into our passions."

Victor reached across the desk and clasped Wilde's hand. "Ditto, mon amour. The thought to be otherwise never crossed my mind. Tu es le seul vrai amour de ma vie."

"Tu aussi."

Victor put down the paper and said, "You know, there have been rumors about your favorite romantic lead, Rock Hudson."

Wilde shook his head. "No bloody way."

"I've seen stories about some mysterious illness that he might have and that he's been visiting clinics in Europe. Last photo I saw of him in the paper showed that he was kind of thin and a little gaunt."

"Not possible. He's so ... manly. I won't believe it."

"I hope it's not true. I hope they find out what causes that insidious disease and find a cure."

"Amen to that." Wilde looked up at a knock on the door. Quint entered. "Ah," Wilde said in his inimitably sarcastic way, "our company fashion plate graces us with his presence."

Quint dropped down into a chair. "Not a suit person like some anal-retentive people I could name." Victor and Wilde were garbed in three-piece suits (jackets currently off), but Quint was wearing worn jeans, a blue-checkered shirt, and a leather belt with a horseshoe buckle. Of course, he had on his usual cowboy boots but had thankfully eschewed the occasional spurs. His long black hair had a touch of silver at both temples, which had the effect of making the forty-year-old look very dashing.

Quint handed Wilde a sheet of paper, which the senior partner scanned. He frowned. "Really?" Wilde said as he handed the sheet to Victor. "Thayer's resigning? She say why? The letter's generic."

"Apparently, she's had enough of the desert and west coast and wants to go home to New Hampshire. She met someone from back there and they've been having a long-distance relationship, her doing long weekends back there and him coming in town for the same a few times. They've decided to move in together and start a small P.I. firm of their own."

"Is he a cop?" Wilde asked.

"I think she said he had some law enforcement background, and he was a lawyer. I wasn't paying too much attention since she was running off his list of amazing characteristics nonstop. He's a fantastic litigator, he likes camping, he's a martial arts master, blah, blah, blah. Oh, he's *sooooo* wonderful."

"I'll miss her humor." Victor laughed. "But I can understand wanting to go home."

"She'll be missed," Wilde agreed. "So, that leaves a possible opening. Damn shame Iris decided to go back to being a fibbie. Even worse, a lawyer." Iris was waiting for her results from taking the bar, but everyone expected her to pass with flying colors.

"It's funny," Quint mused as he snagged the last piece of French toast on Victor's plate, "but last week when she dropped off a document at our home, after she left Alex said that she'd be leaving soon, and that she'd never be back. He was pretty definitive about that."

"The kid picked up any new languages recently?" Victor laughed.

"Not yet. I think English, French, and Japanese are enough for any seven-year-old. He has been acting a little weirder than usual lately, though. He won't go into his closet and refuses to use any bathroom except the master. He says the others make him feel closed in. Del and I are humoring him for a bit, but that ends this week. We might have to have him see a therapist. Storm's has openings."

"You're gonna need another job to pay for all that head-shrinking," Wilde said.

"With half of our offspring lying on couches babbling about their inner feelings, yeah, I may need to revisit that caddy job at the golf course." He noticed the newspaper Entertainment section in front of Victor. He nodded. "I read about that actor. You know, one of his old forties' films was on TV last week. He was pretty good in it. Very realistic in his love scenes with that luscious Tracie Burnett."

"Whatever happened to her?" Victor asked, trying to visualize the actress, but only getting a sense of someone with expansive breasts and shoulder-length dark hair.

Quint laughed. "She was on an episode of *The Love Boat* a few weeks ago. Not her best work, and about fifty pounds heavier than when she was shrieking in terror in *Horror in Beverly Hills.*" The little gem of a horror movie from 1945 had put the actress on the map and had made producer Charlie Gold a real player in Hollywood after his never-mentioned career in porno films. Quint shook his head at the irony; Tracie had wound up fat on *The Love Boat*, and Charlie had committed suicide after his pedophilia had been revealed to the world.

"That show makes me cringe," Wilde offered, scowling. "Tripe. Will it never go off the air?"

"Not as long as there are old-time actors and actresses needing a job," Victor said sardonically. He arched a telling eyebrow at Quint. "Most of them aren't hearty enough to carry a set of golf clubs."

"How do you say 'prick' in French?" Quint replied tartly.

"Ask your son. I've taught him the important aspects of the language."

"So, to go back to the issue at hand, do we replace Thayer or what?" Wilde asked. "We're bursting at the seams with new cases ever since our revisited notoriety after Murphy's demise. Turner is swilling down too many caffeine products while he's balancing his three cases, and Fox and Shayne are spending twelve-hour days on their cases. Shayne's blowing out her weekends studying for that last course she needs before she can graduate law school and take the bar. Belzer's upped his part-time work to full time when he's not slyly courting Pamela Munch. That's not to mention what the four of us are handling. Raine won't be back at work until after the honeymoon, and even then, she's our techie and has limited understanding of how to investigate otherwise. Not sure if she's interested in becoming a real P.I. We need to hire someone."

"Or two someones," Victor added. "You know, Tucker did some good research during his past work here. Now that the kids are older maybe he can divide his time between nannyhood and private dickness."

"Is that even a word?" Wilde asked.

"For our intents and purposes it is. Quint—you brought up the subject before about adding a real security sector to our business. I think we should discuss that and consider whether or not to move forward."

"Agreed," Quint said. "Also, I've been talking to my occasional bodyguard who's still keeping an eye on my house for another week or so. He's got a great background and isn't overly attached to his current position. If we go for developing a security team, he might be a good catch. And, just maybe it could be a two-fer—Rafe and Tucker starting out and building from there."

"I like it," Victor said. "What's the guy's background?"

"Lee Jernigan recommended the firm," Quint replied. "Lee used the crew for a hairy legal matter a few years ago. The head of the firm was a Korean War vet, and all his people have been in the service, more than half of them ex-Green Berets or Rangers. The guy I've kept on part-time, Raphael Caleb Spencer, was a flight lieutenant in the Navy. He got shot down shortly before the war ended and spent six months in the Hanoi Hilton. He stayed on in the Navy until 1979, then went into civilian life. Divorced, no kids. Had a couple of gigs before joining Manitou Security Solutions in 1984. According to his boss, he's top-notch, but does have an occasional problem with authority."

"Which explains why you can relate to him," Wilde chuckled.

"Obviously," Quint said, ignoring the jibe. "Natch, I did a background check on him and his buddies before I hired them, but I suggest a more through exploration of his past and character before we decide to go ahead."

"Let Tucker do it since you're envisioning him as part of that team. Fox can assist," Victor offered.

"Agreed," Wilde said. "Oops—I forgot—we need to have the witch in on this before we can push forward."

"I broached the subject with my wife already, and she's on board, but, yup—we need to have her in on this conversation." Victor hit his speed dial and a moment later Deliverance came in and perched her shapely butt on the edge of Victor's desk.

"I agree," she said off the bat. "A security team is building for the future."

"How …" Wilde began, then shook his head. "Never mind. As long as you're good with it."

"I am. My caveat is that I want Tucker to lead that team, not Quint's bodyguard."

"I'm not sure about that that," Wilde began slowly. "I adore Tucker and thoroughly respect his courage and talent with a gun, but that was an isolated incident and Rafe's got far more long-term experience."

"Let's do this," Victor said. "We establish a team and right now one of us will 'lead' it, and then make a decision based on observation and discussion. Ultimately, whoever 'leads' the team will always be accountable to us partners. Hey—how about this—Union Jack Security Solutions?"

Quint put his hand up. "Second the motion."

"Aye," his partners said simultaneously.

Deliverance added, "This presupposes that Rafe will actually want the job, ditto Tuck."

"You can be unbearably persuasive," Victor said.

"Gruesomely so," Wilde added.

Deliverance slowly slid off the desk, gave her men a stark stare that would freeze a tsunami, and left without a word. She didn't even slam the door behind her.

"We're screwed, aren't we?" Victor opined.

"Like a short, slender, sharp-pointed metal pin with a raised helical thread running around it and a slotted head embedded into studwork by one pissed-off carpenter," Quint said.

CHAPTER SIXTEEN

Eleven Days Until Retaliation

Deliverance opened the front door and was surprised to see Don and Laurel Bollmeier standing there. The married couple were thin and pale, but there was an animation to their faces that made her think they were more than just coping; happy, even.

"May we come in?" Laurel asked with the barest touch of hesitation in her voice. She gave a cursory glance to Deliverance's hands, relieved to see that she wasn't holding a cup of anything cold. Or red.

"Oh, sure," Deliverance replied, moving aside to allow them entrance. She was spending the morning home alone, working in her den on some company statements and paying personal bills. She relished these rare moments of peace and quiet, too few on any given day. Being a wife, mother of four, college student, P.I., and business partner carved their demanding niches out of her daily routine, and she rarely had any true "Deliverance time." Still, she wouldn't have it any other way. "Can I get you some tea?" she asked.

"I'd love some," Laurel said, smiling. She and Don followed Deliverance into the kitchen and sat down at the breakfast table.

"I love your house," Laurel said.

"That's right," Deliverance said casually as she put the tea kettle on. "You've only seen it through the windows as you went poking around."

Laurel blushed. "I'm sorry. I was just doing my job. Deliverance, I'm genuinely sorry that I've tried to invade your privacy."

Deliverance turned from the stove and fixed her knowing eyes on the woman. "But, you'd do it again, right?"

Laurel hesitated for a few seconds, then nodded. "In a heartbeat. Like I said, it's my job. But … maybe I'll be doing it a little differently since I've learned what it means to be the recipient of that kind of … attention." Laurel had been bombarded by the media as early as the second day of her hospital stay, including extremely annoying badgering by her rival, Judie Sutphin. Reporters for all the major west-coast and east-coast newspapers as well as the major TV networks (including that hot newish cable channel, CNN) had tried to interview her and take photographs. She couldn't prevent the latter despite all the precautions she, Don, the police and the FBI took, but she hadn't granted a single interview and was very cagey about when she might. She would love to have a full *60 Minutes* program devoted to her experience, or even *20/20*. The best would obviously be a Barbara Walter's special.

Fox Newberry was a terrier in his efforts to get her manuscript back (as well as the floppy disks on which the text was saved), but the police made it clear that returning the document wouldn't happen until the case was officially closed, and that was still many months away as every aspect of Pete Murphy's life and career was investigated. Even so, Laurel had been writing down what she remembered as well as what had happened during and after her rescue. This book was going to send her literary career into the stratosphere. She had agreed to have Fox as the intermediary between her and potential publishers, and he was already fielding offers and contracts with Random House, Simon & Shuster, and Doubleday. She was going to take her time in selecting the best offer, but she was savvy enough to understand that she had to strike while the iron was hot.

"Fair enough," Deliverance said as she set down the teacups and teabags. She took milk out of the fridge as well as a lemon-poppyseed pound cake she'd baked the night before. She withdrew a cake knife from the island drawer and handed it to Don, who cut a piece for himself, a big one for Laurel, and by instruction a small one for their host. As they waited for the water to boil Deliverance sat down and impulsively reached for Laurel's hand. She asked sincerely, "How are you doing?"

Laurel smiled wanly and shrugged even as she grasped the hand that was offering her solace. "I'm getting there. I had my session with the therapist yesterday and she thinks I'm making progress. Progress," Laurel snorted, "as though I'll ever be rid of the memories and feelings. They'll be there inside my head forever."

"But Dr. Waring thinks she'll come to terms with the memories and find a way to … compartmentalize them and move forward successfully," Don said. He gently stroked his wife's cheek. "I'll be there forever to guarantee that."

"Are you going back to work?" Deliverance asked Don.

He nodded. "In another two weeks. I'm a cop—it's what I do. And, Mike is having conniptions with his new partner, Swansey, so I'm pretty sure he and I will be back to semi-normal in our patrol car. Some other unlucky dude will get Swansey." He cast a guilty glance at his wife, knowing that Swansey had been one of her inside sources.

"I expect you've had a lot of sessions with the Tucson police and the FBI about what happened?" Deliverance said.

Laurel nodded. "Too many. I keep telling them the same things over and over again. There's nothing left to tell—at least before my book comes out. You know, I'm putting in a special dedication to Union Jack for pursuing the case and leading to my rescue. I am so grateful to all of you—and especially my saviors, Victor and Wilde— for ending the hell I went through and resolving the whole case."

"Do we get any royalties?" Deliverance laughed as the teapot screamed and she rose to turn off the stove.

"Well, um ..."

"Just kidding! I do want an autographed copy, though," she said as she poured the water then sat down. "And," she added, arching her eyebrows dangerously, "no photos of us that we don't approve of. And none of our children, period. Deal?"

"Deal," Laurel said enthusiastically as she poured an ounce of milk into her cup. Don had already finished half of his cake. She said hesitatingly, "I don't suppose Tucker or Iris are around?"

Deliverance let out a loud theatrical sigh. "You want to interview them, don't you?"

"Well ..."

"You're never going to change, are you? I expect I'll always have to keep a half gallon of cherry slushies in my fridge just in case you get out of hand." She laughed at the way Laurel paled.

"Dr. Waring said that I need to be true to my intrinsic nature," Laurel replied defensively.

"Dr. Waring," Deliverance mused. "Ah—she's Raine's therapist, too. She's supposed to be very good."

"She is," Laurel nodded. "She's brought out a lot of buried facts and feelings and guided me into accepting and dealing with them." Laurel frowned; she was obviously thinking hard. "Something ..."

"Something what?"

"Something that just came back to me. When you said Raine's name. Psycho Pete was furious that people thought he'd abducted her. He wrote this furious denial, like, a half dozen times and made me read and critique each one, and then type the final version." She shivered. "Nutjob. He smacked me across the back of the head hard when I mistyped the first draft. But ... he was babbling on and on about how people misinterpreted him and didn't appreciate him, blah, blah, blah, and then he said something odd that just came back to me."

"Something about Raine, Honey?" Don asked.

"Kind of. He said something about 'those men that were watching the Quintana house and their fuckin' friends.'"

"Are you sure he didn't say 'man?' Kensington was the only stalker that was haunting Raine's life," Deliverance said.

"I guess ... no, I'm sure he said 'men.' Plural. That doesn't make sense."

"He was a whackjob, Hon—you can't take anything he said as being realistic or reasonable," Don said.

"I know what I heard," Laurel said stubbornly. She looked at Deliverance. "Do you think I should tell the cops what I remembered?"

"Of course. It may mean nothing, but it's still part of the puzzle and should be relayed and documented. Can you remember anything else related to the 'men' reference?"

Laurel took a sip of tea and played with her poppyseed crumbs. "I don't think so. You know, I could be wrong. I was in a pretty bad state then."

Deliverance sat back and absently sipped her tea. "What if you're not wrong?" she said slowly. "What if there's someone else out there?"

Raine hated lying on the therapist's couch even though it was roomy and plush. She felt ill at ease, and the prone position made her feel less in control. Dr. Waring said that of course she could sit up during their sessions, and she'd tried that, but ultimately her expectations and assumptions necessitated her comfortable horizontal position. And, it did relax her. She opened one eye and checked on

Sasha, who was asleep in the baby carrier beside the couch. She closed her eyes again.

Dr. Honora Waring crossed her legs as she sat in the chair beside the couch. She had been seeing Raine Sinclair since two weeks after her rescue, and they had made significant progress in establishing a baseline for remembering and dealing with the experiences the young woman had survived. Waring thought that her patient was one remarkably strong woman to have survived the horrific kidnapping, rape, and near murder and still have gone on to rebuild her life, have a healthy baby, and set the wedding date to the man she loved. Honora had been a psychologist for fourteen years and had seen too much of what one human could do to another. Some of the victims never recovered. She'd had two who were still staring at walls in hospitals after their vicious rapes.

One was in Phoenix, and one was in a nursing home in her hometown of Hartford, where she and her brothers, Howard and Zeke, had grown up in Stowe Village, a public housing community in the city's north end; they were one of the first families to move in when the development was built in 1953. Their single mother scrambled to provide a decent life for them, working two jobs, one at Travelers Insurance and one at Pratt & Whitney. Hollis Waring badgered them into the best education possible, but only Honora and Howard had graduated from Weaver High School; Zeke dropped out at fifteen and began running drugs—he was dead at seventeen from an overdose. That prompted both Honora and Howard to seek out careers in the medical field. Working multiple jobs (she had spent nearly ten years working afternoons, Thursday evenings, and Saturdays in the Brown-Thompson department store; he had worked on tobacco during the summers and in an Italian bakery on Front Street, among other part-time jobs) and on partial scholarships, Howard had graduated the University of Connecticut Medical School and was practicing at an ER in a San Francisco hospital, and she had graduated Trinity College with a Bachelor's, Master's and then PhD in Psychology. She'd tried her hand in her brother's new city, but found it too big and crowded, and after a brief stint in Phoenix wound up in Tucson. She loved the city, she loved her new life, and she loved her job. About to hit forty, she was as content a professional woman as one could ever find. She loved helping people, and perhaps a little too often was drawn too deeply into their personal demons. She made a conscious effort to withdraw to a more objective level, and she was usually successful.

She acknowledged that she was a bit too immersed in Raine's therapy, but she felt deeply about the woman's experience since she had been raped at seventeen while walking home one Thursday night from her job. She was nearly halfway home when someone came up from behind her and dragged her off Main Street and into the Old North Cemetery where she lost her virginity and her innocence. The police basically blew the crime off, and her attacker was never caught although he might have been responsible for several other assaults in Keney Park. She was cautious around boys and men after that, and an early marriage while she was studying for her PhD imploded after only three months. She was happy being single, and she had her three long-haired chihuahuas to keep her company—Abby, D-O-G, and Mandy were the furry, spoiled little loves of her life.

Honora and Raine had discussed the end of scheduled therapy sessions, and after eight months they both agreed that Raine was ready to move forward without her psychologist crutch. That didn't mean that she couldn't come back if she needed to, but they thought that Raine had remembered and dealt with all her bad memories. Still, Honora wanted to run through the basic facts one more time before signing off on their final session. She ticked off each fact on a linear timeline, and Raine responded verbally that the data was correct and to the best of her recollection. Still, there was one area that Honora wanted to revisit just to make sure.

"You say you didn't hear anyone come up behind you before everything went black," Honora said, pen poised.

Raine took a deep breath and nodded, then said, "Yes. I mean, no, I didn't hear anything."

"And when you woke up you were tied up and lying on a floor."

"Yes."

"Nothing in between?"

"No, we've gone over this. I was out like a light. I didn't see or hear anything in between getting out of my car and waking up tied up and with a headache pretty much on the level of an A-bomb."

"You say didn't hear or see anything. What about feeling anything? A touch? Warmth? Cold?" Honora shivered—an unbidden memory of her attacker's hands brutally grabbing her arms to drag her into the cemetery flashed back for a split second. She made a mental note to schedule an appointment with her own therapist.

"Nothing."

"A hand or foot, perhaps?"

Raine's voice was gruff. "No, nothing, really, just their hands ..." She paused, and her eyes snapped open. She looked at Honora. "Hands pulling me out of the car trunk." She rubbed her hands up and down her arms. "Cold air. Then they carried me in quickly, I think, before I lost consciousness again." She sat up suddenly. "I remember him carrying me in for a few seconds. I guess. Time ... it wasn't real. Like ... a dream."

"Actually," Honora began slowly, "you didn't say 'him.' You said 'they.' 'They' carried you in. 'Their hands.'"

"I must have misspoken. Everyone knows it was just Barry that was involved in my abduction. There's no reason to believe he was acting with the Beguiler. No one's found any evidence in Barry's personal effects or the Beguiler's that they ever knew one another or acted in concert. In fact, Murphy was adamant in that note that he had nothing to do with what happened to me. There was certainly no one in the cabin when I was conscious."

"Still ..."

"Still nothing, doctor. I misspoke. Period. And don't you think if someone else was involved I'd want them caught?" Raine checked her watch. "Time's just about up." She swung her legs over the edge of the couch and reached down to touch Sasha's soft cheek. "We both agreed that I'm ready and this is our last session. Let's please not muddy the waters." She and Honora stood at the same time.

"Raine, I'd really like one more session, and a special one."

"Define 'special.'"

"I'd like to hypnotize you and see if we can draw out any last remnants of your experience."

"I don't think so, doctor. Really. There's nothing else, and I don't want to elongate these sessions. I'm getting married in four days and I don't want that joy clouded and certainly not in any way postponed." She picked up the baby carrier and slung her shoulder bag over her arm. She stuck her hand out and Honora reluctantly shook it.

As Raine moved towards the office door Honora tried one more time. "Hypnosis has been proven to be effective, I think—"

Raine whirled around with a deep scowl. "Bugger, woman— give it a rest. Please. I'll let you know if I need your services again. Thank you." With that she fairly stomped out of the office.

Honora sat down at her desk and dictated her notes for transcription. She hadn't missed the confused look on Raine's face. The woman was obviously disturbed by the "misspoken" words and the thought of digging just a little deeper. Honora hoped she would come back.

Wilde had gotten best man Cress LaChoisi to agree to the infamous Bachelor Party today, June 18th, Paul McCartney's forty-third birthday. Cress didn't get the entire Beatles-Stones addiction that Wilde seemed to have, but it was as good a day as any for his brother's event, and since Wilde was paying for half of it Cress thought he should have a say. Wilde's parents, his brother, Danny, and Danny's wife and sons had flown in for the wedding, so the total number of booze-guzzling, raucous men would total seventeen with Wilde, Victor, Quint, Belzer, Tucker, Moon Wolf, Rafe, Fox, Turner, Malachi, Gray, and Dionysus (the Makrises had flown in for the festivities, too, and were staying in a suite at the Westward Dream, right next to the Sinclairs' suites). Beckett had pleaded to come, stating that he was fourteen and plenty mature enough to party with the men. Victor shot him down gently.

Wilde had reserved the largest private dining room in Mariposa Linda's from six to midnight. He had arranged for an open bar and a hot buffet. Cress had arranged for several limousines to take the revelers to and from so that there would be no drinking-and-driving issues. Victor said that he would arrange for the entertainment, and Constantine made him swear to *God* that no strippers or other scantily dressed women would be part of that venue; Victor swore.

The party was in full swing by seven, and by that time everyone had chowed down on the food. Wilde made sure that the offerings ranged from good old southwestern fare (very heavy on the enchiladas) to luscious New Orleans dishes to Italian platters. Wine, beer, margaritas, and single-malt scotch flowed freely. Constantine whooped in pleasure when Victor's entertainment came in: a well-known jazz band from L.A. that played old familiar tunes rampant in the Big Easy as well as new music. They did a rousing interpretation of an old sixties' tune, *Washington Square*. And much to Wilde's delight they played several Beatles songs, including *And I Love Her*, *P.S. I Love You*, and *This Boy*. He hadn't expected his new security man, Rafe, to loosen up since he could be a little bit intense at times, but the man showed an unexpectedly humorous side and did the vocals on all the songs with Wilde duetting on *I Feel Fine*. Rafe had a great voice and had risen several notches in Wilde's estimation.

The guest of honor turned a dark shade of red when a surprise guest came in, courtesy of his father, Dionysus—a very busty, energetic, scantily-clad belly dancer that performed a set of gyrations that had even the gay men salivating. Dionysus intoned very seriously that no bachelor party worth its salt didn't have at least one amazingly "flexible" woman to elicit whistles and catcalls. His son relaxed when Dionysus confessed that he had okayed the lady with Raine, whose only demand was that he take a photo of her on Constantine's lap. The young man in question growled menacingly but under an onslaught of loud, demanding camaraderie let "Jasmine" sit on his lap while his father snapped a few pictures. Jasmine sauntered out of the room after about twenty minutes, much to Constantine's relief. One thing he was certain of—Sasha was *never* going to see those pictures.

The jazz band was paid to perform to eleven but stayed until midnight. They were thrilled to enjoy the open bar and buffet when the gifts-opening began around ten. Constantine was relieved that the first few gifts were nice ones (those that wouldn't embarrass him), but his previous facial reddening was nothing compared to that when he opened Wilde's gift and found a closed white cardboard box that read "Honeymoon Kit"—it contained a large bottle of premium baby oil, an old-style round alarm clock, and a red bell with "Ring For Sex" emblazoned on the front. He cast a guilty glance over at his future father-in-law, but Danny had literally slid off his chair and was on the floor laughing like a hyena as Raine's brothers tried to get their old man reseated.

That "Honeymoon Kit" was only the start of the embarrassing gifts, with others following—Quint's pair of men's top-hat-decorated underwear with the question "Want to See My Magic Wand?" displayed in a strategic place; a pair of dice with each side displaying a particularly explicit verb or body part from Moon Wolf; a knitted, elephant-head penis warmer from Victor for "those chilly island nights;" a matching pair of coffee mugs that said "Hold Me Gently, Kiss Me Softly, & Bang Me Silly" from Malachi; and a set of vividly embroidered sex towels from Cress and Gray. Constantine wasn't sure how many of the gifts he wanted to share with his fiancée, but he conceded that she'd eventually see or hear about them all, and it was better to get the reveal over before the wedding. He would never admit to her that he kind of liked Quint's underwear gift.

The manager of Mariposa Linda knocked timidly on the room door and poked his head in, gently saying that it was fifteen minutes to closing time. His crew would be cleaning up the room, so the celebrating men gathered the gifts and their personal items and filed out of the room at five to twelve. The limos took them all home.

Raine was waiting for her fiancé and demanded to see the gifts. He managed just a slight blush as she studied each one. She grinned widely at the underwear.

He wore the underwear to bed.

And she did indeed see his magic wand …

The Retaliator watched in the darkness as a limousine dropped off Victor, Wilde, Quint, and Tucker. He had been watching the three residences all night. After a half hour all the home lights went out, and he drove off, humming Carole King's *It's Too Late*, the number one song at that key moment in time that had somehow defined all their lives.

He thought the title of the song was ever so apropos.

CHAPTER SEVENTEEN

Seven Days Until Retaliation

Father (Padre) Kino was an Italian-born missionary tasked by the Society of Jesus (better known as the Jesuits) in Spain with colonizing the Sonoran Desert and bringing its indigenous inhabitants to Christ (whether they wanted to or not). His travels brought him through northern Mexico, California, and Arizona. His mission—establishing missions and bringing Christianity to the native peoples—brought him into contact with sixteen tribes: Cocopa, Eudeve, Hia C-ed O'odham, Kamia, Kavelchadon, Kiliwa, Maricopa, Opata, Quechan, Gila River Pima, Seri, Tohono O'odham, Sobaipuri, Western Apache, Yavapai, and the Yaqui.

His most well-known accomplishment, however, was the stunning Mission San Xavier del Bac in south Tucson; also known as "the White Dove of the Desert," the mission was built in 1692 on the land now known as the Tohono O'odham San Xavier Indian Reservation. The mission was named for Francis Xavier, a co-founder of his old religious training ground, the Society of Jesus. The mission was razed during an Apache raid in 1700; the current structure was built between 1783 and 1797 by the Franciscans, who oversaw the original construction as well.

White stucco with an intricate front design reminiscent of Moorish architecture, the mission is still the focal point of the nearby Christian Native Americans as well as non-Indians. A plethora of tourists travel long distances to gawk at its splendid beauty, buy souvenirs, take photographs, and light candles to remember deceased loved ones or offer spiritual support for those still among the living. Every year on the Friday after Easter the San Xavier Festival hosts vendors and offers a parade by torch-light of Yaqui and Tohono O'odham tribal members. Throughout the year vendors of food and arts dot the huge parking lot to sell their wares. Tourists are giddy over the interesting selections of "real Indian art."

On occasion weddings took place in the small chapel, and they were usually restricted to only members of the Native American tribes in the vicinity. Others might marry there but required special permission. Through those rare exceptions Phaedra and Moon Wolf were married there, and their daughter, Persa, was baptized there as well. Their wedding and baptism had been achieved through the efforts of Yaqui artist Julio Banderas, who ran his work through Phaedra's gallery and was distantly related to Moon Wolf. He also paved the way for the wedding between Raine and Constantine. They invited him to the ceremony, but he politely declined, stating he had already committed to his nephew's wedding in Bisbee. He did, however, carve a magnificent fifteen-inch-tall sculpture of an Indian maiden and warrior, and presented it to them as a gift. The handiwork and detail were remarkable.

As famous as the church was, its interior surprised most people since the exterior building loomed large on the stark reservation land. Indeed, the church ceiling was quite high, replete with a balcony, arches, and religious murals and icons; the walls were whitewashed, decorated with colorful renderings and tiles. The pews, however, were relatively few given the importance and history of the church, and the space between them was cozy. Twenty central pews spread down the length of the church to the altar; each could fit five or six people depending on size. To both the right and the left of the central pews single pew-like chairs allowed an individual some privacy and comfort. Both types were wood, with scalloped backs; they were made for spiritual rather than physical comfort.

Raine and her wedding planning committee had made every effort to keep the number of guests down, and by the time the hand-written invitations went out the list was a manageable fifty-two, inclusive of the wedding party itself.

June was a normally not a rainy month in Tucson, with the average rainfall hitting barely a half inch. This June, however, had been an abnormally wet one, and by the time the wedding day rolled around eleven inches had fallen. The average high was 102°F, but it was a "cool" day and would barely break a hundred, if that, due in part to the higher than normal wind that exceeded 20 mph; it was usually only around 8 mph. The sporadic cloud cover added to the dip in temperature, and that was just fine with everyone since the church had no air conditioning and the hot air was alleviated just barely by the fans that whirred and blew. Thankfully, the invitations made it very clear that this was not a formal affair, and people should wear comfortable clothes.

Quint wanted to argue for wearing new jeans, shirt, and belt with his cowboy boots, but he felt obligated as a member of the wedding party to dress in his best navy three-piece suit. He, Wilde, Victor, Gray, and Moon Wolf were groomsmen; Deliverance, Phaedra, Bliss, Shayne, and Raine's mother, Arabella, were bridesmaids. All the men wore dark suits; all the women had specially designed dusty rose gowns and matching wide-brimmed hats. No one would yet know what color Iris had chosen for her matron of honor gown until she preceded Raine down the aisle.

Raine insisted that the actual ceremony be short since it was a Saturday and there would be flocks of tourists waiting to view the church and who would be pissed off if they were denied entrance despite the solemnity of the occasion. She and Constantine had decided to forego writing their own vows and adhere to the time-honored ones used at most of the current as well as past weddings. She made it clear, however, that the word "obey" shouldn't be embedded in the familiar words.

The ceremony was scheduled to begin at 10 AM, and by 9:45 everyone had been seated and were murmuring softly. At precisely 10 AM the traditional wedding music began to play, and the matched groomsmen-bridesmaids began walking down the aisle as all heads turned to watch the gorgeous procession. When they had taken their places near the front pews, Persa appeared with a hand-woven Navajo basket and began tossing fresh rose petals over the floor. Her basket was empty by the time she reached her mother and stood beside Phaedra solemnly. One of Constantine's grad students, an amateur photographer, began snapping pictures from every angle as he smoothly wended his way around the chapel.

Tucker grinned and barely managed to restrain himself from emitting a wolf whistle as his wife appeared in a brilliant vermillion dress. Lowcut with chiffon draping over her bare shoulders, the sleeveless dress was a glorious miasma of silk swirls with a tight, crystal-studded bodice and a full skirt with the barest of trains. Iris was holding a tightly woven bouquet of red roses as she walked slowly down the aisle, smiling and winking at her husband when she approached the priest and took her place to the side opposite Cress and Constantine, who were both decked out in crisp new tuxedos.

All eyes were focused at the back of the church. A moment later Raine appeared on her father's arm. Anyone could see that Danny was about to explode with pride as he walked his daughter down the aisle towards the man with whom she wanted to spend the rest of her life. She looked like a queen as she walked slowly down the aisle holding a packed white-flower bouquet of roses, lilies, and baby's breath. Her train was four feet long, and the veil reached to its very edge under the sparkling tiara that capped the lace and chiffon work of art. Her "something blue" was a London blue topaz necklace and matching earrings set in white gold that her brothers had gifted her. The "something old" was a gold bracelet with a Celtic-knot design that Deliverance had given her, an acquisition from a famous antique shop in Salem where the proprietor swore it had come on the boat from Ireland during the nineteenth-century famine years.

Danny and Raine reached her bridegroom, and Raine's father gently kissed her cheek and whispered something that made her smile. He shook Constantine's hand, then sat in the front pew next to his parents and sons. Alexandra and Dionysus Makris sat behind them, Sasha cuddled in her grandmother's lap. Josette and François LaChoisi were also invited, considering the complex relationship between their adopted children. Josette managed dry eyes, but her thoughts were on her long-dead daughter, Cheyenne, who would never stand before a priest and say her wedding vows. It would have been likely that she would have married Constantine had she not been a stone-cold killer as well as his biological sister. Thank God sweet Cress had survived her deadly machinations.

The audience fell silent as the priest began his ritual with the three important questions of the Catholic ceremony.

"We have come together to celebrate the honorable and sacred marriage of these two people. Be there any objections to the wedding of this man and woman, speak now or forever hold your peace." The couple's family twisted their heads around, and Danny scowled as if daring anyone to respond in the affirmative. After a moment, the priest continued.

"Raine Keaira Sinclair and Constantine Dionysus Black

Wolf, have you come here to enter into marriage without coercion, freely and wholeheartedly?"

"We have," the bride and groom said together.

"Are you prepared, as you follow the path of Marriage, to love and honor each other for as long as you both shall live?"

"We are."

"Are you prepared to accept children lovingly from God and to bring them up according to the law of Christ and his Church?"

"We are."

"Constantine, do you take Raine to be your wife? Do you promise to be faithful to her in good times and in bad, in sickness and in health, to love her and to honor her all the days of your life?"

"I do." Cress handed his brother Raine's wedding ring, and Constantine slipped it onto her waiting finger. "Raine, receive this ring as a sign of my love and fidelity. In the name of the Father, and of the Son, and of the Holy Spirit."

"Raine, do you take Constantine to be your husband? Do you promise to be faithful to him in good times and in bad, in sickness and in health, to love him and to honor him all the days of your life?"

"I do." Iris handed her best friend Constantine's wedding ring, and Raine slipped it onto his waiting finger. "Constantine, receive this ring as a sign of my love and fidelity. In the name of the Father, and of the Son, and of the Holy Spirit." She met her husband's moist eyes and mouthed, "I love you."

The priest cleared his throat and smiled. "As Raine and Constantine have declared their commitment to each other and to God, it is my great joy to pronounce them husband and wife." He waited two seconds before ending with, "Okay, young man—you may kiss your bride."

Constantine grinned as Raine melted into his arms; they were oblivious to the cheers and clapping as their lips validated their hearts and souls. They were both blushing after a long, intimate kiss as they faced their family and friends and began walking back up the aisle as the audience continued clapping and cheering until they reached the door.

The grad student, Charlie Sheffield, slipped past the newly married couple and snapped off photos of them standing under the door arch and as the guests began pouring out of the church. He finished his roll of film with wide-angle shots of nearby tourists that were watching the wedding party in awe. He was thrilled to have the chance to exhibit his talent with a camera, and the extra money would come in handy for his upcoming photography jaunt to Costa Rica.

Many of the guests had driven their own cars to the Mission, but Cress had also hired a small tour bus to pick up others and then take them to the reception venue, the White Buffalo Room at the Westward Dream. He, Iris, and the newlyweds would head back in the white stretch limo where everything was set up for an expansive sit-down dinner of filet mignon, rosemary chicken, and shrimp scampi.

Charlie had rushed to the Dream ahead of everyone to get shots of the empty reception room then shoot the guests and wedding party coming in. His wedding book for his professor was going to be one fantastic history of the entire day. He wished he could go to Maui on the honeymoon to shoot some pictures and make his book even more complete. Well, that and to scope out the well-tanned beach bunnies.

The resort had set up a long table near the picture window and set it with placings for the bride, groom, best man, matron of honor, and both sets of parents. Alexandra turned Sasha over to Deliverance, who was sitting at a round table close by with her husband, Gray, Victor, Beckett, Tucker, Bliss, and Malachi; the younger children were at their own table right behind except for Barnabas, who was on his mother's lap or in a baby carrier at her feet. The string quartet that Wilde had hired was clustered at one end of the bridal table, and they played for the duration of the meal. Danny was a classical music aficionado—much to his rock-and-roll-loving brother's dismay—and had selected the songs from the portfolios of Bach, Vivaldi, and Brahms.

Shrimp cocktails set the stage for appetizers along with triangular slices of spanakopita, and the wine and non-alcoholic beverages flowed freely. Black Wolf Begay threw a short tantrum when his parents cut him off from the cookies, but Phaedra settled him down. Quint was grateful that his raucous brood were behaving themselves although a few times Aislinn gave him heart palpitations when she interacted with other guests. He noticed that Storm successfully calmed her down each time.

Cress stood up after the meal and raised his champagne glass to his brother and sister-in-law. He provided sweet words to the lifelong joy of the married couple and wished them many more children since he was happy as hell being an uncle. Constantine blushed. That was followed by other toasts by Iris, Phaedra, Danny, and lastly by Wilde, who decided to express his thoughts in slightly salacious words instead of classy ones. Everyone roared when Raine threw him the finger (Charlie was hooting when he captured that on film).

The string quartet ceased playing as Raine and Constantine moved to the center of the room for their first dance as marrieds. Wilde had been insistent on choosing the song and medium for the dance, and as Constantine put his arms around his wife, the loudspeakers began emanating the love duet between Roberta Flack and Peabo Bryson, *Tonight I Celebrate My Love For You*. As Wilde scanned the room and saw the tears in people's eyes and the looks of love and admiration, he knew he'd chosen right.

The room burst into applause as the song and dance ended. Constantine backed away and another song played as the father-daughter dance commenced, *Times of Your Life* by Paul Anka. As Paul finished the last lyrics ("Do you remember, baby, do you remember the times of your life?") people began rising from their chairs and hitting the dance floor under the musical selections that Wilde had chosen for that part of the festivities. He absolutely cracked up as his friends formed a line and gyrated to an old '70s tune, *The Hustle*. He knew Quint hated disco, so he made a conscious effort to include some. Quint glared at him but did some impressive dance moves, although John Travolta had nothing to worry about.

The reception broke up after 4 PM, but it took a good half hour for people to leave as hugging and kissing dominated the dwindling guests. Constantine had taken the wedding suite at the Dream so that he and his wife could relax and get some sleep before they boarded their flight to Honolulu in the morning. Raine burst into full-blown sobbing as she cuddled and kissed her baby daughter goodbye before Cress could extract his niece from her mom and take her home.

The huge suite was western-themed, with ceiling beams and rough-hewn bed, tables, and chairs. As he opened the double doors Constantine held Raine back, then swung her up in his arms and carried her inside, kicking the door closed. The door opened a moment later as a hand stuck the "Do Not Disturb" sign on the outside handle.

The next time the newlyweds stepped outside of the room was the next morning, and they were dressed for travel and carrying matching suitcases. Constantine paid their bill and called a taxi, and forty-five minutes later they were checking in at the Tucson airport.

Their boarding was called and as first-class passengers they were amongst the first to hand over their tickets and walk to the plane; the stewardess directed them to seats 1A and 1B. They settled in as other first-class passengers spilled into the plane. They took note that seats 1C and 1D were still unoccupied. There was a momentary pause after the rest of the prime seats were filled, and they expected coach to start boarding.

Raine's jaw dropped as she stared at the last two passengers about to seat themselves into 1C and 1D. Three passengers, really— Cress was holding baby Sasha as he and Gray grinned at the newlyweds.

"What the devil are you two doing here?" Constantine asked in wonder.

"Three of us, big brother," Cress replied as he placed Sasha in her mother's arms. Gray had already buckled himself into 1C and was grinning widely. Cress winked at his sister-in-law. "We figured out that you and my bro, here, weren't going to be able to relax and enjoy your honeymoon if you were missing and fretting about my niece. We also were concerned that you'd cut the honeymoon short and fly back early. Since neither of us has a course to teach this summer, we figured you wouldn't mind if we came along so you'd have access to the little monkey when you needed it, while still lying on the beach, eating primo seafood, and making love as the cool ocean breezes waft through your French doors."

"Meanwhile we'll be having a semi-vacation while we're babysitting. You can see and hold the little one any time you want and have privacy when you need that. We've also seen to our privacy—we took a suite on the same floor as yours, but down the hall. We thought about adjoining suites, but Cress made the good point that we probably wouldn't get any sleep from the noise going on in your room," Gray said.

"Grayson Akihiko Kingston," Raine said sternly. "We wouldn't make that much noise."

"Uh, actually ..." Constantine began.

"Behave yourself and hold your daughter," she commanded as she handed her bundle of joy over to her husband. Her eyes were misty as she looked at Cress and Gray and said, "Thank you."

"What the hell are brothers for?" Gray replied as he nodded and took the glass of champagne from the attentive stewardess. He didn't mention putting the cost of their suite on Constantine's Master Charge. There was time enough for that when they all checked out of the Maui Majestic Resort in fourteen days.

CHAPTER EIGHTEEN

June 29, 1985
Retaliation Day: Morning
8:00 AM

"Butts in gear," Deliverance yelled from the kitchen. Her imps were lagging behind today and they needed to get to their karate class for the 8:30 AM session. She had a few typical Saturday errands to run and planned on keeping as busy as possible so the memories wouldn't come crashing back as they did every year at this time.

She looked through the window blinds and relaxed. The hardly-ever-accurate weatherman had predicted a partly cloudy sky and temps reaching around 109°F; it was already 85°F. Thankfully it hadn't rained since the wedding, and she was hoping for a mid-thirties dewpoint. She needed to take her car in for a tune-up and have them check the air conditioning, which was starting to blow mildly warm air instead of cold. Even so, she usually drove with her window down and often forgot to turn it on. It was the kids who bitched and moaned, but she ignored them—they weren't paying for the cost of maintaining a car in the desert. She had already shelled out sixty bucks for a new battery three weeks ago.

Storm ran into the kitchen; Aislinn was right on her heels and nearly ran into her sister. She scowled at their mother and jammed her fists into her waist as her brother and younger sister came in carrying the backpacks that held their martial arts uniforms—uwagi (shirt), a shitebaki (pants), and the obi (belt). Vikki's obi was yellow (yellow signifies the first beams of sunlight which shines upon the seed giving it new strength with the beginning of new life. A yellow-belt student is given his first ray of knowledge, opening his mind, from his instructors.); Aislinn and Storm had advanced to orange-belt status (orange represents the growing power of the sun as it warms the earth to prepare for new growth in the spring. The orange-belt student is starting to feel his body and mind open and develop.); and Alex had achieved the next level and wore a green belt (green signifies the growth of the seed as it sprouts from the earth reaching toward the sun and begins to grow into a plant. A green-belt student learns to strengthen and refine his techniques.)

"I don't want to go to practice today," Aislinn said defiantly. "I want to go to the zoo."

Deliverance leaned down and gently cupped her daughter's face in her hands. "Oh, I'm sorry, sweetie. Sometimes I just don't make myself clear. Were you under the impression that that was a request instead of a direct order?"

"Screwed," Vikki whispered to Alex, who nodded. He didn't want to seem like a wuss and said nothing, although he didn't want to go, either. He usually looked forward to the sessions, but he felt queasy for some reason he couldn't define. Maybe it was just the date. He felt this way every year although he kept his disquiet hidden from his mother. She was sad enough on the day. He didn't understand why; she just was. Anyway, his favorite instructor at the dojo would be teaching the class today. He adored Bobby and had learned a lot from him.

"I heard that, little miss," Deliverance admonished tartly. "What the hell have I said about swearing?"

"You swear all the time," Aislinn offered. "Why can't we swear?"

Deliverance loomed over her recalcitrant daughter and said firmly, "Because I'm an adult. And if that isn't good enough reason for you, consider the fact that I can tan your adorable behind any time I want until you look like a chili pepper."

"Daddy would never hit us," Aislinn replied, chin up defiantly. In truth, neither of their parents had ever made good on a physical threat.

"Daddy's a big, fat sucker, smart as hell but with a marshmallow constitution when it comes to disciplining his evil brood. I'm not, so bear that in mind. Into the car—*now!*"

"Yes, ma'am," all four muttered as they hiked their backpacks over their shoulders and headed to the garage. They were surprised that Quint's beloved Dodge 400 convertible was there and not their mom's station wagon.

She grinned at them. "I thought you might like a ride with the top down." She clapped her hands over her ears as the kids shrieked and piled into the car. Deliverance hit the garage door opener and then the button that put the car's top down. Aislinn had tried for shotgun, but Vikki somehow beat her to it. Deliverance buckled her youngest daughter into the seat as the other kids fiddled with the belts in the back seat. They knew better than to dawdle since their mother wouldn't back the car out until they were strapped in.

Deliverance endured the nonstop gabbing of the four children as she maneuvered the car down Swan and took a right on Grant. A few streets later she turned north on Campbell and fifty yards later pulled into the strip mall where the dojo had been in business for fifteen years. She had time before her errands, so she decided to finally meet the infamous "Bobby" from whom her son was gaining such proficiency. She followed the kids into the building where the receptionist greeted her as her hellions barely said goodbye before they stampeded off to the changing rooms to put their uniforms on.

"Daisy, does Bobby have a minute? I wanted to speak to him about Alex's progress," Deliverance said as she pulled out a pocket mirror to check her hair.

"Oh, Alex is making great strides," Daisy said enthusiastically. "He's right on the cusp of getting his blue belt. But, I'm sorry— Bobby called in sick today. Jasper Jones is subbing for him. Did you want to talk to Jasper?"

"No, that's okay. Maybe next week. I'll pick them up at ten. Later, sweetie." Deliverance walked out into the bright sunshine and warmth and promised herself that she would be on a better emotional keel today. She had so much to be thankful for. She slipped on her sunglasses, got into the car, and drove off to Bookmans to check out Larry McMurtry's new novel, *Lonesome Dove*. She thought he was an amazing writer and had enjoyed several of his books including *The Last Picture Show* and *Terms of Endearment*. She thought the movies were fabulous, although Quint griped all the way through the latter and they'd had a big fight about his Neanderthal concepts of entertainment. Fortunately for her the man was enlightened enough not to feel threatened by her ambitions, and he enthusiastically supported her college education. She was two courses short of completing the requirements for her Bachelor's degree in Criminology and would finish those by her wedding anniversary if she did both classes over the summer. She needed to focus on that and on the positive and make her morosity begone. It wasn't that she owed that only to her family, but to herself as well.

Alex had finished changing and was the last one to leave the locker room. He almost ran right into Bobby as he exited and his whole face lit up.

"Bobby," Alex exclaimed. "JoJo said you weren't gonna be here today." The tall man with dark brown hair and riveting blue eyes was smiling down at the boy in a conspiratorial way. He was wearing jeans that had a few streaks of dirt on them, and a tee-shirt that had sweat marks under the arms. There were a few scratches on his hands, just like the ones Daddy had when he was puttering around the back yard.

Bobby smiled. "I felt better, and I wanted to show you some special techniques that I don't think the other kids are ready for."

"Cool!"

Bobby took his hand, put a finger to his own lips, and led the little boy into a small dojo room. Alex felt a peculiar tingle when Bobby took his hand for the very first time. As they entered the room Alex felt a wave of icy dread smash over his body like a tidal wave and he tried to pull his hand away. Seconds later, everything went dark.

8:35 AM

Yale Cornell stared down at the dead body bound to a tall, very old tree beside Reid Park's manmade lake. There had been no attempt to hide the body, which was facing the lake and tied with strong nylon rope. The body had been discovered shortly after 6 AM by a fisherman and his ten-year-old son, who screamed for quite a while at the lifeless eyes staring into the water. Within fifteen minutes two patrol cars were on the scene and Cornell was being woken up by his jangling phone and hateful beeper. Baxter was calling, and they agreed to meet at the scene. They preceded forensic tech Josie Ross, who had been bumped up in seniority after Murphy's death and Deuel's murder, by eight minutes. She and her team were walking the grid and photographing and collecting any possible evidence that would give some clue as to who had murdered the young woman tied to the tree. Her face was badly bruised. There was a bloody stain on her chest, right where the heart had once beat, although there was no tear in the shirt. She was fully clothed and there were no immediate signs of sexual assault, but the M.E. would verify that.

"You know," Cornell said as he shoved the last bite of his Egg McMuffin into his mouth, "she looks familiar, even with all of those bruises."

"You bust her once?" Baxter asked as he sipped his cold coffee.

"No," Cornell said slowly, "but I'm sure I've seen her ... and recently." He yelled over at Josie, "Mind if I search her for ID, Miss Pussycat?"

"I wouldn't have had you not used that ridiculous and demeaning nickname," she yelled back. Too many people who thought they were amusing at the station had dubbed her "Miss Pussycat" because of her name—an old TV series on CBS during the early '70s was *Josie and the Pussycats*. The show was based on a comic book of the same name that ran from 1962 to 1983; despite the two-year absence of the comic the nickname had stuck, and she hated it. It didn't help that she was a dead ringer for Pussycat Melody. Men, she thought, sucked.

"Would a sincere apology assist you in making a decision?" Cornell asked.

"A two-parter—an apology and the promise to never say that sucking name again."

"You're killing me, woman, but—okay. I apologize, and I promise to never call you Miss Pussycat again."

"Cornell, don't take this the wrong way, but you're such a dick. Go on—search her but slip these on, please." She handed him latex gloves then returned to a team member and gave him instructions on searching the bank of the lake.

"Are you really going to keep that promise?" Baxter asked as he watch his partner feel around at the back of the dead woman's jeans.

Cornell looked up at his partner and then cast a glance over at Josie. "Do you need an assessment of risk to figure out not to pet a rattlesnake? That's one mean-ass woman, and I think I'll respect her boundaries."

Baxter started to emit a hoot then slapped a hand over his mouth. He leaned down and whispered, "You're sweet on her."

"Fuck off," Cornell replied affably as he withdrew a driver's license from the woman's rear pocket. He looked at it and sucked in a deep breath as he stood. He handed the license to Baxter. "I knew I'd seen her before."

Baxter read the important details. "Thayer Burton. Born June 4, 1952, residence 2010 E. Copper Mine Road." Suddenly he realized and did a double-take. "She's one of Quint's crew. Holy shit. This isn't going to start again, is it? Murphy's dead."

Cornell took the license back and dropped it into a plastic bag he whipped out of his jeans pocket (he always carried at least two for unexpected evidence gathering). "I don't know what the hell this is, but I'll bet my next paycheck that it's not a coincidence."

"You're willing to risk 98 cents?"

"You know, I'm going to come up with a really nasty nickname for you and spread it all over the department. Let's go."

"Where?"

"Union Jack Investigations—where else?"

9:01 AM

Deliverance went nuts and instead of getting just McMurtry's new book, she added *The Handmaid's Tale* by Margaret Atwood, Stephen King's new offering, *Skeleton Crew*, and *The Vampire Lestat* by an author that Deliverance just loved, Anne Rice. She smiled when she thought of Quint, who had built four magnificent alder bookcases for what they called "the library." He understood that his literature-loving wife hadn't grown up with enough money to buy anything other than an occasional paperback, and now that they had a solid, money-making business she could afford to indulge her desire for hardbacks. She said that someday people would read books on a computer, but for her there would never be an option save holding a real book in her hands and listening to the crackle as she turned the pages.

She was balancing her bag of books in one arm as she unlocked the Dodge when her car phone started ringing. She cursed and dumped the bag on the passenger seat as she slid into her seat and grabbed the receiver. She remembered briefly her conversation with Raine about the technology progress being made rapidly as each year went by. Motorola had demonstrated what they called a prototype "cellular phone" in April 1973; they called it a "DynaTAC," and one of the engineers, Martin Cooper, made that call. On October 13, 1983 David D. Meilahn made the first commercial wireless call from his Mercedes-Benz, and the man on the other end made a tag-team call to Germany to a grandson of Alexander Graham Bell, who had flown to Europe just for the occasion. The DynaTAC 8000X became the first mobile phone approved by the FCC. Deliverance had seen photos of the phone dubbed "the brick" because of its huge size and weight; Raine said that in the future the phones would be smaller and have much more power. Deliverance couldn't wait for that day. She certainly hoped that the initial cost of the phone would drastically decreased from its $3,995 price tag.

"Yeah, hello," Deliverance expelled breathlessly. She listened for a few seconds. "Oh, Daisy. Is everything okay? My brood isn't acting up in their class, are they?" She listened against for thirty seconds. She slumped back against the seat and her heart began beating wildly. "Okay, okay. Take it easy. What do you mean Alex wasn't in his class? I saw him head off to the locker room. Some boys saw him there? Then where the *hell* is my son? You people damn well better be searching every nook and cranny. I'll be there in ten minutes. My son better be waiting." She slammed down the receiver and took several deep breaths. He was just being a little pain in the ass. He was probably hiding. She wouldn't put it past Aislinn to help him abscond. If that was the case, she really was going to tan her little hide. His, too. Maybe she should just tan all their hides as a life lesson.

She grabbed the receiver and put in a call to Quint. He didn't answer. She cursed. He had gone to the home and garden store to pick up some cacti she wanted to plant, and rocks to build a small garden near the casita. She dialed Wilde; no answer either. She let loose a colorful string of vulgarities then dialed Tucker's casita number. A wave of relief washed over her as he answered on the second ring.

"Tuck, Alex isn't with you by any chance, is he? I mean, he didn't somehow come home from the dojo just to piss me off, did he?

He didn't. Yes, something's wrong. The dojo called, and he didn't show up in his class even though I dropped them off. No, they're searching the place and I'm heading there now. Couldn't get ahold of Quint or Wilde. Yes. Yes, please meet us there. Try to get ahold of my old man and partners. Thank you. Yes, bring Iris. Love you, bye."

Deliverance tore out of the parking lot and screeched onto Grant. She nearly collided with two cars as she gunned it to the dojo while chanting repeatedly, "No, no, no, no, no."

9:15 AM

Quint made it back to the office after he dropped off the lumber, rocks, and plants he had picked up at Home & Garden Depot. He tried to push away the utter shame of driving around in a station wagon but using his convertible or the Cougar was impractical.

The receptionist was off since it was Saturday, and Quint hadn't planned on coming in, but he was a little behind on some case paperwork, and since Del and the kids would be gone for a few hours he decided to catch up. He and Tucker could start on their gardening project on Sunday.

Still, he felt guilty at not being by his wife's side today. As usual she was a little morose, and he should be there to comfort her. Well, she was occupied right now, and he'd finish up his work and go home to spend the rest of the day with her and the kids.

He saw his answering machine light blinking, but he assumed it was regarding business and thought that it could wait until Monday. He was sipping a cup of coffee and scowling over the invoices for the Catania case when he heard pounding on the downstairs front door. He wanted to ignore it, but the knocking was insistent. He cursed and went down to the lobby where he was surprised to see Cornell and Baxter through the glass doors. He unlocked the door and admitted them.

"This can't be good," Quint muttered as they ascended the staircase to the second floor. He led them into his office. Baxter pleaded for a cup of coffee and Quint grudgingly complied before seating himself behind his desk. "Okay. What's happened?" Suddenly he froze. "My wife and kids?"

"No, no," Cornell said. "This has nothing to do with them. Look, it's bad news."

"Go on," Quint said tensely.

"We were called to a body dump in Reid Park. The victim was tied to a tree out in the open. There was no attempt to hide the body, which is fairly unusual."

"Except for whackjob Murphy," Baxter interjected.

"Who was the body and why are you here?" Quint asked.

Cornell handed Quint the plastic bag containing the driver's license. Quint frowned as he stared at it, then his face drained of color. He looked at Cornell. "Thayer? Oh, my God. She's dead?"

"Yes. Stabbed and beaten. I've seen her before, of course, but I barely recognized her until I found the license. Was she working on a case that might have gotten her killed?"

Quint shook his head in disbelief as he continued staring at Thayer's smiling face on the license. "She resigned earlier this month and her last working day was June 14th. She was moving back to New Hampshire to open a P.I. firm with her boyfriend."

"Know his name?"

Quint groaned. "She called him Robert but if she ever told us his last name I don't remember it. Maybe her family back home would know. I'll get you their number."

"'Preciate it. What can you tell us about her? Did she ever engage in risky behavior that might bring her into contact with someone dangerous?"

"No, no. She was ex-Army and an ex-cop in Frisco before she moved here and joined the firm. Top-notch person in every way. Maybe a little on the romantic side. We were real sorry to lose her, but she seemed to be in love and wanted to give a new life a try." He smiled sadly. "We gave her a helluva going-away party."

"All right," Cornell said, putting away his pad and retrieving the license. "We'll make the notifications and will have to interview all of your people to see if we can uncover any clues. We're heading over to her address to see what we can find." Quint handed him a note with the Burtons' home and business numbers. "Thanks." Cornell was about to say something else when Quint's phone rang.

Quint picked up immediately. "Tucker? What? What the

fuck? Are you sure? Yeah of course I'm on my way." He slammed down the phone and jumped up. "My son is missing from his dojo. I gotta go."

"We'll come with you," Cornell said. He didn't like this coincidence at all.

When Cornell's car was peeling off, Quint was in the back seat, mumbling.

"What?" Cornell demanded.

"I said if anything happens to Alex it will literally kill Deliverance." He paused for a moment. "You don't know this, but when she was a kid she had a baby, a baby boy. He was stillborn. David John Dane. He died on June 29, 1971. He would have been fourteen today."

9:55 AM

The Dane-Quintana daughters were clustered around their screaming mother, terrified at her persona and at the thought of their missing brother. Daisy, Jasper, and several other employees including the dojo owner were trying to calm her down, but since an exhaustive search of the studio and nearby premises had uncovered no Alex, she was on a nonstop tear and was lambasting every single person with sharp words that only Deliverance could spit out with a mixture of eloquence and vulgarity. Tucker and Iris had arrived and were trying to calm her down, but they gave up and Tucker started battering the employees about the kid he thought of as almost a son. Iris flashed her FBI badge and made it clear in icy tones that if the kid didn't turn up within the hour she was going to call in a full-blown kidnapping team and shut the place down. As it stood, all the other children had been sent home early, and the front door was locked.

Suddenly three men appeared outside, and one began savagely banging on the door.

"That's my husband," Deliverance snapped. "Let him in or he'll kick down the door."

The dojo owner rushed over and unlocked the door, just managing to step aside before Quint shoved in and nearly knocked him over.

"Daddy! Daddy!" the girls cried and ran to him, hugging his legs and sobbing. He met his wife's eyes—she was white and terrified. He managed to free himself from his daughters and strode to her, holding her tightly in his arms. She began sobbing against his chest as Cornell flashed his badge.

"When was the last time anyone saw the boy?" he asked.

Jasper answered. "JoJo Carson saw him the locker room just before class started. That's it. Swear to God—we've searched very inch of this place and the stores nearby."

Just as Quint was about to bear down on the quaking owner there was hard knocking at the door and the owner scooted over to admit Victor and Wilde.

"Where the hell's my nephew?" Wilde demanded.

"No sign of him yet," Deliverance sniffled. She found herself strangely calm, as though this was the shoe she'd always expected to drop someday. She shrugged herself out of her husband's arms and frowned. "Jasper, you took over his normal teacher's duties today."

"Yes, ma'am. Bobby called in sick."

"Mr. Massey is rarely late or absent," Moon Choong-Hoon, the dojo owner, offered. He was literally quaking in his shoes as the enormity of what this would do to his livelihood if the situation wasn't resolved quickly and determined to not be his fault.

"His name is Robert Massey?" Baxter asked. He stared at his partner. "Thayer's Robert?"

"I hope that's just a coincidence," Cornell said. He noted Deliverance's querulous look and frozen stance. "Quint can update you. Something?" he asked her.

With a tight smile Deliverance shook her head. "No, nothing. Look—I want to get my daughters home. Tucker, can you take them and stay with them while Cornel and Iris do their cop thing?"

"Yeah, sure, of course," Tucker said. He sensed that she meant right now. "Okay, hellions—let's go."

Storm hugged Deliverance and asked plaintively, "Aren't you coming with us, Mommy?"

"Soon, baby girl, soon. Daddy and the boys and I have to check some things out at the office but then we'll be right along. I promise."

"Please come with us, Mommy," Vikki said as the tears in her eyes brimmed over.

"Soon, Cuddle Bunny, soon. Tuck?"

"Let's go, kids," Tucker said as he firmly ushered the three girls outside and to his car. He knew they were scared and stressed, but he also knew that some of that disquiet would dissipate under the onslaught of a dipped Dairy Queen cone on the way home.

"I'll call you with updates," Iris said gently to Deliverance. "Go home."

Deliverance nodded absently and walked out followed by her husband and partners. They piled into Victor's Cadillac and the ride to the office was mostly silent as she and Quint sat in the back seat holding hands. She, Wilde, and Victor were stunned to hear of Thayer's murder. She knew then that what she suspected was true. She got out of the car without a word and pounded up the stairs to her office, followed by her men. They watched from the door as she withdrew a bottle of tequila from her desk drawer and poured a full glass. She sipped a good amount before she met their curious eyes.

"Robert Massey," she stated flatly.

"Alex's teacher?" Wilde said.

"And possibly Thayer's boyfriend and killer," she said, no inflection in her voice whatsoever. A shiver ran up Quint's spine at her dead eyes. "I'm sure it's an alias, and the alias of someone devious and evil. He'd have to be to carry out this plan of revenge."

"Who the hell are you talking about?" Quint asked.

She didn't answer immediately. Then, she said, "Being from Salem as well as being a Wiccan I've studied every single aspect of that city's past. I was always good in history. Silly as this might sound I had youthful aspirations of being a history teacher."

"You'd've made a great teacher, chère," Victor said as he took the glass of tequila from her hand and moved it far away on the desk. "You don't need this. You have us."

She smiled wanly and sat down behind her desk as her men seated themselves and waited patiently. "Of course, the Salem Witch Trials are world-infamous. There were a lot of so-called 'good Christians' engaged in that horror. Praise be to God, let us torture people and murder them because we're ignorant idiots. Two of the Puritan ministers, a father and son, were part of that travesty. Increase and Cotton Mather. Both men were zealots, but oddly enough both condemned the trials' use of what they called 'spectral evidence.' Increase was enlightened enough to write—and I quote—'It were better that ten suspected witches should escape, than that one innocent person should be condemned.'"

"What a guy," Wilde said. "I feel the love."

"He had his foibles, but he also had a side to him that was rational and progressive. Unfortunately, it didn't stop twenty innocent people from being executed. But to my point, I did a lot of research on the Mathers for a sophomore term paper. Got an A+, by the way. I learned that Increase matriculated at Harvard when he was twelve. He graduated with a Bachelor's degree when he was seventeen and promptly took a boat to Ireland where he entered Trinity College in Dublin and studied for his Master's in Divinity. He gave his first sermon at the age of eighteen. Oliver Cromwell licensed him as a Commonwealth Minister. Fascinating, Huh?

"But that's just a summary of his early years before Salem. The key point is that when he entered Harvard he roomed with and studied under another student. That student's name was Robert Massey." She let that sink in as she reached across her desk for the glass of tequila and took a sip.

"That can't be a coincidence, but—" Victor began slowly but was cut off by Deliverance.

"It's not. Think of Massey's roommate's name."

There was confusion on all three men's faces until Quint leaned forward, his jaw dropping. "Fuck," he whispered. "Fuck."

"Yeah, fuck," his wife agreed. She took another sip.

"I don't get it," Wilde said.

"Winston Goodwin," Quint intoned ominously. "David's father. Winston *Mather* Goodwin."

"Mon dieu," Victor breathed. "But … he has no idea it was us that night."

"Maybe he suspects, or maybe he just hates Del because she made a great life for herself and his turned to shyte," Wilde said.

"He killed Thayer after he seduced her and got close and learned a lot about us from his unknowing girlfriend. Jesus Christ," Quint said. "She said he'd come out and visit her. He must have been watching us for a long time." He looked at his wife. "Your mother said he'd fallen on really hard times. Maybe you should call her and see if she has any more information about him. I don't know if you should tell her about Alex and Thayer, though."

"I need to tell her. She'll sense that something's wrong. She always does. Some privacy, please, gents." Without hesitation her partners rose and left the room, shutting the door. Deliverance dialed her parents' home number.

"This is too flippin' unbelievable," Wilde said as he slugged down a cold beer to calm his nerves. He froze. "Aside from the murder and kidnapping and its consequences for him—and we *will* get Alex back safely—if what we did comes out all four of us will wind up in prison."

"That's the least of my concerns," Quint snapped. "Besides, the statute of limitations has run out, and in addition to there being no proof whatsoever of our actions, he's not going to espouse his suspicions to the cops or anyone else."

"Why not?" Victor asked.

"Because I'm going to kill him." He narrowed his eyes at his partners. "Alone. Neither of you nor Del will be involved. If I have to wind up in the slammer I can do the time if I know you're taking care of her and the kids. No argument."

"That doesn't sit well with me. We'll talk," Wilde said evenly. All heads turned as they heard Deliverance's door open. They were instantly alarmed as she made her way towards them, slowly and slightly weaving, unsteady on her feet.

Quint grabbed her before she could fall. They both went to

the floor as she melted down the wall, her eyes haunted and filled with tears.

"Baby, what is it? What is it?" Quint asked desperately as he squatted beside her crumpled form. Victor and Wilde did the same.

"Mom … Mom," she choked out. "She and Dad went to the cemetery today to put flowers on David's grave. The police were with her when I called."

"Are they all right?"

She nodded, then met his eyes. Hers were full of torment and fear. "Someone broke into his grave, it looks like a few days ago by the grass and earth cuts. Oh, Quint. Oh, Quint—they took his body. They left the coffin in the ground but empty. They took my baby boy. *He* took my baby boy." She began sobbing from the very depths of her soul as her husband and friends remained rooted and stunned. She wailed, "He's going to kill David's brother."

"No," Quint said almost to himself. "I'm going to kill him."

10:49 AM

"Cute house," Baxter commented as he and Cornell pulled up in front of Thayer Burton's rented house. It was tiny, a single-story brick almost hidden by short palms trees and ungroomed bougainvilleas. The street, off Campbell, was laid back and quiet except for kids here and there playing in their yards and invading the street to play kickball when no one was driving by.

Baxter followed Cornell to the front door, which had a thick bunch of dried chili peppers hanging from the top. Baxter checked under a potted barrel cactus beside the door and found the key that Quint said she always kept there. Cornell wished people would find a less common hiding place for their keys. He opened the front door and went inside. He stood in the middle of the tiny living room and surveyed the contents. Nothing out of the ordinary, nothing out of place. Thayer was obviously a neat person.

"You head east I'll head west," Cornell instructed Baxter as they split up to investigate the rest of the house. Cornell was scanning the neat-as-a-pin kitchen when Baxter called out.

"I think we've found the crime scene," Baxter drawled as his partner joined him in the master bedroom. The covers had been

581

swept off the mattress, leaving just the sheet on which was a huge smear of blood.

"Yeah," Cornell agreed as he pulled out a handkerchief and lifted the bedroom phone receiver. He called into forensics to get a team out asap, then hung up and began exploring the bedroom very carefully after he snapped on his latex gloves; Baxter did the same. After fifteen minutes they heard a "Hello?" from the front door and Cornell called out, "Back here." He was surprised when Josie walked into the room.

"You finish up at Reid Park?" he asked.

She nodded. "The M.E. has the body now and I logged all the evidence. I was just about to head over to the Café Coyote for waffles when your call came in. Thanks a lot."

"You could have sent someone else."

"Not as good as me. Move away from the bed." One of her team came in and she said, "Hit the kitchen first and move your way into the living room and—" She looked at Cornell and asked, "Second bedroom?" He nodded. "—then the second bedroom and check out back for a shed. There's no garage or carport that I've seen." The man nodded and left the bedroom with Baxter trailing. Josie began taking out her camera and plastic evidence bags.

"What's the 'Josie' stand for?" Cornell asked.

She scowled at him. "What do you care?"

"Just curious. Josephine? Josette?"

"Drop it, copper," she said as she snapped several photos of the bed. She put a ruler next to the blood stain for perspective and snapped another.

"Josslyn? Joyce?"

She glared at him. "Joyce? I'd rather be dead." She examined the dresser and nightstand, then surprised him. "Jocasta. It's Greek. It means 'Shining Moon.' Jocasta was the Queen of Thebes. She married Oedipus, her own son. My dad emigrated from Greece before I was born and changed his surname from Roussopoulos to Ross. Middle name Andromeda."

"How'd you get the blonde hair?"

"Grandma was from Norway and Mom was from Germany. Happy?"

"Ecstatic. Overjoyed. Beguiled."

"Not a good adjective considering the recent past," she said as she knelt and looked under the bed. She pulled out a duffel bag and opened it. Inside were a few men's shirts and a pair of jeans. She looked up at Cornell in triumph, but her smile faded at the stern look on his face. "What?" she demanded.

"Will you go out with me? I know a great pizza place near the university."

"A pizza place? You want our first date to be at a pizza place? Class act, Cornell. I can't imagine why women aren't beating down your door."

"First date? Are you implying that there may be more?"

"Depends on how good the pizza is. By the way, I'm a vegetarian, and I don't kiss on a first date, certainly not someone reeking of sausage and garlic."

11:35 AM

When Alex opened his eyes, he couldn't see anything. Wherever he was, it was dark and, he sensed, small. Confining. He began touching, and thought that he felt silk, and something like his mother's velour kitty blanket. When he raised his hand it immediately banged into something hard. He moved his hand to the right, his fingertips encountering the same hardness close to both sides. And yet, he somehow knew that there was a pillow under his head.

And a weird plastic mask on his face. He used both hands to explore the mask over his nose and ran his fingers down the length of a tube until he felt something metallic and hard. A canister or something.

Second by second, he was panicking although he tried to meditate and tell himself that he was alive, and his parents would find him. They had to.

He didn't know what would happen if he took the mask off, so he left it on for the time being. With his right hand he felt around his side and touched a small metallic cylinder. He knew what it was—a flashlight. Light. He could have light. He grasped the flashlight and switched it on, bathing him and his surroundings in light. He whined in relief. For a second.

Then he realized where he was. He was in a coffin. And he knew—just knew—that he was buried underground. He was buried alive.

Calm. Calm. Remain calm, he told himself. He shone the light on the big cylinder and read the word "Oxygen" on the side. Whoever had put him here had given him some time yet to live. He wondered how long the tank would last.

He shone the light down the length of the coffin. Like his hands, his feet were unbound. Why wouldn't they be? He saw that he was still wearing his dojo uniform. He closed his eyes and concentrated. How had he gotten here? The last thing he remembered was being at the dojo with Bobby in a small room, where he had started to feel icky. Then, a sickeningly sweet smell over his mouth and nose, and then—here. Bobby did this? Why would Bobby do this—they liked one another.

He forced himself to relax and breathe, and he tried to "send" a message to his mother, as Mariko had sent to him. But Mariko hadn't directed her plea for help to anyone—he just somehow intercepted it. Still, he needed to try. After a few minutes he opened his eyes and hoped that his message had landed on someone. He stretched and felt something close to his left side. He aimed the flashlight to his side and turned partially over. He saw what had been touching his side.

Alex screamed and screamed in absolute panic until his throat was raw as he stared at the tiny skeleton nestled up against him.

For the first time, Deliverance's sons were together.

11:55 AM

Three feet above the entombed brothers Robert Massey—AKA Bobby, AKA Winston Mather Goodwin—threw the last shovelful of dirt on the shallow gravesite. He carried the shovel over to a pile of debris and hid it before he scampered over to his four-wheel-drive jeep, laughing maniacally, thrilled that he could affect such a devastating vengeance on the bitch that ruined his life. He'd thought about killing her, but sometimes living with grief was worse. And, losing two sons would be even more devastating. He wanted her to suffer.

Goodwin had no proof that Deliverance or her spic husband

and their fag friends had anything to do with his abduction and beating. The police had interviewed them when they returned from England, but they had solid alibis considering they were all up in Salem for the wedding. The queers had even stopped in Lynn for a snack on their way up to Salem, and their receipt proved that they were in that area when he was being snatched. The police suggested that it might have been an irate husband of one of the women with whom he'd been cheating. The case was still open, but the statute of limitations had run out both for assault (three years) and kidnapping (six years).

Even if the trashy little bitch hadn't been involved, he hated the fact that she had a wonderful life and his was deep in a cesspool. As it turned out his wife had been cheating with an associate and wound up kicking his cheating ass out and taking most of his assets. Then her father canned him and blackballed him. He couldn't get a job in Boston, and he'd had no luck with applications for other parts of the country except some bumfuck little town in South Dakota. He'd chew his own balls off before debasing himself by taking that job.

After a lot of drinking, disappointment, and failure, he needed to latch onto something that would bolster his spirits. Revenge. Payback. He'd started with his ex-wife, stealing a car and ramming it into her from behind late one night. He rammed her twice; she lost the baby she was carrying. He was ecstatic. He had a rock-solid alibi when the cops came—he was billeted in Danvers at a motel, hoping to visit the city's premiere law firm in hopes of a job. According to the desk clerk his car hadn't moved all evening. He'd snuck out, hotwired a car a mile away, and then abandoned it three miles away off the road in a forest and walked back to the motel; it would take time for someone to find the car, and it was unlikely that anyone would match it to his ex-wife's accident.

But it was Deliverance that he really wanted to hurt. She had had the nerve to think he'd ever consider supporting her bastard—he never thought of the kid as his—and even nervier was her low-class old man who banged on the family door and demanded satisfaction. He was the one who'd hired the thugs to work Blaskó over, not his own father. Even so, his father had been very disappointed in him for banging the witch chick, and old man Goodwin had severely cut his allowance. He'd barely managed any luxuries his last year of college, and the allowance for college only covered his tuition, room, and board at one of the lesser dorms at Harvard. He was humiliated when his father demanded that he pay half of his law school tuition, and he'd had to get a part-time job—*a fucking part-time job!*—to pay his bills.

He'd decided during his second year of Harvard Law School that he couldn't depend on his father's good will anymore, and he sure as hell wasn't going to sweat out a career climb from the bottom up. He made a list of eligible women at Harvard and homed in on a Beacon Hill beauty that had looks, brains, and—most importantly—money. He swept her off her feet, and by the time he graduated with a law degree they were engaged; they married that July. Goodwin took the bar and passed on the second try and joined her father's law firm at an outrageously wonderful starting salary.

Goodwin felt no compunction to be faithful to his wife, and the cheating started on the honeymoon. He was sure she suspected nothing, and he made sure to simulate romantic efforts that made her feel cherished. He had even called in an order for Valentine's Day flowers to be delivered while he was banging a pro in a discreet little hotel in downtown Boston.

And then came that day when his life changed forever. After drinking himself nearly blotto at a bar after work he was shoved into a dark alley from behind, gagged, bound, and blindfolded. Without warning there was a sharp jab in his neck, and that's all she wrote until he wound up dumped in some alley the next day, his arm, leg and five ribs broken, and black and blue marks all over his body. In the hospital the doctor said it looked like someone had worked him over with a baseball bat. He recovered from his wounds even as then police made no progress. Even today he got an occasional leg twinge when he walked, a reminder of that day.

He tried to reclaim his former life, and his wife did stick by him even as she did double duty at the law firm in her role as a junior associate. Still, gradually, he could feel her pulling away, and he went back to his bad habits. They cost him a wife, a job, a home, and any decent prospects for the future. He had gone to a psychiatrist several times after his marriage and career crashed and burned, but he quit the therapy after the doctor offered the opinion that he was a sociopath. His parting gift to the quack was four slashed tires. He was questioned by the cops but convinced them that he was innocent of the crime. People were so stupid.

Deliverance. He flew out to Tucson and began observing her and her family and friends as he tried to formulate a plan in his mind. He needed to know more about the intimate details of her life, so he surreptitiously initiated a romantic relationship with one of the Union Jack investigators, Thayer Burton. That was easy as he began to frequent the bar where she'd blow off steam on Friday nights. She was garrulous, and he learned a great deal. When she said she was from Jaffrey, he pretended amazement and said that he was from Concord and was just out on legal business for a client. He was a lawyer, you see. He made sure that she was impressed with him, and when she mentioned visiting him back home the next time he visited, he was thrilled. Of course, that meant finding out her travel plans a day or two before her flight so that he could beat her there and be ready "at home" to greet her ("home" being a cheap apartment that rented by the week; he had an arrangement with the landlord to have it available whenever he needed it by paying double.). That took a toll on his stamina and wallet (which he had filled with the money from pawning his mother's high-end jewelry; he had perfected breaking and entering as a kid with his equally snotty, entitled buddies and sneaking into his parents' home one night while they were at the opera was a no-brainer). Still, it was worth it. The endgame was worth it.

He had learned that the miserable little Dane-Quintana kids took karate lessons at the Moon Dojo. He had been practicing martial arts for most of his life, and knew that was a way in. He offered his services to Moon Choong-Hoon a few months ago at a reduced rate. He said he was in Tucson for a few months and wanted to practice and teach his skills before he moved on. Moon was thrilled to get him at a low salary and made peace with the fact that he was only present on some Saturdays. Goodwin made sure that neither Deliverance nor her husband ever met him. He was careful but had had a few close calls.

He decided to put his final plan into action on that very special day, the anniversary of the date that the bitch had birthed his dead son. He had felt nothing about the child or its death; the kid wasn't real to him. Alex Dane-Quintana, however, was very real, and would be the linchpin of his final vengeance. So, he created a timeline and actioned it, stealing the coffin from the Merciful Savior Funeral Home and absconding with it in his hot-wired stolen station wagon. He couldn't help himself—he pretended to be a tourist at their friends' wedding at that mission. He laughed when he thought of that excursion, and he was immensely self-satisfied that still no one had any idea that he was the British psychopath's very temporary buddy in the abduction of Raine Sinclair.

And then he scheduled a special romantic evening on June 28th for Thayer. She had finished packing her things for the move back to New Hampshire. He cooked and served a delectable meal by candlelight, then took her to bed and performed, oh, exceptionally well. As she basked in the afterglow of sex, he reached under his pillow, withdrew a butcher knife, and slammed it into her chest. She died with a gasp. He proceeded to beat the hell out of her face before the blood could settle. He slipped out of bed, dressed, took out her driver's license and stuffed it in her jeans pocket after he dressed her corpse. Somewhere around 2 AM he stuffed her in the back of the jeep, drove her to the park, and bound her to a tree. He wanted them to find her. He wanted them to identify her immediately.

He wanted Deliverance to suffer a double dose of guilt and pain.

And now it was time to inflict even more pain and terror.

He gunned his jeep and barreled down the road by which he came.

Judgment day.

CHAPTER NINETEEN

June 29, 1985
Retaliation Day: Afternoon/Evening
1:36 PM

Deliverance was sitting at the kitchen table, idly sipping a Coke while her husband, partners, Cornell, and the phone-trace tech waited anxiously for the phone to ring. Cornell asked her why she thought that Goodwin would call at that time. She told him that she had given birth to David at 1:36 PM on June 29, 1971. If what they suspected was true about his identity and actions, that would be the perfect time to call.

Cornell thought that Deliverance seemed preternaturally calm, and that worried him. It worried him because her natural way of dealing with tortuous matters was to be aggressive, noisy, and on top of her game with wit and resilience. This version of Deliverance made him nervous.

At precisely 1:36 PM the phone rang, startling everyone even though the call was anticipated.

Cornell held up a hand and said, "Remember—keep him on the line as long as you can. Don't say anything to upset him or he might hang up before we can pinpoint him." The trace man turned on the recorder and monitored the trace progress.

"I'm not a fucking moron, Cornell," Deliverance snapped as she smashed her finger into the speaker button and said, "Hello?"

"Hey, Sweet Pea? How's my adorable little witch?" She recognized the voice right away while the others recognized the Boston accent.

"Cut to the chase, Winnie. What's your endgame?" Deliverance said in a frigid tone.

"Aren't you going to ask how your innocent little boy is?"

"How's my innocent little boy?"

"Experiencing a tad of claustrophobia, I dare say."

Quint wrote down a few words and showed it to his wife. *Maybe in a closet? He used the present tense not the past tense—Alex is alive.*

"He doesn't like being kept in a closet," she said.

"Ding-dong—so wrong. Try again." After a few seconds of silence, he went on. "Where else could he be claustrophobic? C'mon, bitch—think hard."

"A car trunk?" she said coolly.

"Really?" Goodwin said in disappointment. "I thought you were smarter than that. Of course, it wasn't your brain I was interested in."

"Get to the endgame, Winnie. Where's my son, and what's it going to take to get him back?"

"What makes you think you're ever going to get him back? And, oh, what I want we'll get to. No more location guesses?"

"No more games. Make your point." Even as she struggled to keep her voice ice cold a bare hint of desperation began to seep in. The trace guy made the stretch-it-out motion with his hands.

"Tucson Police Department Case 0502-850313." He hung up.

The trace guy shook his head.

"Do you know that case?" Quint asked Cornell.

"No, but I will," Cornell said as he headed into the den to use the other line, muttering about how the hell did Goodwin know the case number?

"He'll call back," Victor said.

"I know," Deliverance said. Her hand shook slightly as she finished her drink. She wished she could have put a little rum in it. A lot of rum.

"Querida," Quint said gently, "we're gonna get through this. All of us." He was curious about the case number; as an ex-cop he knew the codes for various crimes, and 0502 was the code for Burglary/Unlawful Entry/No Force. He tried to force back the icy tendrils creeping their way up his spine. "Wilde—would you please check on Tucker and the kids?"

"Sure," Wilde said as he bounced off his chair and left by the sliding patio doors. He could hear the kids yelling in the casita, including his own nephews. He was sure they were safe since both Tucker and Rafe were with them. The rest of the team was at the office voluntarily to see what they could find out about Thayer's life and relationship with Goodwin, AKA Massey. Fox was communicating with the Salem cops about the cemetery desecration, and they were coordinating with the Boston cops about Goodwin's life. Iris was handling the FBI's involvement.

Quint stared hard at the phone as his stomach churned in knots of fear about his son. Deliverance was his heart; the kids were his soul. He looked up at Cornell's appearance.

"You find out something about that case?" Quint asked.

Cornell's face was drawn and ashen. "I did," he said quietly. "Look, this is going to upset you, but you have to focus on—"

"What the flying fuck is case 0502-850313?" Deliverance demanded. "Just tell us."

Cornell nodded. Maybe it didn't mean what he thought it meant. No, that would be lying to himself. "Okay, here it is. The case was opened on June 3rd by the patrol officers that responded to the call. Mike Beckham and, sadly, Swansey. They were called to the Merciful Savior Funeral Home off Broadway." He hesitated as all eyes riveted on his face. He swallowed then told them. "Someone broke in overnight and ... stole one of their coffins. That doesn't mean—"

"Connard," Victor whispered harshly. The motherfucker had put the little boy in a coffin.

Deliverance was frozen to her seat, her eyes unfocused. She didn't say a word as Quint grasped her shoulders and kissed the top of her head. He didn't say a word either, but Victor had a frightening premonition of visiting him in prison where he'd be serving a life sentence for murder.

"He buried him," Deliverance said flatly. "He buried him with his brother."

"We don't know that for sure," Cornell said.

"Yeah, we do," Quint replied evenly just as the phone rang. The trace guy was poised and ready. Deliverance let it ring four times before she opened the line.

"My son is dead," she said evenly.

"Well, one is. The other one—not necessarily. Are you willing to spin the roulette wheel?"

"No."

"What?" The surprise at the other end of the line was genuine.

"You buried him alive. If he wasn't dead when you put the

coffin in the ground, then he was shortly after the first few shovelfuls of dirt. I'm not stupid enough to think for one minute that you'll let him live or tell me where he is. Your plan is to hurt me and giving me back my son wouldn't accomplish that."

They could all hear the smirk in his voice. "Unless he was buried with an oxygen tank that would give him a chance at breathing for a bit. Maybe a flashlight so he could see his big brother."

"You are one sick fuck," she said coldly.

"So, do you want to take a chance on rescuing your last son? Tick, tock. Tick, tock."

Quint was immediately on edge at the strange look on his wife's face. He narrowed his eyes and clenched his hands.

"You're mistaken," she said in an oddly casual tone.

"And why's that, little witch?"

"Because Alex isn't my last son. You blew it, you piece of shit. I've *got* another son … in my womb. So, count your life out in minutes, not days. Because we're coming for you, and mercy isn't on the menu." She hit the speaker button and ended the call. She met her husband's shocked eyes.

"Did I mention that I had a surprise for you?" she said. "Surprise!"

2:36 PM

Iris and Liberty were working the kidnapping on the down low since the situation hadn't been released to the media. Baxter was working with them and he had arranged for a precautionary patrol car to hover around the homes of the Begays and the Dillingers, and two cars to circle the Union Jack partners' homes.

Iris had mercilessly browbeat every employee at the dojo while Liberty interrogated Moon Choong-Hoon until he broke down and cried. Neither FBI agent was touched by the discomfort they were causing; a child's life was at stake. They finally let everyone go at 2:30 PM and left for the FBI office to file their reports.

"Figures that the prick would give Moon a phony address," Liberty said as she smoothly swerved around a stalled car. They were driving back from the address on "Massey's" employee documents—the address didn't exist. "Doesn't leave us much to go on to find his real hidey hole."

"What was the name of that bar that Quint said Thayer hung out at?" Iris asked.

"Um … it's in my notes."

Iris unlatched Liberty's briefcase and pulled out her notebook. She flipped through the spiral pages until she spied what she needed. "Cute. The New England Nugget. Explains why she felt drawn to it." Iris picked up Thayer's driver's license and shook her head. "Wish we had a photo of the perp."

"Hopefully the bartender will recognize her. We have a description of Goodwin, and fingers crossed that someone will recognize him." Liberty turned into the parking lot of the bar. "Nice place. The façade's got that east-coast ocean look."

The women got out of the car and headed to the door.

3:13 PM

Winston Mather Goodwin was so far beyond seething that he could barely focus his eyes as he drove his stolen car up Craycroft.

I don't care. I'll get that bitch. Time for her to die. Time for all of them to die.

He chanted those words to himself nonstop. He suddenly jammed on his brakes, then squealed right into a Shell gas station.

He was inside for five minutes before he came out carrying his weapon of vengeance. For a total of $15 he was going to rock their world, and probably end his, but he didn't give a shit—he was obsessed.

Bitch, bitch, bitch, bitch, bitch, bitch, BITCH!

5:34 PM

Quint opened the door to see Phaedra standing there. She was usually glowing when she was pregnant, but today she seemed antsy and stressed.

"Phaedra, hi," Quint said. "Um, unless this is an emergency it's not really a good time. But, come in for a minute." As she entered he glanced at her parked car and saw that she'd come alone. He'd barely closed the door when she addressed him in a hesitant voice.

"Quint, is something going on here?"

"Why?" he replied tersely.

"All right, this is going to sound weird, but here goes. Cress called me from Hawaii and said that he was getting unsettling feelings."

Quint tensed. "About what?" He saw Wilde come out of the kitchen and stand under the arch, watching.

"He couldn't define it, but he got a sense that, well … one of your kids was in trouble. Is everything all right?"

Quint met Wilde's eyes and his friend nodded slightly.

"Okay, Phaedra. This is strictly confidential. We've got a situation here. Alex has been kidnapped."

"What?" she exclaimed. "Oh, dear God. When did this happen?"

"Early this morning. The cops and FBI are working it."

"Do you know who the kidnapper is?"

"We do. Let's just say it's a ghost from the past. Look—what exactly did Cress say?"

"He said that it felt like something was poking his brain. He said that he got the sense of a closed space and it reminded him of the time he was locked in the cabin cellar. He said he felt words."

"Felt words?"

"He couldn't explain it, but this … prodding was saying 'aidez moi, aidez moi.' That's French for 'help me.' He said that at times it was almost as though someone was in the room with him talking."

"Alex," Wilde stated unequivocally.

"Phaedra, did Cress say anything else?" Quint asked urgently.

"No, that was it. He just got a sense of … doom. He said he felt that way when he was facing death in the cellar. Does this help?"

"Maybe," Quint said. "Look, please don't tell anyone about this except Moon Wolf. I'll call you if we need anything else. Thank you for bringing this to me."

"Of course. God, how's Deliverance holding up?"

"Not great, but we're coping." Quint opened the front door and Phaedra left after hugging him and kissing his cheek. He closed the door. He and Wilde stared at one another.

"Why Cress?" Quint asked. "If Alex was trying to reach out to someone, why Cress?"

"Mariko said she wasn't even thinking about Alex when she was being held hostage. He just sorta ... intercepted it."

"So why would Cress 'intercept' a cry for help from Alex?"

Wilde looked thoughtful. Just then, Victor came into the living room. Wilde said, "Maybe because there was some link that we can't fathom at the moment." He updated Victor on Phaedra's visit.

"C'est étrange," Victor said. "You know, I've been thinking about that whole experience with Mariko."

"Come to any conclusions?" Wilde asked.

"Velcro versus teflon."

"Huh?"

"I think," Victor began slowly, "that Alex and people like him routinely transmit unconscious mind messages that either stick to someone else's mind or senses—like velcro—or slip away before they're recognized—teflon. Cress got the velcro stick this time. We just have to figure out why and what it means."

All three men were silent as they thought and looked at one another. After a minute or so a dawning look passed over Wilde's face.

"Phaedra said Cress had a sensation of a closed space like in the cabin," Wilde said.

"And we know that Alex is confined to a coffin. Besides the obvious claustrophobia, what's the commonality?" Victor said.

Another moment of silence, then Quint said softly. "Location."

"Location?" Victor said.

"The fucking cabin," Wilde shot out in realization. "The son of a bitch buried him at the cabin."

Wilde had barely gotten out the last word before Quint was dialing a familiar number.

5:52 PM

"How long can someone survive on an oxygen tank?" Quint shouted over the noise of the helicopter blades.

"Depends on the size and cylinder structure of the tank," Dr. Dennis Scribner said loudly so his airborne contact could hear him, "and whether it's set up for a continuous flow or a pulse flow. The pulse flow lasts longer. For example, a D Cylinder is about 16.5 inches tall and around four and half inches in diameter. With a flow rate of, say, three, a D can last 2.3 hours with a continuous flow and seven hours with a pulse flow."

"What's the difference?"

"There's a conservation device attached to pulse flow canisters. An electronic circuit opens an electrical valve and meters a precise dose of oxygen. Unlike continuous flow, pulse flow issues oxygen only upon inhalation instead of constantly. But let me be clear—there are several types of cylinders besides the D—the E, the C, the M4, the M6, and the M9."

"Which has the shortest life?"

"The M4 Cylinder. At flow rate three the pulse flow can last less than two hours. If a continuous flow is issued, that drops down to about thirty-six minutes."

"Jesus," Quint breathed. "Any other factors that might impact the duration of the oxygen flow?"

"Of course. The age and size of the user, the health of the lungs, a lot of things. I mean, if there wasn't a lung issue a person probably wouldn't need an oxygen tank."

"Okay. Thank you, doctor. We'll call back if we need any more info." Gray had recommended Scribner as a contact from his association with him in the hospital where he'd recovered from his attempted murder. He'd called Scribner and Josh Wyllys had linked him into his chopper communication, and the good doctor proved to be helpful and patient. Quint hoped that his supposition that Goodwin might have given Alex an oxygen tank was on the mark. It made sense—he'd want to keep Alex alive for a while in case he needed leverage. Quint also knew that his wife's statement about Goodwin never giving away the location or ever having any intention of letting the child live was dead on.

"Good luck," Dr. Scribner said just before Quint signed off.

Quint waved towards the encroaching horizon. "Can't you fly this thing any faster, Josh?"

"It's a helicopter, Quint, not Apollo 13. I'm going as fast as I can." Josh glanced over at his irate passenger. "This is a freebie, by the way. No charge. At this point I kinda feel like I'm one of the family."

"We'll finalize our firm's funding for you when we get back and this all dies down." Quint clasped a strong hand on Josh's shoulder and nodded. He looked over his shoulder at the back seat where Wilde and Cornell were scrunched in. The intensity on their faces bespoke of men on a mission, but Wilde looked as though he might shatter at the least provocation. Quint suddenly realized that Wilde was his goddamn best friend and the brother he'd never had.

A headwind had kicked up, but Josh kept his speed as he occasionally dipped close to the land and swerved around trees and rock cliffs. He knew the way; he had flown Iris and Constantine to the same location to rescue Raine. He hoped to hell that this would be another rescue and not a body recovery. A kid. Jeez. He'd met Alex at Iris's homecoming from the hospital and thought he was smart and nice. *Please let this be a rescue*, he thought desperately.

Quint leaned forward and scanned the landscape as it rushed past down below. Finally, he saw the end of FR 10, the point at which the path to what had been the cabin began. He got his colleagues' attention from the back seat and pointed.

Josh's chopper kicked up dust and debris as he landed it at the edge of the road. The blades hadn't stopped whirring when Quint, Wilde, and Cornell jumped out and began running down the rough, overgrown path towards the cabin that the Union Jackers had demolished after Iris's rescue. Cornell tripped and fell into a patch of three-leafed green plants, scraping his hands. He scrambled up and wheezed to catch up. He came to an opening in the trees and saw the shards of lumber and other home components scattered across the home plot. Quint had hired a crew to remove as much debris as possible, and only a few pieces were left.

"Spread out," Quint yelled as he began searching for any signs of disturbed earth that would signal a grave. Wilde checked out what had been the interior of the cabin and shoved away some remaining boards that had covered the root cellar where Cress had been held captive. He knelt and checked the cellar area, which was partially caved in and clearly held no coffin or anything else except a mother squirrel and her three babies. He thought he saw something and moved a few pieces of wood, uncovering a shovel.

"Quint," Wilde yelled. "C'mere."

Quint rushed over and Wilde showed him the shovel which had fresh clumps of dirt clinging to the spade.

"He's here. He's here somewhere," Quint said desperately as he and Wilde began scanning the immediate area, seeing nothing.

Cornell scoured the area east of the cabin but found nothing. He circled the area when suddenly his foot pushed a little into the ground. He stared down, then backed off. The ground was harder. He dropped to his knees and began clawing at the softer ground. It became clear that the soil was significantly looser.

"Over here," he screamed and a few seconds later Wilde, Quint, and the newly arrived Josh clustered around him. "I think something's buried here."

Wilde was holding the shovel, which Quint ripped out of his hands and began frantically digging. Wilde, Cornell, and Josh were on their knees ripping their hands into the earth and clawing away as much dirt as they could.

Suddenly, down about twelve inches, Quint hit something hard. Wilde leaned down and pulled as much dirt as he could away until a shiny stainless-steel, brushed-blue surface was visible.

"Steel," Cornell said breathlessly. "That's the type of coffin that he stole. Keep digging!"

"No shit, Sherlock," Wilde muttered as he dragged his hands through the dirt, inch by inch exposing the top of the coffin.

The four men worked relentlessly until finally the entire top of the steel coffin was visible.

6:17 PM

A weak pulse of oxygen invigorated Alex's lungs. For the last few minutes he could feel that the strength of the pulse was weaker. The oxygen was running out. He felt dizzy; his eyes kept blinking, and his mind began to wander. He'd used the flashlight sparingly, but even so the battery seemed to be wearing down and he knew that soon both it and he would expire.

He scrunched up his sweaty face and thought very hard,

trying to send out "I love you" messages to his parents. He prayed that they would get to Mommy and Daddy.

He shrugged his left arm and cuddled the skeleton next to him. Somehow, he knew this was his brother. At least they could spend eternity together. He wouldn't be lonely.

He tried to flick on the flashlight. The dim light flickered, then went out completely.

He breathed in one last pulse of oxygen, then closed his eyes and smiled slightly.

It was time to go to sleep.

He took his last breath.

6:19 PM

"There must be some kind of lock on it," Wilde fretted, as he searched for a way to open the coffin.

"There," Cornell pointed. "That looks like a lock."

Quint whipped out a hunting knife from his belt holster and began yelling Alex's name and trying to pry open the lock. It wouldn't budge.

"Bugger that," Wilde exclaimed and shoved Quint away from the coffin. He whipped out his gun, said a silent prayer, and shot at the lock repeatedly. The lock separated and dangled, and Quint and Wilde dropped down next to one another and pulled and pulled at the coffin lid.

It seemed like an hour, but it was less than a minute before the lid popped open and Quint gasped at the sight of his son lying in the coffin, his eyes closed, his arm around David's skeleton. He picked Alex up and whirled around, laying him in the rough dirt.

"C'mon, Scamp, c'mon," he repeated as he searched for a pulse in the unresponsive child. Without another word he began CPR, all the while saying "C'mon, c'mon, c'mon." He tried and tried but got no response. He kept going.

Wilde was standing over the man and child, tears streaming down his face. He met Cornell's equally wet eyes and shook his head.

Quint was sobbing by the time he sat back on his legs.

And then Alex coughed.

"Open your eyes, Alejandro," his father said gently but firmly.

Alex's eyes blinked open and shut, then focused on Quint's face. He smiled.

"Daddy. I knew you'd come for me," Alex choked. Quint took the canteen from Wilde and poured water down Alex's throat. It felt so good. Wilde pulled out his handkerchief, wet it, and washed Alex's clammy face. The faint sent of urine hit his nostrils and he knew that the boy had peed himself at least once.

"Oh, God," Quint breathed as he swept his son up in his arms and yelled at Josh, "Get me to the hospital." He began running down the path with his son clasped tightly in his arms, Wilde and Josh on his heels.

"I'll stay here," Cornell called after them. "Send a team." He frowned and began scratching his arm. He closed his eyes and groaned—poison ivy. He hoped Josie liked spotted men.

Josh pushed his chopper as hard as he could. Wilde was riding shotgun and Quint was in the back seat cuddling and murmuring to his son. Josh called into the hanger where he kept his chopper and gave them Deliverance's phone number and to call and tell her they got Alex and were headed to the Sisters of Mercy Hospital.

People scattered in a wave as Josh landed his bird in front of the hospital. A police car was parked there, and the two uniforms flew out of their car and held back until the bird was on solid ground. Quint scrambled out of the chopper and caught a movement out of the corner of his eye—Deliverance and Victor were bolting out of her car and running towards them at breakneck speed. Deliverance cried out and her husband waited precious seconds for her to catch up. She ripped Alex out of his father's arms and crushed him to her body, crying and crooning as she held her living son. She, Quint, Wilde, and the two cops barged into the ER and it looked like the staff knew they were coming. Two doctors and three nurses surrounded them, and one doctor took Alex from his mother's arms and placed him gently on a gurney as they headed to an examining room. The cops remained in the hall as the medical staff examined Alex under the unrelenting gaze of his parents and uncles, who refused to leave.

One of the doctors was Dennis Scribner, who was gentle and soothing to the child who had just gone through hours of trauma. Scribner performed standard checkups on the boy, then said they wanted to x-ray him to make sure there were no broken bones. He ordered a neurological doctor to check out the boy for any residual effects of whatever had been used to render him unconscious (Scribner suspected it was chloroform). Then, he told Alex's parents, the nurses would bathe him and check him into a room where they could be with him as long as they liked. They rolled Alex out of the room as Deliverance and Quint clutched one another tightly and finally breathed a sigh of relief.

Deliverance sobbed in her husband's arms for long moments before she sniffled and stopped and looked up at him.

"Oh God, he was alive when you found him. It's a miracle," she whispered. She noticed Quint's over-her-head look at their partners. "What?"

Quint cupped her chin and met her eyes. "Honey, Alex wasn't breathing when we got the coffin open. I did CPR and he finally came back. But—it *was* a miracle."

"I can vouch for that," Wilde agreed. "And he was able to focus and speak to us. I think he'll be fine, physically. But he's going to need therapy."

Deliverance nodded. "I'll call Raine's therapist tomorrow." She paused, then asked hesitatingly, "David?"

Quint kissed her forehead. "He was there. When we opened the lid, Alex was cradling his brother in his arms."

"That's my boy," Deliverance said in awe and satisfaction. "My boys."

Quint grinned and rubbed her stomach. "And number three. Thought of any names yet?"

"Yup. I'll let you know when we're home." She broke into a wide, bright smile. "My birthday night in Tahiti proved quite fruitful. Quint, I want all of our boys together."

"David will stay with us forever, Witchy Woman. I promise." He'd once sworn to her that if David had lived and been with her when they came together he'd've raised the boy as his own. He meant it.

The four Union Jackers waited impatiently for a half hour before Dr. Scribner returned and found himself surrounded. He felt like a deer being sized up as a protein feast by hungry wolves. He figured that his audience would appreciate the bottom line.

"No broken bones and absolutely no evidence of sexual assault. He's got a few bruises but nothing extensive. He's severely dehydrated and we've got him on an IV for vitamins and fluids. I want to keep him overnight for observation, but I see no reason you can't take him home in the morning. You've got a tough kid, there."

"We know," Quint said as he shook the doctor's hand.

"I'll spend the night with him," Deliverance said. She saw that Quint was about to protest—he would want to stay, too—but she shut him down. "I'll be fine and there'll be cops with me. You rescued him. This is my job. Your job is to find that cocksucker and bring him to justice." She ducked her head and said to Scribner, "Sorry for the vulgarity."

"Anyone who can bury a child alive deserves all the vulgarity you can heap on his head," Scribner said. "Now, if you'll excuse me, I'm going verify that the tests are done and get him into a room. I'll be back shortly to bring you there." Scribner left and went straight back through the doors from which he'd come."

Deliverance looked up at her husband and issued a single command. "Go."

Quint kissed her and stroked her cheek, then turned to leave. Suddenly Deliverance grabbed his arm and tiptoed up to him, and whispered in his ear, "Wyatt Francisco Nicolae." He grinned at her and kissed her again.

Wilde and Victor followed him after tight hugs with the woman they both loved, respected, and—on occasion—feared. She watched them go, hugging herself tightly as she waited to see her son.

7:49 PM

"They're sleeping," Rafe said to Tucker. "It's early, but they're probably exhausted. Even Beckett dropped off and seems intent on doing a buzz saw imitation." He grinned. "I don't know how you do it, taking care of the three ragamuffins."

"Four," Tucker corrected. "And sometimes five or six depending on how desperate Wilde and Victor are. Doesn't matter—I love 'em all. Hey—Quint called while you were checking the kids. The doctor said that Alex is going to be all right. Deliverance is going to spend the night at the hospital with him, and the guys are going to the office and regroup. He said we should take the kids to the main house and stay there with them. He's going to send Shayne over to back us up."

"Where's Cornell?"

"Still at the burial site. A sheriff's deputy is there along with two uniforms that Josh flew back. A forensics unit is on its way up by the Catalina Highway." Tucker shivered. "Deliverance's son's bones are still in the coffin. Jeez. What a douchebag."

"I guess that means we need to wake the kiddikins up and herd them over."

"I guess so. I'll go drag them out of the land of nod." With that Tucker walked to the large room addition that he and Iris had made their master bedroom.

Rafe looked around the living room and thought that his security teammate had a sweet deal. A great job, employers—no, friends—that loved him, a hot-as-hell FBI agent for a wife, a marvelous home, and an infinite future. Rafe wanted all those things, and maybe with his new position he'd have them someday. The painful divorce was a faded memory, and he was ready to take a chance on life again.

There was a gentle knock at the door. Rafe took his gun out of its holster and flipped off the safety. He checked the peephole and brushed aside the see-through curtain on the window beside the door. The sun had set twenty minutes earlier, but the moon was nearly full, and the porchlight was dim but still illuminating enough to see the person on the doorstep. He relaxed and reholstered his gun. He turned off the alarm and opened the door.

The uniformed officer touched the brim of his hat. "Mr. ...?"

"Spencer. Everything okay, officer?"

"Yes, sir. I was just making my rounds. I haven't heard from the station yet about a timeframe for the return of the Quintanas. I checked their house and it appears deserted."

"They're at the hospital with their son." Rafe frowned at the odd look on the cop's face. "Didn't your people tell you that Alex was rescued?" It was a split second later as the officer responded that Rafe noticed a few drops of what appeared to be blood on his pants leg.

"Apparently not," Winston Mather Goodwin said casually

as he whipped the gun out his holster and shot Rafe point-blank in the stomach. Rafe flew backwards, falling over the coffee table and hitting the floor groaning. Goodwin bent down and retrieved Rafe's gun, stuck it in the back of his belt, and aimed again.

Tucker rushed into the room and took in the sight and froze for a second; his gun was on the kitchen counter. He faced the man grinning evilly at him and knew that this was the psycho that had kidnapped Alex. He whirled around as fast as he could to head back to the bedroom just as Storm was coming down the hall. Beckett was in the doorway with a shocked look on his face. It felt like he was hit by a sledgehammer as the bullet tore through his back shoulder and he crashed down onto Storm.

"Run, Storm," Tucker screamed. The little girl hesitated before scrambling up and torpedoing towards the bedroom where Beckett pulled her back inside. Goodwin stepped over Tucker's prone body and reached the door just as it was slammed and locked. He let out a primal howl and put four bullets through the door.

Goodwin turned around with a snarl and saw that Tucker was trying to crawl towards the living room. He strode past the injured man and slammed the butt of his gun down on the back of Tucker's head, knocking him out. He deliberately stepped on Tucker's fallen eyeglasses as he rushed to the living room and found Rafe trying to crawl to the phone. He kicked him away savagely, then pulled out a bandana from his back pocket and bound Rafe's hands behind his back.

Goodwin opened the front door and took a quick look around. The moon was almost full and bright, but the area was still dark since there were few houses in the neighborhood. He smiled, then bent down and picked up two five-gallon cans of Shell gasoline.

"Push," Beckett growled. He, his brother, and the Dane-Quintana girls were moving the king-sized bed across the floor so they could barricade themselves against the maniac's entrance. "Now that," he ordered, pointing at the four-drawer dresser. He and Bechet each grabbed one side of the top edge and groaned and pulled and pushed until it was shoved up against the bed. One person could never crash his way in. Beckett had turned off the bedroom light and the room was dark, but objects were still visible. "Aislinn," he snapped.

"Get as close as you can to the door and listen for any sounds. Storm—move to the window carefully and see whatever you can out there. Don't get directly in front of the damn thing. Bechet—search the dresser drawers and closet for weapons."

"What do you want me to do?" Vikki asked in a tiny, tremulous voice.

Beckett squatted down and smoothed her hair. "I want you to crawl under the bed and be very, very still. Can you do that, ma douce fille?" She nodded vigorously and scampered under the bed.

Storm was at the window, edging her line of vision to the outside. She could make out distant lights near the Catalinas and the sprawling desert. She whispered, "I don't see anyone."

Aislinn whispered back. "I don't hear anyone. Wait—there's groaning. I think it's Tucker. Why does that policeman want to hurt us?" she asked plaintively.

"He ain't no policemen," Bechet said. "I bet he's the bad guy."

"Thank you, Einstein," his brother snarled. Beckett was sweating. He was almost a man and now these kids were his responsibility. "Did you find any guns or knives?" Bechet shook his head. "Swell. Okay. Here's what we're gonna do. We go out the window and run for our house."

"Not ours?" Storm asked.

"That's the first place he'd look. Maybe … look—I'm going to our house. Plenty of guns there and I'll call the cops—the real cops."

"I wonder what happened to our real cop?" Storm said quietly, thinking that the patrol officer was probably dead.

"Dead," Beckett replied without hesitation. "And we'll be, too, unless you go with my plan. While I'm going to the house you four head to the north and east edges of the property and find a house with lights. Bechet—you're in charge."

"Why is he in charge?" Storm said angrily.

"Because I'm a boy," Bechet said haughtily.

"As Mommy would say, piss on that."

"Both of you shut up and do as you're told. No talking—*quiet*." Beckett moved carefully to the window and looked outside at every angle he could. The creep could be waiting out there for them with his gun, but they had to chance it. He unlatched the window as quietly as possible and pushed it up extremely slowly. The fucker had a screen in front of it, just like his room. He swore silently, paused, and listened for any sounds. Just the usual night sounds, owls hooting, coyotes screaming, small desert creatures rustling through the underbrush, a plane or two high in the sky. There was no way he could loosen the screen without making noise, but they had to go.

Beckett took a deep breath and began loosening the screen. He stopped, listened, then continued as the kids clustered around him. He looked down then said, "Where's Vikki?"

"Still under the bed," Aislinn whispered. "Should I get her out?"

"Duh," Bechet said.

Aislinn dropped down to the floor and grabbed her younger sister's arms and dragged her out while Beckett continued working the screen. He managed to get the bottom and side locks undone so they could slide out. He very carefully pushed the bottom of the screen outward and stuck his head through, swiveling it around to check for "the bad guy." Nothing. He was about to crawl outside when Storm patted him hard on the back.

"What?" he whispered fiercely.

"I just remembered—Iris keeps a .22 in a lockbox in the bedroom. Don't know why I didn't find it."

"It's under the bed," Vikki said.

"Why didn't you say something, dork?" Storm griped. "Argh."

"'Cause Beckett told *you* to search." She hadn't finished her haughty explanation before Storm threw herself under the bed and seconds later came out with the lockbox that was just barely hidden after the bed had been moved.

"It's locked," Aislinn said.

"That's why they call it a friggin' lockbox," Storm hissed.

"And of course, we have no idea where the key is," Beckett said.

Storm pulled a bobby pin out of her hair and chewed off the plastic at the end. She began jimmying the lock, and ten seconds later the lock sprang open and there it was, a .22 revolver with a box of ammo.

"Where'd you learn to do that?" Aislinn said.

"I have no idea," Storm replied, handing the gun to Beckett who was taught to shoot by his uncle.

Beckett checked the cylinder and flipped off the external safety. He stuck the gun in his belt and nodded towards the window. The pack of frightened but determined children clustered around the window. Beckett began to crawl out swiftly and dropped to the ground. He crouched and scanned the perimeter. He saw no one. He stood up and pulled Aislinn out of the window, and then Vikki, who was clutching JuJu in her arms. "Go, go," he said urgently, and the sisters linked hands and began running off into the night.

He'd turned back to pull Storm out when out of nowhere someone wrapped their arms around his waist and brutally threw him to the ground. Goodwin stood over him with gun pointed. Beckett couldn't quite see his face, but he sensed that the maniac was smirking. Suddenly Storm's voice split the night.

"Hey, shitbag—why don't you pick on someone your own size?"

Goodwin whirled around and stared at the young face at the window. The kid was giving him the finger and he made an instinctive move towards her.

The diversion gave Beckett the chance to pull the .22 from his waist and get off a shaky, wild shot. Goodwin yelped as the bullet grazed his shoulder and he turned on Beckett savagely, but the teenager let off a couple more wild shots that missed but scared the man enough to send him running back around the house.

"C'mon, c'mon," Beckett yelled as he pulled Storm out the window and then Bechet. "Go, go," he screamed at them and Bechet grabbed Storm's hand and began pulling her off to the east. Beckett scrambled to his feet and tore off towards his own house a short distance away. He threw one look back over his shoulder but just kept pounding his way to home. He practically crashed through the rear sliders and searched frantically for the usual hidden key. He half expected a bullet to enter the back of his skull, but he made it into the house, locked the sliders, and with badly trembling hands dialed 9-1-1.

Goodwin was infuriated that the goddamn nigger kid had shot him and kept shooting. He was so taken by surprise by that point that he'd fled to the safety of the house. He wouldn't have the satisfaction of barbecuing the kids, but he could burn down the casita and the two injured friends of the rotten bitch, then burn down the Dane-Quintana house. He'd live another day to withdraw and regroup, then make a new plan and someday he would kill the bitch and her whelps.

He cast a glance over at Rafe, who was lying motionless, his hands still behind his back. He looked down the hallway where the so-called nanny was lying just as still, obviously unconscious. He thought about putting another bullet in each of them but decided that burning them alive would be much more … fun. And, the autopsy results would devastate the bitch. "Yeah," he laughed, "you two macho men are going to be turned into briquets. Wish you were awake to enjoy the burn but I'll take a win any way I can get it."

He dragged one of the gas cans over to the kitchen and began sloshing the toxic fuel over the counters and floor. He froze and looked at the end of the sink counter—the gun that had been resting there was gone. He dropped the can and stared down at Rafe, who was still motionless. He heard a noise and whirled around. He found himself staring at Tucker, who was covered with blood from his scalp wound and shoulder wound. Tucker was leaning against the wall and pointing the missing gun at him with both hands. Out of the corner of his eye Goodwin saw his own gun resting on the island three feet away. Without warning he threw himself towards the island, only to scream in agony as Tucker blew part of his hand away. He shirked and stared in disbelief at Tucker, who was moving slowly and unevenly towards him, an expression of utter hatred on his face. He braced himself against the edge of the island, a few feet from Rafe's body.

Goodwin grinned and threw up his hand and a half. His self-satisfied smirk contrasted with his pale face and the blood spilling out of his missing finger sockets and wrist. "All right, all right," Goodwin said quickly. "I surrender."

"That a fact?" Tucker said evenly.

"Call the cops. I'm ready to be taken in and get a lawyer. I have so much to say to him and the authorities."

"About?" Tucker said as he moved closer and eyed Rafe, whose chest was moving up and down slightly. He was still alive.

"Oh, I don't know—my kidnapping, beating, little things like that. I may be headed to a life sentence, but I'm not going down alone. It's prison, baby, for your friends, including the witch bitch. Halloween, 1979—a memorable night for all of us."

Tucker felt a chill run down his spine. He didn't know what Goodwin was referring to, but he sensed something truthful and dangerous about it. Before he could comment Goodwin pulled Rafe's gun out from his back belt with his left hand and aimed it at Tucker, but Goodwin wasn't fast enough, and Tucker blew out his left shoulder; the gun went skittering away across the tile floor.

"Fuck," Goodwin screamed. "You shot me again! I'll get you, too, prick. You and your cunt wife—I *swear* it."

Tucker made a decision that he knew would stay with him for the rest of his life. He kept an eye on Goodwin as he moved carefully over to Rafe and touched his neck for a pulse; Rafe was alive although the pulse was weak. He knew the kids had made it out since he had heard them screaming from the outside. In the distance he could hear police sirens. He only had moments.

He dragged Rafe's unconscious body over to the front door. He turned back and stared balefully at the bleeding animal on the floor. Goodwin was grinning madly. Tucker picked up Rafe's gun and fired two shots into the wall behind him, then tossed the gun to its former location. He met Goodwin's mad eyes with his own determined ones. Tucker felt completely at peace.

"You know," Tucker began, "the Quintanas are my family. I love them to the bottom of my soul. The same goes for my wife. And you took their son and buried him alive and tortured them. You know, I honestly believe that somehow you will continue to try to harm them, and that I can't allow. Did I forget to mention that you planned on burning me and Rafe alive?" He looked around. "I love this casita. It's where my life truly began and where I share it with the finest woman in the world. But it's just an object."

Tucker walked to the coffee table and picked up the book of matches that Goodwin had put there. He looked at Goodwin, whose sardonic smirk had turned to understanding and stark terror.

"No, no," Goodwin whimpered.

"Deliverance told me what she said to you on your last call.

She said that mercy isn't on the menu. Truer words were never spoken. See you in Hell," Tucker said as he struck a match and casually tossed it towards the pool of gasoline on the tile floor.

A mighty whoosh brought on the beginnings of an inferno as the fire roiled towards Goodwin and set him on fire; dropping the gas can had resulted in splashed gas all over his legs.

Tucker had the faintest of smiles on his face as he listened to Goodwin's screams of agony. He hauled Rafe up and opened the door. He looked back once, satisfied that the monster that had invaded all their lives was burning alive. He dragged Rafe out and closed the door. He dragged Rafe as fast as he could away from the casita just as four uniformed policemen were running towards him with guns drawn.

Tucker shouted at the officers, "Get back! Get back! There's gas cans in there." One of the cops slid his arm under Rafe's other side and helped haul him to the back of the Quintana house. Just as they reached the patio and another cop was calling the fire department and an ambulance there was a huge explosion as the full gas can and the open one blew and bathed the night in orange flames.

By the time that the first fire engine arrived the casita was in a conflagration that could be seen for miles from the foothills.

Tucker was sitting down as the EMTs attended him just after another ambulance carrying Rafe raced off to the hospital. His head was killing him, and his shoulder sent shards of agony across his nerve endings, but he was alive. He and Rafe and the kids were alive. Beckett had rushed out and rounded up the kids and they were standing around him, Aislinn and Vikki crying.

The casita was nearly destroyed when Quint, Wilde, and Victor screeched up and ran to the unreal scene. Quint's kids sobbed and inundated him with arms and hugs and kisses. Bechet hugged Victor then Wilde, pretending to be brave but still filled with fear. When he disengaged, Victor and Beckett stared one another before the teenager threw himself into his uncle's arms and chanted, "Je t'aime" over and over again.

As the fire team finished putting out the flames, the casita was a decimated, blackened shell.

"We'll rebuild," Quint said to Tucker.

"I know," Tucker replied as he watched the EMTs wheel up a gurney to take him to the ambulance.

"Any particular design considerations?"

"We'll talk." Tucker hesitated. "I'll tell you everything when we're alone."

"Works for me."

CHAPTER TWENTY

July 19, 1985, Tucson, Arizona

The average temperature for that day of the year was 99°F, but Tucsonians were lucky to have a below-average temperature of 91°F, which some die-hard southwest denizens considered "brisk." The dewpoint was a high 67°F but the wind was a reasonable 8 mph, SSE. Rain and thunderstorms were predicted, and the encroaching dark sky lent credence to that forecast.

Even with the anticipation of wet weather Raine and Constantine were determined to move into their new house that Friday. They had signed the purchase and title documents at the Old Pueblo Title Company; unlike many states lawyers were not involved and the administrative processes were handled by title companies in Arizona. They were a little disappointed to not meet the Prescotts, but that couple had signed earlier and were on their long drive to their new home in San Francisco. Zack Prescott had left a new-home card with the title company for them and wished them a happy life and that he and his wife had left a housewarming gift for them "near the fireplace."

Immediately after the signings the Black Wolfs had driven to their new house where Constantine carried his wife and daughter over the threshold. They roamed through the rooms and were in awe of the housewarming gift the Prescotts had left—an original oil painting by famed southwestern artist Amado Peña, a member of the Pascua Yaqui Tribe who was born in Laredo, Texas in 1943. His art was bold and characterized by sleek lines, with images of Native Americans as well as cowboys, and his reputation as an artist of vision and merit began in the 1970s and was growing by leaps and bounds as more and more people discovered his talent.

The painting that the Prescotts had left hanging over the great room fireplace was a background of the New Mexico mountains with two Native American women in profile in the forefront. It was colored with vivid reds, blues, oranges, greens, and a wide variety of secondary hues, and not just a little reminiscent of Picasso's style. Raine and Constantine loved the painting and decided to leave it just where it was on the stark white wall.

Luckily the Prescotts not only left the house in mint condition, they'd obviously had the rugs steam-cleaned and the tiles scrubbed to near-new quality; the kitchen was spotless. The house was move-in ready, and the Black Wolfs started moving in some personal effects that night. Constantine had his condo on the market and there were two competing offers, so they wanted to move in as soon as possible. They knew that some of their family and friends planned on helping them, but were astonished and touched when the entire Begay, Dillinger, and Dane-Quintana families showed up at the condo along with Cress and Gray. They helped box and get the furniture ready, and when the truck and the entire posse arrived at the new house they found that Victor, Wilde, their kids, Tucker, Iris, the Union Jack associates, and new "family members" Rafe Spencer and Josh Wyllys were waiting for them. Constantine could smell the delicious scents of roasting chicken and ribs and laughed when he saw that Wilde had set up two gas grills on the back patio alongside cases of soda, beer, and water. A boombox was emitting the sounds of the newly released album *Heart*; currently, the rocking sounds of *What About Love* were blasting out.

The entire morning and half of the afternoon took up moving in boxes and furniture and hanging some prints on walls that Constantine just knew were going to be moved again when his wife decided that she'd positioned them too hastily. He was smart enough not to impart that to her.

The movers left at eleven, and the entire burgeoning crew took a break at twelve and chowed down in the kitchen and back patio. Everyone was able to relax and enjoy each other's company and ruminate on the events during and after the end of the last threat to their circle.

Unlike the aftermath of the ax murders, the Union Jackers didn't need the outside counsel of Barnaby Lucas from San Francisco—they had Fox and Shayne, who had finished her law courses and was studying for the bar (as a surprise to everyone Shayne mentioned that she and Fox were moving in together). Fox proved to be far tougher than anyone thought he was as he grabbed the bull by the horns and refused to let Tucker give a statement to the police before they talked. Tucker told Fox that he managed to grab his gun when Goodwin was outside trying to intercept the kids, and they had a shootout in the casita where Tucker got the best of him, unfortunately not before Goodwin dropped the lit match he managed to strike thus setting off the fire that killed him and destroyed the Townsend home. Fox grilled him about every detail, and when he was satisfied that Tucker's story could withstand police interrogation, he allowed the police to interview him in the hospital. Cornell did the interview and pretty much soft-balled the questions, ending the interview with a recommendation that no charges should be brought against Tucker; his actions were a matter of self-defense. The D.A. went along with the recommendation and Tucker was cleared.

Only Quint and Deliverance knew the whole truth. Tucker had a private conversation with them when he was discharged, and he and Iris moved into their guest room until their new home was erected. The four of them closeted themselves in the den with the door closed and locked. It was there that Tucker confessed that he deliberately set the fire, and that Goodwin's death was a murder and not self-defense. He told them what Goodwin said and that he was certain that if the bastard lived he'd find some way to continue hurting the family. He couldn't allow that, especially after what Goodwin had already done.

Tucker said he'd understand if Deliverance and Quint didn't want him around their kids anymore and if they wanted to fire him, he'd be fine with that. He looked over at Iris and said if she wanted to divorce him, that was fine, too.

Quint told Tucker that he was an idiot if he thought they were going to let the best nanny and bodyguard in the world get away; in fact, Deliverance said, they were giving him a "humongous" raise to correspond with his actions and his position as the permanent head of their security team. Quint said that as far as a moral compass went there were many directions and not all of them were wrong; Tucker's was pointing due north. And, point of fact, he was a member of their family and family stuck together no matter what. *And*—it *was* a matter of self-defense of others by preventing potential future murders.

Iris said that he was far worse than an idiot if he thought he could get away from her so easily—then she kissed him like he had *absolutely* never been kissed before until Quint and Deliverance cleared their throats. All four linked hands and swore that this was one secret that would never be revealed. Later that day when he and Tucker were alone, Quint told him the story of October 31, 1979. Tucker nodded sagely and said Goodwin had mentioned that date, and it was further justification that Tucker had done the right thing. Both agreed that this was something Iris didn't need to know.

Then they sat down and scoped out a design for a new much-larger casita farther behind the Dane-Quintana house. Insurance would pay for most of the rebuilding, and Tucker and Iris demanded that they pay for the rest—*IF*, Iris said pointedly, a garage was part of the deal. Quint hemmed and hawed but agreed. The debris had been cleared away for a week and the blueprints for the new home were drawn up.

Victor and Wilde were sitting together closely and talking and laughing about the changes in their lives over the past year. They had become surrogate parents to an adolescent and a teenager who redefined the word "difficult," but then slowly came around to solidify a true family that cherished and nourished one another. Victor asked Beckett and Bechet to stand beside him as "best men" when he and Wilde handfasted in October, and the boys excitedly agreed; Beckett even asked Victor if he could throw a bachelor party for him. Victor said he'd think about it but made it clear that if there was some raucous event Beckett couldn't attend because of his age. That put a damper on Beckett's idea. The four of them were now discussing what Beckett's college desires were even though he would only be starting his sophomore year in high school in the fall. He had offered up that he wanted to graduate college with a Criminology degree and go into law enforcement. Wilde sniped that he'd better brush up on his shooting capabilities since he'd only barely wounded Goodwin. Becket huffed and groused about it being too dark to aim properly; Victor calmed him down and said they'd spend more time at the shooting range, and yes, Bechet could come with them. No, neither boy could have a gun until he was eighteen. Yes, they were going out tonight to see that new flick, *The Legend of Billie Jean*, at Plitt Foothills 4 Cinemas. Beckett had fallen head over heels for the lead actress, Helen Slater, who just the year before had starred in *Supergirl*.

Cress had a full glass of wine as he meandered through his brother's new home and admired the house structure and the furnishings and art. Constantine had put the beautiful acrylic painting of the Grand Canyon by Red Hawk Begay over his bed, and his Redbird and Mullan framed prints in the den. He wandered into Sasha's room and smiled at the baby stuff occupying the place haphazardly until Raine could decorate it properly. As much as he loved his nieces and nephews, he was sad that he'd never experience true fatherhood, and he knew that Gray felt the same way. There seemed no way to have a child biologically, although Gray mentioned that he'd read several articles on surrogacy. There was only a snowball's chance in Hell that they'd ever be allowed to adopt as a gay couple; virtually all countries refused to allow same-sex couples to adopt, and in quite a few countries same-sex activity was illegal. In vitro fertilization was still in its infancy, with the first in vitro baby, Louise Brown, making her appearance in 1978 in England. Since then, only a few dozen such efforts proved fruitful. Still, with a donor egg, the possibility of a blood child for either him or Gray was a possibility.

So, they piled their love and attention on their growing dog family. He did envy Victor and Wilde for having non-canine children in their household.

Cress was anxious for his handfasting. He had commissioned Moon Wolf to create a special pair of rings that incorporated their various ethnic backgrounds and found out that Victor and Wilde had done the same. They may not be legal wedding rings, but they symbolized the same kind of love and commitment. He sensed Gray behind him and turned, smiling. They stood together looking around the baby's room, then Gray said, "How would you feel about a French Bulldog?" Cress laughed and said he wanted a black one.

Iris had invited Liberty to the moving event and she eagerly agreed since she didn't mind seeing Turner again, and he didn't mind seeing her. She and Iris were cloistered in the kitchen alcove sipping lemonade and discussing the recent events. Iris scowled and said the inimitable Laurel Bollmeier had cornered her at the hospital when she was visiting Tucker and tried to push her way into the room. Iris intercepted her, and none too gently shoved her back into the hall where she told Laurel in no uncertain terms that if she bothered

Tucker again Iris would use every legal trick in the FBI catalog to rain vengeance down on her. Laurel got the message but persisted and Iris agreed that she and her husband would sit down with Laurel for an interview—*when* they were good and ready.

Actually, Iris said, she and Laurel had a nice talk for about ten minutes after their coming together of minds, and Iris was genuinely glad that Laurel was putting her life back together. She had put on weight and her mental faculties were as sharp as ever. Laurel confided to her that she was seeing a therapist and probably would be for months to come but getting back to work at the *Sentinel* and working on her returned manuscript was medicine for her soul. She excitedly told Iris "in *absolute* confidence" that she was going to be interviewed by the journalistic goddess herself, Barbara Walters, on an ABC special. And she had been approached aggressively by Random House and her lawyer, Fox Newberry, was negotiating a helluva deal with a huge advance. This book, renamed to *Beguiling Death in a Southwest Town* from *Epicenter of Horror*, was going to stay on the *New York Times* best-seller list for months! Laurel lamented that although she was able to persuade Quint and Deliverance to grant her an interview (in their own good time, sigh …) they had also granted an interview to that miserable Bruce Peterson from the magazine *Seraphim*. Apparently, Quint was tight enough with the husband of the mag's owner, Norah Maguire, and that had greased the wheels. She wished she could be the only interviewer, but she'd take what she could get. And, she had the advantage of having up-close-and-personal contact with the Beguiler. She whispered a secret that no one else knew in hopes of softening Iris up for the kill—the Beguiler had another name for himself when he started killing. He called himself "the Surrogate Scourge." She wasn't certain of his origin of the ridiculous appellation, but she could make a few guesses and they'd be in her book.

Iris let the Union Jackers know, and they all had a good laugh at Murphy's pathetic attempt to brand himself with a cool nickname. The police hadn't found any evidence of the nickname when they had minutely examined his house and office. With determination and a little luck, she and Liberty had uncovered Goodwin's hidey hole and their team tore it apart looking for evidence and clues. Iris was shocked when she went into his bedroom and found all the walls plastered with photos and newspaper articles about Deliverance and her family. Goodwin had obviously been following them for many months and had taken the candid shots himself. Deliverance's items covered at least 80% of the walls, but there were other pictures and articles about his ex-wife, including her accident and the miscarriage; Goodwin had drawn a smiley face on that article. Iris had provided that insight to the Boston police who were going to reopen the accident and explore Goodwin's possible involvement. Iris also found a jarful of diamondback rattles, and she knew then that it hadn't been Storm who had killed those snakes under the bush but Goodwin. She shivered to think how many times he'd been so close to the kids.

Iris noted that on one of Deliverance's photos Goodwin had drawn a date in red ink—October 31, 1979. Iris knew that that was the Dane-Quintanas' wedding date, and the day on which Goodwin had been kidnapped, drugged, and beaten. Quint had hypothesized that Goodwin was bitter about the way his life had collapsed while the life of the girl he had seduced and betrayed was a full, rich one filled with happiness and promise. Iris had called the Boston police detectives that had investigated his case, but they offered no clues as to his attackers, and the case had been closed once the statute of limitations had been reached; the kidnapping statute was set to expire in four months. She wondered about Goodwin's motivations, but decided to close her inquiries into his past. She had her suspicions but decided to let them rest in lieu of what he had done. The case was still open, but she anticipated that it would be closed in a few months.

Moon Wolf watched his sons and daughter playing in the back yard. He was munching on a burger as he sat next to his wife and had his arm around her shoulder. He loved the feel of her. Her pregnancy was beginning to show and they both hoped for a daughter so Persa could be a big sister and enjoy girlie play. Persa was a clever little girl, smart in school and athletics. She seemed to find biology fascinating, and twice they'd caught her with an anatomy book in her room as she dissected first a frog and then a Gila monster. She said she wanted to be a doctor, then a veterinarian, then a doctor again, then an archeologist, then a writer. Phaedra was a regular customer at Bookmans and bought all kinds of books to satisfy her daughter's intellectual pursuits. Her sons were hellions in training and loved sports, which their father eagerly played with them in the back yard. Right now, they were kicking a soccer ball with fury and talent that would scare Pelé.

Moon Wolf had the commissions for the two sets of handfasting rings, and he was preoccupied now with designing them in his head. He had a pretty good idea about how to design the rings for Cress and Gray, but he was less certain about Victor and Wilde. He wanted the rings to be perfect. Suddenly he thought about embedding a stone into the rings besides carving an unusual design. Their birth months were all different, but … he grinned at his wife when he knew exactly which stone to embed. Phaedra looked at him curiously. He leaned over and kissed her, then rubbed her belly.

Bliss smiled at the sight of the two loving Begays as she held Barnabas in her arms, humming an old lullaby. She had enjoyed teaching Angel about Wicca, tarot, and psychic powers, and she would now have another child to indoctrinate into her religion. Malachi had made gentle noises about perhaps baptizing the baby into his Protestant religion, and she agreed much to his joy. It didn't matter whether the kids were baptized and raised partially Christian, but it wouldn't stop her for showing her kids the true way. Deliverance was raising her kids to be educated about Wicca and Catholicism, and they seemed to be fine. They had discussed the latest hints of Alex's abilities, and it was clear that he was "special" and needed to be guided. Deliverance asked her for help, and she was happy to give it. Currently, Alex was in therapy with Dr. Honora Waring, who had helped both Raine and Laurel Bollmeier.

Bliss gazed over at Del and her family and thought they looked peaceful. Deliverance caught her eye and winked, and the two longtime friends shared a warm smile.

Quint was juggling Vikki on his lap and trying to eat a sloppy loaded burger. His youngest daughter was antsy and getting a little crabby from the long, exhausting day, but she was quieting down, and he knew she'd fall asleep soon.

Deliverance had been scolding her kids about their riotous antics, and when they, too, seemed to be scaling back their fun she sat next to him and took a dozing Vikki from his lap.

"The kids okay?" he asked as he took a swig of cold beer.

"Yes," she said. "They're showing remarkable resilience for kids that were terrorized and almost shot and burned alive."

"Remarkable doesn't quite cover it. Still ... I'm worried that Alex seems to be handling it too well. I think he's suppressing some of his feelings and that's not good."

"I agree, and I've spoken to Dr. Waring about it. Even so, he's just in the infancy stages of therapy. He has a long way to go."

"I think we all do." He gave her an owlish look. "That includes you."

"I know. Are you suggesting that I make an appointment with her, too?"

"Not the worst idea you've ever had. I mean, you've taken a lot of psychology courses, so you know the signs of trauma and the road to get healthy."

"Maybe we should transfer Storm to her care, and then with me on the couch, too, we could negotiate a family rate."

"You're a financially rapacious little critter, aren't you?"

"You bet your sweet Hispanic ass."

"You're obsessed with my Hispanic ass."

"It is luscious. Perhaps if I'm in the mood I can explore it tonight."

"I'm not sure it's right and proper for me to take advantage of a pregnant chick's horniness. By the way, I love the name you've picked out. Sure it's a son?" There was no answer as he withered under her baleful gaze. "Of course you are." He leaned close to her and crooned a few words of his favorite Steve Miller Band song, *The Joker*. "Really love your peaches, wanna shake your tree."

"Shaking my peaches is what got me into the throes of morning sickness."

"And who stopped taking her pills without any discussion?"

"I want what I want when I want it. It's part of my countercharm."

"Well, a baby is one thing, but I sincerely hope you never want a Ferrari."

"We don't have garage space."

"I'm sure you could figure out a way around that."

Deliverance grinned and adjusted the sleeping child on her lap. "I was thinking of dying my hair pink again, like when we first met."

"I can live with that," Quint sighed as he polished off the last ounce of Bud.

"And maybe put a pink streak in our girls' hair."

"The term 'no fucking way' comes to mind."

"This from a man who once looked like Don Johnson with copper streaks."

"A momentary lapse in judgment. Leave their hair alone—and don't even consider for a *nanosecond* streaking our son's hair."

"Hmm. Now that you mention it ..." She burst out laughing at the horrified look on her husband's face. "Maybe purple. Boys look good in purple."

A loud rumble of thunder boomed over the city, and several sharply defined lightning bolts lit up the sky as though to punctuate the lives of the people celebrating a family's new life.

EPILOGUE

Saguaro National Monument West, Thursday,
October 31, 1985, 6:00 PM

The sun set at 5:34 PM, an unfortunate sign of the rapid approach of winter. The full moon was waning but still bright and robust. At a higher elevation than Phoenix Tucson was much cooler than the capital city and at this time of night in the month it was hovering around 60°F and dropping rapidly as the darkness encroached.

Bliss would have preferred the ceremony up in Sedona, which was saturated with mystical vortexes, but with the number of people attending the ceremony and the feast afterwards it was impractical to drive a caravan nearly two hundred and fifty miles. So, Bliss spent a few weeks exploring ideas and finally selecting a spot that had meaning for everyone involved. The spot had bad memories associated with it, but it was the linchpin site where they had all seeded and grown their special bonds.

In 1977 the late ax murderer Cheyenne LaChoisi had left her first victim under a huge saguaro in the western section of the split desert monument. That action and its consequences had brought all the celebrants together in some way, so it was the best option although Bliss understood that it would make some people uneasy. Nevertheless, she planned to have a warm, intimate ceremony that would hopefully dispel some of the disquiet. She had broached the site with the two couples, and they agreed to go with it; Cress had been the queasy one since it was his sister that had committed the swath of murders years ago.

Bliss had dragooned Deliverance into participating in the plans and they worked tirelessly to design the event. Both women would be celebrating legal wedding anniversaries that day, Bliss's seventh and Deliverance's sixth; Bliss had performed Deliverance's handfasting in March 1978 while she was in the hospital after giving birth to the twins, and Deliverance had returned the favor for Bliss.

Unlike Deliverance's legal wedding in Salem, her hometown, the guests would not be required to dress in Halloween costumes. Del had dressed as a flamenco dancer and Quint had dressed as a mariachi. Victor and Wilde were Quint's best men and had stood beside him dressed as vampires, complete with faux fangs. Bliss made it clear to everyone that they could dress as they wished—formal, casual, naked—although she would be dressed in an elaborate Wiccan priestess robe. Deliverance told her that she, too, would wear the garments of their religion (which would hide her six-months-pregnant belly) but Bliss should expect to see Quint in faded jeans, a checkered shirt, cowboy boots, and a bolo tie. Alex would most likely mimic his father's garb, but Deliverance was considering making her daughters Wiccan robes, too.

The women in their clique were volunteered to create a tasty feast for the group that would eat afterwards in the Westward Dream event room where Raine and Constantine had their reception. Naturally, Bliss ordered some special dishes from a prominent catering service to supplement the home cooking. She couldn't fully restrain herself from expressions of Halloween, and part of the decorations on the walls and the eating tables presented tastes of bats, witches, and spider webs. She had a brilliant idea to have the webs made from edible cotton candy, so guests could nosh on sweets while they were gobbling down jambalaya, gumbo, enchiladas, refried beans, Spanish rice, bangers and mash, fish and chips, gyoza, yakizakana, vegetable tempura, and more varieties of food that covered Cajun, Japanese, English, and down-home American dishes. Mariko Kingston had come down two days early to begin preparing the Japanese dishes while her husband golfed. They were staying with Gray and Cress and their (now) four dogs; Tiger Lily was being intimidated on all fronts and spent a lot of time growling.

Even with stringent red pens etching on the possible invitee list Bliss and Deliverance had only whittled down the attendees to around forty. She had called Cress's parents and Constantine's parents, but the latter weren't able to come although they did send genuine warm wishes and a beautiful gift that Deliverance stockpiled with the many others sent by friends and families. She'd also called Wilde's parents, who were expected to attend although business kept Wilde's brother Danny away.

And now as the day arrived for the commitment ceremony everything was in place and there were no surprises—yet. Fingers crossed. Deliverance had pursued certain other potential attendees and had sent them a letter and a map but so far, no word of any kind.

Quint rented a small bus to take many of the attendees to the site and then to the reception venue, the same as for Raine's wedding. Even so by the time that everyone arrived around five-thirty there were ten cars plus the bus hugging the side of Kinney Road. Quint was embarrassed to drive his wife's station wagon, but with her advanced pregnancy and four rambunctious kids dressed like Wiccans and howling at the moon (just to annoy him) he certainly couldn't drive his convertible or Cougar. He hadn't disabused his wife of her earlier prediction as to his garments. But, he thought, at least the designer jeans and cowboy boots were new.

Cress and Gray arrived with Gray's parents. The two men were wearing Armani jeans they'd picked up in Goldwater's, and matching casual navy jackets over silk dress shirts, both open at the neck. Black Oxfords were the shoe of the day. Gray's parents were dressed more formally, his father, Grayson, in a spiffy navy three-piece suit and his mother, Mariko, in a beautiful designer dress from the current Versace collection. Charlotte Blackledge was also in attendance and was the height of New York City style.

Victor chose to wear formal attire from a small but respected tailor in Los Angeles; charcoal with a crisp pale-blue cotton shirt, the suit made him look like (as Wilde put it) "a bloody barrister." Wilde had his parents bring him a tailored suit from the famous Burton Menswear store in London. Gun-metal gray, the suit was complemented by a pale lavender silk shirt. Wilde wore a Rolex watch that his father, Davey, had given him as a gift; Davey had bought it in 1941 to celebrate Wilde's birth. Victor was wearing a retro-looking watch made by the new designer company, Fossil Group. Quint and Deliverance had given it to him and said it was to remind him that he was a fossil at fifty-two. He scowled at them but loved the look and the sentiment.

A few other guests were wearing suits or formal dresses, but most of them had gone the casual route. Bliss and Deliverance, of course, were dressed as Wiccans, Bliss in a spectacularly embroidered gold robe and Deliverance in an equally elaborate vermillion one. The Dane-Quintana girls were wearing modest robes of cerulean blue, and Alex was a miniature version of his father. Bliss was wearing very sharp and elaborate metal finger covers that prompted Deliverance to ask, "Where'd you get those? The medical supply store for S&M gynecologists?" Bliss made a clawing motion at her friend.

At 6 PM sharp Bliss called out to the congregation that they were beginning. Everyone clustered around Bliss and the two couples, who were standing under the infamous ax murder saguaro, about five feet away. Charlie Sheffield had been hired to photograph the wedding and reception, and he was holding an expensive camcorder to video tape the events. He'd do stills later.

Bliss began the ceremony after everyone lit the candles they were holding. "Handfasting is the eternal joining of two people in love. It is a sacred ceremony of commitment, not to be entered into lightly. In the ancient religion of Wicca, it is no different than the legal marriage ceremony of this century. Unlike modern marriages it recognizes that the joining need not be between a man and a woman, but between two human beings, period. We are here today to join two couples in these fasted bonds and to send them onto the rest of their lives together."

She turned first to Wilde and Victor. "Please express your commitment to these, your family and friends."

Wilde looked at Victor and said, "I thought about trying to build coherent sentences that could express my feelings, but it's not my strong suit, so I decided to plagiarize some lyrics from Air Supply."

"Seriously, dude?" Deliverance exclaimed. Quint shushed her, and Wilde went on.

"I know just how to whisper, and I know just how to cry. I know just where to find the answers and I know just how to lie. I know just how to fake it and I know just how to scheme. I know just when to face the truth and then I know just when to dream. And I know just where to touch you and I know just what to prove. I know when to pull you closer and I know when to let you loose. And I know the night is fading, and I know the time's gonna fly, and I'm never gonna tell you everything I've gotta tell you but I know I've gotta give it a try. And I know the roads to riches and I know the ways to fame. I know all the rules and then I know how to break 'em and I always know the name of the game.

"But I don't know how to leave you, and I'll never let you fall. And I don't know how you do it, making love out of nothing at all. You can take the darkness at the pit of the night and turn into a beacon burning endlessly bright, I've gotta follow it 'cause everything I know, well, it's nothing 'til I give it to you. And, mon cher, I give you all of me forever."

Quint handed Wilde the ring, a masterpiece of silver on which Moon Wolf had carved and entwined the Union Jack flag of England and the New Orleans flag symbol of a fleur-de-lis. In the center of the entwined images was a tiny but perfect oval opal, the birthstone of October. The engraving inside was one simple word—"Wilde." Wilde slipped it on Victor's finger.

"Victor?" Bliss prompted.

"I have no songs except the one in my heart at the thought of spending the rest of my life with you. You awakened in me feelings and dreams I thought were long dead. You enriched my life. You've stood by me in every way. You claimed love and responsibility for my nephews. Although I think I know every iota of your heart and soul, I know that I'll spend the rest of my life mining the nuances of a remarkable human being." He paused for a second. "I just don't know why you chose that song instead of something by the Beatles." Everyone laughed, and Wilde blushed.

Victor nodded to Beckett who dug into his pocket and extracted the other ring. The design was the same as Wilde's save that the name etched inside was "Victor." He slid it onto Wilde's finger and they linked hands.

Bliss withdrew a red silk cord from her robe and wrapped it around their wrists in a figure-eight infinity pattern.

Bliss said, "Now we will hear from our other committed couple. Gray, please begin."

Gray and Cress held hands, and Gray at first puzzled everyone with his Japanese speech, except his parents and Alex. "Watakushi wa kono dansei to kekkonshi, fufu to narou to shite imasu. Watakushi wa kenkouna tokimo, soudenai tokimo, kono hito o aishi, kono hito o uyamai, kono hito o nagusame, kono hito o tasuke, watakushi no inochi no kagiri, kataku sessou o mamoru koto o, chikai masu." Gray switched to English and translated the vows. "This man, I marry no matter what the health situation is. I will love this person, respect this person, console this person, help this person until death, protecting fidelity, I swear."

Malachi handed Gray the ring, which like the other set was silver, hand-carved and engraved. The names on the rings followed the same pattern, but the entwined carvings on the top of the band and around the oval opal overlapping were a samurai sword and a feather, the first representative of Gray's Japanese heritage and the second representative of Cress's Native American blood. Gray slipped the ring on Cress's finger and stared deep into his eyes, both momentarily oblivious to their surroundings.

"Cress?" Bliss prompted. "Yo—*Cress!*"

Cress was startled out of his trance and smiled shyly. "Tu fais partie de mon âme, l'autre moitié de mon cœur. Vous êtes le co-parent de mes chiots. Vivez avec moi pour toujours. Je serai toujours fidèle à toi. You are part of my soul, the other half of my heart. You are the co-parent to my puppies. Live with me forever. I will always be true to you."

Constantine handed his brother the ring and Cress slipped it on Gray's hand. "Je t'aime," he said, finishing his short but heartfelt vows.

Bliss bound their hands with another silk cord, then offered a Wiccan handfasting blessing.

"May the loving protection of the Lord embrace you. May the light of the Lady shine upon you. May the memories of this day forever touch you. Because love is a light to guide you, and love is a blanket to warm you, and love is a wonder given to you to cherish and hold forever dear." She smiled beatifically at the two couples in front of her. "You have pledged your love and commitment to each other. By the power vested in me as a Wiccan priestess, I do pronounce you handfasted forever. Well, dudes—what are you waiting for?"

The audience started clapping as each couple sealed their vows with a kiss then turned to face their audience.

Victor was grinning widely as he scanned the faces of his family and friends, then suddenly his gaze caught on a couple at the back of the group and the grin turned to jaw-dropping disbelief.

Wilde saw his face change and looked towards the back. He, too, was shocked.

Victor's parents, Sabine and Bastien Renard, were standing closely together holding hands. Although neither was smiling, both faces showed no disapproval or tension. Everyone could see that something was going on with Victor as he slowly held Wilde's hand and led him thorough the throng to where his parents were standing. He stopped three feet in front of them as everyone watched the scene being played out.

"Maman, Papa—you came," Victor said with a tremor in his voice.

Sabine reached out a shaking hand to touch his cheek. "Oui. Nous sommes tellement désolés. Pouvez-vous nous pardonner pour ce que nous avons fait?"

"Oui," Victor answered quietly, surprising himself but knowing instinctively it was the right move.

She looked at Wilde with tears in her eyes. "Et vous?"

"If he forgives you, I can forgive you," Wilde said. He felt Beckett come up behind him and put a hand on his shoulder. He craned his neck to face the teenager. "This your doing?"

"Mais non," Beckett said. "I believe Madame Deliverance should get the credit." Victor and Wilde looked over at Deliverance, who winked at them and mouthed, "Surprise!"

"Okay, okay—a little later for the family reunion," Deliverance admonished. "You guys get over to the cactus for still shots." She impatiently waved Charlie over as the two newly handfasted couples took their places in front of the saguaro. Charlie took a dozen shots to make sure he got it right, several of the four men together then the rest of each couple alone. Candles were blown out, hugs were exchanged, and people began hustling off to their cars or the bus for the trip to the Westward Dream

The resort had handled all the last-minute decorations and settings perfectly. The setup was similar to the reception for Raine and Constantine. It wasn't ten minutes before the food and drinks began flowing, but over an hour before the toasts began. A half dozen people stood up to make toasts, and all but one or two were humorous. Quint quipped about Wilde's odd English slang and got a stern middle-finger flashing for his efforts. Grayson's toast was the sweetest, and brought tears to a lot of eyes, especially his son's and his new "son-in-law."

People danced, laughed, gave congratulations, swilled down food and drink, and had a wonderful time. Deliverance had changed the seating to allow the Renards to sit at the table with their son and grandsons and changed her kids' child-section seating to a table that just held Dane-Quintanas.

They all partied hearty for the entire evening. At 10 PM Quint clinked his champagne glass to get everyone's attention. When the room was quiet (sort of) he and Deliverance each took one of Storm's hands and led her to the middle of the floor.

"As you all know," Quint began, "this young lady entered our lives in a most peculiar manner, then went about changing our family forever." He bent down and kissed the top of Storm's head before continuing. "That word—forever—has a special meaning today. My wife and I and our three and a half other kids all stood together in a judge's chamber where he signed the legal adoption papers to make Storm our official daughter. Ladies and gentlemen, I want to introduce you to Storm Destiny Grace Dane-Quintana."

The entire room stood up and clapped and cheered as the little girl blushed and tightened her grip on her father's hand. Destiny—she had chosen that from Quint's crucial words to her self-esteem and sense of security—"Your destiny is to be our daughter."

Quint picked her up in his arms and she surveyed the crowd of people of whose world she was now a permanent, integral part.

She smiled slightly. She didn't know who she had been once upon a time—and might never know—but she knew who she was and always would be—Quint's and Deliverance's daughter.

Nothing in the whole damn world could be better than that.

Excerpt from

Devil Cholla,
Volume Three of the Arizona Trilogy

the upcoming novel by Gloria H. Giroux

BOOK ONE

*"Few western wonders are more inspiring than the
beauties of an Arizona moonlit landscape; the silvered
mountains in the distance, the strange lights and shadows
upon hog back and arroyo, and the grotesque details of the
stiff, yet beautiful cacti form a picture at once enchanting
and inspiring; as though one were catching for the first time
a glimpse of some dead and forgotten world, so different
is it from the aspect of any other spot upon our earth."*

Edgar Rice Burroughs, "A Princess of Mars," 1917

Devil Cholla, Carefree, Arizona

631

CHAPTER ONE

April 19, 1995, Mount Lemmon, Tucson, Arizona

The sheer rock face of the cliff on Mount Lemmon spanned nearly four hundred yards from the nearly even, flat ridge that capped the dangerous cliff, down to the gently sloping floor of the gorge. The immediate landscape at the foot of the drop was cluttered with scrub brush and cacti and large clusters of sharp rocks, which angled up like huge, deadly spikes; more than one careless or unfortunate climber had met his fate impaled on the vicious projections. Only the most well-trained and savvy adventurer had any business attempting either a climb or a rappel down. Dozens of men and women per year made the effort; few were able to scale or descend the cliff for the full measure of its impressive height. Nevertheless, some amateurs succeeded with sheer force of will and determination.

Storm Dane-Quintana tightened the cinches on her harness as she rested her expensive hiking boots flush against a point on the sheer rock down about a hundred yards from her starting point at the top. The smooth, unforgiving surface was more intimidating than she had thought when she evaluated this latest goal in her carefully designed personal regimen. She had promised herself that she would succeed in conquering this great challenge by her sixteenth birthday, but she was already a year behind that goal. She loathed failure, particularly her own. Lithe and athletic at five-foot-eight she prided herself on her physical strength and resiliency and refused to be constrained by social expectations of what a seventeen-year-old should be and do.

She leaned back slightly and looked up towards the edge of the cliff. The imposing, sheer width of the rock loomed over her but didn't block out the bright sun due to the early hour. The warm sunlight felt good on her face. Her long reddish, chestnut-brown hair was clasped back tightly with a silver and pearl barrette, but she could feel a slight trickle of sweat run down the back of her neck, and on both sides of her expressive face even though her head was covered with an Arizona Cardinals cap. She glanced to her right and saw that her younger brother had just dropped down to her level and was grinning at her. Wyatt was athletic from the get-go and had been badgering her for six months to take him along ("As an observer—I swear!"), and she had

632

the last three times on smaller rappels, teaching him about harnesses, dropping, emergency procedures, and other tidbits that would protect him from "falling to your death and pissing off Mom and Dad."

"Stop there and take a drink of water," she ordered him. Wyatt nodded and took a deep swig from his canteen as his sister did the same. "Ready?" she asked. He nodded. "Three more drops and we stop again." She had taken extra precautions with her brother and had a tether linking them together.

She blew out a deep breath and tensed her strong, lean arms and legs and began rappelling down the next section of cliff. She let the slack out exactly the same length each time she dropped and hit, dropped and hit, and paused again thirty yards farther down. They both sipped and continued back down. During the next drop her right foot didn't hit quite right, and she slipped and hit the rock face awkwardly, banging her right knee. She groaned and paused and studied the rock carefully to see if any difference in texture might have caused her gaff. Nothing about the rock was different; she had simply made an awkward, inappropriate move that could have caused her more damage had she not been as agile as she usually was. She cursed herself silently, angry at her stupid mistake. Her ears burned red at her brother's laugh; the little rat was as sure-footed as a mountain goat and even though this was his first try he was doing remarkably well, better than she had at his age. She threw a deadly scowl at the boy, who laughed even harder.

She tightened her grip on the tether and kept going, a little more slowly.

Drop and hit, drop and hit. She gave a quick glance down and saw that they had about thirty yards to go. Not too bad. They'd be done before by ten and be back at home in time to help their siblings prepare for their mother's fortieth birthday celebration.

She looked down carefully and raised her eyebrows over her mismatched green and blue eyes as she spotted the small forms of her parents standing a quarter mile away from the base.

Deliverance and Quint stared up at the tiny figures on the rock face, which grew larger moment by moment as their children descended the sheer rock. They were standing together with binoculars aimed towards the siblings. Storm made a hand signal to Wyatt and they continued their descent.

Storm hit a flat ledge two yards from the ground and her brother descended to that same point seconds later. One more drop and she expelled an involuntary whoosh of breath as her feet hit solidly, and she realized that she had accomplished her goal. Wyatt joined her on safe, solid ground and grinned widely. They unfastened their harnesses and freed themselves from the confining apparatuses. She let her tether dangle as she turned around and walked over to her brother, helping him with one stubborn clip. She saw a very slight flicker of sun glinting off her parents' binoculars. She smiled to herself, knowing that they were undoubtedly watching their kids' dangerous progress with tense minds and hearts. They were far too overprotective of their various offspring, but in truth, she never minded, especially considering her family's history.

As she reached her brother she inclined her head ever so slightly and spoke in amusement. "Our parents are out there watching," she said casually as she checked his pulse rate.

"Yup," Wyatt sighed. "I saw a few glints myself. They're predictable, aren't they? Endearing, but predictable." He grinned saucily. "Should we wave to them?" Wyatt had his mother's luminescent amber eyes and dark red hair that their father said came from his Irish mother, Aislinn Ryan. Where he got the cleft chin was anyone's guess considering his diverse ethnic ancestors—English, Romanian, Mexican, and Irish.

"Why not?" The siblings turned towards the glints and jumped and waved wildly and hooted loudly.

"They saw us," Quint sighed as he lowered his binoculars and gave his wife an appropriately guilty look.

"Of course they saw us," Deliverance replied in exasperation as she lowered her own device and raised an eyebrow at her husband. "You aren't exactly the paragon of discretion. How could they possibly miss us?"

"I was simply concerned for their safety. That cliff is one of the most dangerous in the area. You saw how she slipped and banged her leg into the rock. She could have lost her grip on the tether and wound up banging some more dangerous portion of her body against the cliff. I know we gave them permission to do this damn thing, but that doesn't mean I'm going to kick my feet up on the recliner and watch soap operas while my kids are out there defying death."

"Our daughter is a nearly grown woman. She's seventeen with the mind of a thirty-year-old. And you know she's careful, methodical, and not given to unconsidered actions in any part of her life. We can't protect her from everything. We must allow her the freedom to choose her own pursuits, however they may give us heart flutters or sleepless nights. And, she would die rather than let anything happen to Wyatt—you saw that she had a double tether and made him wear a helmet and padding so that he looks like the Michelin Man. That kid ever fell he'd bounce into New Mexico."

"I know. You're right, as usual," Quint responded in a semi-annoyed tone as he sighed heavily and started walking back down the path where they'd parked their 1994 Ford Explorer. They both turned as they heard yelling from behind them. Storm and Wyatt were running towards them carrying their harnesses. A minute later the brother and sister collapsed at their parents' feet, laughing.

"What's so funny?" Deliverance asked as she fixed her face into a definitive mock scowl.

"You guys," Wyatt crowed. "We're not babies."

"You're nine years old, little boy," his father intoned seriously. "And point of fact, we'll be your parents and worry when you're fifty. So—I suppose you want us to drive you back up to the cliff so you can get to your car without too much effort?"

"That's the plan, man," Storm laughed.

"Five dollars," Deliverance stated.

"Five friggin' bucks," Wyatt exclaimed, then when he saw the disapprovingly looks on his parents' face he mumbled, "Sorry."

"It just went up to six," his mother said. "And it's coming out of your allowance."

"Suck it up, Grasshopper," Storm said. "Ain't no way we're in shape to hike back up." She looked at her mother and stuck her hand out. "It's a deal."

As Deliverance took Storm's hand she elaborated. "Each."

"The f—," Storm started to say then cut off her favorite curse word and nodded. "Okay, deal."

"I thought so," Deliverance said, nodding in satisfaction. "Follow us to the car."

Storm whispered loudly to Wyatt, "Mom's been particularly

crabby ever since this birthday sneaked up on her. Old people—jeez." The parents refused to turn around so the kids could see their wide grins.

The four Dane-Quintanas reached the car and the kids parked themselves in the cramped back seat of the Explorer. Quint slid into the driver's seat and before Deliverance got in she reached into a small Igloo cooler and took out two ice cold cans of Coke. She handed them to her kids who popped them open and drank the sweet cola down without taking a breath.

Quint jackrabbited and pushed the Explorer hard through rough terrain around the base of the cliff and farther afield as he reached a pothole-ridden offshoot road that they climbed to get to the Cougar parked above the starting point of the rappel. Quint smiled as he looked at the 1972 Cougar that he'd had since 1978. Wilde had bought the car when he and Deliverance sprang Quint from jail in San Francisco. Quint just loved that car and despite its age he kept it in tiptop condition all these years and bequeathed it to Storm on her sixteenth birthday. He still had his '83 Dodge 400 convertible, but years ago they had traded in Deliverance's Plymouth station wagon for this car. They'd had to build a fourth garage bay to hold the fire-engine red '90 Mitsubishi Mirage that the twins, Aislinn and Alex, shared grudgingly.

He stopped the car and Storm and Wyatt got out and began stuffing their gear in the trunk. Storm turned to her father and said, "We'll follow you home."

"Tailgate me like the last time and you lose the Cougar for a month," Quint warned.

Storm froze and saluted pertly. "Yes, sir."

"She gets her irreverence from you," Quint accused his wife who just sat there with a cat-that-ate-the-canary smirk on her heart-shaped face. He shoved the gear into low and made a U-turn, satisfied that Storm was following him at a safe distance. He picked up speed once he reached level ground and whisked the Explorer towards the route that would take them to Sabino Canyon Road. Once they hit the road it was a quick trip down until they came to the turn to their home on Fire Water Lane.

Quint hit the garage door remote and drove smoothly into the bay, followed by his daughter, who parked her car next to his. The

Dodge was in the singular third bay, and he could see that Alex had washed and waxed it that morning. The Mitsubishi was also likely newly washed and sitting in the fourth bay. Aislinn rarely lifted a finger to clean their cars, but Alex was meticulous and consistent.

The kids ran into the house, hungry for a bite to eat. Quint and Deliverance followed and entered the kitchen, which was empty. They could hear the TV playing loudly from the family room. Quint grabbed an orange juice and followed his wife into the room where his kids, Tucker, and four-year-old Brennan were sitting at the edge of their seats, staring at the TV. Quint and Deliverance stood behind the couch and watched the special report on CBS. High camera angles of a decimated building flashed as some reporter summarized what was happening.

"Where is that?" Quint asked, stunned.

Alex looked up at his father. "Oklahoma City. Someone bombed the federal building about twenty minutes ago. Half the building is gone. They don't know who did it or how many are dead, but they think hundreds."

"Dear God," Deliverance whispered in stunned disbelief. She looked at her husband. "It's two years to the day that the Branch Davidians went up in flames in Waco. Judie Sutphin had an article about that this morning in the *Sentinel*." She noticed that Tucker was as white as a sheet. "Alex, take Brennan into the kitchen, please."

Alex nodded and extracted the boy from Tucker's arms and hurried away.

Deliverance sat next to Tucker. "Tuck—what is it? What's wrong?"

Tucker looked at her, absolute fear spread all over his face. "Iris … Iris was in Dallas for a conference. She … she called me last night and said she was flying to Oklahoma City at 6 AM for a side meeting with the ATF." He turned and stared at the shocking images on the screen. He spoke the words they already knew.

"The ATF offices are in that building."

...

Coming in 2019

637

CPSIA information can be obtained
at www.ICGtesting.com
Printed in the USA
BVHW03*1205310718
523166BV00004B/23/P